A DARKER SHADE

A DARKER SHADE

Ever since Steig Larsson shone a light on the brilliance of Swedish crime writing with his phenomenal debut thriller **The Girl with the Dragon Tattoo,** readers around the world have devoured the dark and compelling genre of Nordic noir. Containing seventeen stories, never before published in English, **A Darker Shade** brings together Sweden's best crimewriters, and illuminates this beguiling country and its inhabitants as never before.

A DARKER SHADE

Edited by

John-Henri Holmberg

Magna Large Print Books
Long Preston, North Yorkshire,
BD23 4ND, England.

British Library Cataloguing in Publication Data.

Edited by Holmberg, John-Henri
   A darker shade.

A catalogue record of this book is
available from the British Library

ISBN   978-0-7505-3991-3

First published in Great Britain in 2013 by Head of Zeus Ltd.

Translation copyright © 2013 John-Henri Holmberg
Introduction copyright © 2013 John-Henri Holmberg

Cover illustration © Joanna Jankowska by arrangement with
Arcangel Images Ltd.

Published in Large Print 2014 by arrangement with
Head of Zeus

Magna Large Print is an imprint of Library Magna Books Ltd.

Printed and bound in Great Britain by
T.J. (International) Ltd., Cornwall, PL28 8RW

CONTENTS

INTRODUCTION

JOHN-HENRI HOLMBERG

This book is, in its small way, a landmark. It is the first overview anthology of Swedish crime fiction published in English, and consequently – given today's global culture – the first one accessible to readers around the world.

It presents seventeen stories by twenty Swedish writers. Several are original to this book. None has ever before appeared in an English translation. They cover a wide range of styles and themes: you will find examples of fairly traditional detection, of police procedure, regional tales, stories carried by social or political concerns, as well as stories written primarily to entertain. One story is historical, set in a fairly recent past of which few of today's readers even in Sweden are aware; another is set in the future.

The choice of authors is similarly diverse. You will find a story by the writing team Maj Sjöwall and Per Wahlöö, whose ten novels, originally published from 1965 through 1975, brought international attention to Swedish crime fiction and totally transformed the way in which that form of literature was written and perceived in the authors' home country. You will find another by Stieg Larsson, whose three Millennium novels have made him the most translated and read

Swedish author of all time. You will find stories by many of the most highly regarded and award-winning Swedish crime authors of today – all told, the authors represented in this book have won twelve of the twenty best crime novel of the year awards (called the Golden Crowbar, and consisting of a miniature gilded crowbar) presented since 1994 by the Swedish Crime Fiction Academy (also translated as the Swedish Academy of Detection), as well as five of the eight annual Glass Key Awards for Best Nordic Crime Novel ever given to Swedish authors. But you will also find a surprise or two – the first professionally published story by Eva Gabrielsson, Stieg Larsson's life companion and otherwise an architect and non-fiction writer, and a story by Sara Stridsberg, currently perhaps Sweden's foremost literary author – but not one ordinarily associated with crime fiction.

In all, my aim has been to present as wide-ranging and eclectic selection of stories and authors as possible in the hope of giving a fair reflection of the diversity, vitality, and concerns of current Swedish crime writing. One item of note: a few of these stories contain references to customs, places, or other peculiarities known to most Swedes but probably unknown to most non-Swedes. In my introductory notes to the stories, I have tried to provide the brief explanations I think may help non-Swedish readers to fully appreciate each story.

That this book is possible is, of course, due to the enormous interest in Swedish crime fiction shown by international – and not least American and British – readers during the last five years or, more precisely, since the first of Stieg Larsson's novels, published in English in early 2008, became a publishing phenomenon. During the forty years between the first Sjöwall and Wahlöö novel and the first by Stieg Larsson, a number of Swedish crime authors were translated, but most of them only in other continental European countries. To English-language readers, only a very few authors – primarily Henning Mankell, whose work has been translated into English since 1997 – were available. But of course Sweden had crime writers before Sjöwall and Wahlöö, as well as between them and the present. For those readers interested in the development of crime fiction writing in Sweden and its current and possible future state, I offer the rest of this introduction as a fairly brief historical and critical overview, with a few personal attempts to explain the specific directions in which Swedish crime writing has developed.

Crime fiction is a wide literary field, encompassing numerous, very different kinds of stories. You have the classical stories of rational deduction written by Edgar Allan Poe and fifty years later by Sir Arthur Conan Doyle, still later by Agatha Christie, Dorothy L. Sayers, Ellery Queen, and so many others. You have the hard-boiled private-eye stories of Dashiell Hammett, Raymond Chandler, Mickey Spillane, Ross Macdonald, Walter Mosley, Sara Paretsky, and Dennis Lehane. You have the psychological thrillers by such writers as Daphne du Maurier, Patricia Highsmith, and Ruth

Rendell. An equally well-established category is the spy thriller, possibly created by W. Somerset Maugham, later with Ian Fleming and John le Carré as its most famous writers, but in Sweden with so far only one major practitioner, Jan Guillou, whose thirteen novels about Swedish secret agent Carl Hamilton have been immensely popular since 1986 but have so far had virtually no competition. For this reason, Jan Guillou and spy thrillers are excluded from the following discussion. You have most of noir literature, although my conviction is that noir is in fact defined emotionally, not by plot elements; even so, most major noir writers, from Cornell Woolrich through David Goodis and Jim Thompson to Roxane Gay, do include crimes in their bleak stories of alienation and hopelessness. You have the many depictions of police at work, where the earliest notable writers were John Creasey and the unsurpassed Ed McBain; the serial killer thrillers, from Robert Bloch's *Psycho* to Barry Malzberg and Bill Pronzini's *The Running of Beasts* to Thomas Harris' *The Silence of the Lambs* and innumerable later works. And we haven't even mentioned courtroom stories, financial thrillers, political thrillers...

Most, if not all, of these various subgenres within the field of crime fiction initially appeared in either Great Britain or the United States. The detective story, the hard-boiled private eye story, the police procedural, and most of the other dominant kinds of crime fiction are initially Anglo-Saxon developments. But just like science fiction, another of the important literary traditions first established in the nineteenth century, crime fiction also quickly became popular in other countries and is today read and written throughout the world.

In fact, not only today but for quite a while.

Sweden is a case in point. Forty years ago, American and British crime readers suddenly became aware of the existence of Swedish crime writing when the ten police procedural novels featuring Detective Inspector Martin Beck and written by Maj Sjöwall and Per Wahlöö were translated and became bestsellers. They are still in print, and Henning Mankell achieved considerable recognition in English translations, so perhaps it is unreasonable to say that Sweden was again quickly forgotten and remained so until only six years ago, when in 2008 the first novel in Stieg Larsson's Millennium trilogy was translated as *The Girl with the Dragon Tattoo* and became the next worldwide Swedish crime fiction bestseller. This time, however, the appeal of Stieg Larsson's talent and sales led to an increasing number of other Swedish crime authors being introduced in English translations, something that did not happen in the wake of Sjöwall and Wahlöö's success.

What virtually no one will remember is that if Stieg Larsson followed forty years after Sjöwall and Wahlöö, they had also followed forty years after the first internationally successful Swedish crime writer: the pseudonymous Frank Heller, who enjoyed considerable popularity not only throughout Europe but also in the United States during the 1920s.

But, even if Frank Heller was the first Swedish

writer of crime fiction to achieve success in translation, he was far from the first Swedish crime author, and indeed stories of crime and detection have been a flourishing part of Swedish literature since at least the beginning of the twentieth century. But most of this tradition is entirely unknown to non-Swedish readers.

Most Swedish experts place the birth of Swedish crime fiction in 1893, when a novel called *Stockholms-detektiven* (*The Stockholm Detective*) was published. The author's name was Fredrik Lindholm, but he chose to publish his novel under the pen name Prins Pierre and, during the next decades, several other early Swedish crime writers also wrote pseudonymously. Individually, they may have had different reasons for this, but, collectively, a major reason was almost certainly that they shied away from being associated with what most critics and intellectuals at the time considered vulgar trash. We will get back to this a bit later.

Although *The Stockholm Detective* was hardly a bestseller – indeed, the novel was almost entirely forgotten for many decades until it was finally republished to coincide with its centenary – several other early crime authors were enormously popular. In 1908, a vicar named Oscar Wågman, writing as Sture Stig, published the first of two collections of parodic Sherlock Holmes stories; both clever and funny, his work remains the earliest still-readable Swedish crime fiction. One of his readers, according to his own statement, was the young Gunnar Serner (1886–1947), a brilliant scholar who entered Lund University at the age of sixteen and received his doctorate (on a dissertation written in English and entitled *On the Language of Swinburne*) at twenty-four. However, due to his family's relative poverty, Serner was forced to finance his studies by short-term loans, and in the end found himself with no other alternative than to forge a number of bank letters of acceptance; in September 1912, he fled Sweden. Trying to make his fortune at the Monte Carlo Casino, he instead lost everything and decided to try his hand at fiction. Surprisingly, he succeeded and quickly began selling stories under a variety of pen names – in Serner's case an absolute necessity, since he was wanted by the Swedish police.

In 1914 Serner's first book was published, establishing the name Frank Heller – from then on his only pseudonym. Until his death, 'Heller' published a total of forty-three novels, story collections, and travelogues; he also edited anthologies of crime fiction as well as fantasy and science fiction, and he wrote poetry. Several further short story collections were issued at a later time. Heller became not only a bestseller in Sweden, but also Sweden's internationally most successful entertainment writer of his time. His inventive, humorous, and exciting stories of swindlers, gentlemen adventurers, and criminals were bestsellers throughout Europe and the basis for five feature movies; in the United States, eight of his novels were published by Crowell during the 1920s. With a single exception, the work of Frank Heller is the best Swedish crime fiction written during the first half of the twentieth century and is still both readable and interesting.

That exception is a short novel called *Doktor Glas* (1905; translated as *Doctor Glas*) by Hjalmar Söderberg, generally acknowledged as one of the major Swedish twentieth-century authors. *Doktor Glas*, however, was not viewed as crime fiction; it is a psychological novel of a young doctor who decides to commit murder, and it is still both chilling and convincing in its careful and empathetic portrayal of a good man convincing himself to do evil.

Other early authors include Harald Johnsson, writing as Robinson Wilkins, whose master detective, Swede Fred Hellington, was employed by Scotland Yard and so solved cases in England. Samuel August Duse, writing as S. A. Duse, who published thirteen novels about lawyer and genius detective Leo Carring, silly, racist, and snobbish entertainments, though with sometimes innovative plots (in a novel called *Doktor Smirnos dagbok*, *The Diary of Dr. Smirnos*, Duse already in 1917 lets the murderer record a police investigation in his diary without revealing, until the end, his own role. This contrivance became world famous when repeated by Agatha Christie in her 1926 novel *The Murder of Roger Ackroyd*). Julius Regis, often signing himself Jul. Regis and born Petersson, was immensely popular for his ten crime novels, most featuring journalist and detective Maurice Wallion.

These were the major Swedish crime writers until the 1930s. Most detectives had un-Swedish names; so did most major criminals. The crime story was perceived as a non-Swedish literary field, and so native authors chose to make their stories more international by importing both their protagonists and their adversaries. 'Frank Heller' was the exception, writing primarily about Swedish heroes – but on the other hand, virtually all of his stories are set outside of Sweden: his method was simply the opposite, since he chose to export instead of import his detectives.

The reason for this is obvious. Foreign crime writers were voluminously translated and quickly became popular. The Sherlock Holmes stories began appearing in Sweden as early as 1891; they were followed by translations of work by Maurice Leblanc, G. K. Chesterton, R. Austin Freeman, Agatha Christie, Dorothy L. Sayers, Freeman Wills Crofts, and the other major British and American writers. During the 1930s, early crime-fiction pulp magazines also began appearing in Sweden. These were quite different from the American pulps of the same period, and in fact more similar to the German popular-fiction magazines: generally of small size, stapled, and usually presenting a single long story rather than many short works. Most were translations; when written by Swedes, they were mostly disguised as translations by being set in England or the United States and published under English-sounding pen names. The pulp crime magazines lingered in Sweden until the beginning of the 1960s, but had for a decade largely been replaced as a primary source of crime entertainment reading by low-priced original paperback novels and translations.

Meanwhile, the first Swedish crime writer to firmly place his stories in Sweden and also create thoroughly Swedish detectives with unmistakably Swedish names was Stieg Trenter. Most of his novels were told by photographer Harry Friberg, but the problem solver is primarily Detective Inspector Vesper Johnson, a friend of Friberg's. Trenter is generally considered one of the finest literary chroniclers of the growing Stockholm during the postwar years. He published twenty-six books from 1943 through 1967, the last few cowritten with his wife, Ulla Trenter, who after his death published a further twenty-three crime novels until 1991, many still featuring her husband's protagonists but with markedly weaker plots and little of his trademark depiction of Stockholm settings.

Stieg Trenter can be said to have been the author who made crime fiction accepted by Swedish critics. He had followers during the 1940s and 1950s, most notably Maria Lang, a pen name for Dagmar Lange (1914–1991), though as her novels always featured not only romantic but often erotic subplots, they were often dismissed as 'women's romances' with detective intrusions. Nevertheless, Lang's first novel remains interesting; *Mördaren ljuger inte ensam (Not Only the Murderer Lies*, 1949) was extremely daring in sympathetically depicting a murderer who turns out to be a lesbian killing the woman who scorns her passionate love. The shocked reactions to this book may well have contributed to the fact that Lang minimized her discussion of serious issues in her following forty-two adult novels; she had her social standing and position as a high school dean to worry about. Even so, the scorn heaped by male critics on her output seems out of proportion: the fact that the leading female characters in her novels (though the primary detective is always male) actually concern themselves with commenting on men's looks, potential as partners, and sex appeal – things male protagonists in novels from the same period written by men constantly do about women – seems to be one of the primary so-called failings of 'Maria Lang.'

The first Swede to write only about professional policemen was Vic Suneson, a pen name for Sune Lundquist, who published more than thirty novels and story collections from 1948 through 1975. Many of his novels are experimental, with shifting points of view, told in a nonlinear fashion, or combine depictions of criminal investigations with psychological portrayals. After Suneson, the last of the major Swedish crime writers before the 1960s published his first novel in 1954. H(ans)-K(rister) Rönblom wrote about historian and teacher Paul Kennet, who reveals killers not primarily to serve justice but to make certain that the historical record is set straight. Rönblom was in a sense the first recognizably modern Swedish crime writer, since his novels are also insidiously critical of the small-town life they portray: below the idyllic day-to-day life is seething corruption, religious intolerance, sexism, racism, narrow-mindedness, and self-righteousness, all brought to life by the meticulous, rigorously honest Kennet. Rönblom, a journalist, began writing fiction late and died early (1901–1965); still, he managed to publish ten novels.

Crime fiction became popular in Sweden first in

translation. With the exception of the very talented Frank Heller, the relatively few Swedish crime authors writing before the 1940s were highly derivative and were considered unworthy of critical notice; Heller himself, though often praised for his prose, erudition, and inventiveness, was also often accused of 'seducing the young' by glamorizing his amoral swindler heroes. Gradually, however, translated stories of clever detectives, primarily those of Christie and Sayers, later those of Ellery Queen, John Dickson Carr, and Georges Simenon, gained acceptance and were openly read as entertainment by the middle class. This paved the way for Swedish authors to write in the same style: Trenter, Lang, Suneson, and Rönblom dominated Swedish crime fiction for twenty years with their novels of murder within the upper middle class. With the partial exception of Rönblom, despite their storytelling and literary qualities, their novels were as conservative, unchallenging, and devoid of social criticism and daring themes as those of Agatha Christie. These were the writers published in hardcover by reputable Swedish publishers; one latecomer must also be mentioned, the hugely talented Kerstin Ekman, whose first six novels (1959–1963) were pure stories of detection, but who later mainly wrote contemporary literary fiction, though she often includes crime elements in her work and published two later novels which can reasonably be categorized as crime fiction. In 1978 she had the distinction of being the only author of initially popular fiction, and only the third woman in its then 192 years of existence, to be inducted as a life member of the Swedish Academy.

Simultaneously, an undercurrent of what Swedish critics and intellectuals referred to as 'dirt literature' (yes, honestly) also began appearing in the period between the wars. At first this form of entertainment fiction was published in adventure weeklies and in small-size pulps, then starting around 1950 in original pocket-book lines sold only through newsstands and tobacconists, never in bookstores – and for that reason, absurdly, not considered to be books at all. By the mid-1950s several hundred such paperbacks had appeared, and with them the hard-boiled crime fiction of the 1930s and later had arrived in Sweden. Peter Cheyney, Mickey Spillane, and James Hadley Chase were bestsellers during the first years of the 1950s – but never mentioned in reviews or overviews, since they were published outside of the established and respectable book trade, as were the few but existing Swedish authors trying to imitate them. Swedish encyclopedias still claim that 'pocket books first appeared in Sweden in 1956,' since that was the year when one of the major publishers first began issuing pocket-size books to be sold in bookstores.

Consequently, an extreme double standard existed: blue-collar workers, teenagers, and presumably more than a few white-collar readers (though one can suspect without admitting it) consumed hard-boiled crime, but the only crime stories officially published in the country were of the traditional armchair detective variety. In fact, such crime novels are still written and published in Sweden, and have had leading practitioners continually: Jan Ekström, whose first novel was published in 1961, may be the most meticulous of all Swedish puzzle crime writers; his closest competitor in later years is probably Gösta Unefäldt (debut in 1979), though his detective is in fact also a policeman; a current practitioner is Kristina Appelqvist, who published her first novel in 2009.

The first authors to dramatically break with the Swedish upper-class drawing room crime tradition were also the first Swedish crime writers in forty years to become successful outside of the country: Maj Sjöwall and Per Wahlöö, who published the first novel in their cowritten, ten-volume police procedural series, The Story of a Crime, in 1965. This novel, *Roseanna*, was by no means an immediate success in Sweden: critics found it too gritty, too depressing, too dark, too brutal. However, gradually the Sjöwall and Wahlöö series began to be hailed as a unique literary experiment and became a bestselling phenomenon. They achieved this success largely due to the political message of their novels. Where earlier Swedish crime writers had been politically conservative or liberal, Sjöwall and Wahlöö were both left-wing activists and consciously planned their ten novels to become more overtly political. The motives behind the crimes gradually become connected to the social background of the victims and of the criminals; the later books in the series directly address issues like fascist tendencies within the police, the betrayal of the working class by the purportedly socialist government, the emptiness of the capitalist-bourgeois lifestyle.

Swedish political life since the mid-1930s was

dominated by the Social Democrat party, to which all government heads from 1932 until 1976 belonged. Beginning in the 1930s, the party gradually transformed Swedish society into a centrally planned welfare state, though at a much slower speed than its rhetoric usually promised. A consequence of this was that many Swedish intellectuals, as well as a growing number of young people, began to view the Social Democrat party as derelict in its dedication to socialist ideals. Thus, during the 1960s, social criticism in Sweden tended to come from the radical left, and the Sjöwall and Wahlöö novels changed the way in which many leading intellectuals viewed crime fiction: what had once been dismissed as a pointless bourgeois pastime could be turned into a force for political analysis, education, and change. Suddenly reading, and even writing, crime stories became respectable among left-wing Swedes; interestingly enough, this coincided with the coming of age of generations of young readers who had grown up not on their parents' Agatha Christie-inspired novels, but on the hard-boiled crime novels published in the disreputable 'kiosk books' lines, and this combination of circumstances quickly transformed Swedish crime fiction as a whole.

Of course, the success of Sjöwall and Wahlöö, and the following tide of crime novels written from a politically radical perspective, did not extinguish the more traditional or purportedly apolitical kinds of crime fiction. They had their readers, and continued to be published; indeed, one of the most popular writers of the 1968 through mid-1980s period was the pseudonymous Bo Balderson who, in a total of eleven novels, poked fun at Swedish government circles from a clearly conservative point of view. Other new writers, considerably more accomplished than Balderson, proved that the more traditional kind of detective novel could still be written brilliantly; among the foremost of these were psychiatrist Ulf Durling, with his first novel in 1971 and his sixteenth, and so far latest, in 2008, and the very prolific Jean Bolinder, whose first crime novel was published in 1967. Even so, around the time when the tenth and last of the Sjöwall and Wahlöö novels was published in 1975, most of the new authors were writing about police collectives, and most were combining their crime stories with an underlying political agenda. Some of the most notable authors of this generation were Uno Palmström, K. Arne Blom, Olof Svedelid, and most particularly Leif G. W. Persson, a professor of criminology who published three novels in 1978–1982, then returned with a fourth in 2002, and has since written a further six crime novels; their intricate plots, often based in actual Swedish crimes (his trilogy *Between Summer's Longing and Winter's Cold*, 2002, *Another Time, Another Life*, 2003, and *Falling Freely, as in a Dream*, 2007, dealing with the unsolved 1986 murder of Swedish prime minister Olof Palme, is an impressive case in point), their careful atmosphere and obvious literary merits have made him one of the foremost Swedish crime writers; he is one of only two three-time recipients of the Swedish Crime Fiction

Academy's Best Novel of the Year Award, the other being Håkan Nesser.

Persson, indisputably not only one of the best but also one of the most influential Swedish crime writers, also helped set the tone of social criticism in Swedish crime fiction. His background – as a criminologist with the national board of police, as an influential government adviser, as an expert adviser to the Swedish minister for justice – gives a unique weight to his novels, which are often extremely critical of Sweden's rampant police inefficiency, of the legal system, and of the political and bureaucratic establishment, whose primary aim seems to be to perpetuate and extend its own power and privileges.

Parallel to Persson, similarly critical views of Swedish society also played a central part in the novels of Kennet Ahl, pen name for journalist Christer Dahl and later writer and actor Lasse Strömstedt, who had spent eight years in prison. They wrote seven novels from 1974–1991, adding inside knowledge of the prison system, police brutality, the narcotics trade, and the precarious existence of addicts. Also important was the already mentioned Uno Palmström, originally a journalist, later a publisher, whose nine novels (1976–1990) also expressed fundamental doubts about Swedish society, which Palmström viewed as largely a corporate state where the unholy alliance of politicians and financiers repressed the population in order to further its own interests. Lawyer and naturalist Staffan Westerlund wrote a series of novels where a common theme was the inhumanity of both big business and big government; he wrote about the meddling and callous outrages perpetrated by Swedish authorities and the indifference towards individuals shown by medical, chemical, and energy corporations in their quest for profits.

By the late 1980s and early 1990s, this trend of social criticism was not only firmly established but further enhanced in the work of important new authors. Journalist Gunnar Ohrlander published a first thriller in 1990, chosen Best First Novel of the Year by the Crime Fiction Academy, and Henning Mankell published his first crime novel in 1991, chosen Best Novel of the Year by the Academy; these two were the first Swedish authors to seriously treat the subject of Swedish racism and anti-immigrant feelings in literary form, and they did so in crime novels.

When Stieg Larsson's novels were translated in 2008 and on, many critics seemed surprised at their negative depiction of a Swedish welfare state swollen to a monstrosity willing to sacrifice the rights, liberty, and lives of its citizens in order to preserve its privileges and power. This, to readers in the United States and Britain, seemed a dramatic reversal of the earlier, rosy picture painted of modern Sweden as a wealthy, liberal welfare society, characterized by openness, tolerance, and compassion. In fact, the bleak view of Swedish society set out in the Millennium trilogy was a direct continuation of the social criticism of the Sjöwall and Wahlöö novels, and thus established as central to Swedish crime writing since almost forty years.

We have already touched on the reasons why so many – though, as we shall also note, not by any means all – of the Swedish crime writers came to express strongly leftist political views. In brief, Maj Sjöwall's and Per Wahlöö's novels had broken entirely with the earlier tradition in Swedish crime fiction: they chose a much more realistic approach both to crime and to crime solving, they wrote from an underdog perspective, they were often critical of both the efficiency and motives of the police and of the close ties between the legal system and the political establishment, and they examined the social and economic factors contributing to crime. This made their novels not only acceptable but required reading for intellectuals sympathetic to their views, which created a whole new readership for original Swedish crime fiction. At the same time, their novels were published when the Swedish political landscape was being radicalized. The 1968 youth revolt throughout much of the western world also had a considerable impact in Sweden, where opposition to the Vietnam War became a unifying symbol to a number of radical groups: the Marxist-Leninists, the Maoists, and the few but intellectually significant Trotskyites. By taking control of the anti-Vietnam War movement, the Maoists and in some cases the Trotskyites managed to influence a generation of Swedish high school and college students. Very consciously, these groups also encouraged their members to choose professions which would give them the opportunity of influencing others; many became entertainers, actors, teachers, social workers, and certainly not least writers or journalists – for a number of years, the Stockholm College of Journalism was popularly called the 'College of Communism.' That a number of them also chose to follow in the footsteps of Sjöwall and Wahlöö by expressing their views and concerns via crime novels is hardly surprising, and indeed many of the major Swedish crime writers of the last decades have a background in the radical groups of the late 1960s and 1970s. Stieg Larsson was a Trotskyite; Henning Mankell is a Maoist, as was Gunnar Ohrlander; these three have spoken openly of their affiliations, which is why they are named while others are not.

Let me add, for clarity, that my point here is not to denounce these writers, but to give an intelligible background to the specific direction in which Swedish crime writing has developed: already in their teens or early twenties, the writers maturing in the 1960s and 1970s learned to view society from a principled standpoint, in a dialectical manner, and to attribute both social problems and individual actions to political and economic factors. I have no doubt that very similar forms of social criticism would have appeared if a number of leading Swedish writers had been guided by equally strong liberal or libertarian views, but such views are seldom part of the consensus-driven Swedish political discourse. On the other hand, there are certainly examples of politically conservative writers using crime fiction to criticize Swedish society.

By the mid-1990s, a new generation of leading writers had established itself, with Mankell,

Håkan Nesser, who began writing crime in 1993, and Åke Edwardson, with a first crime novel in 1995, as its most important authors. Both Nesser and Edwardson to some extent broke with the social realist tradition. Nesser placed his highly literary novels in a fictitious city, Maardam, in an unnamed country which is a composite of Sweden, Germany, Poland and the Netherlands, with his emphasis largely on the psychology of his main characters, not least his police protagonist Van Veeteren. Most of Edwardson's novels feature his Gothenburg Detective Inspector Erik Winter, but Edwardson as well has chosen to deal primarily with existential and psychological issues, also in a highly literary fashion. Mankell, Nesser, and Edwardson brought the Swedish crime novel to a level of literary accomplishment that made it not only accepted as potentially serious fiction, as indeed it already was since the 1960s, but viewed as a potentially important part of contemporary Swedish literature.

What was largely lacking, however, were female authors. With the exception of psychiatrist Åse Nilsonne, virtually all of the foremost Swedish crime writers were men. The turning point came towards the end of the nineties, when Inger Frimansson, Liza Marklund, Helene Tursten, and Aino Trosell all published their first novels in 1997 and 1998. They also brought a much needed renewal to the forms of Swedish crime writing. Frimansson from the start concentrated on psychological thrillers with few recurring characters; Marklund wrote about a journalist investigator, Annika Bengtzon, and Aino Trosell featured crime-solving female 'anti-heroes' in her largely proletarian realist novels. Of the four, only Helene Tursten, a registered nurse and dentist, writes about a police officer, Detective First Irene Huss at the Gothenburg police.

Despite this, the police procedural is alive and well in Sweden. Among those still writing in that tradition, the most important newer writer may well be Arne Dahl (penname of Jan Arnald), who introduced his fictitious 'A Group,' specialized in internationally related violent crimes, in 1999 and, after eleven books, in 2011 began writing about Opcop, a fictitious secret operational unit within the European police organization. Other impressive police procedural writers include Anna Jansson, who introduced her police protagonist Maria Wern in 2000; Mons Kallentoft, writing about the brilliant but damaged and heavy-drinking Detective Inspector Malin Fors since 2007; Carin Gerhardsen, who began writing about the police in Hammarby, a part of southern Stockholm, in 2008; and Kristina Ohlsson, with protagonists Fredrika Berman and Alex Recht, introduced in 2009.

Nowadays, however, many of the most highly regarded Swedish crime novels fall outside the police procedural field. Camilla Läckberg published her first novel about writer Erica Falck and her police boyfriend Patrik Hedström in 2003, and quickly became one of the most popular authors in Sweden. Her novels, as do those of many of her later followers, emphasize the personal lives and relationships of her main characters while the crime story, though central to the plots of her novels, is not always the most important element in them. This kind of 'crossover' between relationship novels and crime fiction has become a standard part of Swedish crime writing, in a sense harking back to the structure used in Maria Lang's 1950s novels, but written in a decidedly more realistic fashion. Others successfully writing in this vein include Mari Jungstedt and Viveca Sten; it also has attracted male writers like Jonas Moström.

Among those writing about lawyers, Åsa Larsson may be foremost. Her first Rebecka Martinsson novel was published in 2003 and was considered that year's finest first novel; two of her later four books have won the Crime Fiction Academy award for Best Novel of the Year. In her novels, regional traditions and religious and psychological conflicts play major parts; she is among the most accomplished, as well as original, current Swedish crime authors. A recent lawyer writing about a lawyer and using her novels to criticize or question aspects of the Swedish justice system is Malin Persson Giolito, daughter of the previously mentioned Leif G. W. Persson, who published her first crime novel in 2012. Among the finest of current crime authors are also Anders Roslund and Börge Hellström, writing together since 2004. Roslund is a journalist and previous TV crime reporter; Hellström a former criminal, now engaged in helping criminals readjust to society. Their novels are closely tied to the Swedish tradition of using crime fiction to discuss and criticize social problems, and have a traditional police protagonist, but rise above most similar work through their literary skill, their wide range of themes, and their level of ambition – all of their six novels vary greatly in plot, form, mood, and style.

In 2005, the first of Stieg Larsson's novels was published in Sweden, and by the time the second appeared in 2006, their success was already enormous. By the turn of the century, crime fiction in Sweden had been a thriving field, with a growing number of new writers adding diversity to what for almost thirty years had been a form strongly dominated by male authors writing about largely male police collectives. After the Stieg Larsson novels, the annual number of original Swedish crime novels has increased to an unprecedented number, currently around 120. A negative aspect of this is that since the total number of crime fiction titles remains largely unchanged, a diminishing number of foreign crime novels are translated into Swedish, making Swedish readers miss out on important new writers and trends, as well as depriving Swedish crime fiction writers not conversant in other languages the inspiration of new literary and thematic developments. On the other hand, by now it also seems obvious that the Stieg Larsson novels themselves led to lasting changes in Swedish crime writing.

Since the early part of the twentieth century, Swedish literature as a whole was dominated by the notion that, to be taken seriously, a literary work should be realistic, deal primarily with either psychological or social issues, and show restraint in its portrayals of characters and events. This view of literature spread also to include 'good' entertainment literature, while works not conforming to it were more or less automatically considered inferior by reason of their insufficient realism. Perhaps one result of this is the fact that science fiction never managed to get a lasting foothold in Sweden; by not dealing explicitly with the here and now, it was viewed as primarily 'escape' fiction, which was by definition neither good art nor worthwhile literature. When applied to crime fiction, the result of this view was that the field as a whole can be characterized by its restraint and by its lack of imaginative freedom: in a field where social concerns and down-to-earth realism are primary virtues, there is no room for villains like Hannibal Lecter, heroes like Jack Reacher, or plots like those of Mickey Spillane.

Perhaps it took a writer like Stieg Larsson, whose favorite reading was American and British science fiction and crime fiction, and who paid no particular heed to the traditions upheld in the Swedish literary establishment, to write a work so completely *un*-Swedish – in its main characters, its action, its graphic sex and violence, and its sheer joy of imaginative storytelling – as the Millennium trilogy. The critical and popular triumph of the novels meant that later writers were suddenly freed from many of the previous taboos, which in fact hark back to the early-twentieth-century modernist rejection of the linear plot structure, heroism, moralism, and romanticism of earlier literature, which the modernists considered outdated and unsuited to cosmopolitan and urban civilization.

Consequently, in the last few years, Swedish crime fiction has suddenly been enriched by innovative authors writing in totally new ways. Karin Alfredsson and Katarina Wennstam, publishing their first novels in 2006 and 2007, write on the subjects of men's subjugation of women and homophobia, and are perhaps the two current writers whose main concerns are closest to the underlying theme of Stieg Larsson's novels; Alfredsson, using her physician protagonist Ellen Elg as a unifying link in her first five novels, has examined the horrifying situation of women in five different countries; Wennstam, in her highly accomplished crime novels, has dealt with trafficking, police brutality towards their domestic partners, sexual harassment in the movie business, and homophobia in sports. Lawyer Jens Lapidus, writing since 2006, is stylistically and thematically inspired by James Ellroy in his depictions of gang violence and corruption in the Stockholm suburbs, and has brought a unique voice to Swedish crime fiction. Johan Theorin, whose first novel was published in 2007, is a highly literary writer often combining crime plots with both regionalism and elements of fantasy, mythology, and horror. Dag Öhrlund, making his debut in the same year, writes violent crime thrillers much in the American hard-boiled tradition, and has created the first genius serial killer in Swedish crime fiction. Starting in 2009, the writing team Alexandra and Alexander Ahndoril, under their joint pen name Lars Kepler, write fast, imaginative, and moody action novels featuring both heroes and villains larger than life. Security expert Anders de la Motte's crime novels, starting with [*geim*] in 2010, are characterized by intricate, mazelike plotting and by a nerdy, half-criminal, and computer-savvy slacker protagonist who is anything but typically Swedish. Håkan Axlander Sundquist and Jerker Eriksson, under their joint pen name Erik Axl Sund and debuting in 2010, have so far published only one huge, three-volume novel; an intricate, hypnotically enthralling story of obsession, vengeance, psychoanalysis, and redemption which is an unmistakably central work in current Swedish crime fiction. Even later, Christoffer Carlsson is a highly unconventional, noir-inspired author whose three novels so far show huge promise, while writer team Rolf and Cilla Börjlind published their first crime novel in 2012: dark, atmospheric, and with one of the most original protagonist couples since that of Stieg Larsson; the Börjlinds, in creating their two detectives, are both playing with, parodying, and rising above the conventions of the form.

Given the proliferation of new writers; its sudden freedom from earlier restraints on themes, style, and elements; and its great popularity among readers, Swedish crime fiction today is at both an enormously exciting and a chaotic stage of its ongoing development.

Ancient controversies have resurfaced – how much graphic description of violence, murder, or sex should be 'acceptable' in fiction; how much literary experimentation should be 'condoned' in a crime novel; how much adherence to the field's traditions of rational deduction should you 'demand' of a crime novel; can supernatural events or plot elements be part of a crime novel? This makes for often heated and fascinating discussions, not least in the awards committees of the Swedish Crime Fiction Academy.

But despite the controversies, and despite the fact – not previously stated, but nevertheless fundamental – that the majority of crime novels in Sweden (as in all countries) remain both fairly undistinguished and are written in one or other of the already established traditions of the field, the future of Swedish crime fiction seems bright. And considering its sudden global appeal, there is also reason to believe that it will continue to attract talented, innovative, and original writers who will widen and enrich it even further.

After that optimistic thought, I won't keep you any longer. In the following pages, you will meet many of the writers who have shaped the Swedish crime fiction field as it exists today and a few who I believe will help shape it tomorrow. I hope you will enjoy getting to know them, and reading the stories they have to tell.

John-Henri Holmberg
Viken, July 2013

REUNION

TOVE ALSTERDAL

She steps out of her car and slowly walks down towards the lake. It draws her. The paved walkway disappears between a couple of birches and becomes a path. A dizzying feeling of time rushing off, back to then.

Its black waters.

It is the same lake, the same time of summer as it was then. Just before midsummer, before the heat has permeated the ground and the greenery is still tender and young. The water as dark and tempting as in the nightmares she has had ever since. Not always, to be fair. There have been weeks, even years, when she has managed to sleep calmly, as when Lisette was just a baby.

'Ohmygaawd, it's been so long! Marina! Piiiaaaa!!'

'Agge!'

Two other cars have driven up and parked next to hers. The women yell loud enough to make the famous birdlife flutter up from lake pastures and reeds, take cover deeper into the woods.

She forces a smile and turns to meet them.

'Jojjo, is it really you?' Marina takes the last few steps at a run and hugs her. Watches her face, pushes back a strand of hair. 'Shit, you look just the same. You haven't changed a bit.' She turns to the others, who are unloading baskets and bags full of food from their cars. 'Have you seen who's here already? Johanna!'

They laugh and shout and soon she is wrapped in everyone's arms, they hug and agree that all are just as they were.

And it's fabulous to meet again! After thirty years! And you don't look a day over twenty-five! Well, neither do you! They laugh at absolutely everything. And as they tumble into the tiny scout's cottage she thinks, how great that I decided to come after all. That I didn't give in to that feeling of just wanting to hide. There is a warmth between them she had forgotten. They have known each other since such an early age that those thirty years are shed in just a moment. Or so it feels at that particular moment when they are jokingly chattering about who slept in the upper beds that time.

Johanna watches them and wonders which one of them actually came up with the idea of a reunion. She has just assumed that Marina did. Her parents had some kind of connection to the scout organization that owns the cottages. Marina, her hair almost black, though by now she surely must dye it – there are only slight touches of gray that paradoxically make her look younger. Almost more beautiful than she remembers her.

'Didn't you bring a sleeping bag, Jojjo?' Agge asks when the others are throwing their overnight things on the bunk beds.

'No, I'm not sure if I can...' She feels all of their eyes. It was a long time since anyone called her Jojjo. 'I have to get up early and...'

40

'What are you saying, aren't you going to stay the night? Wasn't that the whole thing?' Agge's deep voice, always sounding as if something was self-evident. She has put on at least sixty pounds and it's still impossible to disagree with her. 'I've got blankets in my car,' she says, 'it'll be all right.'

Johanna nods and smiles. Why did she agree to this? Her first reaction on seeing the invitation was a ringing NO. And yet. Just that someone invited her, remembered her. Pia already has the coffee-maker going. Just as back then she slides in without saying much but still ends up at the center, the prettiest of them all. Tiny, attractive wrinkles around her eyes when she laughs.

'What the hell,' Agge says, 'let's have some champagne.'

And the cork bounces against the ceiling.

The fire is burning, a genuine campfire. Their faces glow. The mid-summer dusk is blue and transparent. They pull their sleeping bags around themselves. She knows that she is drinking too fast and too much.

Marina's idea: that they toast each other, all round. They have toasted Marina's new executive position at the staffing company and Pia's new lover who has proposed, third time lucky! They have toasted that Marina has run the women's six-mile race and that Agge has retrained as a gardener; at last she is living her dream! Here's to our dreams! Marina has been married for eighteen years and still loves her husband – *skål!* – and Pia has gotten new tits after her pregnancies – *skål* to them! – and to all their kids who are all doing

41

so well in school – *skål! skål! skål!* – and particularly to Agge's eldest who has been picked for the junior national swim team.

'And what about you, Jojjo, out with it!'

She knows it was a mistake to come here. Her life is nothing you hold up for inspection at reunions. She manages a toast to her daughter, Lisette, getting a job after graduating high school, then slips away, saying that she has to take a trip into the forest.

Nowadays there are toilets behind the cabins, but she does it the way they did back then. Squats down behind a spruce.

A little urine squirts on one of her shoes. Between branches she sees the fire die down to embers and the silhouettes of the middle-aged women around it.

What else could she toast? That she's divorced and has been unable to find someone new? That her apartment is mute now that Lisette has moved out? She can't even do Internet dating, since it makes her feel like the last passenger on the late-night bus going home from town, where everyone is desperately grabbing whatever is offered. And she knows that thousands of people are finding love on those sites, so of course it's all her fault. Like missing the last night bus and being left standing outside in the cold. A toast to that! She sleeps badly, because there will be more cutbacks and nobody knows who will be laid off. And here's to the body going downhill while time runs out, *skål!*

As she is pulling her pants up she hears a sound. Branches creaking. Somewhere down by the lake.

She breathes silently and stands immobile, her hand on her zipper. Seems to see a shadow between the spruces, a shift in the weak light.

A voice. And everything within her is suddenly cold as ice.

'Have you saved me anything to eat?'

Someone is standing where the spruce forest ends and the shoreline begins. Thin and short. Her hair a flowing blonde tangle. Her green sweater.

'What is it?' Lillis says, laughing. Her face is unnaturally pale. As it was already back when they were playing with death. 'Didn't you think I'd show up?'

I'm dreaming, Johanna thinks, I'm more drunk than I think. It can't be the same sweater!

'Don't you want to talk to me?' The figure steps closer to her, head a little askance. 'And I always thought we were friends.'

Johanna steps back. 'I'm going back to the others,' she says, half running through the forest, a branch scratching her face.

She doesn't turn round until she is sitting by the fire again. Then she stares at the forest, so long that the others also have to turn around.

'But what the hell...' Marina stands. 'Lilian! I didn't even know ... who managed to get hold of Lillis? Why haven't you said anything?'

Johanna doesn't even realize that the question is put to her. She sees the woman come closer. A smile animating her face. Now all the others are standing. Johanna feels that she has to stand as well.

Lillis' body is cool and thin in her arms. A quick

43

hug. A darkness sweeping in from the lake and night has fallen.

'God, how great to see you.'

'Where did you go? Didn't you disappear even before we started our senior year?'

Distantly she hears them toast Lillis, as if inside a glass jar. Now, for the first time, she actually sees the others. They aren't at all as unchanged as they fancied; they have aged. Their skin has lost its grip and is hanging loosely from their chins; the years have dug furrows even in Marina's once-perfect face. You can tell that they all dye their hair. Only Lillis is still young, entirely smooth and as dangerously and strangely beautiful as she was then. That tiny little squint.

'My God, you haven't aged a day!' Agge yells. '*Skål* to that!'

Johanna sees their mouths move and laugh. Lillis' face is so white that it shines, despite the embers having gone out and everything is cold.

Can't they see that it's wrong?

Lillis, who for a short while was her closest friend. The unreachable whom she incomprehensibly reached, the great happiness of being seen and being allowed in. Lillis, who was an adventurer and a center, one of those around whom the moon and the earth and the boys revolved, while Johanna was a vapid planet at the rim of the solar system. Vaguely she had understood that Lillis needed her, or someone, anyone, by her side. Johanna had never entered the competition, just followed. The first cigarette, the first high on beer and aspirin, the play in the hut where Johanna mostly waited outside while

44

Lillis was making out inside, but anyway. Afterward she was allowed to share her secrets.

Johanna feels the scream grow inside of her, it wants to burst and escape, but she can't, it isn't possible. The silence is too huge. It has lasted for thirty years.

Wants to tell the others: But can't you see, don't you get it?

She pinches her arm, hard, and it hurts. It's no nightmare, it's happening. She has to project it when she looks into Lillis' pale-blue and slightly squinting eyes. Project her words, silently, across the dead fire that is now all ashes.

You don't exist. You're dead.

And then she can't stay there any longer, because she is sucked into the pale blur and it makes her shiver. She has to rise and walk down to the lake.

There is a story about the Upper Lake. Have you ever heard it?

It is Lillis' voice, but is it then or now? They have walked along the water's edge, away from the others, because Lillis is tired of the endless competition between Marina and Pia. Johanna is thinking that Lillis is also competing, but she never says it out loud. They are sixteen years old and will sleep in the cabin all the weekend and tomorrow – Marina has asked some boys – they'll have a party.

Come on, let's swim. Aw, come on, now! We'll have to see if it's true what they say about the Upper Lake.

45

That somewhere out there, there's a bottomless spot. Where those who have drowned live. They say that if you go down deep enough you can be caught in their trailing hair. Down there are those who died willingly, the suicides, and they're all women, unhappy and full of despair. Men shoot themselves, but women drown themselves, that's how it's always been. It's their hair you can feel under your feet, if only you dare swim out there.

Lillis throws her clothes into the high beach grass and starts wading out in the lake. Johanna has to do the same. Everything they share becomes meaningful and the more dangerous it feels, the more alive they become. Lillis has taught her that. They often play with death, strangle themselves with scarves until they pass out. It's become an addiction to them, an obsession, they have to do it every day. Johanna is panicky as she pulls the noose tight, yet she pulls it until all air is gone, her temples start throbbing and it feels as if her eyes were forced out of her skull. She sees pinpoints of light and outside sounds disappear and then everything goes black. There's no danger as long as you don't make a knot in your scarf, Lillis has promised her, since it loosens when you pass out. Before you die.

There is a moment in every person life when you decide whether to walk with the living or with the dead. That time is now, before we go rigid. After, it is too late.

She can see that Lillis has started swimming out

46

there and is pulling away. They are closing in on the middle of the lake. The cool water caressing her skin, so present and naked. She thinks that some boy may be standing somewhere on the beach, watching them, and it feels exciting, and then just a little bit shameful as she thinks about Lillis naked under the water maybe thirty feet ahead of her, her strokes powerful even though she is so thin and so cute, but it's not like that. Nothing sexual, that is, between them, or that's what she constantly tells herself even though it sometimes feels that way when Lillis snuggles into her arms on the couch or wherever. Like a puppy, sort of. But that's how Lillis is, without any boundaries against what is dangerous.

And they're alone under the sky, in the night, and they don't give a rat's ass for anyone else.

We have to know something about death to be able to choose, right? Otherwise, we'll just be victims.

She doesn't perceive it when it happens. Just sees that the surface of the water is suddenly smooth. You're kidding, Johanna thinks, and swims to the spot where Lillis' blonde head was just visible, swims around in circles, where the hell are you? She dives under to look, but it's dark and impenetrable. All she sees is water and you can't see water and she loses her sense of direction, of what is up or down, and she panics. That's when she feels it. Something moving down by her feet, slithering around her legs. Fear overwhelms her and she has to get up right now, up to the surface. She kicks and hits something below, there really is something down there, and in her head

47

she sees all the images of the dead, of eels slithering out of eye sockets, and that thing that is tangled around her feet is still there, pulling at her, and she kicks wildly and brandishes her arms, up, up, and she has no air left, must get away from there. She doesn't breathe until she is at the shore. Doesn't think until she has stood up. The lake is glittering and black. She shakes so hard that it takes forever to get her clothes back on. Next to her are Lillis' clothes, spread out on the grass.

Time just passed, or perhaps it stopped. Finally she had to rise and walk back.

'Have you been out swimming? Where's Lillis?'

Johanna doesn't know where the lie came from. She had meant to tell them what happened, that Lillis swam out and disappeared. But then she would have to lie about the rest. About her being out there herself. About the dead in the water and her own panic, how do you tell someone something like that? About the sensation under her foot when it hit something soft and at the same time hard, and what she hadn't even dared to think through: that it was Lillis' face. Lillis, who just intended to scare her, that it had all been part of a plan, the stories about the dead and their silly hair. Lillis, who always trained to be able to swim farther underwater than anyone else in the public baths.

'She just split, I don't know. Maybe she got upset about something.'

In the morning she had gone back to that place

48

and picked up Lillis' clothes, buried them. Cried and dug. It was too late for the truth. It was the summer when everything changed. In the fall they all disappeared in different directions, knots being untied. Marina would attend high school in town, the others started different courses. Johanna quit after a single semester, then graduated from a folk high school up north in Ångermanland. Lillis' father was a heavy drinker and there never was any serious investigation. The police had appeared once to put their questions, and Johanna had described how Lillis was dressed when she disappeared: the sea-green angora sweater (stolen from H&M). They believed she had run away from home. She probably had reasons to.

The tree growing more or less alone at the edge of a grove. Johanna believes she recognizes the place and starts digging on the lake side of the trunk. Is it possible that fabric and angora wool are still there after thirty years in the ground, or do they decay? Sneakers? She digs, and there is nothing. Is it the wrong spot? Perhaps the wrong stretch of beach, new trees grown up, she has no idea of how much a forest can change over thirty years. Lillis is standing at the edge of the woods, looking at her. Johanna doesn't dare turn, but she can feel her presence as something cold in her neck.

We had a deal. A deal about secrets and betrayal, have you forgotten that, Johanna?

She has dirt under her nails, reaching far up to

her elbows.

That's why she walks down to the water and kicks off her shoes, she tells herself. When she bends down to wash off the dirt she sees herself in a brief reflex, her adult self. She has never stopped being sixteen – it's just new ages added, like layers in a cake. Then the moon disappears behind a cloud and she is gone. No, not gone, there she is: pretty far out in the water already, where it's deep. She swims, still fully dressed, towards the middle of the lake, because she must. Closes her eyes and swims on, tries to find the power within her body, but there is only the awkwardness of her wet clothes and the fat that has lined her stomach; she can feel her own weight. At the middle of the lake she stops, treads water, looks around. It was here, just here. And she dives down, as deep as she can, looks and sees nothing, fumbles around and gets a grip. Something trailingly soft, and she seems to hear it whisper and sing. *There is a moment ... to walk with the living or with the dead...* Now it is all around her, entangling her in its threads until she is caught and dragged down into the whispering darkness where no light will be and no dread to wake up to, just a quiet song, is that how death really is? She lets herself sink. Let me go, she wants to scream, I don't want to die. *Do you call that life*, it whispers, *that thing you believe yourself to be living?* Now she has no air left, and she sees dots of light all around. Is it Lillis' face she can see down below? Or someone else's?

No, she sees herself, and she is young again, and will do anything to be allowed to belong. No, she

50

wants to scream, NO, I DON'T WANT TO ANY LONGER, but she has no air and there are no sounds in the water. She kicks, grabs the hair entangling her legs, tears it loose and rises towards the surface, and there is air, cold and clear.

Deep into her lungs she pulls life and power and a sense of reality. What the hell is she doing out here in the lake? She swims as well as she can manage, breathless and exhausted, towards land. Untangles her fingers from something in her hand.

Lisette, she thinks. *She needs me, even if she doesn't want to admit it.*

'Are you out of your mind – have you been swimming fully dressed?'

Pia is removing her makeup. Rubbing her face with expensive creams. Agge is snoring in her upper bed. Johanna looks around in the small scout cottage. No sea-green sweater.

'I was thinking about Lillis,' she says, guardedly. 'I thought I saw her out there.'

'You must have drunk a lot. I didn't think anyone had any contact with her since she got out of here. And come to think of it, I never understood why you hung out with her. Want some tea?'

Johanna finds her scarf and dries her hair with it, it's still dripping. They sit down, each with her mug of tea. She has taken her wet clothes off and borrowed dry ones from the others. Seaweed, she thinks, the only thing out there is seaweed or some other kind of water plant. She is grateful her head is no longer spinning.

51

'What do you mean, why I hung out with Lillis?'

'You were cool, you were smart,' Pia says. 'You never needed to pretend or act. I was always so impressed by you. And then you let yourself be used by her.'

Johanna stares at them, one at a time. A quick sensation of being visible, as if she suddenly was more clearly delineated. Was that really how they perceived her?

She gets one of Agge's blankets and wraps it around herself.

'You know, before, when we were sitting around the fire– ' she starts. 'I didn't think I had anything to contribute... I mean, my life is ... it's okay, but I guess no more than that.'

'Isn't that enough?'

'*Skål,*' Marina says, raising her teacup.

That's when the tears come, burning and overflowing. She rubs them away, sniveling, but they keep flowing. Suddenly she can't remember what's so wrong about her life. And she thinks that all of it was just nightly imaginings, nightmares; she knows drinking too much makes her feel unwell.

Pia puts her arm around her and the crying abates. While light is growing outside, Marina starts talking about her uncertainties: that feeling that they'll discover what a failure she is as an executive, and Pia tells them that deep down she really isn't sure of loving this new guy. Finally they fall asleep, each in her own bed.

The next morning they say good-bye, outside the cabin.

'Thanks for setting this up,' Johanna says, hugging Marina. The ghosts of the past night certainly seem childish in the morning light, the sun already high.

'What are you talking about? You were the one inviting us.'

Marina exchanges glances with the others.

'We were pretty uncertain all of us, but then we thought, what the hell, get away from hubbies and kids for a weekend, why not?'

A few strands of mist have remained since night and are dissolving on the lake. Marina holds up her cell.

'It says here for anyone to see that you created this page. Is anything wrong with you?'

Johanna grabs the phone from her hand.

She recognizes the Facebook page. 'Return to Upper Lake.' At the top it clearly says that the group was created by Johanna.

She feels a taste of lake water in her mouth. A stinging sensation in her cheeks, a swaying unreality.

She hadn't even logged in to Facebook in half a year. Doesn't know why she's on it at all, but on the other hand she doesn't want to be left out. When the message arrived in her mailbox, nobody had contacted her in more than six months.

When she returns the cell phone her hand feels numb.

'We've got to do this again,' Agge says. 'Same time next year?'

'Sure.'

She remains standing there for a while after the others have left. Remembers a strand of hair entangled in her hand. The lake has turned a pale blue. The air is so still that the images of the trees on the water seem as real as the forest around her.

'There really is another story about the Upper Lake,' she says, slowly, into the air. 'Have you ever heard it? I think it's about those trying to live, despite all.'

Just as she steps into her car she feels a sudden chill on her neck. A wind creeping across her cheek, a quick caress. And the leaves are immobile.

HE LIKED HIS HAIR

ROLF AND CILLA BÖRJLIND

He still had time to pace the room, that simple and measured surface that was his home. A word he never used. To him it was a surface, not a space. He had put in a couch and a table, and had a wooden balsa model of the Dakota on his windowsill. There was no carpet on the floor and the narrow mirror by the kitchen door was hung too low. He hadn't put it there himself. When he wanted to see how his mouth looked he had to bend down; all he could see was dead meat. He had no relationship with his face, his eyes met the gaze of a stranger and he wondered why the nose was crooked.

He liked his hair.

It was the one thing he admitted as his. Brown, and slightly curly, it reminded him of his mother, the woman who had no hands. Her hair had been brown and curly, and her laugh – when she was finally told – was his only memory of her voice. But it made time pass.

That, and his pacing.

He was a night person, his biological clock set to night. That was when he came awake: when darkness fell, when he could escape being seen and could avoid seeing, when he could be in-different to his surroundings, cut out, when he could walk from one neighborhood to another without knowing where he had gone.

Often, at night, he walked from one point to another and back along a different route. And always with the same purpose. It made time pass and it made him tired. And made it possible to fall asleep before light caught up with him.

That was important.

He had to fall asleep before it became light and sleep until it grew dark again. Sometimes he failed, woke out of a strange howl and stared out at the light, unable to go back to sleep.

Those times were when he missed it.

That which could lower him back into darkness. Which they had taken from him and which he had to get back.

In one way or another.

He began pacing the room, from wall to wall and back. For how long he didn't know. He had no watch; usually he felt from his body when he was done, when he could go to sleep. Tonight it took a long time. He sat down on the edge of his bed, felt his body. He ought to be tired by now, more tired than he was.

It bothered him.

He went to his window to look out. Nothing moved; all was as usual. In the corner of his eyes he was aware of the charred hands on his window ledge, two of them. They lay there every time he had to go. Not every time, it struck him, just the times he had to lower himself into darkness.

Then they lay there, as a reminder.

He opened his window, carefully, watching the hands. It was quiet outside. On some nights he could hear a blackbird not far away, a blackbird singing in the middle of the night. He never saw it but he knew what it looked like. Its beak was the same orange-yellow color his mother had had when she was told.

And they had the same black eyes.

He closed his window and went to the shelf above the mirror. The small blue-and-white box stood where he had put it four nights ago. He stuffed it in the pocket of his long, dark gray coat and left the room.

He had to.

Outside a soft rain was falling.

He liked rain, he liked something to happen while he moved between the buildings. Not pelting rain, but a monotonous, quiet drizzle. Tonight the rain was perfect. He knew the address where he was going and was in no hurry. He kept to empty streets; if he met anyone he crossed to the other side.

He never looked back.

When he came to the right part of town he stopped, not far from a green container. He stood quietly, for a long time, hidden in the darkness of a broken streetlight. He thought about a sentence he'd read (where, he couldn't remember) about a man standing on a bridge casting switched-off light across the water. Switched-off light, he liked that, as if your pocket was full of darkness and you could spread it when it became too bright.

Perhaps that was what he could do?

Switch off?

After all, he had the box in his pocket.

He turned to the container near him, having seen a movement, a woman alone pulling herself up to drop an unmarked plastic bag into the container. He watched her tired body and wondered what was in the bag. Perhaps a black wig and a tube of lip gloss? He watched her disappear in the darkness and remained standing. There were nights when he followed people walking alone, often on the opposite side of the street, followed until they disappeared into a doorway or a bar. He conceived of it as having company.

Tonight he wanted to be alone.

He twisted around.

The dogs were whistling down by the bus stop.

Sometimes he imagined that, that the dogs were whistling, late at night when shadows were his only company. The dogs nobody knew about, long, crooked, narrow bodies suddenly just there, out of nowhere, crossing a darkened street to disappear, then suddenly breathe right next to him and disappear again.

He heard them whistling to each other, the dogs, and he knew what it was all about.

Him.

It was connected to the third puppy, the drowned one. The one he pushed into the bucket many years ago and that fought for its life under the sole of his boot. A life it had just been given and that would be taken away from it, because it was the third and was deformed, lacking a fully developed spine. Sometimes he thought about it, being deformed. The animal was deformed and would have died anyway. He just did what the dog owners ought to have done; he took care of it. But

58

the way the animal struggled under his boot left its trace in him. He had thought it would be quick.

It wasn't.

And while the animal fought and twisted under the sole of his boot there was time for him to start thinking. That wasn't a good thing. Suddenly he was thinking about what he was doing and about what moved under his foot. What had been only a quick decision to rid the world of pointless suffering turned into something else. The deformed animal refused to give up and forced him to make an entirely different decision.

He had to kill a puppy.

He might have lifted his foot and said that it didn't work, the pup didn't die, then give it back to its owners. But he didn't. That was what he considered now, in the soft rain. Himself as hostage to a situation he had created and that forced him to kill. Or confess that he was unable to do it.

He killed the pup.

That's why the dogs whistled to each other those special nights when he walked in the company of shadows and knew that he was a hostage again. And had to kill.

Or confess.

He waited until the lights went out in the stairwell and all sounds ceased. Then he pulled on his rubber gloves. In darkness he climbed one floor up and rang the bell by the door of the one he had chosen. It took the old woman a while to open.

'Yes,' she said. 'What's it about?'

'I'm looking for Ester.'

'Yes, that's me?'

'I'm sorry.'

Later, when he sat on the kitchen chair watching the thin, white cotton thread hanging from her mouth, he wondered about that. About why he had said, 'I'm sorry.' It was nothing he had planned, it just came to him spontaneously at the doorway. As if he apologized for what would happen.

It confused him.

The duct tape was the first thing he pulled out in the foyer. Putting it over the thin woman's mouth made quick work. When he lifted her into the kitchen he noticed how slight she was. Almost like a scarecrow he'd built once, just as fragile and wiry.

If he were to build a new scarecrow now he would name it Ester.

With a few blue cable ties he fastened her thin feet and arms to a kitchen chair. In the cupboard above the stove he found a glass. He filled it with water from the faucet next to the stove. He saw the woman's eyes follow his every movement and wondered what she was thinking about. Who he was? Probably, or perhaps more about what he intended to do. He put the glass down on the table in the middle of the kitchen and took out the blue-and-white box. A second before he would open it he hesitated and looked up at the old cobbler's lamp hanging from the ceiling. The light from the filament was soft. He watched the lamp. It was the kind of light he could stand, artificial light you could turn off at will.

He opened the box and pulled out a tampon. He put the thin plastic wrapping in his pocket; he disliked untidiness. With his left hand he pulled the tape from the woman's mouth. She opened it wide to scream, he had no idea for whom. He pushed the tampon down her air pipe to drown her yelling. Now she was silent. He grabbed her jaws with one hand and poured half a glass of water into her mouth before closing it.

Now he was done.

He pulled up another kitchen chair and sat down, almost directly opposite the old woman. He knew that the tampon was swelling inside her throat now, and there was nothing for him to do but to wait. He glanced down at the chair he was sitting on, an unpainted wooden chair. He liked wooden chairs, simple, functional furniture without any frills. His mother had five chairs around their kitchen table, all wooden and all unpainted. For a while they were four in the family, but never five. He never wondered about the fifth chair.

Then.

Now he did. For whom was it intended? He looked at the bound woman in front of him. Her knees were shaking, she no longer could breathe, her eyes bulged a bit. Was the fifth chair intended for visitors? But they never had any visitors. He supposed it was one of his mother's secrets, an extra chair for something unexpected. He smiled slightly. Now the woman's head sank down to her chest, she had stopped shaking. He bent forward

61

and saw the thin white cotton thread hanging down from the corner of her mouth. It would soon be still. He wondered what was flashing through her mind right now. Where was she going?

We know so little about those things, he thought.

Soon he would leave.

He was on his way back, on foot, to his carefully measured surface. The streets were empty, his steps followed the edge of the gutter; he never needed to raise his eyes. At this time there were no movements in this part of town. A couple of hours ago homeless people had shambled past, carrying sacks full of empty cans; drunken teenagers had hunted for cabs or drugs; lonely hookers had tried enticing customers by lowering prices – everything had been drawing to an end. He had seen it a thousand times and another thousand.

Now it was all empty.

Now there were only gulls picking at the pools of vomit and the echo of distant sirens. Nobody saw him. Or perhaps at a distance? Perhaps a sleepless elderly man stood in a costly window a block away looking down at him? Perhaps the man wore a dark green smoking jacket and held a black cheroot in his hand? Perhaps he was listening to the Vienna Boys' Choir? The man who had come to his mother one night and tied a purple bow around her neck had done so. She didn't know that he was sick; she listened to 'O Tannenbaum' and let the man stitch a veil of rapture to cover her eyes.

Then the man waved at the young boy.

He raised his head to glance up at the well-to-do building fronts. Perhaps he might glimpse the man?

The faucet water was freezing. He always washed his hands when he got back, held them under the running water until they grew numb, disappeared, until he could bite them without feeling anything. It made him calm. The day before he put a picture up on the wall above his bed. It was the only picture in the room. It pictured a young boy pushing a strange metal funnel under the skirt of a kneeling woman. Both wore medieval clothes. In the background two liveried men were sharing a melon. The picture was in color. He liked falling asleep to the picture and waking up to it. The only thing he lacked in the picture was sound. It looked as if the two men in the background were talking to each other; he would like to know what they said. Was it about the melon? Or about the strange funnel?

Now he lay in bed watching the picture. He was lowered in darkness and knew that he would be able to fall asleep. All he had to do was to ponder the question to which he always fell asleep; why didn't anyone ask for help? He often wondered about that. He could stand in a park, perhaps hidden by a maple, and watch faces walk by, silent, expressionless, as if nothing had happened.

It was very strange.

People ought to be more careful. Once he had stretched out a hand to a young boy walking past. He had wanted the boy to feel the pain in time.

The boy had run away.

Since then he had never tried contacting anyone.

Now he was on the verge of slipping away. His eyes let go of the picture on the wall; he hoped he was slipping in the right direction, not towards the interface. He hoped to be here still when he woke up.

He is dreaming.

In his dream he is walking as if he really existed, walks across low, warm heather, through a sparse fir wood, towards dunes of sand; he wants to reach the sea. He has heard that it's supposed to be calm today. He is just a young boy and has never seen total calm, never seen the sea all shiny and smooth. He never gets there. A large, dark bus pulls up in front of him, blocking his way. The door to the bus opens and the shape behind the wheel waves to him. He doesn't want to enter the bus, but there is nobody close he could call out to. He opens his hand. Only moments ago he caught a ladybug; he blows at the red-and-black insect until the ladybug flies away. He doesn't want it to come along into the bus. When the door closes behind him he runs to the seat at the very back of the bus, hoping that he'll be able to hide. The bus lifts from the ground and soars above the fir wood; he glances out and sees a small house far below. In a hammock behind the house a woman is lying; she waves to him. He presses a hand against the window. When the bus stops it is dark outside, green neon light pulses in through the windows. He sees darkened houses on both sides, houses of stone. It has taken him to a city. The figure behind the wheel turns around

towards the back seat and brings out a microphone.
He can hear the figure start singing.
He knows the song.

He was still there when he woke up.

He lay in bed for a very long time, trying to decide how he felt. Sometimes he didn't know if he was still inside his dreams; sometimes that's what he believed, that he was still in another world. That he was someone else.

But not this time.

He raised his hands and pushed them through his brown, curly hair. Even his hair was still there.

That made him feel calm.

Two nights in a row he stayed in his room. He didn't open the window, didn't touch any of the pills on his table, fell asleep without pacing his surface. He didn't know what this meant. Perhaps he wouldn't have to go out any more? In that way? That would be a relief. He didn't like the fact that it had dragged on the way it had.

That wasn't how he had first meant it to be.

At first it had just been a woman. Anyone of the right age.

And just one.

But it wasn't enough. He had thought that one would be enough, a single one, to lower him into darkness once and for all.

It wasn't that simple.

The light caught up with him again.

Now he didn't know when it would stop. That worried him; he already felt a tinge of weariness. The first time there had been a streak of

65

excitement. Not because of what he would do, or did, but because of the chance of reaching the darkness. The second time the excitement had gone, it was more like a preliminary to what he really wanted; to what enveloped him when he saw the white cotton thread grow still in the corners of their mouths and it was done with.

Then he wished for the darkness never to end.

But it did.

He went over and opened the window. It was still night outside and the window ledge was empty, no charred hands, no singing blackbird.

There was no reason to go outside.

He sat down by his wooden model and thought about people in other places. I'll never meet them, he thought. Sometimes he gave them names, taken from plants or animals. On his wall he drew kings with saucer heads and completely ordinary people with long, extended noses, noses like slim roots, three feet long. You could see that they were prying into things they shouldn't. It was danger-ous. Already in the sandbox there were children prying, small, round children with noses already long. He learned to recognize their kind.

He went up to his long coat and pulled out a slim brown leather glove from one of its pockets. It had probably belonged to a woman. He had found it on his way to Ester. It happened fairly often that he found lost gloves on his nightly walks. If they were made of leather he brought them back with him and boiled them in a steel pot, for a long time, until they had shrunk. He hung them on a clothesline stretched across the

66

kitchen. Almost a hundred shrunken gloves hung there now, fastened by small wooden clips. He viewed it as a row of pennants.

He let the glove fall into an empty pot.

In good time he would boil it.

He glanced at the door to his apartment. Sooner or later there would be a knock on it, he knew that, if he still remained in who he was. It was a wooden door and there was no doorbell; someone would knock on the timber. He tried to imagine the sound and the hand that made it. Whose hand was it? At best it would be himself knocking, at worst someone who wished him ill. Someone whose long nose had discovered him.

He wouldn't open at once. First he would remove the picture of the funnel from the wall and hide it under his pillow; then he would hold his hands under the freezing faucet water until they were numb.

There would be another knock.

Then he would say something through the door, explain that he couldn't open it since he had no hands. What would happen after that he didn't quite know; perhaps they would fetch someone who could pick the lock or perhaps they would just break down the door.

He would have to be prepared for the worst.

He went over and took his long coat from the hanger. Soon it would become light and he wasn't tired; soon the light would come. He felt that it came too fast. He had paced his room for many hours and still wasn't tired. He ought to be.

He ought to sleep.

He ought to be more careful.
He went out.

Gunvor Larsson was seventy-eight years old and lived alone. Her husband had died from an intra-cranial hemorrhage four years ago. She missed him, on one level, as a life partner should, but at the same time she was relieved. Their last years had been marked by the immense bitterness her husband felt about his life, a life he viewed as ruined by many different things. Those few times Gunvor had carefully tried to suggest that, after all, they had loved each other and stayed together for all of their lives, he had started to weep.

That was almost the worst of it.

But now he was gone and Gunvor was in good health, given her age. Her only problem appeared at night; she always woke up after only a couple of hours and found it difficult to relax again. She had tried almost everything, from medications with strange names to books on tape with just as strange tales. One of her grandchildren had tried to get her to start meditating and made her make up a mantra, a special word which after being repeated interminably would make her relax and be able to go back to sleep. She had chosen the word 'ocean.' On the first few nights she had mumbled 'ocean' for ten or twenty minutes and then brewed a cup of tea to pass the time.

Tonight was the same again.

Shortly after two she woke and got out of bed, wrapped in her worn, pale blue dressing gown. She put some water for tea to boil and sat down by the kitchen table. During the last few nights she had taken out some of her old photo albums – she had quite a few – and looked through them, image by image, to pass the time. Pictures of children and grandchildren, of trips abroad and summer houses and pets and people whose names she had forgotten. Now she held the last of her albums on her knee, the one from last year. Another of her grandchildren had printed out a number of digital pictures on paper and gifted her the album.

She had reached a photo of her single great-grandchild when the doorbell rang.

'Tonight you will dance.'

The phrase from the lovely song floated to the surface of his mind. 'Tonight you will dance.' People sang it on bright midsummer nights when he was tied inside the greenhouse. He heard them trying to sing in parts, heard their wobbly voices searching for each other. Everyone was in high spirits, many were children. Later they would come in to weep in front of him and feel bad. When they loosened the harness it was almost dawn; his mother had put sour milk out on the steps. He never knew if it was intended for him or for the hedgehog.

He had time to think all that before the door in front of him opened. An elderly woman peered at him through the crack.

'Yes?'

'Is it Gunvor?'

'Well? I don't want to buy anything.'

'Neither do I.'

He looked at the photo album on the kitchen table. It was spread open. He stretched his hands out and took it. The two open pages were crammed with pictures of children. He let his eyes move across the images until they stopped on a small boy down by the corner of the page. He looked at the boy for several minutes, his brown, curly hair, his tight mouth. Finally he held the album out to the woman bound opposite him and pointed at the little boy.

'Is that your grandchild?'

The woman's face was dark blue, her eyes wide, her head shaking violently. He couldn't make out if she said yes. He turned the album back towards him and opened the next spread. It too was full of pictures of children; children hugging adults and children holding flowers. All of them looked cheerful and happy; none of them were harnessed. His mouth narrowed to a bitter streak; he knew that in time those children would grow very long noses. He turned the pages back to the picture of the little boy down by the corner; that boy's eyes were searching for his, he thought, perhaps as if he wanted to appeal to him. He felt something wet rise under his eyelids.

Suddenly he shut the album and watched the woman in front of him. It seemed to take much too long. He was impatient. He wanted what he had come here to find. He was on the verge of rising before she had died but remained seated. Finally her body went limp. He watched her and waited for his reaction.

For the darkness.

It didn't come.

Nothing happened inside him.

He poked lightly at the white cotton thread at the corner of her mouth. It hung slack and immobile. Everything was as it should be, but even so it was all wrong.

He remained sitting in his chair for several minutes, close to despair.

He had a feeling.

Suddenly he rose and threw the photo album across the floor. His heart beat unnaturally hard.

He kicked his chair aside and rushed out from the kitchen.

In the stairwell he felt his throat constrict in a cramp.

He left the house without giving a thought to remaining unseen. It meant nothing any longer. He tore off his heavy coat and started to run. It was still dark and he chose the nearest way. He noticed that he met a few nightly walkers; a couple of cars had to swerve. He continued straight ahead. He knew what was happening and he wanted it to happen where there was no one else. He had to make it back to his crypt.

He began screaming long before he had reached the door to his building.

Now his heart had calmed down, the scream had gone silent, his body had slowed down. He stood leaning against one of the walls of his room. He knew it to be the calm before pain. He had experienced it before, how everything went still for a little while before it began in earnest.

As if there was compassion.

He looked around his room to remember it, the

71

couch, the table, the wooden model; his eyes caught at the wooden door in the wall. Inside it was a wardrobe. He knew that there were clothes in the wardrobe that weren't his. He didn't know whose they were, but that didn't matter to him.

Particularly not now.

He started by taking the picture down from the wall, the one with the funnel and the melon. He folded it, carefully, and put it under his pillow.

If he returned he would know where to find it.

He went over and opened the window. The window ledge was empty. He brushed his hand over it. He would miss the charred hands, those that never touched him.

Suddenly he heard the singing, the blackbird, far away out in the darkness. He tried to see it without succeeding. He pursed his lips to whistle but refrained from doing it. He didn't want to disturb the past.

He stood at the window for a long time.

When he closed it he felt tiny, rolling movements across his cheeks. He went to the mirror, bent down and saw a face.

Is that how I look?

He regarded the face in the mirror. He recognized it. He recognized certain features, those particular cheekbones, those arched eyebrows, the mouth he had never seen before. He leaned against the mirror and let his mouth touch the mirror mouth. Then he brushed away the things trickling down his cheeks and felt that it was time.

He lay down on top of the bed.

His time had run out, for this turn, it was pointless to try to fight it.

72

The first few times he had done that, tried to remain in who he was.

It never worked. He screamed and cut his own body not to lose touch with it. In vain; whenever he began slipping in the wrong direction there was no return.

Nowadays he just slipped along.

He lay stretched out on his bed, his hands clutching the blanket tight; his whole body began shaking. He knew what would follow. He knew that there were a few seconds, sometimes ten or fifteen, when he was right in the middle of the interface, inside the zone, on his way from who he was to something he couldn't even imagine.

Or someone.

A few seconds that brought an unbearable physical pain.

The first time it happened he was unprepared. He slipped into the zone and didn't know what would come, not until he saw the executioner. A shadow with no face and with a long object in its hands. He stared at the shadow and never had time to react; the glowing scythe cut through the base of his skull, down through his body and through his groin.

There everything ended.

Now he was going there again, into the zone, slipping, just at the verge of letting go when he heard it.

Or them.

The knock, on his door.

The one he knew would come.

He stopped himself.

Would he walk to the door or slide away? If he

73

slid away they would never find him as who he was now. What they would find he didn't know. Perhaps a dead blackbird on his pillow. Or two charred hands under his blanket. He ought to stand up.

He ought to rinse his hands in the freezing water and walk to the door.

But he didn't do what he ought to do.

When the knock sounded again he closed his eyes, hid his tongue at the back of his mouth cavity, let go and slipped away.

Into the zone.

NEVER IN REAL LIFE

ÅKE EDWARDSON

She listened to the weather forecast and he concentrated on driving. He was chasing the tracks of the sun. A brief flash was enough, or a shadow. He was prepared to turn any number of degrees. U-turns had become his specialty.

She read the map. She was actually good at it. They drove farther and farther away from civilization, but she never missed a turn.

'It's as if you grew up around here,' he said.

She didn't reply, just kept her eyes on the map covering her knees.

'There's a tree-road junction in about half a mile,' she said, raising her eyes.

'Uh-n.'

'Go left there.'

'Will that get us to the sun?' he said.

'It's supposed to be better in the western part of the county,' she said. 'The local station just said so.'

'So a better chance to find the sun,' he said.

He could see a crack opening in the slate-gray sky far to the northwest, as if someone had stuck an iron lever into the clouds. Maybe it's God, he thought. Maybe we'll finally get some use out of Him.

'There's the junction,' she said.

75

When they drove through the town, the sky was incomprehensibly blue.

'So that's what it looks like when the sun is out,' he said, pulling out his sunglasses. 'Maybe there is a God after all.'

'Do you believe He's thinking about us?' she said.

'Maybe He even *believes* in us,' he said.

'That's verging on blasphemy,' she said.

'I don't think He cares. He's got His hands full building up air pressure.'

'How do you know it's a he?' she said quietly, but he heard.

'And don't talk too much about God to people around here,' she added. 'This is a religious community.'

'Isn't that where you're supposed to talk about God?' he said.

'There are different ways of talking.'

'Aren't you suddenly the expert. On both people and God.'

She didn't reply.

'In any case, we'll stop here,' he said. 'When we've been chasing the sun this long we sure won't leave when we've found it.'

He turned right in the center of town, at another tree-street junction. A small church stood on a hill. It was plastered white and a thousand years old. Most people around here belonged to some non-conformist religion, but even so they took good care of their ancient state churches. Though maybe that had nothing to do with religion.

A man in a peaked cap was mowing his way

76

down the hill on a riding mower. The engine sound was soft, almost like the buzz of a bumblebee. The grass was thick and succulent; no sun had burned it. Perhaps they've waited for weeks to mow the grass here, he thought. A couple of days more and they would have had to use a scythe. Go get the guy with the scythe, he thought, smiling.

The man in the cap raised his eyes as the car passed, then looked back down, without any greeting.

'Maybe there's some small place where you can swim around here,' she said.

'If there is, we'll make camp,' he said.

They were alone by the lake. Or the pond, or whatever it was. The creek ran past here and the townspeople had dammed the stream, creating their own small lake. He saw the dike on the opposite side of it, only some three hundred feet away.

The swimming nook had a table with two benches and two changing rooms, one for men and one for women.

'I haven't seen any of those since I was a kid,' he said, nodding at one of the two red sheds. He stood in the middle of the grass. The water glittered in the sunlight. Suddenly the air was very warm. It was like suddenly being in another country.

This is where I belong, he thought. I hope nobody else finds their way here.

Close to the swimming pond was the campground, or whatever it might be called. At any rate there was a small wooden bench for washing and doing dishes, with two water faucets, an outhouse built from the same kind of wood, room for car and tent. What more could anyone wish for?

She looked up from their luggage.

'We have to go shop somewhere. All that's left in the cooler is some bottled water.'

'I know, I know,' he replied. 'But we'll put up the tent first.'

The closest town was less than twelve miles away, if it could be called a town: a closed railway station, closed shops with empty display windows, an empty main street directly beneath the sun. *If a display window no longer displays anything you really can't call it a display window, can you?* he thought.

But there was a cooperative store and a state liquor store.

What more do you need on a vacation? he thought.

'I'll do the liquor store if you do the Co-op,' he said.

'Can't we shop together?' she said. 'We're not in any hurry.'

He didn't answer.

'It's what you're supposed to do on vacations,' she went on. 'Take your time.'

'Yeah, yeah,' he said.

The inside of the store was cool, verging on chilly. As far as he could see they were alone in there, apart from the girl at the cash register whom he glimpsed at the far end. Not a single customer. He had seen nobody in the streets as they drove through the town. Perhaps everyone had escaped before the sun finally arrived. This district was more or less midway between the east and the west coasts of Sweden. In the end people had lost their patience and went off to chase the sun in the west or in the east. He had done the opposite and it had paid off. The sun was up there to stay. Once high pressure had settled over the interior of the country, nothing could budge it.

'The chops look great,' she said.

In the endless dusk he enjoyed himself. The sun just didn't want to sink beyond the treetops, now that it was finally allowed to show itself. He had drunk a small glass of whiskey while preparing the marinade and the chops, then another small glass while he assembled the grill. Life was wonderful. Look at him: Dressed in only a pair of shorts in the eighty degrees heat of the evening, the wonderful scent of the forest and another wonderful scent from the water and a wonderful scent from the whiskey and soon a wonderful scent from the grill!

He lit the grill and sipped another small one.

'Are you sure you don't want one?' he asked and held up his glass. A sun ray hit the liquor and there was a flash of amber. A lovely color.

'No, the wine is enough for me,' she said, nodding toward the bottle of wine that waited uncorked in the shade beyond the camping table where she was mixing a salad.

He had wanted to uncork two bottles directly, but she had felt that they could open them one at a time. And they both agreed not to buy box wine since they were on vacation, not even in this out-of-the-way spot. He had always thought that box wine lacked style. And you must always have style, no matter what. People who drank wine from a box might as well use a paper cup to drink it. And eat their food from paper plates with plastic cutlery. And generally go to hell, he thought, smiling, and emptied his glass. The whiskey was great. Everyone could go to hell. This is my vacation and my sun and my lake and my camping ground. At least there's something good about this fucking country. You can put your tent up wherever you like without some fucking farm yokel shooting your head off.

Maybe I ought to run up to the road crossing and take down the sign advertising the lake, he thought. This is our place. I do have my box spanner. Suddenly the idea struck him as brilliant, but he also realized that the whiskey was pushing it. Some damned hick might pass by on his hay cart and wonder what he was doing and that would be no good, just lose him a lot of time unnecessarily.

He held his hand over the grill to feel the heat.

'I'll put the chops on now,' he said.

Later on he sat in what might be called darkness during some other season, but not now. The sun was just down, waiting beyond the horizon of firs. The water was still. He could see the outlines on the other side. It was like a jungle, a jungle three hundred feet away.

Suddenly he saw a light.

'What was that?'

He turned to her, pointing across the water's surface. She had said that she would go to bed, but she was still sitting there. Typical. Said one thing, did the opposite. He would have loved sitting here alone for one last hour. Enjoying the silence, the peace. Now it seemed as if she was watching him. Yes. Watching him. He had felt that continuously more often lately. As if she studied him.

But now she was staring across the lake, as if she was doing it just because he did.

There was the light again, like a flashlight.

It blinked. One-two-three short blinks.

'There it is again!'

'Where,' she said.

'But don't you see it?'

'Was there something blinking?'

'You bet your ass there was!'

'Maybe I saw something,' she said.

'Maybe? It was someone with a flashlight.'

'But couldn't it be some reflection?'

'Reflection?' he said. 'Where would that come from?'

She shrugged.

'The sun won't be up for a couple of hours.' He tried to see something moving within the contours of jungle, but now everything was still. 'There was someone over there.'

'Maybe someone out for a walk.'

'Mh-m.'

'No, I'm off to bed now.'

'You sure aren't worried,' he said. 'Back home you hardly dare sleep with the lights off.'

'It's different here,' she said.

In the morning all the vague contours were gone. Everything was sharp and brilliant under the sun. He went directly out into the water, amazed at how clear it was, and how cold. He threw himself forward and felt the cold envelop him and when he returned to the surface he had rid himself of his hangover even before he had noticed it.

This was vacation!

He saw her walk out of the tent, stretch, yawn, screw up her eyes and peer at the sun, peer at him.

'Aren't you going to jump in?' he said, splashing his hand down on the surface of the water.

'In a while,' she said and walked off to the outhouse.

'Didn't they have a bakery in that hole-in-the-wall town?' he called to her.

She turned around.

'Yes, I think so.'

'I'm fucking dying for some fresh rolls. And a Danish. I'll drive down and get us some for breakfast.'

He began swimming towards shore.

'Are you sure you can drive, Bengt?'

'What do you mean?'

'The whiskey.'

'Fuck, that was yesterday. And I'd bet a hundred thousand there isn't a cop within fifty miles.'

'We don't have a hundred thousand,' she said and turned her back again.

He turned left at the swim sign and left again at the three-way junction in town. The church plaster gleamed so brightly that his head started to ache despite his sunglasses.

Three hundred feet ahead of him a pickup was parked across the road.

A man in a baseball cap stood in front of the car. He raised a hand.

What the fuck.

He rolled down his window. The man leaned down.

'What's happening?'

'A large family of moose is crossing,' the man replied.

He spoke in a vaguely recognizable dialect, an intonation he'd heard somewhere but couldn't place.

'I can't see any.'

'It's a bit further on. We don't want people to get hurt.'

'You're really on it.'

'It's our job.'

'I thought your job was to shoot the moose,' he said and gave a short laugh.

'So it is,' the man said, smiled and straightened. 'But this time of year, it's all about the moose safaris.'

'Yeah, sure, like on all those signs.'

'Did you see them?'

'Hard to miss them.'

He had seen the blue-and-white signs at two of the exits from the town: the words MOOSE SAFARI, a fat, pointing arrow and a picture of a moose.

'So have you ever seen a moose?' the man asked.

'Lots of times.'

'Really?'

'In photos,' he said, giving another short laugh. 'But never in real life.'

The man smiled again.

'Wouldn't be hard to fix.'

'How do you mean?'

'We're going out tonight, at dusk. I can guarantee you'll see something you've never seen before.' He smiled again. 'In real life.'

'Well, I don't know.' He tried looking past the pickup, but saw no moose. If he had seen any, it would have been easier for him to decline this offer, or whatever it was.

'What are they really?' he asked. 'These moose safaris?'

'We're a small group of people who know where the moose usually can be found in these woods. So we bring people out there and show them those places. It's as simple as that.' The man bent down again. 'And of course we bring some food along, and some beer and schnapps. We have a lean-to where we set up a barbeque late in the evening.' The man smiled again under the beak of his cap. You couldn't make out his eyes. 'Mostly we have a pretty nice time.'

Lean-to, barbeque, woods. Wild animals. It really sounded like an adventure, a very modest one, but still. Beer and schnapps. His throat was already dry, as were his lips. He could see himself by the fire, a glass of colorless liquor in his hand. Guys all around. A world of men, damn it.

'We do a pentathlon, too. Most people like it a lot.' The man smiled again. His teeth were dark. Perhaps just from the shade cast by his cap. 'Usually it's pretty wild.'

'What ... what do you charge for it all?'

'Five hundred kronor. But as much meat as you can eat and as much liquor as you can drink is

84

included. Along with the moose.'

'What time?'

'We set out at seven. We meet up on the church green,' the man said, nodding in the direction he had come from. 'Just before the intersection.'

'Will there be a lot of people?'

'So far five, six if you join us. It's just enough – too many people worries the woods.'

Worries the woods, he thought. Well put. As if the woods had a life of their own. Maybe they had. Perhaps the winking lights he had seen last night were the eyes of the forest.

'I'll be there,' he said.

When he returned she was just getting out of the water.

'That felt good,' she said.

'So I told you.'

'Did you get the rolls?'

'You bet your ass!'

'So what's made you so happy all of a sudden?'

'Anything wrong with that?'

'No, no.'

'How about being a tiny bit grateful that I drove off to get you fresh rolls, and Danish?'

'Well, it was your idea.'

'So there's no reason for you to give a fuck, is that what you mean?'

'That's not what I said.'

'Maybe I should just have stayed here instead?' He hefted the paper bag in his hand. It felt heavier now than when he had carried it out of the bakery. 'Maybe we'd just as well not have these for breakfast?'

'Bengt, please don't be silly now.'

'Silly? So now I'm silly?' He took a step towards her. 'Are you calling me silly?'

He saw that she flinched. As if he was going to hit her. It had happened before, but he knew that she understood why he had to do it that time. Or those times. She had gone too far and he hadn't been able to stop his hand, or his arm. They'd talked about all that. She got it. But what he didn't get was that it seemed that she still didn't get it. She called him stupid. On their vacation. When he'd been shopping, really exerted himself. Just as he'd started to feel relaxed.

When he was going to see real, live moose. Would she call that silly too?

He hefted the paper bag in his hand. He threw it as far away as he could.

It was heavy enough to fly pretty far out over the lake.

He saw it float with the current.

He heard her give a sob but didn't turn. So it went when you didn't appreciate what someone did for you. If you didn't there would be no fresh-baked buns. There would be hell to pay instead.

She was silent at lunch and that was just as well. He only drank two beers with his food. Any other day he would have had a couple of schnapps as well, but it would be a long evening.

He had told her and she had nodded, almost as if she'd already known. At least that was the funny feeling he got. He had told her about the moose safari and she had nodded and looked away, at the lake and the opposite shore, towards the place where the lights had winked last night. As if someone was standing there. But it was just her way of taking in what he'd said. She knew that it wasn't her place to object. Christ, it was his vacation as well, wasn't it? Shouldn't he too be able to have some fun?

'Will you ... spend the night?' she asked after a few moments.

'No, no. We'll break camp sometime after midnight.'

He liked that expression. Break camp. There was something robust about it, between men. Breaking. Camp.

'Where is that ... lean-to?'

'Out there,' he said, pointing to the woods all around them. 'That's all you need to know.'

Again, she looked away.

He drank the last of his beer and stood up.

'Enough of this, I'll have a dip.'

He went straight in and let his body sink through the water. It was much warmer now than it had been this morning. He took care not to swim out. He had heard somewhere that it could be dangerous to swim after eating; you could sink like a stone. He didn't want to become a stone. There were enough of them on the bottom of this lake, on the shore.

He saw her stand up and walk into their tent. After a minute or two she came back out and went off to the washing bench to get a plastic tub for the dirty dishes. If she had just taken it easy for a while he would have had a chance to offer to take care of the dishes. Now it was too late.

He lay on his back to float on the surface. It was easy, as if there was at least a little salt in the water. He smelled the fragrance of the forest and the beach and the water. This swimming spot was really something. The only strange thing was that they were the only people who'd come here. It was true that this was a deserted part of the country, but this was vacation time, and even the deserted places were filled with people from all over half of Europe. He had heard German spoken when he walked into the bakery. The Germans ought to have found their way here. The main road was a blacktop and the swim sign was easy to spot. There should have been more tents in the camping ground. Thankfully there weren't, but still. And some people from town ought to come here to swim. There must be kids on the farms. There were several farms nearby. And the fucking yokels themselves at least ought to come here to wash off the hay after a working day.

But nobody came.

Maybe it was too hot, he thought. Maybe the kids had all gone to some summer camp by the sea. But hardly. In any case it was more probable that a few kids from the city should have come here for the summer. Summer kids. A funny expression, as if those kids existed only during the summer, were kids only as long as the summer lasted.

She had been a summer kid. He couldn't remember when she had told him, or if somebody else had. Whoever that might have been. But surely she had spent a couple of summers in the country when she was a kid? Maybe somewhere similar to this, he thought. He couldn't remember where she had been. But she never became a farmer's wife. The only thing left since then was a strange remnant of some strange dialect, a single word or two now and then. Strange, like that baseball cap guy, the moose safari guy. Maybe all hicks sounded the same, maybe it was a universal thing.

He smiled, kept on floating.

At five to seven he parked his car below the church green. The sun was still very strong. He locked his car and walked up the hillside. At some point during the evening she would come here on foot to pick up the car. It wasn't more than two or three miles to the camping ground and the lake. She had suggested it herself. He'd like her to come up with more ideas as good.

The church looked almost fluorescent in the white sunlight. Everything here was white: the church façade, the grass and the graves against the light, the sky all above him. In an hour or so the blue evening light would lower from the sky. That was the best time of the day.

He stood in front of the iron gate. The grave-yard inside was quite small, just some twenty graves bearing witness that few people lived here, or rather had lived here. Few had led their lives around here and so only few had died. He wondered briefly if he would be able to live here. The answer to that question was a simple no. Sure, it was okay when the sun was shining, but when it didn't? This was the uplands. In the middle of winter it must be around twenty below.

Even the thought almost made him shiver. He looked at the graves again. Could he die here? Hardly. If you didn't live here you didn't die here, did you? He smiled. He heard the sound of a car motor behind him and turned. The pickup truck drove onto the gravel and the man with the baseball cap stuck his head out the driver's window.

'Jump in,' he called.

He went down to the car and jumped in on the passenger seat.

'Where are the others?' he asked.

'Waiting out in the woods.'

'I thought we were supposed to meet here.'

'They were early. My partner drove them out.'

He asked no more questions. They drove back the same way he had arrived. The wind blew warm through the open window. He saw grazing cows on the pasture to his right. Their udders were swollen. It would soon be milking time. The cowboys would come riding to drive the animals in. *Movin',* *movin', movin'.* Many years back he had watched some TV show, and the theme song had stuck. That show could have been set here. Nothing seemed to change here, except for the horses having been replaced by pickups. But there were still plenty of riding horses in the fields.

They drove past the turning to the lake. Or at least he thought they did.

There was no longer any sign there.

He turned back when they had passed.

Yes, no doubt it was their turning. He recognized a twinned spruce about a hundred feet down the road to the lake. He turned to the driver.

'The sign is gone.'

The man in the baseball cap gave him a brief glance but didn't reply.

'The swim sign for the lake. I've put my tent up down there.'

The man raised his glance to the rearview mirror.

'Sign?'

'Yeah, sign. Blue and white. An ordinary swim sign.'

'Yeah. You're right,' the driver said, his eyes still on the rearview mirror. 'I think there used to be one of those.'

'It's not there any longer.'

'Well. Maybe they took it down to fix it or something.'

'In the middle of vacations?'

'Well, how should I know?' The man threw him a brief glance. 'Does it matter?'

'No, I guess it doesn't ... I just think it's fucking strange.'

The man gave no reply. He suddenly swung onto a forest road impossible to make out even a few seconds ago. There was no sign.

The road was no road, more like a broad track. Maybe a moose thoroughfare, he thought. Here they calmly walk along, without any apprehension, while the yokels sit waiting up in their moose towers, aiming their guns. He glanced at the driver. Better be careful. He had a hick beside him. Wouldn't do any good if he suspected what he was thinking. He looked like a tough bastard.

They arrived at a three-way forest junction. The road split like a crooked poker and he suddenly

91

remembered the late-night barbeque. The schnapps and the beer. He hadn't even had his afternoon whiskey and he was starting to feel it. His throat was dry. His tongue felt like something not quite belonging in his mouth. I'll never again waive my afternoon whiskey, he thought.

The pickup bumped up a slope. The forest thinned out and disappeared entirely at the top. The driver stopped and turned off the ignition.

'Here we are,' he said and climbed out.

Up here it was like standing on the roof of the world, or at least of the county. You could see for miles. It was like the middle of an ocean, the tops of the spruce forming the horizon all around you. The sun had finally started to sink towards the western horizon. Your eyes could follow it all the way down until it turned yellow as a firebrand, then follow it as it rose again if you just stood there long enough.

But it was time to move.

'There are the others,' said the man in the baseball cap.

A few people came strolling out of the edge of the forest below them. He counted four men. They were dressed in sturdy jeans and plaid shirts, rough boots and baseball caps, just like the man standing beside him. They all looked to be from around here. He himself didn't look like a local. He had a blue linen shirt tucked into a pair of chinos. And Top-Siders, by all means sturdy, but still. He didn't have a baseball cap.

The man in the baseball cap introduced him to the others, as if he were the only stranger. Perhaps he was, he thought. Perhaps five hundred kronor is a lot of money to these hicks, a hundred each. With that money they can drive down to the farmers' co-op and buy a few sacks of whatever the hell they need.

But nobody has asked me for any money yet, he thought.

'All right, let's take positions,' the man with the baseball cap said. He thought of him as the man with the baseball cap even though they all had baseball caps. The expression was a bit strange: Let's take positions.

The man in the baseball cap walked ahead to a kind of watchtower that looked newly built. It almost seemed unnecessary to have such a thing up here, but perhaps it gave a still better view of the moose. Perhaps the idea was not to disturb them.

It was higher than it looked from the ground, but then that was always the case. He always got that feeling when he stood at the top of a diving platform, but it was a long time since he last stood at the top of a diving platform. Or any kind of tower. Suddenly he felt that it was a long time since he had done anything at all. Mostly he had existed, whatever that might be. He hadn't climbed any tower, as he did now. Nor lit any fires. He had drunk liquor, but then you could do that anywhere. He believed that he had lived in reality, but this was reality.

Up there he felt the wind.

He felt both large and small at the same time.

'Look down there,' he heard one of the men say.

He looked.

Something moved below among the spruce. He could see the branches shake, rise, fall. He saw something brown, or black; it was difficult to see any colors now since the sun had begun sinking beneath the horizon and that meant that colors had begun sinking into the ground.

He saw the moose walk on to the three-way junction down there, or the three-track junction, and walk on east. The moose! His first moose! They looked like a family, even though from up here all the moose seemed to be about the same size. They appeared as if to order. For a moment he thought that they were trained to show themselves just when people had climbed the tower, but that was just too impossible to believe. Though you never knew. People in this back-woods might well communicate better with animals than with city dwellers like himself.

The moose walked on east, without hurrying. A couple of times they stopped to nibble the branches, as if to check on their freshness and taste. Their movements were jerky and a bit clumsy, but at the same time there was something magnificent about them. Kings of the forest, and queens. Suddenly he wished that his wife had been standing here beside him. He surprised himself with that thought. He thought that everything might have been different. They might have been a family, a real family.

Like the moose down there.

Now they were disappearing, walking back into the forest again. The moment was past. He had had his moment in reality and now it was gone, slowly walking east.

He looked around and saw that all the men were watching him. Watching his reactions. He was fairly certain of being the only one here paying, but that didn't matter. He had had his moment.

He had become someone else.

He wanted to tell her that, do it at once. But that wouldn't be possible. He wouldn't be able to find his way back, nor walk the whole way back, and the other men would have to give him his money's worth. To them it would be a matter of honor and if he demanded to be driven back already he would insult them.

The man in the baseball cap took the lead again and they climbed down the ladder.

Down there the man dragged a large wooden crate from under the tower and began taking something out. He couldn't see what it was since the man was standing with his back to him.

He moved closer and saw the silhouette targets the man had laid out on the ground, the hunting targets, the shooting targets. They depicted moose, close to life-size. The man in the baseball cap stood one of them up. It looked almost alive.

One of the other plaid shirts had walked back to the pickup truck and returned, arms full of rifles.

The man in the baseball cap shook the moose.

'Right, let's do some hunting.'

'How ... do you mean?' he asked.

'We put the targets up down at the edge of the woods,' the man in the baseball cap replied, smiling. 'Then we plug them!'

'I've ... never shot,' he said.

95

'High time, in that case.'

The man in the baseball cap nodded to one of the plaid shirts, who handed him a gun. He supposed it was the kind called a moose-hunting rifle. He had heard that expression. He accepted the rifle, felt its weight. Suddenly he thought of the weight of the paper bag full of rolls and Danish he had thrown out over the lake. He regretted having done it. Suddenly he regretted that more than anything else he had ever done. Standing here, with the damned gun in his hand and the fucking hicks around him, it felt as if he had done something unforgivable in throwing the paper bag. He didn't know why he thought so at this particular moment, but it felt as if he had crossed a line in doing it. A final line. A final line in their relationship. He had crossed the final line.

A few times she had wanted to take another direction, away from him. Towards another line. But he hadn't allowed her to take even a single step. She had known what would happen if she tried to leave him.

'Let's put the targets up,' said the man with the baseball cap.

He really didn't know what would happen if she tried to leave him. Perhaps she knew more than he did. Knew more about him. What he would do to her if she tried.

Christ, let me get away from here. I want to get away from here before it's too late. Soon it will be too late, he thought, wondering at the same time why he would think so.

He stood still while the men placed moose at

different ranges down by the fucking edge of the woods. Some of them were visible and some weren't visible, as if he was supposed to just shoot into the forest. But he wouldn't shoot, for him the adventure was over. He wanted to get away from here, back to her. He was someone else now.

The men were standing around him, their guns in the crooks of their arms. They looked as if they'd been born with a gun in their arms. Which he supposed was more or less the case in regions like this.

They were looking at him as if they expected him to fire the first shot. Whoever fires the first shot, he thought, almost smirking. But nobody had even shown him what to do. They hadn't even given him any bullets, or whatever the fuck they were called.

'I think one of the targets has fallen down,' the man in the baseball cap said, nodding at him. 'Could you walk down and raise it back up?'

'I?' he replied.

The man in the baseball cap nodded again.

He carefully put his gun down on the ground, as if it had been loaded, and started walking down to the edge of the forest.

He couldn't see any moose-shaped target lying flat on the ground. If there had been one it was gone by now, just like the sign pointing to the lake.

'A bit to your left,' he heard the voice of the man in the baseball cap somewhere behind. 'On the other side of the juniper shrub.' And suddenly he recognized the dialect.

It was the same melody she sometimes spoke in.

This was where she had been a summer child.

Right here.

She knew these men.

They had also been children here, though not just in the summers.

She had read the map.

It felt like a hundred summers since.

She had guided them here.

In real life, there was no camping ground.

Now he saw the target on the other side of the juniper. It was upright. The moose leered at him from the corner of its eye, or maybe it leered at something behind him. He turned. He saw the plaid shirts, the baseball caps, the boots. The guns. Now they were raised. They pointed at him. You're fucking supposed to aim at the moose, he thought before understanding. Truly understanding. He heard a sharp, metallic sound from the guns, a sound he couldn't identify. But he knew what it was. There are certain things you recognize the first time you encounter them, he thought.

Beyond the men the sky was flame colored. He saw the tower as a silhouette outlined by fire. He saw the figure standing at its top. He wanted to wave. He wanted to cry out. He wanted to explain all. He wanted to run up the ladder. He wanted to fly. The evening breeze suddenly took hold of her skirt and blew it out like a black banner.

IN OUR DARKENED HOUSE

INGER FRIMANSSON

Doctor Rosberg was an old man, so old that he really shouldn't be practicing medicine any longer, Inga-Lisa had told her.

'But who cares,' she had laughed, loudly enough for the makeup on her face almost to crack. 'That's why I see him. He gives me anything I want to get, just a short lecture and then he pulls out his prescription book.'

Inga-Lisa was her newest acquaintance. She had met her out in Hovsjö. A woman of around fifty, fresh and loud. But with a heart of gold. They had met coming home from the mall, same suburban bus, same apartment house entrance.

'What the hell, do you live here, too?'

She cussed constantly. And she knew people everywhere. Jannike did neither. One evening, while they were sitting in Inga-Lisa's cosy kitchen playing the two-player version of whist, she told her about Doctor Rosberg.

'I've seen him for years. He prescribes for me. Whatever I need. He knows I can hardly fucking sleep. It's my arthritis and my fibromyalgia. Stuff you get when you're an old hag. He's one of the few doctors who'll go to bat for a woman. Last time he gave me pills that would kill an ox ... if you're not careful.'

She kept thinking about that. Kill an ox. Nothing was clear to her as yet, no plans or anything of that kind. But perhaps that was how they began taking shape.

Now she was standing outside the door of his office and had to press the bell hard and long, so long that she was at the verge of giving up. But finally she heard stumping from inside and the door opened. A lined, wrinkled male face appeared.

'Miss Linder? Is it you?'

'Yes,' she mumbled.

'Welcome, Miss Linder. Please step inside.'

His hands were long and so thin that they looked as if the veins lay on top of his skin. She didn't like the idea of having to feel those hands on her body. But she would have to. She had to play along.

'How do you do,' she said and put on an expression of suffering while she made her breaths heavier and strained.

'Please sit down and wait. I will call you in a moment.' He made a gesture towards a group of chairs and disappeared down the hallway.

His office was part of a huge apartment in the Östermalm part of town. Heavy, plush furniture, stained cushions. Inga-Lisa had said that as far as she knew, he lived alone in the apartment. She had never heard of any Mrs. Rosberg, nor had she ever seen any nurse. On the couch was a small stuffed dog, its fur made from crocheted silk strings. Its nose was almost entirely worn away, only loose remnants of black, torn yarn. She imagined a child hugging it, holding it up to ward off the smell of ether and the metallic clattering and the tiny screams now and then penetrating from the examination room.

She put her fake fur coat on a hanger and unwound the long, striped scarf that had covered her head and warmed her ears. Cold had arrived already in late November along with several inches of snow that for once hadn't melted but remained as on a Christmas card. She supposed they were talking about that snow right now at work as they sat around the coffee table. The highlight of the day, when they were all gathered in the tiny canteen. Two candles would be lit, for next Sunday was the second in Advent. She supposed Sylvia as usual would have gotten hold of some bog moss for the Advent wreath and bought candles. She would have been down in the cellar to get all the electric candles and the red tablecloth with Santas that usually covered the table for all of December and part of January until someone, mostly Evy, brought it home and washed it. Surely they had also bought gingerbread biscuits and a saffron ring. She could still hear the crackle from the small sugar granules when you crushed them under your feet in the canteen. However carefully you tried to cut the saffron ring and put the pieces on plates, there were always crumbs on the floor. Sometimes someone put up an angry sign by the sink. YOUR MOM DOESN'T WORK HERE. CLEAN UP YOUR MESS! It usually helped for a while.

Jannike sank down in one of the armchairs and reached for a magazine. They were popular women's or family weeklies, *Allers* and *Husmodern*, but at least fifteen years old and thumbed to shreds. She looked at the photos of celebrities with outmoded clothes and hairstyles. Mullets and shoulder pads. It looked weird. After a short while she heard the door of the examination room open. The old man cleared his throat.

'Your turn, Miss Linder.'

As if his waiting room had been full of patients!

He had slid down in the chair behind his gigantic, worn desk. Papers and documents piled high almost hid him from view. He had to lean forward to be able to look at her. To his left, on a smaller table, stood a skeleton made of plastic or bone. Its naked teeth grinned at her. She shook herself.

'Well, Miss Linder, so tell me why you're here.'

'Well … a friend recommended you, Inga-Lisa.' She was suddenly unable to remember Inga-Lisa's last name, and it disturbed her.

The man lifted a bunch of papers out of a suspension file lying on his table. She got a glimpse of notes written in a shaky, sprawling hand. She started to cry. She didn't know why, the tears just came, like a strong swell of despair. Embarrassed, she covered her mouth with her hand.

His eyes turned towards her. The skin beneath them was slack and baggy, as if his eyeballs might fall out at any moment. She fumbled for a handkerchief.

'I'm in such awful pain,' she whispered.

He regarded her sadly.

'Where does it hurt?'

'Here and … here. All over.'

'Hmm.' Again he thumbed his papers. 'Have you

102

seen a doctor previously?'

'No-o.'

'And why not?'

'I just thought... That it's part of it, sort of.'

'Part of it?'

'Yes, my mother has it and my aunts and my grandmother as well. They've told me it's part of it, it's just something women get. Something with fibro... There's no point, they've told me, doctors just don't care. But then I met Inga-Lisa. We're neighbors. She told me about you, Dr. Rosberg, how kind and considerate you are. That you hate to see people suffer.'

He put his papers down and looked out the window. His nostrils twitched slightly.

'I have to examine you, as I'm sure you understand.'

'Of course.'

'I can't just go writing prescriptions left and right without knowing what I'm doing.'

'No, of course not.'

'I'm an old man. I'll very soon close down my office.'

'Oh,' she mumbled. 'I'm sorry to hear that.'

He snapped his bony fingers.

'Yes. It's sad. But sooner or later everything in life comes to an end.'

He asked her to undress down to her underwear and lie down on the examination table. The paper covering was wrinkled and torn. She saw that it was the last piece of the roll. She was freezing, but she undressed as he had told her and lay down. He had turned his back to her while she got ready, stood fingering the skeleton. Tapped its arms, which rattled.

'Are you ready, Miss Linder?' he asked after a short while. She was lying on her back and felt goose pimples on her stomach.

'Yes.'

'Then I'll be with you.'

She turned her eyes up to the high ceiling. Far above a lamp dangled on its cord. She saw wafting thread and spiderwebs. The doctor was leaning over her. He had a stethoscope, pressed it hard to her chest and listened.

'Mm,' he muttered. He touched her body with his cold, smooth hands, he pressed, squeezed, pinched. He was so close that she saw the coarse hairs growing from both his ears and his nostrils. He smelled vaguely of acetone. She felt a floating dizziness.

'Yes,' he said. 'Being in constant pain is no holiday. It can dull your entire existence.'

She nodded slowly. Her tears began flowing again, down her cheeks and into her hairline. He patted her head. His sad cheeks were sagging.

'Just stay calm, now, please be calm. We'll fix this, don't you worry.'

While she dressed he went back to his desk. She felt suddenly uncertain. What if he had seen through her.

But he hadn't.

'I'll give you a prescription for something called Dextromordiphene. But I must also inform you of the risks.'

'So?'

'The truth is, this medication is really too strong to use as a first treatment. But you have a family history of the same illness, going back for generations as I understand it. And so I plan to give you a radical cure.'

Jannike held her breath.

'However, I must ask you to be as careful and as circumspect as this medication warrants.'

She didn't really understand what he was saying, but she nodded.

There was a watchfulness in his misty eyes as he handed her his prescription.

'Do you have a driver's license, Miss Linder?' he asked.

She shook her head.

'I ask because you are not to drive while taking this medication. Doing so is illegal.'

'I understand.'

He stared at her, seemed to look straight through her.

'And how about alcohol?'

'I'm sorry?'

'Imbibing even a mouthful of an alcoholic beverage when you have taken one of these pills can cause suspension of breathing. Or, in fact, not *can*, but *will*. Do you understand what I'm telling you, Miss Linder? I'm talking about an acute, life-threatening condition. At first the patient will notice nothing. But after around thirty minutes... And by then, it is often too late. It is almost as wily as the mushroom poisons. But faster. Much faster.'

He fell silent and turned his gaze toward the window.

Jannike swallowed.

'I understand. I would never dream of... Well,

I'm honestly not very fond of strong drink, you see.'

His lips curled very slightly.

'Very sensible of you. And one thing further. Do you have any children, Miss Linder?'

'No,' she whispered.

'Nor any you are in close contact with? The children of siblings, or of neighbors, for instance?'

'Why do you ask?' she managed.

'Lock away your medicine. Never let any child come near it. The fact is, it tastes far from unpleasant.'

She took the commuter train to Södertälje. When Arthur left her she had also lost her home. Well, or his, if you had to pick nits. His condo in the Tantolunden area of Stockholm. A two-room apartment with a breathtaking view. He had more or less just thrown her out. Jannike had gone back to her mother and lived with her for a few days, but they had rubbed each other the wrong way. Her mother had managed to get her the second-hand lease on the single-bedroom apartment in Södertälje.

'How old are you now, Jannike? Thirty-six, isn't it? Won't you ever grow old enough to stand on your own two feet?'

Jannike knew that deep down her mother was relieved that she and Arthur had split up. He was a Muslim, and not only that; he was black as well. Her mother had never been comfortable with anything that was different.

She looked out on the snow-covered suburb and

remembered the first time they had met, her mother and Arthur. The sudden aggressiveness. 'Do you want to put a burka on her as well?' Arthur had remained silent; he was a quiet man. He carried most things within, but at the end he had been unable to take any more. He had put his coffee cup down on the table so hard that its little handle had broken. Grandma Betty's cups, the ones with the ivy. She had had to run downstairs after him, all the way out on the yard. Beg and beg.

'Don't be mad, she can be so clumsy sometimes, my mom. She didn't mean it.'

Though deep down she knew that what she said wasn't true. Her mother had meant every word she'd said. And as far as she herself was concerned, she had no other alternative than to choose. Arthur or her mother.

She picked Arthur. He was kind to her and took care of her, comforted her when she was sad. He was good in bed as well. She had never been as satisfied with anyone else as she was with Arthur. And when she lost her job, or at least during the first period after it happened, he was there for her. Bought delicacies on his way home from work. Spoiled her. Got in touch with the union and asked them if Swedish law really allowed someone to sack a conscientious employee without any cause at all.

There were negotiations. And then of course the reasons why she had been laid off crept out. Fucking Gunhild and her lies. She and Arthur on one side of the table, Gunhild on the opposite and between them, at the short end, the trade union representative. Gunhild the hag had taken off her ugly, old-fashioned glasses. Her hands shook, you couldn't miss it. You might wonder who actually had liquor problems.

'Your girlfriend has been intoxicated practically every day during the last several months. We have been patient with her, very patient. But … we simply can't take it any longer.'

Jannike heard Arthur draw a breath.

'I'm sorry, but I don't believe you to be quite full of truth.' He spoke Swedish well for being an immigrant, but sometimes he made mistakes. Right now she wished that he'd be silent and not meddle in this.

'Indeed? And what do her colleagues have to say about it?' The union representative was jiggling a bottle opener. He seemed tired and aloof.

Gunhild, the hag who had been her boss, opened her briefcase and pulled out a rolled paper.

'This,' she said. Slowly, and without taking her eyes off Jannike, she slid the rubber band from the rolled paper. The paper was full of signatures. Ten of them. All of her fellow workers. Even Marja, whom she had liked so much. Who had been her confidante.

The train was entering the commuter station in Södertälje. Jannike stood up and stepped out. She rummaged in her knapsack and thought about the prescription she had had filled at the Scheele pharmacy, two boxes of fifty capsules each. Her chest grew hot and she felt her heart flutter. Everything would be fine. Soon there would be an end to her suffering.

Her apartment was on the ground floor and,

because people could so easily look in her windows, she always had the curtains drawn. Sometimes kids were running about outside, banging her windows or sometimes throwing dirt and mud. Telling them off was pointless. The best you could do was to turn a blind eye to them. Four or five kids were standing outside the door to the building. They didn't move as she approached. One of them stuck his tongue out. She thought of the capsules, of their taste which was 'far from unpleasant.' She pushed herself past the children and opened the door. She felt a little dizzy.

Inside her apartment, she had to lie down at once. Hear heart was thudding, sweat ran from her pores. She closed her eyes, moaning. After a while she got up and walked into the kitchen. Poured a glass of silver rum and emptied it. At last the world steadied around her. But the images returned, the images from the meeting with the trade union.

Sustained abuse of alcohol at her place of work. Nothing had helped. Neither reprimands, warnings or confidential discussions with her hag boss. Arthur grew more and more quiet as the meeting progressed. His silence spread like cold and it scared her. In the evening, when they had returned home, he had to go to work. He was a ticket salesman at the Old Town subway station, one of the hardest places to work on the line. That's where the skinheads hang out, on the helipad nearby. Sometimes they felt like fucking with someone. Despite his skin color his lips were pale when he turned to her.

'I want you out of here when I get back home.'

'What? What do you mean?'

'Pack your things and get out!'

'But Arthur, you can't…'

He raised his hand and for a moment she thought he would strike her.

'You've lied to me. What you've done is worse than if you'd been unfaithful.'

'It's all of them lying!' she cried. 'That fucking hag Gunhild, she's made it all up, you have to believe me. I love you.'

His face was tense and closed.

'And the name lust?' he said in a hard voice.

List, she thought, but it wasn't funny; sometimes she could joke with him and laugh when he said a word wrong. He had used to laugh too, and topple her onto the bed. 'Just you wait and see what I'll give you for daring to tease me.'

He looked like a stranger standing there in his subway uniform. She had thought it made him look sexy but now all of that was gone, only despair remained.

'She's written those names herself, she hates me. I'm a threat to her, I'm so much younger. She can't stand me.'

He took his shoulder bag. His sketch pad stuck up out of it; when things were quiet he liked to draw.

'It's enough now, Jannike.' The exact words the hag cunt had said to her, that last day at work. 'You know what we've talked about before, you and I. And now it's enough.'

Jannike had started laughing, a strange, gurgling sound.

'And just what do you mean by that?'

Red blotches had appeared on Gunhild's wrinkly chest. 'Don't pretend to be stupid.'

'I don't. I don't understand what you're talking about, you're imagining things. Making things up. You're a mythomaniac, that's what you are.'

She was happy about that word; it had come to her at exactly the right moment.

'If you prefer I can get all the others in. Hold a staff meeting. But I suspect it wouldn't be very enjoyable for you.'

She felt strong and indifferent. She cut her laugh off, as with a knife.

'Let me tell you something,' she said, smacking her palms together. 'Nothing at this place has been very enjoyable. Ever! And as I'm sure you know, it's always the boss who sets the mood.'

Then she walked out.

The pharmacy bag was on the kitchen sink. Her dizziness had passed. She took out the two cardboard packs and looked at them. The angry red triangles that meant danger. Dextromordiphene. She pronounced the word aloud to herself, moving her lips very deliberately. Carefully she opened one of the packs and pulled out a blister strip, each cell containing a little pink, oval pill.

To be swallowed whole, she read.

She took down two tumblers. Her mother had given Jannike her old ones, the chipped ones. She had decided to throw them away but when Jannike moved out they came in handy. In one glass she poured hot water. In the other a little silver rum. While she fingered two of the pills out of their protective foil she felt her mouth go a bit dry, but nothing more. One pill in each glass, a spoon to stir. Wait for a little while, two minutes, ten.

Yes!

She shouted the word standing in her kitchen. YES! It worked. The pills were entirely dissolved, both in the water and in the rum. No trace of them left, nothing at all.

But of course, she thought. Of course they have to dissolve, how else could your body absorb them?

That night she slept well for the first time since moving to the apartment. She dreamt of flying, of Arthur and her sailing around above downtown Stockholm, dressed in white shifts. It was delightful.

A couple of days after he had thrown her out she had gone to the Old Town to look for him in the ticket booths. She couldn't find him. She asked a young guy in one of the booths.

'Excuse me, do you happen to know when Arthur's shift is supposed to start?'

He gave her a cold stare.

'Why don't you ask him yourself?'

She fell silent. Lost her words.

'You're holding up the line,' he said. 'Do you want a ticket or not?'

She felt like grabbing hold of his booth and toppling it. Could it be that Arthur had warned his coworkers about her? 'If some skinny broad comes looking for me, don't speak to her.'

Was that what had happened?

For a moment her anger turned towards Arthur, writhing within her, but then it stilled and again

112

centered on her place of work. Gunhild and her former fellow workers. The list of names. Their hands holding pens, quick, flourishing movements. All of it on the sly, to push her away.

She hurt when she thought about it. And even Marja. Her name had been there, at the bottom of the list, as if she had hesitated until the very last moment but then finally had signed after all. Marja Hammendal. Marja, with whom she'd sometimes had gone to the movies. Marja, who had cried herself out at her place when she had quarreled with her husband.

Those times she had felt motherly. Sat there holding Marja's hand, pulling out tissue papers for her.

'It'll pass,' she had comforted her. 'You'll be friends again tonight.'

Marja, who at last had started laughing. 'You're so kind and wise, such a wonderful pal, what would I do without you?'

Even Marja.

She went four times to the Old Town subway station. Arthur was never there. He had been transferred. Systematically she began checking all the inner city stations. It was an unreliable method, since she didn't know his work schedule. But finally she succeeded. At the Rådmansgatan station and at two twenty-five in the afternoon. Coming down the stairs she already saw that it was him. She waited for a moment while the hallway emptied. Then she walked up to him and showed herself.

His beautiful, beautiful face, his mouth. Those

113

eyes that had regarded her with so much love. Not now. No longer.

'Where do you want to go?'

As if he'd never before seen her.

'But Arthur, love... It's me.'

They had all let her down. Deserted her. In a sudden jerk she lifted one of the two glasses and emptied it down the drain. Then the other. Ran the faucet at full.

At that moment the doorbell rang. At first she thought not to open. Then that crazy, wild thought that it might be Arthur.

It wasn't. It was Inga-Lisa. She had on a black turtleneck sweater that made her face seem older. Her eyelids shone, green metal. She looked like a snake or a lizard.

'Hi, honey. So you're back now.'

Jannike stepped aside and let her in.

'I just wanted to hear how it went. Was the nice doctor real good to you?'

'Yes. He gave me the same as you, Dextro-mordiphene.'

'Great. Then you'll soon feel better.'

'Yes.'

'How about coming along to my place for a cup of coffee? I was just going to make some.'

Jannike accepted. Her friend's apartment looked as if a tornado had just passed. The place was full of boxes filled with Christmas decorations, candle-sticks, Santas, ornaments made from straw and crackers. One box was overflowing with different-colored tinsel.

Jannike made place for herself at the very edge

114

of the couch.

'What are you doing?' she asked.

'Just sorting some stuff. You end up with so much junk. I sure won't celebrate another *Fanny and Alexander* Christmas.' She took a painted ceramic Santa with furiously red cheeks. Held it out to Jannike. 'Ever seen an uglier thing?'

Jannike smiled uncertainly.

'Got it from my mother-in-law. A hundred and eighteen years ago. I've kept it all, can you imagine? But now it goes.'

'What? Are you going to throw it away?'

'Well, I've always believed the kids might want it. But no fucking way. I never even hear from them any longer. Can hardly remember if I ever had any.'

Jannike had heard it before. Inga-Lisa had two grown children, a son and a daughter. They didn't seem to put a high priority on keeping in touch with their mother.

Inga-Lisa pressed her lips together.

'The fuck with all that. I won't torture you with any more old nostalgia. I'll carry it all down to the garbage room. And then I'll be rid of it. Unless you happen to want it?'

Afterward she thought it had been part of the plan. As if some divine director sitting up among the clouds had pointed a knobby finger. Do this. Do that. While Inga-Lisa poured the coffee and chain-smoked cigarettes Jannike rummaged about in her boxes. She found several things that could be useful to her. Small things, which wouldn't be hard to carry. And best of all, a Lucia nightgown which fit her perfectly and a Lucia crown to go with it. Inga-Lisa was carried along by her enthusiasm and got her a new battery for the crown. She put it on Jannike's head and twisted one of the electric candles.

'Yes. It works.'

'Can I still take it? Are you really sure?'

'Of course, honey. Everything you don't want is for the garbage bin.'

She didn't ask what Jannike wanted the Lucia outfit for. She was great in that way, a true friend and comrade. As opposed to Marja and the others.

Early on Saint Lucia's Day she fixed the mulled wine. She warmed it in a pot she had borrowed from Inga-Lisa and poured it into a large thermos jug. She had borrowed that as well. It looked like one of the thermos jugs at work. Once she had jokingly painted eyes on it, making it look like a mad penguin. Of course Gunhild had failed to appreciate the humor. 'We're having a board meeting, are you out of your mind?' As if the board members didn't need something to laugh about.

Over the weekend she had washed the Lucia gown and ironed it and the wide, red sash that went with it. The one said to symbolize the blood of the saint. She folded it neatly and put it in a paper shopping bag. In another she put her ten small Christmas presents. They were things Inga-Lisa had let her take from her boxes, nothing remarkable, but still. Santas, candlesticks, stars made from straw. She had taken great care and the presents had turned out beautifully, with ruffled strings and labels where she'd written the names of her ex-colleagues and the words *Merry Christmas* in her very best hand.

She put the thermos with the mulled wine upright into her knapsack and braced it with towels so it wouldn't fall over and start leaking.

Later, as she sat on the commuter train, it felt as if she was now one of them, one of all those going in to the city to work. Tired, pale faces, the aisles full of slush. The outside temperature this Lucia's Day morning was just around the freezing point and wet snow was falling. She took one of the free dailies and since she got on at the first station she got a seat. She leafed through the paper disinterestedly while some school teens with glitter in their hair were messing about, having celebrated all night. She smiled at them. As opposed to them, she was absolutely sober.

Thank heaven, the lock code remained the same. She took the elevator to the top floor of the building and continued up the half stair to the attic door. Up here, behind the elevator's control cubicle, she changed her clothes. She had been shivering from the cold while she walked from the train station. Now she no longer felt cold. She put her garments in one of the paper bags and pushed it close to the wall. Then she tied the red ribbon around her waist and put the crown of lights on her newly washed hair. In the glass pane of the elevator well she could see her own reflection. She twisted one of the candles and the crown lit up. So far everything had gone according to plan. She cleared her throat and sang softly.

Then in our darkened house,
Walking with gleaming lights...
After that, she glided slowly downstairs.

There was a wreath of boxwood on the door to her former place of employment. The smell of cat pee was persistent. It had been the same way all the previous years. That they never learned, that they didn't get lingonberry wreaths instead. They didn't smell at all.

It was a quarter to nine in the morning. Jannike steadied her grip on the thermos bottle and rung the bell.

Marja opened. Sudden worry flashed across her face.

'Who ... oh! It's you!'

'Hush!' Jannike put a finger across her mouth. 'I'll leave in a few minutes, I just wanted to...'

She held out her paper bag with the small presents.

'I wanted to ask all of you to forgive me,' she mumbled and managed to make her voice sound just as thick and full of regret as she had planned. 'I brought some mulled wine as well. Please, Marja, help me out.'

Marja's bad conscience. It radiated from her. It came to her help. It was Marja who went out to the others and convinced them all to come to the conference room. All of them were there, all ten of them; it hardly happened every day, but on just this day it did, everything went her way. It was also Marja who went to the canteen to get ten cups.

Jannike stood straight and calm. She paused for a moment on the threshold of the conference room, watched all of them sitting there, her former

118

coworkers. Gunhild looking stiff and wary, Sylvia in a new hairdo. Evy, fatter than before, her breathing a dull rattle. Someone had lit the tea lights and the Advent candles. The room smelled of dust and old papers.

Jannike had intended to give a short speech, but it didn't work out that way. And perhaps that was just as well. Perhaps it was more striking this way. She passed from chair to chair pouring her mulled wine, without trembling or spilling a drop.

'Cheers, and Merry Christmas,' she said and saw them lift their cups and drain them. They smacked their lips and smiled cautiously at her.

'And please forgive me for all the things I've done.'

Marja said:

'But how about you, dear, aren't you going to have some mulled wine yourself?'

She looked Marja straight in the eye.

'No, you see, I've quit,' she said softly.

Then she brought out her gifts, passed them out one by one.

'I wish you a wonderful Christmas,' she said, leaving the office with the empty thermos cradled in her arms.

PAUL'S LAST SUMMER

EVA GABRIELSSON

Perhaps the upward slope to the churchyard was a little too steep after all. But Paul Bergstrom stubbornly set his jaw and continued walking, firmly if slowly and a bit unsteadily, supported by his cane. In honor of the day he wore his best tweed jacket and a trench coat bought in the 1970s, which he used in the summer.

'What your head lacks your legs better make up for, as they said when I was young. But now both my legs and my memory are going. Being eighty isn't easy. The down slope of life but still you have to go uphill, nothing fair about it,' he grumbled to himself.

Finally he was on the graveled path winding among the graves, stepping carefully, his bouquet in a firm grip. 'Now where is Emma's grave,' he mumbled, trying to find the red granite stone somewhere among the linden trees. In the greenery, nothing seemed familiar. He stopped to get his wind and get a better look. The white stone church blinded him. 'I'd really appreciate a tiny bit of revelation right now,' he said hopefully.

Sitting in the cool church vestry, Louise Alm was considering her Sunday sermon. She lit a candle, wound her long hair around her index finger,

121

chewed her pencil, and finally began noting down random thoughts.

Her congregation was a mixture of young and old. Lately, they had begun worrying markedly more about the future. More of them had asked to see both her and the lay worker. It was a time of life crises for persons of all ages, and unfairly enough many of them seemed to land simultaneously on the same weary and insignificant person, as she saw herself. Louise felt insufficient. She was only forty, with much less life experience than many of the older members of her congregation. While the younger lived lives she was hardly able to comprehend, despite her two children. She was constantly uncertain about her own role. How was she supposed to be a shepherd to this flock of wildly careening individuals? Perhaps what she had felt to be her life's calling was hopelessly out of date in this era of egotism.

The candle suddenly fluttered as the doorway was blocked by an elderly man, clearly lost and with a bouquet of flowers in his hand. There were tears in his eyes.

'Can I help you in some way?' Louise asked, putting her pencil down.

He really looked desperate.

'Could you come?' he said. He held out a trembling hand, dropping his flowers.

'I'm sorry. My name is Paul Bergström.'

'You are very welcome. I'm Louise Alm and I'm the vicar. We have met before, though perhaps you don't remember it right now.' She stood, went up to him and shook his hand. Then she picked up his flowers.

Together they walked out in the churchyard and up to a small red granite marker with room for more names than the three already cut into it. Next to the red stone stood a smaller black one. They looked at them silently for a long while. Louise waited, uncomprehending, next to Paul. His breathing was rapid.

'I visit more graves than people nowadays,' Paul said when at last he had regained some of his composure. 'But even so I don't think anyone should have to visit his own grave while still alive.'

'I'm sorry, I don't understand,' Louise said.

'That black one,' Paul said, pointing. 'It has my name on it, though no dates.'

'That can't be. How strange. Maybe it's been delivered here by mistake,' Louise tried.

'Oh, no. I haven't even ordered it,' Paul said.

Squaring his shoulders, he searchingly tapped his cane on the stone, as if to see if it was real. It remained, immobile, dark and frightening.

'And I'm not even supposed to rest here once the time comes,' he went on. 'I'm to be buried with Adele, my wife. And Emma is here, as she should be, with her husband and their daughter.'

'But then why on earth is your stone here?' Louise said.

'I have no idea,' Paul said, and started to cry again. 'It frightened me.'

'Please calm down, Paul. I'm sure there must be some reasonable explanation,' Louise said. 'Let me walk you home. Somehow I'll get to the bottom of this.'

'Thank you,' Paul said, wiping his nose. 'That's very kind of you. Could you hand me Emma's flowers? After all, it's for her sake I went here.'

Louise stopped to admire Paul's wooden house and its garden, full of apple trees.

'I built it myself, back in the nineteen fifties,' Paul said. 'Had to do it all on weekends and holidays, of course. Then I married Adele. But she died ten years ago.'

'I remember you from Emma's funeral,' Louise said. 'That's when we met. And I knew she wasn't your wife.'

'No, she never was. But we lived together for five years. Both her husband and her daughter died in a car accident eight years ago. Only her granddaughters are left now. Nice girls. You can see them in the photos on my living room bureau.'

On the kitchen table was a pile of junk mail, a few magazines and a smaller pile of letters, some of them left unopened for more than a month, to judge from the postmarks. On the windowsill, a forlorn geranium wilted in abandonment. If anyone had had green thumbs, it must have been Emma. Louise pushed the piles of paper aside to make room for the coffee and cinnamon buns Paul began to set out. In the middle of it all the doorbell rang. Paul went off to the door and returned with more mail and a large parcel.

'That was Johan, the mailman. He usually checks to see if I'm in, so I won't have to walk out to the mailbox if I should get heavy or unwieldy things. It's hard to carry things nowadays, when

I need my stick and often get a bit dizzy.'

'What service,' Louise said, while Paul sorted the new mail into the piles for junk, advertisements of interest, and letters. He put the parcel in a pile of its own. Most of his mail seemed to be bills.

While they had coffee, Paul praised his kind mailman. 'Though one thing was a bit strange,' he said. 'Johan wondered about my lodger. But I've been alone here since Emma died.'

'Yes, time must seem to run slow nowadays,' Louise said. 'How are you doing?'

'Well, when I don't speak to Emma's photo, I mostly talk to the birds in my garden. It does get a bit monotonous. Adele and I never had any children, you know. But of course I see my brother's children. And while Emma was still alive, her girls looked in on us fairly often.'

'Maybe your mailman was suggesting that you should get a lodger, not saying that you already had one,' Louise said.

'Oh, no. He said that someone is having his mail forwarded from my address.'

'He couldn't be talking about Emma's mail?' Louise said.

'No. He didn't mean her. I asked him about that. But he couldn't remember the name,' Paul said. 'But I suppose they have too much going on at the post office nowadays to remember every small thing.'

Louise suspected that Paul must have misunderstood what the mailman had said. Or misheard. Or simply was getting a bit senile. Which might explain the tombstone as well. But she felt that those things should wait until he seemed ready to talk about them. Meanwhile, they could always deal with his mail.

'Maybe we ought to open your letters?' she said, taking a bun.

'Yes, I suppose so,' Paul said. 'I simply haven't been able to do a lot of things since Emma passed. To think it's already been three months. Time flies, it really does.'

There were a few bills that ought to have been paid weeks ago, solicitations from various charities, a few letters of condolence from Emma's relatives and a letter addressed to someone named Carl-Edvard Palm.

'Well, isn't that what I said,' Paul said in a firm voice, putting the letter aside. 'They have too much to do at the post office nowadays. No question about it. Carl-Edvard doesn't live here, now does he?'

'I seem to remember his name. Didn't he go to Emma's funeral as well?' Louise asked.

'Oh, yes, Emma was his mother-in-law. He used to be married to Emma's daughter, the one who died in a car accident. He lives in the house they had at the other end of town, but with his new wife. So the post office really has messed up,' Paul said.

'Well, at least that's one mystery solved,' Louise said.

Fortified by two cinnamon buns and very strong coffee with cream, Paul was clearly in better shape. He walked into his bedroom and returned with a binder full of receipts and account state-

126

ments from his bank. To Louise's surprise, he said thoughtfully:

'Well, as you can see, there was no unopened bill for any tombstone. But I thought perhaps you might help me look through this binder as well, just to make sure that I haven't mixed anything up. Could you spare the time?'

'Of course,' Louise said, impressed, and dismissed the idea that Paul might be senile. She began leafing through years of orderly bills and receipts.

After half an hour they were in complete agreement. There was no invoice for a tombstone, and the bank statements for the last seven months were in complete accordance with the bills accounted for in the binder. Nor were there any unexplained bank drafts or payments that could account for the 10,000 or so kronor such a stone would have cost.

'Well, that didn't make us any the wiser,' Paul said.

'It really is very strange,' Louise agreed.

'The stone wasn't there two weeks ago,' Paul said. 'So it must have been ordered fairly recently. But not by me, as I've said. And I certainly haven't paid for it either.'

'No, I'm sure you haven't. I just don't quite know how to proceed with this,' Louise said, 'but if you want me to, I can easily find out which companies deliver tombstones to my church. Do you want me to give it a try?'

'God bless you,' Paul said.

It was the first time Louise saw him smile.

Not until she got home that day did it strike her that the letter to Carl-Edvard Palm had been printed with the unmistakable logotype of the tax authority. And the tax authority, if anyone, should have the correct address of whomever they wanted to communicate with. After all, they were responsible for the national registration of citizens – if they had a wrong address for someone, that person might even get out of paying taxes. And the government certainly didn't allow that to happen. She suspected there was at least one more phone call for her to make.

Two days later, Louise returned to Paul. She stopped at his mailbox to pick up his mail before ringing his doorbell. Today it seemed his friendly mailman had been too rushed to bring Paul's mail to his door. Paul was in, waiting for her.

'Hello again,' she said, 'and here you are. Today's crop, but mostly advertising.'

'Thank you,' Paul said. 'Come on in. I hope you have something to tell me.'

Louise did. According to the tax authorities, Carl-Edvard Palm really was registered as a resident at Paul's address. The change had been made two months ago, and it was Carl-Edvard Palm himself who had requested it. At the same time, according to the mailman, whom Louise also had talked to, he had put in a request to the post office that all his mail should be forwarded from Paul's address to the house where he lived with his wife.

'Carl-Edvard never told me anything about this,' Paul said.

'I can't understand it either,' Louise said. 'But the mailman has done nothing wrong, except delivering that letter from the tax people here instead of sending it on to Carl-Edvard's house.'

'It's very strange. I suppose I ought to call him about it,' Paul said.

'Wait a bit,' Louise said. 'I have more to tell you.'

Paul suddenly looked frightened, and his eyes shifted warily. Louise suspected that the thought of the tombstone was haunting him.

'I'll fix some coffee,' she said. 'You just sit back and relax.'

But Paul refused to be distracted. He sat rigidly and didn't move until Louise brought the coffee. Then he fetched a small bottle of schnapps from the corner cupboard, put a lump of sugar in his cup, added some schnapps and topped it with coffee.

'Today I need something stronger,' he said. 'It's all right now. Please go on.' He lifted his cup and drank. 'I'm sorry, I really am a bad host. Would you like some as well?'

'No thanks,' Louise said. 'I'm fine with just coffee.' Though truth to tell, she, too, would have preferred something stronger. For what she knew filled her with uneasiness. She began talking. Since she was the vicar, the stonecutters had been very forthcoming.

'The fifth stonecutter I talked to delivered the stone with your name on it in early June. They remembered it well, since they'd thought it very peculiar not to put any dates on it.'

'So I was right when I said I never ordered it,

even if I've been a bit muddled,' Paul said.

'Yes, you were right. It was ordered and paid for by a small company right here in town,' Louise said, trying hard to sound calm.

'But what do I have to do with them?'

'Nothing at all, I gather,' Louise said.

The stonecutters had sent her copies of all the paperwork. Everything seemed perfectly all right. Yet it was all wrong. She wondered how to tell Paul what she had found out.

'Actually,' she said, 'I think you should get someone to help you with this.'

'Well, I suppose I could always ask one of my nephews,' Paul said.

'Great. This sort of thing can be very demanding.'

'Yes. But I'd really appreciate getting this thing fixed,' Paul said.

While he went out in the hallway to make his phone call on the landline telephone he kept in his old-fashioned way on a low teak bureau, Louise got out an envelope where she had put the photocopies of the invoice and the payment receipt she had received from the stonecutter, as well as the copy the tax authorities had given her of Carl-Edvard Palm's change of address. She quickly wrote a short explanatory note, adding her greetings and her phone numbers. The company that had ordered the tombstone was a real estate agent, and she had found out who owned it. But she preferred not to tell Paul. It was a matter for his nephews to take care of, not something to upset an already upset old man with.

'If you just give me his name and address, I can mail this to him,' Louise said when Paul returned.

'Please. My nephew Gunnar will take care of it for me. He's always willing to help out when I need it,' Paul said.

A few days later, Gunnar Bergström phoned Louise and asked her what really was going on. His uncle Paul hadn't been able to explain it very well.

'I'm afraid I probably can't explain it either,' Louise said.

'Well, anyway, thanks for sending me those copies,' Gunnar said. 'It seemed pretty nasty. We've asked the stonecutters to remove the black stone. They'll pick it up today, and if there's any more trouble, they will have it out with Carl-Edvard Palm.'

'Good. Nobody will miss it,' Louise said. 'Does Paul know that it was Palm who had it set up?'

'No, I just told him there had been some mistake,' Gunnar said. 'And I've called the tax people and told them that Palm doesn't live in Paul's house, or at his address. Now it's their job to sort it out. I called Palm as well, but I couldn't get him to say anything sensible. He gave me some kind of tribute to Emma and Paul and their great love. When I asked him to explain in what way the tombstone and his address change were connected to the great affection for Paul he professed, he got abusive. But I don't want to talk about him. Mostly I wanted to thank you for caring about my uncle.'

'It was no trouble at all. He is a good man. Let's keep in touch,' Louise said.

Less than a month later, Louise had to prepare a funeral. In her world, life was in constant turmoil, beginning and ending without notice. Paul had passed away, and his nephews had asked her personally to officiate. When Gunnar Bergström called, she was in her vestry. He was cleaning out Paul's house.

'I know that my uncle came to care for you. If it feels right, you are very welcome to come by and pick out something to remember him by,' Gunnar said.

'I'll be happy to. And we could talk about the ceremony without being disturbed,' Louise said.

A little later, she sat with Gunnar in the by now familiar kitchen. Habit had made her check the mailbox on her way in, but this time it had been empty. On the other hand, the kitchen table was even more full of papers than usual, serving as storage for all the insurance policies, bills, subscriptions and private documents Gunnar had found in drawers and cupboards.

'It feels strange and a little solemn to be here without Uncle Paul,' Gunnar said. 'So today it seems right to use his best china, the set he only used on special occasions. He kept it in that showcase cupboard. Do you think you could get cups?'

'Of course,' Louise said, pulling up a chair to stand on. 'It's a little rickety,' she added, balancing two cups and saucers in one hand and a carefully sealed envelope in the other. 'This was wedged in

132

next to the plates. I think you'd better take care of it. It says *Deed of gift* on the envelope.'

'In that case I'm pretty sure I know what it is,' Gunnar said. 'Just put it with the other papers.'

When they had finally sat down, begun sipping their coffee from the flowery, golden-handled cups and picking out the hymns to be sung at the funeral, someone opened the door to the house. Carl-Edvard Palm stepped in, camera in hand. He walked straight to the kitchen but stopped at the threshold.

'How do you do,' he said, obviously surprised. 'So you are here?'

'How do you do yourself,' Gunnar said. 'Yes, I'm here with the vicar to arrange some practical things after my uncle passed away.'

'Hello. I'm Louise Alm,' Louise said, holding out her hand.

'A pleasure,' Carl-Edvard said, introducing himself. 'Well. Yes, I suppose there is a lot of paperwork at times like these. Too bad about your uncle, of course. My sympathies.'

He remained irresolutely in the doorway for a moment. Obviously the others intended to stay put for quite a while, he realized. Oh well, he could always return when they had left. Now he just had to make sure not to make a wrong step. But, of course, he had brought his camera.

'Right. Well, I'll just go about my business, I suppose,' Carl-Edvard Palm said, and disappeared into the living room.

Louise and Gunnar exchanged a bewildered look.

Soon they could hear the sounds of furniture being dragged around, interrupted by groaning and moaning.

'He's a real estate agent and seems to be taking pictures of the house,' Gunnar said when they saw flashes of light reflected from the living room. 'Maybe he intends to put it up for sale.'

'I think it's a pity that none of you want to stay in this nice house.'

'Oh, but my brother will move in as soon as the estate is divided up. He took care of keeping it up ever since Uncle Paul grew too old to do it himself,' Gunnar said. 'I really don't know what he is doing here.'

Louise went along with him into the living room. Palm was busy trying to find angles where the photos would show the antique charm of the house.

'Would you mind telling me what you are doing?' Gunnar asked.

'Oh. Yes. Well, I assumed that the house will be put up for sale,' Palm said. 'And I thought it best to be prepared. I mean, so you can get going at the right time of year, when buyers are eager to find something quickly. Next month prices usually fall, when everyone is away on vacation.'

'Right. But our meeting with the lawyer about the inheritance is set for the week after next, so nothing has been decided yet,' Gunnar said.

'Oh. Well, I was only trying to help you out. After all, we're almost family. Or were.'

'I think you'd better leave now,' Gunnar said.

'Well, I can always come back. By the way, who is handling the distribution of Paul's estate? Would that be you, Gunnar?'

'No. It's a lawyer my uncle picked himself,' Gunnar said.

'Indeed. May I ask you which one?'

Gunnar told him, and asked him again to leave. Palm left, obviously disgruntled. Gunnar and Louise returned to the kitchen.

'Palm has always been high-handed rather than helpful,' Gunnar said. 'But taking that kind of liberty is more than I'd expected even from him.' He opened the window, and the slight breeze blew the lace curtains and the scent of apple blossoms into the room. 'Obviously he has gotten hold of Emma's keys to this place,' Gunnar said after a moment. 'I ought to get them back from him. Though God knows how many copies there may be.'

'I could ask Him,' Louise said. 'But I don't think He'll tell me.'

Gunnar laughed.

Louise left, feeling ill at ease despite the little creamer she had picked as a memento. The one she and Paul had used so often during their many talks at the kitchen table.

Gunnar stayed on to clean up and sort through his uncle's papers. Then he phoned a locksmith and took all the relevant documents along to the lawyer.

From his office, a week after Paul Bergström's funeral, Carl-Edvard Palm cheerfully phoned the lawyer who was handling the estate.

'Carl-Edvard Palm speaking. This concerns the estate of Paul Bergström. His nephew Gunnar

135

has told me that you will hold a meeting to shift the inheritance in a few days.'

'Yes, that's correct,' the lawyer told him. 'It's set for next Tuesday.'

'Yes. But the thing is, I don't seem to have received a notice to attend,' Palm went on.

'No, I'm sure that is also correct,' the lawyer said in a neutral voice. 'Since you aren't entitled to any share, you aren't notified. But we have notified your two daughters.'

'What? What! There must be some mistake,' Palm exclaimed. 'Are you sure your papers are in order? Have you looked through his house? Really looked carefully?'

'Certainly,' the lawyer said. 'Everything is being done according to Mr. Bergström's will.'

'Oh, no, I'm not buying that, I know there's something fishy going on,' Palm told him angrily. 'But you'll be hearing from me, be sure of that!'

'Thanks for calling,' the lawyer said. But Palm had already hung up.

'The shit has hit the fan,' he said aloud. 'I'd better check up on it.'

But at the front door of Paul's house, he discovered that his key no longer fit the lock.

The following week, Paul's two nephews and Emma's two granddaughters came to the lawyer's office to attend the shifting of the estate. After the meeting, Gunnar phoned Louise.

'I just wanted to tell you that I and my brother get the house, and that the girls get fifty thousand crowns each.'

'Well, I suppose that was expected. So I hope

everyone is satisfied,' Louise said.

'Not quite everyone,' Gunnar said. 'There is a drama behind it. That envelope you happened to find turned out to contain another will none of us had ever heard about. In that one, our uncle left his house to Carl-Edvard Palm, and a hundred thousand to Palm's daughters. It seemed perfectly legal and was correctly witnessed. It was dated the week after Emma died.'

'I understood that Paul was in a very bad way back then,' Louise said. 'He could hardly have been in a state to make any important decisions. Did he really understand what he was signing, that he was disinheriting both you and your brother?'

'No, not likely. But he often said that he wanted to give the girls some money. Though only money.'

'I'm sure he did,' Louise said. 'But that thing about the house sounds suspicious.'

'So it was. My brother and I went with Uncle Paul to show him that the black tombstone was really gone,' Gunnar said. 'And while we were talking he remembered that Palm had turned up with some papers to sign concerning gifts to Emma's granddaughters. We searched, but couldn't find anything. That made Uncle worried that his deed had been lost, so in the end I went with him to the bank where he wrote a new will and put it in his safe-deposit box. He never showed me what he wrote, and only his lawyer was authorized to open that box. I never saw his will until today, and I didn't know about that other one until you found it, even if I suspected something. But the fact is that Palm's attempt to swindle my uncle failed only by pure chance. Imagine that. Pure chance.'

Gunnar and Louise fell silent. Neither of them felt like saying anything more.

Later that day, Louise stopped for a moment on the church stairs. In the dusk she saw that someone had put fresh roses on Paul's grave. It warmed her heart to know that others also remembered him. There was something deeply hopeful in all these small, visible proofs of concern for others. Louise walked down to the grave. There was a small, unsigned card tied to the bouquet. She read it.

From those who thought of Paul, unlike his greedy relatives who sabotaged his last will.

Louise read the words over and over again. Unbelievable. Did that Realtor imagine that he could abuse the graveyard as his private battlefield? It could hardly be anyone else. She had had enough. She tore the card into pieces, walked away and stopped by the churchyard gates with her hand full of shredded paper. Her heart was pounding in anger. She threw the pieces of paper into the wastebasket at the bus stop before getting on the bus to go home. She was still upset when she reached her house and stood for a while outside her door.

This was far from over, she realized.

A sudden impulse made her go back to the church. She sifted through the wastebasket, retrieving the torn card. When she sat down in her vestry she felt lost. Why had she come back here?

She lit a candle to calm herself. The pieces of paper were spread on the table before her, almost illegible now after being smeared by ice-cream wrappers and the damp remains of some unidentified fruit. She looked at them for a long time. The dirt on them matched the dirty thought behind them.

She thought about the deadly sins, of all the holy scriptures that had warned generation upon generation of what unbridled passion could do to society and to men. That warning was always timely.

She nodded to herself. The flame fluttered in the draft from her hand when she took her pen to start writing her next sermon. She would talk about greed.

Carl-Edvard Palm was sitting on his porch, red both from sunburn and fury. His new wife was equally furious but less red. She used sun lotion. The only ones chirping with joy today had been his daughters.

'Do you know what the girls told me when we had lunch? The old bastard wrote another will just a couple of weeks after I had gone to all the trouble to help him out,' he had told his wife.

'But how could he do something like that?' his wife said incredulously.

'That's what you get for trying to fix things for a senile old childless fart,' he said.

'And you worked so hard,' she said in an injured tone.

'I stood all the costs, I did all the work, and

what did it get me?' Palm said. 'Not a damned thing, that's what.'

'It's really unfair,' his wife said.

'I won't even get the fee for selling the house. It seems one of them actually means to live in it. Can you imagine? It's all come to nothing,' he said bitterly.

But perhaps something could be salvaged, after all. He drove to his office, made a photocopy of the stonecutter's bill and payment receipt for the black tombstone and wrote out a bill. To the sum and his rate for helping out, he added the highest-allowed market interest. It came to quite a decent amount. On his way home, he mailed the bill to the estate of Paul Bergström.

THE RING

ANNA JANSSON

When he saw the beer can tab gleam under the thin ice covering the pool of water he understood that it was the Lord of the Rings. In the magical brightness of the streetlight the secret was revealed to him as it had been when Elrond ruled Rivendell and Gandalf was still called the Grey. Deep within his boy's heart he had anticipated that something like this would happen.

'Today, Tuesday, December the twelfth, Fredrik Bengtsson is chosen to be the Ring-bearer,' he says out loud to himself. At the very edge of his consciousness he can hear the school bell giving its second call to class. The school yard is empty. The ring resting in its coffin of ice looks deviously inconspicuous, but nevertheless it will soon change the world.

Next to the bicycle stand there is a sharp stick. Fredrik is still in pain from the previous recess, when Torsten attacked his back with it and yelled 'piss your pants' so the girls in his class could hear it. The wooden sword is the tool he needs. Liberator of the Ring. With a single stroke, the invaluable power is his. Fredrik takes the Ring in his hand and puts it on his finger in the name of Gandalf and the elves and the surly dwarves. It doesn't feel special, not to start with. But then, when he looks at Torsten's new, cool bike in the stand, with a hand brake, twenty gears and double shock absorbers, something happens within him. His teeth grow sharper and his eyes shrink to small, glowing fires. Rough, black hair slithers out of his hands and his nails grow into claws. The Ring-bearer does something Fredrik Bengtsson in class 1A would never dare. He steals a bike.

Downhill the bike is going much too quickly. The street is all ice. Streetlights pass by dangerously fast. Fredrik tries to brake by pedaling backwards, then in a panic tightens the hand brake and crashes. Thanks to his gloves he doesn't skin his hands on the asphalt, but he gets a tear on his knee. The bike's fender is dented and its enamel is scratched. If he hadn't worn the Ring he would surely have cried from fear and pain, but not now.

The Ring-bearer looks forward. The forest road calls to him. There is a whisper in the frosted crowns of the trees. A whisper of legends. He mounts his steel steed and enters the labyrinth of the black tree trunks. By the frozen flow of the creek is a village of small, gray cottages covered by turf roofs. At the far end, just where the pasture begins, there is a grassy hillock with a small door of decaying wood. That's how hobbit houses look. Now he has to be watchful. Fredrik crouches down behind the compost bin and pulls the bike down with him. There are black riders. You have to be careful. Just as Fredrik pulls off the Ring and puts it in his pocket he sees the door in the grassy hill open and a dark figure emerges and disappears towards the forest. He glimpses a face.

Good or evil? Enemy or friend? He waits for an eternity of shivering seconds. The morning sun quietly filters down through the branches and eats the shadows. Supported by the bike he sneaks closer to look into the earth cellar. The door is slightly ajar. There is no trace of the roundness and friendliness characterizing hobbit homes. The walls are rough and the cold sticks to his body. Fredrik gropes farther in and his foot hits something on the floor. Something looking like a sack of potatoes, yet doesn't quite. He fumbles in his pocket for the cigarette lighter he took from his big brother's jacket earlier in the morning. With the slim flame in his hand he bends down, looking through the smoke of his breath straight into a pale, yellow face. Two eyes stare glassily at him. A mouth gapes with a toothless upper jaw. The dentures have fallen to expose much too pink gums. He stands mesmerized for a few immobile seconds, then runs towards the light. Runs through the forest while his thoughts scatter like frightened birds.

'You're late again, Fredrik Bengtsson.' His teacher has that peremptory wrinkle between her eyebrows. Everyone in class turns towards the door. Accusing eyes follow him to his desk.

'I've been to the boys' room.'

'Piss your pants,' Torsten hisses from his corner by the bookcase.

Detective Inspector Maria Wern watches as the slender woman's body is encased in a black plastic bag. The technician closes the zipper and rises

143

clumsily, one hand to his back. Nobody has spoken in a long while. The silence of the forest makes it feel like a memorial grove. A place where mortality is natural, and yet isn't. The eye is offended by the brownish-red stain on the cement and by the child's bike dropped outside the door of the earth cellar.

'A woman wants to speak to you, Wern.'

Police officer Ek points to a white Saab. The car has driven along the gravel road straight up to the cordoned-off area.

'Her name is Sara Skoglund. She says she spoke to you on the phone earlier today.'

Maria takes a deep breath, tries to chase the images away and calm herself before entering the car with the upset old lady.

'Ellen Borg,' Sara says, pointing to the cottage of the deceased, 'and I live in the same apartment house. We always play bridge on Mondays. Last night she asked me if I could give her a ride to her cottage. She's gone here for the last few months. Every Monday after bridge. We agreed that I'd pick her up today, at two in the afternoon, but I was a little delayed. Ellen doesn't have a phone out here, so I couldn't call her.'

'At what time would you say you got here?' Maria asked, taking out her notepad.

'Almost three, I think. The door was unlocked, so I went in. I called ... but she didn't answer. Mostly she puts her key under the flowerpot on the stairs when she walks down to the village. But this time it was still in the lock. Then I saw that bike someone had left outside her potato cellar. I wondered about it and walked over

144

there. And then...'

The woman's face crumples in emotion. Maria gives her time to recuperate before continuing her interrogation.

Night falls. Fredrik lies in bed, listening to the slowly ebbing sounds. The TV is turned off, but for a while yet he can hear the CD player in his older brother Leo's room. A hoarse voice penetrates the walls. The electric guitar claws at the wallpaper, scratchy, full of sadness, and beautiful. Leo is in love. Therefore he listens to uncompromisingly heavy bass rock ballads. Love hurts, he says, throwing himself down on his bed to stare at the ceiling, and Fredrik tries to understand what is hurting him so. Of course it would have been best if they could have been in love together, just as they both had chicken pox at the same time. He had felt snug listening to Leo reading *The Lord of the Rings*. Fredrik's room feels very lonely, especially when it's dark and Mom isn't at home. But Leo wants to be left alone in his agony. He showed that very clearly when he threw an empty Coke can at his baby brother's head just a short while ago. An Advent star lights up his window. It's at least a small comfort when so much is scary, and soon they'll celebrate Saint Lucia's Day in school. Fredrik has been given a verse he is supposed to know by heart. He practices until his head is spinning. In the whirlpool of sleep he lets go of reality. There are dachshunds under his bed, black slimy spirits of dead dachshunds. If Fredrik puts his legs over the edge of his bed they'll bite him and he'll be infected by death. That's why he's

145

running through the forest without resting. They're snapping at his pant legs. He kicks out to get loose. Runs out into the cold, black water of the creek and jumps downstream on the ice floes. That's when he sees the face under the ice. Gray hair floating like a halo of dust and eyes staring at him from that yellow face, accusing and sly. Fredrik screams but the sound is stuck in his lungs, frozen. On the opposite bank, where his salvation is, he sees Torsten with his broken bike. His fear is greater than he can bear. Fredrik stops struggling, sinks, and is carried towards the dam by the icy creek water. He is so horribly cold that he wakes up. Then it all feels very lonely and wet.

'Leo! Wake up, Leo!' Fredrik shakes his older brother's shoulder.

'What is it?'

'The dachshunds have peed in my bed and I'm cold.'

Maria Wern sits slumped in front of her office window, looking out at the falling snow without seeing it, lost in thought. What did Ellen Borg do in her cottage on Monday nights? The little house lacked every modern convenience. To get a cup of coffee you first had to break the ice, carry water and set a fire in the woodstove. The bedding was raw and damp and the floor cold as ice. Staying there in the summer might be charming, but in the middle of winter? Her musings are interrupted by Ek's voice on the intercom.

'You have a visitor.'

A tall, thin man in a black overcoat tells her his name is Ludvig Borg. His thinning hair is parted

146

in the middle and his eyes, peering behind wire-frame glasses, are very dark blue. Last night, Arvidsson and Ek had performed the difficult task of telling him that his mother was dead. Surprisingly, they had found Borg in his mother's apartment. He was passing through and had walked in using his own key.

Maria asks him to sit down and gets two cups of coffee. Ludvig declines milk and sugar. He wraps his thin hands around the cup for warmth. Despite his woolen coat he seems to be cold.

'She really was murdered?' is the first thing he says when at last he speaks.

'Yes. There is no doubt about it. Someone hit her from behind with a blunt object.'

'A burglar?'

'Perhaps. Do you know of anything in her cabin that might attract a thief?'

'I can't believe there was anything. My mother wasn't well off. She had her pension. It doesn't come to very much when you've worked your whole life in a post office. She could hardly manage when they doubled the real-estate tax on her cottage a couple of years ago. She absolutely refused to sell the cottage. For a while she even considered giving up her apartment to live there full time instead. I don't know how she managed to keep both.'

'Yes, I remember. I read in the papers about the new estate evaluations. It seemed ill advised. Many elderly people had to sell. Do you know if there are any year-round residents left in the village, or are the houses only used in the summer nowadays?'

147

'Only well-to-do people can afford those houses now. The last resident to move out was the old grocer's wife. I don't think she sold her house, but now that she's living in an old people's home she rents it. I believe some nurse is living there in the summer. In the winter, there is nobody at all.'

'I'll kill whoever broke my bike,' Torsten says slowly and looks at the Lucia celebration boy attendees.

They're standing in the schoolyard in their long white shirts, holding their star-spangled paper cone hats in their hands to save them from being wafted off by the wind. Torsten stares them in the eye, one after the other, his own eyes half lidded, sucking his lower lip in to make a threatening face. Fredrik feels his stomach heaving, but tries not to listen. He wasn't able to eat any breakfast, just drank some water. There is a beast living in his stomach, and it refuses to eat human food.

'Whoever took my bike will get a hell of a beating from my dad. He won't be able to walk for a fortnight. They took my fingerprints!' Torsten says and holds out his thumb. 'There's no escape!'

Here is their teacher with the school's Lucia, Ida, and her maids. It's time. The girls flutter in their long white robes. The tinsel coiled in their hair and tied around their waists gleams in the moonlight. With her wavy long hair Ida looks like an elven queen. Her hair must be very soft. Fredrik would like to touch that long, blonde hair, but he doesn't dare. In her crown of lingonberry sprigs, candles burn. Their teacher will sit at the front with a bucket of water. Last year the Lucia set fire to a curtain.

The assembly hall is full of parents and children. But Fredrik's mom can't come. She works nights again. Fredrik raises the stick with its paper star and sings though there is a big, nervous lump in his throat. Then there is silence. This is when he is supposed to recite. His teacher nods. The darkness in the hall is full of gleaming black eyes. Fredrik opens his mouth, but there are no words. Torsten jabs him with his star-boy stick and grins. His teacher tries mouthing something. Fredrik's whole body freezes up. He has to pee, he suddenly feels. The star on Torsten's stick is jabbing his armpit. There is not a sound in the hall and everyone hears the splashing which echoes from the hardwood parquet of the stage.

At dawn, Maria Wern is woken by a two-voiced Lucia song. Krister fumbles for his glasses, wraps the blanket around his naked body and opens the front door. Emil and Linda come padding out into the hallway and listen raptly to Krister's pupils, who stagger in more or less unsteadily after a night of revelry. Maria puts on coffee to serve them. Most of them look as if they need it after their sleepless night. One boy throws up on the stairs to the house, two of the girls fall asleep locked in the bathroom and a third suffers from frostbitten toes in her much too thin pumps.

'Is there really any point at all to teach class on December thirteenth?' Maria asks her husband in the kitchen once the Lucia train has left them to haunt other victims among their teachers.

149

'Someone has to look after them. Lots of things happen on Lucia nights that need daylight soul-searching and emotional processing. Conflicts become open, love turns sour, they have fights and get drunk. It's a busy day for teachers. As for cops, I suppose. I suspect you'll have your hands full today,' Krister says and caresses her cheek.

'I wouldn't be surprised.'

Maria helps her children dress while tidying the living room. She gathers a whole pile of forgotten items – a sweater, a CD, a bag of chips and a lot of tangerine peel. Emil is to be dressed as a gingerbread man and Linda will be a Lucia. At the day care center all the girls get to be Lucia. Linda's wire crown is a little too big. When she pushes it to the back of her head she looks more like a deer or an elk than a queen of light. Emil has a battery candle. When he puts it in his cheek it glows red through his skin. Linda tries to do the same with her crown, gets one of the candles down her throat and throws up on her white, newly ironed gown. Quickly and despite her loud objections she is turned into a Santa. Maria puts together the flower arrangement she is giving the day care staff, puts it on the washer, feeds the cats, and turns on the dishwasher, and they finally leave, still in darkness.

Detective Captain Hartman passes around the plate of saffron buns and gingerbread. It's been a reasonably calm night. No traffic accidents. A drunkard smoking in bed has been hospitalized with burns. Two teenagers are sobering up in the drunk tank. Their parents have been contacted. Bredström's jewelry has suffered a broken shop window, but nothing's been stolen. On the whole a calm Lucia night. Ek throws himself onto the staff room couch; the surge of the cushion almost makes Maria drop her coffee cup. He looks a bit hungover. No doubt the night has been personally rewarding.

'What did Ellen Borg's apartment look like?' Maria asks and puts down her coffee cup at a safe distance from Ek.

'Ordered and clean. A hell of a lot of knick-knacks. A couch full of embroidered cushions, you know. She had a telescope mounted in her bedroom, pointed at the bedroom window of the apartment opposite hers. Want to bet if she knew everything there was to know about her neighbors? Then we found money. She had cash hidden away everywhere in her apartment, in the most unbelievable places. All in all, close to a hundred thousand.'

'Her son says she was living at the edge of starvation. Are the forensics guys done out in Bäckalund?' Maria asks.

'Yes.' Hartman holds the thermos in his hands. 'Are you going back to her cottage?'

'Yes, right now.'

The forest road is black and cheerless. Huge drifts of snow have fallen overnight, but here and there the branches of the trees have caught the snow and the ground is bare. The contrasts create a feeling of mystery. Maria steps out of her car and shades her eyes against the rising sun in the east. Why did

151

Ellen Borg suddenly start going to her cottage on Monday nights, in the middle of October? Did she go here to see someone? According to Sara Skoglund, Ellen didn't have many friends, but this was where she was born and grew up. Perhaps there was someone here her friends in town didn't know about. She's a little odd, Sara had said. She doesn't get along at all with her daughter-in-law. Ludvig always comes to see her alone. How does it feel to leave an active life at the post office, where you know most things about most people, to become a pensioner? To sit in a one-room apartment with your newspaper and see very few people?

Maria is just about to step over the police tape when she catches a movement behind the curtains in the neighboring cottage. It's the one Ludvig pointed out, the one belonging to the grocer, a larger log cabin with a porch. A woman's bike is leaning against the gatepost. Maria walks over and knocks on the door. The ice crystals of the snow crust glitter in the sunlight. Snow crunches under her feet. The door is opened by an attractive blonde, at a guess just over twenty-five. She is enveloped by warmth. Maria hears crackling from the woodstove.

'Maria Wern. I'm with the police. Could I ask you some questions?'

'Lovisa Gren. I'm a school nurse.' The woman's handshake is firm. 'It's cold outside today. Please come in. I suppose it's about that awful thing that happened to Auntie Ellen.'

'You're right.'

Maria enters and brushes snow from her feet.

They sit down by the kitchen table next to the woodstove. It's an unpainted gateleg table, adorned by a pewter tankard full of dried rowanberry twigs. On the wall above is a hanging edged in blue. The artfully embroidered letters reproduce an old proverb: A SMALL TUFT WILL OFTEN OVERTURN A BIG LOAD.

'When did you last see Mrs. Borg?'

Lovisa leans her chin on her hands, thinking.

'I honestly don't know. Probably sometime last summer. Yes, it must have been on Midsummer's Eve.'

'When were you out here last?'

'At midsummer. Then I went abroad. Here it just rained all the time.'

'Does anyone other than you ever come to this cottage?'

'No, I would hope not. I rent it all year.'

Maria unbuttons her coat to let the heat reach her body. Her hands are red from the cold. It feels good to hold them out to the fire.

'How would you describe Ellen Borg? What kind of a person was she?' Maria asks.

'To me she mostly talked about illness. Sometimes I wished I had never told her I was a nurse.'

'I can imagine. And now you've come to your cottage?'

'Yes. I read about the murder in the paper and wanted to make sure nobody had broken in.'

'And all is as it should be?' Maria looks around with a friendly glance. Lets her glance take in the bedroom and the tousled bed.

'Yes. I slept here,' Lovisa says apologetically. 'And I haven't made up the bed yet.'

'You're not easily scared. Have you ever met Mrs. Borg's son?'

'Ludvig. Yes, he was here last spring. He comes to plant potatoes for her. She hasn't been able to do it herself for a long time, but she did want fresh potatoes for midsummer.'

'So what did you think about him?'

'I don't really know.'

'You can tell me,' Maria says. 'I couldn't miss that undertone.'

'I guess he's a bit of a show-off,' Lovisa says with a laugh. 'You know, always the shiniest car. Wants you to know he's done well. He is some kind of financial wizard.'

Ellen Borg's little cabin is all tidiness and orderliness. The spice jars have handwritten labels and stand in perfect lines. The towels underneath the embroidered towel-rail cover have been ironed with perfect creases. The plastered brick hood above the fireplace is perfectly white, as if no fire had ever been set. Everything is in order, except for a single detail. There is a pair of binoculars on the kitchen table. The instrument lies at an angle to the tablecloth. Did the old woman spend her summer spying on her neighbors? Perhaps, but what could there have been to see in the middle of winter? Maria puts the binoculars to her eyes to check the definition. Through the kitchen window she can see clearly all the way to the main road. Not bad. Since Ellen Borg's cottage is the last one in the area, her kitchen window overlooks all the other houses. Maria walks through the cottage again, returns to the fireplace in the living room.

Wouldn't she have used every source of warmth, given how cold it was outside? Maria gives in to a sudden impulse and puts her arm up inside the fireplace. Feels the bricks. One of them is loose and can be pulled out. She brings it along to the window. Underneath the brick, a black notebook is tied in place with string.

Fredrik hides his wet clothes under the bathtub, quietly so as not to wake his mother, who sleeps in the room next door. The blush of shame still burns his cheeks. Perhaps it's a burn he will have to carry all of his life. How will he ever be able to go back to school after this? Will they let you have home schooling if you've peed your pants? They ought to. There was a guy in third grade who had home schooling after breaking his leg. Peeing your pants is much worse. There is a great loneliness in that realization. Fredrik puts his hand in the pocket of his dry pants, feels the cold surface of the Ring against his fingertips. In a sense he is in an emergency. So he puts it on his finger. Evil doesn't overwhelm him all at once. He hardly even notices it creeping in as he thinks about what to do next. His thoughts veer off on a forbidden tangent, pull him in through the closed door of Leo's room. For a while he stands in the persistent deodorant smell, staring at the new poster that has appeared on the wall. A girl in string panties on a motorbike. Fredrik thinks it's a funny picture. She looks like a giant baby with a too-small diaper. She peers at him over her shoulder, her eyelids half shut and her lips open and pouting, as if someone has just grabbed her pacifier.

Leo's cell phone is on the aquarium. It has a tiger-striped shell. Fredrik takes it, weighs it in his hand and almost feels a little like a grown-up. Hello, this is Bengtsson speaking, Fredrik Bengtsson. In the contact list there are girls' names. Fredrik keeps punching and suddenly someone answers. It feels as in a horror movie. She can't see him. He is evil. Evil people pant in telephones to frighten girls. He's seen that on TV.

'Hello, is anyone there?' She actually sounds scared.

Fredrik pants heavily and shudders at his own awfulness. And there is a pleasure in frightening someone, a feeling of power. It makes you want more. When the first girl hangs up on him he goes on to the next and the next again until only his grandmother's number remains. Then he quits and puts the phone back on the aquarium without looking. Where he had thought would be glass is open water and the cell slowly spins down to the bottom like a hunting tiger shark. It looks cool. The doorbell rings.

Miss Viktorsson and Mom are in the kitchen and have closed the door. Fredrik looks at his watch. It's ten. Mom has slept for only two hours after her night shift. That's not good. He knows that from experience. She is speaking in her night voice, the soft, whispering voice they use at the hospital. His teacher, on the other hand, speaks loudly and clearly. She uses words like difficulties and concerned. Then she says ill and school nurse. Fredrik doesn't need to hear any more. What do you do at the school nurse's office? You have an injection or

156

someone is counting your balls. Both are equally horrible. What if you did that to all the old men in parliament, had them line up alphabetically and ... they'd be sure to write about that in the paper. Just as they did about murders. Fredrik doesn't want to think about the dead lady. Or about the bike. Or about who had come out of the earth cellar. The beast in his stomach moves again. It doesn't want to be disturbed by those kinds of thoughts. Sickness fills him so quickly that Fredrik can't get to the bathroom fast enough. He throws up on the blue hallway carpet. All that comes is some acid yellow water. Now the kitchen door is opening. He can't stay here. Quickly he grabs his jacket and steps into his boots.

'Fredrik. Freeeedrik!' His mother's voice echoes in the stairwell.

But he doesn't turn. His feet hardly even touch the asphalt while he flies away into the forest. Once he is hidden by its darkness he removes the Ring from his finger. It's cold. He didn't get his mittens, or his cap. It would have been simpler to walk on the forest road. But someone might find him there. It's better to move among the trees, where there are places to hide. His feet ache from cold in the thin rubber boots. Thin smoke is rising from one of the chimneys down in the old village, but he can't see anyone. A longing for warmth overpowers him. Fredrik runs down to the little cottage with the porch. The door is locked. But out here nobody is in the habit of locking for real; people just lock their doors to let visitors know if they're in or out. The key is under the juniper twigs on the stair. When he silently sneaks into the hallway, the heat envelops him. For a moment he stands immobile, his back to the wall, listening. Then he slides into the room. On a chair is a rolled-up sleeping bag. Fredrik takes it and makes himself a small nest on the floor under the bed.

Detective Captain Maria Wern pulls her long, blonde hair into a ponytail and climbs into the patrol car. Hartman is already seated behind the wheel.

'So how do we proceed from here?' he says, eyes in the rear mirror. The Bäckalund school shrinks as the car accelerates, then disappears behind trees.

'We'll take two of the absent pupils. The two Bengtsson brothers. One of them is in high school, the other in first grade. The older has a cold and is at home, the other one disappeared during the Lucia pageant. His teacher thinks he had something wrong with his stomach. Do you know the way to Lingonstigen?'

'Yes, I do. Anything else new?'

'I talked to the forensics guy this morning. He found surprisingly little. No fingerprints. No murder weapon. The ground outside the earth cellar was frozen, and it didn't start snowing until the afternoon on December twelfth. So the only footprints to be found are Sara Skoglund's, and they fit in with what she told us. Time of death has been fixed at just after eight in the morning.'

'What about that notebook you found? Anything in it?'

'Numbers, just numbers. I suspect it might be

158

time listings – dates, hours, minutes. None of the numbers are higher than fifty-nine. Then there are some kind of symbols. They look more or less like the ones used to indicate curses in Donald Duck comics, if you know what I mean.'

'Do you think any of the numbers relate to December ninth?'

'I think so. We'll have a full analysis in an hour or so. But Hartman, there's one detail that doesn't fit. Maybe it means nothing, but I just can't let go of it. Let's go to Bäckalund.'

The sound of Leo's voice wakes Fredrik. At first he believes he must be at home, in his own bed, but the smell is all wrong. He smells dampness, mice droppings and resin and something else, something cold and unknown. Before answering his brother he looks around. Sees two pair of feet, very close to each other.

'You can't phone me. I thought we agreed about that,' the woman says peevishly, wagging her right foot.

'I haven't phoned!' Leo says in a surprised tone of voice.

'Really! Then who was panting on the line when the display showed your number?' she says angrily, her voice rising.

'I don't know. I forgot my cell at home this morning, so I haven't had it all day. I tinkered with my car down in the garage. Maybe Fredrik has sneaked into my room.'

'Anyway we can't keep meeting like this. I hope you understand that,' the woman's voice says.

'But I have to see you, Lovisa. I love you,' Leo

159

whimpers in a voice Fredrik has never heard before.

The smaller feet take a step back. The larger ones follow.

'You're just horny. It'll pass. Go now and forget about me.'

'I can't!'

'You have to. A school nurse isn't allowed to have a relationship with a student.'

'But you said you loved me,' Leo says, hopelessly.

'Maybe I did, but it's over. And Ellen Borg saw us. She had a little black book where she wrote down every time we met here. She wanted money to keep quiet about it.'

'But she's dead now.'

'Right. And if you ever say a word about any of this to anyone, I'll tell them you did it. Tell them you killed her. In a very safe place I have a hammer with your fingerprints and Ellen's blood on it. Whenever I want to, I can plant it somewhere and tip off the police. And do you really think anyone would believe anything you might say after that?'

'You can't. I never thought... How could it have my fingerprints?'

'You put them there when you helped me put up the hanging.'

'But how could you just ... kill her?'

'You have no idea what I can do.'

The feet belonging to Leo move across the door. The house echoes from the sound of the door being slammed. Fredrik tries to be quiet but the sobs in his throat force themselves out. A hand grabs his hair and pulls him out on the floor while the sound of Leo's car dies away. She grabs him by the scruff of his neck as if he were a kitten. A stream of words pour out of the school nurse, but he can't make them out through the roar of the waterfall inside his head. Passively he goes along with her movements and lets himself be led down through the hatch in the floor into the damply cold cellar darkness. He hears her lock the hatch. There is only darkness. And cold. And silence.

Detective Captain Maria Wern knocks again at the door and waits. Behind her, Hartman steps back and slaps his arms against his sides for warmth. Smoke is rising from the chimney of the gray cottage with the porch.

'What do you want this time?' Lovisa says when she opens the door.

Her cheeks are very red.

'Is it a bad time?'

'No, it's all right.'

Lovisa leads the way in. Her movements seem nervous and jerky to Maria. They sit down at the kitchen table. Lovisa bites her lower lip. Maria waits for a moment without speaking.

'So what is this about?' Lovisa says in a shrill voice.

'Did you pick these rowanberries yourself?'

'Yes, I did. What's that got to do with anything? What do you want?'

'You said before that you hadn't been here since midsummer. Was that true?'

Lovisa stares at the table, rubs her hands against

161

her thighs. Then she meets Maria's gaze. 'I may have been here once or twice in October. I'm not really sure.'

Maria is silent. So is Hartman. Lovisa lowers her eyes.

'Was that all you wanted to ask?' she says with a strained smile.

'Yes, for now. We may be back again later.'

Maria rises without haste. Glances out the window at the white-rimed trees. A half-eaten red apple is lying on the snow, abandoned by magpies. Long icicles hang from the edge of the roof. Then she turns to nod at Hartman, who follows her into the hallway. Lovisa remains sitting. Suddenly she gives a jerk. There is a scratching sound from below them. A weak, small voice is calling for mommy.

'If it's easier for you to tell me that way, you can put on your Ring and become invisible,' Maria Wern says and turns on the recorder.

'But what if I slip away?'

'I trust you,' Maria says, and her eyes are kind and very serious.

'I don't think I want it any longer,' Fredrik says. 'You can have it.'

THE MAIL RUN

ÅSA LARSSON

Bäckström's assistant never quite became himself again afterwards. Before it happened he had been a cheerful type. One of those who sang while he worked. Throwing two-hundred-pound sacks on his back while winking at the girls and tucking snuff under his lip. He became more serious afterwards. Surly, even. Never joked with the girls at Hannula's general store when he came to pick up goods. Began to lose half his pay at cards. Bought liquor from the bootleggers at Malmberget and sold it to the miners, young boys with more money in their pockets than sense in their heads.

But about this thing that happened. It was December 14, 1912. Bäckström, the hauler, and his assistant were on their way to Gällivare. Their sled was full of grouse intended for the train to Stockholm. But the train didn't run between Kiruna and Gällivare due to the amount of snow on the tracks. The snowstorm had lasted for three days and was only now starting to abate. But the restaurant keepers in Stockholm didn't want to wait.

Bäckström delighted in the winter evening. Huge, soft stars of snow fell slowly from the heavens. Almost sleepily they came to rest one by

163

one on top of the outer pelt of his wolf's fur coat, gathered on top of his Russian fur cap like a white hillock.

The moon found a rift between the snow-filled clouds. It wasn't particularly cold out, though of course his assistant was freezing, dressed as he was in only rough homespun and knitted clothes. But the hauler's assistant wrapped the reindeer skin around himself and was soon shouting his love to the mare, who really was the best in the world. Lintu, which means *bird* in Finnish. And wasn't she just like a long-necked crane? So beautiful! Now and then he gave her an encouraging lash when she stepped off the wintry road and risked sinking into the deep drifts. The sled remained right-side up, but all the newly fallen snow made it hard going. The mare steamed from exertion, though her load was light.

Hauler Erik Bäckström let his eyes follow the falling snow upwards, to the sky. A faint smile played over his lips as he thought that perhaps God's angels were a bunch of women doing needlework. Not very different from his own dead mother and the women in his childhood village. Perhaps they were sitting there crocheting in God's old cabin, dressed in their long skirts, their long hair pinned up and covered in head cloths. They had certainly been busy at needlework while alive. No matter how many socks and sweaters, caps and mufflers they made, it was never enough. They had spun, knitted, woven and mended. But now, carefree in the hands of the Lord, they could knit snowflakes. With gnarled hands that had carried well water to the cows during painfully

164

cold winter mornings and had rinsed washing in holes cut through the ice, they were knitting all these stars, absently letting them fall to the floor.

Which is no floor, the hauler thought philosophically, but the vault of sky above our heads.

'What are you smiling about, sir?' the assistant asked, panting.

He had jumped off the sled and was trudging through the snow beside the mare, who was the light and joy of his heart, to help her manage an uphill slope. In his pocket was a cube of sugar, which he gave her.

'Nothing, really,' Bäckström replied, happy about the freedom you enjoyed in your own mind, after all. Even a workingman who was also a businessman like himself could think the most girlish thoughts without risk.

His assistant jumped back up on the sled. Brushed the snow from his pants. Wrapped his muffler around his head all the way up to his ears.

Aside from occasional snorts from their horse, the silence was as deep as it can only be in a wintry wood during snowfall. The runners slid soundlessly over the soft, new snow. Only just before meeting the other sled did they hear the horse bells.

Both Bäckström and his assistant immediately recognized the mail sled.

They called a loud greeting to the postman, whom they both knew very well indeed.

'Hello, Johansson!'

There was no answer. The postman, Elis Johansson, sat deeply hunched over in his sled and

165

gave no reply no matter how loudly Bäckström and his assistant called.

The mail horse trotted on in the opposite direction and Bäckström and his assistant continued on towards Gällivare.

'Was he drunk?' the hauler's assistant asked, looking back over his shoulder. He could no longer see the mail sled, only the black silhouettes of trees in the weak moonlight that managed to escape between the snow-laden clouds.

'Nonsense,' Bäckström replied angrily. Johansson, never. He was a deeply devout Laestadian and a teetotaler.

'Maybe he was deep in prayer,' the assistant said mockingly.

Erik Bäckström did not reply. Shame over his recent fanciful speculations about God stopped him from defending Johansson the way he should. But he knew that Johansson was a hardworking and capable man. His faith was serious and grounded in scripture. He would never speculate freely about heaven the way Bäckström just had.

And Johansson kept his faith to himself. He never said a word if others had a drink, for instance. Many of his Laestadian brethren dared to do just that. They might be a guest in someone else's home, decline a swig but then glare indignantly at those who accepted the bottle. 'That shot will soon feel lonely,' they'd preach. 'It wants company, so they get to be two. Then they start arguing and a third is sent down to intervene. And then it's boozing.'

No, Johansson wasn't like that. He left others to

166

their own. Bäckström felt an urge to smack his young assistant.

But the assistant soon got going again. Talked a blue streak about all the hypocrites and liars and drinkers among the Laestadians. Everyone knew it. There were those who went to prayers and asked forgiveness of God and their brothers just to keep sinning as usual come Monday. And really: What, if not strong drink, could make a man sleep so deeply while seated in a sled?

His harangue was interrupted when the horse suddenly stopped dead. She shied backwards a step. Her neck stretched and her eyes rolled back.

'Easy, girl,' the assistant cooed.

'What's gotten into her now?' Bäckström wondered, swinging his whip.

The horse didn't move. Her nostrils widened. She snorted. Muscles hard as steel wire under her skin.

The hauler's assistant put a hand on Bäckström's arm to stop him from delivering yet another lash with the whip.

'Lintu is a good horse,' he said softly. 'Sir shouldn't whip her in anger. If she stops like that, there's a reason for it.'

He was right. Erik Bäckström dropped the whip, fumbling for his rifle under the box. *Wolf pack* is what he was thinking now. Or a bear that had been wakened from its winter sleep.

He prepared himself for the mare suddenly kicking over her traces. Turning round to bolt. Maybe tipping the sled over. And if he fell out of the sled and was left alone with the wolves, he sure wanted his gun for company.

167

'Is there anything up there?' the hauler's assistant said, peering through the falling snow.

'What?' Bäckström said. He couldn't see a thing.

'It's a man! Wait a moment.'

The assistant jumped out of the sled and ran on for a few paces. Now Bäckström too could see that there was something lying across the road.

The assistant ran, but then stopped himself and walked slowly the last few feet to the body lying across the middle of the road.

'Who is it?' Bäckström called.

The body was lying on its stomach, face down in the snow. The hauler's assistant bent down low and looked from the side.

'It's Oskar Lindmark,' he called to Bäckström, who was now standing in the sled, peering up ahead. 'And I think he's dead.'

Oskar Lindmark was mailman Johansson's twelve-year-old errand boy.

'What do you mean?' Bäckström called back. 'Has he fallen from the sled and broken his neck, or what?'

'No, I think…'

The handyman leaned down over the body and fell silent. Was it blood, all that black stuff? All colors disappeared in the faint, weak moonlight. Snowflakes fell in the dark puddle and dissolved.

'Hey, there,' he said, putting his hand on Oskar Lindmark's back.

Then he resolutely turned the body. Pulled on an arm until Oskar Lindmark flopped over on his back. Still thinking that Oskar might not be dead. That he needed air.

Oskar's face was as white as the snow itself. Eyes open, mouth as well.

Is it blood? the hauler's assistant wondered, pulling his mitten off and touching the black on Oskar's forehead.

Yes. Maybe. It was wet. He looked at his fingertips. Rubbed his index and middle fingers against his thumb.

Suddenly Bäckström was standing beside him.

'Is he dead?' the assistant asked. 'I think he is.'

'Oh Lord,' Bäckström said in a choked voice. 'Of course he's dead. Can't you see that his skull is completely smashed in?'

And that's when the hauler's assistant saw. He stood up quickly. Backed away from the body.

Bäckström turned in the direction of Jukkasjärvi.

'Johansson,' he called desperately into the forest.

The snow caught his voice. It carried nowhere. They could stand there yelling in the forest to their heart's content.

'Put the boy in the sled,' he said to his assistant, who was shaking with terror, steadying himself against a birch tree so as not to fall down.

'I can't,' the assistant trembled. 'He's all covered in blood. I can't touch him.'

'Get a grip on yourself, boy,' Bäckström roared. 'We have to turn the sled around and catch up with the mail run.'

Then together they dragged the dead boy and laid him on top of the grouse. Bäckström thought that the blood would seep through the sacks and stain the white birds. Then he thought that the

169

restaurant keepers down in Stockholm never needed to know what kind of blood it was.

In the Kiruna police station, county sheriff Björnfot and his acting parish constable Spett were sitting at opposite sides of a desk. Outside, snow was drifting down in the glow of the electric street lamps. The police station was equipped with a proper tile stove and Spett had been feeding it birch logs all day. On a rag carpet on the wooden floor, his dog Kajsa was chewing on an elk jawbone.

Sheriff Björnfot was writing up the day's events in his log. It didn't come to many lines. He was the older of the two men, had served for a number of years in Stockholm, where he had met his wife, and moved back to Kiruna with her and their two daughters only a year ago. He was a sensible man and didn't have anything particular against writing up records or taking down witness interrogations, tasks that had seldom been performed during the time when Spett alone had been in charge of the station.

Spett, who was unmarried, was darning a sock. On the tile stove damper, another pair of his socks had been hung to dry. Björnfot overlooked this. When he had taken up his duties in Kiruna, Spett and Kajsa had been living at the police station. In order to keep the peace he turned a blind eye to certain habits that remained from those days.

They were both broad-shouldered men of considerable strength. Spett was wiry, while Björnfot had an impressive stomach. 'Diplomatic talents

170

and physical strength' was what the mining company, which paid the salaries of the town police force, wanted in its servants of justice. The ability to break up troublemakers, in other words. Because there were a lot of those in town. Socialists and communists, agitators and trade union organizers. Not even the religious people could be trusted. Laestadians and Bible thumpers, always on the edge of ecstasy and senselessness. In Kautokeino, a group of newly converted Laestadians – in their eagerness to put an end to sin and liquor sales – had killed both the sheriff and the local shopkeeper, set fire to the vicarage and beaten the vicar and his wife. This happened before the sheriff was born, but even so, people were still talking about the Kautokeino uprising. And then there were all the young men, navvies and miners, just kids, really, migrating here from all over. Far from their fathers and mothers, they spent their wages on drink and behaved as could be expected.

But for the moment, the cell in the corner of the room was empty and Björnfot closed his log and thought of his wife, who was waiting for him at home.

Kajsa rose from the carpet and barked. A second later, there was a knock at the door and Erik Bäckström, the hauler, stepped in. He didn't even take the time to say hello.

'I've got postman Johansson and Oskar Lindmark in my sled,' he said. 'They're as dead as can be, both of them.'

Parked in the courtyard were the mail sled and

171

Bäckström's sled. Bäckström's assistant had draped blankets over the horses. Johansson lay in the mail sled and young Oskar Lindmark in Bäckström's sled.

Spett swept away a few curious passersby who had stopped at the opening to the courtyard.

'There's nothing to see here,' he roared. 'Keep moving, before I lose my temper!'

'...so when we found Oskar Lindmark lying in the snow we realized that something must have happened to Johansson,' Bäckström said. 'We put Oskar on the sled and turned around and caught up with Johansson. His horse was just trotting along. Of course it knew the way from earlier trips. Good Lord, when we halted it and saw that Johansson was shot...'

He shook his head. Looked at his assistant who stood a few steps away, pale as paper and holding Lintu's reins. She exhaled calmingly on him, as if he were her half-grown colt. Don't be frightened, my boy.

'So we tied the mail horse to our sled,' Bäckström finished. 'And came here at once.'

Sheriff Björnfot climbed up on the mail sled and took a good look at Johansson. Turned him over.

'Shot in the back,' he said thoughtfully. 'And you found him sitting up.'

'Yes.'

'And young Lindmark on the ground?'

'Yes. With his face in the snow.'

Björnfot felt in Johansson's pockets. Looked around in the sled.

'Where is his pistol?' he asked. 'I'm not saying

172

he wasn't a peaceful man, but he must have been armed when he was traveling on duty.'

Bäckström shrugged his shoulders.

'We didn't see any gun,' he said.

'And the letter box is broken,' sheriff Björnfot went on. 'So it was a robbery. But it seems strange to think that someone would shoot him with his own gun.'

He switched sleds and examined the wound on young Oskar Lindmark's head. He leaned down over the boy, holding his lantern very close to his face.

'It's snowing,' he said. 'Was it possible to see any tracks?'

'No,' replied hauler Bäckström. 'But of course it was dark. And we were upset.'

'Come here and take a look,' Björnfot said to Spett.

Spett came closer.

'Now this looks like frozen tears,' Björnfot said, touching Oskar Lindmark's face with his finger. 'And look at his muffler. Given the light clothes he has on, he should have used it to cover his face.'

'So?' Spett said.

'What I'm thinking,' Björnfot said, 'is this. Perhaps the killer shot Johansson, and the boy ran. Crying. And pulled his muffler away from his face to be able to breathe more freely while he ran.'

'Maybe so,' Spett said thoughtfully. 'But why wasn't he shot as well?'

Björnfot pulled his hand over his face in a gesture that meant that he was thinking. His hand

173

passed over his large mustache and down over his mouth. His fingers and his thumb followed the opposite sides of his jaw until they met at the tip of his chin.

'We have to talk to the postmaster,' he said. 'Ask what kind of mail they had to deliver. And then we have to tell Johansson's widow. And Oskar Lindmark's parents.'

Spett regarded him silently. Kajsa also quit her sniffing around the runners of the sleds, sat down in the snow and gazed at him. Her tail struck a pleading rhythm against the ground. Björnfot knew what their looks meant. They didn't want to bring mournful tidings to crying widows. They wanted to follow the trail of blood.

'Yes, yes,' Björnfot sighed, turned to Kajsa. 'You talk to the postmaster, I'll talk to the families.'

At that, Kajsa gave a happy bark. She rose on all four and ran to the archway. When she was out in the street, she turned and gave her master a summoning glance. Her pointed ears were turned forward.

Come on, she seemed to be saying. We have a job to do.

Hauler Bäckström had to smile despite the harrowing events of the evening.

'Look at that,' he said to Spett 'Before you know it, she'll be ironing your shirts.'

'She's too smart for that,' Björnfot commented, watching his younger colleague disappear into the street, following his dog.

When Björnfot arrived home shortly after eleven

174

that night, the lights had been turned off and the sheriff's house was dark. He found his wife sitting at the kitchen table.

'Hello,' he said, carefully. 'Are you sitting in the dark?'

He immediately felt stupid. Of course he could see that she was sitting in the dark. She often did. Said it saved them expensive kerosene. Now she slowly turned towards him. Smiled, but only as though her polite upbringing compelled her to.

Björnfot thought of Spett and Kajsa. How simple that bachelor life seemed. He lit the kerosene lamp hanging from the ceiling as well as the one on the table.

She didn't reply. Instead she asked:

'Would you like something to eat?'

She got out bread and something to put on his sandwiches. Set a fire in the stove as well. That disturbed him. It was as if she was telling him that there was no need for a fire just for her sake. He asked about the girls. She told him that they were asleep.

'What's that?' Björnfot asked, nodding to a parcel on the sideboard.

'Sheet music from my mother,' she replied without looking at it.

'Aren't you going to open it?'

'I don't have anywhere to play,' she said without emphasis. 'I can't understand why she would send them to me. Will three sandwiches do?'

He nodded without finding anything to say. He wanted to remind her that she was welcome to use the piano at the community center whenever she felt like it. As well as the piano at the company school. But what good would it do? She had answers to everything and he was tired of hearing them. One of the pianos was too out of tune for her to stand it. The other was guarded jealously by the headmistress of the company school, who always found it convenient to appear just as Mrs. Björnfot sat down on the piano stool. And since it was the headmistress who played at commencements and gave lessons, her interest in the keyboard took precedence. Always.

'You could at least open it, take a look,' he tried. 'Wouldn't it be nice to see what it is? And I'm sure your mother has written you a letter.'

'Open it if you want to,' she said, still in the same light tone. Thin as autumn ice on cold, black water.

Björnfot looked at the parcel. Would it lie there all through Christmas, spreading malaise? He was seized by a longing to throw it in the fire.

Instead, he chewed his sandwiches dejectedly. His wife watched him with vacant eyes. Not in an unfriendly way, but he still felt that he was being punished. He just didn't know for what.

He thought of Elis Johansson's widow, whom he had visited. Her silent reaction when he had delivered the news of her husband's death. Six children in a two-room apartment. The ones old enough to understand had gathered around her. Stared at him, dressed in dark fabrics, as the Laestadians usually dressed themselves and their children. Eyes like deep wells when he told them. Mrs. Johansson had stood there before him, she also simply dressed in a long, gray skirt, a kerchief and a simple cardigan. Nothing ostentatious. No

176

frills. Their home had also been simple, no curtains, no pictures on the walls. She hadn't cried. But he had seen her mouth and the wings of her nose widen in fear.

What will become of her now, he thought. Will she be able to support the children on her own? Will she have to give up some of them? Of course they wouldn't be able to stay on in the apartment, since it belonged to the Postal Administration. She had asked if he wanted some coffee, but he had declined. Her frightened eyes were more than he could stand. And the sobs of Oskar Lindmark's parents were still ringing in his ears.

He had longed for home, for Emilia and the girls.

Now he wished he had returned home earlier. So that the girls had been awake. They enlivened things.

Why can't you be happy? he wanted to ask.

The girls were healthy. They had food on the table. Dresses of bought fabrics. She had recently purchased new lace curtains. How could she feel that everything was so miserable all the same? When the Female Lecture Association had courted her and offered her membership, she had declined on some pretext he could no longer remember.

'I'm not the pioneering sort,' she had said at some point.

You don't know what a pioneer settlement is, he had wanted to answer. In this mining town we have streetlights, shops. A public bath! But he had kept quiet. The words between them were growing more and more scarce.

After they had gone to bed, he lay awake for a long time. Stared up at the darkness under the roof and thought about Oskar Lindmark's crushed head. About postman Johansson's widow. He longed to touch his wife, but refrained for fear of being rejected.

'Are you asleep?' he asked.

She didn't reply. But he could tell from her breathing that she was awake.

When he woke up it was still dark. It took him a while to realize what had awakened him. Someone was throwing snowballs at the window. The pocket watch on his nightstand showed a quarter past five.

Spett and Kajsa were waiting for him. They were accompanied by hauler Bäckström.

'Get dressed and come along,' Spett called. 'Bäckström has something to show us.'

They walked together in the falling snow through the town. Kajsa was sometimes ahead of them, sometimes behind them. Plowing her pointed nose through the snow, which was light as down. Sometimes she snorted and took a small, joyful leap.

Björnfot felt frozen in spite of his winter uniform and coat. Even so, it wasn't as cold as it could be in December.

Lights were lit in many homes already. Women had risen to light fires. Now they were preparing breakfasts and lunch boxes for their husbands. After that, they had their own jobs to go to. The insides of the kitchen windows were fogged up.

When they arrived at Bäckström's property, the

hauler led them into the carriage shed. They went up to one of the sleds inside.

'An hour ago, one of the mares arrived home alone dragging this sled. Someone had borrowed her without asking permission and then just left her somewhere. But she found her way home on her own. Stood outside the stable in the cold, waiting to be let in. And when I took a look at the sled...'

He finished his sentence by pointing at the floor of the sled.

An axe. Spett bent to pick it up. The blunt end of the axe blade was covered in blood and hair.

'Who is capable of doing something like that?' Bäckström wondered. 'And besides, I also found these.' He held out his hand, showing little red pieces of a broken seal.

'Is that a mail seal?' Spett asked.

'We'll bring them to the station to have a closer look,' Björnfot said. 'Did you speak to the post-master?'

'Yes,' Spett said. 'He said that Johansson had a very valuable delivery in his sled. It was insured for twenty-four thousand kronor. Probably worth twice that. And he was armed. The postmaster was certain of that.'

'Someone has driven this horse to the limit,' Bäckström said. 'Her back has been beaten and she had sweat so much that a sheet of ice covered her coat of hair. My assistant has rubbed her off and covered her in blankets. I'll be glad if she doesn't fall ill and die on me.'

'Yes,' Björnfot said, thoughtfully. 'The horses have been through quite a lot since yesterday. I wish they could speak.'

'That they can,' hauler Bäckström said. 'Though perhaps not of such things.'

At that moment, the door to the carriage shed was opened and a boy poked his head in. He was around ten years old. Dressed in an oversized leather jacket. A running nose poked out of a knitted gray scarf. Clumps of snow hung like grapes from his knitted mittens.

'There you are, sir,' he said to sheriff Björnfot and managed something that resembled a bow. 'Your wife told me... I ran there first, then here... They've caught you a robber, Sheriff. They're waiting for you outside the police station.'

In the street outside the police station, four men were waiting for sheriff Björnfot and acting parish constable Spett. They were all around twenty years of age. Three of them wore heavy clothes against the cold. One was dressed only in pants and shirtsleeves. Two of the heavily dressed men were holding the thinly dressed one. One of them was twisting his arm up behind his back. The other had pulled his mitten off and was holding the lightly dressed man's neck in a firm grip.

The last one, who had both hands free, called out in greeting as soon as he caught sight of Björnfot and Spett.

'And here comes the police authority. We've brought you a present.'

The speaker was a big man, easily as large as the arriving servants of justice. He was blond. His eyes shone, blue as spring snow.

The man being held captive was delicate, almost

spindly, with shoulders like a bottle. He had brown, greasy hair. His eyes were dark and full of terror – like swamp water in his pale, frozen face. His lip was swollen and split. One of his eyes was swollen shut and his nose was red and puffy. It seemed as if the man in his shirtsleeves had tried to stop his nose from bleeding, because the sleeve of his white shirtsleeve was stained red all the way up to his elbow.

'Here's your murderer,' the big man said, shaking hands. 'My name is Per-Anders Niemi. I work at the post office. The postmaster told me what happened last night. So all I had to do was to think it over a little. Who knew about the valuable delivery? And when Edvin Pekkari didn't show up to work on time this morning, I thought … well, why not surprise him with a visit?'

'Are you Pekkari?' Björnfot asked the man being restrained by the others.

'Answer,' the man holding the spindly one by the neck said and punched his temple with his free hand.

Pekkari didn't answer.

'That he is,' Per-Anders Niemi said. 'He works at the post office, too. As a mail carrier. As I said, he knew about the insured letter. And we found this at his place.'

He hauled a pistol out of his pocket and handed it to Björnfot.

'It's Johansson's,' he said. 'I recognize it.'

'But what about the money?' Björnfot asked.

'We didn't find it,' Per-Anders Niemi said. 'But then we didn't look all that carefully. We were more interested in turning him over to you.'

181

'Did he resist?' Spett asked, scrutinizing Pekkari's battered face.

Per-Anders Niemi and his two friends smiled crookedly and shrugged their shoulders.

'We'll lock him up,' Björnfot said. 'After that, we'll search his place.'

Pekkari gave him a frightened look.

'You can't lock me up,' he croaked. 'I'm innocent.'

Per-Anders Niemi turned quickly and hit him in the stomach.

'Shut up,' he screamed. 'Goddamned killer bastard.'

Pekkari sank to his knees in the snow.

'We can watch him for you,' Per-Anders Niemi said to Björnfot.

'There won't be any watching,' Spett said resolutely and snatched Pekkari as if he had been a sack of potatoes.

He walked into the police station, holding Pekkari by the scruff of his neck. Kajsa stood guard outside. After a while he came back out. Locked the door from the outside and demonstratively put the key in his pocket.

'He should be hung right now,' Per-Anders Niemi growled.

'If anyone as much as touches the door while we're gone...' Spett warned.

'All right, boys,' sheriff Björnfot said diplomatically, 'now I'd like to take a good look at Pekkari's place. Not waste my time imposing fines on such splendid specimens of our citizenry as yourselves just for disobedience to the police. So if you'd be so kind...'

182

He finished his sentence by making a considerate gesture asking them to leave.

The men muttered a moderately insolent goodnight and slunk away.

Edvin Pekkari's apartment was on the second floor of a wooden house on Järnvägsgatan. A stuffy smell of boiled reindeer meat, old smoke and wet wool greeted sheriff Björnfot and acting parish constable Spett when they entered the house.

'Here it is,' the landlady said, opening the door to a tiny room just under the sloping roof. She looked askance at Kajsa, but said nothing.

'Who does he share with?' Björnfot asked.

'He doesn't share,' the landlady said. 'Asked special when he moved in back in October. And since the windowpane is broken and the window is boarded up, he got it cheap. No, he doesn't know anyone and lives all lonesome. Is it true he killed Johansson and his waggoner lad? You'd never have believed it. He never made a fuss about anything. Paid his rent on time.'

A bed, a chest of drawers, a small chair and a shaving mirror. Nothing more would fit in the room. It was quick work to search it. Björnfot went through the chest, pulling out all the drawers. Checked the coat hanging on a hook in the wall, felt its pockets. Spett kicked aside the rag carpets on the floor to check for a loose floorboard where you might hide a wad of bills. They found nothing.

'Hang it all,' Spett said as they went back into the hallway.

'Are you done?' the landlady asked. 'You can

183

tell him from me that I'll be renting the room at once.'

'What's up there?' Björnfot asked, pointing at a hatch in the ceiling.

'Nothing,' the landlady said. 'Just an attic.'

'That we want to see,' Björnfot said.

Spett got the chair from Pekkari's room, put it under the hatch and opened it. He folded down the ladder made fast to the hatch. They asked the landlady to bring something to light their way and she returned with a simple flashlight. Björnfot climbed the ladder, lamp in one hand.

When he had climbed a ways up the ladder and placed the flashlight on the attic floor, something suddenly rustled up there.

A rat ran across his hand on the edge of the hatch and he heard numerous others start running back and forth. Their shrill squeaks cut through the dark. He quickly backed down the ladder.

'Rats!' he exclaimed. 'Nasty devilry!'

The landlady smiled, amused. Afraid of rats. Such a big man.

'Move over, Sheriff, and we'll let Kajsa up,' Spett said.

Spett lifted the bitch and carried her up the ladder under his arm. Set her down in the dark. He stayed on the ladder, holding the lamp.

Suddenly the hunt was on in the attic. They could hear rats scurrying across the floor. As well as Kajsa's heavier but rapid steps. Then a mortal scream as she bit the back of one of the rats. After that silence, broken only by the crunching and slurping from Kajsa, eating her prey. The other

184

rats had escaped and wouldn't dare show their ugly noses for quite a while.

The servants of the law climbed up into the attic. Kajsa swaggered about on the double flooring, fawning and swaying to the praise of her masters.

'You're really something, girl,' Spett said proudly, but he wouldn't let her lick his mouth. It had been a rat, after all.

And Björnfot said that he was going to order a uniform for her the next morning.

They searched the attic. And this time they didn't have to search in vain.

'It's time to confess!'

Sheriff Björnfot was standing outside the cell in the police station, talking to Edvin Pekkari. In his hand he held a cotton bag, adorned by the Postal Service emblem.

'We found this in the attic above your room,' he went on. 'There is five thousand kronor in it. Can you explain how it ended up there?'

Edvin Pekkari didn't answer. Just sat on the farthest corner of the cot.

'You can improve your position by cooperating,' Björnfot continued. 'The examining magistrate is arriving tomorrow. If you hand over your haul and confess, it will count in your favor. There was supposed to be fifty thousand in the sack. Where is the rest of the money?'

'Listen to the sheriff,' said acting parish constable Spett, who stood with his back turned, picking his dry socks from the tile stove damper and stuffing them into his pockets. 'What good

185

will the money be to you if they chop off your head?'

'I'm innocent,' Pekkari said in a low voice. 'I've already told you...'

Acting parish constable Spett turned around violently. Kajsa stood up, barking passionately.

'Johansson had six children!' he roared. 'God knows what will happen to them now. Oskar Lindmark was twelve years old. Johansson's gun was found in your room. The sack with some of the money in the attic above your room. You knew about the money. I want you to tell me... Tell me how you stole the sled from hauler Bäckström, how you shot Johansson with his own gun, how you killed Oskar Lindmark with the axe. I can't take any more of your damned lies, so shut up until you want to confess.'

He grabbed his uniform coat and his fur cap.

'I'm going out,' he said to Björnfot. 'I need some fresh air.'

He pulled the door open and a man standing outside, on the verge of raising the knocker, lost his balance and stumbled into the police station. Spett caught him in his arms and kept him from falling down. It was a tall man with an impressive mustache. Borg Mesch, the town photographer.

'Mister acting parish constable!' the photographer exclaimed. 'Now only the music is missing! But which of us should lead? You or me?'

Spett lost his ill humor and laughed. He put his coat back on its hook and let Kajsa out the door to take her evening walk on her own. Mr. Mesch dragged in the heavy cases holding his equipment. Then he put his hand in between the bars

186

to introduce himself to Edvin Pekkari.

'May I take your picture?' he asked.

Pekkari pulled his hand back.

'No,' he said. 'I'm...'

He glanced at acting parish constable Spett and fell silent.

'Perhaps I could show you some photos,' Borg Mesch said eagerly, anxious to break the silence.

He opened his briefcase and pulled out a bunch of black-and-white photographs. They were neatly wrapped in tissue paper and he showed them one at a time. Before showing the next picture, he carefully rewrapped the previous one.

'This one,' he said, 'just look ... it's King Oscar II after the inauguration of the ore line up to the border. This is from the royal dinner with managing director Lundbohm. Important gentlemen. I photograph important gentlemen. That's my profession. Well, what more could I show you ... oh, yes, this one ... just look ... the Kiruna Athletics Club...'

Spett and Björnfot had to come closer to look at the strong men of the athletics club, posing with folded arms in their black vests, with broad leather body belts and light-colored tights. On the floor in front of them were round iron weights with handles or fitted on steel bars.

'The one with the medals is Herman Turitz,' photographer Mesch said. 'Isn't it great that we have such an outstanding and versatile athlete in town...'

He fell silent and looked with interest at Pekkari.

'You actually resemble him a little. Would you

be kind enough to turn your head a little away from me ... no, in the other direction... Do you see, gentlemen? Can you see the resemblance?'

The photographer kept talking while, with surprising speed, he unpacked his equipment.

'Mainly it's your forehead. And your jawline. You have a phrenologically interesting forehead, Mr. Pekkari. A sign of inner strength, did you know that? So I told Mr. Turitz when I took his portrait. That in his case, one might have expected a herculeanly developed occiput. Which is what you find in most physically strong persons. But no, it's his forehead. Too bad, I should have brought his portraits along. You would have found them most interesting. Perhaps next time. I told Mr. Turitz that inner strength is more important to an athlete than bodily qualifications. It's his inner strength that makes him submit to the constant practice, the self-sacrifice necessary to win all those medals. The other day I heard that he had run through the deep snow all the way to Kurravaara for a training session. If you could ... if you'd allow me to take a picture ... perhaps you could come a bit closer to the bars. Yes, that's it. No, no need for you to look this way, keep your eyes down a bit just as you did. I can see a sadness in your expression, which I hope to do justice. Now, please hold...'

The flash was lit and burst.

Borg Mesch put a new glass plate in his camera and replenished the magnesium powder in his flash.

'Perhaps now you might come a little closer,' he went on. 'I would like to see your face here, between the bars. Just so. Do you think you might take hold of the bars as well? One hand high, the other below. Exactly. I don't doubt that you could have become an actor if you had wanted to, Mr. Pekkari. Just a moment now…'

Photographer Mesch quickly walked up to Mr. Pekkari and arranged the sleeve of his shirt so that all the bloodstains were clearly visible.

'Open your eyes a little more, Mr. Pekkari. So! Just so! You're a mind reader!'

Sheriff Björnfot watched Mr. Pekkari while he was being immortalized.

Now he was truly posing in front of the camera. He stood there, seeming to want to burst out of his cell. Eyes wide and hands clenched around the bars as if he were shaking them. Blood on his sleeve, a black eye and a swollen lip.

Kajsa barked outside the office. Spett let her in and she immediately sought out her moose jaw, lay down in front of the tile stove and began gnawing it. Photographer Mesch offered everyone Turkish cigarettes.

'Who is it now?' Spett wondered when the knocker sounded. 'What an infernal running.'

Photographer Mesch looked out the window. Dusk had returned. It was that time of year when daylight lasted only briefly at midday and the sun never managed to clear the horizon.

'Watch your language,' he said with a wink. 'For here comes the servant of the Lord.'

The Eastern Laestadian preacher Wanhainen was simply dressed in black pants, a black worker's vest and a woolen coat. He was a working man,

189

drove water around town on weekdays. The preachers were not like the priests who lived off the toil of their brethren. No, a Laestadian preacher supported himself. He was not superior, was not a burden to his siblings in faith, never leafed through Scripture with tender fingers looking for cloudberry-sweet words as did the state church priests.

He walked into the police station closely followed by the father of the murdered errand boy, Oskar Lindmark.

Wanhainen greeted them the Laestadian way, giving a half embrace with his left arm while simultaneously shaking hands in the Swedish fashion.

'*Jumalan terve.*'

God's greetings, in Finnish.

Björnfot and Spett both grew stiff and uncomfortable. It was the preacher's way to hold a handshake for so long, his eyes staring unflinchingly into those of the one he was greeting, that it seemed as if he had the penetrating eye of God. And to that came his way of ending his embrace with pat on your back that was slightly too hard.

Borg Mesch kept his good humor, even responded to the greeting, though Spett thought that his reply sounded like a teasing '*Jumalalle terveisiä,*' Greetings to God.

Oskar Lindmark's father also greeted them, but mostly kept his eyes on the floor.

The preacher turned to Pekkari.

'The boy you killed,' he said, 'his father is here to forgive you.'

He put his hand on the father's back, pushing

190

him towards the cell.

'As I myself have been forgiven,' Oskar Lindmark's father said in a thick voice, 'I want to forgive you.'

'Are you ready?' the preacher asked in an unctuous voice. 'Are you willing to let go of your thoughtless life and receive redemption from your brother? What is bound on earth is bound in heaven and what is released on earth is released in heaven.'

Edvin Pekkari was drawn to the bars by a power he was unable to resist.

Maybe what he saw in the teary, sincere eyes of the father was the image of his heavenly maker.

He was unable to stop himself from seizing the knotty hands of Oskar Lindmark's father. And while he held them, tears streamed down both their faces.

Borg Mesch rigged his camera and immortalized the moment.

'God's forgiveness,' the preacher said. He too seized Pekkari's hands through the bars.

In that moment, the door burst open. In strode the Western Laestadian preacher Jussi Salmi. East and West were adversaries in faith ever since the Laestadian congregation had split in two. Preacher Jussi Salmi in a roundabout way had learned what was happening in the jailhouse and had therefore brought the widow of postman Johansson, who belonged to his congregation. His red cheeks and the fact that he had removed his mittens showed that he had been in a hurry. He greeted the policemen with the same embrace and a 'God's peace.'

Johansson's widow also mumbled a 'God's

peace.' Spett noted that she showed the same interest in the floorboards as had Oskar Lindmark's father.

'*Jumalan terve*,' preacher Wanhainen said, carefully wiping tears from his cheeks with a cloth handkerchief. 'This evening, Pekkari has been absolved of his sins.'

His statement made preacher Salmi grind his teeth. It was ignominious to arrive late and also to have lost the race to redeem Pekkari. But he refused to let himself be disheartened. He tore off his coat and pointed at Johansson's widow.

'This mother,' he said tremulously to Pekkari. 'This woman, who has lost her husband. This mother of fatherless children has come here to forgive you. She has not traveled as a gentleman, in a sled with bells...'

Here he made a brief pause while his opponent Wanhainen blushed in vexation.

Preacher Wanhainen and Lindmark's father had indeed arrived in a horse-drawn sled. And it was true that Lindmark's horse had a bell around its neck. What pride. Vanity of vanities!

'...but tonight she has left her little ones to walk on foot through darkness...'

What followed was a soulful sermon on the widow who had suddenly lost her provider and who would now have to trust to God and, of course, her congregation siblings. The sermon rambled this way and that, touching on the widow's mite and the camel and the eye of the needle and that many are too great in their own eyes to enter the Kingdom of Heaven, but the true God was the God of the poor, indeed, the

God of the widow. And Now Here She Was.

Preacher Wanhainen mostly looked as though he had a mind to throw both the Western preacher and the widow out into the snow. Oh, if they had only walked, in the fashion of pilgrims.

'To lose your only son...' he tried.

But his words fell on bedrock. Now the hands of the widow and of the murderer had also met between the bars.

He asked her to forgive. And without being able to make herself meet his eyes, the widow whispered that if indeed he was truly sorry, she forgave him. Then she turned to her congregation preacher and said that the little ones were all alone at home. That she must return.

Through the window, acting parish constable Spett saw her enter the street. In the glow of the streetlight he saw her bend down and wipe her hands on the snow, as if she wanted to wash them clean. Then she hurried off.

Back by the cell, the preachers were now deep in a dispute concerning the vanity of the world and the fact that East Laestadian women were permitted to wear hats.

Spett turned around.

'Out,' he roared. 'It's bedtime for converts and sinners both. You are welcome to return tomorrow after the hearing.'

When all visitors had disappeared, Spett leaned against the bars and spoke to Pekkari.

'Now that you have received absolution from God, perhaps you might tell us where the rest of the haul is hidden.'

Björnfot, who was busy shining his boots in

193

preparation for the next day's trial, stopped rubbing the leather and raised his head.

But young Mr. Pekkari gave no reply. Without a word, he backed into the corner of his cell and lay down on the cot, his back to the two policemen.

The trial was held the next morning. It had stopped snowing but the wind had picked up during the night and now a storm was brewing. It lifted the newly fallen snow, whipping it madly across the mountain and along the streets in town. You could hardly see your own hand in front of your face. The wind took your breath away.

In spite of this, people had plodded down to the courtroom. Word had spread about the atrocity. Everyone wanted to get a look at the murderer, as well as hear more about the shudder-worthy deed. And watch the shiny buttons, uniforms and store-bought boots of the servants of justice. The kind of footwear poor folk could only dream about. The crowd wore large, homemade shoes of reindeer skin, which they stuffed full of hay.

The presiding judge, Manfred Brylander, regarded his courtroom. Today's audience was filling it to the brim; people were even jostling one another outside in the hallway. And it was growing warm, of course. The usher had been feeding the stove all morning. The steam was rising from wet woolen coats and furs. On the floor, snow had melted into small lakes. You could smell the odor of sour fat from peaked shoes. A number of dogs lay at the feet of their owners, adding to the musty smell of poverty filling the room. Manfred Brylander wiped sweat from his brow, banged his gavel and called upon women, children, and youths to leave. So they did, but the crush grew no less. Some of those in the hallway managed to squeeze in. The women and children remained in the hallway, out of his sight.

He glared at the audience. There were the Laestadian brethren, like gloomy ravens on the branches of a spruce. The Eastern brothers looked askance at the Western and vice versa. There was the indignant public, Lapps, Swedes, and Finns, all wanting to see the murderer pay with his life.

Per-Anders Niemi and his friends sat in the front row. They had caught the killer and enjoyed admiring glances and slaps on the back. A few people even snuck them a coin, or a piece of dried meat.

'Will it ever begin?' Per-Anders Niemi called out, well aware that he would never be ordered out of the room.

Kiruna, judge Brylander thought. A town of rebels and agitators. The room seemed full of an electric power. Something vibrating, waiting to be let loose. He could see it in their burning eyes. He feared that the mere sight of the accused would make the entire crowd explode. He looked at sheriff Björnfot and acting parish constable Spett. Dressed in uniform and stiff-legged, polished and brushed. The sheriff let his hand rest easily on his service gun.

'Any outburst and I'll clear the room,' judge Brylander warned, but without looking at Per-Anders Niemi.

195

The district police superintendent, Svanström, was serving as prosecutor. There was no defense attorney. After all, the accused had declared himself willing to confess.

The prisoner was brought in. His hands and feet were chained and he rattled a bit when taking his seat at the place of the accused. His large prison uniform made him look smaller than ever.

The proceedings began. Svanström presented the strong evidence pointing to Pekkari. Johansson's service gun, which had been found in Pekkari's room, and the mailbag with part of the stolen money, found in the attic above his abode.

'Do you admit,' asked the judge, 'that on December fifth, and without leave, you borrowed a sled from hauler Bäckström, that you drove it in the direction of Gällivare, that in cold blood you shot mailman Johansson and killed his errand boy Oskar Lindmark with an axe? That you then broke open the mailbox and stole an insured parcel?'

Pekkari whispered something inaudible.

'Louder!' the judge urged.

Pekkari said nothing. Then a man in the audience stood up. It was Oskar Lindmark's father. He remained silent. Just stared at Pekkari until the judge ordered him to sit.

But then Pekkari began to speak.

'I confess,' he said in a steady voice.

'This is a most serious crime, and I must urge you to reply honestly to the questions of the court,' judge Brylander admonished him. 'Did you perform your actions alone?'

'Yes,' was the answer.

'Did no one accompany you in the sled?'

'No one but the devil!'

There was a ripple through the audience. Someone blew his nose, someone gestured quickly with his hand. Someone else muttered something and half rose in his seat. It was like drifting snow pushed across the frozen crust by a gust of wind. Judge Manfred Brylander had heard of the religious ecstasy of the Laestadians, their *liikutuksia*. He had never seen it with his own eyes. What did it take for something like that to start in this flock of ravens? Had it already begun? He lifted his gavel but didn't strike the table in front of him.

'Did you not have anyone else with you?' he asked the accused.

'No one except the devil,' Mr. Pekkari said.

Now his voice rose and he called out from the stand like a preacher.

'I obeyed him. At Tuolluvaara I wanted to turn back. But he whispered in my ear. Urged me on. I had not yet found safety in the blood of the lamb.'

Now the flock of ravens was sobbing in the benches. Embracing each other. Giving God's redemption to the brother closest to them.

'I did it,' Mr. Pekkari called out, raising his shackled hands and shaking them to heaven in despair. 'Young Oskar Lindmark. He was on his knees before me, begging for his life. He spoke of his mother. He clasped his hands. He turned his face towards me and I beat him to death.'

Sheriff Björnfot leaned towards acting parish constable Spett.

'Come along outside for a while,' he said curtly.

Out in the street, Björnfot began walking quickly. The storm hit them. The wind whipped along the streets. When Spett called to Björnfot to slow down and wait, his mouth filled with snow. Turning his collar up and buttoning his coat was a chore. Snow blew in at his neck and between the buttons. Kajsa ran along behind him, sheltered from the wind by his legs.

'He didn't do it,' Björnfot yelled.

Although they walked close together, his voice was lost in the wind. Spett had to strain to hear him.

'What do you mean, sir?' Spett called back.

Björnfot pulled Spett into a doorway. They stood inside, in lee of the wind. Snow had already formed a hard crust on their clothes. Kajsa was biting her paws, ridding them of clumps of snow.

'Damn it, Pekkari is innocent,' Björnfot said, out of breath. 'You saw Oskar Lindmark. He was wearing mittens. There's no way he could have kneeled and clasped his hands and talked of his mother.'

'Well, Pekkari is exaggerating. I suppose he enjoys the attention, now that…'

'Right,' Björnfot said. 'He enjoys the attention, as you put it. The back of Oskar Lindmark's head was crushed. He was hit from the back. If he'd been on his knees, facing his killer, he would have been hit here.'

He pointed to his forehead.

'Pekkari's lying. Why doesn't he say where the rest of the money is?'

'I suppose he's hid it and hopes to get away with life. Then maybe to escape...'

Björnfot shook his head. The icicles in his mustache jingled.

'He doesn't know. It's that simple.'

'Then why would he confess?' Spett wondered distrustfully.

'I don't care!' Björnfot snapped. 'But who else knew about the insured parcel? Who...'

'Who found the gun in Pekkari's room?' Spett asked with clenched teeth. 'Per-Anders Niemi did.'

They remembered Per-Anders Niemi and his friends, delivering the badly beaten Pekkari to the police station.

'I'll rip his head off his shoulders,' Spett growled. 'It'll be a deliverance for him to confess. And those tail-wagging friends of his...'

'But first, we'll take a look at his room,' Björnfot said, opening the door.

The wind tore at it. Kajsa looked at the two men.

Do we have to go back out into that? she seemed to be saying.

Postal assistant Per-Anders Niemi rented a room in an unplastered brick house on Kyrkogatan.

'He shares it with a friend,' said the landlady who opened the door for Björnfot and Spett.

'Was he home on the evening before last?' Björnfot asked as he stepped into the room.

'Don't think so,' the landlady said. 'He spends most of his time with his fiancée. She rents a room of her own.'

199

She gave the policemen a knowing glance.

The rag carpets on the floor were overlapping to keep out the cold. The two beds were separated by a hanging piece of cotton. There was a washstand with a bowl and a jug. Next to a portrait of King Oscar II on the wall hung a shaving mirror, brown with rust. Beside each bed stood a valet stand. A yellowed undershirt and a pair of socks hung on the one by Per-Anders Niemi's bed.

Spett and Björnfot tore the covers off both beds. They lifted the pillows and the horsehair mattresses. They rolled up the rag carpets and examined the floorboards just as they had done in Pekkari's room. When they'd turned the room upside down, they searched the attic. And found nothing.

'Are you finished?' the landlady asked, glaring at the mess in the room. 'Can I make up the beds again?'

Björnfot seemed not to hear her. He was gazing out the window at the white curtain of snow. He had been so certain. Now he suddenly felt unsure. Perhaps Pekkari was guilty after all. Perhaps he just didn't want to admit killing Oskar Lindmark from behind. That was a base deed, after all. Perhaps he wanted to add drama to what had happened.

Kajsa settled down on the floor with a disappointed sigh.

'I suppose we'll have to take a look at where his friends live,' Spett suggested.

Björnfot shook his head.

'I don't think he's the kind of man who trusts his friends...'

He turned to the landlady.

'What's the name of his fiancée? Where does she live and work?'

Majken Behrn was the fiancée of postal assistant Per-Anders Niemi. She was nineteen years old. A girl with round cheeks and curly hair who attracted customers to Hannula's General Store, where she worked as a sales clerk. When Björnfot and Spett asked her to put on her coat and hat and come along, Björnfot knew that they were on the right track.

She didn't ask what it was all about. Hurried to get her coat on. Didn't even take the time to remove her apron. As if the wife of shopkeeper Hannula might forget that she had been picked up at work by the police if she was just quick enough about it.

'Perhaps you can guess what this is about,' Björnfot began as they started off along the street.

But it wouldn't be quite that easy.

Majken Behrn wound her scarf several times around her neck as protection against the snowstorm and shook her head.

'Your fiancée, Per-Anders Niemi: did he spend the evening before last in your company?' Björnfot yelled over the wind.

'Yes,' she yelled back. 'I'll swear to that.'

Then, quickly, she added: 'Why do you ask?'

'It's regarding a double homicide,' Spett said bitingly. 'And I'll ask you to remember that, miss.'

They fell silent and struggled on through the storm to the house where Majken Behrn lived.

201

It was a pleasant room, Björnfot thought as he looked around. Woven curtains with knit fringes. Between the outer and the inner windows, Majken Behrn had put *Cladonia stellaris*, the white lichen beloved by reindeer, against the damp. In the lichen, she had placed little Santa Claus figurines made of yarn. On the wall in the bedstead alcove hung a paper Christmas hanging depicting a farmyard house elf feeding red apples to a horse.

There was a plain wooden chair on each side of a drop-leaf table covered by a spotless embroidered tablecloth. A coffee pot stood on an iron stove with a hotplate. Over the pot handle a small, crocheted kettle-holder hung neatly.

Kajsa shook off snow to the best of her ability. Then she found a tub of water on the floor in the alcove and drank noisily. Spett and Björnfot searched the room. Looked in drawers and everywhere. Nothing.

She doesn't even ask us what we're looking for, Björnfot thought. She knows.

Spett called for Kajsa to come. When she didn't appear, he went over to the sleeping alcove.

'What's that she's drinking?' he asked.

He saw that the tub held a piece of clothing put there to soak.

'I hope you haven't put any lye in the water,' he said.

'No, no,' Majken Behrn assured him, suddenly blushing. 'It's just. It's nothing…'

'What are you washing?' Björnfot asked when he saw the color rise in her cheeks. Spett pulled the garment out of the tub. It was a pair of men's breaches. Even though they were wet, you could see that the legs beneath the knees were stained with blood. Björnfot turned to Majken Behrn. If her face had been red a moment ago, it was now white as linen.

'Those are your fiancée's trousers,' he said sharply. 'And it's Oskar Lindmark's blood.'

Majken Behrn was breathing harshly. She fumbled blindly for something to hold on to.

'Tell us everything,' Spett said. 'If you do, you may save yourself. Otherwise you'll be sentenced as an accomplice, I can promise you that.'

Majken Behrn said nothing. But she turned slowly, pointing to the iron pipe leading to the stove.

Spett dropped the wet pants on the floor. He hurried to the stove and grabbed the iron pipe with his huge fists.

'How?' he said.

Majken Behrn shrugged.

'Don't know.'

Spett tugged at the stovepipe and the middle part of it came loose.

'There's something stuck inside,' Spett said, peering down into the loose pipe.

Majken Behrn turned in alarm to Björnfot.

'Don't tell Per-Anders. He'll kill me.'

'He won't be killing any more people,' Björnfot said calmly as Spett began unfolding a thick wad of bills with his sooty hands.

Majken Behrn was standing by the window. She looked at her engagement ring. At the white frost ferns on the windowpane.

To know something, yet not know, she thought. How could you explain that?

The night before last she had suddenly awoken. Per-Anders was standing by the iron stove. He was twisting the pieces of the stovepipe together. 'What are you doing?' she asked. 'Just go back to sleep,' he said.

Then he came to her in bed. He was cold. His hands like two winter pikes. 'Soon, now,' he whispered in her ear before she went back to sleep. 'Soon I'll buy you a fur coat.'

In the morning, he had awakened before her. Told her not to light a fire in the stove to make coffee. She mustn't touch the stove for a few days, he said. And his pants were soiled. He asked her to wash them for him. 'I helped the cobbler with his Christmas pig,' he said. 'He sure bled all over me. I asked if I could have the head to bring you.'

She laughed and pretended to shudder. Later, when she heard about the two murders, she stopped laughing. But she said nothing. Perhaps didn't want to know. Lit no fires in her stove.

'And he, Edvin Pekkari,' she said to herself, forgetful of the presence of Spett and Björnfot, 'he was such a nasty man. Never said a word. Didn't even say hello when you went into the post office. But stared at me as soon as he thought I wouldn't notice. In that way, you know. The whites of his eyes all yellow. It could have been him. It should have been him.'

Sheriff Björnfot threw open the courtroom door. Judge Manfred Brylander lost his way in the

204

middle of a sentence. People turned their heads.

'Pekkari is innocent,' Björnfot called out, striding up to the bar. 'Release him!'

'What are you talking about?' judge Brylander exclaimed.

He had grown vexed and worried when Björnfot and Spett left the courtroom. His thin hair now lay sweaty and flat on his head. He was gasping for air like a clubbed fish.

'I've got the money from the robbery in my hand,' Björnfot called, holding high the parcel he had found in Majken Behrn's stovepipe.

'And this,' he went on, lifting his other hand, 'is the murderer's trousers. Stained by Oskar Lindmark's blood.'

All the spectators gasped in unison. Theirs was a joint inhalation of horror at the sight of the wet pants in Björnfot's hand, and perhaps an inhalation of rapture at the amount of money known to be in the parcel he held.

Per-Anders Niemi rose quickly. Before anyone managed to stop him, or even realized that he ought to be stopped, a few quick steps had brought him to the side door at the front of the room, the door through which the accused Pekkari had been brought in only an hour before.

'Stop!' sheriff Björnfot roared, but by then Per-Anders Niemi was already out of the room.

Outside the doorway he ran straight into the hard fist of acting parish constable Spett.

It took only a second or two. Then Spett walked in, holding Per-Anders Niemi by the scruff of his neck.

Björnfot looked around for the men who had

helped Per-Anders Niemi bring Edvin Pekkari to the police station. One of them was crouched down in his seat like a sinner at the altar. Björnfot grabbed his hair and pulled him to his feet.

'I'll talk,' he whimpered.

'You'll shut up!' Per-Anders Niemi yelled, trying to pry himself loose from Spett's closed hand.

'No,' his friend cried in desperation. 'I want to speak. I haven't slept since it happened. Per-Anders told me about the money. Said we should rob the mail sled. But only that. He never said anything about killing anyone. We took the sled since the hauler was gone. We stopped at Luossa-jokki, turned the sled over and pretended that its runner had broken. We had mufflers up to our ears and caps pulled down low. They'd never have recognized us, we didn't need to... Per-Anders hid behind a tree, since the postman knew him. They stopped to help us. Oskar jumped out of the mail sled and bent down to look at the runner. Postman Johansson stayed in the sled, holding back the horse since it wanted to go on. Then Per-Anders slipped out from behind the tree. He jumped on the sled and shot Johansson in the back.'

'With Johansson's gun?' Björnfot asked.

'No, with his own. We found Johansson's later and pretended to discover it in Pekkari's room when we rushed him. Even Pekkari though we found it in his drawer. Tried to tell us that someone else must have put it there. Sneaked in while he was sleeping.'

'But after that,' Björnfot said. 'Out in the woods. When Per-Anders Niemi had shot mailman Johansson.'

206

'The shot made the horses go crazy. Our horse reared up and tried to run, but the sled was turned over and stuck in the snow. The mail horse bolted. Per-Anders Niemi was standing in the sled, holding on, and called out to me. The boy, he said. Get him!'

Per-Anders Niemi's friend tottered. In his mind, the scene was played out again. The sheriff had to grab hold of him to keep him from falling down.

Oskar Lindmark's face is pale blue in the moonlight. He is kneeling by the sled to look at the runner that is supposedly broken. Eyes wide. He hasn't understood what has happened, though the shot has been fired and the mail horse has neighed in panic and bolted. The mail horse is running, though not very fast in the loose snow. Per-Anders Niemi is standing in the mail sled, yelling:

'I have to break it open to get the money. The kid! Get him. Don't let him get away!'

They stare at each other, Per-Anders Niemi's friend and Oskar Lindmark. Frozen in fear of this deed that lies before them. The grown man's mind calls out: I can't!

Their horse rears up, trying to get loose. And suddenly Oskar Lindmark jerks. He gets to his feet. Stumbles, but doesn't fall. Runs off like a hare in the moonlight.

'Get him,' Per-Anders Niemi roars. 'If he escapes in the woods we're done for.' His friend takes the axe. And goes after the boy.

The snowflakes dance so beautifully in the air.

As though they can't make up their minds whether to fall or rise. Clouds float across the moon. Like a woman's behind in a smoking sauna, fat and shiny. Hiding and revealing itself in a dance of veils. The shadows of the trees on the snow are now sharp and black, now soft and almost invisible. Not even if the moon is entirely hidden by clouds will Oskar Lindmark get away. It's easy to follow his footprints in the snow. But still Per-Anders Niemi's friend runs so hard that he can taste blood. His feet sink down in the snow, but since he can run in Oskar's tracks he is gaining on him. And he is just a little boy. Oh, God. Per-Anders Niemi's friend has soon caught up with him. He raises the axe and strikes the boy's head before he manages to turn around. The boy mustn't look at him; he wouldn't have been able to endure it. Now Oskar Lindmark lies before him, face down. His feet are still running, like those of a sleeping dog.

The man hits him over and over, because of those feet.

Per-Anders Niemi's friend kept his eyes on Björnfot.

'Lindmark ran. But I caught up with him quickly. I hit his head with the back of the axe. He died in the snow. I walked back to the sled and managed to get it right side up on the road. Held the horse until Per-Anders came trudging up with the money. He had Johansson's pistol. My pants were bloody. It drove me insane, that blood, so Per-Anders said we could switch. He put on my bloody pants and gave me his clean ones. Outside town we jumped off, lashed the horse and walked home, each to his own place. The snow was coming down heavier. We knew all the tracks would soon be gone.'

The third man who had come along when they took Pekkari to the police station suddenly stood up.

'It can't be true!' he exclaimed, looking in horror at Per-Anders Niemi and his friend who had just confessed to the awful deed. 'You damned bastards. I believed you. When you came to me and said we should search Pekkari's room. When you said that you suspected him. You bastards!'

The room grew deathly silent. Then Spett spoke up.

'Out, all of you,' he cried. 'There will be a new trial here tomorrow. But now. Get out! Get out!'

People rose from the benches, as if stunned.

Nobody spoke. They had sat there, willing an innocent man's death. Guilt pulled a thick blanket over the courtroom. The Laestadian brethren looked awkwardly down at the ground. Nobody looked at Edvin Pekkari.

Pekkari, who stood up by the bar, still in chains, and who called out:

'But I did it. Can't you hear me? I am guilty. I AM GUILTY!'

The snowstorm lasted for three days. Then it went on its way to ravage other places, leaving Kiruna in peace under a soft, white blanket. Horses pulled snowplows and drifts cracked fences. Birch tree branches bent all the way down to the ground under their snowy loads.

Björnfot and Spett stood at the railroad station, watching Edvin Pekkari board the southbound train. The mining company had ordered men to shovel snow from the tracks. People were moving back and forth over the platform, passengers and goods.

Pekkari with huddled shoulders and a knitted cap. He carried all his belongings in one suitcase. Nobody was going with him. Nobody had come to see him off.

'So, I guess he's moving out, then,' Spett said.

Björnfot nodded.

'Why the devil did he confess?' Spett wondered.

'Who knows,' Björnfot said. 'Perhaps the attention,' he said. 'He became famous overnight. And before that he was a loner nobody wanted to know.'

He thought of when they had searched Pekkari's room. Not a single letter in any of the drawers. Not a single photograph.

'He would have had his head cut off,' Spett protested. 'It's senseless.'

'The evidence pointed to him. Perhaps he imagined that he had done it. That what everyone said was true. Who can know?'

Spett snorted incredulously, then laughed at Kajsa who was greeting the train conductor and trying to invite him to play. She ran a few crazy turns, spattering him with snow.

'Well,' Björnfot said, stroking his moustache. 'People talk about the mystery of God. But I'd say people can be just as great a mystery.'

'I thought that only applied to women,' Spett said.

Speaking about women made sheriff Björnfot remember to check his watch. He had arranged to meet his wife at one o'clock. It was time to get going.

'But admit that it's strange,' Spett said before Björnfot hurried off. 'The Laestadian brethren, I mean. They could forgive Pekkari for being a cold-blooded killer. But they couldn't forgive him for being a simple liar.'

'People are a mystery,' Björnfot said again and bid him good-bye for now.

She stood waiting at the street corner as he came panting up the hillside. Her dark, wide eyebrows under the ermine hat. Her hands in the white muff. Her long, black coat had a rim of snow.

'Just wait!' Björnfot said cheerfully and linked his arm through hers.

The walk to the new music pavilion took only three minutes. He had borrowed a key. On the stage up front was a Steinway grand piano.

'It's yours every Thursday from two till half past three,' he said. 'Nobody will disturb you.'

She looked at the grand piano. Felt herself lured into a trap.

She thought of her first trip up north to Kiruna. In Gällivare, the train conductor had come up to her and inquired whether she had someone to 'answer for her.'

'What do you mean?' she had asked.

'You can't travel to Kiruna by yourself,' he had replied. 'You must have a man to answer for you.

Or at least a certificate stating that a man will meet you up there and answer for you.'

'Answer for me?' she had exclaimed, but at that moment Albert and the girls had entered the compartment. They had just been outside, taking a walk on the platform during the stop.

The conductor had excused himself, checked their tickets and gone his way.

Albert had defended him.

'It's not like Stockholm,' he had said. 'It's a mining town. But they don't want it to turn into another Malmberget, full of drunkenness and...'

He had stopped talking and glanced at the girls, who were following their discussion with rapt expressions.

'...and women who oblige with this and that,' he said. 'They want to keep that kind of women-folk out. There's no need for you to take offense.'

'In Finland, women are allowed to vote,' she had said. 'Here, we're not allowed to take the train.'

Kiruna was a town belonging to men. The gentle-men and their businesses. And of course the sheriff was always invited when this or that was to be discussed.

How he polished his boots when he was invited to visit managing director Lundbohm. Spat and buffed. The director himself sometimes turned up for meetings dressed as a navvy.

She had expected something else from this town of the future. Something that felt modern. But the women here sighed devoutly in front of the altarpiece painted by Prince Eugén.

And she suffered poverty badly. All those women and children whose cheekbones stuck out from their faces like mountain-tops. From hand to mouth, all the time. All those women whose men came to harm in the mines. The child auctions. They had them in Stockholm as well. But here, it was all so close. It affected her badly.

Albert had a five-year contract as sheriff. She couldn't understand how she would bear it. Nowadays she could hardly stand him either. His heavy breathing when sleeping. His table manners had begun to annoy her. She felt ashamed of herself. But what did that accomplish? Sometimes she wished that she would come down with some illness. Just to escape it all.

He opened his uniform coat and pulled out the parcel with the sheet music her mother had sent her.

'I can't,' she said. 'My fingers are frozen stiff.'

He dropped the music. Took her hands in his.

'You don't want to?' he said, pleadingly. 'Don't you have any feelings left for me?'

She gave in. Loosened herself from his hold and sat down at the piano. Struck a chord. Hoped for it to be out of tune. It wasn't.

I'll drown here, she thought.

And at that moment, her fingers dove down onto the keys.

They landed on the opening chord to Debussy's *La Cathédrale Engloutie*.

The piano can't lie to Debussy. The first tones sound one by one. But the grand piano keeps the promise it made from the start.

213

Now the cathedral bells are ringing down in the depths of the sea. She strikes each key distinctly. Oh, these pealing sounds. The storm tears the surface. Waves rise high. The bells below toll and ring out.

Her touch is hard and demanding. Furious.

Her fingers aren't long enough. Her arms aren't long enough. Her coat arms are tight as a straitjacket. She sweats. Her back hurts when she stretches.

Then she looks at Albert. He is smiling, but below that smile is worry. He doesn't understand this music. It frightens him. She frightens him when she shows him this side of herself.

Abruptly, she stops playing. Her hands land in her lap. She almost wants to sit on them.

'Go on,' he says.

Why, she wants to ask him. You don't understand.

And as if he could see right through her, he says:

'I'm a simple man...'

His voice thickens. The thought of his crying scares her half to death.

'...but if you knew how proud I am of you, my songbird. When you play. I wish I could... I'm really trying...'

He is unable to go on speaking. His lips compress and the muscles under their skin twitch.

She looks out the window. A squirrel runs along a branch. Snow loses its grip and falls to the ground. It is light outside. Beyond all the white, the sky is colored rose.

Her heart is not as heavy as before.

214

I'll try to be happy, she decides. Thursdays from two until three-thirty. Maybe that's what I need.

She smiles at him. Then she puts her hands on the keys again and begins to play. She picks Schubert's Impromptu in G Flat Major. It's lyrical and she knows that he likes it very much. She looks at him and smiles. Goes on playing tunes he appreciates.

Now he is smiling back at her, his heart happy. As if she were the returning sun.

He is a good man, she thinks. He deserves better.

She is miserable in Kiruna. Sometimes she thinks she'll go mad.

But he is a good man. And soon it will be Christmas.

BRAIN POWER

STIEG LARSSON

Mr. Michael November Collins
Sector 41
Aldedo Street
8048 New York 18-A-34

Mr. Michael November Collins, that's me, and the letter with my name and address on its envelope arrived in the morning, dropping from the mail tube to the breakfast table.

Judith, my wife, picked it out of the basket, read my name and handed it to me. Even before opening the letter I saw that it wasn't an everyday one. There was no postage on it, just a stamp informing me that postage was paid by the government – or the taxpayers, whichever you prefer. My getting mail from the government was hardly a common thing. It had only happened a single time before, two years ago when I'd managed to run myself into a gold medal at the Olympics and the President had sent me his congratulations. That was in 2172. Now was 2174, but the world record I set then still held.

I slit the envelope open.

Michael November Collins 46-06-18

Mr. Collins is called upon to report for medical examination at the office of Dr. Mark Wester, Boston University, State Research Facility, on 74-08-24. This is a Governmental request.

That was the entire text of the letter, apart from an illegible signature above the single word 'Assistant.'

I was still staring in confusion at the letter when Michael Junior and Tina came to say goodbye before rushing off to the school lift. While I was hugging the children, Judith came up, took the letter from me and told the kids to hurry.

'What's the meaning of this?' Judith asked.

'No idea, honey. I guess I'll just have to go there and find out.'

'But why would they want you to have a medical examination?'

I pulled her close, smiled and gave her a kiss.

'Maybe it's something about my fitness. I do hold a few world records, you know.'

'But why at the government's request?'

'Your guess is as good as mine.' I shrugged. 'But I guess in time they'll tell me why.'

'Doctor Mark Wester,' I repeated.

I was standing by the information desk in the central rotunda of Boston University, speaking to the attendant.

'Where can I find him?' I asked impatiently.

'I'll phone his secretary. It may take a while. As you perhaps don't realize, Boston University is no ordinary university, but a state research center, and formalities usually do take a few minutes.'

'No, I didn't know. Perhaps you can enlighten me by telling me why I've been asked to come here?'

'For a medical examination. It says so in your letter.'

She picked up her phone and tapped a number. 'Mary? Hi, it's Information. You're expecting a Mister Michael November Collins today. He's here now.'

Silence.

'Oh, okay, I can send him right up.'

She gave me a smile and pointed to a uniformed man seated inside a glass booth. 'Talk to the man in there. I'll give him a call, and he'll show you to Doctor Wester.' She lifted her phone again, and I began walking across the hall. I saw that she'd finished her phone call before I was even halfway across. The uniformed man rose, left his cage, came to meet me and shook my hand.

'I understand you're here to see Mark Wester.'

'That's right.'

'Fine. I'll show you to him. Please follow me.'

While walking along in his footsteps, I began feeling a steadily growing apprehension. My imagination was telling me that something was wrong. I couldn't put my finger on exactly what made me feel that way, but that only added irritation to my unease. Twice along the way we had to stop when uniformed guards asked us for access permits, but both times my guide sent them away by pointing to me and saying, 'He's here to see Doctor Wester.'

I grew steadily more bewildered, and finally couldn't refrain from asking him why I had been requested to see Wester. But the man knew nothing more than the girl at the information desk. Finally, we arrived.

An assistant, whom I assumed to be Mary, asked me to sit down on the couch and said that Doctor Wester would see me in just a minute or two. After three minutes, a man of around fifty came out of an inner office. He was fairly heftily built, and all of his visible skin was darkly tanned – a real tan, I mean, not the disgusting coloring you buy at the chemists. He looked to be in great shape.

'Thanks for coming in,' he said and held his hand out. I shook it.

'Perhaps you'd like to tell me why I'm here,' I asked.

'Didn't they put that in the letter? You're to have a medical examination.'

'That's what they wrote. I just don't understand why.'

'Oh, that. Well, you'll understand why in a short while. All depending on the results, of course.'

'Oh. Really? Well, in fact I'm not sure if I have any great wish to be checked. I'm extremely fit. In my line of work, I have to be.'

'Certainly. I know you're incredibly fit, but what I want to find out is how your innards are doing.'

He laughed, patted me on the back, and showed me into his office.

'I didn't know Boston University is a state research center. Don't you have any students at all any longer?'

'Yes, but we're all about specialized education nowadays. Not much of what we do is known to the general public.'

'So what are you doing?'

'I really shouldn't tell you, I suppose, but I suppose you could sum it all up by saying that we're doing biological research.'

'And what's that got to do with me? Where do I come into this?'

'Unfortunately, I'm afraid I can't give you any details until we have finished testing you.'

'Really? Well, how about getting started at once, in that case? I'd really like to get this over and done with, so I can get back to Judith and the kids again.'

'Oh, that's true, you're married, of course,' Wester said, scratching his head.

'So I am. To the most wonderful woman in the world,' I said, smiling.

'Good for you. Personally I have neither wife nor children, and I suppose I'm getting too old to start thinking about those things. At any rate I'm happy that you agree to our examinations.'

'So when can we start?'

'Tomorrow.'

'Tomorrow? I had believed it could all be done today.'

'We're talking of extremely thorough and complex examinations, and I'm afraid the procedure will take some time. But don't worry. We have arranged a private room for you here at the university. And you can always phone your wife.'

'Exactly how many days are we talking about here?'

'It's difficult to say. But it might be up to a week. It depends on if everything works out as it should.'

'A week! What kind of examinations are we talking about here? I want to know what this is all about. Why am I here? How are you going to test me? And why?'

'I've already said that I can't tell you until we have the results.'

'In that case I'm not going to go along with any tests at all,' I said firmly.

Wester smiled.

'Please, there's no reason to get all worked up about this. I assure you that the tests will be absolutely harmless.'

'That doesn't change anything,' I said. 'I still want to know the reason for them. That's not negotiable. I won't cooperate otherwise.'

'You've misunderstood, I'm afraid. It's not a matter of cooperating or not. You *will* cooperate. That's an order.'

'Whose order?'

'The government's.'

'Damn the government,' I said and grew angry. 'I'm not cooperating.'

'You don't have a choice.'

'I certainly do. I'll simply stand up and walk out the same door I came in.' I stood up and walked away from him.

'Please take a look at this paper,' Wester said just as I was grasping the doorknob.

'Why should I?'

'Because it's of great concern to you.'

'So long,' I said, opening the door.

'It's an order signed by the president...'

I hesitated.

'It demands your absolute obedience. If you refuse, you will be arrested for obstructing the government.'

'Is this some kind of joke?'

'Hardly. You can be punished by up to twenty-five years in prison and fined twenty-thousand dollars.'

I stared at him, mouth open.

'I don't believe you.'

'Read it yourself.'

Slowly, I closed the door. Slowly, Wester had adopted a threatening attitude.

'Well, how about it?'

'It doesn't look as if I have much of a choice, does it?'

'No, not really.'

'Can I phone my wife?'

'Of course. You are free to do whatever you like.'

'As long as it doesn't contradict what's in your orders, you mean?'

'Exactly. Someone will escort you to your rooms.'

'Where I'll be under guard?'

'Just to ensure your safety, of course.'

'Of course...'

Mark Wester certainly hadn't exaggerated when he told me that the tests and examinations to be performed were complex. For four days I did nothing except be shuffled from one room to the next, in each of which different doctors did their best to discover any ailments. In vain I tried to explain to them that I was as fit as a fiddle – to use an old and tired cliché. Nothing helped. They examined me from top to toe, from the inside and out. The first day they put me to a number of physical tests and fitness tests. They checked, double-checked, triple-checked and then, just to be sure of not having overlooked even the slightest detail, did a final check.

The second day I was X-rayed; they tapped my spine and asked me to stick my tongue out and say, 'Aaaah!'

That was all they did that day, and so I actually got a short breathing pause. They had given me a luxurious suite of rooms, and I was truly living just as comfortably as I normally spent my time wishing I could live. I phoned Judith every night and tried to explain to her that I had to stay put for a while. I never mentioned Wester's threats about jail time and fines. She kissed me over the phone and wished for me to come back home.

From the first time I was taken to my suite of rooms and for my entire stay at the university, two hefty uniformed guys from the university security force had stuck to me like glue. Just to ensure my safety, of course.

If I'd been hoping for the rest of the examinations to be no harder than those during the second day, I was hugely mistaken. During the third, fourth, and fifth day they practically turned my entire body inside out, scrutinizing every nook and cranny. They checked me for everything from athlete's foot to lung cancer.

On the sixth day it was finally all over, and Wester came to my rooms to tell me that I would be allowed to go home over the weekend, but that I had to return on Monday.

'Why?' I asked. It had become a routine question.

'We'll take your appendix out.'

I turned in my hospital bed, discarding my half-read comic book. I really didn't like my situation. The operation had been performed twelve days ago, and since then the doctors had pumped me full of vaccines against every conceivable illness.

I was bored and mad as hell. Mad because they more or less forced me to do whatever they felt like. Mad because I no longer felt like a free citizen of the United States. Mad because they refused to tell me what it was all about.

I sighed and picked up my comic book again.

In the afternoon, Mark Wester entered the room and sat down on a chair by the bed. His face was serious, and I realized that something must have happened, something that meant that everything was no longer going according to his plans – whatever they might be.

'You'll be discharged from this ward tomorrow.'

'Hooray,' I said, cheerful, for once.

He remained sitting, silent, hardly saying a word for perhaps five minutes.

'I guess you'd like to know what all this is about,' he said at last.

'Man, that was the smartest thing I've heard you manage since I came here.'

Wester took no offense.

'Have you ever heard of Hans Zägel?'

'Professor Hans Zägel, you mean?'

'Yes.'

'Could anyone have failed to hear about him?'

Professor Hans Zägel was the foremost scientist of our time. He was born in Germany, but when the Russians occupied Germany in 1936, he escaped to England, later on to the United States. There could hardly be anybody not aware of Hans Zägler, and I felt slightly insulted that Wester had asked me if I had heard of him. Compared to Zägler, Einstein was a nobody.

'No, I suppose you can't have failed to hear about him. Do you know how old he is?'

'Around eighty-five, I guess,' I said.

'He's eighty-six. Do you know what kind of research he is doing?'

'This and that, if you are to believe the news. He seems to know most everything within all areas of natural science. I suppose physics is his field of specialty. After all, he did build the first photon spaceship.'

'True, physics is his main subject, but for the last ten years he has mainly concerned himself with biology.'

'Hold on. What does Zägel have to do with me?'

'I'll tell you in a moment. Do you read any science fiction?'

I gestured towards the pile of magazines I had spent the last few days reading.

'Have you read anything about brain transplants lately?'

'I guess the idea pops up in some story now and then. Why?'

'What do you think about brain transplants in reality? Do you think they might be possible to perform?'

'No way,' I laughed. 'That's impossible.'

'You're wrong. Hans Zägel has performed several successful brain transplants. The first one six years ago.'

'But, dear God, that's impossible. There are just too many nerves that would have to be spliced together. It's just not possible!'

'Professor Zägel has performed one hundred forty-five transplants, forty-six of them on humans. With the help of his computer, he has developed a risk-free method. A computer, incidentally, that he himself constructed.'

'I find this very hard to believe.'

'I understand your doubts, but I assure you it's all true.'

'How?' I asked, still doubting him.

'Professor Zägel makes the necessary incisions. Opens the cranium, and so on. After that, he performs the rest of the operation aided by his computer. It keeps track of all nerves that have to be spliced and makes sure that none of them are forgotten. The nerve splices are performed with a laser.'

I scratched my head.

'If he's really managed all that, he's even more amazing than I thought. But why haven't you published anything about this?'

'That's what Professor Zägel wants until his work is entirely done.'

227

'And when will it be done?'

'In nine or ten years' time.'

'Now I'm not sure if you're pulling my leg or telling the truth, but I certainly would like to see some kind of evidence. Would it be possible for me to meet Professor Zägel?'

'No, unfortunately not.'

'And why not?'

'He is dying. He is an old man. His heart is giving out.'

I lay back in bed without answering, feeling sorry for Zägel.

'And where am I supposed to enter this?' I asked at last.

Wester slowly stroked his beardless chin.

'I assume you'll agree that Zägel's brain is the most distinguished on earth, possibly the finest ever known?'

'Sure,' I nodded. 'He's brilliant.'

'And would you agree that when such a brain is put at the service of mankind, that brain becomes the most important one on earth?'

'Yes, of course. Too bad he's going to die.'

'Now listen. To speak plainly, the world can't afford to lose a brain like Professor Zägel's.'

'Everyone has to die sometime.'

'Professor Zägel's work is almost finished. He needs, perhaps, another ten years. That's all the time he needs.'

'And where do I enter into all this?' I repeated patiently.

'Professor Zägel needs another ten years to finish the greatest work ever performed in the history of mankind.'

'And...'

'What we wish for is to find someone willing to give him the time he needs.'

'Where do you want to get with all this? Nobody can stop death.'

'No, but it can be postponed. We want you to let Professor Zägel's brain borrow your head in order for him to finish his work. We want you to be his new heart and body.'

I just stared stupidly at him. There was a long pause before I managed to reply.

'You're insane,' I whispered hoarsely.

'To Professor Zägel, it's a matter of life or death.'

'What about me, then? What about my life? I'll never agree to it!'

'You have to. Professor Zägel has no more than a week left to live.'

'The answer is no. To me, Zägel is welcome to die this instant, if that's what he wants. My life is more important to me than his. How could you even suggest something like this?'

'You have no choice in the matter. Professor Zägel is too important.'

'You can't force me!' I stood up and grabbed Wester's jacket.

'Pull yourself together, for God's sake!'

'Pull myself together?' I cried back at him. 'Do you really expect me to commit suicide just to save Zägel's life?'

'Professor Zägel's knowledge is of paramount importance to all of humanity.'

'I won't do it. Is that why you've been testing me these last weeks? What made you pick me instead of anyone else?'

'That's self-evident. You are as fit as anyone on earth. Your physique is phenomenal. Professor Zägel himself picked you out three months ago...'

'So he's picked me. He's chosen his own salvation. I'm supposed to save Zägel's life by means of his own discovery. But you'll never make me do it.'

'You have no choice. The president himself has approved the plan.'

I sat silent for a few seconds, then shot up and tore the door open, attempting to get out of the university. But I didn't manage more than five steps before the guards posted outside my door had caught me. I yelled and cursed, kicked them to make them release me. One of them twisted my arm hard behind my back, and the pain made me scream.

'Don't hurt him!' I heard Wester call out.

So I did have one small advantage. They couldn't hurt me, but I had no scruples as far as they were concerned. When all is said and done, I am one of the world's foremost athletes. I aimed a kick at the stomach of one of the guards, and hit home perfectly. He doubled up, and before the other one had a chance to stop me I kicked him again. The second guard held me in a hard grip around my body, locking my arms to my sides, but I slammed him hard against the wall. I heard him moan when the back of his head struck the marble, but I was unable to pity him. I was fighting for my life. He refused to let go, but when I threw myself down, his body flew forward, above my head. Now my hands were free, and with all my strength I drove my fist against his temple.

Jumping across the first guard, who had started to rise, I ran towards the exit. Wester tried to catch hold of me after a couple of steps, wanting to stop me, but I pushed him violently aside. 'Bastard,' I cried, and ran out the revolving door.

I ran along the hallway and down the stairs until I reached the ground floor, where I paused for a second or two while trying to remember if I should go left or right to get out of the building. I decided on left and was halfway down the hall when I heard the loudspeakers warn that I was escaping. They urged everyone to try to stop me, but warned people to be careful not to harm me. Suddenly I was back in the rotunda and saw the huge glass doors leading to freedom.

I began running but was immediately seen by the receptionist at the information desk. She stood up, yelling at me to stop, but of course I ignored her. She screamed for the uniformed guard who had helped me find my way on that first day to stop me, and I saw him closing in on me at an angle. He was closer to the doors than I was, but I was faster. I knew that if I could only make it out the doors, I could outrun anyone who tried to catch me.

Perhaps being a champion runner wasn't such a bad thing after all. The guard almost reached me, but missed by a few inches.

I threw myself out the doors and began running across the lawn. I was dressed only in my pajamas and was barefoot, so I had to choose the lawn. I made it out of the campus block. I ran across the street and saw a man just getting into his car. He was putting his key into the ignition lock when I threw the door open and tore him out on the pavement.

'Sorry, buddy, but this is life or death,' I told him.

The car didn't start on the first turn of the key, but on the second try it began spinning. The guards were sixty or seventy feet away when I started accelerating and I assumed that they noted the plate number. I drove for six blocks, then turned towards the main road. I had to stop for a red light, and while I waited for traffic to pass by I realized that I was shaking from fear. I felt empty inside, unable to realize how I – I, of all people – had ended up in this nightmare.

'Fuck you, Mr. President,' I muttered. 'And to think I voted for you. Next time I'll vote for the Democrats ... if there is a next time.'

When I woke up, Wester was leaning down over me. The shock from the injection they'd given me was slowly abating, and I was able to start thinking again. I tried to rise, but found that leather straps tied me to the bed, so I let my body relax.

'What ... how?' I asked.

'The police caught you. You shouldn't have tried to run.'

'No, of course not. I suppose I should just urge you to operate as soon as possible?'

'The operation will be tonight. We don't dare let Professor Zägel fight his body any longer. He might die at any moment.'

'Let's hope. Is there really no way you could

pick someone else?'

'No. It's too late, and regardless of that you are the one we need. Your excellent physique makes your chances to survive the operation better than anyone had during any of Professor Zägel's previous procedures. And besides, this time I'll be operating, and it will be my first time. I want the best chance possible to succeed, particularly given the importance of this operation.'

'My life is important to me. I have a wife and two children. I'm responsible for them and have to take care of them!'

'Don't worry about your family. The state will take care of them in the best way possible. They'll want for nothing.'

'But I don't want to lose them. I don't want to die!'

'I'm sorry, but there really isn't any alternative.'

'But why try to stop the inevitable? Zägel will die anyway, sooner or later. Even at best, I won't live for more than fifty or sixty years.'

'Professor Zägel can put those fifty or sixty years to immense use. And please let me ease your mind. You won't feel anything at all during the operation.'

'And what will you do with my brain afterward?' I asked him ironically. 'Donate it to medical research?'

'No, of course not. We plan on freezing it. In a few years, perhaps when Professor Zägel has perfected his method, we'll try to find a suitable body for it. Maybe you'll even get your own body back, though I doubt the government will agree to that.'

'I doubt it, too. Zägel will still be important. And what will you do when my body wears down? Find him another?'

'Perhaps. That will depend on how worn-out his brain is becoming.'

'Don't you have any feelings at all?' I didn't even try to hide the loathing I felt for him.

'You have to understand why we're doing this. Look at it from our perspective. We do what we truly believe is best for the state. In addition to his medical work, Professor Zägel is also engaged in designing robots to cancel the Russian defense shields.'

I spat at him, but Wester didn't even react.

'I'll leave you now. Next time we meet will be in the operating room. Your wife has been permitted to see you for two hours. You will be entirely undisturbed during that time, and how you spend it concerns nobody else.'

Wester opened the door. Two guards entered the room. They undid my restraints and left before I had time even to rise. After a few minutes the door opened again, and Judith walked in. She had tears in her eyes and threw herself into my arms.

'Michael,' she gasped. 'Why, Michael? Why you?'

'They just picked me. Do you know what will happen?'

'They've told me. But they can't do it, Michael, tell me they can't do it!'

I sighed. 'I'm afraid they can. I did my best to get out of here, but I only got a few blocks away before the cops picked me up.'

'But the police are supposed to protect people's lives.'

'They do exactly as the government tells them. And in this case, Zägel's life is more important than that of an athlete. Judith, promise me to take care of Junior and Tina. Make sure they get the best of everything.'

'Oh, Michael, can't you stop it somehow?'

'How?'

She made a helpless gesture. I held her close and kissed her. For the first time I realized how unbelievably lucky I really had been to find a wife like Judith.

'Where are the kids?' I asked her.

'They weren't allowed to come. They're too young to understand this kind of thing, they told me.'

'Too young...' I felt bitter.

'I'll take care of them.'

I pulled her down on the bed.

'Michael ... Wester, that man out there, he says they might be able to freeze your brain and wake it again later.'

'But my body will be ten years older, or even much more than that. At the very least I'll have lost years of my life. And besides, I don't believe they'll give me my body back even when Zägel has finished his work. He would still have maybe fifty years left to live in it, and I suspect the government won't feel like wasting those years on me.'

I kissed her again, softly at first, then hard and demanding.

'We have two hours. Would you? One last time?'

I began undressing her. We touched and teased each other, fondled and urged each other on.

Finally we tumbled down on the bed and made love more tenderly and intensely than ever before. It was my last time, and I had never before felt a greater passion, never before realized how much I truly loved living. My last time. I could hardly assume that Judith would live in celibacy for the rest of her life because I was no longer there. Perhaps she would marry again. In that case, who? I couldn't bear thinking about that.

We melted together.

Afterwards we lay talking. Judith smoked one of her cigarettes. I caressed her thoughtfully. Strangely enough, neither of us felt any despair or fear despite what would happen. We were both very calm and spoke mostly of things in the same way we used to do when I was going off to some training camp and would be gone for a couple of weeks. We talked just as if I would be back after a while.

They let us stay together for more than two hours, but after three, one of the guards knocked on my door, stuck his head in and told us to get ready to say goodbye. We dressed, or at least she did, and we said our goodbyes. Then we sat holding each other until they came back in through the door.

They closed the door behind Judith, and one of the men stayed inside trying to talk to me. I didn't want to. I just lay on my bed, staring at the ceiling, remembering Judith's lips.

At half past four the other guard came back and told me to make myself ready. I had half an hour. He wondered if I would like to talk to a priest, but I told him no. Then a nurse came and shaved my head.

I was hungry, but they wouldn't allow me to eat. At five sharp a nurse rolled in a hospital bed and asked me to lie down on it so she could roll me off to surgery.

'The hell I will,' I told her. 'I've got legs to walk on, and if this is my last trip, at least I'll walk it myself.'

None of them objected. I stood, put my shorts on and followed the nurse. The guards walked behind me. When we stepped into the hallway, I thought of trying to escape again, but I knew it would be pointless. They would have caught me in a few minutes. So I stepped into the lift instead. Another hallway, more swinging doors. Then I stood in the operating room. There were half a dozen people, all of them busy preparing for the operation.

Mark Wester came up to me. He nodded and asked me to lie down. There were two operating tables in the room. A man already lay on one of them. I assumed him to be Zägel, and for a second or two I was filled with the thought of rushing up to him, crushing his head, beating his brain to a pulp. Wester broke the spell by grabbing hold of my arm and walking me to my table. I lay down and someone covered my body with a mauve sheet.

'Let me thank you for all your assistance and cooperation,' Wester said. 'Thank you.'

I felt the sting of a needle in my arm.

The last thing I remember was hating him. Hating him. Hating...

AN UNLIKELY MEETING

HENNING MANKELL
AND HÅKAN NESSER

Suddenly Wallander realized that he no longer knew where was. Why couldn't she have come to Ystad instead? On the freeway, somewhere north of Kassel, he had doubted if it was even possible to drive on any longer. The snow had come down very heavy. Already then he had known that he would be late for his meeting with his daughter. Why did Linda have to suggest that they should spend Christmas together somewhere in the middle of Europe?

He turned on the roof light in the car and found his map. In the beam lights the road stretched empty. Where had he made a wrong turn? Around him was darkness. He had a sudden premonition of being forced to spend Christmas night in his car. He would drive blindly along these unknown continental roads and he would never find Linda.

He searched the map. Was he even anywhere at all? Or had he crossed some invisible border to a country that didn't even exist? He put away his map and drove on. The snow had suddenly stopped falling.

After a dozen miles he stopped at an intersection. He read the signs and searched the map again. Nothing. He made a sudden decision. He would have to find someone to ask. He turned off towards the town the road signs claimed to be closest.

The town was larger than he had expected. But its streets were deserted. Wallander stopped outside a restaurant that seemed to be open. He locked his car and realized that he was hungry.

He stepped into the dusk.

The restaurant was a breath of a Europe that hardly existed any more. Frozen in time, a strong smell of stale cigar smoke. Deer heads and coats of arms shared the brown walls with beer posters. A bar, also brown, empty of patrons; shaded booths, similar to the pens in a barn. At the tables shadows leaned over glasses of beer. In the background, loudspeakers. Christmas songs. Holy night.

Wallander looked around without finding an empty booth. A glass of beer, he thought. Then a good description of how to drive on. Then a phone call to Linda. To tell her whether he'd make it tonight or not.

One of the booths was occupied by a single man. Wallander hesitated. Then made up his mind. He walked up and pointed. The man nodded. It was okay for Wallander to sit down. The man sitting opposite him was eating. An old, sad-faced waiter appeared. Goulash? Wallander pointed to the other man's plate and beer glass. Then he waited. The man opposite went on eating with slow movements.

Wallander thought that he might start a conversation. Ask about the way, ask where he was. He took the opportunity when the man pushed his plate away.

'I don't mean to disturb you,' Wallander said. 'But do you speak English?'

The man nodded noncommittally.

'I've taken a wrong turn somewhere,' Wallander said. 'I'm Swedish, I'm a policeman, I'm on my way to spend Christmas with my daughter. But I'm lost. I don't even know where I am.'

'Maardam,' the man said.

Wallander recalled the road sign. But he had no memory of having seen the place on his map. He told the man his destination.

The man shook his head.

'You won't get there tonight,' he said. 'It's far. You're off course.'

Then he smiled. His smile was unexpected. As if his face had cracked.

'I'm a policeman, too,' the man said.

Wallander gave him a thoughtful look. Then he held out his hand.

'Wallander,' he said. 'I'm a detective. In a Swedish town called Ystad.'

'Van Veeteren,' the man said. 'I'm a policeman here in Maardam.'

'Two lonely policeman,' Wallander said. 'One of them lost. Not the most amusing of situations.'

Van Veeteren smiled again, nodding.

'You're right,' he said. 'Two policemen meeting only because one of them has made a wrong turn.'

'Things are as they are,' Wallander said.

The waiter put his food on the table in front of him.

Van Veeteren lifted his glass, toasting him.

241

'Eat slowly,' he said. 'You're in no hurry.'

Wallander thought of Linda. Of his having to call her. But he realized that the man who also was a policeman and who had a weird name was right.

He would spend his Christmas Eve in this strange place called Maardam and which he suspected wasn't even marked on his map.

Things were as they were.

Nobody could change that.

Just as so many other things in life.

Wallander placed his call to Linda, who of course was disappointed. But she understood.

After the call, Wallander stayed on outside the phone booth.

The Christmas songs made him sad.

He disliked sadness. Particularly on Christmas Eve.

Outside, the snow had begun falling again.

Van Veeteren remained sitting in their pen, his eyes fixed on two crossed toothpicks. How strange, he thought. I almost could have sworn that I wouldn't need to exchange even two words with anyone until the Christmas dawn's early gleaming ... and then this guy suddenly turns up.

A Swedish policeman? Taking the wrong road in a snowstorm?

Just as unlikely as life itself. And that he himself was sitting here certainly wasn't the result of any planning. Quite the contrary. After the obligatory Christmas lunch with Renate and the afternoon best wishes telephone call to Erich, Jess and the grandchildren, he had crawled into a bubble bath

242

with a stout beer and Handel turned up full. While waiting for the evening to come.

Christmas Eve chess with Mahler at the society. Just like last year. And the year before that.

Mahler had called shortly before six. From the hospital up in Aarlack, where the old poet was stuck with his even older father and a broken thighbone.

A pity for such a vital ninety-year-old man. A pity considering the gambit he had thought of while taking his bath. A pity all things considered.

When despite all he had finally arrived at the society in the whirling snow he had also realized that it was no use to him without Mahler. He had driven on a few blocks towards Zwille and finally walked into the restaurant without any expectations. Regardless of everything else he had to eat. And perhaps drink.

The Swedish policeman returned with a sad smile.

'Did you reach her? What did you say your name was, by the way?'

'Wallander. Yes, it's fine. We just postponed everything until tomorrow.'

There was a sudden soft warmth in his glance and there could hardly be any doubt about its origin.

'Daughters aren't such a bad thing to have sometimes,' Van Veeteren said. 'Even if you can't find them. How many do you have?'

'Only one,' Wallander said. 'But she's all right.'

'Me too,' Van Veeteren said. 'And a son too but that's something else.'

'Doesn't surprise me,' Wallander said.

The sad waiter appeared, asking about what was to follow.

'Personally I prefer beer when alone,' Van Veeteren said. 'And wine with company.'

'Ought to think about where to spend the night,' Wallander said.

'I've already done that,' Van Veeteren stated. 'Red or white?'

'Thanks,' Wallander said. 'Red it is, then.'

The waiter again disappeared into the shadows. A brief silence fell at the table while an Ave Maria of unknown origin began playing from the speakers.

'Why did you become a policeman?' Wallander asked.

Van Veeteren studied his colleague before answering.

'I've asked myself that question so many times by now that I can't remember the answer any longer,' he said. 'But I'd guess you to be ten years younger, so maybe you know?'

Wallander gave a half smile and leaned back.

'Yes,' he said. 'Though I'd have to admit that there are times when I have to stop to remind myself. It's all this evil; I'm planning to exterminate it. The only problem is that it seems we have built an entire civilization on it.'

'Or at least some major supports,' Van Veeteren said, nodding. 'Though I would have thought Sweden to be spared at least the worst aberrations ... your Swedish model, your spirit of consensus ... well, it's what you read about, anyway.'

'I used to believe in all that, too,' Wallander

said. 'But that was a few years ago.'

The waiter returned with a bottle of red wine and a few pieces of cheese, courtesy of the house. Ave Maria ended and muted strings began playing.

Wallander raised his glass but stopped in the middle of moving, listening hard.

'Do you recognize that?' he asked.

Van Veeteren nodded. 'Villa-Lobos,' he said. 'What's the name of it?'

'I don't know,' Wallander said. 'But it's a piece for eight cellos and one soprano. It's damned lovely. Listen.'

They sat without speaking.

'We seem to have some things in common,' Wallander said.

Van Veeteren nodded contentedly.

'So it seems,' he said. 'If you play chess as well I'll be damned if I believe you're not just something someone's made up.'

Wallander drank. Then he shook his head.

'Damned badly,' he admitted. 'I'm better at bridge, but hardly a champion at that either.'

'Bridge?' Van Veeteren said and cut off a third of the Camembert. 'Haven't played that in thirty years. Back in those days we used to be four.'

Wallander smiled and gave a slight nod towards another table.

'Back there are a couple of guys with a deck of cards.'

Van Veeteren leaned out of the booth to check.

Wallander was right. In a booth a few yards away two other men were flipping cards back and forth, looking bored. One of them was tall, thin and slightly stooped. The other one was almost his opposite: short, heavy and with a dogged expression. Judging from wrinkles and hair they were both close to fifty years old.

Van Veeteren stood.

'All right,' he said. 'It's only Christmas once a year. Let's make our move.'

Less than ten minutes later the bidding was under way and after a further twenty-five minutes Wallander and Van Veeteren had won a doubled bid of four spades.

'Vagaries of chance,' the shorter of the two men muttered.

'Even a blind hen sometimes finds a grain of corn,' the taller one explained.

'Two,' Van Veeteren said. 'Two blind hens.'

Wallander shuffled the cards with slightly unpracticed hands.

'And what do you two do for a living?' Van Veeteren asked, accepting an offered cigarette.

'Writers,' the tall one said.

'Crime novels,' added the shorter one. 'We are fairly well-known. At least back home. Or at least I. We lost our way – that's why we happen to be here.'

'Many have lost their way tonight,' Van Veeteren said.

'Crime writers often lose their way,' Wallander noted and began dealing the cards. 'I suppose that's another pretty rotten line of work.'

'I don't doubt it,' Van Veeteren said.

They were about halfway through the next hand – an undoubled three no trump contract

with the fairly well-known author as declarer –
when the waiter appeared unasked from the
shadows. He looked pained.

'Might I just inform you,' he said subserviently,
'that we'll be closing in ten minutes. It's Christmas Eve.'

'What the heck...?' Wallander said.

'What the hell?' Van Veeteren said.

The tall crime writer coughed and waved a
dismissing index finger. But it was the short,
well-known one who spoke.

'In that case, might I just in turn inform you,'
he said without the slightest tone of subservi-
ence, 'that there is at least one advantage to being
a writer...'

'...even one who has lost his way,' the tall one
interjected.

'...and that is that we are the ones writing your
lines,' the short one continued. 'So I'll ask you to
damned well repeat that entrance!'

The waiter bowed. Disappeared and after only
a few seconds reappeared, armed with a bunch of
keys. Bowed again and cleared his throat.

'On behalf of the host I would like to wish you
all a Merry Christmas. Please feel free to serve
yourselves from the bar, and should you feel
hungry, there are cold cuts in the refrigerator.
Lock up whenever you leave, but please don't
forget to put the keys in the mail slot.'

'Excellent,' Van Veeteren stated. 'Perhaps there
is some common sense and good in the world
after all.'

The waiter retired for the last time. When he
disappeared through the entrance they briefly

heard the whistling of the snowstorm, but then the winter night again enfolded the little restaurant in the town that was missing from the map.

Common sense? Kurt Wallander thought, sliding a trey towards the king and jack already on the table. Good?

Well, if there was, perhaps on Christmas Eve.

And in the company of fictitious poets.

Poets, my ass! he thought after a second. Eight novels and not even a fucking line of blank verse!

Tomorrow, he would see Linda.

AN ALIBI FOR SEÑOR BANEGAS

MAGNUS MONTELIUS

They were alone in the small interrogation room. The defense lawyer regarded him under heavy eyelids. His face was red and bloated and his hair a bit unruly. It had probably been a tiring holiday. Welcome to the club, Adam thought.

'So you mean,' the lawyer sighed, 'that you are absolutely innocent of these charges.'

Adam nodded.

'But you did make a complete confession to the police?'

'It's complicated.'

The lawyer looked even more tired. He obviously didn't believe Adam, nor was he in the mood for any complicated stories. But even so, Adam thought, he had to tell him what really had happened. And start at the beginning.

Señor Banegas carefully sipped his wine toddy and glanced around appreciatively. He and Adam were the only guests in the Hotel Reisen bar, not particularly strange since, after all, this was the night before Christmas Eve.

'It's not a bad plan, is it?'

Adam couldn't get a word out. Actually, it was the most idiotic idea he had ever heard.

Banegas smiled crookedly. 'Of course it entails

a certain amount of inconvenience. And to me, personally, considerable cost. But love, my dear friend, is worth any sacrifice.'

Señor Banegas was the Honduran secretary of state for infrastructure, a successful retailer of favors and favors in return. He had arrived with a delegation a little over a week ago. The absurd time of year had been chosen to coincide with Christmas shopping, and the delegates had all brought their wives.

Banegas twisted his grizzled mustache. 'Adam, I tell you this most seriously. We never know where and when a great love will overwhelm us.'

But Banegas was strangely reticent about the object of his passion.

Adam felt as if the minister read his thoughts. 'We are gentlemen, you and I. So I know that there is no need for me to name the young lady. That is well. As I have told you, my wife is the problem.' He sighed. 'She is crazy, and I use the word in a strictly clinical sense.'

Adam was prepared to agree. During his trips to Honduras he had met Mrs. Banegas at receptions. A round woman with staring eyes who seemed to watch every movement her husband made.

'When I told her that we would stay on an extra week, just she and I, to celebrate Christmas in Stockholm, she was at first overjoyed. But then she became jealous and suspicious. Why had I decided on such a thing? Was I going to meet someone? I tell you, she is crazy.'

'Well, not totally off the mark, anyway. And is this where I enter the picture?' Banegas spread his arms.

'Exactly. I explained that it would unfortunately not be possible for me to spend all my time in her company, no matter how happily I would have done so. But that my good friend Adam Dillner laid claim to part of my time for meetings concerning a transaction between the Honduran government and the company represented by him. And that I could hardly refuse, which she also realized. In my country, this would have been entirely normal. Not here, naturally. But she doesn't know that.'

He was right, of course.

Banegas fished a paper out of his inside pocket and put it on the table. 'I took the liberty of writing the schedule you have set me, since I thought it would add a nice touch. I used your company letterhead.'

Where had he gotten hold of that? 'If I may say so, this looks like a very busy schedule.'

Banegas solemnly put his right palm over his heart. 'My friend, I am in love.' In a more subdued voice, he went on: 'I must implore you to stick entirely to our little subterfuge. Explain to your family that you are meeting an important client and, of course, stay away from home during the periods set out in the schedule. As I have told you, my wife is unstable and might very well decide to check on your absences from home. It is a most reasonable precaution.'

Adam looked at the schedule. In fact it was highly unreasonable that he would have to spend such a large part of the days between Christmas and New Year's shuffling around in the snowstorm to prevent Mrs. Banegas from breaking her unfaithful husband's alibi. There were more conventional ways of making business contacts with Central American customers that worked perfectly well. Still, right now Banegas' insane wife happened to be just what Adam needed.

'Grampa, Grampa, Grampa!'

Max and Ada ran a set course around the living room, through the hallway, past the kitchen, and back again. Adam walked up to the kitchen island to pour himself some more wine.

Kattis gave him a glance. 'Adam, we'll have a nice evening tonight.'

His mother-in-law entered the kitchen, an empty wineglass in her hand. She stumbled on the carpet, muttering under her breath, bent to the bag-in-box wine container and wrinkled her nose. 'Don't you have anything Spanish? A Rioja?'

The plane she was on had lifted off from Málaga less than ten hours earlier.

Kattis removed a baking sheet full of gingerbread from the oven. 'Adam, would you look?'

But his mother-in-law had already forgotten it all and refilled her glass. 'I think I'll make some toffee tonight, by the way. The poor little ones have hardly had any Christmas candy at all.'

'We're trying to cut back on sugar.'

'Adam, dear, you really shouldn't jump on board every new health bandwagon.'

'It's hardly– '

Kattis let go of her rolling pin. 'That's a great idea, Mother!'

Grandma called out to the living room: 'What

do you say, kids, do you want some of grandma's toffee?'

They screamed back. Hopelessly, Adam verified that they were always willing to sell their souls for some melted cane sugar.

'There, you see,' Grandma said, staggering back into the living room.

He turned to Kattis.

'Adam!' she growled.

In the living room, Grampa was in the middle of playing something with Max and Ada while Grandma was leafing through some old Swedish family magazines Kattis had put out for her. When they entered, Grampa poured a whiskey and sat down in the couch, arms spread across its backrest. 'Katarina told us about your Mexican, Adam,' he said.

'Honduran.'

His father-in-law waved an impatient hand. 'That's what I said.' He glared at Adam. 'What I don't understand is how anyone, a husband, can abandon his wife almost the whole Christmas holiday just to play tourist guide to some Colombian.'

'Hond–'

'When he has two small children and his wife's parents have come to visit–'

'Daddy, it's okay. Adam and I have talked about it. It's his work.'

'Haven't we come any further despite all our talk about equality? And Adam, what's so important about this – Honduran?'

Adam hesitated. 'We are trying to get a road project, the new highway from Honduras to

253

Nicaragua. This Banegas fellow–'

His father-in-law slowly shook his head. 'Adam, Adam, Adam. That's so out-of-date. Why don't you build a railroad instead?'

Grandma put her magazine down and turned to Kattis. 'Daddy is the chairman of the Torremolinos Environmental Club. We have become activists.'

'That's great, Mother!'

Adam half-heartedly began to describe the infrastructure of Honduras, but his father-in-law interrupted him again.

'They don't need a new road to Nicaragua, Adam. What they need is a road away from climate disaster.'

'God, how well you put that, Göran!' Grandma exclaimed. 'Why don't you write it down, Adam?'

He rose slowly. 'I think I'll lay the table.'

When he stood in the kitchen, he heard his mother-in-law's voice. 'He never listens to a word we say.'

Tomorrow was Christmas Eve, but according to Banegas' schedule he would still be away for a few hours to explain the traffic solutions used on the Southern Link expressway. He could hardly wait.

Thanks to the Banegas scheme, he could spend several Christmas Eve hours in a coffeehouse on Nybrogatan. He brought a book he had given himself for Christmas, but most of the time he just sipped his coffee and looked at the last-minute shoppers rushing past outside. As for himself, he had no more shopping to do, no other tasks to perform than to serve as an alibi for a horny minister of infrastructure.

On Christmas Day, Banegas hadn't dared make any entries on his schedule, and Adam spent the entire day with his family and in-laws. It was worse than usual. Kattis' family had introduced so many traditions that the holidays became rigidly directed performances. Every detail was sacrosanct and their order must not be changed.

Mostly it was all about games. After ten years, Adam was still unable to see any point to them. They played Hide the Pig Santa, the Almond Race, and something which seemed mainly to involve everyone hitting everyone else's head with tiny sandbags his mother-in-law had dragged along from Spain for the occasion. He wanted to refuse to get involved but knew from experience that everything would just get worse if he didn't join in. Since he was the only one unaware of the rules he always lost, to his father-in-law's undisguised delight. Adam sadly observed that as opposed to himself, his children always joined in with great enthusiasm.

The evening ended with a quiz on the lives of members of the clan. Though he always got what the others considered unusually easy questions, he had so far never managed a single correct answer.

'But Adam,' his mother-in-law exclaimed, 'you had the same question about Aunt Lotta's rusty old Audi last year!'

Tomorrow was the day after Christmas. That was when they were supposed to have their traditional waffle breakfast in front of the TV. Followed by a combined outdoors walk and new quiz competition, then a lunch with Kattis' sister in Australia attending via a computer link, and after that a family game called Where Is the Krokofant, named for a disgustingly sweet candy bar.

Luckily, Banegas had a full schedule.

Adam decided to install himself in the cafeteria of the Museum of the Mediterranean. According to the schedule, he was showing Banegas biogas refueling stations. In the evening they were doing something even more silly; he didn't remember what. It didn't matter.

He was deep into his book when his phone rang. It was Banegas.

'Adam, we have a problem. It is extremely important that we meet at once.'

Every protest and demand for further explanations was met by hissed objections.

'We really must meet, I'm waiting at the Hotel Reisen bar.'

Adam plodded through the snow on the bridge to the Old Town. What had he gotten himself into?

Banegas seemed perfectly calm and sat comfortably with a wine toddy. His whole demeanor suggested that it was far from his first. He went straight to the point.

'We have a problem with tonight's activity.'

We?

Banegas went on. 'I chose the visit to the Hammarby Lake City since my wife refuses to travel by boat. Now it turns out that you can go there by land. Which you failed to tell me.' He glared at

Adam. 'And of course my wife has found that out and insists on accompanying me.'

Why, oh why had he gone along with Banegas' plan?

'Adam, it just won't do. And so at the last moment you have changed our schedule and instead arranged for us to go to the opera.'

'Opera?'

'My wife hates opera. As an extra precaution I have also decided that Señor Harald Thorvaldsson of the Export Council will join us, and that after the performance we will have supper at the Gyldene Freden restaurant to discuss business.' He held up Thorvaldsson's calling card, as if it were a winning lottery ticket. 'That's when he gives me this, which will further strengthen the credibility of our story.'

It was hard enough to get hold of any of the Export Council functionaries during normal office hours; to convince one of them to spend the day after Christmas at the opera with a Honduran secretary of state would probably be humanly impossible. But, as Banegas would probably have said if Adam had bothered to object, his wife didn't know that.

Banegas pulled out their schedule. 'So I would like to ask you to make the necessary change to our little program.' He gave Adam a pen and added kindly: 'You can do it by hand.'

As in a trance, Adam struck out the visit to Hammarby Lake City and wrote in the opera performance according to Banegas' instructions. 'Don't forget to write that Señor Thorvaldsson will accompany us.'

257

When that was done, Banegas conjured up a ticket to that night's performance of *Don Giovanni* and ceremoniously tore it apart along the perforation. 'Here's your ticket, Adam, I leave nothing to chance.'

'Is that really necessary?'

'I insist.'

Outside, Banegas embraced him. 'Adam, how will I ever—' The Honduran was cut short as they both lost their footing. Arms around each other, they bounced down the snow-covered steps to the sidewalk. Adam managed to loosen his grip and keep his balance, but just as he imagined all was well he felt one of his feet crack the ice on a pool of water and his shoe immediately filled.

'God *damn* it!'

Banegas gave him a reproachful look. 'My dear friend, I don't know what that was all about, but there is no need to worry. Here we both are, and none the worse for wear.' He glanced down at Adam's feet. 'Well, sorry about your shoe. But I assume you must agree that it's a minor problem.' He checked his watch. 'Sorry, I really can't chat any longer. Remember that according to our schedule we are having supper after the performance. Make sure not to get home earlier than midnight.'

The minister hurried off towards Kungsträdgården park.

Back at his house, the windows glowed in the night. Adam hid behind the snow-laden lilacs. According to the program he shouldn't be here, but there was no helping it. His foot felt frozen

258

stiff. In the washroom there were rubber boots and a laundry basket with warm socks; the key to the cellar was in the third right-hand flowerpot in the greenhouse. Perfect.

Then he saw it. The door to the cellar was open. The kids must have been playing down there again. How many times had he told them... And besides, there had been a lot of burglaries in the area lately. Silently he sneaked across the lawn, cursing under his breath every time the cold water in his shoe splashed his toes.

He walked soundlessly through the cellar and was just about to start digging in the laundry basket when he saw the man. His heart skipped a beat and he had to bite his lip not to scream. Wasn't that... Yes, something metallic gleamed in the thief's hand! Adam's eyes flickered wildly around the room and stopped at a board left over from their renovation. Perfect. He grabbed it, slipped forward. His temples throbbed. I'll fucking show you!

Slap that thing out of his hand with the board. Get the bastard. He lifted his arm, felt his foot slip on the floor. He lost his balance but completed the blow. No, a little too high, straight to the head. And much too hard! A nasty, dull sound and a jolt he could feel all through his arm and body. The man collapsed to the floor and made a rattling sound.

Fuck, how bad had he hit him? He couldn't... A thin, red trickle of blood ran from his ear and joined the blood on his cheek. Adam frantically looked for some sign of life. He couldn't... Warily his shaking hands turned the body. That's when he recognized the familiar face, burned hazel by endless hours on the golf courses in Torremolinos. An unlit flashlight rolled from a slack hand. He felt his cartoid artery. Nothing. No no no, say it isn't true! Anything, just not this! Suddenly he heard the rhythmic yells of his children upstairs.

'Where's the Krokofant? Where's the Krokofant?'

Get rid of the board, find socks, put on boots. Fuck fuck fuck. He ran across the lawn, through the woods, to another subway station. Just to be safe. Threw his shoes in a building-site container. Then he threw up on the platform. It just couldn't be true. At the pub in the main railway station he downed a pint of beer and immediately ordered another. At least it made his hands stop shaking. What had he done? But it was an accident! Sure, but still!

While running through the wood he had promised himself at least to consider it. But halfway through his third pint he made up his mind. What good would it do? Confessing wouldn't bring Göran back to life. But it wasn't the thought of jail that frightened him, it was the reactions of his children. What would they think of him? He would forever be the man who had killed their adored Grampa. And Kattis? No, no, he would keep silent.

The two police officers waiting in the living room were dressed in civilian clothes and unobtrusive. The body had already been removed, the older one whispered, a kindly man who reminded Adam of his company's personnel officer. His colleague was a younger woman who wore an inscrutable expression and her hair in a ponytail. She scrutinized Adam from head to feet. Did he have any stains? He had checked so carefully! The personnel officer cop took him aside.

'A horrible thing. I understand you are all in shock.' He went on to explain the circumstances with which Adam was already much too familiar. 'We have had reports of a number of burglaries in this area. Your father-in-law must have left the door open and been surprised by them. He was playing some game with the children, aah...'

The young police woman checked her notes. 'Where's the Krokofant?'

'Exactly,' the policeman went on. 'These international burglar gangs are no Sunday school boys. They used as much violence as necessary to be sure of getting away. Unfortunately they may already be out of the country.'

Adam slowly shook his head, angrily clenching his jaws to hide his relief.

'Of course we hold no preconceptions,' the young woman added. Adam said nothing. He much preferred her older partner.

Adam spent the rest of the evening trying to comfort Kattis. His mother-in-law took care of the children and managed to be both strong and tender despite her own grief. Had he misjudged her all these years? Before the police officers left they had wanted to know where he had spent his evening. Just routine, the man assured him self-consciously. Adam told them about his visit to

261

the opera and showed them the ticket Banegas had given him. The policeman excused the necessity for such formalism. The woman said nothing but carefully noted the seat number in her little book. No, Adam didn't like her at all.

That night he got no sleep at all. Would the police contact Banegas? And what had that police-woman been looking at all the time? He had to get hold of Banegas before the police got to him. At eight in the morning he sneaked out into the garden to call Banegas' cell. No answer. He called again, several times, until nine-thirty. He didn't dare phone their room at the hotel, given how suspicious Mrs. Banegas was.

Finally he decided to go to the Grand Hotel. He waited in the lobby for at least an hour. Suddenly he got a glimpse of Mrs. Banegas, hurrying out alone through the revolving doors. Strange. Ac-cording to their schedule, there were no imaginary educational field trips until three o'clock. At this hour, Banegas ought to be keeping his wife company. Could he be busy with the police?

Nonchalantly, Adam stepped into an elevator. On the third floor he found room 318.

'Señor Banegas,' he hissed while knocking. 'Señor Banegas, it's me. Adam.'

No reply. Adam tried again. 'Héctor! Open, it's important.'

He waited for another minute and was just about to knock again when he heard someone clear his throat behind him. A tall man in the hotel uni-form, buttons gleaming.

'Are you looking for someone?'

Adam made a half-hearted attempt to explain.

'Hotel policy is that all callers must announce themselves at the reception. And your friend doesn't seem to be in. If you give me your name, I will inform him that you have been here to see him.' He gave Adam a strange look. 'Your *full* name.'

Adam thought for a second and decided on 'Jonas Lindgren,' an old classmate who had always gotten into trouble. The uniformed man followed him all the way out to the street.

Kattis had decided to leave for Spain that day, bringing her mother and the children. They had to get away from the house for a while, she said. Adam told her that he understood and promised to take care of all the practical details, whatever they might be. When he had waved them off in the departure lounge at Arlanda airport he felt sweat begin to seep out on his forehead. But not because of what Banegas might say; what filled his mind was the memory of the blood trickling from Göran's ear. It was an accident, he mumbled, a little too loudly. People around him seemed to look suspiciously at him.

When he got home he was unable to eat and instead poured a large whiskey. He had heard that some of the neighbors were going to start patrolling the area at night after what had happened, but that they didn't want to ask him to join. Nobody wanted to ask anything of him. Out of sympathy. His conscience was surging over him and he began pondering whether he should begin building water mains in Sudan, give all his money to homeless or join a monastery. But it passed. What did any of that have to do with Göran's death? Maybe he could just sign up to be a Homework Help instructor with the Red Cross. It had just been an accident, after all.

He lay down on the couch, pulled a throw over himself and tried to read. When the doorbell rang, he didn't know how long he had slept. It was the two police officers. Something seemed to have changed. Now the young woman stood in front while her male partner stood to one side behind her, his head slightly bent. And it was she who spoke first.

'Could we come inside, we have a few more questions.'

They asked about his evening with Banegas, about the opera and the supper. Adam answered to the best of his ability and kept to the schedule. What might Banegas have told them?

'Have you spoken to him?' Adam tried to smile. 'He can be a bit confusing sometimes, maybe the Swedish police would make him nervous if...' He fell silent. Something was obviously wrong, enormously wrong. The two police officers exchanged a glance. The woman cleared her throat.

'He is dead.'

'Dead?' At first, Adam felt immensely relieved. His worries about what Banegas might say had been totally needless.

'Banegas was found murdered on Kastellholmen,' the police woman said. 'Beaten to death with a blunt object. We estimate the time of death to between ten p.m. and midnight. In other words, shortly after you left the opera.'

Adam had nothing very satisfactory to say and chose to give an uncertain nod.

'There are a few details we find confusing. We thought you might help us fill in the blanks.'

Was this when he should insist on having a lawyer present? Or was it too early? Would it seem suspicious instead?

Before he had reached any conclusion, she went on: 'Maybe we could do this down at the precinct.'

They took turns questioning him. The older policeman seemed anxious to explain that it was all just routine, nothing to worry about. He had a kindly smile.

His female partner didn't. She pulled out Banegas' schedule. 'Do you recognize this?'

Adam nodded.

'What happened to your supper? At the Gyldene Freden they have no memory of you, and there was no reservation made in your name.'

Adam managed to strain out an answer he felt reasonably satisfied with, about having forgotten to reserve a table and that anyway it had turned out Banegas had preferred to go for a walk on his own. If he had said anything else earlier, he must have mixed things up. She silently wrote down what he said. Then her partner took over and explained that of course this was no interrogation, but would Adam consider helping them out by staying on for a couple of hours?

In fact, only around three-quarters of an hour passed before the police woman returned. 'Your schedule says that Harald Thorvaldsson at the

Export Council was supposed to join you at the opera.'

Damn it!

'However, when we spoke to Mr. Thorvaldsson he denies that any such thing was ever even considered on his part. In fact, he dismissed it very firmly.'

The answer Adam managed this time was less satisfying. She put a few resulting questions, and Adam got himself still more entangled. After a while she suggested that they could take a break and continue later. He declined to have a lawyer present.

When he was brought back into the room, the kindly policeman was gone and the woman in the strict ponytail questioned him alone. As before, she wasted no time on small talk or smiles. 'We have had an interesting conversation with a member of the Grand Hotel staff. The day after the murder someone tried to gain access to the room where the Banegas couple stayed. That person acted nervously and gave a name that turned out to be false. However, you were identified from the photo we took in connection with out other investigation.'

Adam's efforts to explain were torn to shreds by her furious counterquestions. He needed to sleep and clung to the single point which seemed to speak in his favor. 'But why would I have anything to do with Señor Banegas' death? It's absurd!'

'Actually, we've learned a reasonable motive from his widow. It seems that you have spent a long time discussing some major road construction project. But Banegas had already given the commission to some American consortium. He was going to tell you before leaving for home.'

What a bastard! 'But you don't kill anyone because–'

But she wasn't interested in Adam's reasonable objections. They let him go home to sleep but brought him back again the next morning. At first, the atmosphere seemed more relaxed. The kindly policeman said that they accepted Adam's statement that he had left for home immediately after the opera. Adam said that he was glad to hear it, and the policeman seemed pleased as well. But the female officer remained silent and resolute throughout. Without any warning, she asked:

'So could you tell us why you didn't get home until two hours later? And wearing rubber boots?'

Suddenly the interrogation veered off on a new, horrible track.

The lawyer looked up from his notes. 'So that was when you decided to confess to the murder of Banegas?'

Adam nodded. 'I just can't bear to be convicted of murdering Göran, my father-in-law.' He thought of Kattis and the children and closed his eyes. 'This way I get an alibi for that.'

'But now you claim that you had nothing to do with Banegas' death?'

'That's what I've been telling you. But on the other hand–'

The lawyer held up a deprecating hand. 'One thing at a time. Let us focus on the crime you have been arrested for.'

He summed up the situation in a few tired platitudes and looked at his watch. 'We'll see,' he said. 'Complicated. Must consider strategy, consult my colleagues.'

A police officer arrived to return Adam to his cell. He was led along a corridor and past the open door to a room. In the room was a sobbing, rotund little woman dressed in black. She was leaning her head against the shoulder of a woman officer, but despite that Adam immediately recognized Mrs. Banegas. She glanced up at him. Her sly eyes shone triumphantly and her mouth curled in a superior smile.

She really was crazy.

SOMETHING IN HIS EYES

DAG ÖHRLUND

The scream burst from Lenya the moment she lost contact with the balcony rail and fell.

It seemed strange to her that so many thoughts could pass through a brain in only a few seconds. An icy wind burned her cheeks.

Her life became a movie. As a small child she toddled around with Azad. Of course they squabbled, like all siblings, but she didn't love anybody else the way she loved her big brother.

He was God, and Love, and everything else, even though she wouldn't truly understand that until much later.

Would he ever forgive their father, after this?

A second or two later, her thoughts ceased as her head hit the asphalt.

Lenya Barzani died instantly.

If any angels lamented, her father's howl from the balcony drowned them out.

Detective Captain Jenny Lindh's fingers tightened on the steering wheel as she fought back nausea.

Her car was stuck in traffic on the Essinge freeway leading downtown. The line of cars inched forward a few feet at a time through the heavy snow, and the wipers were hard put to keep the windshield clear.

269

Right now, Jenny hated everything.

She'd gotten the call a few minutes earlier. A patrol car had been sent to an apartment building in the suburb of Tensta after a witness had reported seeing a lifeless girl lying on the ground. In the midst of the blizzard, they were scarce on patrol cars, field investigators and everything else.

So Lindh got the job.

As if I didn't have enough problems, she thought.

Her life, as the 'burbs kids would say, had gotten *totally fucked* over about a week ago.

That night.

Jenny had felt sick during the night shift. She excused herself by saying she must have caught a bug, and left for home several hours early.

She didn't want her colleagues to know she was pregnant.

At least not yet.

She managed to grab a Kleenex just in time, catching the small gob of vomit that came up as the images returned to her mind.

Cursing under her breath, she rolled down the window, threw out the slimy tissue and was blasted in the face by a whirl of snow.

Daniel and ... the whore.

Yeah. She had looked like a whore. Blonde, a bit too fat, in a lace bra and black garters, moaning and riding Daniel on the bed.

Their bed. *Her* bed.

The nausea that had been tormenting her for hours was forced aside as she stood immobile in the doorway. It was replaced by rage, kindling in her stomach and working its way up her throat to her mouth.

270

She had screamed. Seen the slut's eyes bulge as she slid off Jenny's husband's cock and tried to cover herself. Seen Daniel sit up, raise a hand in some kind of defense.

'Jenny, it's not what you think...'

The stupidest fucking sentence she had ever heard.

That was when she had drawn her gun.

It had been a funny sight: Daniel and the whore, practically naked, racing out of their home as she aimed at them. Tumbling around in the snow outside as they tried to get dressed.

For no discernible reason, the line of cars slowly dissolved. Jenny Lindh pulled out a cigarette, lit it and wondered if she had any pain relievers in her handbag. She had been up drinking whiskey until two in the morning, and her head was pounding.

Yeah, sure – she shouldn't drink while she was pregnant.

Yeah, sure – she had taken up smoking again two days ago, even though she knew better.

Who cared? She would have an abortion. Her marriage was over. Her picturesque life had ended. Her dream of a good life with another cop had turned into a pathetic game of roulette where her money was on the wrong number.

Clara, her only support, had made the difference between extinction and survival. Tough, smart Clara, who had always been there. Who always had answers, could comfort and encourage. And who had an outlook on men and relationships that was completely different from Jenny's.

Everlasting love is fucking bullshit. So I'll help

271

myself, get laid, have fun and move on!

Clara was one of a kind.

Smacking her hand against the wheel, Jenny shot the car into the left-hand lane and sped up. Her right hand fumbled for the rotating blue light, managed to get it up on the roof above her and turned it on.

Get the hell out of my way!

Sixteen minutes later, she stood outside the blue-and-white police tape and observed the scene in front of her.

The first thing that struck her was the ugliness of the building, and she wondered who had thought it up.

Had *anyone* been thinking?

Roughly forty years ago, the politicians of a small country called Middle-of-the-Road suddenly realized there weren't enough homes.

One million apartments.

It took them ten years to build that million, and here in front of her was one of the results.

It looked awful.

The first patrol on the scene had cordoned off an eighty-by-eighty-foot area. The forensics team's gray-blue Volkswagen van was parked just outside the police tape. A tent had been erected close to the building to cover something that had to be the body, in order to stop the press photographers from taking pictures.

A man dressed in a coverall and boots came plodding up to her through several inches of snow. As he approached, she recognized him as Björkstedt. A reliable workhorse who had been investigating crime scenes since forever.

272

'Hi. You can come in if you want.'

'Thanks, Anders.' Jenny lifted the tape and slipped under it. 'So what have we got?'

'Balcony girl, model One A.'

'Which means?'

'No footprints, no other tracks anywhere near her. She must have died from the fall alone. The neck is bent at an unnatural angle.'

'So, broken?'

'I'm no medical examiner, but yeah, I'll bet my next paycheck on it.'

'Anything else?'

'She wasn't wearing outdoor clothes, just jeans and a T-shirt. Her cell phone fell out of her pocket. It's crushed; must have ended up under her body when she landed.'

'Can I have a look at her?'

'Sure.'

Björkstedt turned and walked ahead of her through the snow. She had to crouch to enter the tent, where a strong lamp cast a cold light on what, until recently, had been a living teenager.

The girl was on her stomach with her head turned to one side. Her face had stiffened into an expression that was anything but peaceful. There were scrapes and bruises on one cheek, but the rest of her face was unmarked.

Lindh pointed to the marks. 'What do you think?'

Björkstedt shrugged. 'She hasn't been moved. You can see that the snow has been pushed aside by her cheek, and there's blood. So she could have gotten the scrapes when she hit the asphalt, but they could also have been caused before she

273

fell – I can't swear to either.'

'Do you know anything about her?'

Björkstedt jerked his thumb at the building. 'I talked to our colleagues. Lenya Barzani, seventeen years old. Lived on the fourth floor. The uniforms are up there.'

She nodded. 'Thanks.'

'Sure.'

Jenny left the tent, her boots leaving a straight track in the snow up to the police tape closest to the main entrance.

My husband cheated on me with a whore. In our bed.

A seventeen-year-old girl is dead, maybe murdered. Gotta focus. Damn, it hurts!

Head pounding, she took the elevator to the fourth floor while fumbling for painkillers in her pocket. From inside the shaft, she could hear a commotion that got louder the higher she rose.

She opened the elevator door and stepped out into chaos, pushing aside a woman who flailed her arms and cried. Distressed neighbors spoke loudly in a language she didn't understand. Uniformed colleagues patiently kept them from entering the apartment they were guarding.

Lindh showed the colleagues her badge, pushed through the throng of upset people, and stepped into the hallway where she was met by yet another uniformed policeman.

'Hi. Jenny Lindh, criminal investigations. What have we got?'

The officer consulted the small notebook in his hand.

'The dead girl is Lenya Barzani, seventeen. A

274

Kurd from northern Iraq. Her father Schorsch is in the living room. Nobody else was here when we arrived. We've had a look around. The living room and balcony are a mess; one of the techs is out there now.'

'Thanks.'

Jenny walked past him, into a long hallway. A bedroom door stood open to her right; she paused and looked inside.

It was a typical girl's room. A Justin Bieber poster on the wall; a vanity table with a laptop squeezed in between lipstick, deodorant and perfumes. A speaker with an iPhone dock; a teddy bear and pink pillows on a sloppily made bed. A pair of jeans, a spaghetti top and some underwear discarded on a chair.

Lenya's room?

She kept walking. The doors to the other rooms were closed, and the hallway led her into the living room.

The man on the couch might have been sixty. He was dressed in brown pants, a beige shirt and a brown knit sweater. He sat slumped over with his head in his hands, sobbing. Next to him sat a female cop, her hand on his shoulder, trying to speak calmly to him.

He's barefoot. The floor by his feet is damp. Why?

Lindh gave the policewoman a quick nod, saw the kitchen doorway and walked in. She dug a couple of aspirin out of her pocket, put them in her mouth, turned on the faucet and filled her cupped hand. The unpleasant taste filled her mouth as one of the tablets dissolved, and she gazed at the small pool of water in her hand as if

275

it were a mirror.

We should have had an entire life together. We were happy. We had bought a house. We were going to have a baby.

You betrayed me. So I wasn't good enough?

With a jerking motion she threw the water into her mouth, then refilled her palm, shut her eyes and swallowed. She stood there for several seconds, her eyes closed, while the water ran from the tap and the policewoman spoke softly to the man on the couch.

Focus, Jenny.

She pushed back a stray strand of hair and looked around.

An ordinary kitchen, except for the large fabric decorations on the walls. Images, probably of some religious significance. Writing she didn't understand. Kurdish? She went into the living room. The policewoman was still there, her hand on Schorsch Barzani's shoulder. Through the window, she could see the squatting technician working outside. Jenny opened the door, and he looked up at her.

'Hi. Jenny Lindh, criminal investigations. What's it look like?'

He swiped a plastic-gloved hand across his forehead.

'Well, there seems to have been some kind of scuffle. The snow's been kicked away, and a couple of flowerpots have fallen and broken. That chair has lost a leg. Right now I'm taking casts of the shoe prints. And I've bagged a few fibers.'

She nodded, and was just about to close the door. Then:

276

'How long would you say it takes to fall from here to the ground?'

The technician's eyes lost focus and stared into space.

'Fourth floor ... maybe nine seconds.'

'Thanks.'

She closed the door.

Nine seconds.

Her head was still pounding, but the pain seemed to be abating. Jenny sat down opposite the man on the couch. She met the policewoman's gaze.

'Has he said anything?'

The woman shrugged. 'That she jumped of her own volition. He's devastated. He tried to stop her.'

'Had they argued earlier?'

'No, not according to him.'

Oh, really. So a smiling, carefree Lenya had walked past her father on the couch and told him she was going to jump. He had stood up, followed her and tried to stop her, but his strength hadn't been enough to restrain a seventeen-year-old girl.

In fact, he hadn't even had the strength to drag himself down to the courtyard where his daughter lay dead.

'I want him detained for interrogation on reasonable suspicion.'

Jenny leaned forward.

'Schorsch...?'

No reaction. She tried again.

The man slowly raised his head. His face was red, swollen from crying. His eyes were wet, his gaze both empty and despairing.

'Schorsch, you'll have to come with us to police headquarters. I want to have a little chat with you there. Do you understand me?'

He made a resigned gesture.

'Why no talk here?'

'For practical reasons.'

'You cannot think...'

'I don't think anything, but I need to talk to you where we won't be disturbed.'

She went on.

'Where's the rest of your family?'

Again the resigned gesture. 'Azad is at a friend's...'

'Who is Azad?'

'My son.'

'And your wife?'

'She and Lara are with my cousin Naushad.'

'Who is Lara?'

'My daughter.'

'How old is she?'

'Fourteen.'

Something in his eyes when he mentions her name.

'Okay, I understand. Now, would you please come with us...'

The police building at Kronoberg is colossal. Covers a whole block. Gray and ugly. It holds more departments, corridors and officials than most people could ever imagine. In one of the interrogation rooms, somewhere near the middle of the building, Jenny Lindh is sitting at a table opposite a sixty-two-year-old Kurdish man.

The man looks weary and worried. He twists his hands. He stopped looking around a long

278

time ago; his empty stare is fixed in front of him.

Jenny Lindh has activated the recorder, has pointed the microphone at Schorsch Barzani.

She intends to conduct a short routine interrogation in accordance with paragraph 24, section 8 of the penal code, then ask the prosecutor to arrest Schorsch.

But their conversation drags on, and it makes Jenny feel ill at ease. Neither an interpreter nor a defense attorney is present. She would have felt better if there were.

Schorsch doesn't want to stop. They talk for almost an hour. About Lenya. Schorsch. The whole family. About their escape from Hawraman in northern Iraq. About their request for political asylum, and how they were allowed to stay, many years ago. About their life since then.

Lindh is still suffering from a dull headache. She tries to push her personal problems aside, tries to understand what Schorsch is telling her.

It's bullshit, of course. The same old nonsense. Of course he was the one who threw his daughter from the balcony, like other Muslim men have done to their daughters or sisters. Because the girls became real Swedes after they came here – no longer wanting to live by Muslim rules, they went to dances, lit cigarettes, fell in love with boys. Broke all the rules.

That's obviously what happened. Schorsch Barzani murdered his daughter because she broke his rules. Shamed her family.

The police have seen it before. A hundred times. Famous cases have been debated in the papers. Fadime Sahindal, a twenty-six-year-old Kurdish

279

woman from Turkey, had been threatened and beaten by her father, who finally killed her with two shots. Being in a relationship wasn't her only crime: she had also let the public know how Kurdish men treated their women.

Pela Atroshi, a nineteen-year-old Kurdish woman living in Sweden, had been murdered on a visit to her family's home in Iraq, for besmirching the family honor. Her father's brothers got a life sentence, but years later her father confessed that he was the one who killed her.

Jenny Lindh makes a face. She hates the concept of *honor killing*, and cannot for the life of her understand why both politicians and feminists use it. To her, the word *honor* has a positive connotation, and she thinks it should be called culture killing, or even ignominy killing.

There is no honor in killing someone. Least of all in killing your own daughter.

It's unacceptable in a modern, Western society. Maybe *they* put religion and respect first, but *we* put the law above all.

Jenny Lindh realizes that after all her years of police work, she is full of prejudice, based on what she has seen and experienced. It's what they do to their women, those Muslims. Force them to obey and to veil themselves. Forbid them from showing their faces and loving whomever they choose.

She looks back at Schorsch, who has fallen silent after a long story about himself, Lenya and the rest of the family.

He keeps repeating that he loves her. That he has loved her since she was born. That she can't be dead.

That he did everything he could to stop her.

Jenny lets his words sink in. On her recommendation, the prosecutor has already decided to arrest Schorsch. She studies him for a few seconds before calmly saying:

'Schorsch, you'll have to stay here for a while. Right now, you're suspected of murder.'

Barzani meets her eyes, in surprise and despair.

Then his expression changes.

And there is something in his eyes that she doesn't understand.

A few hours later she learns that Magnus Stolt has been assigned to lead the investigation, and with a grimace she drives to Solna to find him at the west Stockholm prosecutor's office.

Stolt barely even looks up when she enters his office and greets him.

Asshole.

He's well-known among the police, and most of them think that Dick would be a more suitable last name. Magnus Stolt is the man who gave bitterness a face and nurtures his preconceptions as if they were vulnerable hothouse flowers. He is generally disliked, not particularly successful in court, and Jenny Lindh wonders why he gets to stay, when there are so many good public prosecutors.

'Hi.'

'Hello. Take a seat.'

He shuffles through plastic folders and papers. As if to show her how busy he is. Finally he takes the top folder from the pile, pushes his glasses

281

onto his forehead and looks at her.

'It's Tensta, right?' He glances at the printed-out interrogation protocols. 'Scho ... well, Barzani, right?'

Lindh nods without speaking.

Stolt gives her a crooked smile.

'I see that he's denying all charges. And, as we know, they always do. But – I'll have him put in custody and then you can keep working at your leisure.'

His voice is nasal and his tone is superior. She can understand that he rubs people the wrong way.

Stolt stands up, closes the office door and sits back down. Twirls the arms of his glasses between his fingers.

'Conduct a formal interrogation at once. But make sure his lawyer and an interpreter are present, or the defense will be screaming their heads off later. What more have you done?'

'The technicians are working hard out there. We've impounded the girl's laptop and given it to forensics. Operation door-to-door is in full swing, and we're waiting for the rest of the family to come home so we can do preliminary interviews with them.'

'I see. And how many are they?'

'The wife and Lenya's sister and brother.'

Stolt raises an eyebrow. 'That's all? There's usually at least seven or eight of those people.'

Those people.

'I think...' Jenny pauses midsentence.

'Yes?'

She thinks Stolt looks annoyed. That bothers

her. Right now she would like to have his support.

'...he's innocent.'

'Why?'

Jenny shrugs. 'A gut feeling.'

His glasses fall back onto his nose as he keeps shuffling through his papers. 'Tell your gut to calm down until we have the autopsy report and the results from forensics.'

Jenny Lindh stands up and leaves the prosecutor's office.

In a fourteen-by-eight-foot holding cell, Schorsch Barazani pounds his fists against the wall until they start bleeding, and howls in pain and despair.

That night, Jenny Lindh drinks too much again. She wanders slowly through her house, *their* house.

This was where the love of her life should have flourished.

This was where their child should have grown up.

The drunker she gets, the more aggressively she declutters. Furious, she tears his clothes from the closets and throws them on the floor, rips pages from photo albums, dumps framed photographs and small mementos into a cardboard box.

Deep in a closet drawer, she finds the dildo they shyly purchased from a sex shop a long time ago. In disgust she flings it in the garbage without removing the batteries.

She feels sick, throws up in the toilet and drinks more wine before she continues getting rid of everything that was her, their, life for five years.

Everything has to go.

Him. The child. The house.

Jenny Lindh has no idea what will happen next.

The next morning, she has an impulse. She returns to the apartment, which has been sealed off. The family had to spend the night somewhere else.

Where do you stay when you've been thrown out of your home? With friends? A homeless shelter?

Jenny takes a deep breath. She's got a long day of interrogations ahead of her.

The crime scene technicians have combed the apartment, and Jenny doesn't actually know what she's doing here. She won't find anything they missed.

She just wants to look. Feel. Try to understand.

At ten o'clock, she conducts a long, investigative interrogation of Schorsch. He's been saying all along that he doesn't need a defense attorney, because he is innocent, but they appointed one anyway. He also declined help from an interpreter, but nevertheless one is sitting beside him.

Magnus Stolt enters the room just before they begin.

Jenny drinks cold water from a plastic cup to ease her sick feeling. She starts the interrogation coolly and calmly, as usual. As time passes, she notices more and more signs of the prosecutor's annoyance. He sighs deeply, occasionally tapping a pencil against the table. Schorsch Barzani is distraught and worn out. His eyes are red and what little gray hair he has left is standing on end.

He sticks to his story.

All he did was try to stop Lenya from jumping.

As he utters the words, Stolt makes a sound like a snort, and the defense attorney looks at the prosecutor in surprise.

Barzani answers every question and the interpreter never needs to intervene. Yes, of course Schorsch has kept his daughters on a tight rein. Forbade them to get piercings or tattoos, told them to be proud of their origins and to live by the *Book*. He has tried to restrain himself, allowing them to dress as they liked, listen to pop music and even go to dances. But he has used his right to choose whom they will marry.

'What *right?*' Stolt suddenly asks.

Barzani looks surprised, spreads his hands and explains the duties of a father. The prosecutor sinks down in his chair, drags a tired hand across his face and fixes his gaze on a point far away.

Jenny continues asking questions in a calm voice. No, Schorsch really has no idea why Lenya was so upset. When she was on her way to the balcony he had asked her why, and she had said that it was none of his business. She had opened the balcony door in her stocking feet, letting in the cold, and he had followed her. Lenya had grabbed the railing and begun heaving herself up. Schorsch had grabbed hold of her and pulled her down. She had clawed his face, hit him and kicked wildly so that the flowerpots broke. In vain, he tried to hold her, but she had been stronger.

She'd heaved herself up – thrown herself over.

Schorsch bursts into tears again, and Jenny lets the next few questions wait. She throws a quick glance at the prosecutor, who rolls his eyes before leaning across the table and making a half-hearted attempt to hide the irritation in his voice.

'Wouldn't it be better just to confess, Barzani? This doesn't look good, and it's such a relief to just come clean.'

The interpreter translates and Schorsch Barzani shakes his head, burying his face in his hands.

'I ... I loved her,' he sobs. 'I would never...'

The interrogation ends at 11:42.

Early the next morning the lobby guard from the police station calls Jenny Lindh to tell her that a group of men want to talk to her.

'It's about Schorsch Barzani.'

She asks what they want, but the guard doesn't know. According to him she has two choices. She can either come down and try to calm this perturbed bunch or he'll have to request some uniformed officers.

Jenny sighs and takes the elevator down.

The guard was right. The men, five Iraqi Kurds who are friends of Schorsch Barzani, are very upset. They can all swear that Schorsch had indeed done everything to defend the Barzani family honor, but he was certainly no murderer and should be released immediately.

Patiently, Jenny tries to explain to them how the Swedish justice system works.

She gets no response. The men tell her that they want to talk to the *man* in charge of the investigation.

Jenny tells them that she is in charge and is

greeted by incredulous stares. The men confer quietly for a moment in their own language and then demand to speak with the *man* who is her superior officer.

Jenny tells them that her superior officer is Lena Ekholm – a woman.

This doesn't diminish their agitation. Once again they call for the immediate release of Barzani. When Jenny firmly explains that they will be moving forward with the investigation, the group becomes more strident and starts shouting in a mixture of Swedish and their own language and Jenny can no longer subdue them. Some uniformed officers enter the building and there is a bit of a scuffle as the Kurdish men are forced outside. One of them resists so violently that he is arrested.

She slowly shakes her head.

Why does it have to be this way?

Three weeks later Jenny Lindh is sitting in a one-bedroom apartment in a new suburb, thinking about life.

Everything's happened so quickly. The house was sold. She left almost all the furniture in it behind; the mere thought of keeping anything that might remind her made her sick. With the help of friends, a van and IKEA she put together a new home in a few days.

The rest wasn't as easy.

The abortion.

It was mandatory that she speak with a psychologist first, and of course she broke down. A five-year relationship, promises of undying love, memories of adventure and intimacy – it all came together as she faced the decision of whether or not she really wanted to get rid of the child in her belly.

The child.

When it was over she steeled herself, took only a couple of days' sick leave while the bleeding was at its worst.

Better to bury yourself in work than to stare at a wall wallowing in memories that aren't worth remembering anymore.

Daniel had made some awkward attempts to contact her. He had used words like *respect* and *adults* and said that they should at least try to talk to each other.

Jenny texted him saying that he a) could take his whore and go to hell, and b) should contact her lawyer if he wanted anything else.

Very mature, Jenny, she thinks and bites her lip, as she stands in front of the mirror trying to put on her makeup. Her tears smear her mascara and she has to redo it.

It's high time she spent an evening drinking wine with Clara.

At work she downs cup after cup of strong coffee and winces at the burning sensation in her stomach.

Once again she carefully sifts through the material surrounding Lenya Barzani's death.

The CSI and computer forensics reports are coldly formal, just like the autopsy report from the pathologist and the evaluations from SKL, the state crime lab.

The technicians indicated that they found footprints from both Lenya and Schorsch Barzani in the snow on the balcony, and that there were numerous signs of a struggle. They found traces of Lenya's blood. After scraping her fingernails they detected evidence of her father's skin under them. Samples taken on the first day Schorsch was examined showed traces of Lenya's DNA in wounds on his cheeks. Jenny searches for the major points in the pathologist's long report. Lenya's neck was broken, her skull and brain sustained injuries. Her face was swollen where there had been bruising. Her left arm was broken. The pathologist was unable to determine whether all of these injuries happened simultaneously or in brief intervals. Theoretically she may have sustained some of her injuries before falling from the balcony. Her lungs indicated that she was a smoker, but apart from that the girl was healthy. Neither drugs nor alcohol were found in her blood or any traces of semen inside of her.

The computer forensics experts easily accessed Lenya's laptop and went through her files, e-mails, and Facebook account. Their report included an attachment of about a hundred pages of documented conversations between the girl and her friends, as well as a printout of something that looked like a diary.

Jenny spent hours absorbed in reading the printouts. The email exchanges between Lenya and her friends revealed that Schorsch had been very strict with both Lenya and Lara. Granted – just as he had admitted – he had allowed them a certain amount of freedom in choosing their clothes and activities, but he made himself very clear when it came to the most important thing of all: their choice of boyfriends.

There was no mistaking that Lenya was in love with a boy named Joakim. The e-mail exchanges between him and Lenya were intense, and she gushed over him to her girlfriends.

Meanwhile, she expressed her deepening distress in her diary. Several years earlier, her father had explained that she was to marry Rawand, his cousin Naushad's son. The fact that her chosen husband lived with his father in Badinan, in northern Iraq, did not make things less complicated.

In a private Facebook exchange, Lenya had told her friend Ebba that her father had discovered her relationship with Joakim and gone ballistic. He had subjected Lenya to a long and rigorous interrogation. After that he grounded her and said she could not go anywhere at all without either her father or Azad as chaperone.

And not only that. Her diary also disclosed that Schorsch had ordered his wife, Runak, to bring Lenya to Haval, an Iraqi in Tensta who claimed to be a doctor. The purpose of this visit was to determine whether or not Lenya was still a virgin.

Lenya described the encounter as disgusting. Her appointment with Haval took place in an ordinary apartment, and Lenya got no impression that he was actually a trained doctor. Her mother had looked away as the man poked around her genitals with his fingers. Lenya described the experience as both painful and deeply humiliating.

In her text messages, she told Ebba that she had never had sex with Joakim or anyone else, but that her hymen had broken a year or so ago during ballet practice.

When Schorsch received the 'doctor's' report he had become even more furious and grounded Lenya indefinitely. This took place about a week before her fall from the balcony, and during that time, Lenya's brother had met her at school each day to walk her home.

Jenny put the papers down, drank some coffee and sighed deeply. Would she ever get used to these cultural differences?

Lenya's mother, Runak, and an interpreter are sitting across the table from Jenny.

Runak, weary from lack of sleep and worn out from crying, answers Jenny's questions only briefly. She knows Schorsch well after all these years. He loves his daughters and would never harm a hair on their heads. Runak wants to know when Schorsch can come home and cries hysterically when she gets no definite answer.

Two hours later, at Jenny's second interview with fourteen-year-old Lara, instead of an interpreter, a woman from social services in Tensta is present.

Jenny gets no clear answers to her questions. She leans across the table, and smiles at the girl.

'Are you afraid of something or someone, Lara? I promise that nothing is going to happen to you.'

The girl is silent for a moment. Then she shrugs her shoulders, looks Jenny in the eyes and says:

'How can you promise anything? You don't

291

even understand what this is all about.'

You're right. How could I ever understand?

'Then tell me, Lara. Explain it to me so I can understand.'

The girl just stares down at the table, silent.

Her interrogations of Azad Barzani don't go much better. He replies laconically to some questions, and answers others with a shrug of his shoulders or not at all.

'But, Azad, do you think that Lenya was afraid of your dad?'

'Why would she be?'

'Is it true that recently Lenya wasn't allowed out by herself? That your father told you to meet her at school every day, to make it impossible for her to see Joakim?'

'Who's Joakim?'

'Lenya had a boyfriend named Joakim, didn't she?'

'She didn't have a boyfriend.'

'But we've already spoken to Joakim, and he said that he and Lenya were in a relationship.'

'He's lying.'

Not once during the questioning did Azad meet her gaze, and Jenny knows that he will never tell her anything.

Another world. A world of men with a concept of honor that differs from the Swedish one. For a moment she considers letting some male colleague take over the interrogations.

But – no way in hell!

She is Detective Captain Jenny Lindh.

The next day, Jenny questions Lenya's best friend,

292

Ebba Green. Ebba isn't afraid. She confirms much of what Jenny has already learned from the computer printouts.

Lenya was definitely afraid of Schorsch. Her father had a terrible temper and was constantly setting up new rules for Lenya. She was hardly allowed to use makeup, always had to wear pants instead of skirts and having a boyfriend was out of the question – she was set to marry the older man, Rawand, in Iraq. Ebba said that they had talked about this a million times and Lenya wanted nothing more than to get away from home. But how would she do that? She was seventeen, a high school student, with no other place to live and no job. And besides, even if she had escaped, Schorsch, his friends and his relatives would have found her and brought her back home.

According to Ebba, Schorsch was a family dictator, and both the Barzani sisters were afraid of him. Lenya had even said that she feared for her life, that her father would kill her if he discovered that she had a boyfriend. And her mother, Runak, would never dare to stand up to Schorsch.

After all, she was only a woman.

The interrogation transcripts were typed out and entered, along with all the other investigation reports, into the DurTvå system – a computerized log of pretrial investigation material.

Shortly before lunch the next day Jenny gets a call from the prosecutor who curtly tells her she should report to his office immediately with an update. Slightly annoyed, she drives to Solna again, hurries along the corridors to Magnus Stolt's office and takes a seat in his visitor's chair.

The prosecutor pushes his glasses up on his forehead. 'Did you get anything from the door-to-door?'

'Hardly. Nobody seems to have seen or heard anything. It was midmorning when it happened. I suppose most people were at work.'

He gives a short laugh. 'Work? People in that area are hardly known for working themselves to death, are they? You know the type – the ones who are said to enrich our culture.'

His voice drips with sarcasm. Lindh has heard it before, in paddy wagons, in the corridors of police headquarters. *Cultural Enrichers. Camel jockeys. Dune coons.*

If the police, with their special training, can't accept these people as citizens, then how can the rest of the population be expected to do so?

Jenny has seen on the news that populist, right-wing extremist parties have gained considerable support in recent years. Jackboots.

She shudders.

You can't hate people just because of their origin.

Stolt shuffles through his piles of paper and pulls out some that are marked with a yellow Post-it note.

'You're saying that nobody has seen or heard anything. But here's a transcript from a witness named Pettersson who says that he heard shouting and arguing, and that he saw the father and daughter fighting on the balcony.'

'That's true. But for one thing, that man is obviously an alcoholic. He reeked of liquor when we spoke to him. And for another, he keeps changing his story around. You can see from the

294

transcript that he's confused.'

'But it says here that he even saw the father throw his daughter from the balcony.'

Jenny takes a deep breath.

'But if you read on, it says later that he isn't sure about that. I suspect the defense would rip him to pieces pretty fast if you put him on the stand.'

Stolt looks irritated and puts the papers down.

'Do another door-to-door. Without any witnesses or supporting evidence I won't be able to charge him with murder.'

'But what if he didn't do it?'

The words slip out before she's had time to think.

Jenny notices a small muscle twitch near his eye. Stolt pulls his glasses back down over his eyes, leans over the desk on his elbows and fixes her with his stare.

'If he *didn't* do it? Get a grip, Lindh. Read the interview with her best friend. Lenya feared for her life. This is just one more honor killing and I'm gonna put Barzani away for life. Stone Age behavior is not acceptable in this country.'

Jenny Lindh stands up. As she leaves his office she hears him say quietly: '*Fucking Hajjis.*'

She turns around and looks at Stolt.

'Did you say something?'

He forces a smile.

'No, no. It was nothing.'

The next morning Jenny interrogates Schorsch Barzani again. As she is about to start, in comes the prosecutor, out of breath and with his face showing clear signs that he's under pressure. Both the morning papers and the tabloids are still headlining Lenya's death so maybe Stolt has been fielding phone calls from police headquarters as well as from politicians. Jenny's heard what can happen when a case becomes politically sensitive. The next election is closing in. The center/right-wing coalition government is under attack from the opposition and will resort to any tricks to stay in power. Statistically significant opinion polls show that support for the populist, anti-immigrant party has reached two-digit percentages. Not only does that mean that it will become more influential, but it will likely continue to hold the balance of power in parliament in the little country called Middle-of-the-Road.

A political disaster.

And now an immigrant girl is dead. Again.

Her father is suspected of murder. Just like so many fathers before him.

The result of this trial could have major political consequences.

Will the small, but democratic country allow immigrants from different cultures to murder their daughters in order to 'protect their honor'?

It seems to Jenny that Schorsch has become smaller, hunched over. When she asks her questions about that particular day, the point at which Lenya died, he sticks to the same story as before.

He had been watching TV when she walked past. He followed her onto the balcony and yes, there was a fight when he tried to stop her from jumping.

As before, she asks why he didn't leave the apartment and run down to the courtyard after Lenya fell.

He shakes his head slowly.

'It was like ... I paralyzed. No could move. I just sat, no could understand.'

Prosecutor Stolt squirms in his seat, gives Jenny an irritated look that says: *Get going damn it – c'mon, sink him!*

But she asked her questions again and again and received the same answers. Asked about the family's escape to Sweden, about Lenya's childhood, about how Schorsch thought his daughters should conduct their lives. Asked what he was doing during the minutes and seconds before she fell. Asked why he was barefoot.

And sure, he is a cliché that would make any xenophobic Swede smirk. A typical *Muhammad*, dominating his wife and daughters, writing his own laws and administering whatever punishments suit him.

But then they return again and again to that moment when Lenya walked out onto the balcony.

And Schorsch gets that look in his eyes.

Jenny is becoming increasingly more convinced of his innocence.

Granted – through his dominance and tyranny, she feels certain that he made Lenya afraid of him. Maybe even systematically broke her spirit, contributed to her suicidal thoughts. If the prosecutor can prove that, it might lead to Schorsch's conviction. Jenny doesn't know if any similar case has ever gone to trial before.

297

But she does know that there is a world of difference between *causing someone's death* and *murder*.

Jenny Lindh gives it one last try. She makes an effort to sound more determined, looks Barzani in the eye and says:

'Schorsch, isn't it time for you to confess? You threw Lenya from the balcony, didn't you?'

The tired, gray-haired man looks at her in surprise. This woman who had been so kind to him up until now. After a few seconds he bursts hopelessly into tears.

The defense attorney lays a gentle hand on his shoulder, and between sobs Schorsch manages to reply:

'No ... I ... loved her...!'

Magnus Stolt closes his notebook irritably and quickly leaves the room.

And Jenny Marina Elisabeth Lindh covers her eyes with her hand and wonders why the hell she ever became a police officer.

The pressure on her is increasing. Stolt wants a report at least twice a day and Jenny has little news to give him. Operation door-to-door number two yielded no better results than the first one. The witness Pettersson has been questioned again, numerous times. And every time there are discrepancies in what he's seen, heard, and experienced. It is obvious that he greatly enjoys the attention and loves responding to questions. The problem is that he gives a different answer each time.

And that he reeks of booze.

Jenny questions Joakim Merker, the boy who was supposedly Lenya's boyfriend. She had spoken to him previously a few times on the phone; now everything is formal and official.

Joakim is eighteen years old, a senior in high school majoring in media studies. He gives a calm and quiet impression, and Jenny likes him from the start.

He tells her that they met in school about six months ago. Then one thing led to another, they continued seeing each other, they took walks, went for coffee, talked – *like things we usually do.*

And it turned into love.

Of course Joakim can't tell her the exact day he fell in love with Lenya, or she him. He remembers certain days and dates when they said or did something special. Like the time he wanted to buy her a ring from a shop at Hötorget in Stockholm, but she couldn't accept it for fear her parents might see it and ask what it meant.

The boy tells his story. Every once in a while, Jenny tosses in a question or two. She is absolutely convinced that he is telling her the truth.

Yes, they had hugged and kissed, eventually made out a little. In doorways, on footpaths, in places where they could avoid being seen. Even in the basement of Joakim's house. And yes, Lenya had come with him up to his room, but his mother or siblings were always at home, so ... no, they had never gone any farther.

Yes, they had wanted to. But Lenya wouldn't dare.

Before Lenya, Joakim had had two girlfriends, both of them Swedish. He had had sex with one of them. Lenya had told him that she was a virgin, sworn that she would happily give herself to Joakim, that she loved him and wanted to live with him for the rest of her life.

But then she also told him about the rest, and sorrow clouded their romance.

If Schorsch found out that she had a boyfriend, both Lenya and Joakim could end up in big trouble, she had said. And if her father discovered that they had had sex, she'd be killed.

Maybe Joakim, too.

At first, he hadn't believed her.

Slowly, she convinced him to believe her and helped him to understand.

But she couldn't make him accept it.

How do you kill love when it's at its strongest? How do you say good-bye because someone else refuses to respect your love?

How, when you're only seventeen or eighteen?

You can't.

They had continued meeting in secret. Hugged, kissed, caressed.

But nothing more.

Joakim had been happy and somewhere deep inside he hoped that one day, all of it would be resolved. He had even suggested to Lenya that they could explain everything to Schorsch, and Joakim could ask him for his daughter's hand.

That day, the look on Lenya's face was filled with sorrow and she just shook her head as tears welled up in her eyes.

That had only been a few weeks ago.

One morning she had arrived at school completely beside herself, pulled Joakim into a corner and told him what had happened. Somehow – she didn't know how – Schorsch had found out about their relationship. From now on she would be watched and they could no longer see each other. Azad would pick her up at school every day, so all they could do was communicate secretly via cell phone texts and e-mails – unless those things were also taken away from her.

Joakim had comforted her as best he could, but he felt a burning pain in his chest as he watched Azad walk away with Lenya after school, without so much as a glance back from her.

The next day, during their first break, she told him what her father had said the evening before:

If he found out that they were seeing each other outside of school, both she and Joakim would die.

He had been shocked, not wanting to believe what she'd said. Then he had thought about it and discussed it with his closest friends. Wondered if he ought to report Schorsch to the police or what? After all, this was Sweden in the year 2012.

After the interrogation, Jenny shook hands with Joakim and thanked him. She told him that he would be called as a witness at the trial.

After he left she made a cup of strong coffee and felt grateful that she was no longer seventeen.

Then thoughts of Daniel and the whore came back to her, and once again she hated everything.

Ebba Green sat on a park bench, staring at nothing while she took quick, nervous drags on her cigarette.

Old son of a bitch. Asshole.

The trial had ended a week ago. She had been called to witness and told them everything she knew. So had Joakim.

Then came that neighbor, the guy who said he'd seen the old bastard hit Lenya and throw her down.

The bastard's lawyer had tried to break the guy, but this time he was sure of himself.

He had witnessed the fight and seen how Lenya's father heaved her over the railing.

This morning she had read online that the bastard had been convicted of murder and sentenced to life.

Serves him fucking right.

Slowly she pulled out the crumpled piece of paper she had been keeping in her jacket pocket for weeks.

Lenya's letter.

It had arrived the day after Lenya died. Ebba had been more than surprised to see the neat handwriting on the envelope.

Lenya's handwriting.

Usually they kept in touch only via texts, e-mails and chats, and in fact Ebba couldn't recall ever having received a real letter, a paper letter, from any friend before. She read it for the thousandth time:

Ebba, I love you! I love you and Jocke and Gusse and Anna and Mariana and Linnéa, but I can't take it any longer!

My old man is never going to change. There's no hope for me, they'll force me to go to Iraq and get married. Just can't take it! I want Jocke and no one else.

There's no other way out than what I'm about to do. Not sure if I'll cut myself or jump or what. But I'll do it. Sending you this as snail mail since I know you'd try to stop me otherwise.

Love you forever, give this to my darling Jocke afterward, I've written to him on the back.

XOXO, Lenis

She had let Joakim read the letter. He remained silent for a long time afterwards. Finally he said that they would have to take it to the police. Lenya had committed suicide after all, but now her father had been convicted of murder.

Ebba tore the letter from his hand and ran away.

She'd never let the bastard get away with it.

She pulls out her lighter, watches the flame flutter in the wind, then catch hold of the paper, obliterate it.

Ebba drops the letter on the ground, witnesses the flame devour Lenya's handwritten lines. Tears come to her eyes and when only ashes remain she rubs them into the ground with the sole of her shoe.

Jenny Lindh has taken some time off, is sitting in the silence of her apartment and looking out the window.

The trial had been tumultuous at times and in the end the judge had to remove the Kurdish men who continued to protest loudly as the prosecution presented its case.

303

She had listened to all the witnesses and been very surprised by the neighbor, Pettersson. He had appeared on the stand in a clean shirt and suit, was clean shaven and did not smell of liquor. Now there was no doubt in his mind about his testimony. He had seen a violent fight that ended with Schorsch Barzani lifting up his daughter and throwing her over the balcony railing.

And when the verdict was handed down, she had observed Schorsch Barzani very closely. As if he had felt her gaze, he turned to face her.

There was something in his eyes...

Translated by: Angela Valenti and Sophia Mårtensson

DAY AND NIGHT MY KEEPER BE

MALIN PERSSON GIOLITO

There was no fragrance of cinnamon, of sealing wax, of bubbling toffee or grilled ham. Only of stressfulness and rancid calories. The wind brought sounds from a tombola booth and a shrill, electronic version of 'Jingle Bells.' The cloud cover was sagging with repressed rain.

The woman held her daughter's bare hand in one of hers and a pen in the other. Her son sat in his stroller. At the entrance to the city amusement park, and at a couple of popular museums, they gave you little ribbons to fill out and fasten around the wrist of your child. They called them identification bracelets. But they had nothing like that at the Christmas market. Writing your phone number on the hand or arm of your child instead was a tip the woman had found in a parenting magazine.

I shouldn't be here, she thought. It was a mistake. But the kids had been quarrelsome, teasing, snatching each other's toys. One of them had pulled the other one's hair, they had yelled in chorus and she had decided that they must do something, or they'd all go mad. Stroll for a while among happy families, buying cornets of homemade fudge and letting the kids gorge themselves on sweet buns. It could have been an excellent idea.

Now she longed for home. Longed to get back to the apartment, lie down on the couch and nap while the kids watched the children's channel.

Instead they were here, and returning home without pushing the walker even once around the square would feel like failure. Besides, her baby boy would probably fall asleep on the bus and if she allowed him to sleep now she would never manage to get him into bed tonight. She tightened her grip on her daughter's hand. It was hard to write on the girl's thin skin and she had to press down pretty hard to get the ink to stay. When the child protested her mother yanked her arm.

'Be still...' she muttered. But she couldn't think of anything more to say. She went on writing. A muscle twitched under one of her eyes and she blinked.

One turn. Just a single turn around the square, then she could go back home. With a bit of luck they'd fall asleep early. Then the evening would be all hers. A few hours of peace and quiet. She deserved that.

When all ten digits of the phone number were done the mother drew her thumb over the ink. It was already dry. And as soon as she let go of her daughter's hand, the child's chapped thumb found its way into her half-open mouth. The girl hardly sucked, just let her thumb rest in the corner of her mouth. Her mother shook her head but said nothing.

'Mommy,' the boy in the stroller complained. 'Moommyyy!'

The woman's son was only a little over a year old. In a crowd like this, there was no way for her to let him rove on his own. But he hated his stroller, hated every second of sitting still. Now he twisted with all his strength, furiously trying to escape the harness that tied him down, bumping up and down in his seat. The stroller swayed. The girl stood by, thumb still in her mouth, while her mother pulled a couple of clasps tighter and tried to force the boy down on his seat. He kept trying to squirm free. His mother gave up, started walking and shook the stroller hard a couple of times to make her son slide back down.

The girl's boots were both too hot and too big. Her heels scraped the gravel when she walked. Her snowsuit zipper was pulled down and her collarbone showed. The pale, blue shadow of a vein fluttered with her heartbeat.

'Walk properly,' her mother said. 'Can't you lift your feet?'

'One turn around the square,' she repeated under her breath. 'Just one turn.'

If only the square hadn't been so crowded. The rock candy stand was far away, the waffle stand looked closed. But on a two-foot-high platform maybe thirty feet away sat a middle-aged man with a flopping false beard and a bright red felt cap. Next to his easy chair stood a stuffed reindeer. The prop animal had black eyes of glass and a basket full of smoked sausages hung like a saddlebag across its back. A handwritten sign proclaimed that the sausages cost twenty kronor and that Santa wanted to know what all good children wanted for Christmas.

With a vague sense of relief, the woman halted the stroller. Her daughter no longer believed in Santa Claus, and her son probably had no idea of who he was or what miracles he supposedly worked. But this was better than the alternative. She dug out a painkiller from her handbag and swallowed it dry. It stuck in her throat and she closed her eyes against the pain, putting her fist to her chest.

This is when it happens. They stand in line. The woman tries calming her son with a cracker she's found at the bottom of her handbag. But the boy refuses to be coaxed. Instead he snatches the cracker, sharp nails scratching his mother's wrist, and throws it at the man standing in line before them. And when his mother has brushed crumbs from the stranger's coat and apologized fervently, her daughter is gone.

The woman turns around. Many times. Looks in all directions. Calls out, first in a low voice, then louder; the third time her throat hurts.

Where is she, she thinks. She can't be far; she was here a moment ago. Just a few seconds, can it even be a minute since she saw her last?

At first she is irritated. Angry.

'Be still!' she screams at her son. Her handbag keeps sliding off her shoulder, she claws at it. And she feels very tired. Exhausted. 'Why,' she whispers to herself. Not frightened, just dejected. 'Why, why, why?' It isn't fair. What's she supposed to do now?

She asks the man in line next to her to take care of her stroller. Her son's wide eyes watch the stranger while she squeezes through the crowd, calling and calling, jumping high to be able to see farther ahead.

Which direction should she choose? She chooses them all, a dozen feet this way, a dozen that. But she finds nothing and then she has to return to her boy and already on the way back fear sneaks up on her, suddenly pushing everything else away, her angry thoughts, her tiredness and gloom. Fear hugs her close, envelops her with its poisoned smoke.

Where is the girl? Where is her daughter? How can she just be gone? Why can't she find her?

And when she fumbles her phone out to be certain of hearing its signal when someone calls the number written on her daughter's hand, she sees that the display is all black. The battery has run down. It's dead.

She presses a few buttons, shakes it, but it's pointless. Her daughter is gone and the phone won't ring and fear has to duck because now terror runs up her back, with sharp talons and pointed teeth.

My daughter is gone, she thinks. Swallowed by the sluggish crowd of shoppers and by something totally unknown.

Her son starts twisting in his stroller again. But less furiously. His mother's terror is infectious. High above the clouds finally loosen their grip. The rain pours down. The crowd disperses as people hurry off, take cover by the stage and close to the canvas roofs over the stands. The mother remains in the open, looking into the gray curtain of water. But no girl is left in the rain. No child remains on the square. She is gone.

Her name is Petra, the mother who has lost her child. She is dressed in jeans and a thin down jacket. Her hair is dyed. She is on parental leave from her office work. Actually she isn't really a single parent, or at least wasn't supposed to be, but her boyfriend has left her and she doesn't know how to find him. He left almost four months ago, and when she phones his cell he never answers; all she gets are his parents or some friend, and once his brother. They all say the same thing: he needs to be left alone and that he'll be in touch as soon as he can. What they mean is that they want nothing to do with her. She and her kids should leave them alone, all of them. She has had to pay her rent alone since he left and she hates him, hates his parents, his whole family and every one of his worthless slacker friends. She couldn't call him. Not even if her phone worked.

Where is the kid? How is it possible to disappear so quickly?

Petra doesn't know what to do. Where should she turn? Whom should she talk to? She needs help. But how to ask for it? Should she try to seem calm? Would anyone listen to her if she did? Will she have to scream or at least cry to make them understand that it's serious? Before she has made her mind up she feels a hand on her shoulder. She probably looks frightened, for the man who stood in line in front of her offers to help search. He tells her to ask the Santa Claus for help.

'Tell him what's happened,' the man says. And

he says, 'It'll be all right.' He must see that she needs to be calmed. 'Don't worry,' he says, 'she'll soon be back.'

But there's no need for her to worry; she does that without any conscious effort. The images appear faster than she can explain what has happened to the false-beard Santa. They trip over each other, those pitiless images. Her daughter is little, only four years and nine months; she still wears a diaper at night, still stubbornly sucks her thumb.

Is there any deep water close by, Petra thinks while Santa Claus, whose real name is Magnus, phones someone who will put out a call on the improvised speaker system in the square.

'My daughter's name is Emma,' she says.

'Emma,' the loudspeakers crackle. 'Your mother is waiting for you beside Santa Claus.'

'She can't swim,' Petra whispers. A lake, a canal, a river or just a creek? The water doesn't even have to be deep. A child can drown in eight inches of water.

But they're in the middle of the city. Where could she drown here? The fountain is turned off during winter and she can't get down to the harbor; it's much too far, more than an hour's walk. Of course Emma can't walk that far on her own and, even if she could, someone would find her before she got that far.

Still the images crowd Petra's thoughts. There are no limits to the disasters possible, no end to the number of accidents that can happen. Falling down? Easy to see her daughter lose her balance, see her body fall headlong, perhaps from a height.

An empty playground, a tree, a slippery swing, a wall, a rock, a jungle gym. Or down a manhole in a street, the darkness below swallowing the child, silencing her wordless cries. Squeezed to death, beaten to a pulp, bones crushed, chest caved in, suffocated in some cramped space. Death is always quick, even if dying can be painful, excruciating, drawn out. There is no merciful transition from living child to no longer breathing child, from growing child to decaying corpse.

The rain has abated and the crowd is moving again. Another announcement rasps from the speakers. 'Emma, who is four, is looking for her mother. Emma is dressed in a blue snowsuit and has blonde hair. Her mother is waiting by the main stage.'

The man who has helped her search is back. He looks sad, but now his children are hungry and tired and he has to go home.

'It will be all right,' he says again and leaves Petra. Her mind runs on, her thoughts wild.

The square seems small. The crowd, the stands – it's such a limited area. Why would her daughter want to stay here? Only a few feet away the wild city begins. The parking places, the streets, the cars, the badly lit thoroughfares. Has Emma walked there? It isn't very far. In the throng it's not easy to see if a child is alone.

Run down, run over, dusk is early this time of year. Her reflector disc, a luminous rabbit, is stuffed in the pocket of her dark blue snowsuit. Emma will never remember to pull it out so drivers can see her. Why should she? She hasn't learned to watch for traffic before crossing streets. Emma can't judge distances, can't find her way. If she starts walking you have to tell her to turn around, or she'll just keep going straight ahead. How could she ever find her way back to a place she's left? She is only four.

Magnus, the Santa, has stopped asking about presents, turned his chair over to Emma's mother and rid himself of both cap and beard. Nobody stands in line in front of his stage; they've all switched to the Social Insurance Office grab-bag stand. Dark has fallen, the streetlamps are lit. The lanterns outside the Red Cross stand flutter forlornly.

Magnus is staying with Petra. They are waiting for the police. A couple of adults have left their stands to help search. Magnus paces, feels worried. The boy, Emma's brother, has fallen asleep in his stroller and Emma's mother sits frozen in her chair.

They don't talk of the things that can happen to a lost little girl. There is no need. Those thoughts live their own lives. That statistics and probability and experience all say that Emma will soon be found means nothing.

Petra just sits there. Is it shock that makes her immobile, Magnus wonders. He clenches his hands, opens them. His joints feel swollen. He thinks of his own mother. She was always worried. Always.

Is it her thoughts that make her like this? The stories she's read and heard and can't fend off, of what really does sometimes happen? Is she thinking about the children who never return home? Or who are found but harmed for life, with invisible scars that never heal? The children abducted, away from cars and precipices but into hidden recesses, locked up by someone they should never have met. Human monsters with strong arms, heavy bodies, cellars, incomprehensible desires, and strangling hands.

Why isn't she searching, Magnus wonders. He feels an urge to shake her, slap her. She is just sitting there, staring. He clears his throat. Leans towards Petra, crouches down, puts a hand on her knee. Tries to sound authoritative. Decisive. His voice quavers as if it were breaking. Petra doesn't even raise her eyes when he says that Emma won't return on her own. He knows how important it is to act quickly, the first hour has already passed and they are approaching the steepest part of the slope to disaster. Yet here she sits, the child's mother, letting the minutes pass.

'I have to charge my cell phone,' is all Petra says.

And Magnus takes out his own, puts in her SIM card instead of his own. They watch the phone while it searches for a provider. But there are no missed calls for Petra, no texts. Instead the police arrive.

There's a routine way to do this. It tells you which questions to ask and which observations to make. Police officer Helena Svensson even has a checklist in her pocket. She could pull it out and mark it off, but instead she squats down beside the chair where the mother, Petra, is sitting. She

314

speaks in a low voice. Unless she manages to keep the mother calm, she won't get any answers. And right now nothing is more important than for her to get reliable information.

Helena Svensson takes this seriously. She asks about Emma's length and weight and what she wore. Petra doesn't have a photo of her.

'It doesn't matter,' Helena soothes her. 'I'm sure we won't need one.'

Then she takes Petra's arm, stands with her and asks her to show her exactly where they were when Emma disappeared. Six of Helena's colleagues are already searching the area. The dog patrol is busy elsewhere but has promised to come as soon as possible. The square is badly lit, but the flashlights of the police are sweeping the ground, their swaying beams of light dissolving the December dusk. When Petra tells her that she doesn't know where Emma's father is, that she hasn't heard from him since he left four months ago and that she doesn't even know if he still has the same phone number, Helena excuses herself to step aside. A phone call later, her colleagues at the precinct have been informed.

Helena knows the statistics. Statistics are held in high esteem at the police academy. Around seventeen hundred children are reported missing each year. Helena knows that most of them turn up. Even before the police arrive at the scene most return by themselves, without any drama at all. Occasionally it takes longer, and that makes it important to act before the cold gets too severe, the darkness too impenetrable. Children can get lost in the night, fall asleep and freeze to death.

And Helena also knows that if a child is in fact abducted, it is almost always by one of its parents.

Helena wants to know more about Emma's father. She can hardly contain her excitement. What happened when they separated, does his family live in Sweden, what's his profession, what does he do or not do. At that Petra gets angry. Almost screams at Helena not to be such a fucking idiot, does she really believe Petra doesn't get what she's after?

'Emma's dad hasn't kidnapped his daughter,' Petra spits. 'If he'd wanted to see her I sure wouldn't have stopped him.' She breathes. 'I do it all on my own, it's all on me. He doesn't contribute a dime, never changes a diaper, it sure isn't him wiping vomit or cooking, picking them up or dropping them off, dressing them and undressing them. If he wants her he can have her for as long as he wants.' Petra is getting breathless. She is falling to pieces. 'Take her, I'd say if he ever asked, just take her and keep her.'

Helena nods to calm Petra. She's worried; there's nothing odd in her screaming, anyone this scared would scream. But Petra refuses to calm down, she's losing control. And her loud voice wakes her son.

'I have to get home,' Petra says when the boy tenses against his harness and tries to rise. 'You have to call me when you find Emma, but I've got to get home. I can't stay all night. He has to have a new diaper and I have to feed him and I can't stay any longer to answer your stupid questions.'

Helena is surprised. It's true that you can very seldom predict how anyone will react to extreme stress. She learned that at the academy, but nobody has prepared her for this. Nobody has told her how to cajole a mother to help look for her missing child.

But Helena finds a new diaper in the stroller and offers to change the boy. That calms Petra down a bit. Someone gives the boy a banana to eat and when that's finished a female Salvation Army soldier gives him a sweet bun. Petra sits down in Santa's chair again, sipping hot coffee, and Helena walks off to call in. She wants to know if they've got hold of Emma's father.

But Helena never makes the call. People start calling to each other and though she can't hear what they're saying she knows it from their voices and their bodies. Then her colleague Stefan is walking towards her, holding a child in his arms; he is smiling and she returns his smile. Now they're all smiling, all gathering around Stefan. Applauding. The darkness seems to recede. Maybe they weren't truly worried as yet, but now they feel happy in a way they had hardly expected.

He found her less than thirty-five feet from her mother, deep under the improvised stage. He had to crawl in with his flashlight and backing out was even harder, but he managed and got Emma out. She had fallen asleep and her snowsuit smelled of pee. When he started pulling her out she woke up but didn't cry.

Helena feels a lump in her throat. She laughs again, calls out to Petra.

'Let's go to Mommy,' she whispers to Emma.

'Mommy is waiting for you.'

When Stefan steps up on the stage with his smile and his precious burden, Petra rises from the chair. But she takes no step towards him, just puts her arms around herself. She can see that he has her daughter. But she asks nothing, not is she fine, is she hurt, is she alive. Nothing.

'She was asleep,' Stefan says. 'But she's fine. I guess she was just hiding.'

Emma has turned her face and sees her mother. But she doesn't hold out her arms to her. Instead she turns back, pressing her nose to Stefan's chest. He tries coaxing her, doesn't she want to go to Mommy? She doesn't. Her thin arms are tight around the strange man's neck and Helena's smile stiffens.

But it's not really strange, she thinks. The girl must be frightened; she just woke up, everything is scary, she's so small. Not strange at all.

Petra is no help.

'Damn kid,' she growls. Her eyes are black. Then at last she lets go of herself and tears the child from Stefan. Emma starts to cry. She fists her little hand and puts it in her mouth and there is no sound, but tears trickle down her cheeks. 'Have you peed?' Petra says when her fingers feel the wet snowsuit.

'I didn't mean to, Mommy,' her daughter whispers. 'I didn't mean to.'

'Let's leave,' Stefan says, taking Petra's arm. Helena Svensson agrees. It's perfectly natural that the girl is afraid, with the high-powered flashlight shining into her hiding place and all the strange adults looking at her; it must be overwhelming.

And Petra is in shock, of course she is numb. People react differently to extreme stress. Helena learned that at the academy. None of this is really out of the ordinary. Nothing is strange, everything is quite normal. Petra will soon calm down.

Now the boy too has started to yell. He screams very loudly but it's good that they're crying; children who cry and scream are seldom badly hurt. When they're silent is when there's cause for alarm.

'Have you peed?' Petra says again and this time she almost screams and Emma starts crying harder and now they have to get away from here, have to get into a warm apartment, and the children must get some food and dry clothes because now it is raining again, hard. Helena feels her pulse racing, her hands sweating. How could anyone calm down in this chaos? And if she gets this upset, is it strange that their mother can hardly contain herself? It must be a thousand times harder on her.

It's been a tough afternoon, Helena thinks, and everyone is jumpy.

'Let's go to my car,' Helena Svensson says at last. 'I'll drive you home.'

But the mother doesn't seem relieved. She wants to fend for herself, take the bus home. 'Why do you want to tag along?' she asks. 'I can manage on my own. Don't you think I can manage? Anyone could lose a kid for a little while. She's back now. You don't have to check up on me. I'll manage, I always have.'

Helena Svensson has to insist. When they get to her car someone has called an ambulance. It's

319

parked next to Helena's patrol car and Helena asks them to turn off their flashing blue lights. One of the paramedics takes a look at Emma and certifies that she doesn't seem to be harmed, doesn't need any treatment. She has scratches on one knee and a few bruises, one over her ribs and a couple on her arms. But nothing is broken. And she is hardly black and blue. She confirms it herself: it doesn't hurt.

Petra is standing beside the girl while she's examined.

'I guess she must have hit something crawling around in there,' Petra says, glaring at the bruises. Then turns to Helena. 'It makes no difference how many times I tell her. She never listens. And she's so clumsy. Always running into things or falling down. If she'd just listen…'

The bruise on her ribs is yellowish, not even blue any longer.

And Helena thinks: Those aren't recent bruises, she didn't get them today. She glances at the paramedic. But he just slides his hand across the girl's downy back, pulling her shirt back down. Then he pats Emma's cheek. The examination is done.

Children always hurt themselves, Helena thinks. Always. At day care, for instance. She must have hurt herself at the day care center.

'I'll help you get settled,' Helena says to Petra. 'You could use some help.' And for some reason she can hardly understand she goes on, to forestall any protests. 'There are some questions I have to ask you for my report, and if we can do it at your place you don't have to come down to the

320

precinct. I'm really sorry I have to; I know you'd prefer to be left alone, but those are the rules.'

Petra just nods. Now she looks tired again, exhausted.

Helena's partner drives. Petra and the children are in the backseat. When they arrive, her partner waits in the street and Helena enters the building with Petra and the children. The apartment is small but tidy. You can see all the rooms from the hallway. A bar of butter is lying on the sink in the kitchen but the beds are made, the living room floor is empty of toys.

Both children run off when their shoes and snowsuits are off.

'I'll shower her after you leave,' Petra says, calmer now, and puts Emma's snowsuit in the laundry basket by the apartment door. 'Take your jeans and panties off,' she calls to her daughter.

Helena nods. The apartment is neat. Warm. Ordinary.

Helena shuffles her feet. Mumbles a few questions. Petra replies. She doesn't ask her in. Walks into the living room and Helena hears her turn the TV on. She considers following her, but doesn't.

'I'm hungry, Mommy,' Emma calls from the TV couch and Petra walks into the kitchen. Helena stands on the threshold, watching Petra pour frozen meatballs into a frying pan.

Helena can't think of anything more to say and retreats into the hallway. They agree to talk again next day. Just to follow up.

'Bye, then,' she calls to the children.

'Bye,' they say.

She can hear their mother lock the tumbler and

put the door chain in its slot.

Helena Svensson walks down the stairs and out in the street. It isn't relief at having left that makes her turn around and look up at the apartment building, trying to find the windows of the apartment where Petra and her two children live. It's a different feeling. A jarring one.

Her partner waits in the car. He is older than her. At least fifteen years on the force. He wants to get home. As soon as he's let her off he will. Have dinner. Watch TV. Be with his family.

'What did you think of her?' Helena asks carefully. 'The mother. Didn't she seem a bit ... angry?'

'Who the hell wouldn't be angry?' her partner asks. He laughs and Helena feels her cheeks redden. He thinks she is silly, it's unmistakable. 'Kids getting lost. Anything could have happened. She might have been stuck down there under the stage. Unable to get out, what do I know? And I guess she was embarrassed, too. Got half the cops in town out just because her kid fell asleep thirty feet away. Of course she felt ashamed.'

Helena nods. Of course she did.

'Just let it go.' Her partner turns in at her street. 'We did something good today, Helena. Think about that instead. It sure doesn't happen every day. Now let's go home. It's fucking Christmas. Smile and be happy. This was one of the good days.'

Police officer Helena Svensson goes to bed early. A large cup of tea on her bedside table. She leafs through a glossy magazine. A recipe for gingerbread cupcakes, a home decoration article full of embroidered silk cushions. A famous actress talks about her family Christmas traditions. She wants to teach her children the joy of giving.

Helena turns pages, reads, starts over again when she is done. She is wide awake. Unthinkingly reads the same article again and again, unable to concentrate on how to make a sugar-frosted Christmas garland out of spruce twigs. Her mind is full of dirty yellow bruises and a little girl clinging to Stefan's neck.

Even at the police academy they talked about it. About the worst threat to little girls not being a dirty old man with his pockets full of candy and an imaginary puppy in the trunk of his car. The dirty old men are few. Many more children have mothers who can't take it any more, have fathers who never help out, are always told that they are hopeless and clumsy and stupid. And get bruises even if they never dare climb a tree.

The apartment where Emma lived was warm. Her mother wasn't a drunk. She cooked meatballs and kept a laundry basket by her door, had bought detergent and booked the laundry room.

Let it go. That's what her partner had said. And why shouldn't she? Petra already led a tough life. Alone with two kids. She certainly doesn't need to get social services on her back. And Helena has other things to worry about.

Tomorrow was another day. Her shift would start at eleven and the weather forecast said it would be cold. Cold drove the homeless to places where they became visible, into stairwells where landlords complained about their smell and into shopping malls where they didn't fit in with the Christmas decorations. Tomorrow would be a hard day and tomorrow night even worse. She can't worry the small stuff like this. She'll burn out before finishing her first year.

Helena throws the magazine on the floor and switches off the light. She turns on her side and kicks at the covers to get her foot free.

Let it go? Is that really what I'm supposed to do? Is that really how it's supposed to be? When it's soon fucking Christmas. Was this really one of the good days?

THE MULTI-MILLIONAIRE

MAJ SJÖWALL AND PER WAHLÖÖ

A few years ago, we made the acquaintance of a dollar multi-millionaire. You don't meet multi-millionaires every day. Particularly not in dollars. When all's said and done, there is something special about dollars.

If you consider the place where we met, perhaps the occurrence wasn't all that strange. It happened on board the *Queen Elizabeth* – the real *Queen Elizabeth*, the one nowadays moping around as a hotel somewhere in Florida – and not only that, but in first class, where they probably had more than one millionaire. There were also a lot of blue-haired American ladies and tottering English lords. But we particularly remember our man because he told us a story. A story complete with a moral.

From the poop deck we watched as we sailed out to sea under the Verrazano-Narrows Bridge, and when Ambrose Lighthouse had disappeared in the sun haze we went to the bar and that's where we first saw him.

He sat alone at a table, his back bent in its light-blue cashmere pullover as he brooded over a double whiskey. It was fairly early in the morning. He gave us a cursory glance as we each climbed on one of the bar stools. The three of us and the man behind the bar were the only ones in the room and it was still more than an hour to lunch.

The man looked close to sixty; later we learned that he was forty-two.

At the same moment we were ordering drinks the man dropped his pack of cigarettes on the wall-to-wall carpet. Then he fixed the bartender with his violet-blue stare and said: 'Please hand me my cigarettes.'

The barman went on mixing our drinks.

'My cigarette pack fell to the floor. Please hand it to me,' the man on the couch said.

The bartender vigorously stirred our drinks and pretended not to hear.

'Shall I blow my top?' the man asked.

Unconcerned, the bartender rattled the ice while the man on the couch sat immobile, staring hard at him with his truly conspicuous violet eyes.

We started to get interested and awaited further developments.

The man in the light-blue pullover slammed his glass down on the table and said, 'Okay, I'll blow my top.'

So he did. Which meant that he got furious. He stood up, heaped abuse on the bartender, behaved like a hysterical five-year-old and left the bar with quick, mincing steps, leaving his pack of cigarettes on the carpet. The bartender didn't bat an eyelid. After a while a bar assistant arrived and put the cigarettes back on the table.

'A loathsome man,' we said.

The bartender's face was sphinxlike.

For this trip we had been seated at the table headed by the purser and the ship's doctor. At the table we met the man from the bar again. Not at lunch, when his chair was empty, but at dinner. He was in a bad mood, since he had been expecting to sit at the captain's table. After all, he was a multi-millionaire.

The crossing took four days, fifteen hours and twenty-five minutes.

This isn't a very long time, historically speaking, but aboard a large ship it can feel rather long.

Since there were relatively few first-class passengers on the trip and meals tend to be many and long and we also sat at the same table, we came to talk a lot to the man who was a multi-millionaire.

We even learned his name: McGrant. That he was an American there was no reason to doubt for even a second.

When we asked him where he lived, he raised his eyebrows in great surprise and said, 'In McGrant, of course.'

And so it was. He came from a town called McGrant somewhere in Mississippi or Kentucky or whatever state it was in. His great-grandfather was a Scot and had come there and founded the town and then it had been passed on to his heirs. Quite simply he owned the town that bore his name: the bank and the department stores and most of the buildings and, indirectly, also almost all of the land. It was a fine town, he said, of around ten thousand inhabitants, and they all lived in their own houses and were white, even the servants, and of course he also had control of the local party organization.

He liked his Bentley, he said, but he liked his Rolls-Royce better, even if both of his Cadillacs were more American, and he regarded us as friends of his since we shared our bread and our salt and Cunard's peculiar desserts, which looked like swans made from jelly pudding, and sat at the same table.

He threw indignant glances at the elderly, stodgy peers at the captain's table and said that of course he couldn't have known we would end up at the same mess table that first time in the bar when he delivered his first fit of rage and let his pack of cigarettes fall to the long-suffering deck in the old *Queen*'s barroom.

We listened to him in badly hidden amazement and watched his antics in sadness mixed with terror.

He never opened or closed any door, never sat down in a chair unless someone pushed it under him and never retrieved any of the objects that with regular and usually very short intervals he let fall from his hands. And however fast the servants were he would tell them off. That was part of the system, an integrated component of his method.

If any of us, or any other passenger, in some way tried to help him along, he was put off.

Somehow that was inappropriate.

We wondered: How can any person become like him?

328

And he must have read that question in our eyes, for that was when he told us his strange story.

The beginning wasn't so strange. The story of the single son of an inhumanly demanding father. And the son, who within a year would take it all over but who first had to prove himself capable of making his own way. What was strange was the rather particular method.

Suddenly one day his father had said: Here's a ticket to San Francisco. Go there and stay for a year and fend for yourself and come back and take over the town of McGrant. (He ought to have added that he himself would probably die from heart failure within that year, and so indeed he did, that is, die.)

McGrant junior had no other choice than to do as his father demanded. With a couple of dollars in his pocket and a bag with the bare necessities of clothing he took the train to San Francisco. It was a very long way and he had never before been on the West Coast and he knew nobody in the city.

'But I made do,' McGrant said. 'Of course I made do. And more than that, I lived well that whole year in San Francisco.'

'So you got yourself a job there,' we suggested.

'A job?' said McGrant, flabbergasted, and looked unsympathetically at us with his round, violet-blue eyes.

It was the third day, a stormy day, and in the afternoon through our binoculars we had sighted

329

Fastnet Rock far away in the northeast quadrant. The swell of the Atlantic was heavy and green and pitiless and manropes had been stretched all around the ship.

We three had been the only diners in the mess – rumor had it that even the ship's doctor was seasick in his bathtub, where he observed the swell of the sea by watching the water in his bath rise and fall – and now we were having coffee and brandy in the very thinly populated salon.

'No,' McGrant said. 'No, I certainly didn't get a job, but I did learn how to live in San Francisco. And since you are friends of mine I will tell you how I did it. Perhaps knowing it will come in handy at some point.'

And we listened.

'So I arrived in San Francisco without a cent in my pocket,' McGrant said.

'Without a cent?'

He raised his eyebrows in a very surprised manner above his violet-blue eyes and said: 'Don't you really know how to do it?'

No, we said. We truly really didn't know.

And so he told us:

'I came to San Francisco without a cent in my pocket and I had only one chance.'

'San Francisco,' he said, 'is one of the toughest towns in the States, and that makes it one of the toughest towns in all the world.'

'Really?' we said. 'And how do you get ahead there,' we said.

Questioningly.

And then he told us his story.

It went like this:

'So as I said, my dear father sent me to San Francisco without a cent in my pocket.'

'And then what happened,' we said.

'It was morning, early morning, when I arrived in San Francisco,' McGrant told us. 'I was broke and hungry and since I wasn't used to either I didn't know what to do. I walked out of the railway station and saw the line of cabs and it felt strange not to be able to get into one of them and go to the best hotel in town. I stood there with my little bag and I thought: You're all alone now, and you have to manage this.

'But I didn't know how.'

'That's when I caught sight of him. A short, shabby man stumbling along on sore feet along the opposite sidewalk. He was carrying a sign saying: EAT AT FRIENDLY – THE FRIENDLY RESTAURANT!, and below that, in smaller letters, it said: *TRY OUR GREAT HOMELY FARE – IF YOU'RE NOT SATISFIED, YOU DON'T PAY!*

'As I already told you, I was hungry, and the little money my father had given me for travel expenses I had already out of old habit spent on drinks in the dining car. I decided to do as the sign suggested and I decided that I would certainly not be satisfied. As it turned out, the friendly restaurant happened to be just halfway down the first block on the next crossing street. The dining room was huge and full of breakfast eaters. I sat down at the back of the room and ordered a square meal of ham and eggs, toast, butter, cheese, jelly, juice, coffee, well, basically all I could think of. Now I should mention that I really don't eat much, as you may have noticed already, being my friends at the purser's table. I eat like a bird, always have.'

We nodded. He certainly hadn't indulged much in the way of solid food during these few days.

'At any rate, all the things I had ordered were brought to my table and when I'd just tasted a small sampling of each I was absolutely full. So I called to the waitress, pointed to my seemingly untouched breakfast and declared that it was the worst meal I had ever been served. She got hold of the head waiter. He was sorry that I wasn't satisfied, assured me that of course Friendly would stand by its promise and asked me to sign my name to the check. I wrote the first name that popped into my head: G. Formby. I've always liked the banjo. When I walked to the door, full of food and happy, I noticed that many of the guests had left their tips on the table, you know, coins half hidden under a plate, the way we do back in the States. It was an easy thing to snatch those coins on my way out.'

'Well, it wasn't a bad start. The money I found under the plates was enough to rent a room. And can you imagine how surprised I was when I glanced out the window and the first person I saw was an old man carrying exactly the same sign as the one I'd seen outside the railway station: EAT AT FRIENDLY – THE FRIENDLY RESTAU-RANT! *TRY OUR GREAT HOMELY FARE – IF*

YOU'RE NOT SATISFIED, YOU DON'T PAY!

'Naturally I went to a phone booth and to my considerable delight I found that Friendly was a huge chain of restaurants with at least a hundred outlets in the San Francisco Bay area. I immediately realized the enormous possibilities hidden within this fact. Obviously I became a faithful patron of these eateries, and the coins I found under most plates meant that I never needed to be penniless. On the contrary, my capital began growing, slowly but surely.

'One day a man at the table next to mine spoke to me. He was a shabby creature whom I of course hardly could start talking to. What he said was:

'"This is a great trick. Too bad you can only pull it a couple of times a year. The checks you sign are collected in some office somewhere, and they keep track of the names. If you sign too often they put you on their blacklist, and they just won't serve you any longer." I stared at him. Most probably he was an imbecile. After watching me sign the check with a dignified and dismissive expression, he sadly wiped his mouth and said:

'"I know another good trick, but you can only do it once a year. At Parsley's. They give you a free cake on your birthday. And then you can sell it. But you have to be able to document that it's really your birthday."

'Without dignifying him with a glance I rose to leave, increasing my capital with a further five quarters on the way out.'

'I was now faced with a problem, but solved it immediately. I could hardly get in touch with my father, but instead I could write the authorities in McGrant and tell them to send me a hundred identity cards with my birth date left blank. In McGrant, that kind of thing was handled by the sheriff, and since he was up for reelection only half a year later, I had the cards in three days. He had mailed them special delivery.

'After that, everything became much easier. I picked my cakes up at Parsley's, which was also a major trade chain, and sold them to those Friendly restaurants I had already used up.

'Perhaps I haven't told you that I genuinely dislike walking, while at the same time disdain on principle so-called public transportation, possibly, and I really mean just possibly, with the exception of this kind.'

McGrant fell silent and made a sweeping gesture encompassing the *Queen Elizabeth*'s lounge, where the fifth Earl of Something, strongly marked by age, senile decay and general stupidity, was just giving a lecture on Lord Nelson and the Battle of Aboukir to a sparse audience of commandeered ship's officers twisting uneasily in their seats. The old man seemed totally oblivious of the swell.

'Well,' McGrant continued, in passing letting his coffee spoon fall to the floor, 'in brief, this is what I did. I phoned all the major car retailers in town and told them that my aunt had asked me to buy her a car. A luxury car, but that she wanted it thoroughly tested. Then I set up meetings with the salesmen in the lobby of one of the largest hotels. After that I let myself be chauffeured around for a week or so, taking in the nearby sights. When the salesman began to seem nervous and started hinting that I ought to make my mind up, I would of course have come to realize that his particular car just wouldn't do for my discriminating aunt. After that, I turned to the next outlet. At one point, I believe when I was riding a Daimler, I had already been driven around for ten days and had to let my poor aunt pass away from a heart attack on the eleventh.'

'Yes, my friends, that's how I lived during my year in San Francisco, most brutal of all great cities. And if you should ever happen to find yourselves there, at least you know how to cope. When the year ended I took a train home, and you can trust me when I tell you that this time I had plenty of dollars in my pocket. Unfortunately my father never got to see my proud return, since he had died a week before.'

McGrant was a careful man. At an intimate moment he showed us his medicines – around a hundred – and his cash. In spite of his checkbooks and bank accounts and credit cards and the fact of his trip being prepaid, he always carried a wallet full of bills in large denominations and from every Western European country.

'You never know what may happen,' he said.

And of course that's true.

He disembarked at Cherbourg and on the quay a black, chauffeured limousine waited for him.

The last piece of advice he gave us was:

'Don't tip the bootblack when you get to Southampton.'

We last glimpsed him as he minced out from the dining room, on his way palming a few dollar bills left under a plate by some gullible American.

Otherwise, the trip was as such trips usually are. Schools of flying fish and porpoises and a whale blowing. By the way, the captain was named Law.

And we won a prize in designing the funniest hat in a competition. Everyone who entered did. McGrant didn't enter. He was up on deck, telling off the cabin steward for allowing his suitcases to be wrongly packed. Incidentally, it wasn't his cabin steward.

DIARY BRAUN

SARA STRIDSBERG

The curtains let in light but no images. The land-scape outside is a desert. The rhythm of the train is convincingly and seductively lulling. He has written you that you must pull down the curtains in your compartment when the train passes the places you have talked about. So you pull down the curtains or you lean your head against the window glass and watch the other passengers in the compartment and their luggage when the train pulls close. A woman alone with cheap luggage and her face turned to the corridor. A man with an armful of sunflowers in a paper bag. The compartment is sun-faded with burnt-through leather seats that must once have been elegant, but which are now splitting along their seams and letting out spongy upholstery. Politics bores you, always has bored you to death. The sun-bleached curtain separates you from the world and the earth. You are going back to the house on Berghof. Insubordinate sunbeams sneak in through tears in the fabric. A patch of blue, bulging sky. The beauty of this country. Wheat and roses.

How should I describe you? Sweet as a box of chocolates. A kind of dreamy beauty, an expensive small piece of jewelry. The Munich girl falling for a pair of famous blue eyes. For a long while you were retouched out of all public photographs since your love has the notion that he shouldn't be seen in public with any women. So. Your rabbit fur disappears from the image. Your ash-blonde hair, your mother-of-pearl nails, all your devotion will afterwards be retouched out. As if you had never been there or as if you are a ghost who on her own has invented your decade-long love. Occasionally a single woman's hand is visible on his forearm, but the body belonging to it is gone. As late as June of 1944, the British intelligence service believes you to be his secretary.

Further descriptions of you from literature: mild, naïve, dreamy, romantic. I add your longing for death to the catalogue. Since it must be there. Your inclination for the underworld. Absolutely.

'About twenty-four years of age, brunette, attractive and unconventional in her dress. Occasionally wears Bavarian leather shorts. In her spare time, walks two black dogs. Protected by operatives of the RSD during her walks. Always without makeup, on the whole gives an impression of inapproachability.'
–*From a Special Operations Executive document*

The spring smells of ashes and greenery just come into leaf. Long, lonely walks, rambling conversations about the weather and the dogs, sleepless nights. Obersalzberg, the small set piece, a utopia of purity and beauty. Still no public displays of affection. Hamburg transformed into a sea of fire, its people ashes. It's your birthday. Money in an envelope. No greetings, not a kind word, nothing, but your entire office looks like a florist's shop and smells like a funeral chapel. You ought to make use of the shelter, but instead you stay in the house, dancing with your mirror image, get up on the roof after each raid to see if any fire bombs have fallen. The crowns of the trees bend down towards the water as if in prayer. You write: *They say that my country is burning. All will be well. It will be all right. Dragonflies dive down at our picnic. My bathing suit is gold and silver.*

You have never been as happy as now. After all the years of waiting he is finally yours. He has grown strangely old and stern, but at least today he is cheerful. Blondie sings like Zarah Leander. She sounds like a mad wolf. It's snowing even though it is April and throughout the night you drink wonderful champagne, full of promise, toasting his last birthday. The next day all of the presents from the ranks of the people are sent away due to the risks of poison. You wear the dress he loves, the navy-blue sequined silk one. When you are dead, a German journalist writes of it: 'Her taste now was more mature and she could carry off clothes that were chic, not just lovely and youthful.' Then Munich falls and he is off again to the underworld.

You and your silly little cousin wait every day in your bathing suits for the mailman in Obersalzberg who drives you down to the lake and the beaches, the happy waterfall, the fairy-tale beach by the ice-cold blue lake. Sometimes you take off your bathing suits to swim nude between alps. You imagine the officers doing nasty things to themselves while they watch your naked body.

That thought appeals to you. The assassination attempt in Berlin fails, but all the sunlight disappears. Days pass. All the tender letters and carrier pigeons. *Pull the curtains down my dear when the train passes the places we talked about. Pull the curtains down my dear...*

You order a new dress for Christmas. It's to be something special and more, something to amaze everyone. Miss Heise nags you about her perennial bills. It would be best if they could be obliterated once they are paid. It would be best if they just disappeared. You don't want anyone afterwards to study your correspondence with your seamstress. Your dresses are your secrets. You hold a slip and a diamond brooch up against death. Snow falls like sugar cubes on the city. There is no longer any hope for a future.

A cherished meeting with a sister in Wassenburgerstrasse. A few pieces of jewelry handed to Gertraud when you are both temporarily in the shelter beneath the house, a necklace and a bracelet. You say, 'I don't need them any longer.' The decision has been made; we leave all of this together, where you go I will go, where you are buried I too want to be buried.

His birthday gifts for your last birthday: a Mercedes, a diamond bracelet, a pendant set with topazes. You have a birthday celebration in the marbled room. I don't know which dress you chose to wear for this last night in the house, but I imagine it to be extravagant, I imagine you in cream and embroideries and throughout with a brandy snifter in your hand. You pick clothes and jewelry to bring along from your enormous

340

closet, the rest you will have to give away now. You make sure that the dogs will have somewhere to live. One last time, trying out everything, once more enjoying your image in the huge, mirrored bathroom. The flocks of jackdaws take wing from your heart, leaving it empty.

The sheets in the night train sleeper are white and fragrantly clean. Outside are the wastelands. When you arrive at Berghof there is still snow. The train to the underworld will leave at 8:14 p.m. He can no longer stop you since you are not afraid of death, since you long for it. The only thing frightening you is that your body will be disfigured, violated by strangers once you can no longer defend it, dress it, adorn it. Now you leave the window of your compartment naked despite his warnings. Anyway it's dark outside. Earlier in the day a weak sun was shining. Ominously weak.

The lack of natural light underground amazes you. That disgusting neon light, artificial and sinister. From now on it is always claustrophobic night. You dream of huge scenic windows. In your dreams strange tropical animals roam in slow motion through the garden above. Your miniature suite next to the chart room comprises a bedroom, a closet, a bathroom and toilet. Even Blondie has a small room to herself and her pups. It isn't far to the climbing roses in the garden and yet you can't go there because of the grenades. The cities are gray and wasted now, dead and crushed, occasional shreds and climbing roses, people resembling clouds.

The apartment underground smells of marmalade and metal. You watch movies, drink sparkling wine, eat fruits and sweet cookies, you prepare for death, write wills. A black sunlight radiates through the windows. The night is a tomb. Not all birds sing. In a letter to your sister, you write, 'Destroy all my private correspondence, particularly the bills from my seamstress, Heise. Bury the blue leather notebook. Wait until the last to destroy the films and the albums. The telephone lines are all dead now. I hope Morrell landed safely to bring you my jewelry.'

You order Moët et Chandon. You order cakes. Cocaine drops for his bad eye. New promotions. The pretend war goes on. Paper swallows across the office floor illustrate devastation. You call into the wind. Mrs. G. is given a brooch. Afterwards it is still pinned to her dress. It looks like a fallen butterfly. Now death is keeping you busy, it is your only conversational subject. To do: Change dress. Fix nails. Paint mother-of-pearl. Life is a beauty pageant and you are the foremost exhibit underground where you have free access to his luxurious bathroom. A. still washes and irons your clothes. You change your dress several times a day, always wearing elegant, gossamer underwear. You dance alongside the dead. A brimstone butterfly gone astray into the tunnels.

The silver-fox stole gleams like a cloud in darkness. How you have loved that stole. A garment made for a movie star. A boa for the future. For all your silly dreams. You give it away, too. It has lost all value for you. You put it in the arms of a secretary, Miss T., convincingly say, 'Take it. Use it. Enjoy.'

The best way to die is to shoot yourself through the mouth. Memorandum: *My husband dislikes being seen in the nude. For that to happen would be a defeat to him. Please bear this in mind*

The underground wedding resembles none of your dreams. But yet. An elegant, navy-blue sequined dress and black suede Ferragamo shoes. No flowers, no songs, no incurable diseases, but champagne – the cellar is still full of fabulous, immortal drops. For the very last night you are dressed in carbon dioxide and night. Thirty-six hours of marriage under the earth. A political testament in four blueprints. The bride of night in poisoned veils. Your closet is like your love, a black circle without end. The king's first and last wife.

And I want my death to be painless. Nothing of all I wished will turn out as I wished, but that I do want. A painless death. I thought about dying in my silver-fox stole. I think about this and that. Everything passes, everything ends.

Thirty-six hours after the wedding all that remains is a last, dizzying farewell. The patterned fabric of the couch under your nails, your favorite couch. In the distance the sound of a diesel-powered fan, and the scent of his sweat. You sit like children, legs up in the couch. You listen to his continuously more disjointed talking, his chest close to your ear and in it you can still hear the beating of his heart. How you loved him, dizzyingly much. The garden, fire, love, the underworld.

The dress with black roses will be your last dress, the one leading to eternity. There are thirty-seven roses, you have let him count them one last time. One rose for every hour you were a wife, and one extra. For nothing. For all you will now never be. The pink curlers are thrown on the floor of your bedroom. Hair newly set. Just a whiff of powder and a little lipstick, since he still hates makeup. You have showered in perfume to drown the odor of sweat.

A last, flaring memory. You are riding your bike through the woods to meet him by a lake. You are young and his eyes are blue like gemstones. A box of cookies on your baggage carrier. A dead pheasant smeared across the road. The feeling that a cloud is following you. A light in those blue stones you will never afterwards be able to forget. Afterwards your bodies will be burned outside in the garden. The small brass tube that held the cyanide looks like a discarded lipstick. A glass phial full of dark-brown fluid. The searing smell of bitter almonds. Breaking the glass phial between your teeth and swallowing the dark-brown fluid. Soviet grenades fall around your burning bodies. And Blondie. Doctor Stumpfegger takes care of her. Your loved one was unable to do it himself. He put the glass phial into your mouth, in bewildered trembling tenderness, but he was unable to do it to her.

REVENGE OF THE VIRGIN

JOHAN THEORIN

Gerlof woke in a cramped and cold wooden house. The walls and windows shook and rattled. The house was his own, his old boathouse, and it moved when gusts of wind pushed up from the beach to howl like a lost, unholy mare.

When he lifted his head from his camping bed he also heard the sound from the waves at the beach. It wasn't a roar, not yet, just a rhythmical rattle when they broke on the gravel.

There would be a storm today, it seemed. Gerlof didn't worry about his boathouse – his grandfather had used it for twenty years, then his father for thirty and now he had used it another ten years. He knew that the house and its foundation of stone would stand, no matter what winds blew in across the coastline. So the best thing for Gerlof would be to just stay inside. He had a day off from the sea. His boat was moored in Borgholm harbor, waiting for a new anchor.

But Gerlof had to get up. He, John Hagman and the Mossberg cousins had put quite a few nets in the strait last night, and they had to be emptied as soon as possible. Otherwise the storm would blow the nets out into the strait – along with all the fish that had been caught in them overnight.

Only one thing to do. Sighing, Gerlof sat up in his boathouse.

'Up ev'ry day, bad weather or fair,' he muttered to himself and put his stockinged feet on the linoleum.

The floor was icy. The fire in the small iron stove at the foot of the bed had gone out during the night.

'John?'

Gerlof bent to the other narrow bed and shook his friend's shoulder. Finally John raised his head.

'Wha'?'

'Wake up,' Gerlof said. 'The fish are waiting.'

John coughed, blinked his eyes and looked at the window.

'Can we put out?'

'We have to. Or do you want to lose the nets?'

John shook his head.

'We shouldn't have laid them yesterday ... Erik was right about the weather.'

'Just a lucky guess,' Gerlof said.

'Might well go and get stormy tomorrow,' fisherman Erik Mossberg had said in his dialect the evening before, when he'd come down to the beach. His cousin Torsten waited with Gerlof and John by the boats.

'Really?' Gerlof said. 'Did they say so on the radio?'

'Nope. But on the way here I stepped across a viper. It lay on the stairs and hardly wanted to leave.'

'I suppose it had eaten its fill,' Gerlof said. 'Are

346

snakes supposed to become experts on what happens in the atmosphere just because they lie still?'

'It's proven true before,' Erik said. 'I've seen snakes before when there was a storm brewing, and more than once.'

Gerlof just shook his head and put the nets down on the floor of the boat. He believed neither in portents nor prophecies.

But a little later, when they had launched their two wooden crafts on the glassy water and begun to lay their nets over the railings, Gerlof had peered north at the Blue Virgin on the horizon and seen that the granite cliff had changed its color. It had darkened from blue gray to black and seemed to have risen above the waters of the strait, as if it floated in the air.

The weather was still fine. The sun shone on the sea and the May wind was soft and almost warm, but when Gerlof had thrown in the last of the net floats he realized that Erik had been right. A storm was coming. He didn't believe in vipers, but the changed appearance of the Virgin had told him so. And when he rowed back to shore the cliff was no longer visible – it had disappeared in a pale, white mist.

Harder winds were coming.

Half an hour after they woke up the next morning, John and Gerlof were down at the beach along with Erik and Torsten.

The boats were ready, but despite the gale drawing closer John and the two cousins persisted in smoking a cigarette each on the beach before setting out.

Gerlof checked his watch in irritation, but the smokers just smiled.

'If you smoked too, you'd be less cranky in the mornings,' Erik said, blowing a white cloud into the wind.

'Tobacco isn't healthy,' Gerlof said. 'Pulling a lot of thick smoke into your lungs? Sooner or later, doctors will start warning people not to do it.'

The other three smiled at his prophecy.

'I'd be bedridden without my cigarettes,' Torsten said. 'They keep me healthy ... they rinse out your throat!'

After their smoking break they walked down to the boats. Gerlof and John pushed their old Öland gig onto the water and stepped down in it. Then they pushed out past the breakers, each using one oar, and finally raised the small spritsail.

As the wind caught the cotton canvas and the seventeen-foot gig began making way across the sea, they heard a dull whining behind them, as from a large, bad-tempered bumblebee. Erik and Torsten Mossberg had started their new outboard. The motor made their rowboat speed up and determinedly plow straight ahead, white foam mustaches at its prow.

Gerlof didn't want an outboard, not while there were oars and sails. They used no gas and the long-keeled gig was easy to sail. It lifted effortlessly from the waves, kept a straight course and beat to windward as steadily as a Viking ship, which the Öland gig was, in a way. At least they were related.

When John and Gerlof had reached their nets they let out the sail and let the boat drift freely. Their three nets were north of those of the cousins, who had laid four on the night before. The cork floats holding the nets up were called *läten* on northern Öland and were marked by small, white pennants fluttering hard in the wind.

Gerlof pulled up the first *läte*, then began hauling the net on board with long, even strokes. The net twisted around his legs, coiled down like wet hawsers into the wooden crates.

The catch was good this morning. The first struggling flounder appeared after only a couple of yards, followed by many more. But the wind increased and while he pulled up the nets Gerlof was continually forced to try to stand steady in the rough waves lifting and pulling down the gig.

He felt relieved when the nets were all out, lying like huge balls in their crates. The balls moved, for the flounders kept struggling.

Gerlof gently worked loose a fourhorn sculpin that had managed to get stuck in the loops of yarn and threw it back in the water.

'How many did you make it?'

'Eighty-six,' John said.

'Really? I made it eighty-four.'

'Then I guess it's eighty-five.'

That was fine – Gerlof's wife Ella in Borgholm had wanted flounders for the weekend, and their daughters liked them, too. Time to get back to land and home to the family.

The wind had risen steadily, as had the waves. Of course, here in the strait they never grew to the steep hills of water and pools of spray Gerlof and his boat had met farther out on the Baltic, but they were closer together and made the gig's broad planking shudder.

He would have preferred to turn the boat and get back ashore as quickly as possible, now that the nets were up, but when he put his hand to the tiller he felt John's touch on his shoulder and heard a question through the wind:

'What's that over there? In front of the Virgin?'

Gerlof turned his eyes northward and saw something narrow and black move in the strait, around a nautical mile from the Blue Virgin – an object seeming to roll helplessly in the foaming sea.

'Looks like a rowboat,' he said.

'Yes,' John said, 'and it's empty.'

Gerlof shook his head. He couldn't see a head sticking up out of the boat, but he had seen enough small and large crafts at sea to know when one of them was loaded or not, so he said:

'Not quite empty. There's something in it.'

Or someone, a human? His glass was still lying in the wheelhouse on the boat down in Borgholm, but when the waves lifted the rowboat he could still make out something long and light within it. At this distance, it looked like a person who had lain down, or fallen, and been covered by a tarpaulin.

Without saying anything more Gerlof set the spritsail again and set off to northwest. John sat in the bow and didn't object. Every Ölander knew that if someone in a boat was ill or in distress that person must be helped, no matter how hard the wind.

Fifteen minutes later they were within hailing distance of the rowboat, which now and then disappeared in the waves. Gerlof cupped his hands.

'Ahoy,' he called. 'Ahoy over there!'

Nothing moved in the boat, but Gerlof saw that the tarpaulin was dry. That meant the rowboat couldn't have drifted for very long in the strait.

Behind them, a rattling outboard came closer. 'What's up?'

The Mossberg cousins had followed and reached them. Erik gave more gas, yawed narrowly across a wave and went up alongside the rowboat. Gerlof was envious at how easy it was with the outboard.

Torsten stretched out his arm and caught hold of the boat's railing. In the calm of a trough he crossed to the rowboat, stood up and threw a rope to his cousin. Now the two boats were tied together.

Finally Torsten bent down, lifted the tarpaulin and looked at what was underneath it.

'It's just rocks!' he called to the others.

'Rocks?'

Gerlof turned his gig round. It closed the distance to the rowboat a bit, and he saw that Torsten was right: in the bottom of the rowboat was a large pile of rounded rocks. They looked like water-smoothed beach stones.

Gerlof had no more time to consider their strange find. A huge wave broke against his boat, drenching both fishes and fishermen in ice-cold spray.

He shook himself and blinked at the wind. Now

351

the waves had grown to sloping walls. There was a storm in the Kalmar strait, no point in denying it.

Gerlof tried turning his gig around to catch the waves on the aft quarter, but suddenly there was a short bang and an extended, tearing sound. The boat straightened and the sail lost all power. When he raised his eyes there was a large tear in the canvas.

'*Pöt!*'

John cursed in the Öland dialect and held on to the gunwale as the boat heaved on a wave. He rushed forward to take in the torn sail.

At the same time, Gerlof let go of the tiller for a couple of seconds to get the oars in. When he was done, John took over between the oarlocks and started rowing, but it was hard work for him to make steerageway.

'The waves are steering us!' Gerlof yelled through the wind.

'What?'

Gerlof cupped his hands.

'It's too late to turn back... We might as well make the Virgin, until it lulls.'

'What about this one?' Torsten called from the rowboat. 'What do we do with it?'

'Tow it!' Gerlof said.

After all it was a solid boat, and Ölanders have taken care of lost property adrift on the sea since time immemorial.

Laboriously they made their way north and saw the Blue Virgin grow in front of them, immobile and heedless of the storm.

Gerlof was always amazed that the strangely round island cliff rose here, just a few nautical miles from the coast of Öland. The Blue Virgin was older than Öland, millions of years older.

The island of witches. And indeed the waters around it looked like a boiling cauldron.

It was to this island the witches came at Easter, according to popular belief, to revel with Satan himself. The place had been in bad repute for centuries. In fact it had another name, an older name than the Blue Virgin, but saying it out loud meant bad luck. Gerlof didn't intend taking any such risk, for out here on the waves he was more superstitious than ashore.

He turned the tiller to make the gig run parallel to the steep rock, dancing in the water. John stayed on the seat, fighting the oars.

'Can we make landfall in this wind?'

'Not here!' Gerlof said. 'The east side is better.'

There were no natural harbors on the Virgin, just rocks plunging into the sea – but on the opposite side of the island the wind was less hard. The sea was calmer there as well, though choppy and foaming close to shore.

Gerlof had taken the oars and both steered and paddled, closer and closer to the granite. The gig rolled back and forth in the water, but John was used to waves and managed to jump from the prow at the right moment. He landed, kept his balance by the heels of his boots and was ashore, almost dry-shod and with a rope to make fast the boat.

Shortly after him the Mossbergs' boat reached the shore thirty-five feet away and its outboard fell silent. Now there was only the deep rumble of the storm above the cliffs.

Well ashore, Gerlof blinked against the wind and looked searchingly up at the spruce growing on top of the island. No people were to be seen. Had the abandoned boat in the strait come from here? That's what he suspected. But who would have picked the island as their goal on a day like this? In bad weather, nobody willingly set off for the Virgin.

'Give me a hand.'

The four fishermen managed to get their boats higher up on the rocky beach, then lifted out their nets and their catch and turned the hulls on their side against the wind, supported by a few driftwood planks.

They sat down in the lee of their boats to take a breather.

'Fine,' was all Gerlof managed to say.

Before darkness fell, he realized, they would have to get up to the forest to get some spruce twigs in order to be able to sleep comfortably on the rock under their boats. Unless the wind fell.

After a while John got up to untangle the nets and take care of their catch. There were matches in the boat, as well as salt and ground coffee and a can of drinking water, so surviving on the island wouldn't be a problem.

At least not for the first week, Gerlof thought. He remembered an old legend he'd heard about three shepherds who hundreds of years ago had spent a summer on the Virgin, but who had been trapped there by a prolonged storm in the strait.

First they had slaughtered their animals to survive, and when all the sheep had been eaten two of the shepherds had dined on the third.

He walked over to the cousins who were already picking the fish from the nets. They had let the abandoned rowboat remain bobbing in the water, tied by a piece of rope in its prow. The boat was too heavy to drag out of the sea while the pile of rocks remained in it, but if the wind turned the waves would quickly slam it to pieces.

'Should we bring the boat home?' Gerlof said.

'Sure, it could come in handy,' Erik said. 'But the stones should remain here.'

'They make fine ballast.'

'True,' Erik said, 'but they bring bad luck. The weather will never improve as long as they're still in the boat.'

Gerlof sighed at the superstition.

'I guess I'll have to empty it, then.'

He pulled the rowboat to a small cove and jumped down in it. Then he folded back the tarpaulin and began lifting out the stones. They were round and quite beautiful, pale gray and polished to large egg shapes by the water. He became even more convinced that they actually had come from the Virgin. Just as when he'd pulled up the flounders earlier in the morning he counted the stones before throwing them ashore: *one, two, three...*

Stone followed stone over the railing, back to all the others.

Twenty-nine, thirty, thirty-one...

He had put his hand out to the thirty-second stone when he stopped himself. It was round and grayish white, but didn't quite look like the others. He turned it over and froze.

'Erik,' he called into the wind. 'Come take a look at this.'

Both the cousins stopped gutting flounders and walked down to the water's edge.

'What?'

'Look at this,' Gerlof said again.

What he held up to them wasn't a round granite rock.

It was a skull. A human skull, pale gray and with deep, black sockets. The lower jaw had fallen off, but the upper smiled broadly with white teeth.

Nobody on the beach said a word.

Gerlof carefully handed the skull to Erik Mossberg and looked down at the pile of stones in the boat.

'There's another one down there under the rocks,' he said quietly. 'And bones.'

The cousins looked but said nothing. Erik silently accepted the second skull and put both of them on the flat rock, out of reach of the waves. Then he and Torsten and Gerlof together picked all the bones out of the boat and put them beside the skulls.

When they were done, two almost complete skeletons were laid out on the rock. Tall enough to have been adults, Gerlof saw. They had been dressed when they died, since there were pieces of pant fabric around their hips.

The mood on the beach was even more subdued than before.

'How old can they be?' Erik said.

'Difficult to say,' Gerlof said. 'What's left of their

clothes looks modern ... but I don't think they're really fresh.'

'What should we do with them?' Torsten said.

Gerlof had no answer. He looked out across the empty sea, then glanced back at the island. He sniffed the wind and thought that he caught a whiff of smoke. And hadn't he seen something move as well, at the corner of his eye?

Now he saw nothing. He slowly walked over to John Hagman, who had quickly turned his back on the dead and gone to deal with the nets. Gerlof knew that John had a thing about dead bodies, as who hadn't?

'Are you okay?' he asked.

John nodded. Gerlof glanced back up at the Virgin and opened his mouth.

'I thought I caught a smell of...'

Then something clicked up on the cliffs and he heard a brief, whistling sound a few feet over his head.

'Down!' he yelled.

He made John duck. A second later another shot rang out from the cliffs – it really was a gunshot, no doubt about it. Gerlof even imagined seeing the second bullet hit the water not far from the shore, like a white strip of bubbles.

He also saw that the Mossbergs had heard the shots. They were lying down behind the hull of their boat now, while he and John were entirely unprotected on the cliffs. Gerlof quickly slid away towards a couple of mulberry bushes. Unworthy but wise. John followed him, and they stayed down.

'Someone's moving up there,' Gerlof said in a

low voice.

John stayed pressed to the ground behind him but tried to look.

'Can you see who it is?'

Gerlof shook his head.

'Stay here,' he said softly. 'I'll move a bit.'

The bushes grew closer together there and, hidden by them, he slowly crept a couple of hundred feet north along the edge of the water. From there he went on, behind pines and boulders.

From a distance, the Virgin looked round and smooth, but close up the granite was full of cracks and steep rock faces. Gerlof certainly didn't mind; they gave him protection.

The wind blew cold and the island felt more dangerous than ever. There were no more shots, but Gerlof didn't relax. He moved in a wide circle towards the western side of the Virgin.

There he found an unknown rowboat pulled ashore. He saw it near the water from a long way off – it was made from pinewood and couldn't be missed. But no owner was in sight.

Gerlof went on at a crouch. A hundred feet above the boat he came to a precipice, and on top of it he found trampled-down lyme grass and a fresh cigarette butt.

He looked up at the forest and saw, or believed that he saw, a dark flow of hair billowing in the wind and disappearing among the firs.

A woman?

He thought of the mythological sea warden of the Blue Virgin, she who ruled the waters and the winds and who punished those who mocked her.

That legend was older than those about cursed stones and witches' revels, but of course Gerlof believed in none of them. The sea warden would hardly sit on the grass smoking cigarettes.

He went faster, but tried to move as quietly as possible.

Then he was inside the forest, a labyrinth of boulders and twisted firs. Here were both tangled hazel shrubs and deep crevices, and it was easy to lose your way.

He stopped again to listen. Then he moved quickly, stepped around a thick maple – and almost collided with the person hiding behind the trunk. A woman in dark clothes. She sat looking down, and Gerlof was able to sneak up very closely behind her.

'How do you do?' Gerlof said calmly.

The woman gave a scream. She twisted round, saw that she had been found and threw herself forward, fists raised.

'Easy!'

Gerlof roared and stood his ground on the cliff, but didn't hit back. He just raised his palms.

'Take it easy!' he shouted again. 'I won't hurt you.'

Finally the woman lowered her arms, stopped fighting. Gerlof could ease his breath and take a step back. He saw that she was around thirty-five and dressed for a visit on the Virgin, in a warm woolen sweater and heavy boots. Her eyes were tense and nervous – but at least she didn't hold a rifle in her hands.

'What are you doing here?' he said. 'Why are you sneaking around on us?'

She stared back at him.

'Who are you?'

'I'm from there,' Gerlof said, pointing across his shoulder at the coast of Öland. 'We've been out fishing and came here to get away from the storm ... we're harmless.'

The woman slowly relaxed her tense shoulders.

'I'm Gerlof Davidsson,' he went on. 'Do you have a name?'

She gave a short nod.

'Ragnhild,' she said. 'Ragnhild Månsson. I'm from Oskarshamn.'

'Good, Ragnhild... How about us joining the others?'

She nodded without speaking, and Gerlof led her around the island close to the water's edge. He kept looking up at the top, watching for movement. If Ragnhild wasn't armed, someone else had fired the shots. But he couldn't see anyone up there.

When they got back to the eastern side, John and the Mossberg cousins had sat up behind the boats. They were smoking again, throwing nervous glances at Gerlof.

The woman looked at them without speaking, then at the bones and skulls placed on the cliff. Her eyes were still worried, but Gerlof saw no surprise in her face.

'We found those in the strait. At the bottom of a rowboat.'

'An empty rowboat?' Ragnhild said.

Gerlof nodded.

'Have you seen them before?'

'I don't know who they are,' she said finally.

Gerlof realized that she hadn't denied anything.

'And the rowboat?' he said, nodding towards the water. 'Do you recognize it?'

Ragnhild Månsson looked at the boat bobbing by the beach and paused for a while before answering.

'It's Kristoffer's,' she said at last. 'My brother. It's his boat.'

'And where is your brother?'

'I don't know.'

The woman sighed, sat down on a boulder, then suddenly became more talkative.

'I came here for his sake ... we were supposed to meet here today. I took my own motorboat from Oskarshamn and landed on the western side. Kristoffer was supposed to come from the opposite direction. He lives on Öland.'

'The rowboat was out in the storm when we found it,' Gerlof said. 'Did he have a life belt, or a life vest?'

'I don't think so.'

The cliff was silent.

'I think we could get our spirit stove going and make some coffee,' Gerlof said. 'Then we can talk.'

Fifteen minutes later they had newly brewed coffee with biscuits. Gerlof handed a cup to Ragnhild and met her eyes.

'I think you should tell us more now, Ragnhild,' he said. 'My guess is that you know some things about the bones and the stones in your brother's boat. Or don't you?'

'Some,' she said.

'Fine. We'll be happy to listen.'

Ragnhild looked down into her coffee mug and drew a breath. Then she began talking in a low voice.

'My elder brother Kristoffer was a bird-watcher when he was young, or rather a bird lover. Back in the thirties, when we were teenagers, our family lived on Öland, near Byarum ... closer to the Virgin than anyone else, I believe. So Kristoffer used to row out here to the island to look at the eiders and guillemots and all the other kinds of birds. Autumns and springs there was almost never anyone here. But when Kristoffer got here one morning he found traces of other visitors... And they were horrible traces, trampled nests and broken bird eggs on the rocks. People who hated birds had come to the island.'

She fell silent, drank some coffee and went on.

'We didn't know who they were, but Kristoffer wanted to stop them. He brought me with him. That autumn we came often to the island, wanting to watch over the birds. It was a kind of an adventure. But one Sunday when we got here there was a strange boat moored by the old quarry. Kristoffer put ours beside it and then we sneaked up on the island. We heard loud screams from the birds ... that wasn't a good sign.'

Ragnhild turned her eyes upward to the cliffs.

'Up on the cliffs we met the people who were tormenting the birds. They were two young men, not much older than Kristoffer. Immature idiots. They had collected stones and broken branches and were throwing them at the black guillemots that were flying in flocks around them, terrified.

362

The birds they hit fell with broken wings on the beach and in the water ... I was heartbroken when I saw it. So I forgot to be scared, I just ran up to them and screamed that I would call the police. Which of course was a stupid thing to say out here. They just laughed, and one of them grabbed me.'

She lit a cigarette and continued.

'Kristoffer yelled at them and then they caught sight of him as well. When they heard him they forgot about me for just a moment. So I tore myself loose and began running back down to the water, with Kristoffer beside me. They came after us and threw rocks at us, but we knew the terrain and were faster. Down at the beach we pushed their boat out, then jumped into our own. And then we rowed back to Öland, ducking the stones those guys on the shore were throwing at us. The last we saw of them was that they were standing like fools at the water, staring at their boat, which was drifting away from the island.'

Ragnhild blew out smoke.

'We rowed back home to Öland,' she went on, 'and even before we got back a storm was rising in the strait. I remember thinking that the angry wind came from the Virgin, that it was the island that had called it up to take revenge on the bird haters. The storm increased almost to a hurricane during the evening and lasted for more than a week, nine or ten days. The Virgin was invisible in the mist, nobody could go there or get away from there. Kristoffer and I stayed inside, and we didn't dare tell anyone that there were people on the Virgin.'

She lowered her eyes.

'Finally the wind in the strait slackened, and then we rowed back here. Kristoffer had brought one of our grandfather's old rifles. But the guillemots were calm and silent and there was nothing threatening left on the Virgin any more.'

Ragnhild was silent for a few seconds.

'We found the two men almost at the top of the island. One of them lay sheltered by a large fir and the other one nearby, close to a boulder. The birds had pecked them ... they no longer had any faces.'

She was silent again.

'Do you know how they died?' Gerlof said.

She shook her head.

'I don't know if they had starved or froze to death, but dead they were. And then we panicked, I and Kristoffer. We felt like killers who had to cover up our crime. So we pulled their bodies down into a deep crevice and put a lot of beach stones on top of them. We carried stones for hours to fill that crevice. Then we rowed back home again ... and a couple of days later we heard that two young men from the mainland were missing since the storm. They had taken their boat out, and police believed that it had gone down in the strait.'

She sighed again.

'We tried to forget what had happened, but of course that was impossible, and I've been thinking about it for almost twenty years. And nowadays there are just more and more tourists coming to the Virgin every summer ... sooner or later they would be found. So I and my brother decided to get the bodies today and sink them out in the strait in a tarpaulin weighted with stone. That's what we planned to do. But I was delayed on the mainland this morning, so I guess Kristoffer began without me. He must have fallen from his boat, or...'

Ragnhild fell silent and looked sadly at the empty rowboat. She had nothing more to tell.

But Gerlof did. He felt a smell in the air and looked up at the top of the Virgin.

'There is someone else on the island.'

'How do you know?' John said.

Gerlof pointed to the middle of the island.

'There's a fire burning up there, and earlier someone shot at us.'

'Shot at you?' Ragnhild said.

'Someone shot to warn us off.'

'He said he would bring the rifle,' Ragnhild said in a low voice. 'Kristoffer, I mean. Just as a precaution.'

Gerlof nodded.

'In that case your brother might still be here,' he said, 'if the sea pulled his boat out without him. I think we should take a look at the top of the island.'

Ragnhild nodded quickly and stood up.

'But carefully,' Gerlof added. 'Make sure he knows who you are before he starts shooting again.'

John and the cousins stayed down by the water and let him and Ragnhild start climbing to the top of the island.

As much as he could, Gerlof kept in the shelter of thickets and trees while he led the way up to the largest of the caves on the island. He had been there on earlier visits; it was called the Virgin's Chamber and lay on the east side of the island's highest cliff. The chamber was like a small church room hollowed out of the mountain and gave good protection against the winds.

Silently and carefully, Gerlof drew close to the opening. He hid behind a boulder to look into the chamber. It was dark inside, but the floor of the cave rose slightly and inside the narrow opening he saw a flickering light.

He stayed on behind his boulder, irresolute and still remembering the shots by the beach, but Ragnhild slipped closer and called out.

'Hello? Is anyone there? Hello?'

For a few seconds, all was quiet. Then an echoing reply came from the vault, a tired male voice.

'Hello yourself.'

Ragnhild flew up and hurried into the chamber. 'Kristoffer?'

Fifteen minutes later Gerlof returned to the edge of the water, alone. Torsten, Erik and John stood smoking between their boats. They looked hard at the Mauser rifle Gerlof was holding, its barrel pointing to the ground.

'Her brother had this,' he said. 'I thought it better to take care of it.'

'So her brother is here?' John said.

Gerlof nodded.

'He took shelter from the storm up in the Virgin's Chamber. He had loaded the stones and the skeletons in the morning, but his rowboat had drifted off in the storm. When he saw us on the beach he shot a couple of warning shots. He was upset, wanted to scare us off... I guess we'll have to try to understand.'

The others nodded, not very willingly.

'And what are they doing now, those siblings?' John asked.

'They'll be leaving soon.' Gerlof nodded to himself and looked at the two skeletons on the cliff. 'My thinking is we bring these back with us to Öland and tell the police that we happened to see some bones sticking out of a deep crevice here on the Virgin. That way maybe we can solve an old disappearance without getting anyone else involved. Is that all right by you?'

The other three nodded again.

'You can hardly accuse an entire island of murder if someone happens to die there,' John said. 'Not even the Virgin.'

The other fishermen dragged thoughtfully on their cigarettes.

'It's just one thing I don't understand, Gerlof,' Erik said. 'How you could be so sure there were others here on the island. Do you have second sight?'

Gerlof thought of praising his intuition or perhaps blaming the movements of vipers, but told them the truth.

'It was the smells.'

'The smells?'

'I didn't notice any smells at all,' John said, dropping his butt between the stones.

'You should have,' Gerlof said. 'I caught the smell of Ragnhild's cigarette smoke from the very beginning, down on the beach ... and then the smell of her brother's fire up in the Virgin's Chamber.'

'You did?'

'Oh yes, very clearly.'

The three fishermen silently regarded Gerlof, but he just pointed at their glowing cigarettes.

'I told you to stop that...The tobacco is ruining your noses.'

MAITREYA

VERONICA VON SCHENCK

Stella Rodin sipped the champagne in her glass and looked around at the exhibition room. The slate-gray walls showed off the colorful modern art covering them like an old quilt. The dark suits of the male guests showed off the colorful dresses of the female guests. The overall effect was attractive and the room was filled. At the center of the show was Stella's father, Emmanuel Rodin. His glow competed with both his guests and his exhibits; he wore a light tweed suit with a burgundy vest, matching bowtie and pocket handkerchief. This was his favorite moment. To rule absolutely but with mild joviality one of the year's most important showings and auction afterwards. To introduce with flattery and generosity his experts to interested and inquisitive customers possessing extremely well-stuffed wallets. To personally extol the quality of paper used in Warhol's serigraphies. As for Stella, she loved art as passionately as did her father, but she hated this world. She had always been a black sheep, ever since day care. A girl as pretty as a doll and with a searing intelligence, who neither in day care nor since had had the sense of hiding her brain's capacity and hunger for knowledge and truth. Definitely unattractive. She had a way of shaming, irritating or frightening most of the people she met. Mainly because she had never quite learned to keep her big mouth shut when someone stated an obvious lie. Her school years had been understandably painful, but had provided her with a hard shell. Instead of working in the family company atmosphere of flattery and hypocrisy *(We do this just because of our passion for art, not at all to make money, of course not!)* she had chosen to become a police forgery expert. It had made it possible for her to work with the art she loved, but in an environment a bit more tolerant of her abrupt personality and in her view at least slightly less hypocritical. But since her parents and her older brother, to whom she was close, still ran the auction house, here she was, reluctantly moonlighting as a poster girl for the family business. Her father had resolutely bribed her to do it. A beautiful, burgundy vintage dress with a tight waist, a boat neck and a flowing skirt with several petticoat layers. From the fifties. Dior. She stroked its crisp fabric. It was a bribe she had simply been unable to resist.

Stella walked up to her father and lightly kissed his cheek.

'Hi, Dad. An hour and a half, okay?'

'And what's so important for you to do then? Do you have a date?' he asked in a kindly but irritated voice. This was a discussion they had had innumerable times. It usually started with some disparaging comment about her choice of profession – working in a police laboratory wasn't her father's idea of a successful career for his daughter.

'Yeah. With a good book and my bathtub.'

He sighed.

'Do you even understand how condescending that sounds to me? Don't you know how hard I – all of us are working for all this? The least you could do is to smile and act a little friendly, at least this one evening. It can't be all that hard.'

Stella sighed.

'Okay, okay, I'll stay on.'

After a full hour's worth of kissing cheeks and smiling, Stella was dead beat. She wasn't made to stand this much uninteresting human contact in a single day. She turned to the paintings to escape further platitudes, at least for a moment. She stood for a long while watching a Picasso all in shades of gray, for one of his pieces a strange but surprisingly anatomically correct portrait of a young woman named Françoise, if the title was to be believed. If she had happened to have an extra 50,000 dollars she would happily have made a bid for it, but considering her police salary she ought to be happy if she managed to put that much aside during her entire working life. She straightened the frame minutely; it had slipped slightly to one side. Earlier in the day she had helped her brother Nicholas hang the pictures. Even if she didn't work here she enjoyed helping him create the exhibitions, and he enjoyed having her there. It had almost become a tradition. She loved art intensely. Loved the craft of it. Was fascinated by the hours of single-minded energy and pure love given by artists and artisans to their work, by the combination of deep sorrow and exultant joy coexisting in a truly successful work of art.

Nicholas came up to her and put a hand on her shoulder.

'Someone named Carl Andreasen wants to talk to you. He's at the entrance. Isn't he your boss?'

With a worried frown, Stella looked searchingly towards the door. Yes, that was Carl, all right. A tall, gray-haired man with a crew cut and a lined face wrapped in a gigantic scarf he was trying to untangle himself from.

'Yes, it's him. What the hell is he doing here?'

She wove through the throng of visitors and reached him.

'Carl. What are you doing here?'

'I've got a job for you.'

Stella caught her father's disapproving glance from the opposite end of the room.

'Okay. Come along,' she said, pushing him ahead of her, away from the nosy, curious glances of the guests. Carl looked more like an aging soldier turned homeless than as a guest slightly late for the party.

Stella turned, snatched a second glass of champagne and brought Carl up to the library before he had time to object. She gave him the new glass and pointed to a chair. Carl sat down and Stella took the chair beside his.

'I never knew you were playing daddy's girl during weekends.' His voice was scornful and he put his glass down without touching it.

'So now you know.' Stella smiled, amused at his lame attempt at provoking her. He usually did better. She and Carl were joined by a love-hate relationship to each other. She thought his thinking too traditional and formalistic, though despite

372

that a good policeman. And he, as far as Stella could tell, considered her a troublesome pain in the ass who ought to keep her mouth shut, do as she was told and not stick her nose where it had no business to be – but despite that a good forgery expert. 'Now tell me what you need my help with that's panicky enough for you to come looking for me yourself even in a place that's so obviously uncomfortable to you.'

'I want you to go to another cocktail party tomorrow. I hope that's not overtaxing your talents.'

Stella raised her eyebrows but said nothing. He sighed and went on.

'We have a guy who's worked undercover for a long time in a smuggling ring. He's finally been invited to a party given by the head of the organization, an informal auction of what we believe to be illegally imported works of art. Our guy needs a girlfriend.'

'Doesn't sound too hard. Don't you have lots of boobsy police officers who could help you out? It's been a long time since I did any police work outside the lab, as you very well know.'

'It isn't your police field experiences I'm interested in. I want you to do what you do in the lab. Take a look at the art and tell us what it is and whether it's genuine. So simple even an academic like you ought to manage.'

'But – if the guy you're after is in the antiques business, he might know who I am. I might blow your whole operation.'

'I grant you your daddy is pretty famous. But I don't think my guy has gotten his stuff from your auctions.'

373

She drank some champagne and gave him a searching look. He was far from as biting as usual. He must be really desperate. She was far from certain that it was quite as simple as he made it out to be, but the idea of doing something outside of the lab for once sounded like fun. She gave him a brief nod.

'But what has your undercover guy been doing? I don't believe it's mainly about antiques. In that case you'd either have talked to me about it before, or your guy would know enough about it for you not to need me.'

Carl looked vexed, leaned back in his chair and swung his foot.

'Mostly it's about drugs. And weapons. The antiques are just a sideline.'

Stella watched him carefully for a moment. What he'd just said wasn't the whole truth either. She shrugged her shoulders.

'Okay, I'll do it.'

'Good girl.'

Stella followed him to the door – she didn't want to risk his starting to talk to any of the guests. A cold gust of wind, full of dancing snowflakes, sneaked in when she opened the door for him. Stella shivered and looked thoughtfully at her boss when he crouched down against the wind and slowly disappeared into the darkness.

'So what did your boss want on a Saturday? I imagined police forgery experts only worked weekdays.' It was Nicholas.

'He wants me to play cop for real – do an undercover job. There's a private auction of illegal antiques of some kind tomorrow night,' Stella said, her eyes still fixed somewhere far off in the wintry night.

'Cool.'

Ali opened the limousine door for her. His black suit was a perfect fit and his smile was broad. He looked just as disgustingly healthy as always, Stella noted, with black curls, slim hips and broad shoulders. Those hips she remembered particularly vividly. They were very attractive when covered only by briefs. Without briefs as well, in fact.

'You look great, as usual.'

'Hi, Ali. Long time. Good to see you.'

Many years ago they had belonged to the same class at the police academy and been a couple during their years of study. But when she decided to go for forensics while he went for investigative work, they separated. Though whom did she think she was fooling? The simple fact was that she had never been able to make any relationship work in the long run. He had been no exception.

'Jump in. I'll tell you about the party while we go there.' He made an exaggerated bow, helped her into the back of the car and stepped in beside her. Another cop in civilian dress had been given the honorable job of driving them.

'Great. Where are we going?'

'Djursholm. The stronghold of snobbery and wealth.'

'And here I was thinking we were bound for one of the dangerous hoods, given the badly concealed gun you're carrying under your tux.' She snaked a hand in behind the small of his back to adjust his leather holster.

'Thanks,' he said with an apologetic grin. 'Did you see my mike as well?'

She studied him carefully but caught nothing suspicious.

'Nope, all fine – you're as handsome as ever.'

'Thanks.'

The sky was inky black when they stopped outside an enormous yellow mansion on a low hill. Stella walked carefully up the sanded path in her stilettos, holding Ali's arm. She savored the cold air, which brought her the scent of his warm body. He smelled of spice and recently showered skin. She snuck her arm deeper under his. He smiled, but she was very aware that his body revealed apprehension rather than any other emotion. She knew that he was not given to worry. On the contrary, he had a definitely exaggerated belief in his own abilities. Like most males, for that matter. Again, she was convinced that this assignment was far from as simple and harmless as Carl had wanted her to believe. Thick walls of chalk-white snow rose on both sides of the path. Lit torches were stuck in the drifts, their softly flickering light casting dancing shadows on the snow. It had stopped snowing only an hour ago.

'It'll work out fine,' Stella said in a clumsy attempt at sounding calm.

Ali gave her an amused glance.

'Sure. But be careful with Peter. Don't irritate him. He's fucking unstable.'

'Don't irritate him? How would I do that? I don't even know the guy.'

'Please, just don't be yourself. You see…'

'Shut up and smile, you mean?' She was amused. A little put off deep down, but she certainly wouldn't let him see that.

'Right. And show him that magnificent chest.'

'Got it. Smile. Flash tits. Almost makes you wonder why I spent seven years in college to get where I am now...'

'Seven!'

'Sure. Police academy, art, a few courses in England–'

He gave her a weak smile, shook his head and raised a hand to make her stop. 'Sorry for asking.'

Stella punched his arm.

'Hey. That hurt.'

They had arrived at the house and a grave doorman let them in. They left their overcoats with another strict and unsmiling man. Stella heard a murmur of voices. On their way to the living room they passed a pedestal with a cracked and badly worn urn. Mediterranean. Roughly two thousand years old, she couldn't be more specific without inspecting it more closely. There were still traces of sand left on it. Beautiful and dignified in its pale patina.

'I understand why I'm here,' Stella whispered to Ali and kissed his neck to make her whisper seem less suspicious. Or actually just because she felt like it. He shivered slightly.

They stepped into the huge living room and the rigidly directed performance began again. A nod here, a glass of champagne there. Twice in the same weekend was definitely too many for Stella. Shallow exchanges of pleasantries conveying nothing, meaning nothing and impossible for anyone to remember. Laughter and charming smiles but ice-cold eyes. Superficiality. Stella hated it, but she was a pro. At least tonight she had a job to do. As soon as the tenth smiling male with a forehead unlined as a baby's bottom had finished his platitudes and turned away, she pulled Ali over to an object placed on a smooth, white pedestal by one of the walls. The wall was made of glass. You could vaguely distinguish the fluttering torches on the terrace outside, but beyond them was only the impenetrable blackness of night. As she came close to the pedestal, Stella's heart beat faster. She saw an eight-inch-tall bronze statue. Its surface was black, dark with a satiny sheen, but the details were perfect. It depicted a crowned man sitting cross-legged. His right palm was raised to the viewer. His left rested on his thigh, holding a water pitcher. The almond-shaped, half-closed eyes were inlaid with silver and watched Stella kindly along his narrow nose. The statue was perfect. So beautiful that it stole her breath. She had to stop herself from grabbing it and trying to run off with it. She carefully caressed the curves of the statue and felt that there still were remnants of sand at its hollow base. Fury began to seethe in her.

'Ali, let me introduce you to Maitreya.'

'Mai ... who?'

'The next Buddha. This is a statue made in the first decade after Christ, I'd guess. Probably dug up somewhere in Afghanistan. And very recently.'

'How do you know that?'

'It hasn't been professionally cleaned. There are still traces of sand on it, and there are scratches made by the clumsy fools who dug him up.' She slid a fingertip across a deep scratch. It was impossible for her to understand how anyone could do something like this. It was an insult to the country, to history and to the present.

Stella saw Ali stiffen and look at someone behind her. Probably the famous Peter. She put on her most simpleminded smile and slowly turned around. Behind her was a tall man with an almost unbelievably huge stomach hanging from a body that seemed to suffer under its extra weight. He was dressed in a perfectly tailored gray suit and the hand holding his champagne flute was adorned by numerous golden rings. He looked at her, or rather at her plunging neckline, in the same way a cat looks at a herring before sinking its teeth into it. Stella pushed her chest out some more. After all, that was her task tonight.

'Ali, I see you've brought a little tidbit along tonight.'

Ali gave a hearty laugh and put his arm around her waist. He seemed impressively at ease in this kind of situation, Stella noted.

'Absolutely. This is Stella, my girlfriend.'

'So nice to see you at last.' Stella held her hand out. He took it, pulled her close, and kissed her cheek instead. He smelled of liquor and expensive cologne, with a vague undertone of acrid sweat.

'I see you're admiring the statue. Are you going to bid for it, Ali?'

'It seems Stella has fallen in love, so I probably don't have a choice.'

'It's adorable. Is it Indian?' Stella chirped in her most naïve and imbecile voice.

'You might say so. This little baby is around two thousand years old. It won't be cheap.'

'Oooh, is it really that old?' Stella said with what she hoped was a surprised look and leaned closer to the statue. So at least he knew what he had, she noted.

'Oh, yes. There aren't many in this little shithole country that can compete with this collection,' Peter said, then turned to Ali. 'So what happened yesterday, did you get anywhere?'

'It's beginning to come together. They wanted us to talk about the last details tonight, if that's okay with you.'

'Business on a night like this?' His eyes were suddenly hard; then he began laughing. 'Why not? Tonight is all about great deals anyway, isn't it? Just remember to leave Stella with me when you abandon her for business. I'll take care of her, okay?'

Stella smiled and preened a bit while suppressing a sudden urge to throw her champagne in his face and respond with a couple of impolite words. She really appreciated the fact that normally her work didn't entail meeting a lot of people, she thought. She just wouldn't be able to handle that.

'How do you think he gets hold of things like these?' Ali asked her when Peter had walked off. Their eyes followed him as he moved away among his guests, like a good-natured absolute ruler among his subjects.

'Afghanistan has been more or less systematically plundered of its art objects during the last decade. Items like these are being sent abroad to

380

finance the war. If he is in direct contact with people in the country and doesn't need any go-betweens, he's probably gotten treasures like this one very cheaply.'

Ali sighed deeply. Stella took another look at the beautiful Maitreya. 'The problem is that it's almost impossible to prove. A real auction house couldn't sell things like this, since we demand documentation of provenance. But how are we supposed to prove that it hasn't belonged to his family for a century? All he needs to say is that the paperwork was lost, or destroyed. Nobody can prove anything at all.'

'Disgusting. At least I'm happy that we'll soon have enough to get the bastard for other things.'

'His drug deals?' she asked.

'Yes. That's what I'm going to talk to him about later. With just a little luck he'll make me an offer. They're going to give me a job with the organization. We've beaten about the bush long enough.' Ali glanced back at Peter. So this is what scares him, she thought, and almost immediately one of the waiters came up to Ali.

'Adam wants a word in his office on the upper floor.'

'Back soon,' he said to Stella and nodded at the waiter.

'Good luck,' Stella said, squeezed his forearm slightly. He responded with a warm glance, then gave her a long, hard kiss. She responded. A little surprised, but why not, she thought.

'How about reliving some old memories later tonight, Stella?'

'Sounds fine.'

He nodded and she studied his back while he disappeared toward a large, curved staircase. When he was gone she turned to the next pedestal. She spent a long time looking at the objects for sale. The room contained a veritable general store of epochs, religions and styles, with the fact that she felt convinced that most of these things had been dug up by clumsy idiots somewhere in Afghanistan during the last few years as their only common denominator. She also studied the buyers and realized that she recognized some of them. They were accomplished collectors, knowledgeable in the history of art. She kept as far away from them as possible. The risk of any of them recognizing her as Emmanuel Rodin's daughter was small but real – and if any of them whispered something about it in the fat man's ear, the entire operation would break down. She sent Carl an angry thought. When Ali had been gone an hour, Stella began feeling restless. She went out on the terrace and took a deep breath of the painfully cold air. A waiter offered her a fur-lined blanket, and she gratefully wrapped it around her shoulders. A small group of people was outside, smoking in the flickering torchlight. The quiet was music to Stella's ears and she lowered her shoulders, trying to relax. Her cell rang in her purse. She walked farther out on the terrace to escape other guests possibly listening in, and took out her phone. The display told her that the call was from Ali's cell. She put on her wireless headset and answered.

'Ali, where the hell are you?'

The wet gurgling sound ran like a cold wave

through her body.

'Ali, what's happened?' she whispered. The sound went on for a few seconds, then stopped.

Shakily, Stella replaced the phone in her purse without ending the call. She pulled her hair over her ear to hide her headset and went back inside. Without seeming to hurry she wove through the crowd. Behind her relaxed smile she could feel her heart beat hard and fast. She climbed the stair to the second floor without being challenged. The house was enormous. Carefully she opened the doors to a few rooms just enough to glance in. One of them held an intimately occupied couple, but she saw no signs of Ali. Just as she was going to round a corner she heard footsteps. She opened the door closest to her, silently slid in and closed it behind her while praying to the beautiful Maitreya downstairs that nobody had seen the door move. She held her breath and heard them clearly as they walked past.

'Take the body out with the kitchen garbage when the party's over. Just let it be until then.'

When they were gone, Stella waited for two minutes before returning to the hallway. She still seemed to hear weak, rasping breaths through the headset. She must find him. Before it was too late. She continued in the direction the two men had come from and stopped when she saw a small, almost black mark on the floor outside one of the closed doors. Blood. Almost certainly, and put there by someone's shoe. She opened the door very slowly. The dark inside was impenetrable. As soon as the opening was wide enough for her to slip through she slid in, closing the door behind her. She turned on the light. A twisted body lay on the floor. Ali, a large, open wound in the middle of his chest. Blood had formed a pool on the floor around him. Stella went down on her knees beside him, feeling the sting of vomit in the back of her throat. She felt his neck, but there was no need. His eyes were staring blindly at the ceiling. Probably she had just imagined those last breathing sounds from her phone. Stella closed the call and carefully took Ali's iPhone from his hand. She put on the long, black gloves she had worn when they arrived, stretched her hand under his body and felt along his waist, underneath his jacket. Warm blood enveloped her hand. There it was. His gun. She pulled it out, took off her bloody glove and used it to wipe off the gun. She might need it before the evening was over. With a last look at Ali, Stella rose and went over to the window. Standing in darkness, she looked out into the black night. Inside she was cold and hard. She had no time to feel. Later, not now. She saw the fluttering flames of the torches on the terrace below. At last she drew a deep breath, took out her cell and phoned Carl. He answered almost immediately.

'Ali is dead. Shot,' she said straight out.

'What? What are you saying?'

'What the hell have you put us up to?' she asked. 'I want to know it all. Right now.'

'We'll be there as soon as possible.'

'No. Hell no. We have no evidence of anything. You'll never be able to prove a damned thing. We'll never get either Ali's killers or the damned fools who are plundering Afghanistan.'

'Afghanistan? What's that got to do with anything?'

Stella gave an exasperated sigh.

'The antiques they're selling here tonight are invaluable art treasures from Afghanistan, dug up by assholes whose only thought is to get money to wage war. I'll get you evidence.' She spoke quickly but with exaggerated clarity.

'It's too dangerous.'

'You have to trust me. I know what has to be done. I want a backup force in place at a quarter past midnight. Not a second earlier or later. Okay?'

'Stella...'

'Did you understand me?'

'Yes. Okay. But...'

Stella heard footsteps in the hallway outside and ended the call. She stood immobile, breathing slowly. There was nowhere to hide in the room. The steps faded. Stella felt a rush of relief. She weighed Ali's gun in her hand and pulled out the magazine. It was fully loaded. Good. She wondered where to hide the gun. It was true that she did have large breasts, but nowhere near large enough for her to be able to hide a nine-millimeter pistol in her bra. On the other hand she wore enormous, flesh-colored 'tummytuck' panties under the wide skirt of her 1950s dress. She slid the gun up inside her panties and carefully checked that it would stay there. It did. Peter's cell phone she put in the inner compartment of her purse, along with her bloodstained gloves. She put on more lipstick and straightened her shoulders,

385

then crouched down beside Ali's body for the last time. Stroked his cheek. He looked very calm. She remembered his bubbling, ringing laugh. His special way of twisting his fingers in her hair to kiss her neck.

'I promise to find the bastard who did it,' she whispered to him. Not only that, she would personally make sure that he regretted what he had done. Then she stood up, straightened her dress and went back down to the party, without looking back. Gladly accepted a new glass of champagne and sat down on a bar stool. Carefully, so that the gun wouldn't fall to the floor. She took out Ali's cell and sent the identical text to the last five numbers he had spoken to. 'I know,' she wrote. Then she let her eyes roam, trying to find someone just receiving a text message. She looked for a long time but saw no one. She resent her message. Peter was in the middle of the room, a giggling girl on his arm. Stella studied him, her anger carefully hidden. Instead she hoped to look vaguely admiring. He was at the top of her list of suspects. She looked searchingly at him. He was large, boisterous and extremely pushy, particularly towards the female guests. He behaved as if he owned the place. That made Stella suspicious. Hold on, now, she thought. If he really did own the place he wouldn't have felt the need to behave as he did. Of course, the house might actually be his. But someone else was more powerful. Who?

Stella sipped her champagne, carefully weighing everyone in the room, one by one. At last she found him. A thin man of average height, light-skinned, with black hair and dark eyes. He was

386

absolutely calm and relaxed. Polite but without the least interest in impressing anyone. He reminded Stella of her black tomcat, Sherlock. He, too, acted just that way: friendly, relaxed and condescending, as if he owned the world. In this case it might well be true. Both the dark-eyed one and the gray-haired man he was talking to turned toward her and looked at her. The dark-eyed man raised his glass to her in a silent toast. She returned the gesture and simultaneously recognized the gray-haired man. He was an art collector. One of Rodin's regular customers. Her cover was blown. Hell!

Time for a new plan. Stella slid off the stool, in the same movement returning Ali's phone to her purse. She too knew how to look as if you owned the world. It came easier to women. Tits out, sway your hips and you're fine. She crossed the floor, went straight up to the dark-eyed man and put out her hand.

'Stella Rodin. I want to attend the auction.'

His velvet eyes smiled at her. His eyelashes were so dark that they looked painted. He took her hand, pressing it slightly.

'Markus From. Aren't you already at the auction? I assume you have an invitation.'

'No. I came with someone else. I had hoped to be more discrete, but that plan didn't seem to work out. I represent a client of the Rodin auction house. Someone who is prepared to pay well for your objects. The Maitreya by the wall, for instance, would fit my client's collection perfectly.'

'And how am I to know that you are who you claim to be?'

'I assume you already know.'

Their eyes locked for a long moment. Stella's patience began to run out.

'You're very welcome to phone our office to get confirmation, if you want. I believe my brother is still in.'

She could see that he already was familiar with Rodin and that the man beside him had told him who she was. Hopefully he only knew that she was Rodin's daughter, not that she was a cop. It was hardly something her father boasted about. On the contrary. And if the man had known and told velvet eyes, she would already be locked away or dead, so it was probably all right. It made her furious to stand here and hint that she or her father would ever buy invaluable antiques stolen from a country torn by war, but in this situation she had no choice. The dark-eyed man watched her searchingly, slightly amused. She appreciated the fact that he at least showed her respect enough not to try to pretend that he wasn't in charge here. She kept eye contact and hoped fervently that the white-hot anger and grief burning inside her didn't show.

'Give the number to Daniel.' He gestured to a man who had been standing a few steps behind him and had probably listened to every word they'd said. 'Have another glass of champagne, and I'll see that you get your answer shortly.'

Stella nodded briefly, gave the office number to his assistant and walked toward the terrace. Again she gratefully accepted the heavy blanket one of the waiters offered her at the door, and wrapped it around her shoulders. Now her life might very well depend on if Nicholas realized what was happening and proved a convincing liar. It would be pointless to try to warn him. She had seen the assistant, Daniel, begin to dial as she turned away. Stella thought of Ali's body upstairs, then immediately forced herself to stop. If she wanted to grieve, she could do it later. First revenge. For Ali and the Maitreya and the rest of the war spoils inside. She spent the rest of her wait making new plans. There was still plenty of time before reinforcements would arrive. After a short while, the man called Daniel came to fetch her.

'Stella Rodin? Everything's in order; the auction will start in ten minutes.'

Stella thanked him and locked herself in the rest room to prepare. She slipped her iPhone inside her bra to get the best possible sound reception. She carefully wiped Ali's cell with toilet paper, then tried to fix his gun against her thigh in a more comfortable position. She couldn't find one. Giving up, she set the cell phone between her breasts to record, then rejoined the throng outside. This time she carried Ali's phone in her purse. At the door to the auction room two forbidding but polite men were collecting cell phones from the audience. She had counted on that. They surely didn't want anyone to record this auction. She smiled a friendly smile, put Ali's phone on the table and put the number tag in her purse. The room, otherwise probably a large dining room, was furnished with numerous chairs turned to a podium, just as at Rodin's. Peter took the floor and spread his arms.

'Ladies and gentlemen. Welcome to this informal auction. I realize that you all want to be certain that the items we offer you are genuine.' A slide presentation began on the wall behind him. Desert and caves. Close-ups of items being dug out of the ground with rough hatchets and shovels. 'All objects for sale today have been discovered in Afghanistan. All of them have been found during the last year and are absolutely unique. In age, they vary from around one thousand BC to around five hundred AD. For reasons I'm sure you will understand, no documentation will be provided, so what I now tell you is the only guarantee you will have. However, we do have an expert on the relevant period present.' He pointed to an elderly man who gave the audience a friendly nod. Stella recognized him; he sometimes helped Rodin's by authenticating objects. 'Please make use of his expertise, and after the auction you are welcome to ask him anything you may want to know about the objects you have purchased. Now, let us begin.' He spread his arms and stepped down from the podium. Another man stepped up in his place.

'The first post is this beautiful collection of silver dinars, minted during the fifth century AD.'

The bidding became brisk. Stella bid on a couple of objects, but made sure not to win any of them. The atmosphere was so tense that you could cut it with a knife. Just as at a Rodin auction. Nobody even glanced at anyone else; everyone stared as if mesmerized at the auctioneer and at the objects for sale. Everyone wanted to win. The room was simmering with passion, happiness, anger, frustration, but nothing could be heard or seen on the surface. When the magically beautiful bronze statue was finally displayed, Stella stubbornly bid until the Maitreya was hers. After all, it was just pretend money anyway – once the police arrived, everything would be impounded.

Once the auction was over and all arrangements about how and when money would be exchanged had been made, Stella retrieved Ali's cell. And finally held the Maitreya in her hand. She went back to the rest room to check on the recording made by the phone between her breasts. The important part was what the dark-eyed man had said. She hoped fervently that it would be evidence enough, but she knew how extremely difficult it was to get anyone convicted in cases of this kind. She mailed the sound file to Carl and added a text. Now only one thing remained. To find Ali's killer. It was eleven-thirty. She had forty-five minutes left. If she hadn't identified him when the police arrived, it was all over. She sat down by the bar again. Took out Ali's cell and sent a new text to the five last numbers on his log.

I know. The terrace at midnight.

That was all she wrote. She remained by the bar, watching the crowd. After a short wait she got two replies, which she immediately discounted. Obviously none of them had any idea of what she was talking about, nor were they at the auction. It was a quarter to midnight. She began to feel very stressed. At last she saw it. One of the guests discretely took out his cell, then put it back in his pocket and looked around. His forehead seemed damp and his hand shook almost imperceptibly.

He hadn't been present at the auction. She slowly weaved through the throng to get closer to him. She was in luck. The expert on Afghan antiquity was standing almost directly next to the man she suspected of being the killer. She talked politely to him about the bronze she had just bought, meanwhile studying her suspect. All of his features were strangely colorless. She tried to come up with some way of taking his picture and sending it off to Carl, but realized that there was no way to do it without being seen. The man had an expensive suit, but it fit him badly. When he turned to look at his watch she saw it. Three small, black, round stains on the cuff of his shirt. Blood. Good. She went out on the terrace. It was freezing cold, even with her blanket and the heaters set up. She liked the cold. It honed her brain. Waiting, she caressed the cool bronze of the Maitreya. Five minutes to go. At the stroke of midnight, the colorless man stepped out on the terrace. At the sight of him, Stella again set her cell to record. He looked around, realizing she was the only other person there. She gave him a warm smile and stepped closer, put her head on one side and lightly put her hand on his arm.

'Why? It's really all I want to know. After that, I'll leave you alone,' Stella said.

He looked at her. Surprised. Uncertain how to react. She held her Maitreya in front of him. It was cold as ice. Stella spoke calmly, softly.

'We're all in the same boat here, so to speak. I don't want to know who you are. Just why you shot Ali. If I don't know why, I'll never be able to let go of it. I'll chase you forever just to learn why.

So just tell me, here and now, and we'll go our separate ways.'

Stella knew she had just fifteen minutes before Carl would arrive with his backup force. If she hadn't been able to make him talk before then, it was all over. But she hadn't dared risk that he would tell the dark-eyed man about her questions before more police arrived, so she had cut it as close to the raid as possible without risking the entire operation.

He looked uncertainly at her, gave a small, disdainful laugh and shook his head. Looked down at the ground. She stepped even closer.

'Why?' she whispered. 'Why?'

'He asked too many questions. He wanted to take over. Tried to get close to Markus. I had to stop him. He– '

The silence of the black night was shattered by the sound of cars. Many cars. There was movement in the shadows. Steps crunched through snow. They had arrived. Stella glanced at her watch, realizing her mistake just a moment too late. The man had seen her gesture.

'Hell! You've called the fucking cops!' he yelled, pulling Stella to him with a sudden twist of his arm. Her head was thrown violently to one side. She felt a sting of searing pain. He held her neck locked hard in the crook of his arm. 'Bitch,' he spat in her ear. She felt her throat constrict. She couldn't breathe. Sparks lit up in front of her eyes. She felt panic rising within her. In a desperate attempt to break loose before fainting she grabbed the heavy, cold Maitreya in both hands, slamming the base of the statue up as hard as her fear and anger allowed. There was a crunching, thudding sound close to her ear. The man screamed and let go of her. She felt hot blood running down her cheek. She spun round and looked at him. His left eye was a mess of blood and flesh. She glimpsed the white bone of his eye socket. He fell screaming against the terrace railing, through it and into the snow below that immediately began turning red. Stella stared at him, frozen. Why in hell had the police come this early? She clawed her gun out from under her skirt. They weren't supposed to be here yet. A movement in the corner of her eye made her spin around. A man ran out on the terrace, the gun in his hand aimed at her. Before she could even react there was a loud bang behind her and the man fell headlong. Another man in a black uniform, helmet, and a bulletproof vest ran up to her. The police backup. With thick, black gloves he took hold of her arm, carefully but firmly pulling the gun from her hand. He looked searchingly at her through his protective glasses.

'Stella Rodin?'

She nodded limply and stared dully at the pink stain spreading through the snow around the man with the torn face. He had stopped screaming and lay silent. His warm blood had started to melt the snow under him. To her despair, she realized that all she felt was satisfaction at having had her revenge.

'Are you okay?' the policeman asked, much too distinctly. Stella shook herself to make the world around her return. She heard sounds of uproar, saw police officers in black uniforms and surprised, frightened and upset guests everywhere.

'Yes, I'm fine.'

He nodded and ran off to help his colleagues. Stella stayed on the terrace, waiting while the first phase, that of pushing people against walls and screaming at them, was going on. She saw paramedics lift the colorless man's body out of the snow. He was dead. She had killed him. When the screaming began to abate she walked back into the house, still with her blanket wrapped around her. A tall, angular man came up to her.

'Did you find Ali's body?' she asked.

'Yes.'

'Good. That one is the most important.' She pointed at the man with the dark eyes. 'His name is Markus From. Then you should talk to this guy, and those two.' She walked through the room, pointing out those she knew had been involved. 'Here's Ali's cell.' She handed it over. Saw that her hand shook. She felt that just seeing his phone threatened to break all the floodgates and let out the grief and shock she had kept locked away. 'I'm off.'

'But–'

'If there are more questions, I'll be in tomorrow morning. You won't need me right now. Carl has everything I know and all the evidence I could get.'

'Okay.'

She walked quickly to the cloakroom and got her coat. Walked down the long, sanded path with short, careful steps. The torches had gone out. The sky was turning the color of ashes. The damp cold made her shiver. Her throat hurt. She crossed the

395

road, down to the pedestrian walk along the beach. Looked out at the smooth ice covering the bay. First she sent a short e-mail from her iPhone, then she called Carl. He sounded tired and worried.

'Hi, Stella, I'm–'

'You have my resignation in your e-mail.'

'But what the hell? You're overreacting.'

'You lied to me about how dangerous this was. You forced me to involve my family. And as if that wasn't enough, you didn't trust me and it seems you can't even tell the time. It's your damned fault I had to kill him.'

'Now just calm down and stop being silly.'

'I'm totally calm. Beginning today, I'm free of both you and the Swedish police department and your arrogance and damned incompetence. I've had it.'

'And what do you intend to do instead? Run back home to daddy?' Carl was angry.

'It's none of your damned business.'

Stella broke the connection, put her cell in her coat pocket and walked on along the beach. She saw no one, heard nothing in the sleeping suburb. The sky slowly shifted color from black to indigo to violet. Stella cried until her tears made little icicles in the fake fur lining of her coat. Cried until no tears were left. The ice-cold Maitreya rested in her pocket, both comforting her and accusing her.

TOO LATE SHALL
THE SINNER AWAKEN

KATARINA WENNSTAM

'Who the hell phones in the middle of Donald Duck.'

Her phone is lying on the dining table and gives its urgent summons, an embarrassingly selected tune cheerfully calling to mind a pop song competition four years ago. Every time she hears it, Charlotta wonders why she never remembers to change it. Agneta glares at Charlotta's phone but immediately turns her eyes back to Cinderella, slips a piece of marzipan between her lips and sinks back against the couch pillows. The phone keeps playing its little tune.

'Why don't you answer it!'

'On Christmas Eve?'

'It's got to be your job.'

'I suppose so.'

Charlotta hurries to the phone, almost but not quite hoping that whoever is calling will give up. Hidden number. Charlotta takes a deep breath to confront whoever may be disturbing her in the peace of her home at twenty past three in the afternoon on December 24, of all days.

'Charlotta Lugn.'

The phone is silent. She can hear that there is someone at the other end of the connection, but

397

seconds pass. Nobody speaks.

'Hello? This is Charlotta Lugn. Who is it?'

'Hello... How are you? I'm sorry. I ... I didn't mean to disturb you.'

'No problem. What's it about?'

Charlotta looks at the couch, the lit candles, the Christmas tree and the TV showing dancing mice and small birds. Agneta on the couch, her legs comfortably beneath her. The bowl of Christmas candy beside her on the couch. She is sucking the bottom of a paper toffee mold to get the candy out, puts it in her mouth accompanied by Cinderella's singing. *Hurry, hurry, hurry, hurry, Gonna help our Cinderelly, Got no time to dilly-dally.*

Charlotta closes her eyes and knows already before she hears the voice on the phone that she will have to leave her Christmas peace behind.

Call it female intuition, call it twenty-six years of police experience, call it grim realism. Nobody making a work call on Christmas Eve does it just to wish a Merry Christmas.

'Oh, and Merry Christmas, by the way. I'm very sorry to disturb you like this. But it's important. I really had to phone you today.'

'I'm sorry, but I still don't understand what this is about. Who are you?'

A small laugh at the other end of the connection. Indulgent, slightly embarrassed.

'No, of course not. You couldn't recognize my voice. It's been forever. I'm very sorry. Of course I should have... Well, you meet new people all the time, of course there's no way for you to remember... I just thought...'

The woman on the phone lets her sentences trickle out in endless silence. In some strange way she seems both stressed and very calm. As if she possessed some inner peace while at the same time being worked up, wanting to say too much in too short a time.

'Hnh. I understand. But couldn't you help me along a bit and tell me your name? That would make everything so much simpler.'

'Oh, of course, how right you are. What would you say to doing it this way – do you remember Erik Granath? I'm his mother.'

Hearing those words, Charlotta Lugn is absolutely certain that this Christmas Eve will resemble no other.

While still holding the phone to her ear she silently sneaks back to Agneta, kisses her forehead softly, soundlessly, and gives her an apologetic look. There's no need for more; Agneta understands.

Her expression is far from happy, but their agreement is old and they're both used to it. Charlotta's job doesn't end even when it's a holiday, or when it's night or someone's birthday or the flu is at its worst. How often she has rushed away from dinner parties, shopping rounds and quiet evenings at home.

But still, Christmas Eve... They had looked forward so eagerly to this evening. Their first Christmas in the new row house. Their first without any of their children. Their first without mothers, siblings or cousins. Just the two of them.

Charlotta caresses Agneta's cheek and her

mouth soundlessly forms, 'I'm sorry.' And she walks out into the hallway. Puts her feet into her curling shoes without bothering with the heel zippers, pulls her heavy jacket across her shoulders.

'I'm on my way. How do I get there?'

Charlotta Lugn picks the downtown route. Takes a short cut across the Sahlgrenska hospital grounds, almost collides with a rattling streetcar at Wavrinsky Square. She can hardly see it, in the dark and heavy rain visibility is awful. Temperature is down to thirty-two and at any moment the rain can turn to sleet. The streetcar driver signals at the last moment. Those endless streetcars.

The streetcar snakes its lonely way up the incline towards Guldheden. Charlotta can see three people within, all of them dressed in black and seated far from each other, looking out the rain-whipped windows. Hopefully they're all on their way home to someone. She can hardly bear the thought of all those who are abandoned at Christmas. She wants everyone to be safe, warm, surrounded by their loved ones.

She knows better than most that it doesn't work that way. Least of all at Christmas.

As much as she loves Bing Crosby, shiny red wrapping paper, saffron buns and the smells of sealing-wax and mulled wine, she also intensely hates Christmas with all of its drunken and violent traditions. Regardless of how hard she tries to burrow down into her own and Agneta's married bliss, how hard she tries to glut herself with Christmas pottering and glittery garlands. Still the damned Christmas season remains the worst time of year to be a police officer.

All the other days of the year she loves her work, but at Christmas it stinks. She still remembers working her first Christmas night, when she had inaugurated her fairly new police boots by slipping in the blood of a woman beaten to death by her blind-drunk husband.

He had sat in a corner of the kitchen, mumbling. 'She fell, the fucking cow. I swear, can't understand how she can be so fucking clumsy.' The table was laid with their Christmas ham. Charlotta can still see the five slices cut from it on the plate. He had used the same knife on his wife's face.

Other Christmases she has cut down lonely souls hanging from telephone cords, their staring eyes still forlorn. She has cried secret tears into the soft hair of a little terror-stricken girl who had seen her mother beaten to a pulp by her raging, aquavit-stinking stepfather while 'Ferdinand the Bull' was playing on the TV. Year after year she has been forced to face what everyone in fact knows but refuses to acknowledge while they're opening their gifts and watching their children's eyes glitter along with their Christmas tree lights.

No wonder Detective Captain Charlotta Lugn hates Christmas just as much as her private self loves it.

Charlotta arrives at St. Sigfrid's Square and turns in behind the Russian Embassy. The guard outside stands immobile with a face that

401

gives no smallest hint either of the heavy rainfall or of the fact that the Soviet state disappeared long ago.

She drives on toward the luxury apartment buildings in Jakobsdal. Squeezes the car in between two others outside the last building on the cliff, where the view encompasses all of downtown Gothenburg. For a moment Charlotta stares at the play of light from the millions of small bulbs decorating the trees of the Liseberg amusement park at Christmastime, but the bitter wind wets her hair and bites her naked throat. Shivering, she enters the door code and steps into the building.

'Just walk straight in. I'll leave the door unlocked for you. I'm in the last drawing room and don't always hear the doorbell. You're very welcome.'

Erik's mother, Lovisa Granath, has both given her careful directions and carefully explained why she specifically wants Captain Lugn to visit her this particular afternoon.

'I want to tell you what happened. I'd be very grateful if you could possibly listen to what I have to say.'

Charlotta Lugn has waited twenty-six years for those words. But to be honest she never believed that she would really know. Somehow she has learned to live with the fact that her first major murder case is also the only one still unsolved.

What older colleagues have said about similar defeats in the end has made her understand that everyone's past includes cold cases. All of them at least once have had to accept that some mysteries remain unsolved. Have learned to live with the fact that not everything hidden in snow is revealed by thaw.

But what Lovisa Granath had said promised more.

'I know who killed Erik and I've kept silent much too long.'

It feels strange, almost forbidden to open the door of a private home she has never visited and just walk straight in. Charlotta met the Granath family during the murder investigation more than twenty-five years ago. And even though they didn't live in this apartment back then, the feeling now is the same as it was then. Heavy furniture, objects of the kind you can call heirlooms, ugly paintings in colors so stifled that their subjects are difficult to distinguish.

With so much money you should be able to make things look a little brighter, but this home breathes of dull sorrow, uneasiness and restrained emotions. At the time, Charlotta had believed that it was all due to the sorrow and shock of having lost a child, but a quarter of a century later the feel of the Granath home is identical.

From the hallway she can see huge candelabras and lamps lit on side tables and writing desks, she feels cold and only very reluctantly hangs her rain-heavy jacket in the cloakroom.

'Hello,' she calls towards the rest of the apartment, even though Lovisa Granath has asked her to just walk in without announcing herself. No reply.

From beyond the dining room and a farther room she feels certain is called the library, or possibly the smoking room, she hears a soft sound of music. The wallpaper is dark plaid, and giant leather armchairs are placed around a table with a cigar box and an ashtray. The walls are covered by full bookcases.

Charlotta Lugn walks through the rooms and finally enters the drawing room. Lovisa Granath sits by the window, watching the lit trees of Liseberg.

'Oh, there you are. I'm happy to see you. Please have a seat.'

Lovisa Granath doesn't rise, doesn't shake hands, hardly even moves in the pale blue-striped armchair where she is sitting. The sitting room is a dramatic contrast to the rooms Charlotta has passed through. The wallpaper is light, the curtains hanging down to the floor are certainly heavy, but lime-blossom green and pulled open. The corner room is framed by four windows and in their deep recesses grow beautiful white cyclamen in the eight-edged pots designed by Prince Eugen.

Lovisa Granath holds one of her hands raised, immobile, palm up, fingers slightly bent. She is offering Charlotta Lugn a seat in a dainty couch.

'Please sit down. I took the liberty of making some tea before you arrived. I never have coffee this late in the afternoon. And I'm not at all fond of mulled wine... Would you like a cup of tea? Perhaps it would...'

Lovisa Granath again lets her sentences hang unfinished in the air. It seems to be a bad habit with her.

Charlotta Lugn shakes her head and sits down. Looks at the mother of Erik Granath, at how she looks twenty-five years later.

What is it they used to say, Charlotta thinks. Life hasn't treated her gently. The years have begun to tell. Consumed by sadness.

The expressions all fit the old woman. Charlotta remembers Lovisa Granath as genial, a woman who seemed out of place in the somber upper-class home. Today she fits in more naturally, as difficult to decipher as the dark paintings in the dining room and the library. On the verge of undernourishment, with sharp furrows around her lips and eyes. Ugly. From grief.

Lovisa Granath drinks her tea in small sips and meets the searching eyes of her guest. All at once the whole thing comes rushing back to Charlotta.

December 1981, the night of Lucia Day, Kungsport Avenue in central Gothenburg. Trouble and racket, kids in tinsel glitter and noisily drunk. Vomit at every street corner. For once snow, perhaps that's why there were so many people about, so much rowdiness.

Charlotta Lugn was a police assistant and, at least now, when glimpsed in the rearview mirror, as green as a newly sprung spring leaf.

Erik Granath was the high school kid found beaten to death on Geijer Street, a stone's throw from the revelers on the always crowded Kungsportsavenyn. People all around but no witnesses. Newly fallen snow, but no decent tracks of the murderer. A nineteen-year-old boy, already dead

405

and gone.

Most indicated a drunken brawl gone too far, or a robbery. That Erik Granath was a victim of pointless street violence, something then a fairly new phrase as well as a new phenomenon. As if violence and murder weren't always pointless.

Drunkenness, many teenagers in the streets, no wallet and proximity to the entertainment area all supported the assumption, as did the absence of anyone who had seen anything of value. Not even back then, in the 1980s, did anyone care about two youths fighting in an alley.

But there was one thing both puzzling and pointing in another direction.

Erik Granath had worn a gold crucifix around his neck, a piece of jewelry he wore every day since his confirmation. It had been torn loose from its chain and was missing.

But it hadn't been stolen along with his wallet and money. During the autopsy, it had been discovered – forced deep down his throat. The throat which had shown dark lilac marks from the unknown killer who had strangled the young party-dressed man and left his body to be covered in silent snow.

Given that symbolic message from the murderer, the investigation spun off on a religious tangent, parallel to the robbery theory.

Additionally, the boy's family was deeply devout as well as active in a free church congregation. They were socially prominent, the boy's father a businessman linked not only to the free churches but also to Lions Clubs and Rotary International.

The question that had confounded the police at the time seemed simple but was impossible to answer: why had Erik Granath been killed? Was the motive related to his religion?

Many of Erik's friends were also Christians, friends from the youth seminars at his Pentecostal congregation as well as the children of his parents' friends from church. Charlotta Lugn particularly remembered how quickly they had discovered that the seemingly pious and devout teenagers drank and partied just like most others of the same age. But it had been almost more difficult to get them to talk about their drinking habits and sex life than to get them to share their suspicions about who might have wanted to see Erik Granath dead. The congregation had in many respects been a closed world, as difficult to penetrate and understand as the various criminal gangs she had encountered over the years.

Erik had had no girlfriend at the time of his death. No enemies, no known quarrels. An upfront guy, nice to the point of being dull. In spite of a large circle of acquaintances it seemed as if most of his friends hadn't known Erik Granath particularly well. Not deep down.

None of their leads turned out to get them anywhere. The feeling that there was some motive they were unable to see was inescapable, but in spite of that it remained possible that it was just a robbery that had turned bad. A perpetrator who had left a strange message entirely without meaning, done it in sheer panic and without any ulterior purpose. Such things had happened.

What tips they were given also petered out, and after eight months of futile investigations the case was shelved. Occasionally over the years it had been brought up from the archives, the tabloids had written about it, a new tip gave rise to a few news stories a couple of years ago.

But nothing new came to light and Erik's killer was still unknown, still at large.

And now. Christmas Eve. Twenty-five years had passed. So obvious. The statute of limitations had just ended. Charlotta Lugn smiles at Erik Granath's mother, but inside she is cursing the hag. All this time you've stayed silent. Who is it you've been protecting?

And how has she been able to keep quiet? After all, it's all about her own son. Her murdered son.

But Charlotta's lips display only a small smile. Her face neutral, she looks at Lovisa Granath with eyes concealing nothing. Tell me. Trust me. Charlotta knows how to conduct an interrogation. Nowadays.

'There was something you wanted to trust me with. I'm here now. I'm listening.'

'I'd like to start by telling you why I phoned you personally. It suddenly felt so... Why I finally decided to reveal it all. But only to you.'

Charlotta wrinkles her brow but tries not to let her feelings show.

Lovisa Granath bends toward the little side table to wrap her fingers around the wafer-thin teacup. Her little finger straight out, she carefully sips the hot brew. Smells the fragrance of the tea and seems to enjoy its taste. Charlotta Lugn is getting irritated with the woman's long-winded and slightly superior manner. She bites her tongue to keep from urging her on.

Lovisa Granath remains silent and Charlotta Lugn starts to look at the room around her. She notices a little porcelain statue on a side table. She truly doesn't appreciate that kind of knick-knack, but there is something attractive about the fragile little girl in her bonnet and wide skirts. Without thinking she reaches out to take the figurine. It feels surprisingly cold in her hand.

'I would appreciate it if you didn't touch that.'

'Oh, I'm sorry, I wasn't thinking. Is it valuable? It's exquisite.'

'No, not particularly. But she is my favorite. I don't want her dirtied.'

A strange choice of words. Charlotta Lugn doesn't like the undertone of what Lovisa Granath says. But she holds her tongue. She's good at that. She wants to hear what the woman called her here to tell her.

Lovisa Granath puts her teacup down.

'Actually I don't understand why you couldn't see what it was all about already back then. You were... I haven't forgotten you in all these years. Sometimes I've thought that if I'll ever tell someone, it must be you. Because if anyone would understand, it would be you. I really think that you did realize what it was all about. But you were too inexperienced. Not stupid, but afraid to trust you own intuition.'

Charlotta Lugn suddenly realizes that she must

look like an idiot. Her open look has been transformed to a dropped jaw. What is she talking
about?

'I don't quite understand. You must know that I
wasn't in charge of the investigation, I was just...'

'I know. But you were close to something
nobody else even had a hint of. You put all the
right questions, but never quite seemed to really
listen to the answers you got. Do you remember
when you came to our home, to the house we
lived in then? The day after Erik died?'

Charlotta nods. And remembers. Erik's father,
Lennart Granath, had greeted them at the door
of their house in Örgryte, fully decorated for
Christmas and cocooned in lovely snow. Icy cold
inside as well as outside.

She remembers that he kept clearing his throat,
particularly when Lovisa was talking. It was
horribly irritating, but who will tell a father who's
just lost his son to stop sniveling? She interpreted
it to mean that Lennart Granath suffered from a
severe case of macho ideals and would do anything to stop himself from bursting into revealing
tears.

But it spoiled the whole interview. Both
Charlotta Lugn and her much more experienced
colleagues were repeatedly put off balance and
lost their thread of thought by that wet hawking.
It sounded as if Lennart Granath was trying to
draw a huge wad of phlegm from his throat, and
even now Charlotta shudders at the memory of
the disgusting sound.

'Where is he, by the way?'

'He?'

'Your husband. Lennart.'

'He's... He went to buy a newspaper. He'll be back soon.'

It sounds silly, verging on the ridiculous on this particular day. As if the man at any moment might appear at the door dressed as Santa. It also doesn't sound very likely. Is Lovisa Granath lying to her?

Charlotta lets it rest. She wants to know more about the leads she should have seen twenty-five years ago.

'Please go on. What did you mean when you said that if anyone had understood, it should have been me?'

'What was the first question you asked?'

'Back then? I'm sorry, but I can't possibly remember that. It's more than twenty-five years ago.'

'Try. The first question you yourself asked, not your colleagues. What did you ask?'

Charlotta Lugn closes her eyes for a second and suddenly that moment returns to her. How she leaned forward, almost interrupting her partner. Actually she had put two questions to them, or perhaps asked the same thing in two different ways. Was he at home the night before the day he was murdered? Do you know where he slept?

Neither Lovisa nor Lennart Granath had answered. Lennart coughed and hawked, and Lovisa sat staring down at her lap. Charlotta suddenly sees the scene in front of her, as if it all happened yesterday. Why didn't she react to the fact that they didn't reply?

411

And now she asks the same question again.

'Where did Erik sleep on the night before the day he was murdered?'

'I truly don't know. But we had our suspicions... Lennart said...'

She falls silent again. Sips her tea and draws a loud breath.

'I made my mind up almost a year ago. That's when I decided to tell you. Finally. When I read about you in the newspaper. I hadn't understood before that you were ... well, that you were ... well ... I mean you were such a nice and pretty girl – how could I have even thought that you needed to be with other women?'

Charlotta knows all too well what Lovisa Granath is talking about. At the beginning of the year, the morning daily *Göteborgs-Posten* had published a major profile of her. With a provocative heading and an intrusive photo. 'Lady, Law Enforcer, Lesbian.'

When Charlotta Lugn assumed her new position, her sexual orientation suddenly became highly interesting. Despite her having been open about it for fifteen years. Despite her hardly being the only lesbian on the force. But she was the first lesbian detective captain. To her, it doesn't feel like some major thing, but on the other hand she didn't shy away from the attention it gave her. If she can help someone else to step out of the closet, or even just to feel a little less weird, she'll be happy to do so.

But she doesn't understand what Lovisa Granath is after. What does this have to do with the murder of Erik Granath?

412

'I don't understand. What...'

'You realized. You were asking about motive. You understood what it was all about. Really about. And I suppose you have to be ... well... You were asking so insistently about Erik's girlfriends, if he'd had any romances that might have made him enemies, about where he'd slept the night before... It took someone like you to realize...'

Someone like you.

Charlotta turns a blind eye at the hidden insult, it doesn't stick to her. She's used to it, even if it always stings. Curiosity dominates and the pieces of the puzzle begin to come together. Homosexual. Someone like you.

It takes one to know one.

'Was Erik...'

'Are you asking me if my son was a faggot?'

She asks her return question in a hard voice and her small, tight mouth spits out the last word. Lovisa Granath holds her teacup in her hand and Charlotta can see that her hand trembles slightly.

'Was he a homosexual?'

'Of course he was. That you never realized that! The way you were snooping among his friends, the way you were digging and prying. Didn't it tell you something that you could never find any girlfriends, that a good-looking boy like him never... Didn't you understand? And you ... who are also ... and you were right there, poking around, getting so close with those questions. But Lennart...'

'Lennart?'

Lovisa Granath goes silent again. Her gaze drifts

to the window and for a moment she doesn't just look tired, but entirely absent. Her eyes fixed on something far away. The Gothia Towers Hotel high-rise downtown, the rain whipping the windowpane, or perhaps some inner image reflected in the black glass.

She smacks her mouth loudly, and it feels uncouth and almost obscene coming from the finely dressed and strict woman. Her mouth seems dry; she sips her tea and finally meets Charlotta's eyes again. Is she drunk? Her gaze isn't as sharp as a moment ago. Her eyes are rimmed in red, but there are no tears.

It is obvious that this is hard on her, that her story is stuck deep inside her. That the words both want out and remain hidden in the dusk of secrecy.

'Would you be kind enough to put some more music on? The record seems to have ended. It feels a little easier to talk when the music...'

Lovisa Granath doesn't finish her sentence, just points to a stereo on a side table against the wall. The Christmas tunes greeting Charlotta on her arrival felt like such an ordinary backdrop that she didn't even notice the music stopping.

'Of course. Will the same record do?'

Her unaccustomed fingers grip the pickup. How strange that CD players have already made the gramophone feel like an ancient phenomenon. When her hand touches the black vinyl record she feels nostalgia for the pop records of long-gone days. Mahalia Jackson. 'O Holy Night.' Not a particularly timely choice for a Christmas record, but perhaps not unexpected in

414

the Granath family.

First a scratching sound, then a second of silence, then the music begins. The organ roars and Mahalia's powerful voice fills the room with Adam's Christmas song.

'Tonight is Jesus' birthday. Tonight we must be grateful for the gift of God. For his coming to this world as a human being, as a naked child in the arms of a poor woman. Mary held him new-born and naked in her arms. We must be... Jesus is here with us tonight, as all other nights and days. All these nights I have... Oh, Jesus, what have I done? Forgive me, God. Forgive me, Erik.'

Lovisa Granath sits back in her armchair, her eyes closed. She babbles incoherently. Charlotta Lugn remains standing by the gramophone, staring at the woman. Listening.

'I asked for it. I forced it. I settled on Lennart because he was... He was so clear in his faith, so strong and so uncompromising. I despised those other weaklings, all those who imagined that you could pick and choose among the words of the Bible and still call yourself a Christian. Those who thought that you could accept what fit and just... I wanted such a man. I wanted definite answers, I wanted a man to lean on, a firm ground to grow from... One who told me what to do. Who appreciated me as a woman and who was a real... Lennart was a real man. He truly was. Not a weakling. His father had raised him with equal parts love, rules and punishment. Spare the rod and spoil the child. And that's how he wanted to raise Erik as well, our weak, soft, damnably soft... Erik wasn't like other boys. Of course we knew that. Didn't want to be a part of our family, our community, our faith. He broke...'

She falls silent again. Shuts her eyes hard and sips her tea again. The final drops. She makes a disgusted grimace.

Charlotta Lugn feels her heart beat wildly. She wants to hurry Lovisa Granath on, but she also wants to hear every uncomfortable detail. She knows better than to interrupt with questions or leading statements at this point. But the woman's slurred speech worries her. She seems to have had a stiffener or two too many, and...

Charlotta Lugn is suddenly conscious of the empty teacup in Lovisa Granath's hand. It sits loosely in her slack hand which now rests on her lap. Damn!

'Lovisa. Lovisa! Listen to me! Have you done something stupid? What is it you've been drinking?'

Charlotta Lugn crosses the floor to the woman and puts her hands on her shoulders. Her body feels slack and Lovisa Granath turns her face up to her. Smiles happily. She looks more at peace than Charlotta has ever seen her before.

'It's too late. You can't do anything now. I've been drinking this poison all day. And to tell you the truth, it tastes like hell.'

Her hand goes automatically to her mouth, as if to stop the profanity before it crosses her lips. She smiles apologetically.

'It's up to you. Phone for an ambulance if you choose, but they won't make it in time. Or do

416

you want to hear the end of... I really do want to tell you. I don't want ... you must be my confessor. Even if I don't even believe in the penance of confession. Nothing can save a sinner like me, someone who has... Please sit down, won't you?'

Lovisa Granath's eyes briefly become hard. She wants to be obeyed.

'Are you out of your mind?'

Charlotta gets her phone out; she carries it in the back pocket of her jeans. The emergency service center is preprogrammed on a priority number. After four seconds she is talking to a colleague. Subconsciously she counts while speaking. Twelve seconds. A car will be on its way in ... call it thirty seconds. At worst a minute, it's Christmas Eve. It's a fairly long drive from Eastern hospital. Is there any chance that they'll be in time?

Her last words to the emergency center: 'You better fucking hurry!'

As if paralyzed, Charlotta Lugn sits down, as close to the old woman as possible. Unconsciously she holds her hands out to her and Lovisa Granath's thin fingers meet hers. She folds her warm hands around the cold and bony ones. Just sits there, looking hard at Lovisa.

'Lennart used to follow Erik on weekends and evenings. At first I thought it was just fine, a bit like those Dads on the Town they've got nowadays. He was involved in what his son was doing, and wanted to... We didn't know who he met, you see, we noticed that sometimes Erik lied to us about where he had been. He didn't go

417

straight home after his church meetings. But Lennart became obsessed. Sometimes he didn't even go to work just to keep track of Erik. He followed him, watched every step. It was ... it was sick, it really was. Then of course I understood why.'

Lovisa Granath clasps Charlotta's hand. She is surprisingly strong. Lovisa looks her straight in the eyes.

'You really must understand. I and my husband hate homosexuals. It's a sin. It's fornication. Against nature. God in his wrath will smite those who live in such sin... Who believes it can ever be the same as between a man and a woman. Who lies down with a man as a man lies down with a woman will suffer the wrath of God. And our son ... our only son. An abomination. A degenerate. A ... freak!'

The words make Charlotta shrink back. She tries to take her hand away, but Lovisa holds it firmly.

'I don't say these things to hurt you, my dear. I say them because I want you to understand. Understand why Lennart in the end could see no other solution. He knew that Erik would never... Erik was such a weak soul. And so easily led. He met the wrong people, they made him... God will forgive us in the same way He ... God let His only son die on the cross to show His real... God will...'

Lovisa Granath is panting, as after a long run. She has talked so much and so fast and her strength seems to be fading. She licks her lips. They are very dry and Charlotta Lugn knows that it's only a matter of minutes. She glances at her watch. Almost three minutes since she phoned for an ambulance. It ought to be here by now.

She asks her heart if she's doing something wrong, if she ought to do more to try to stop this insane old woman from committing suicide. But what more can she do? Other than listen.

But there is one more thing.

'Lennart?'

'He has left. He knows you won't be able to ... that you can't get ... can't prosecute him. But I told him I would tell you the truth. That it was time. That God wanted to hear me speak true words, no more lies. He is already far away, abroad... He doesn't want... The shame. Everyone will... And I don't want to either... I want to be with Erik. It's the only thing I want.'

'One more question.'

'Uhnn...?'

Lovisa goes ever deeper into her fog. She no longer looks at Charlotta, but she seems to hear her. And she can't refrain from asking.

'Why did he kill Erik? I mean ... even if you hated his sexual bent. Did he really have to die for that?'

Part of her wants her to lean closer to Lovisa and slap her face. A good slap. You fucking nut. Kill your own son. Protect a murderer. Just because of God... She feels pure rage. Charlotta doesn't believe in all the drivel about abominations and words of God. It's just words. But obviously there were those who accepted the words as their law, as demands that had to be

419

obeyed. Regardless of consequences.

'Do you see... Snow. It's snowing. The angels are no longer crying. Rain ... it doesn't rain. Snow... Erik loved the snow. It's he who is...'

'But why kill him? Wasn't that going too far?'

'Uhnn...?'

'Did anything special happen that night? That Lucia night?'

'Nothing special ... or, I don't know ... no, he ... Lennart had been angry for so long ... hateful ... mad with rage. He thought Erik was fucking around. That's what he said... That Erik... Erik was a... He was out. Sinning. With some new boy. Lennart had followed them the night before. That's where he slept. And he supposed Erik was going there again ... and, well...'

There is silence.

A minute passes. Lovisa's eyes are closed and Charlotta fears it is all over.

Where is the damned ambulance?

A quiet peace spreads over the woman's face, softens the hardened features and makes her look young.

'Lovisa?'

'Mhmm...'

'Is there anything more you want to tell me?'

'Mhmm... No. I... Thank you.'

She whispers the last few words. The sirens can be heard outside, softly but getting closer. Charlotta envisions the car going up the hill at high speed, braking outside the building. But it's too late.

Charlotta Lugn feels Lovisa Granath's hold on her hand loosen, sees her thin fingers letting go.

At the corner of her eye, she glimpses the white snowflakes.
 Falling quietly outside.
 Snow is falling from heaven.

ACKNOWLEDGMENTS

For their help, advice, and support during my work on this book, I owe thanks to a number of people. In particular, I would like to acknowledge:

• Otto Penzler and Morgan Entrekin, who believed in this project from the start, and particularly Otto, long-time friend, publisher, editor, and crime fiction expert extraordinaire, not to mention a great guy to go log-riding with;

• The authors with which I worked on many of these stories, and in particular Åke Edwardson, Eva Gabrielsson, Veronica von Schenck, Maj Sjöwall, and Dag Öhrlund. In this context, my thanks also to Jerker Eriksson and Håkan Axlander Sundquist, who but for unfortunate circumstances would have been in this book, and who were a joy to work with;

• Those others who helped above any call of duty, and in particular Astri von Arbin Ahlander, for translation assistance; Magdalena Hedlund, for her support and suggestions; Dag Hedman, whose efforts, though as it sadly turned out were in vain, were greatly appreciated; Per Olaisen and

Johan Wopenka for suggestions and for generously sharing their expertise.

• Finally, but as always most of all, my thanks to Evastina, first reader and critic, whose views, comments, suggestions, and encouragement remain vital.

John-Henri Holmberg
Viken, July 2013

PERMISSIONS

The publishers hope that this book has given you enjoyable reading. Large Print Books are especially designed to be as easy to see and hold as possible. If you wish a complete list of our books please ask at your local library or write directly to:

Magna Large Print Books
Magna House, Long Preston,
Skipton, North Yorkshire.
BD23 4ND

This Large Print Book for the partially sighted, who cannot read normal print, is published under the auspices of

THE ULVERSCROFT FOUNDATION

THE EVOLUTION OF THE
BRITISH EMPIRE
AND COMMONWEALTH

THE EVOLUTION OF
THE
BRITISH EMPIRE
AND
COMMONWEALTH

SIR JOHN A. R. MARRIOTT

*Honorary Fellow (formerly Fellow and Lecturer in Modern History)
of Worcester College, Oxford.   Late M.P. for the City of York.*

1939
NICHOLSON AND WATSON
LIMITED LONDON

First Published in 1939

Printed in Great Britain by
Hazell, Watson & Viney, Ltd., London and Aylesbury.

PREFACE

A PREFACE is the only opportunity permitted to a writer, professedly scientific, of addressing some personal words to the friends to whom he is known only through the written word. Of these I am happy to believe I have some in all parts of the English-speaking world— not least in India: to them, and not *urbi et orbi*, my Preface is exclusively addressed.

This book, whatever be its defects, is not the fruit of a recent or casual attachment, carelessly begotten and prematurely born. On the contrary, it represents the fulfilment, if inadequate and tardy, of a hope cherished for more than half a century. My interest, historical and political, in the British Empire was first aroused by reading, in 1884, Seeley's stimulating lectures on *The Expansion of England*. In 1886 I was instrumental, together with the late Warden of Merton (the Hon. G. C. Brodrick), Professors James Bryce, A. S. Napier, Montagu Burrows, and others, in establishing at Oxford a branch of the Imperial Federation League. The first course of lectures I ever delivered under the auspices of the University Extension Delegacy was on *The English Colonies* (1887), and since then I have delivered scores, if not hundreds, of lectures on the subject in all parts of England and Wales, and have even lectured on it in Germany! I was, I believe, the first lecturer for the Modern History School at Oxford to offer a course of lectures on the Colonies, for the students of that School. Since then I have devoted many chapters in many books and many review articles to one or another aspect of the same problem. Yet never before, confessedly to my own surprise, have I devoted a complete book to the subject. To my previous books and articles I have made, with, it is hoped, all becoming modesty, frequent references in the notes. This was done partly to save space, and partly by way of acknowledgment to the

v

publishers of the said books and articles (detailed in Appendices A and B), from which I have not scrupled to borrow freely. It is, I fear, unlikely that any readers will recall or identify such borrowings, but if they do, they will, perhaps, condone them. My obligations to the published works to which I am consciously indebted have, I hope, been fully acknowledged, either in the notes or in the bibliographical appendix; but in studies extending over so long a period as half a century it is likely that some obligations have escaped my memory. If such there be, I can only crave the pardon which generous workers in the same field will hardly refuse to an old man.

There are other debts recently incurred that should be more specifically acknowledged. I am grateful for courteous and helpful replies to enquiries addressed to several official quarters which for obvious reasons prefer to remain unmentioned. My gratitude is also due to Professor F. J. C. Hearnshaw, who has read the whole of the book in proof, and corrected several slips, to Major Sir Humphrey Leggett, D.S.O., who, with great knowledge of Africa, both historical and practical, has read those portions of the book dealing with that Continent, and made many valuable suggestions, and to Mrs. Jean Barnes, who not only gave me much clerical help, but discussed with me many points that arose in the correction of the proofs. Not least is gratitude to my publishers and their printers, who have lavished meticulous care upon the material production of this book. The index I owe to hands to which I owe more than many indices.

J. A. R. MARRIOTT.

March 15, 1939.

CONTENTS

CONTENTS

CONTENTS

CONTENTS

CONTENTS

CONTENTS

LIST OF MAPS

Chapter One

Prologue

EMPIRES: ANCIENT AND MODERN. BRITISH COLONIZATION

THE cumbrous title of this book corresponds to historical facts. General Smuts once remarked that the man who found an appropriate name for it would be doing real service to the Empire. He himself was responsible for the title " British Commonwealth of Nations." That title represents a reaction against the implications involved in the use of a word properly descriptive of military dominion. An Emperor was, in ancient days, invariably an autocrat, ruling over the peoples of his Empire by force. But those who adopt the more recent term *Commonwealth* (unless they carefully restrict its application) fall into error less venial than those who prefer the older term. The truth is that the British Empire, including, as it does, the British Commonwealth of Nations (but much else besides), is a unique phenomenon in politics. On the stage of human history it stands apart, alone. No precedents exist for the guidance of its rulers; any parallels that are suggested are less helpful than misleading.

With the great Empires of the ancient world the British Empire has little if anything in common. *Imperium* signified originally the right possessed by a Roman magistrate to employ force to secure obedience to his orders. The great Empires of antiquity conformed to the type suggested by that word. The Empires of Egypt and Babylon, the Assyrian Empire and the Persian, were military autocracies. Founded by soldiers, they were sustained by the sword.

Whether the hegemony attained by Athens, after the defeats she had inflicted on Persia at Salamis and Marathon, can properly be described as an " Empire " is disputed.

" Empire " and " Commonwealth "

The Athenian " Empire "

B   I

Thucydides specifically disclaimed for Athens the character of Empire (ἀρχή) and insisted that she enjoyed only the first place (ἡγεμονία) in a league of autonomous States. By her confederates, Athens was accused of having constituted herself a " Tyrant city," and the accusation, the most serious that a Greek could prefer, undoubtedly precipitated the Peloponnesian war which brought the Athenian " Empire " to an end.

Upon the hegemony of Athens there followed the brief supremacies of Sparta and Thebes. If, then, Empire be the goal of political evolution, Greece must be pronounced a political failure. But failure, as Mr. Baldwin once said, " is a more potent teacher than success, and the tragedy of her failure only throws into more radiant relief the debt we owe her in those arts wherein she was supreme." The Empire of Greece was not political: it was spiritual and intellectual. Immune from mortal decays, it was eternal. The consequence is that Greece still dominates the mind and the spirit of man.

None the less must we emphasize the truth that Greece failed to solve the problem of Empire. Nor is the cause of her failure far to seek. The political ideal of the Greeks never went beyond the perfection of the City-State. Their passion was for civic autonomy. When emigrants went forth from Greece to establish colonies overseas, they established city communities, on the model of the City-States they had left behind. Hence the Greek word for colonies, ἀποικίαι—homes away from home.

Macedon

What Athens failed to do was accomplished by Philip and Alexander of Macedon. Thanks to those great rulers Hellenism, hitherto constricted in sphere though intense in operation, entered on a new and more vigorous life: it extended its influence over an infinitely wider area. Alexander, the pupil of Aristotle, was even more of a Hellene than his father. Yet, though heir to the culture of Greece, Alexander's temper and ambition were oriental. He did in fact diffuse Hellenic influence over a considerable part of Asia, but the Hellenizing of Asia was accomplished at the

2

price of orientalizing Hellas. Nevertheless, alike in his conceptions and his achievements Alexander is justly called the Great. He aimed at nothing less than world-empire, and he went far towards attaining his goal. In addition to Macedonia his Empire consisted of twenty-two provinces, extending from the Adriatic to the Sutlej, from the Black Sea to the Indian Ocean. By no contemporary man, as Grote justly says, had any such power as Alexander's been even conceived. But Alexander's rule was essentially personal. It is true that he left on the world an impress so profound that (as Dr. Hogarth says) " very little that he had done was ever undone." Yet as an Empire his Empire practically perished with him: within twenty years of his premature death four kingdoms had been established on the ruins of his Empire. Yet Alexander bequeathed to the world the idea of world dominion. His ultimate legatee was Rome.

Rome was originally a City-State of the Greek type. By the third century B.C. she had made herself mistress of Italy from the Straits of Messina to the Arno. Another century and a half (264–105 B.C.) sufficed for the conquest of the lands bordering on the western Mediterranean. When Christ was born Rome was mistress of the greater part of the known world, and under the Emperor Trajan (98–117) the Roman Empire reached its widest extent, stretching from the Solway Firth to the valley of the Nile, from the Atlantic to the Caspian Sea and the Persian Gulf. Gibbon put the population of the Empire at 120,000,000; modern research has halved that figure. *The Roman Empire*

The methods employed by Rome for the administration of this vast Empire are of peculiar interest, especially to Englishmen. They were in striking contrast to the colonial policy of the City-States of Greece. The Greek colonies were homogeneous in race, language, culture, and religion, but were connected with their mother-cities by no political ties whatsoever. They stood to their several mother-cities almost in the same relation as, for instance, Virginia and Massachusetts stood to Great Britain after the acknowledg-

3

ment of American Independence, though the cultural ties were stronger.

The Roman Empire was as heterogeneous as the British, but the policy Rome pursued in relation to the subject communities was as generous as it was successful. Just as in an earlier stage Rome extended the rights and duties of citizenship to all the Italians whom she conquered, so, at a late stage, she gradually opened the doors of citizenship to all the free inhabitants of her vast Empire, without distinction of colour, language, or race. " Never any State," wrote Bacon, " was in this point so open to receive strangers into their body as were the Romans. . . . Their manner was to grant naturalization (which they called *jus civitatis*) . . . not to singular persons only, but likewise to whole families, yea to cities, and sometimes to nations. Add to this their custom of plantation of colonies, whereby the Roman plant was removed into the soil of other nations; and putting both constitutions together you will say that it was not the Romans that spread upon the world, but it was the world that spread upon the Romans; and that was the sure way of greatness." [1]

Colonia

The last sentence points the contrast between a Roman *colonia* and a British colony. Roman colonies differed, one from another, as much as English colonies. But what the Roman generally " planted " was a military outpost; the colonists were mostly retired soldiers who in payment for garrison duty received grants of land. " Little Englanders," however, had their counterpart in " Little Romans " who did their utmost to arrest the rising tide of Imperialism. Their efforts were vain. " Rome," as Lord Cromer justly observed, " was equally with the modern expansive powers . . . impelled onwards by the imperious and irresistible necessity of acquiring defensible frontiers."

The expansion of Rome was progressive certainly up to the time of Trajan, perhaps beyond it; but Gibbon maintains that the basis of the structure was essentially artificial, and that it must needs cause surprise that the structure

[1] Of the true greatness of Kingdoms and Estates. *Essays* (ed. 1822), p. 112.

endured so long. How long it can be said to have stood is a matter of controversy, but at the lowest computation it lasted for five hundred years.

Marvellous as was the Imperial administration of Rome, it had one irremediable weakness. Wide as it opened the gate of citizenship, citizenship conferred no right of participation in government. The rule of Rome was despotic. Inevitable, under the circumstances, the defect became progressively operative with every extension of the Empire. As Gibbon in a famous passage wrote: " The decline of Rome was the natural and inevitable effect of immoderate greatness. Prosperity ripened the principle of decay; the causes of destruction multiplied with the extent of conquest, and as soon as time or accident had removed the artificial supports, the stupendous fabric yielded to the pressure of its own weight! " [1] *Decline of the Roman Empire*

The decay, first manifested at the extremities, had before the end of the fifth century reached the heart. The Barbarian invasions culminating (410) in the capture of Rome brought the Western Empire to an end.

Rome had stood for world-unity, and the idea did not wholly perish with the fall of the Western capital. The legacy of the Roman Empire was inherited by the Catholic Church. The Papacy may have been, in the mordant phrase of Thomas Hobbes, "the ghost of the deceased Roman Empire sitting crowned on the grave thereof." But until the Reformation of the sixteenth century the Catholic Church preserved to the world a semblance of unity. The Papacy did indeed set up a rival to itself when in A.D. 800 Pope Leo III placed on the brows of the great Frankish King Charlemagne the Imperial crown. But that institution derided by Voltaire as neither " Holy, Roman, nor an Empire " was far inferior as a unifying force to its progenitor. Though it lingered on for a thousand years the Holy Roman Empire had long since ceased to exercise any influence upon world affairs.

The Protestant Reformation which destroyed the oecumenical authority of the Catholic Church was almost exactly *Modern Colonization*

[1] *Decline and Fall*, vol. iv, 403.

coincident with the geographical Renaissance. At the end
of the fifteenth century a group of intrepid mariners discovered a new world in the West, and opened up a new path
to the old world of the East. In that work of discovery and
exploration England, as a nation, took no part: the rewards
of enterprise fell consequently and properly to Portugal and
Spain. Even France and the newly United Provinces of the
Netherlands were ahead of England. The tardy awakening
of England will be explained in the next chapter. For the
moment it must suffice to say that when in 1603 Queen
Elizabeth died there was not a single Englishman living
under the English flag in any land overseas. King George
VI is Sovereign Lord over nearly 500,000,000 subjects dispersed throughout five continents, and occupying one-
fourth of the whole land-surface of the globe.

The First
British Empire
To describe and explain this stupendous development is
the purpose of this book. It will discuss the causes which
delayed England's start in the colonial race as well as those
which led to the great outburst of maritime activity in
the latter half of the sixteenth century. Elizabethan seamen were not themselves colonizers but they prepared
the way for actual colonization in the coming century. In
the course of a century and a half (1607–1763) England
founded, mainly by peaceful settlement, but partly as a
result of wars with Spain, Holland, and France, a colonial
Empire in North America and the West Indies. In the
East Indies English traders were expelled from the rich Spice
Islands by the Dutch, but before the seventeenth century
ended they had established trading factories in Madras,
Bombay, and Bengal.

Then came the prolonged contest with the French. The
contest extended to three continents, and resulted in the
defeat of the French both in India and in North America.

On this brilliant success nemesis quickly followed. Relieved from all apprehensions due to the presence of French
neighbours in Canada and Louisiana the English Colonies
in North America raised the standard of revolt, and with

the help of France, Spain, and Holland established their independence.

The First British Empire was thus broken into fragments. *The Second British Empire* But on the ruins of the First there quickly arose a Second. Warren Hastings, Lord Cornwallis, and Lord Wellesley developed some trading settlements in India into an Empire. The " Empire Loyalists " trekked from the United States into New Brunswick and Ontario and so laid the foundations of British Canada. Advantage was taken of Captain Cook's discovery of Australia to establish on its shores a convict settlement. Botany Bay marked the beginning of British colonization in the southern hemisphere.

Cape Colony, the Mauritius, Ceylon, Malaya—the fruits of our victory over Napoleon secured our communications with the Far East and the Pacific. Thus were laid the foundations of a Second Empire.

The loss of the First Empire had, moreover, taught British statesmen a lesson. They overlearnt it. Determined to avoid the blunders that had alienated the North American Colonies, the leaders of the Manchester School resolved to train for complete independence, by successive doses of self-government, the component items of the Second Empire. " Emancipate your colonies " was the advice of Jeremy Bentham: his disciples were determined to better it.

Before the end of Queen Victoria's reign, all the more *Colonial Self-government* important British colonies had attained the goal of responsible government. As regards domestic affairs they were virtually independent. But before the separatist policy could achieve its final victory, a new era in world-history had opened. Scientific inventions had caused a shrinkage of the globe. As the globe shrank, Europe expanded. The progress of industrialization and urbanization caused a scramble for tropical territory. The British colonists, more especially in Australasia, were alarmed by the advent of European neighbours in the Pacific islands. Their protests addressed to Whitehall were at first disregarded.

But not permanently. With the decadence of the Manchester School a new spirit began to animate British policy.

By a series of Colonial Conferences (1887–1911), leading statesmen from overseas were brought into consultation with statesmen of the homeland. Their consultations emphasized a striking anomaly. Though completely autonomous as regards internal affairs, the colonies were in foreign affairs subject to the autocratic control of Whitehall. Accordingly, they proceeded to claim a voice in all matters domestic or external of vital concern to themselves.

Nor did they shirk the responsibilities involved in that claim. Colonial contingents fought side by side with troops from the homeland in the Sudan, in South Africa, and in many theatres in the World war. But the crisis of 1914 revealed another glaring anomaly. Prompt as the Dominions were in response to the call of the Empire, they could not ignore the fact that they were liable to be involved in war without previous consultation on the policy which led to it. If they were "jointly to wield the sword" they claimed the right "jointly to sway the sceptre." The claim was just, and was promptly conceded. At the end of the war the Dominions attained a new status in the British Commonwealth as equal partners with the homeland.

The Third British Empire — Thus there came to birth what has been described as "the Third British Empire." The new status of the self-governing Dominions was defined at the Imperial Conference of 1926 and was legally enacted—so far as legal enactment could effect it—by the *Statute of Westminster* (1931).

Would the new Constitution of the British Commonwealth of Nations stand the strain of a crisis? The answer came in December 1936. In the Coronation Service in 1937 the new relation in which the Monarchy stood, under the *Statute of Westminster*, to the oversea Dominions, was fully and frankly recognized.

India — But the Dominions, though the most important part of the British Empire, do not form the whole of it. Of the 493,370,000 subjects of King George VI 353,000,000 are in India. In India a great political experiment has been initiated the results of which it were premature to foretell. Another is being tried in Southern Ireland, whose status, for the moment, defies definition. Finally, besides the Dominions and India there will remain to be considered the Dependent Empire, the Mandated Territories, and the Protectorates.

Such are the main outlines of the structure which succeeding chapters will survey in greater detail. But the British Empire is not, in truth, a structure, once for all erected and completed; it is an organism in constant activity and subject to unceasing growth. None can tell how far development may have proceeded before the last page of this book is written. All, therefore, that the historian can attempt is to tell the story of the evolution of the Empire, as it has thus far proceeded from stage to stage, and to record the results of an analysis which, correct to-day, may be falsified by events to-morrow.

Embarrassing, however, as they are to the writer, these conditions should add zest to the reader, giving him the sense of a great adventure. If much of his journey is by well-trodden paths, the high peaks are still wrapped in the clouds of mystery.

Chapter Two

The Opening of the Sea Paths

TUDOR POLICY

The Insular State

FOR more than a thousand years, from the dawn of recorded history to the sixteenth century, England was an insular State. She had, indeed, for some three centuries been a remote Province of the Roman Empire, and, later, had formed part, for relatively short periods, first of the Scandinavian Empire and then of the Norman-Angevin Empire. But with those exceptions, she had been throughout the whole of the Middle Ages " a third-rate isle half lost among her seas," scantily populated, with a negligible amount of external trade, and far removed from the main current of human affairs.

That current had for thousands of years lapped the tideless shores of the Mediterranean. The Empires, States, and Cities on those shores had led the world in culture, commerce, and civilization. On them the traditional trade routes had found their termini.

Mediaeval Trade Routes

Of these routes the oldest was that which, starting from the Persian Gulf and the Euphrates, found its way into Europe through Syria and Palestine. By that route Abraham travelled from Chaldaea, and it was long controlled by his descendants. From the Israelites the control of it passed in turn to the Egyptians, the Syrians, and the Persians, to Macedon, and ultimately to Rome.

A second route, making its way from central Asia by way of the Oxus, the Caspian, and the Black Sea, was commanded by Constantine's great city on the Golden Horn.

A third route, starting from India, was, except at one stage, that of the modern P. & O.; it debouched into Europe at Alexandria.

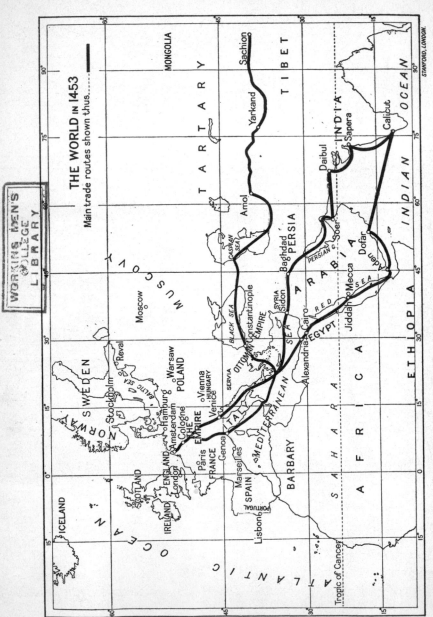

THE WORLD IN 1453

Main trade routes shown thus........

THE WORLD IN 1453

STANFORD, LONDON.

In the latter years of the fifteenth century, and the early *Advent of the Turks* years of the sixteenth, there occurred two series of events which were destined to change the centre of political and commercial gravity, and in particular to revolutionize the position of the British Isles. The first series was due to the advent of the Ottoman Turks; the second followed on what is conveniently described as the " Geographical Renaissance." The two series were not unconnected.

In the middle of the fourteenth century the Ottoman Turks, for the first time, crossed the Bosphorus, and in the course of a century made themselves masters of the Balkan peninsula. In 1453 Constantinople itself fell before the assault of Mohammed the Great. Thus the last remnant of the Roman Empire was extinguished. It seemed likely in the sixteenth century that the Romans would find successors in the Ottomans. Irresistible on land, supreme at sea, the Turks went from triumph to triumph, conquering northern Mesopotamia, Syria, Palestine, Arabia, Egypt, and the whole of the northern coast of Africa. Their Empire reached its zenith under Solyman the Magnificent (1526–1566), whose subjects are said to have numbered 50,000,000 at a time when the Tudors could command the allegiance of a mere 4,000,000.

But the Turkish conquests had a wider significance. As the historian of India graphically said, " the Indo-European trade of the Middle Ages lay strangled in the grip of the Turks." [1] To say that the Turks completely blocked the old Trade Routes may be an exaggeration, but their lust was for war and conquest; trade and traders they despised. Hence the highways which they controlled became manifestly unsafe, and Europe was confronted by two alternatives: the loss of all the luxuries, comforts, and profits that commerce with the East had brought to it, or the discovery of new paths, beyond the control of the all-conquering Turk.

[1] Cf. Hunter: *British India*, chapters I and II. For a more detailed account of the events summarized in these paragraphs see Marriott: *Eastern Question* (3rd ed., Oxford, 1925), chapters III and IV.

The Sea Paths A mere enumeration of dates is in this connection more suggestive than many paragraphs. Mohammed captured Constantinople in 1453. In 1492 Columbus sailed from Spain, hoping by a westward voyage to reach the Far East. He discovered the West Indies: the American Continent barred his further progress towards his goal. In 1497 John Cabot sailed from Bristol, discovered Newfoundland, and explored the northern coast of America. In 1498 Vasco da Gama, the great Portuguese mariner, rounded the Cape of Good Hope, and was thus the first European to reach India by sea.

The Portuguese Empire By that famous voyage, Vasco da Gama not only turned the flank of the Turks but laid the foundations of a Portuguese Empire in the Far East. The prize that fell to Portugal was richly deserved. Prince Henry the Navigator (1394–1460), a son of John I of Portugal and a grandson of John of Gaunt, by setting up at Salgres an observatory, and establishing a school of navigation, had given a great impulse to nautical science. To maritime activity the Portuguese were further stimulated by their age-long crusade against the Moors and their more recent antagonism to the Turks. Madeira they discovered in 1419, the Azores in 1448, and in 1487 Bartolomeu Diaz reached the Cape of Good Hope. The voyage of Vasco da Gama in 1497–1498 was the beginning of an Eastern Empire which, maintained by sea-power and confined to coastal towns, extended from East Africa to India, Ceylon, and even to China. The Portuguese Empire in the Far East lasted for exactly a hundred years, and gave the Portuguese a monopoly of eastern trade until Portugal itself was absorbed by Spain (1580). United with Spain, Portugal became exposed to the fierce competition of the Dutch; Holland succeeded to a large part of Portugal's trade, and for most of the seventeenth century was the leading European power in the Far East.

New Spain While Vasco da Gama, Almeida (1450–1510), and Albuquerque (1453–1515) were establishing the Portuguese Empire in the East, Columbus (1446–1506) and Cortez (1485–1547), Balboa (1475–1517), and Pizarro (1471–1541) were conquering for Spain the West Indies, and great parts of Central and South America. The Spanish Empire in the West was destined to much longer life than the Portuguese Empire in the East; but the defects in its administration were not less obtrusive. With great capacity for conquest the Spaniards had little aptitude for government. From the first they regarded their transatlantic possessions as estates, or rather as a mine to be worked for the exclusive benefit of the Spanish Crown. The mine was a rich one, but its vast output had disturbing effects on the economic condition not of Spain only, but of all Europe. Trade also was treated as a Crown monopoly, and was strangled by the regulations designed to protect it. Feudalism and clericalism completed the ruin of the Spanish Empire. To transport the feudal system into new colonies was a blunder; to introduce into them the methods of the Inquisition was a crime. Between the feudal lord on the one hand and the Catholic Church on the other, the land was drained to the last peseta, and the people were deprived of all incentive to industry and initiative. Consequently long before New Spain had, in the nineteenth century, asserted its independence, it had ceased to be a valuable asset to Old Spain.

In the earlier stages of European colonization England *Backward* had no part. By a Bull issued in 1493 Pope Alexander VI *England* divided the New World between Portugal and Spain. That the claims of England should have been ignored may now seem almost ironical. But there was no reason whatever, at the end of the fifteenth century, why they should have been recognized by the Pope or by anyone else. They did not exist. It is true that, but for an accident to his brother Bartholomew, Christopher Columbus, a Genoese mariner, might have sailed from Bristol under the patronage of Henry VII instead of from Palos under the patronage of the good Queen Isabella of Castile.

In 1496 Henry VII did issue Letters Patent to John *Henry VII* Cabot, a native of Genoa but a naturalized Venetian *and Cabot* resident in Bristol, and to his sons Ludovicus, Sebastian,

13

and Sanctus, authorizing them to search out and to plant the English ensign in any "countries or provinces of heathens and infidals whomsoever set in any part of the World soever, which have been before these times unknown to all Christians." It is noteworthy that the Letters Patent did in those last words implicitly recognize the validity of the Papal Bull of 1493. Still more significant is it that within half a century of the Turkish conquest of Constantinople the two greatest European entrepôts of the old Trade Routes should have so far decayed that their enterprising citizens deserted them for Spain and England respectively. The Mediterranean had become a backwater: the pride of Venice and Genoa was already humbled; their mariners, if eager for employment, must seek it abroad. Truly the "Thalassic" age (in Seeley's famous phrase) had passed: the day of the Oceanic age was dawning: the Mediterranean had already given place to the Atlantic: England had become, geographically, the hub of the Universe.

But England did not yet realize the change.

Cabot, like Columbus, was in search of an open route to the Far East. His precise objective was "an island by him called Cipango, situated in the equinoctial region, where he thinks all the spice and all the precious stones originate." He hoped on the island "to plant a colony and to establish in London a greater storehouse of spices than there is in Alexandria." Precious stones and spices—that was the lure that tempted the adventurers of the fifteenth century. The Turk had cut off the supply: the Turk must be circumvented. "The history of modern Europe and emphatically of England," wrote Sir George Birdwood, "is the history of the quest of the aromatic gum resins and balsams and condiments and spices of India, further India, and the Indian

Mariners and Missionaries Archipelago." That is true; but the commercial motive might not by itself have sufficed to steel the hearts of men against the perils of those early voyages. The adventurers were not merely merchants; they were Christian missionaries. "We come to seek Christians and spices." So said

the first of Vasco da Gama's sailors to land in India. To
" make " Christians would better have expressed their
object than to " seek " them. The Portuguese and
Spaniards " made " them by methods so detestable as to
explain their ultimate failure as Empire builders.

Cabot's motives were also mixed. Those of Henry VII
were not. He sought only profit for the Crown. Any lands
discovered by Cabot and his sons were, under the terms of
his Patent, to be held by them as the vassals and lieutenants
of the King, and to pay twenty per cent of the profits of all
voyages into the Exchequer. But (in striking contrast to
Spanish policy) no custom duties were to be levied on imports from the " Plantations," nor was the monopoly of
trade to be reserved to the Crown; it was granted to the
adventurers.

Cabot sailed from Bristol in the spring of 1497 with one *Cabot's*
small vessel carrying eighteen men. He returned in August *Voyages*
confident in the belief that he had reached the coasts of
Asia and discovered the land of the " Great Cham."

What he had actually discovered is uncertain: but there
is no reasonable doubt that he had touched the American
continent; he may (according to persistent tradition) have
planted the English flag in Newfoundland, and perhaps,
on this or on his second voyage, have surveyed the Atlantic
seaboard of North America.

In May 1498 Cabot left Bristol again with five ships. He
brought back no gold or spices, but his return was hailed
with great enthusiasm in Bristol and in London, and he
received from the King a pension of £20 a year.

Nevertheless, Cabot's example was not imitated by *England's*
Englishmen: his voyages were not followed up. *Tardiness*

In view of subsequent developments this demands explanation. The explanation simply is that England was not
ready. For her unreadiness there were many causes, but
the outstanding cause is to be found in the condition of
affairs when the decisive victory at Bosworth brought Henry
Tudor to the throne. The Wars of the Roses had left
England economically anaemic, socially distraught, and

15

suffering in respect of government from alternations of anarchy and tyranny. " The Lancastrians," in Bishop Stubbs's pregnant phrase, were " weak administrators at a time when the nation required strong government." Moreover, the Lancastrian Parliaments had been guilty of a great blunder. There is no greater blunder in politics than to adopt a form of government which though good in itself is premature. Parliamentary government is, without doubt, the best form of government for England to-day, and for other countries whose traditions are similar to our own; provided that, like ourselves, they have gone through a long apprenticeship in the craft of government. It is not the best, nor indeed a suitable form, for all peoples at all stages of their political and social evolution.

In the England of the fifteenth century Parliamentary Institutions had developed prematurely; they had outrun social and economic development. In the latter part of the fourteenth century England had been depopulated by the ravages of the bubonic plague or " Black Death." At least half of a scanty population had perished, and even in the sixteenth century the English people numbered scarcely 4,000,000 as compared with 12,000,000 in Spain and Portugal and 16,000,000 in France. Moreover, the visitation of the Plague had hastened the break-up of the old social and economic order. The manorial system, the economic counterpart of Feudalism, was already in process of dissolution. The lack of labour consequent upon depopulation hastened the process. The land went down to grass. Sheep took the place of men: wool became our staple product, and with wool of a particularly fine quality we fed the looms of Flanders. London stood in the same relation to Bruges as Melbourne and Sydney to-day stand to the West Riding. For several centuries Englishmen had, indeed, been making rough cloth, but all the finer cloths and all the silks were imported. We had not yet become a nation of shopkeepers: England was a pasture farm. Without shops, we were also short of ships. Froude has summarized the situation in some vivid sentences. " A few merchant hulks traded with Bordeaux, Cadiz, and Lisbon; boys and ply-boats drifted slowly backwards and forwards between Antwerp and the Thames. A fishing fleet tolerably appointed went annually to Iceland for cod. Local fishermen worked the North Sea and the Channel from Hull to Falmouth. The Chester people went to Kinsale for herrings and mackerel; but that was all—the nation had aspired to no more." Mentally inert, England was, in the fifteenth century, socially disintegrated. Of that disintegration, the Wars of the Roses were at once a symptom and the result. Those wars were only accidentally dynastic.[1] They were primarily caused by a social disease. Sir John Fortescue, Chief Justice of the King's Bench (1442–1461) and the leading publicist of that period, ascribed the outbreak of the disease to the malignant growth of " the overmighty subject." Land and power were concentrated in the hands of a few great nobles who, if not aspirants to the Crown, were like the Earl of Warwick, " King-makers." These nobles defied the law and perverted justice. The close of the French wars set free bands of mercenary soldiers. Unused to the ways of peace they readily enlisted under the banner of any nobleman who could guarantee them immunity from the consequences of their lawlessness and outrages. Private wars were prevalent; the Earl of Northumberland waged war against the Earl of Westmorland; the Earl of Devon against Lord Bonneville; the men of Cheshire invaded Shropshire; the students of Oxford fought the men of Oxfordshire, and so on. Wretched was the plight of the middling folk like those Norfolk squires whose life and whose troubles are so vividly depicted in the *Paston Letters*.

Small wonder, then, that the voyages of the Cabots were not followed up. England was not ready. Before it could launch out upon overseas enterprise it must have social order and settled government at home: it called, in fine, for a saviour of society. The saviour appeared in the person of Henry Tudor.

[1] The themes lightly touched in this chapter are developed in much greater detail in my *This Realm of England* (Blackie and Sons, 1938), chapters X and XI.

The Tudor Dictatorship

Henry VII was the founder of the " Tudor Dictatorship." That Dictatorship was of a peculiar type. The Tudor Sovereigns did not supersede Parliament; they dominated it and used it as the instrument of their policy. But their first business was the restoration of social order. A preliminary condition was the establishment of their dynasty. They crushed pretenders to the Throne, and by ruthless methods eliminated all rival claimants. They set up, or strengthened, special tribunals which, like the Star Chamber and the Local Councils modelled upon it, administered justice cheaply, speedily, and impartially. They reorganized local government and by imposing more and more duties upon the Justices of the Peace trained the new nobility and the squirearchy for the part they were to play in Parliament under the Stuarts. By his prudent administration Henry VII restored the finances of the realm and accumulated reserves which greatly strengthened the position of the Crown. But he was specially concerned, by increasing the prosperity of his subjects, to broaden the permanent sources of the public revenue. By administrative action and by legislation he laid the foundations of that mercantile system under which English trade expanded in the seventeenth and eighteenth centuries. His Navigation Laws anticipated those passed under the Commonwealth and Charles II; a merchant navy came into being, and the carrying trade was gradually transferred from foreigners to Englishmen. There are traces also of a conscious policy in regard to currency; the export of gold and silver was restricted, and merchants were required to bring home, in payment for exported wool or cloth, a certain proportion of bullion. The growing woollen manufactures were protected and encouraged.

The Royal Navy

This policy had a perceptible, if gradual, effect upon overseas enterprise. Henry VIII gave a further impulse to it by putting upon a permanent basis the Royal Navy. Within four years of his accession he had added to the seven ships inherited from his father seventeen new vessels. To his successor he bequeathed a fine fleet of seventy-one ships, most of them of an entirely new type, of 11,268 tons in all, with a personnel of nearly 8,000 men and carrying over 2,000 guns. More than that. Henry VIII set aside a regular part of his revenue for the Royal Navy; he appointed a controller and organized the first Navy Board, and founded three colleges for the study of the science of navigation and the art of seamanship. In 1514 he granted its first Charter to Trinity House "for the relief, increase, and augmentation of the shipping of the realm of England." This Guild is still responsible for the maintenance of the lighthouses and other signs of the sea and for the supply of trained pilots.

From 1527 onwards there are records, howbeit very *Sporadic Voyages* scanty, of occasional voyages of discovery. In that year John Rut, a master mariner of London, and Albert de Prado, a canon of St. Paul's and an accomplished mathematician, set out with two ships to renew the quest initiated by Cabot. One of the ships, the *Sampson*, disappeared in mid-Atlantic and was never heard of again. The other, the *Mary of Guildford*, reached Newfoundland, but Rut finding his northward progress barred by ice sailed southward and touched at Porto Rico. He was headed off from San Domingo by the Spanish garrison but returned in safety to England.

Nine years later, one Master Hore with the help of his friends fitted out two ships, and with twenty gentlemen aboard and ninety seamen crossed the Atlantic and explored the coasts of Newfoundland and Cape Breton. But the sufferings of the adventurers, vividly described by Hakluyt, were terrible: many died, some of the survivors took to cannibalism, but were saved by the appearance of a French ship which they sacked, captured, and sailed home in. In pitiable state they returned to England to face the not unnatural recriminations of the injured Frenchmen. Henry, however, "moved by pity punished not his own subjects but of his own purse made full and royal recompense unto the French." [1]

---

[1] Hakluyt: *Voyages*, chapter III, p. 168, and on the whole subject cf. J. A. Williamson: *Maritime Enterprise*, 1485–1558, chapters III, IV, V, X.

A full generation elapsed before the Hores and Ruts found imitators. The perils were too great; the profit too meagre. Less dangerous and much more profitable were the trading voyages made by William Hawkyns, a sea-captain of Plymouth, to Guinea and Brazil (1528–1530). Brazil was, under the authority of the Papal Bull, occupied by the Portuguese, but in 1542 the English merchants, following up Hawkyns's initiative, built a fort on the Brazilian coast. Before the death of Henry VIII, however, the trade died down, only to be resumed in grim earnest, a generation later, by Hawkyns's more famous sons.

Chapter Three

The Elizabethan Seamen

BUCCANEERS AND CRUSADERS.
ATTEMPTED COLONIZATION

SCIENTIFIC curiosity and commercial avidity are powerful incitements to overseas enterprise. But some impulse still more powerful was evidently needed to move the English people out of their insular ruts, to tempt them to explore the new paths opening out to them as a result of the geographical discoveries.

That impulse was supplied by the Protestant Reformation. The cruelties inflicted upon Protestants at home by Mary Tudor, and upon English seamen and traders abroad by her Spanish husband, aroused a new temper in the nation.

Queen Elizabeth was no zealous Protestant; but she came to the throne as the representative of the anti-Catholic and anti-Spanish party. Spain was the enemy not only of English Protestantism but of English commerce. Thus, as Froude truly said, English sea-power was " the legitimate child of the English Reformation." So long as the Bull of Pope Alexander VI was respected in England, English adventurers were deprived of the chance of colonization. From all share in the profits of American trade English merchants were excluded by the colonial policy of Spain. But the final adhesion of England to Protestantism in 1559 made Papal Bulls of no effect; from that moment there was a new birth of maritime adventure.

But Elizabeth, though declining the hand of her brother-in-law, Philip of Spain, was not prepared, in the critical state of European politics, to make war upon him. Peace with Spain remained technically unbroken until 1585. Nevertheless, despite the official " peace," Spanish ships and

Spanish towns were for a quarter of a century perpetually attacked by English privateers. Cordially, though covertly, encouraged by the Queen, the intrepid seamen—the Hawyknses, the Drakes, the Grenvilles, the Raleighs, and the Frobishers—went forth to lay the foundations of English world-trade and world-empire.

These " sea-dogs " were inspired by motives curiously mixed. They were half-buccaneers, half-crusaders, but wholly patriots. The nation was roused to frenzy by the tales brought home by English mariners and merchants. From those tales Englishmen learnt for the first time, at first hand, of the cruelties practised by the Spanish Inquisition, and of the sufferings endured (not wholly without desert) by over-adventurous Englishmen in Spanish ports and Spanish waters. The new temper of the nation, and particularly of the seamen, can be fully appreciated only by those who will read the thrilling tales collected (1582) by Richard Hakluyt, or narratives like that in which Raleigh described Sir Richard Grenville's great fight in the *Revenge*. Hakluyt's prose is, however, reproduced, at times almost literally, by Charles Kingsley in *Westward Ho !* and by Froude in his *English Seamen*. Raleigh's vivid narrative of the *Revenge* has been brilliantly versified in Tennyson's famous ballad.[1] Sir Henry Newbolt has also caught, in his *Admirals All*, the spirit that inspired the Elizabethan sea-dogs:

> " Drake nor devil nor Spaniard feared,
> Their cities he put to the sack;
> He singed his Catholic Majesty's beard,
> And harried his ships to wrack; . . ."

It is significant that moderns who wish to recapture the Elizabethan temper have, as a rule, to resort to verse.

John Hawkyns

Yet there was a prosaic side to the activities of the adventurers. Notably to those of Sir John Hawkyns, whose three voyages (1562–1568) laid the foundations of that nefarious traffic which so long besmirched the annals of English trade. Nefarious it certainly was, when, at the beginning of the nineteenth century, Wilberforce demanded, and Parliament

[1] For the results of recent researches on the Epic of the *Revenge* cf. A. L. Rowse : *Sir Richard Grenville of the " Revenge "* (1937).

assented to, its suppression. Was it nefarious in the sixteenth *The Slave*
century? Froude explains the trade and defends Hawkyns. *Trade*
We may question his logic; we cannot resist his eloquence.

The Carib races whom the Spaniards had found in Cuba
and San Domingo were, from various causes, on the point
of extinction. It occurred to the famous Bishop Casas that
a remnant might be saved if negro labour could be imported
from Africa, with great advantage also to the negroes
themselves: " the negroes would have a chance to rise out
of their wretchedness, could be made into Christians, and
could be saved at worst from the horrible fate which
awaited many of them in their own country."

So the slave trade started. In the humane work of the
Bishop, John Hawkyns was glad to co-operate. Nor was
virtue its own sole reward. In 1562 some citizens of London
formed an African Company and Hawkyns went out as
commander and part owner of three small vessels equipped
by the Company. Hawkyns collected 300 negroes in
Sierra Leone and sold them at an enormous profit in San
Domingo. But the whole of the profits were invested in a
shipload of hides, which were sent by Hawkyns to Cadiz
and on arrival there were confiscated by the Inquisition.

Hawkyns swore vengeance, and in 1564 fitted out a second
expedition in which the Queen herself took shares. This
second venture was in every way successful, and in 1567
Hawkyns embarked on a third. With him, this time, went
his young cousin, Francis Drake. Unfortunately Hawkyns's
luck had at last deserted him, but he and his cousin survived
to tell the tale of disaster, and tempt fortune again with
better results; though not yet awhile.

In 1570 a Florentine banker, living in London, Roberto *The*
di Ridolphi, was plotting with Philip of Spain the assassina- *Ridolphi Plot*
tion of Elizabeth. Hawkyns, learning of it, feigned com-
plicity, and as the price of his co-operation, actually extorted
from Philip £40,000 for the injuries inflicted on him by the
Spaniards on his third expedition, and (what he valued much
more) secured the release of his comrades still in Spanish
hands. The Ridolphi plot was discovered and frustrated;

the Duke of Norfolk and the Earl of Northumberland paid for their treason with their heads. Hawkyns entered the House of Commons as member for Plymouth in 1572, and was presently appointed Treasurer and Controller of the Navy. In that capacity he was largely responsible for the construction and equipment of the ships which, in 1588, destroyed the Spanish Armada.

Where Hawkyns had shown the way there were plenty of adventurous seamen—chiefly from his own west country—to follow. When they were lucky they brought home great treasure; when like John Oxenham, in 1575, they were caught by the Spaniards, they were hanged as pirates.

Francis Drake

Of the " pirates " the greatest, beyond compare, was Francis Drake. He had sailed with his cousin Hawkyns in the ill-fated expedition of 1567 and had sworn vengeance on the Spaniards for the treachery which gave them the victory at San Juan d'Ulloa, and for the barbarities inflicted on the prisoners who then fell into their hands. He made voyages, on his own account, to the West Indies, in 1570, 1571, and 1572, capturing Spanish ships, sacking Spanish towns, winning great fame and amassing much treasure. The Queen herself smiled upon him, and in 1577 accepted a partnership in his venture on terms wholly consonant with her caution and cupidity. Drake's proposal characteristically combined missionary zeal and commercial profit. " Your Majesty must first seek the Kingdom of Heaven and make no league with those whom God has divided from you . . . at sea you can either make war upon (your enemies) openly or by colourable means. . . . Commit us afterwards for pirates if you will . . . you will have the gold and silver mines and the profit of the lands. . . ." [1] In fine, Drake and his fellows would take all the risks: the Queen should have the profits. No one could better appreciate such an

Drake's Voyages, 1577–1580

offer than Elizabeth. In November 1577 Drake left Plymouth in command of an expedition of five small ships with 164 men aboard. Of the little fleet one ship only returned— Drake's own ship the *Pelican*. Aboard her he sailed into

[1] The whole letter should be read in Froude, chapter XI, p. 92.

Plymouth harbour in October 1580, having in those three years circumnavigated the globe. The details of that most famous of all voyages must be read elsewhere.[1] Making first for the Cape de Verde Islands, Drake sailed straight across the Atlantic, passed through the Strait of Magellan, and sailed up the Pacific coast. Taking many rich prizes at sea, and sacking town after town in Peru and Mexico, Drake crossed the Pacific, survived many perils in the Malaccan archipelago, rounded the Cape of Good Hope, and so reached home. Drake's voyage was the greatest feat of seamanship as yet accomplished by man. Nor did it lack material reward. The Spaniards estimated their losses at £5,000,000, in present values. Whatever may be the correct figure there is no question that the amount of treasure brought home by Drake was fabulous. He shared it with his delighted mistress, who rewarded him with a Knighthood, and with further commissions still more to his liking.

Meanwhile, Drake served as Mayor of Plymouth in 1582, and from 1584 to 1585 he sat in Parliament as member for Bossiney. But piracy was more to his taste than politics; he lusted after adventure; the sea was his real home. In 1585 he was sent out, with Letters of Marque from the Queen, in command of another expedition. He burnt Santiago, plundered Vigo, captured San Domingo and Cartagena, and on his way home destroyed a Spanish armament in the harbour of Cadiz (1587).

Even so, despite all these buccaneering raids on Spanish ships and Spanish towns, England and Spain remained technically at peace. Queen Elizabeth had played a difficult hand with consummate skill. Philip, though driven to the verge of frenzy by the daring of English seamen, had thus far been afraid to strike. His hesitation was due partly to the peculiar situation in Europe at large: France though Catholic at home could not be trusted honestly to play the part of the constant friend of Catholic Spain; the Netherlands were in revolt; above all, Mary Stuart represented

---

[1] See Hakluyt: IV, pp. 230 f.; Wagner: *Drake's Voyage Round the World* (1927); and the works of Sir J. Corbett, J. A. Froude, and J. A. Williamson.

French rather than Spanish interests. To dethrone or kill Elizabeth would evidently react to the advantage of the Guises rather than the Hapsburgs. The execution of Mary Stuart in 1587 simplified the situation. In 1588 the thirty years' " peace " was broken; the great Armada sailed.

The Armada   Sir Francis Drake would have anticipated the Spanish expedition by attacking the Armada in Spanish waters. But his mistress refused her consent. She proved right. The Spanish Admiral Santa Cruz, who was to have commanded the Armada, died as it was about to sail. His successor, the Duke of Medina Sidonia, did not like the job, and would gladly have declined it. " My health is bad," he wrote, " and from my small experience of the water I know that I am always sea-sick. . . . The expedition is on such a scale and the object is of such high importance that the person in command of it ought to understand navigation and sea-fighting. I know nothing of either. Nor have I any information, as Santa Cruz had, about the state of England: I cannot tell whom I may trust. . . . If you send me upon this expedition I shall have a bad account to render." His protest availed nothing, but his prediction was fulfilled.

Between the combatants there was no such disparity as tradition has led historians to believe. Recent research has disclosed the facts. The Spanish ships, 120 in number, were much larger than the English, but in the Channel that was a definite disadvantage, and at least half of them were mere transports carrying not sailors but soldiers. Of seamen there were only 12,000 Spaniards against 16,000 Englishmen. Moreover, the Spanish ships were badly handled, the Spaniards' gunnery was bad, and they were short of ammunition. Of the 197 English craft only a small proportion were ships of war: many were privateers. From July 21st to the 27th there was a running fight up the Channel; on the 27th the Spanish fleet anchored in Calais roads; on the night of the 28th eight fireships were floated by the tide into the midst of the Spanish fleet; in panic they cut their cables, but hotly pursued by the English fleet, they were caught off Gravelines, and there on the 29th the great battle was fought. As long as their ammunition lasted the Spaniards fought well, but their ultimate defeat was complete and irreparable. *Deus afflavit et dissipati sunt.* The winds of Heaven completed the work of the English seamen. Three months after the fight off Gravelines some fifty or sixty battered vessels reached Spanish waters. Medina Sidonia's subsequent career did nothing to retrieve his reputation; he died in his bed at the age of sixty-five in 1615.

The British Empire is an Oceanic Empire. In the victory off Gravelines it was begotten. The defeat of the Armada meant, however, much more both to England and to the world than the beginning of England's sea-power. It saved the independence of the Netherlands; it encouraged *les politiques* in France, and it might, had they been prudent, have saved the Huguenots; it confirmed James of Scotland in the Calvinist faith, and Calvinist Scotland contributed to Great Britain, and particularly to the British Empire overseas, a strain of incomparable value. Meanwhile, the defeat of the Armada brought to an end the Tudor Dictatorship. But with its effect upon the English Constitution this narrative is not concerned. With its effect upon English commerce and colonization it is.

These results were not immediate. In the midst of the stirring events recorded above, while Hawkyns and Drake were making England ring with their exploits, a few far-seeing and reflective men were cogitating schemes of permanent plantations in the New World. The sea-dogs had done superb pioneering work. They had defied the Spanish autocrat; they had challenged the monopoly secured by the Papal decree to the Catholic Powers; above all they had given expression to the new spirit, aroused in their own countrymen by the world-shaking events of the sixteenth century. But despite half-hearted attempts by Thomas Stukely and others, there was, as yet, no English settlement on the other side of the Atlantic.

At last, however, a serious attempt was made to plant a permanent settlement in North America. Still the motive was primarily commercial. In 1576 Sir Humphrey Gilbert, another man of Devon, published *A Discourse to prove a passage by the North West to Cathay and the East Indies.* Fired by Gilbert's speculations, Martin Frobisher made a number of expeditions (1576–1578) and landed in southern Greenland. Bringing home some gold he formed a company to exploit his discoveries, but, owing partly to his own domineering temper and brutal conduct, the enterprise came to nothing.

In 1578 Gilbert himself obtained a charter for discovery and plantation, and though his first attempt (1579) to establish a colony hopelessly failed he refused to be beaten. With the aid of his half-brother Walter Raleigh, he fitted out a much more elaborate expedition and in 1583 sailed again. Though he met with little but misfortune he landed at St. John's, Newfoundland, planted the English flag, and took possession of the country in the Queen's name. But of the settlers some were mutineers, others were sick, and many deserted. Gilbert was compelled to abandon the attempt, and on the voyage home the *Squirrel*, in which he sailed, foundered off the Azores. Her consort weathered the storm and brought home the news of Gilbert's brave end and last message: " We are as near Heaven by sea as by land."

Raleigh at once took up his half-brother's unfinished work. " God," said Robert Louis Stevenson, " has made nobler heroes, but he never made a more perfect gentleman than Walter Raleigh." It is true. Of all the Elizabethans, Raleigh most completely embodied the spirit of the age. Statesman, scholar, courtier, warrior, administrator, adventurer, Raleigh touched nothing that he did not adorn. In 1584 he was knighted by his adoring mistress, and without difficulty obtained a renewal of Gilbert's Patent. In that year he sent out two ships on an exploratory expedition under Philip Amidas and Arthur Barlow. Raleigh's captains planted a colony on the island of Roanoke off the coast of North Carolina, and finding the natives " most gentle, loving, and faithful, void of all guile and treason " they took

possession of the land in the Queen's name. Raleigh
christened his colony Virginia, and by that name the whole
coast from Florida to Newfoundland was originally known.
Encouraged by the reports of his captains, Raleigh fitted
out an expedition on a more ambitious scale, and in 1585
seven ships, with 108 intending colonists on board, set out
under the command of Sir Richard Grenville. Having
settled the colonists on Roanoke, Grenville, leaving Ralph
Lane in command, came home for fresh stores. On his
return he found the colony abandoned, but left a small
company, with ample stores, to retain possession. They
were never heard of again. Raleigh, though almost ruined
in fortunes, sent out one relief party after another. To no
purpose. No permanent settlement was effected. In 1595
Raleigh himself made his famous voyage, in quest of
Eldorado, and described it in *The Discovery of Guiana*. Again
without result. A final voyage to the Orinoco was undertaken in 1617 to purchase his release from the Tower.
Thanks to the poltroonery of James I and the vindictive
demands of the Spanish Gondomar, it led only to Raleigh's
unjust condemnation and cruel death.

The Elizabethan era had, indeed, passed away. But the
Elizabethan adventurers had done their appropriate work.
As Mr. Doyle wrote: " The spirit which set on foot raids
against Spanish ports and gold quests was probably needed
as a pioneer to clear the way for colonization, but it was a
hindrance to the actual work of the colonist. . . . The
versatile, restless, enterprising temper which fits men for
the one task is in itself an obstacle to them in the other."

That is true. But to the statement made on page 6
we must now admit a partial exception. It is an exception
that proves the rule. When Queen Elizabeth died there
were Englishmen living under the English flag in a country
overseas. Ireland has always, however, been an anomaly
in the Empire: it was in Ireland that those English colonists
were to be found.

As far back as the twelfth century Ireland had been
invaded by Anglo-Norman adventurers from England; it

had been nominally conquered and partially colonized. But conquest and colonization were alike incomplete; not until Cromwell's day was Ireland ever really conquered by England, or more than partially colonized by Englishmen. The original Anglo-Norman settlers—the barons of the " Pale "—were in fact quickly absorbed into the Irish population, and despite all the efforts of the English Legislature, became in the current phrase, *Hibernicis ipsis Hiberniores*.

Tudor Policy in Ireland

When Henry VII ascended the throne, English authority in Ireland was on the point of extinction. The Tudors reasserted it. Sir Edward Poynings was sent over as Lord Deputy, and the Statute commonly known by his name (1494) made English law applicable to Ireland and brought the Irish Parliament into dependence upon the English Privy Council. Henry VIII made a real attempt to assimilate not only the law but the social customs of Ireland to those of England. His policy had some success until he attempted to bring the two Churches into conformity. The Irish people, though less " Papal " even than the English, were and are devoted to the Catholic faith, discipline, and ritual. The proscription of Catholicism made them Papists.

The accession of Mary brought them relief, but under Elizabeth the Irish " problem," as England has known it for three hundred years, clearly emerged. The problem had three aspects: religious, constitutional, and agrarian. Under Elizabeth, it was the third aspect that was most prominent. The great mass of the Irish people, despite the attempted feudalization of the " Pale," had not yet emerged from the tribal stage; they contended that the land was the property of no " lord," least of all of an alien lord, but belonged to the native tribesmen who were still devoted to their native chiefs. The Irish rebellions against Elizabeth were due to the fear of expropriation; the " Plantation " that followed upon the conquest justified that fear.

" Plantations " in Ireland

Throughout Elizabeth's reign insurrection followed insurrection; confiscation on insurrection; attempted plantation on confiscation. The grantees of the confiscated lands ("undertakers" was their technical description) were mostly of the same breed as the adventurers who went to the Spanish Main. But in Goldwin Smith's grim phrase there was this difference: "The Eagles," he says, "took wing for the Spanish Main; the Vultures descended upon Ireland." Yet among the "vultures" were Sir Walter Raleigh, who received over 40,000 acres of fine grazing land in Cork and Waterford, Sir Christopher Hatton, Sir Richard Grenville, and Edmund Spenser. The most elaborate of the schemes was that devised, after the suppression of the Geraldine insurrection, for the plantation of Munster. Like the others, the Munster scheme hopelessly miscarried: the "undertakers" were busily employed elsewhere; the task of colonization was left to agents. Edmund Spenser, indeed, personally "planted" his property near Cork, and in his *View of the Present State of Ireland* has left a vivid if exaggerated description of the terrible condition of Munster after the suppression of the rebellion. No fewer than 30,000 persons —men, women, and children—were said to have perished in Munster—"not many," in Spenser's words, "by the sword, but by all the extremity of famine which they themselves had wrought."

To the general rule of colonizing failure under Elizabeth, *Ulster* Ireland presented no exception. Not, indeed, until after the flight of the northern Earls, Tyrone and Tyrconnell, and the confiscation of their lands (if theirs they were) in Ulster (1607–1611) was there any effective colonization in Ireland. The plantation of Ulster by English and Scottish Protestants was, indeed, one of the most profoundly significant events in Anglo-Irish history. But the true interpretation of its significance is still a matter of controversy.

Before Ulster was planted with Protestants the Elizabethan era was at an end. Not long before her death, however, the old Queen had planted yet another sapling destined to grow into a mighty oak.

Only at the end of her reign were English merchants moved to emulate the exploits of the Portuguese and the Dutch in the Far East. But in 1591 an English squadron, commanded by Captain (Sir) James Lancaster, sailed to India round the Cape and returned three years later with rich booty. Accordingly, in 1599, a company of London merchants formed an Association for promoting direct trade with the East Indies, and in 1600 obtained a Charter for that purpose from the Queen.

Thus was John Company born. But stupendous as were the results it ultimately achieved, they can be but briefly chronicled in this volume.[1] The purpose of the Company was, in origin, exclusively commercial. There was no thought of colonization or even of territorial dominion. The Company did in fact develop into an Empire; but, if inevitably, unintentionally, and against the express orders of the Directors. Neither has India ever been, nor can it ever be, a British colony—a land for the settlement and expansion of the British race. It is, then, *sui generis*; and it lies outside the main road which this narrative will follow.

The high road to be followed is that of British colonization in lands well adapted to provide a permanent home for men, women, and children of British stock. To such lands the Elizabethan adventurers had shown the way. They failed to occupy them. That task, less exciting but perhaps more exacting, they bequeathed to their successors.

[1] The story is told at length in Marriott: *The English in India* (Oxford, 1931).

Chapter Four

The First Colonial Empire

TRADE AND RELIGION.
THE NORTH AMERICAN COLONIES

WE descend from an age of Poetry to an age of Prose. Romance has, indeed, found appropriate themes in the story of the men and women who laid the foundations of the great American Republic. Nor could the work of those pioneers have been done without the display of qualities truly heroic. But their heroism was of a different order from that demanded from the Elizabethan seamen. Virginia could never have been established, in the face of Indian opposition, had not the settlers possessed great patience and high courage. No Englishman can read, for instance, Mary Johnstone's beautiful story, *By Order of the Company*, without a quickening of the pulses and a deep sense of pride in the exploits of his countrymen. The narratives of Bradford and Prince reveal the indomitable spirit and the religious enthusiasm of those whom we name the " Pilgrim Fathers." Nevertheless, there was between settlers and adventurers a difference of temper which the following pages should make clear.

The primary motive that animated the men who actually *Motives for* " planted " Virginia was identical with that of the Eliza- *Colonization* bethans who failed to found a colony. Like their predecessors, the planters hoped to find gold and silver and, if a north-west passage should give them access to Asia, spices and the products of the East as well. They were straitly charged, too, to send home cargoes of naval stores, timber, cordage, and so forth. Another motive was operative. Parodoxical as it may seem to the inhabitants of an island that now carries 45,000,000 people, the statesmen of the early seventeenth century were alarmed by the prospect of

D   33

Unemployment

over-population. The increase of population in the six-teenth century had not raised the aggregate for England and Wales to more than 4,500,000 at most. Nevertheless, the agrarian revolution—the progress of " enclosures," the dis-solution of the monasteries, and the development of sheep farming—had created a problem of unemployment. The land swarmed with " vagabonds " and " sturdy beggars " evicted by the " greedy cormorants who joined lordships to lordships, manor to manor, farm to farm," and gathered many thousands of acres " within one pale or hedge." The sufferings of the poor caused by enclosures were, moreover, enhanced by the rapid rise of prices due to the debasement and depreciation of the coinage. The State attempted to mitigate the prevalent distress by fixing prices, by enjoining the payment of a minimum wage, and by stimulating private benevolence. Finally, it was compelled to enact the famous Poor Law (1601), which virtually guaranteed " work or maintenance." Before the end of the seventeenth century matters had adjusted themselves, but in the meantime an apparently " superfluous " population had provided the material for emigration.

Religion

A more powerful impulse to emigration was supplied by religious and philanthropic enthusiasm. If New England offered a refuge to Puritans, Maryland was established primarily to afford hospitality to Roman Catholics; Penn-sylvania, though open to all comers, was intended specially for Quakers, while Georgia was founded to give a new start in the New World to the failures of the Old World, and especially to those who had languished for long years in debtors' prisons.

There was, then, in the origins of the English colonies in North America extraordinary variety; and this variety, reflected in religion, in social types, in economic interests, and in political institutions, persisted throughout the whole of the colonial period.

To the details of that period we now turn.

Virginia

Of the thirteen colonies which ultimately achieved in-dependence as the United States of America the oldest is

34

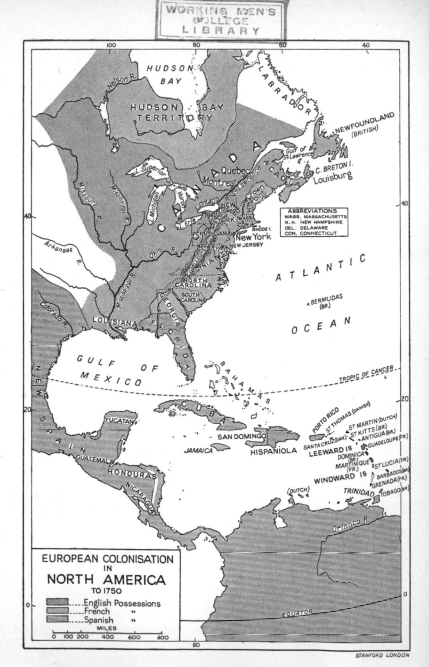

100   80   60   40

HUDSON
BAY

HUDSON BAY
TERRITORY

LABRADOR

Nelson R.

NEWFOUNDLAND
(BRITISH)

Gulf of
St Lawrence

C. BRETON I.
Louisburg

L. Superior
Quebec
Montreal

40

ABBREVIATIONS
MASS. MASSACHUSETTS
N.H. NEW HAMPSHIRE
DEL. DELAWARE
CON. CONNECTICUT

Missouri R.
Mississippi R.
L. Michigan
Huron
Ontario
Erie
Niagara
NEW
YORK
Oswego

Arkansas R.

PENNSYLVANIA

RHODE I.
New York
NEW JERSEY
DEL.

40

ATLANTIC

MARYLAND
VIRGINIA

Ohio R.

NORTH
CAROLINA

SOUTH
CAROLINA

OCEAN

★ BERMUDAS
(BR.)

Colorado R.

LOUISIANA

GEORGIA

FLORIDA

GULF   OF
MEXICO

TROPIC OF CANCER

BAHAMAS

20

NEW   SPAIN

YUCATAN

CUBA

PORTO RICO
ST THOMAS (DANISH)
SANTA CRUZ (DAN.)   ST MARTIN (DUTCH)
ST KITTS (BR.)
ANTIGUA (BR.)
GUADELOUPE (FR.)
DOMINICA
(BR.)
MARTINIQUE
(FR.)
ST LUCIA (FR.)
BARBADOS (BR.)
GRENADA (FR.)
TOBAGO (BR.)

20

SAN DOMINGO

JAMAICA

HISPANIOLA

LEEWARD IS.

GUATEMALA

HONDURAS

NICARAGUA

WINDWARD IS.

(DUTCH)

TRINIDAD

Orinoco R.

EUROPEAN COLONISATION
IN
NORTH AMERICA
TO 1750

0

English Possessions
French   "
Spanish   "

MILES
0   100 200   400   600   800

EQUATOR

0

80

STANFORD LONDON

EUROPEAN COLONISATION IN NORTH AMERICA TO 1750

[35

Virginia. In 1606 the Virginia Company was formed by a number of influential persons, more or less on the model of the East India Company,[1] and on April 10th received a Charter from King James I. The original idea was that there should be two companies, a London Company and a Plymouth Company, each responsible for a colony on the eastern seaboard of North America. The Plymouth Company came to nothing. The foundation of the first English colony on American soil was due to the London Company. Each colony was to be governed by a President and Council of thirteen members nominated by the Crown, and both were to be supervised by a General Council of fourteen members, also nominated by the Crown and permanently resident in London. All jurisdiction was reserved to the Crown, but under the pressure of necessity was largely transferred to the Company under the amended Charter of 1609. All land was to be held of the Crown by homage and on payment of a rent of one-fifth of the gold and silver and one-fifteenth of the copper produced by the mines. The Company was authorized for twenty-one years to levy a duty of two and a half per cent on all goods bought and sold in the colony by Englishmen and of five per cent by foreigners. After that period the custom duties were to revert to the Crown. Under a Constitution promulgated by the King in November 1606 the local Council was empowered to make Ordinances, but they were not to be binding until ratified by the Crown, and all were to be " consonant to the laws of England and the equity thereof "; religion was to be established in accordance with the doctrine and rites of the Church of England under the supremacy of the Crown; land tenure was to follow the English law; the President and Council were to exercise summary jurisdiction in all civil causes and in criminal cases of minor importance, but trials for murder and all the more serious offences were to be by jury. Finally, and as though by an afterthought, the colonists were enjoined to show kindness to the natives and

---

[1] The E.I.C. model was much more definitely adopted in the remodelled Charter of 1609.

use all proper means for their conversion to Christianity. Bancroft is indignant because the Charter conceded to the colonists "not one elective franchise, not one of the rights of self-government." But such criticism is purely doctrinaire: it is based on the pedantry of retrospect. In due course the colonists obtained all the constitutional liberties essential to the development of the enterprise.

On January 1st, 1607, 143 emigrants left England on board a small fleet of two ships and a pinnace, and after a long and perilous voyage 104 survivors landed (April 16th) on the shores of Chesapeake Bay. After a fortnight spent in exploring the country they established a settlement to which, in patriotic duty, they gave the name of Jamestown. "Heaven and earth," wrote John Smith, "seemed never to have agreed better to frame a place for man's commodious and delightful habitation."

So it might well seem to the chronicler of Virginia in retrospect; but if it had not been for Smith's courage and resourcefulness there would probably have been added yet another to the pitiful list of failures. "The people wherewith you plant," wrote Bacon, "ought to be gardeners, ploughmen, labourers, smiths, carpenters, joiners, fishermen, fowlers, with some few apothecaries, surgeons, cooks, and bakers." The original settlers did not, unfortunately, answer to that description. They were mostly ruined "gentlemen of fortune," or rather of "misfortune": gamesters; mere adventurers—in the wrong sense. Among them there were only twelve labourers, four carpenters, and very few men accustomed to work with their hands.

The list of the resident Council nominated by the home Council was not disclosed until the landing was effected, when they elected as President Edward Maria Wingfield, a Roman Catholic gentleman of good family and respectable abilities but vain, pompous, weakly consequential, and autocratic, and wholly lacking in the qualities required for leadership in such an enterprise. After a few months of disastrous rule Wingfield was deposed and, after other experiments, John Smith became (1608) titular head of the colony which he, almost single-handed, had rescued from irretrievable collapse.

Captain John Smith (1580–1631) was a typical soldier of *John Smith* fortune. He had fought in the Netherlands, been taken prisoner by the Barbary Corsairs, and fought in single combat with a Turk in Hungary. Imprisoned by the Turks he had escaped through the good offices of a Turkish beauty, had fled into Circassia, and having travelled widely, fought much, and made a fortune, found himself before he was thirty on his way to Virginia. He was in irons for insubordination when he landed, but his were the qualities most needed by his companions, and by September 1608 his leadership was formally accepted. To his writings we owe most of our knowledge of the early days of the colony, and to his personality the colony itself owed its survival. Doubts have been thrown on the veracity of his narratives, but none upon the value of his intervention. He left Virginia for England in 1609, but subsequently sailed on a voyage of exploration to New England and did valuable service to those who came after by his skill in topography and his industry as a pamphleteer. He died in London in 1631, and is commemorated by a monument and a versical epitaph in St. Sepulchre's Church.

Reinforcements reached Virginia from England in 1608; but the men were still not of the right sort. " I entreat you," wrote Smith to the Council at home, " rather send out thirty carpenters, husbandmen, gardeners, fishermen, blacksmiths, masons, diggers up of tree-roots well provided, than a thousand of such as we have here."

Heed was given to Smith's advice. A public appeal, *A New* influentially supported, was issued in London. Stress was *Start,* 1609 laid upon the opportunity which Virginia offered for the propagation of the Gospel, and for the cure of economic distress in England " by transplanting the rankness and multitude of increase in our people." Nor was a final inducement to subscription forgotten. The " prospectus " held out " the appearance and assurance of private commodity to the particular undertakers by recovering and possessing to themselves a fruitful land, whence they may furnish and provide the Kingdom with all such necessities and defects under which we labour and are now enforced to buy and receive at the courtesy of other princes under the burden of great customs and high impositions." The colony was to contribute to the self-sufficiency of the Empire.

The New Charter
The whole undertaking was, just in time, reorganized. A new Virginia Company was incorporated, consisting of fifty-six city companies and 659 private individuals, among whom were twenty-one peers, ninety-six knights, and many Members of Parliament. The shares were in units of £12 10s., and each settler was credited with one share. The Company undertook to feed, clothe, house, and defend the settlers, and for seven years all profits were to be paid into joint stock. At the end of that period each shareholder, including the settlers, was to receive one hundred acres, in freehold, and a further one hundred on a subsequent division, if justified by an increase of population. One-fifth of all gold and silver was reserved to the Crown and one-fifth to the Company.

Under the new Charter the control of the Company was vested in the stockholders who (after the initial nominations by the Crown) were to nominate the officers and local Council, to whom was delegated all local jurisdiction. But, despite influential and substantial backing, the colony barely survived the attacks of the Indians and the ravages of famine and disease. Though 1,650 persons were sent out between 1607 and 1616, the population in the latter year was only 351, and despite large reinforcements from home it had by 1623 only reached 1,277. John Smith introduced the culture of maize, and in 1612 an early settler, John Rolfe, initiated, to the immediate danger but lasting advantage of the colony, the regular cultivation of tobacco. Rolfe is, however, even more famous as the husband of the Indian Princess Pocahontas, the newly converted daughter of the Indian chief Pouhattan. Rolfe's arrival in England with his bride, in 1616, created no little sensation, but she died in 1617, and Rolfe returned to the colony, where he died in 1622.

Meanwhile, the Company had secured the services, as *Lord De La Warr* first Governor under the new scheme, of Lord De La Warr, a man of high character, of ancient lineage, and of varied experience gained in arms in Ireland under Essex and in the Netherlands. De La Warr reached Virginia with some much-needed reinforcements and supplies in 1610. He perceived at once that the immediate requirements of the settlement were regular supplies of food and a different type of emigrant. " It is not," he wrote, " men of such distempered bodies and infected minds whom no examples either of goodness or punishment can deter from their habitual impieties or terrify from a shameful death, that must be builders in this so glorious a building. But to delude and mock the business no longer, as a necessary quantity of provisions for a year must be carefully sent out, so likewise must there be the same care for men of quality and painstaking—men of arts and practices chosen out and sent into the business.".

So disheartened were the stockholders on receipt of this report that they seriously considered the abandonment of the enterprise. But the arrival of Sir Thomas Gates with more favourable news encouraged them to persevere. Meanwhile, De La Warr enforced discipline and stimulated industry, and when, after little more than a year's residence in the colony, he was compelled by illness to return home, he was able to report that the tide had turned. Brief as his administration was, it had undoubtedly saved the situation.

Even more important were the services rendered to the *Sir Thomas* colony by Sir Thomas Dale, a naval commander who as *Dale* " Marshal " (1609), as Deputy for De La Warr (1611–1614), and finally as Governor (1614–1616) really set it on its feet. Dale's methods were rough, perhaps even unnecessarily rough, but they were effective. His " Code " was little short of martial law. One example must suffice. Failure to attend daily service was punishable by six months at the galleys; similar irregularity on Sundays could be expiated only by the death penalty. Dale was, however, a believer not only in discipline, but in " the magic of property." The profits of tobacco cultivation were so alluring that the settlers, concentrating upon that industry, might have starved, had not Dale assigned to each of them a " private garden " of three acres, two of which had to be planted with grain. Further encouragement to private enterprise and the cultivation of food crops was given by providing each new settler with a four-roomed house and twelve acres of ground rent-free, on condition that they only grew such crops. Dale did a further service by removing the bulk of the colonists from Jamestown, a malaria-ridden swamp, to Henrico and other places higher up the river. He also greatly improved (largely through the intervention of Pocahontas) the relations between the colonists and the Indians. Before he finally left the colony in 1616 the communal period prescribed in the charter of 1609 had expired, and Dale allotted land in severalty to the original settlers.

Argall

After a brief interval Dale was succeeded by another sailor, Captain Samuel Argall. Argall's administration was not merely tyrannical but corrupt, and in 1618 De La Warr was induced to accept a second term of Governorship. He died, however, on the voyage before reaching Virginia, and was replaced by Sir George Yeardley, who held office from 1619 to 1621, and again from 1626 to 1627.

Sir George Yeardley

The first year of Yeardley's administration was doubly memorable. On July 30th, 1619, the first session of a colonial Parliament was opened at Jamestown. " That they might have a hand in the governing of themselves," so runs the *Briefe Declaration*, " yt was graunted that a general Assemblie should be helde yearly once, whereat were to be present the Governor and Counsell, with two Burgesses from each plantation (of which there werc eleven), freely to be elected by the inhabitants thereof, this Assemblie to have power to make and ordaine whatsoever laws and orders should by them be thought good and profitable for our subsistence."

Thus were the free Political Institutions of England transplanted to American soil. From this time onwards the colony was virtually self-governed. Its prosperity advanced by leaps and bounds. Bitter experience had taught many valuable lessons: the emigration of the " better sort " was studiously encouraged; the over-production of tobacco was checked, and schemes were made for the better education of the settlers and for the conversion of the natives. The growing prosperity of the colony was, however, temporarily arrested in 1622 by an Indian massacre which cost the lives of 350 colonists, and in 1623 by a famine which was even more fatal. But the effect of these disasters was temporary. Not so the introduction of African slaves, twenty of whom were in 1619 landed from a Dutch merchantman. Thus were the seeds of social slavery planted simultaneously with the seeds of political liberty. For two centuries and a half wheat and tares were to flourish alongside.

In 1624 a radical change took place in the constitutional position of the colony. Since 1612 it had been administered under a third charter which had amended the constitution of the Company, enlarged its powers of control, and added to its territory the recently annexed Bermudas. Among its directors there were acute differences on policy, and, taking advantage of these, the King called on the Company by a writ of *Quo Warranto* to justify its existence. The courts decided against the Company, the King confiscated the charter, and the government of the colony was henceforth vested in the Crown and administered by a Committee of the Privy Council. A Governor and twelve assistant officials were appointed by the Crown to represent it on the spot and conduct the executive and judicial business of the colony.

Whether the action of James I was instigated by his friend Count Gondomar, the Spanish Ambassador, or was due to his own mistrust of a colonial parliament, or to his detestation of tobacco, is uncertain. Certain it is that its ultimate effect was favourable to the development of colonial independence. The whole principle of chartered companies was, indeed, denounced by Adam Smith, with some lack of historical perspective, in his *Wealth of Nations* (1776). But in the nineteenth century the device was successfully revived, and its value as a transitory stage in the development of a colonial Empire is now generally recognized. The Virginia Company had, perhaps, outlived its usefulness: without its intervention, at a particular stage, Virginia might never have come into existence.

By 1624 the initial difficulties of its establishment were mostly surmounted, and as a Royal Province Virginia made rapid progress. By 1629 it counted more than 4,000 inhabitants. After the King's defeat in the Civil War a large cavalier immigration took place, and between 1650 and 1670 the population leapt up from 15,000 to 40,000. By the end of the century it was 100,000.

Maryland

To the same geographical group as Virginia belong the colonies of Maryland and the two Carolinas, and they also conform to the same social and economic type. Constitutionally, on the contrary, Maryland belongs to an entirely different category.

Lord Baltimore

In April 1632 George Calvert, first Lord Baltimore, received from Charles I a grant of territory to the north of, and partly included in, the original grant to Virginia. Lord Baltimore was a statesman who as a Secretary of State and in other offices had played a distinguished part in English politics under James I. But always interested in colonial affairs he had, in 1621, planted a colony at Avalon in Newfoundland. In 1625 he professed himself a convert to Roman Catholicism, and consequently was not regarded with friendly eyes by the Puritans who had established themselves in New England. He was harried also by French privateers, and after a winter spent at Avalon (1628-1629) determined to transplant his colony to Virginia. The Virginian Government warned him off from the land south of James River. Accordingly, he betook himself to the land to which he gave the name of the Catholic Queen, and in 1633 the first settlement was planted on the northern shore of the Potomac.

The first Lord Baltimore died before he could take possession, but the scheme was taken up by his second son Leonard, a man better fitted for colonial administration than his father, and the Government remained in the hands of the

Calvert family until the declaration of American independence.

As compared with Virginia, Maryland encountered few difficulties. The claims of William Claybourne, a Virginian colonist who had established a trading settlement on the Potomac, gave the Proprietor some trouble, but the Home Government decided in favour of the Proprietor. Claybourne, however, reappeared in 1652, as one of three Commissioners appointed by the Commonwealth to enforce its authority in the colonies, and the rights of the Proprietor remained in abeyance until the Restoration.

Another difficulty arose from the autocratic powers vested in the Proprietor by the original grant from the Crown. To Lord Baltimore and his heirs was assigned absolute lordship subject only to a rent payable to the Crown of two Indian arrows and a fifth part of gold and silver ore. The Proprietor was empowered to make laws with the advice and approbation of the freemen or their deputies, " so nevertheless that the law be consonant to reason and not repugnant to the laws of England." When it was not convenient to summon an Assembly the Proprietor was authorised to make Ordinances so long as they did not affect the life or property of his subjects. *Proprietary Colonies*

The colonists were quick to resent this autocratic Government and asserted their rights, ill-defined in the Patent, to a share in the administration of their own affairs. In the early days of the colony the demand was satisfied by an assembly of all freemen in person, but as the settlement was enlarged the principle of representation was introduced, and, ultimately, the Constitution of Maryland was assimilated to that of other colonies. A bicameral legislature was evolved, one chamber consisting of the Council and other nominees of the Proprietor, a second consisting of representatives elected by the whole body of freemen. The Church of England was established, but there was complete toleration not only for the Roman Catholic co-religionists of the Proprietor, but for all Christians. It is indeed, the unique distinction of Maryland to have been the first community in the Old World or the New to embody in legislation the principles of religious toleration.

"Whereas," so ran the Toleration Act of 1649, "the inforcing of the conscience in matters of religion hath frequently fallen out to bee of dangerous consequence in those commonwealths where it has beene practised, and for the more quiet and peaceable government of this province and the better to preserve mutuall love and unity amongst the inhabitants here it is enacted that no person professing to believe in Jesus Christ shall from henceforth be any waies troubled or discountenanced for, or in respect of, his or her religion nor the free exercise thereof within this province, . . . nor in any way compelled to the beliefe or exercise of any religion, against his or her consent."

Puritan intolerance led to the suspension of this Act during the Commonwealth, but it was re-enacted in 1657, to the glory and advantage of the colony.

The Pilgrim Fathers

In respect of the principle of toleration the Carolinas subsequently followed the example of Maryland, but in the New England colonies it was conspicuous only by its absence. Of those colonies the most important—Massachusetts—was almost exactly contemporary with Maryland. But the first body of Puritan emigrants had established themselves more than twelve years earlier (December 1620) at New Plymouth on the shore of Massachusetts Bay.

" It is no delusion which sees in the foundation of Plymouth a turning point in American history. A new force had been put in motion. . . . The discoverer, the gold-seeker, the merchant, had all attempted the task of colonization with varying success. Now for the first time the religious enthusiast, strong in his sense of a divine mission and of a brotherhood whose foundation was in heaven, sailed out on that sea, strewn with the wrecks of so many heroic ventures and good hopes."

So wrote John Doyle, and truly, towards the end of the nineteenth century. Pastor Higginson had made the same point in the Election Sermon of 1663:

"It concerneth New England always to remember that they were originally a plantation of religions, not a plantation of trade. And if any man among us make religion twelve and the world as thirteen, such an one hath not the spirit of a true New Englandman."

"A plantation of religions." That was, indeed, the original impulse. With the origins and progress of the Reformation in England this narrative cannot concern itself. It must suffice to recall the fact that, after violent oscillations under Edward VI and Mary, a compromise had been reached under Elizabeth and had been embodied in the Acts of Supremacy and Uniformity (1559) in the new Prayer Book and in the Thirty-nine Articles, approved by Parliament in 1571. The intention of the Queen and of Parliament was to make the Established Church as widely comprehensive as possible, and that it did comprehend the vast majority of the nation there can be no question. But the settlement did not and could not satisfy, on the one side, those who were not merely Catholics but Papists, and, on the other, two sections of the large body of people known as Puritans. Of the Puritans many remained within the Establishment in the hope (not dissipated until the ascendancy of Laud) of moulding it to their own views. But another group of Puritans, the Presbyterians, were root and branch opposed to the episcopalian form of Church government, while a third group known as Separatists, Independents, Congregationalists, or to contemporaries more commonly as "Brownists" were opposed to all unified systems of Church government. To them the Congregation was "the Church"; "Presbyter was but old Priest writ large."

It was the "Brownists" who were responsible for the foundation of New Plymouth, and, less exclusively, of Massachusetts.

A small congregation of Brownists had taken refuge in Holland and established themselves (1609) at Leyden, where their Pastor—John Robinson—formulated the Separatist creed. But even Leyden did not fulfil all their hopes; and

Protestantism and Colonization

45

having obtained the King's assent they procured (1619) a Patent from the Virginia Company authorizing them to establish a settlement near the Hudson. Before the intending emigrants left Leyden, Pastor Robinson, who was to stay with the Congregation at Leyden, conducted a service of humiliation and dedication. If his parting words were accurately reported they reflect a mind of singular liberality.

" He charged us before God and his blessed angels to follow him no further than he followed Christ, and if God should reveal anything to us by any other instrument of His to be as ready to receive it as ever we were to receive any truth by his ministry; for he was very confident the Lord had more truth and light yet to break out of His Holy Word. He took occasion also miserably to bewail the state of the reformed Churches; who were come to a period in religion; and would go no further than the Instruments of their reformation, the Lutherans, for instance, could not be drawn to go beyond what Luther said: for whatever part of God's word He had further revealed to Calvin they had rather die than embrace it. ' And so,' said he, ' you see the Calvinists they stick where he left them. A misery much to be lamented. . . .' He, therefore, entreated them to receive (though with care) new truth revealed in His Word. ' For it is not possible the Christian world should come, so lately out of such anti-Christian darkness and that full perfection of knowledge should break forth at once.' " [1]

Well had it been for New England had more heed been paid to the wise words of Pastor Robinson. Yet the initial enterprise of the " Pilgrim Fathers " is rightly regarded as an event of the first importance not merely in American but in world history. An American poet, quoting Robinson's words, has truly said of the Pilgrims:

" And these were they who gave us birth,
The Pilgrims of the sunset wave,
Who won for us this virgin earth
And freedom with the soil they gave.

---

[1] The report of Robinson's address first appeared in Edward Winslow's *Hypocrisy Unmasked* (1646). Prince accepts it as authentic.

" The pastor slumbers by the Rhine,
In alien earth the exiles lie—
Their nameless graves our holiest shrine,
His words our noblest battle cry.

" Still cry them, and the world shall hear,
Ye dwellers by the storm-swept sea,
Ye have not built by Haarlem Meer
Nor on the land-locked Zuyder Zee."

Two small vessels, the *Mayflower* (180 tons) and the *Speedwell* (60 tons), had been chartered and with 120 emigrants on board sailed from Southampton on August 15th, 1620. But before they were out of the Channel the *Speedwell* sprang a leak. Both ships put back into Plymouth, and on September 16th the *Mayflower*, carrying 102 passengers, sailed from that port alone. On November 19th Cape Cod was sighted, but before landing the little company formally constituted themselves a " civill body politick, for (their) better ordering and preservation and furtherance of ye ends aforesaid," i.e. " ye glorie of God and advancement of ye Christian faith and honour of our King and country." They elected as their governor Deacon John Carver, and having spent six weeks in exploring the coast ultimately landed on December 21st at a spot which they christened New Plymouth.

The first winter was one of great suffering. John Carver was among the many victims, and in his stead the survivors elected William Bradford, with Miles Standish as military commander. To Bradford's fine narrative we mainly owe our knowledge of those first days of New England's history. By origin a stout Yorkshire yeoman, Bradford was a man of high character and unyielding courage; he continued, with intervals, to be Governor of the colony until his death in 1657, and to him with Standish and William Brewster its establishment was largely due. When, in April 1621, the *Mayflower* left for England, only twenty full-grown men survived, and so slow was the growth of the settlement that at the end of ten years it numbered in all only 300 souls. But as one of them wrote: " We are well weaned from the delicate milk of our mother country . . . it is not with us as with other men whom small things can discourage, or small

47

discontents cause to wish themselves at home again." The discouragements were neither few nor small, but as an English friend wrote: " Let it not be grievous unto you that you have been instruments to break the ice for others. The honour shall be yours till the world's end."

Massa-chusetts

It will. But in a material sense the Plymouth settlement was insignificant as compared with Massachusetts.

That great colony was due to the initiative of men of substance, rich merchants and prosperous squires who in 1629 obtained a charter from Charles I, and in 1630 sent out a fleet of seventeen vessels, with 1,000 to 1,500 intending emigrants aboard. At that time the prospects for Puritanism in England were very dark. Charles I had (1629) dissolved his third Parliament, and there was a general apprehension that England had seen the last of Parliaments, as France in 1614 had seen the last (until 1789) of its States-General. Ecclesiastical affairs were dominated by Laud; Wentworth as President of the Council of the North ruled the north of England from York, as the Star Chamber ruled it from Westminster.

It was under these circumstances that the great Puritan exodus to New England took place. John Winthrop, having assured himself that Massachusetts would from the first be self-governing, became its first Governor, and with intervals ruled it until 1646. A Cambridge graduate and substantial landowner, Winthrop proved himself in his new sphere to be a man of great power, though not of liberal views. Of all the colonies so far planted in America, Massachusetts was in constitution the most democratic. But the attempt to make of the new Commonwealth a body-politic of saints inevitably resulted in religious exclusiveness. " To the end this body of the commons may be preserved of honest and good men it is ordered and agreed that for the time to come no man shall be admitted to the freedom of this body-politic but such are members of some of the Churches (i.e. Congregations) of the same."

So ran one of the earlier enactments of Massachusetts, and the policy thus accepted and maintained was responsible for the establishment of various daughter colonies which like Providence were afterwards incorporated in Rhode Island.

Providence was founded by Roger Williams, who as a young minister, educated at Charterhouse and Cambridge, had fled from England to avoid religious persecution. He insisted that " in soul matters " there should be no weapons but " soul weapons," and that " no civil magistrate should have any jurisdiction in spiritual affairs." Though selected as Pastor by the congregation at Salem, he soon discovered that Massachusetts was no place for a man of his liberal views. He was brought before the Court to answer for the doctrines he had preached and was sentenced to deportation to England, but avoided that punishment by founding an exile settlement at Providence, on Narraganset Bay. Mrs. Anna Hutchinson, another preacher, was like Williams accused of " antinomian " doctrines and banished. With a band of followers she established herself in Rhode Island, but subsequently moved on to Long Island, where, together with all her children and grandchildren, she was murdered by Indians. *Rhode Island, 1636*

Connecticut, another offshoot from Massachusetts, was recognized by its parent as a separate colony in 1639, and drafted for itself a constitution which, vesting the election of the Governor and Council, as well as the Assembly, in the whole body of freemen, has been described as " the first truly political Constitution of America." *Connecticut*

Several other townships closely connected with Massachusetts were subsequently united in the colony of New Hampshire. Maine, on the contrary, though geographically belonging to the New England group, had a different origin. In 1639 a Charter was granted by Charles I to Sir Ferdinando Gorges, an adventurer who had been associated with Essex in Ireland. He sent out a colony to Maine and, though an absentee, exercised absolute sway over the little settlement. *New Hampshire*

In 1643 Plymouth, Connecticut, and New Haven associated themselves with Massachusetts as " the United Colonies of New England." Each of the four colonies was repre- *The New England Confederation* sented by two members in a federal Council, which was empowered to decide all matters of high policy, though in the event of disagreement they had to be referred to the several legislatures. This Federation refused to admit Rhode Island and Maine, and though itself dissolved in 1684, it anticipated some of the principles embodied in the great Federation of 1787, and on that account is not devoid of interest.

Before the New England Federation came into being, the Mother Country was involved in a civil war which had violent repercussions in the colonies.

Chapter Five

The Commonwealth and the Colonies

THE LATER STUARTS

THE execution of Charles I and the setting up of the Commonwealth created a difficult situation in the colonial Empire. By 1649 English colonies had been established in Virginia and Maryland, as well as in New England and Maine. But between these two groups there lay the Dutch colony of New Netherlands on the Hudson and some scattered settlements of Swedes on the Delaware. There was also a large territory north of Maryland unoccupied as yet by Europeans, but presently to be assigned to William Penn.

The French were firmly established on the St. Lawrence, and Newfoundland, though held to be English in virtue of Cabot's discovery and Gilbert's abortive settlement of 1583, was not effectively occupied until after the Peace of Utrecht (1713). In the extreme south-west the Spaniards had established themselves (1643) in Florida. Guiana had been the goal of a succession of English adventurers from the days of Raleigh onwards; it had been considered by the Pilgrim Fathers as an alternative site to New England (1619), but it was not until 1651 that it was actually settled by Englishmen.[1] British Guiana was exchanged for New York in 1667, and remained in the hands of the Dutch until the Napoleonic wars. It only passed finally into English keeping in virtue of the Peace Treaties (1814–1815).

Events in England, following the fall of the Monarchy, had immediate repercussions in the colonies. The Puritan colonies promptly recognized the authority of the Commonwealth. Not so Virginia and Maryland, or the Bermudas, Barbados, and Antigua, all of which declared their adhesion

[1] Cf. Williamson: *English Colonies in Guiana and the Amazon* (Oxford, 1923).

51

to Charles II. The Bermudas (Somers Islands) had been in English possession ever since Sir George Somers had been marooned on them in the course of his voyage to Virginia in 1609. Barbados had been occupied still earlier (1605), but was first settled like St. Kitts in 1624. It was from St. Kitts that Nevis, Montserrat, and Antigua were occupied (1628–1632).

In 1649 many English royalists took refuge in the colonies which recognized Charles II as King. But Parliament refused to accept this denial of its authority. In 1650 it passed an Ordinance prohibiting trade with the recalcitrant colonies, and in 1651 sent out a strong squadron under Sir George Ayscue, who quickly reduced the Islands to obedience. In 1652 Virginia and Maryland submitted to a Parliamentary commission headed by William Claybourne.[1]

Meanwhile, Prince Rupert had been giving trouble to the infant Commonwealth in home waters.

Sea Power in the Civil Wars

To the success of Parliament in the first Civil War nothing had contributed more than the command of the sea. But in May 1648 a considerable portion of the Fleet declared for Charles I, and after his death was placed under the command of Prince Rupert. From the Irish ports, and from the Isle of Man, from Scilly and Jersey, which adhered to Charles II, there issued swarms of privateers which preyed upon English commerce in the narrow sea. Prince Rupert went farther afield and took rich prizes in the Mediterranean and off the Azores. But Robert Blake, who had been appointed Admiral and "general at sea" in 1649, put an end to Rupert's activities in 1650, and by the end of 1651 had compelled the surrender of the Isle of Man, Scilly, and the Channel Islands, thus depriving the royalist privateers of the harbours whence they had issued.

By 1652 Parliament had completely regained the command of the sea, and its authority was acknowledged by all the British communities oversea.

The Navigation Act

In that year, however, the Commonwealth was involved in war with Holland. The war was provoked by the

[1] See *supra*, p. 43.

Navigation Act of 1651, which forbade the exportation of goods to the colonies or the import thence of goods into England except in English- or colonial-built ships, the property of English subjects, having English commanders, and crews three-fourths of whom were English. Whatever the intention of that famous Act, its effect was gradually to transfer to England the carrying trade, hitherto almost monopolized by the Dutch.

The Dutch made a spirited effort to retain this monopoly, and also insisted on the rights of neutrals at sea. England, practically at war with France, claimed the right of seizing French goods in Dutch ships, while the Dutch insisted that their flag covered the cargo. The war which ensued (1652–1654) was fought, mainly between Blake and van Tromp, with alternating fortunes; but in 1654 a peace was concluded on terms entirely in England's favour. The Dutch accepted the *Navigation Act*, agreed to salute the English flag and to pay compensation for the massacre of English merchants at Amboyna. That massacre, which had taken place as long ago as 1623, had resulted in the expulsion of the English from the Spice Islands and their settlement on the mainland of Hindostan. Neither James I nor Charles I could ever obtain compensation from the Dutch. It was left to Cromwell to extort it in 1654. For by that time Cromwell had expelled the Rump of the Long Parliament: the Commonwealth had given place to the Protectorate.

Cromwell inherited the Elizabethan tradition in foreign and colonial policy. Like the Elizabethans, he was opposed to Spain both as the persecutor of Protestants and as a commercial monopolist. Only on the basis of free trade for English merchants and toleration for English sailors was he prepared to accept the alliance which Spain sought. His terms were too high for the Spanish king. " To ask liberty from the Inquisition and free sailing in the West Indies is," said the Spanish Ambassador, " to ask my master's two eyes." Accordingly, Cromwell put his Ironsides at the disposal of France in the last stage of her war against Spain.

Cromwell and the Colonies

53

Dunkirk was his reward. That seaport would replace Calais and, as Thurloe said, would " serve as a bridle to the Dutch and a door into the continent." Cromwell himself had considered the opening of another door which would also have served as a bridle both on the Spaniards and the Barbary corsairs. Gibraltar, " if possessed and made tenable by us," would, he suggested, " be both an advantage to our trade and an annoyance to the Spaniards." But that enterprise was postponed for half a century. Meanwhile, Admiral Blake was sent to the Mediterranean (October 1654) with one strong fleet. Admiral Penn, with another, was sent, with Robert Venables in command of a land force, to the West Indies. Blake made the English flag respected in the Mediterranean, released a body of English traders held captive by the Dey of Algiers, and inflicted drastic punishment on the corsairs, who had long been a nuisance to English shipping. Penn's objective was Hispaniola, but the expedition was ill found, and though Venables made three attempts to capture San Domingo he failed and the expedition drew off to Jamaica. Jamaica was taken without difficulty (May 1655), and against all the later attempts of Spain to retake it (1658–1660) was held, though at a high cost of mortality, with " grim determination." On balance, however, Cromwell was profoundly disappointed, and though he held on to Jamaica its captors were sent, in disgrace, to the Tower.

Meanwhile, Blake's fleet blockaded the Spanish ports, took much treasure from the Spanish Plate fleets, and, finally, sailing west in pursuit of them, destroyed the entire Spanish fleet in the harbour of Vera Cruz. With this great exploit to crown a wonderful career Blake, already a sick man, sailed for home, only to die aboard his ship as he entered Plymouth Sound (August 1657). His body was buried in Westminster Abbey, but was transferred to St. Margaret's after the Restoration.

The Restoration and the Colonies

Cromwell's body was treated with even greater contumely, but his spirit survived in the colonial policy of the restored Monarchy.

All " Acts " or " Ordinances " passed since January 1649 *Navigation* lapsed at the Restoration, but by a series of Navigation Acts *Acts,* (1660–1672) the policy of the Act of 1651 was maintained, *1660–1672* and in some respects extended. Broadly stated, the accepted policy was to prohibit the trade of foreigners with English colonies except in English bottoms, and to prohibit the export of colonial products except to England, where they enjoyed in some cases a virtual monopoly, in others a substantial preference. Certain commodities not enumerated might be freely exported from the colonies, provided they were carried in English ships.

Restrictive as such regulations sound in modern ears, they were in complete accord with the economic ideas of that time, and, prior to 1760, were economically advantageous to the English Plantations.[1]

Charles II was also responsible for an important change *Committee of* in the administration of colonial affairs. They had been *Trade and* committed by Charles I to a committee of the Privy Council, *Plantations* but in 1643 this was superseded by a special committee, exceptionally strong in personnel, appointed by Parliament. The committee of the Privy Council was restored in 1660, but in 1662 a Standing Committee on Trade and Plantations was set up. Consisting of forty " understanding able persons," it was the ancestor of the Board of Trade which, after various experiments in administration, was established in 1696. Of the Committee of 1662 Lord Shaftesbury was President, and John Locke was for a short time (1673–1674) Secretary.

Shaftesbury and Locke were responsible for drafting the *The* " fundamental " Constitution of the Carolinas—the region *Carolinas* between Virginia and Florida—which in 1663 were granted by Charles II to a body of eight proprietors, among whom were Shaftesbury himself, Lord Clarendon, and Monk, lately created Duke of Albemarle. Locke's constitution, though interesting as the work of a political philosopher, never really came into operation. Purely aristocratic in principle, it proved unsuited to a colonial Settlement, and

[1] See Sir W. Ashley: *Surveys Historic and Economic*, pp. 309 f.

was soon superseded by a constitution of the usual colonial type. Borrowing from Maryland the principle of religious liberty, the Carolinas welcomed immigrants from all sides. A settlement on the Albemarle river was largely recruited from Virginia, and became the nucleus of North Carolina. A number of Quaker exiles from New England also found a home there. South Carolina, with its capital at Charleston, was occupied for the most part by settlers who came direct from England or from Barbados. As a result of the ecclesiastical tyranny of Louis XIV many Huguenots also took refuge in Carolina, where they were welcomed by the Proprietors, though denied, for some time, political rights.

Slavery

The northern settlement did not prosper and was neglected by the Proprietors, who in 1729 sold it to the Crown. Even in South Carolina, with far greater advantages, progress was slow: by the close of the century the population hardly reached 10,000, of whom 8,000 were negro slaves. The great rice-fields and cotton plantations offered specially favourable opportunities for the employment of slave labour, and the planters, growing rich on the profits derived therefrom, left the cultivation of the plantations for the most part to overseers, devoting themselves meanwhile to the amusements and social amenities afforded by Charleston.

Georgia

The southern group was completed, but not until 1733, by the foundation of Georgia. Among the American colonies Georgia was unique alike in origin and characteristics. Its foundation was due to the philanthropic zeal of James Edward Oglethorpe, a Yorkshireman by descent but Squire of Westbrook in Surrey, educated at Eton and Oxford, an adherent of the Stuarts, aide-de-camp to Prince Eugene, Member for Haslemere (1722), prison reformer, and finally founder and ruler of Georgia.

General Oglethorpe

In 1729 this " Paladin of philanthropy " (to use Austin Dobson's description) secured the appointment of a Parliamentary committee to enquire into the state of the gaols and himself became its chairman. The committee gave special heed to the loathsome conditions and corrupt administration of the prisons, such as the Marshalsea, to which unfortunate debtors were committed. As a result of this enquiry the worst evils were eradicated, but, as Oglethorpe pointed out, many liberated debtors were starving about the town for want of employment. Accordingly, he resolved to provide in the New World an asylum for the failures of the Old World.

> " One driven by strong benevolence of soul,
>   Shall fly like Oglethorpe from pole to pole."

Pope did not exaggerate. Oglethorpe's humanity was equalled only by his indefatigable activity. He induced Parliament to vote £10,000 towards his colonial scheme, and to supplement it, later on, by a grant of £28,500 for the specific purpose of building a chain of twenty forts for the defence of the colony against native and European neighbours. Thus Georgia became the first field for State-aided emigration. Sums were also raised by the efforts of Oglethorpe and his influential friends; a charter was granted by the King (1732), and in November of that year Oglethorpe himself sailed with 116 emigrants and " 10 tuns of Alderman Parson's best beer . . . for the service of the colony."

Savannah was selected as the capital of the new settlement, and was carefully laid out. Thus Georgia, though not free from troubles, internal and external, started under the happiest auspices, and was from the first relatively prosperous. South Carolina welcomed the arrival of a neighbour who, with the help of taxpayers in England, could defend it against the French, the Indians, and—most feared of all—the Spaniards in Florida. Religious liberty was a cardinal principle of Georgia, which made a home for Moravians and other continental Protestants, as well as for Presbyterian Highlanders, mainly recruited from the survivors of the Jacobite Rising of 1715. A crowning distinction was, however, denied to Georgia. The High Church discipline of the Wesleys, who joined Oglethorpe in 1735, proved too strict for the colony, and their sojourn was consequently brief and unfortunate. Difficulties of a different order arose from the prohibition of negro slavery and from

57

restrictions on the importation and consumption of liquor. As a fact both slaves and rum ultimately found their way into the colony, where industrial and climatic conditions made slave labour indispensable. But by that time the noble founder of the colony had left it for good (1743), and in 1752 the Proprietors surrendered their charter to the Crown, which set up a government on lines similar to that of the Carolinas.

The Southern Group

Georgia well illustrates that extraordinary variety, in social, economic, and constitutional types, exhibited by the English colonies in North America. Yet it had much in common with the geographical group of which Virginia was the chief. That group reproduced the political traditions and social ideas of Cavalier as opposed to Puritan England. Though religion was "free" the Anglican Church was generally established. Politically, too, the southern colonies were not less "free" than the northern. Whatever their difference in origin, the colonies as a whole were self-governing, with a Council and an Assembly under a Governor who if not quite "constitutional" in the English sense, was not an autocrat. Democracy was, however, of a more robust, more aggressive type in the north than in the slave-owning south. In the south, social distinctions were, moreover, much sharper than in New England; the wealth of the upper classes was derived not as in the north from industry or agriculture, but from great plantations of tobacco, rice, and cotton, worked by servile or semi-servile labour, while the planters themselves dwelt in commodious mansions, living care-free lives and dispensing a generous if rude hospitality. Slavery also intensified the aristocratic tendency to concentrate landed property in relatively few hands. But if the southern colonies exhibited the typical vices of aristocratic societies they did not lack their typical virtues. They produced strong, self-reliant leaders to whom, when the time of trial came, the nascent nation looked for generals, administrators, and constructive statesmen.

New York

Geography has tended to outrun chronology. To return. The southern colonies were separated from New England by the Dutch settlement of the New Netherlands on the Hudson as well as by various settlements made by Swedes on the estuary of the Delaware River. In 1655 the Swedish settlements were absorbed by the Dutch, who in 1664 surrendered their colony, without a blow struck, to a small English force commanded by Colonel Nicholls. Charles II granted the New Netherlands to his brother, after whom it was renamed New York. It was formally ceded to England, in exchange for Surinam, by the Treaty of Breda (1667), but was retaken by the Dutch in 1673 only to pass finally into the possession of England by the Treaty of Westminster (1674). The Swedish settlements were after similar vicissitudes constituted a separate colony to be known as Delaware (1703). Meanwhile, the lands between the Hudson and the Delaware were sold by the Duke of York to Lord Berkeley and Sir George Carteret. In compliment to Carteret, who had made Jersey a secure refuge for royalists in the Civil War, the territory was christened New Jersey. Lord Berkeley, dissatisfied with the results of his investment, sold his share to a considerable body of Quakers who settled in New Jersey, and who subsequently bought out Carteret.

Among the Quaker proprietors of New Jersey the most *Pennsylvania* distinguished was William Penn, a son of the conqueror of Jamaica. Born in 1644, the son showed from early boyhood a strong tendency towards mystical pietism. His championship of the Quakers brought him into conflict with the authorities at Oxford, and in 1661 he was sent down from Christ Church. Committed to the Tower in 1668 for an attack on certain ecclesiastical doctrines he was released through the good offices of the Duke of York, whose proclaimed belief in a policy of toleration he believed to be sincere.

Before long Penn was in trouble again, and accordingly he decided to make a home for himself and his co-religionists in the New World. A debt of £16,000 due to Admiral Penn by the Crown was conveniently liquidated by the grant of some 47,000 square miles of territory west of New York, and extending from Maryland to the shores of Lake Erie (1681).

To the proposed name of Sylvania the King insisted on prefixing the name of a great sailor and his Quaker son.

In 1682 Penn himself sailed with some hundred Quakers for his new property, and on arrival summoned an assembly to whom he promulgated the Constitution, carefully drafted by the Proprietor himself and his friend Algernon Sidney. To Penn the new colony was, like his famous *Essay on Peace* (1694), a " holy experiment." Frankly democratic in form, the government was designed " for the support of power in reverence with the people, and to secure the people from the abuse of power. For liberty without obedience is confusion, and obedience without liberty is slavery." Government was therefore to be based upon consent, expressed through institutions broadly representative. All forms of religion, consistent with monotheism and liberty of thought, were to be tolerated, the sole qualification for citizenship being the profession of Christianity.

One of Penn's first acts was to conclude with the Indians a treaty which, according to Voltaire, was unique in the fact that unsealed by oath it was never broken. Relations with the Indians were, indeed, consistently friendly until 1752, when trouble threatened between the English and French and the Indians were drawn into the struggle that ensued. Great attention was paid in Pennsylvania to education, and the small amount of negro slavery in the colony, eight per cent at most, was purely domestic. British Quakers were predominant in the population, but there was considerable immigration from Germany and some from Switzerland.

From the outset the colony prospered: before the close of the century the population numbered 20,000, only one-quarter of whom were of foreign origin. Philadelphia alone had a population of about 4,000, and by 1750 was, with its 30,000 inhabitants, the largest city in the British colonies in America.

The first phase in the history of those colonies ended with the foundation of Georgia in 1733. Except for the bloodless conquest of the New Netherlands they were the product of peaceful settlement. But the accession of William III to the English throne marked the opening between England and France of the " Second Hundred Years' War." In that prolonged conflict the victor's guerdon was a World Empire.

Chapter Six

European Rivals in Three Continents

THE ANGLO-FRENCH DUEL (1688–1763)

The Revolution of 1688

THE Revolution of 1688 opened a new phase in the evolution of the Empire. Its effect upon the colonies themselves was slight. The power of the Crown, particularly in the proprietary colonies, was somewhat increased, but the effect of the change of Sovereign was negligible as compared with the disturbances which followed upon the abolition of the Monarchy in 1649. William III was, indeed, too deeply absorbed in European affairs to pay overmuch attention to the Plantations.

William III and Louis XIV

That absorption supplies the key to the period which opens with the Revolution. William III was primarily a great European statesman; his pre-eminent concern was with the balance of power in Europe, and in particular with the preservation of the independence of the Low Countries as a means to that end. Towards the constitutional conflict in England his attitude was on the whole reactionary. To any transference of the Executive to a Parliamentary committee he was not less strongly opposed than Charles I or Cromwell. If he made any concession to the Whig theory of government, it was solely because the Whigs were more ready than the Tories to support him in his contest with France.

Extension of the Conflict

In that contest three continents were involved. Hitherto international relations in Europe had only trifling repercussions in colonial affairs. The circumstances attendant upon the accession of Queen Elizabeth had led Englishmen to fight Spaniards whenever they encountered them; yet England and Spain remained for thirty years officially at peace. Cromwell's alliance with France against Spain brought England the rich prize of Jamaica; the Dutch war under Charles II gave us New York and lost us Guiana.

But the most serious conflict between the English and the *The East* Dutch occurred not in the West but in the Far East. The *Indies* East India Company received its charter from Queen Elizabeth on December 31st, 1600. It was thus about two years older than its Dutch rival, which was incorporated in 1602. But the Dutch Company started under better auspices and made more rapid progress. " The English Company," as Sir William Hunter picturesquely put it, " was the weakling child of the old age of Elizabeth, and of the shifty policy of King James; the Dutch Company was the strong outgrowth of the life and death struggle of a new nation with its Spanish oppressor." Down to 1610 the English Company had sent out to the East only seventeen ships, the Dutch had sent out 134. The earlier rivals of the Dutch were the Portuguese. The Dutch inflicted a series of defeats upon them; they conquered the Moluccas and Java (1607), and Malacca (1641), and so succeeded to the dominant position which for just a century the Portuguese had held in the Far East. That position was further guaranteed by the conquest of Ceylon (1638–1658) and by the occupation (1652) of the Cape of Good Hope, pusillanimously abandoned by James I in 1620. Meanwhile, English merchants had endeavoured to establish themselves in the Spice Islands, but were driven out by a series of outrages which culminated in the murder of ten of their number and the torture of others at Aboyna in 1623. The results were happier than the process. The Dutch remained masters of the Archipelago and drew from their monopoly vast profits; the English were compelled to concentrate their activities upon the mainland of India.

For ten years or more after their first arrival in India the *The English in* chief factory of the English was at Surat, high up on the *India* Malabar coast. In 1639, however, the Company, having purchased a site from the local Rajah, built Fort St. George, destined to develop into the capital of the Presidency of Madras.

The marriage of Charles II with Catherine of Braganza brought Bombay into the possession of the Crown. The King was glad to sell that little fishing village to the Company for an annual rent of £10, and in 1687 the Company made it the capital of their western Presidency in place of Surat.

Factories were also opened in several towns in Bengal, and in 1686 the English merchants moved down the river from Hoogly and laid the foundations of Fort William. Job Charnock, English agent in Bengal, purchased some of the adjoining villages from the Mogul Emperor and thereon laid, in 1697, the foundations of Calcutta.

Thus, by the end of the seventeenth century the English merchants had established themselves in the three great Presidencies of modern India. The English capture of Ormuz, the great naval base established by the Portuguese in the Persian Gulf, had marked the end of Portuguese ascendancy in the Far East as long ago as 1622. The rise of the Portuguese had been astonishingly rapid; its decline if less astonishing was even more rapid. Of the monopoly which for a century they had enjoyed much the largest share passed to the Dutch. But the Dutch, in pursuit of trade, preferred to dominate the rich Spice Islands, rather than involve themselves in the maelstrom of Indian politics.

The French in India Not so the French, with whom the English Company was compelled, in order to maintain their position as traders, to enter into a protracted contest for political supremacy in India. The duel fought in India by Dupleix and Clive was, however, only one aspect of a struggle that extended to three continents.

It was under Louis XIV that France attained the zenith of her greatness. Not content, however, with the position secured to the French monarchy by a succession of great kings and sagacious ministers; not content with the security which, thanks to Henri IV and Sully, to Richelieu and Mazarin, to Colbert and Vauban, France at last enjoyed, Louis XIV was determined to dominate Europe. That ambition brought him into conflict with William III and with the country whose resources, after 1688, William could command.

With the European aspect of the conflict this narrative is *The Anglo-* not immediately concerned. It must suffice to say that *French Duel* England was at war with France from 1688 to 1697, from 1702 to 1713, from 1744 to 1748, and from 1756 to 1763. From the standpoint of the overseas Empire the Treaties concluded between the two countries in 1713 at Utrecht and in 1763 at Paris were of primary importance.

Though the world conflict with France was integral, its factors must be broken up; the story, though a connected whole, must be told in parts.

In the Far East France was an even later arrival than *India* England. Between 1604 and 1664 several companies were chartered in France for trade with the Indies, but each was more short-lived and less successful than its predecessor. In 1661, however, Colbert came into power, and with the foundation of his East India Company (1664) the success of French enterprise in India really began. French factories were established at Surat, Masulipatam, and Chanderna-gore, and (1674) at Pondicherry, destined to become the capital of French India.

From the first, French ambitions in India were less com-mercial than political. Support came from the Govern-ment, not from the merchants, whose profits, compared with those accruing to the English and the Dutch companies, were negligible. To give further security to their position in India the French occupied the Isle of France (the Mauritius) in 1690, and some years later the Isle of Bourbon. Had Colbert's naval ambitions been fulfilled a great French Empire might have been established in India, but European domination in the East inevitably passed to the Power which held command of the sea. By that Power, after desperate struggles culminating at Trafalgar, supremacy was retained.

Yet in the middle of the eighteenth century every indica- *Dupleix* tion pointed to the triumph of the French. Down to that time the English traders had scrupulously avoided any inter-ference in the domestic politics of India. From embarrass-ing attentions on the part of the Marathas they deemed it prudent to secure immunity by purchase rather than force.

F   65

Two things made it impossible to maintain that policy. The first was the political anarchy which ensued upon the break-up of the Mogul Empire. The second was the determination of the French to take advantage of that anarchy and establish themselves as the dominant political Power in India.

Beginning under the Emperor Aurungzeb (1658–1707), the dissolution of the Mogul Empire proceeded, after his death, at an accelerated pace. Assailed from without by Persian (1739) and Afghan invaders (1747–1761), the degenerate descendants of Akbar and Aurungzeb became mere puppets in the hands of their own ambitious viceroys at Hyderabad, in Oudh, and elsewhere. The ruin of the Mogul Empire was completed by the assaults of the Sikhs and Marathas.

The first European governor to enter into closer political relations with the native Powers was M. Dumas (1735–1741), but his success, though striking, was far eclipsed by that of his successor François Dupleix (1741–1754), the most brilliant pro-consul who ever served France in India.

Dupleix seized with avidity the chance offered in 1744 by the outbreak of war between France and England. In 1746 a French fleet, commanded by Admiral Labourdonnais, Governor of Mauritius, appeared off the Coromandel coast and captured Madras. Boscawen failed to retake it, but by the Treaty of Aix-la-Chapelle (1748) it was restored (in exchange for Louisburg) to the English Company. Dupleix, though greatly disgusted at the rendition, persisted in his policy, and put his candidates on the thrones of Hyderabad and Arcot. But real power remained in the hands of Dupleix, who was declared Governor of southern India, and ruled, with absolute power, over a country as large as France.

Clive With the advent of Robert Clive the tide turned. Appointed a writer in the East India Company in 1742, Clive soon exchanged the pen for the sword, played a brilliant part in the siege of Pondicherry (1748), and in 1751 won undying fame by the capture and defence of Arcot. From that

66

moment the French prestige waned; English prestige waxed. Dupleix was recalled in 1754: and ten years later he died, poverty-stricken and neglected.

Clive returned to England in 1752, but went back to India in 1755 as Governor of Fort St. David. Hardly had he settled down before news reached Madras of the outrage inflicted by Suraj-ud-Daula, the young Nawab of Bengal, upon English men and women in the memorable Black Hole of Calcutta.

Within forty-eight hours a relief expedition from Madras *Plassey* was planned, and in December 1756 Clive at the head of it reached Bengal. The native garrison holding Fort St. William was routed, Calcutta recaptured, Hoogly stormed and sacked. Suraj-ud-Daula, having sued for and obtained peace from the English, then began to intrigue with the French at Chandernagore. Clive, with a small force, promptly attacked the perjured Nawab and inflicted on him a crushing defeat at Plassey (June 23rd, 1757). Plassey decided the fate of Bengal if not of India. Suraj-ud-Daula was killed and Clive's puppet, Mir J'afar, replaced him on the throne of Murshidabad. Mir J'afar's gratitude, if at first excessive, was evanescent. He intrigued with the Dutch traders at Chinsura, and they summoned their friends from Batavia to help them to expel the English. Things turned out otherwise. Clive attacked and captured Chinsura, destroyed its fortifications, and disarmed its occupants. Henceforward the Dutch remained in Bengal only as traders and on English sufferance.

A similar fate awaited the French in Madras. On the *Lally and* outbreak of the Seven Years' war (1756) Count Lally was *Eyre Coote* sent out to renew in the Carnatic the contest with the English. At first he carried everything before him, but on June 21st, 1760, Colonel Eyre Coote, commanding the English troops in Madras, inflicted on Lally a crushing defeat at Wandiwash. A year later Pondicherry itself surrendered, and though it was restored at the Peace to the French, it was only as a commercial settlement. With the destruction of their military establishments went all French hopes of political ascendancy in India. Coote's victories were as decisive in Madras as Clive's in Bengal. Of the other Provinces the English Company became virtually rulers. To England's victory in these wars several reasons contributed. Sea power and sound finance were at the root of it. But there were two reasons special to India. One was the contrast between the French and English Companies: the former the creature of the Government and looking to the State for sustenance; the latter a vigorous outgrowth of private enterprise, governed by non-official directors and sustained out of the profits resulting from commercial success. The second reason is to be found in the defective political strategy of Dupleix. On the plains of northern India, not in the heel of the peninsula, the political fate of India had always been decided. Dupleix made a fatal blunder in looking for the key of India in Madras; Clive found it, if accidentally, in Bengal.

The French in North America The crucial struggle between England and France took place, however, not in the East but in the West. To appreciate the relative positions of the combatants when that struggle began we must look back from the eighteenth century to the sixteenth.

The West Indies French privateers were beginning to prey upon Spanish shipping in the West Indies shortly before the Elizabethan seamen made their first appearance in those waters. The French, being mainly Huguenots, were, like the English, inspired by mixed motives; they went forth as crusaders no less than buccaneers, but as regards territorial acquisitions their efforts were more richly rewarded. Before the end of the seventeenth century the French were established at Guadeloupe, Martinique, St. Lucia, and Grenada; they shared St. Kitts with the English and Hispaniola (San Domingo) with the Spaniards.

Nowhere in the colonial field were the French so successful as in the West Indies. In 1664 Colbert established, in addition to the East India Company, a Company of the West to control all the French possessions in North America, the West Indies, and Africa. Although he imposed stringent conditions upon the Company, the sugar plantations, worked by African slaves, became a source of far greater wealth to Frenchmen than were the English islands to Englishmen. Frenchmen have always excelled as administrators and merchants rather than as colonists. Colour is less of a bar to them than to Englishmen, and consequently they have mingled more easily than have the English with natives. Their adaptability in this respect has not been an unmixed benefit to them as colonists, but it has eased the task of administration, and has led the French to prefer tropical plantations to colonization in temperate climates.

In pioneering work, however, they achieved brilliant *Canada* success. As early as 1524 Francis I employed one Giovanni da Verrazano, a Florentine, to survey the coast of North America from Carolina to the Gulf of St. Lawrence. The result of the survey was the annexation of the whole continent as New France, but Verrazano himself was hanged as a pirate by the Spaniards.

To substantiate the claim made on his behalf by Verrazano the French King sent out Jacques Cartier to explore the continent. Cartier, gratefully commemorated as the founder of French Canada, made three expeditions (1534–1540) to the West. He visited Newfoundland, set up, as a sign of possession, a wooden cross with the fleur-de-lis on the peninsula of Gaspé, and sailed up the St. Lawrence as far as Quebec. On his last expedition he took out two hundred emigrants, and attempted, with the help of the Sieur de Robeval, to plant a colony on the banks of the St. Lawrence. This first attempt failed ; but it was several times renewed under Henri IV, and at last (1608) Samuel Champlain built some wooden sheds on high ground on the northern bank of the St. Lawrence. That was the beginning of the great city of Quebec. Montreal was founded as a refuge for converted Indians in 1640. In the meantime Champlain had carried out a series of explorations on the Ottawa River and in the region of the Great Lakes. His work was interrupted in 1629 when Sir David Kirke, in command of an English squadron, captured the French foodships and starved

Quebec into surrender. But in 1632 Charles I restored Canada, including Acadia [1] (Nova Scotia) and Cape Breton, to France. Champlain was forthwith reinstated as Governor, but died in 1635. He had found the key to the Far West, and had left upon French-speaking Canada an impress that has never been obliterated. Champlain was said to have " esteemed the salvation of a soul worth more than the conquest of an empire." He called to his aid Franciscan and Jesuit missionaries, and it was they who carried, into the barren regions of the Great Lakes and the Ohio Valley, the Cross of Christ and the Empire of France.

Louisiana

It was a Jesuit Father, Marquette, who, accompanied by a small band of Frenchmen and Indians, set out from Lake Michigan to explore the Mississippi. Marquette reached the Arkansas River, and in 1682 La Salle, a fur trader, carried on the work, tracing the course of the great river from its source to its mouth. La Salle annexed the region on the delta of the Mississippi, and in honour of *le roi soleil* christened it Louisiana. A fleet of four vessels with 280 emigrants on board left La Rochelle in 1684; the colony of Louisiana was launched, and in 1717 New Orleans was founded.

Anglo-French Wars

Four years earlier the signature of the Treaty of Utrecht had marked the close of the second round in the duels between England and France.

The duel had actually begun in 1689, and the first round ended with the conclusion of the Treaty of Ryswick (1697). But that Treaty represented no more than a truce. Both combatants wanted their hands free to deal with the important, and seemingly imminent, problem of the succession to the Spanish Throne. In the colonial field the Treaty of Ryswick led to a mutual restitution of almost all the conquests made in the war. The French thus recovered Pondicherry from the Dutch and Acadia from the English, and in addition they retained all the forts taken in the Hudson Bay territory, except Fort Albany.

[1] Acadia is geographically a loose expression, sometimes signifying Nova Scotia only, sometimes including New Brunswick, which was definitely separated from Nova Scotia in 1784.

The second round (1702-1713) had far more definite and, from an English point of view, much more satisfactory results.

The Treaty of Utrecht, by which it was brought to an end, was immensely significant. Louis XIV did indeed realize a life-long ambition when he put his grandson, Philip V, on the throne of Spain, but England's position in the Mediterranean was secured by the retention of Gibraltar, captured by Sir George Rooke in 1704, as well as of Minorca. *Treaty of Utrecht, 1713*

Not less satisfactory to Great Britain was the settlement in North America. The strong position won by Champlain, and confirmed by the Comte de Frontenac (1672-1698), might well have been fatal to the fortunes of the Hudson's Bay Company. It was not until 1670 that an English Company had been formed to promote the fur trade in the country discovered in 1609 by Henry Hudson, but it quickly developed a flourishing business, which it sought to protect by a series of fortified posts. Except Fort Albany it lost them all, in 1697, to the French. *Hudson Bay*

By the Treaty of Utrecht they were restored, and the English Company maintained its hold upon the Great North West until in 1870 their territories, covering an area almost as large as Europe, were transferred to the recently federated Dominion of Canada. Under the terms of that surrender the Company retained their posts and their trade, they received £300,000 in cash compensation, and retained certain rights and immunities. The native Indians were placed in Prairie Reserves, and 1,200,000 square miles of territory was assigned to half-breeds.

By the Treaty of Utrecht France had also to restore Nova Scotia (Acadia), though without any precise definition of boundaries, and the British claims to Newfoundland were confirmed. France, on the other hand, retained Cape Breton Island and other small islands in the St. Lawrence estuary, as well as the right to " catch and dry fish " upon part of the Newfoundland coasts. The fishery rights continued to be a constant source of friction between Great Britain and France until the agreement concluded in 1904.

Retrospective criticism discerns in the Treaty of Utrecht an important landmark in the history of the British Empire. The Whig politicians of the day viewed it otherwise. Lord Bolingbroke and Lord Oxford, the Tory authors of the Treaty, were impeached. The Whig critics were right in asserting that the Treaty gave the Bourbons a position of dangerous predominance on the European continent, but the control of the Mediterranean and the settlement in North America proved of far greater value to England than the " erasure of the Pyrenees " to France.

The Assiento Nor can another item in the peace terms be ignored. Nefarious as the traffic in slaves was ultimately acknowledged to be, it was commercially valuable, and by the *Assiento* the right of supplying the Spanish colonies with slaves was for a term of years assigned to the English South Sea Company. Charles II had attempted but failed to get the concession in 1667 for his new Royal African Company; in 1701 it was granted to a French Company; its transference to the English Company was, therefore, hailed with delight by English traders. The Company (which had been founded in 1710) acquired at the same time the right to send yearly one ship of 500 tons with general cargo to Spanish South America.

Jenkins's Ear The English merchants having got an inch seized an ell. Under cover of these concessions a large and lucrative but illicit trade was developed. On the other side the Spanish Guarda-Costas exercised high-handedly and not seldom with brutality their right of search. A *Return* made to Parliament in 1737 specifies no fewer than fifty-two seizures of British ships in the South Seas. The case destined to make history was that of Captain Jenkins, commanding the *Rebecca*. Jenkins's ear was cut off and sent with an insulting message to the British Government. His story and his ear were got hold of by the Opposition, and became the subject of a dramatic debate in the House of Commons. Doubts were cast upon the story: it was said that the ear had been procured as an " exhibit " from St. Thomas's Hospital, but the story has been substantiated, after critical examination of

72

the evidence, by modern historians.[1]   Nor was the outrage an isolated one; dozens of such cases had occurred; excitement in England rose to fever pitch, and in 1739 the peace-loving Walpole was forced into the war against Spain, popularly known as the " War of Jenkins's Ear."

The war, commercial and colonial in origin, quickly widened out into a war in three continents, known in Europe as the war of the Austrian Succession, or alternatively and more accurately as the First Silesian war.

War of the Austrian Succession

In Europe, England fought as the champion of Maria Theresa against Frederick the Great, who was supported from diverse motives by France, Spain, and Bavaria.   Not, however, until 1744 did France formally declare war on England, though, as the allies of Bavaria and Austria respectively, their armies had already encountered each other at Dettingen (1743).   But with the successive phases of the European war this narrative is not concerned.

The contest between the French and the English Companies in India has been already described.   The critical contest was in America.

The policy pursued by the two great Bourbon Powers, in particular the " Family Compacts " of 1733 and 1743, had gone far to justify the fears of William III and his Whig disciples.   In America, at any rate, France and Spain presented a united front to Great Britain.

Between 1739 and 1763 war, sometimes formal, sometimes local and unofficial, was almost continuous.   In 1739 Admiral Vernon captured Puerto Bello but failed to hold it.   Nor were his attacks upon Cuba and Cartagena more successful.   Admiral Anson was at the same time despatched to the Pacific.   With an ill-equipped squadron he rounded Cape Horn, raided some Spanish towns on the Pacific Coast, captured a rich treasure ship, and ultimately returned home by the Indian Ocean and the Cape of Good Hope.   He had accomplished nothing.   But the terrain of the decisive conflict between Great Britain and the Bourbon Powers was in North America.

[1] E.g. Sir J. K. Laughton: *English Historical Review*, IV, pp. 741-749.

The Seven Years' War

The position of the combatants at the opening of the contest must be realized. France was firmly established on the two great rivers, the St. Lawrence in the north and the Mississippi in the south. Spain held the peninsula of Florida. Great Britain held, besides Newfoundland, the Atlantic seaboard from Nova Scotia to Georgia. But the English strip was a narrow one, and the French were determined to confine it to the east of the Alleghenies. Could the French in Canada have joined hands with their brethren in Louisiana this object would have been achieved, and the whole of the vast hinterland from the Alleghenies to the Pacific would have been French. The gap between the Great Lakes and the northern limits of Louisiana was not wide, and the French sought to close it by building a series of forts. Despite strong opposition from the Indians they built a fort at Niagara (1720), to which the English responded in 1727 with a fort at Oswego on the southern shore of Lake Ontario. In 1731 the French built on Lake Champlain a fort known to them as Fort Frederic and to the English as Crown Point.

Louisburg

Actual fighting began in 1745, when a force from Massachusetts achieved a brilliant success by the capture of Louisburg, the " Dunkirk of North America." At the Peace of 1713 the French had retained Cape Breton Island and on it had built that great fortress to command the southern entrance to the St. Lawrence. Its capture gave immense satisfaction to New England and was, indeed, of great importance. The more bitter, then, was the disappointment of the colonists when by the Treaty of Aix-la-Chapelle (1748) it was restored to the French in exchange for Madras. But the Treaty was no more than a truce. Of the points at issue in Europe, India, and America, the war had settled none.

The Ohio Valley

Even the truce was ill-kept, especially in the Ohio Valley, where the French were bent on completing the scheme already begun. But Virginia, and in lesser degree Pennsylvania, awoke to the danger involved in the French claims. Between 1748 and 1751 at least three companies were

74

formed to promote English settlement and trade in the disputed region. The French response to this activity was the arrest of English traders on the Ohio and the building of several more forts, notably Fort Duquesne in a key position on that river. In 1754 Dinwiddie, Governor of Virginia, despatched a force to warn the French off. The force was commanded by George Washington, a young man of one and twenty, and though he established a fort at Necessity in the Alleghanies he could not hold it.

The position was serious. The English colonists in North America outnumbered the French by over 1,000,000 to some 52,000, but that might well have seemed to contemporaries their sole advantage. Strategically the French were well placed, and had they commanded the sea, and been able to complete, unhindered, their chain of forts, their position would have been well-nigh impregnable. They enjoyed, moreover, unity of command, while among the thirteen English colonies there was the utmost diversity of opinion and little community of interests. So much was this the case that not a single colony except North Carolina would send help to Virginia when the position in the Ohio Valley became critical. Realizing the defects thus revealed, the Home Government directed the colonial Governors to summon a conference to consider a remedy. The Conference met in 1754 and was attended by Indian chiefs as well as by a majority of the Governors. A scheme for a Federal Union, with a President appointed by the Crown and a General Council elected by the taxpayers of the colonies, was laid before the Conference; but though approved by the Conference it was rejected by all the colonial Assemblies. The author of the scheme, destined to fame as one of the authors of the Declaration of Independence, was a brilliant Bostonian, Benjamin Franklin. Yet not even imminent danger could persuade the several colonies to unite. In 1755 two regiments were despatched to Virginia from England under General Braddock, but Braddock fell into an ambush and with half his force was killed. The news caused consternation in England. War was declared in 1756, but opened disastrously. In the Mediterranean, Minorca surrendered (June 28th, 1756). Admiral Byng was made the scapegoat and shot. From Calcutta came the news of the tragedy of the Black Hole. Lord Loudoun, commanding a British force in the Ohio Valley, not only failed in his attack on the French but was compelled to surrender Oswego to the French Commander, the Marquis of Montcalm.

Pitt

In England, affairs were in complete confusion. The Duke of Newcastle, a man " not fit to be Chamberlain in the smallest of German Courts," was in power, solely by virtue of his enormous borough-influence. Popular indignation naturally fastened upon him. " To the block with Newcastle and to the yard-arm with Byng !" was the cry that resounded throughout London. In despair Newcastle besought the help of Pitt, sometime leader of the " Boy Patriots." Pitt refused " to cover Newcastle's retreat." Newcastle consequently resigned (November 1756). Pitt came in under the nominal leadership of the Duke of Devonshire. He was the idol of the populace: but popular support could not sustain him in office. It soon became clear that without Newcastle's countenance and the votes of his nominees no Ministry could survive. In April 1757 Pitt was dismissed, and for eleven weeks, at the opening of one of the most momentous of our wars, England was without a Government.

At last the inevitable happened. Pitt came to terms with Newcastle. The former was to have place and patronage: Pitt was to have power. He " borrowed Newcastle's majority to carry on the Government." For four years he carried it on with brilliant success. " I am sure that I can save this country and that nobody else can." That was his confident boast: his confidence was justified. " I want to call England out of that enervate state in which 20,000 men from France can shake her." From John o' Groat's house to Land's End the nation responded to his call. With Pitt's accession to power the tide at once turned. From India came the news of Plassey and presently of Wandiwash. Our ally Frederick the Great won two great victories, at Rosbach and Leuthen (1757).[1] Boscawen's brilliant victory off Lagos and Hawke's in Quiberon Bay (1759) established the supremacy of the British navy. But it was in North America that Pitt made his greatest effort and reaped his richest reward. Thither he despatched Admiral Boscawen, General (Lord) Amherst, and General Wolfe. Fort Duquesne was captured (1758) and rechristened Pittsburg. Cape Breton Island, with its great fortress Louisburg, surrendered in July of the same year. Ticonderoga and Crown Point fell to us in 1759, and Wolfe's great victory on the Heights of Abraham compelled the surrender of Quebec. Neither its defender nor its assailant survived. In death Montcalm and Wolfe, heroes alike, were not divided. A year later the Canadian campaign reached its conclusive close. Three British armies moved on Montreal: Amherst from Oswego, and thence down the St. Lawrence, Murray up the river from Quebec, and Haviland from Ticonderoga. Montreal surrendered on September 8th: French Canada passed into the keeping of Great Britain.

Nearer home the year 1759 witnessed the victory of the allies at Minden and Admiral (Lord) Hawke's naval triumph in Quiberon Bay. Truly, as Macaulay said, " the ardour of Pitt's soul had set the whole kingdom on fire. It had inflamed every soldier who dragged the cannon up the heights of Quebec and every sailor who boarded the French ships among the rocks of Brittany."

In 1760 George III came to the throne determined to " be King." There was no room for Pitt. Thwarted in his desire to declare war on Spain, he resigned (1761). " As an organizer of victory Pitt," says Grant Robertson, " has no superior in British history." Has he had an equal?

Pitt was well aware that the Family Compact between *Peace of Paris* France and Spain had been renewed in 1761. Consequently he refused to make peace with the Bourbon Powers and even

---

[1] The diplomatic revolution effected in 1755–6 had brought Frederick the Great into alliance with England against our former ally, Maria Theresa. The two constant factors in these wars were the world rivalry of England and France and the European rivalry of Prussia and Austria Hungary.

his successors were unable to conclude it until 1763. Though violently criticized at the time, the Peace of Paris was perhaps the most splendid Great Britain ever made. The broad result was that France was, politically, driven out of India and North America. She retained her fishing rights off Newfoundland and regained Martinique, St. Lucia, Guadeloupe, and Goree; but Canada, Nova Scotia, and Cape Breton Island were ceded to England, who also retained Grenada, St. Vincent, Tobago, Dominica, and Senegal. France restored Minorca in exchange for Belle Isle, and gave up Louisiana to Spain, who ceded Florida to England. The dream of a French Empire in North America was finally dissipated: to the westward advance of the English colonists there was no longer a barrier: from the Atlantic to the Pacific the vast continent was open.

Yet in victory so complete, in a Peace so brilliantly achieved, danger lurked. The next chapter will reveal it.

Chapter Seven

The Great Schism

DISRUPTION OF THE FIRST EMPIRE

"ENGLAND will soon repent of having removed the only check that could keep her colonies in awe. They stand no longer in need of her protection. She will call on them to contribute towards supporting the burdens they have helped to bring on her, and they will answer by striking off all dependence." That prediction was made to an English traveller in Turkey by the Comte de Vergennes. Vergennes was French Ambassador in Constantinople (1755–1768), and was perhaps the most distinguished French diplomatist of the eighteenth century. So precise and accurate to the last detail was his prediction that it is difficult to believe that it was not apocryphal.

But it was not only disappointed Frenchmen who foresaw the danger. There was acute controversy in England about the wisdom of retaining "a vast barren and almost uninhabited country, lying in an inhospitable climate, and with no commerce except that of furs and skins." This view was strongly emphasized by the sugar interest, who would have preferred to retain Guadeloupe and Martinique and to restore Canada.[1] Nor was it doubtful that, at the moment, the West Indian islands commercially were of far greater value to England than was Canada. But the strongest arguments against the retention of Canada were political and strategical. "The possession of Canada," said a distinguished advocate of rendition, "far from being necessary to our safety, may in its consequences be even dangerous. A neighbour that keeps

Canada v. Guadeloupe

---

[1] On this question cf. L. Grant: "Canada *versus* Guadeloupe" (*American Historical Review*, Vol. XVII).

us in some awe is not always the worst of neighbours."[1]

There was, however, enough of incipient imperialism in England to withstand these specious arguments. Guadeloupe and Martinique were given back to France; Canada was retained by Great Britain. The danger apprehended by the defeatists seemed in 1763 too remote to be seriously considered. Benjamin Franklin, for example, ridiculed the idea of a union of the colonies against " their own nation," which " they all love much more than they love one another." The lack of union among the thirteen colonies was notorious, and, as we have seen, was strikingly demonstrated in 1755. Nor was it surprising. Between each colony and some section of society or opinion in England the ties were very close. But between this colony and that there was, in many cases, little except English blood in common. Massachusetts, for instance, was rigidly Puritan in creed, stern and austere in character, mainly agricultural in pursuits, and intensely democratic in outlook. Virginia and Carolina were on the contrary Anglican and aristocratic, leisured and loyal, deriving their wealth from slave-worked plantations, the land of great mansions, wide hospitality, gracious social life, loyal to Church and King; not less " free " than Massachusetts or Maine, but exercising their freedom more gracefully, less defiantly.[2]

Colonial Defence

Colonial disunion had compelled the Motherland to assume the main burden, military and financial, in the recent wars. Nor were conditions greatly altered by the conclusion of peace. A fierce attack upon the British position was made in 1763 by a powerful Indian confederacy, and only a small force of British regulars saved Virginia and Pennsylvania from invasion and devastation. Such attacks were likely to recur. If successful they might well encourage the French to attempt to dominate the American continent.

Grenville's Dilemma

In 1763 George Grenville replaced Lord Bute as Prime

[1] From a pamphlet said to have been written by William Burke, a kinsman of Edmund's: quoted, with other passages, by Lecky: *Eighteenth Century*, III, pp. 268 f.
[2] Cf. e.g. P. A. Bruce: *The Social Life of Virginia in the Seventeenth Century*, New York, 1907, and (of course) Thackeray's *Virginians*.

Minister. Reviewing the situation Grenville decided that a small standing army, 10,000 men, must be stationed permanently in America. How was it to be maintained? The financial resources of Great Britain had been severely strained by the series of wars. The National Debt had more than quadrupled since the Treaty of Utrecht and now exceeded £133,000,000. Taxation was high, and there was much distress. That the colonies should make some contribution towards the expenditure on their own defence seemed entirely reasonable. But how was their contribution to be assessed and levied? For the method actually adopted George Grenville has been severely criticized. Grenville was not, indeed, a great statesman, but he was an honest and painstaking politician confronted by a dilemma. " I do believe," said Burke, " that he had a very serious desire to benefit the public. But with no small study of detail he did not seem to have his view carried at least equally to the total circuit of our affairs. He generally considered his objects in lights that were rather too detached." Burke was strongly opposed to Grenville's policy, but no more subtle or more just estimate of the man was ever made.

The problem confronting Grenville was this: granting the necessity for a standing army—and it could not be denied, assuming that it was reasonable that the colonies should contribute towards its maintenance—how was the contribution to be raised? Each colony had its own Government, more or less representative in form, but there existed no central body competent to legislate for the colonies as a whole, still less to impose taxation. How little the several colonies were disposed to make any sacrifices for a common purpose had been recently demonstrated. Only Great Britain, then, could impose, collect, and administer a common fund. The attempt to do so cost us the thirteen colonies.

Grenville's plan was twofold: the enforcement of the Trade Laws, and the imposition of a stamp duty. *Grenville's Policy*

The administration of the laws regulating colonial trade was so scandalously slack that the revenue derived therefrom fell short by £5,000–£6,000 a year of the bare expense of collection. Smuggling had become the staple trade of the colonies, especially the Puritan colonies. Grenville was resolved to put a stop to it. In 1764 he revised and extended the tariff, but on the long-accepted principles. He also gave notice of a stamp duty, which was passed almost un-*The Stamp Act* noticed by the British Parliament in 1765. The *Stamp Act* was estimated to produce only £100,000 a year, one-third of the cost of the standing army in America, but the principle involved—internal taxation imposed by a Parliament in which the colonies were not directly represented—was admittedly new.

Rockingham and Burke What happened ? It was the Trade Laws that the colonies detested; it was the *Stamp Act* they resisted. So stoutly, indeed, that in 1766 Lord Rockingham, Grenville's successor, repealed the *Stamp Act*, though the repeal was accomplished by a *Declaration Act* affirming the right of the British Parliament to tax the colonies. Burke, who was Rockingham's private secretary, declared that his chief's policy was entirely successful: " America in various ways demonstrated their gratitude. I am bold to say that so sudden a calm recovered after so violent a storm is un-paralleled in history."

Pitt and Townshend The calm was delusive. Burke and Rockingham had not touched the root of the trouble. In 1766 Rockingham fell, and was succeeded by Pitt. But Pitt was a sick man; by his acceptance of the Earldom of Chatham he had lost much of the popularity attaching to " the Great Commoner." Nor was there any cohesion among his colleagues. His Ministry was (in Burke's phrase) a " mosaic " consisting of " patriots and courtiers, King's friends and Republicans, Whigs, and Tories, treacherous friends and open enemies." The strongest man in the new Government was the Chancellor of the Exchequer, Charles Townshend, a man as reckless as he was brilliant. By him its American policy was dictated.

To the principle of Grenville's commercial policy Towns-hend strictly adhered, but he extended it by imposing new duties on tea, glass, and other articles. Moreover, the new duties were avowedly intended to produce revenue. But the revenue, though collected by British officials, was to be expended in and for the colonies, and the distinction they had drawn between internal and external taxation was respected. Since 1764, however, their views had advanced. Massachusetts led the way in an agitation against the new duties. One colony after another pledged itself to import no goods from England until Townshend's obnoxious measures were repealed. Townshend himself died before the end of 1767, and was succeeded at the Treasury by Lord North. Chatham resigned a year later. In 1770 the Ministry broke up, and to the delight of the King, Lord North became Prime Minister. During North's Ministry the power of the Crown was at its zenith : "everybody," said Horace Walpole, " ran to Court and voted for whatever the Court desired." North continued in office until 1782. Before he resigned the American colonies had been lost.

For three years after North's accession to office there was *Lord North* a lull in the agitation, due mainly to the partial repeal of *(1770–1782)* Townshend's Revenue Act. The lull was delusive. In 1773 the rupture came. The immediate cause was Franklin's [1] publication of certain letters written by Hutchinson, Governor of Massachusetts, to a private friend in England. The letters recommended that the colonies should be reduced to obedience by force of arms. How Franklin got hold of the letters remains a mystery; the result of the publication was disastrous. In December 1773 the Boston tea ships were boarded by " Mohawks " and their cargoes flung overboard. Philadelphia and New York refused to receive the tea consigned to them. The crisis had come. Concession or coercion was the only alternative. The British Government decided on coercion. The port of Boston was blockaded; the charter of Massachusetts was remodelled in an anti-popular sense; and a Bill was passed for bringing criminals, in important cases, for trial to England. Simultaneous with the coercion of the British colonies was a

---

[1] Franklin was at that time agent in England for Massachusetts, New Jersey, and Georgia.

notable concession to French Canada. The Quebec Act (1774) guaranteed to the French Canadians the maintenance of French law (save in criminal trials), the feudal land tenure, and the social institutions and customs with which they were familiar; it virtually established and in perpetuity endowed the Roman Catholic Church, giving to the clergy a parliamentary title to their landed property and to tithes and dues paid by Catholics. It defined the boundaries of Canada, assigned to it Labrador, and in the west reannexed to it the region between the Ohio and the Mississippi. This timely and statesmanlike concession, though deeply resented by the New England Puritans, undoubtedly secured the loyalty of the French Canadians in the coming struggle, if not, indeed, for all time.[1] The attempt to coerce Massachusetts had failed. Resistance spread. A non-importation agreement was widely subscribed, and, in September 1774, delegates from all the colonies except Georgia met in congress at Philadelphia.

The Philadelphia Congress frankly admitted the right of the English Parliament to regulate external trade and even to legislate for the American colonies, but it endorsed the resistance of Boston and asserted the exclusive right of the Provincial Legislatures over internal taxation. It demanded the repeal of eleven obnoxious Acts, asserted the illegality of a standing army, and concluded by a solemn protestation of loyal attachment to Great Britain. The protestation was sincere. " I am well satisfied," said Washington (October 1774), " that no such thing as independence is desired by any thinking man in all North America; on the contrary, that it is the ardent wish of the warmest advocates for liberty, that peace and tranquillity on constitutional grounds should be restored and the horrors of civil discord be prevented."

Opinion was, however, stiffening in England: a General Election in 1774 had shown the country to be almost unanimous in support of the King and his policy of coercion. North did, indeed, though with great difficulty, pass a resolu-

[1] See also *infra*, p. 105.

tion that if any colony would contribute to Imperial defence and provide regularly for the support of its civil Government it should be exempt from all Imperial taxation for purposes of revenue. The proposal was ten years too late. In April 1775 a skirmish at Lexington aroused the temper of New England. In June General Howe took Bunker Hill, but at such cost as to inspire the colonists with fresh hope. Meanwhile, a second congress had met in May 1775 at Philadelphia, and was attended by all thirteen colonies. North's conciliatory proposals were rejected as inadequate; bills of credit were issued, and it was decided to raise an army. The command-in-chief was entrusted to George Washington.

The war thus begun lasted until 1782, but it falls into two *The War of* distinct periods. From 1775 to 1777 it was a straight fight *Independence* between Great Britain and her colonies; from 1777 onwards it became increasingly a struggle of *Britannia contra mundum*. To follow the course of the war in detail is unnecessary. During the first period, the British army, despite the amazing incapacity and lethargy of its Commander, General Howe, on the whole held its own. Twice indeed Howe had a chance of compelling Washington to surrender. Twice he missed it. In 1776 New York and Rhode Island were taken by the British, who in 1777 won a decisive battle at Brandywine and captured Philadelphia. Before the end of that year, however, General Burgoyne, marching down the Hudson from Canada to join Clinton in New York, was hemmed in and compelled to surrender at Saratoga.

Saratoga marked a turning-point in the war. France, *French Inter-* who had for some time been sending unofficial help to the *vention* English colonists, formally came into the war on their side. To France the revolt of the English colonies offered an irresistible temptation. For three-quarters of a century England and France had been almost continuously at war. In the Far East as in the Far West, war had issued in triumphant victory for England. The revolt of the American colonies gave France a chance of revenge. It was naturally taken; but before the French formally came in they

insisted that the colonists should take an irrevocable step and declare their independence. On July 4th, 1776, the famous Declaration was adopted by Congress. The Declaration was actually drafted by Thomas Jefferson, John Adams, Franklin, and one or two others, but Cobbett was probably right when he said that whoever may have written the Declaration its author was Tom Paine. In 1776 Tom Paine published a famous pamphlet, *Common Sense*, in which, though its language was extravagant and scurrilous, the argument for independence was presented with great vigour. The pamphlet produced a marked effect. Nevertheless, the Declaration of Independence was obviously inspired less by English models than by French philosophy. The opening sentence ran: " We hold these truths to be self-evident, that all men are created equal, that they are endowed by their Creator with certain unalienable Rights, that among these are Life, Liberty, and the pursuit of Happiness. That to secure these rights, Governments are instituted among men deriving their just powers from the consent of the governed." It is true that these abstract declarations are followed, in the English mode, by a list of specific grievances alleged against " the present King of Great Britain," but the opening words are significant of a Parisian inspiration which, if indirect, can hardly be mistaken.

Britannia contra Mundum
France signed a Treaty of Commerce and Alliance with the Americans in February 1778, and forthwith plunged into a maritime struggle against England. Spain declared war in April 1779, and the combined fleets of France and Spain obtained, for a time, command of the English Channel. In 1780 Hyder Ali of Mysore, England's most formidable rival in India and the cordial ally of France, invaded the Carnatic, and in the same year Frederick the Great of Prussia avenged himself for England's " desertion " in 1761 by forming a League of Armed Neutrality in protest against England's enforcement of a blockade against neutrals. The League was joined by Russia, Sweden, Denmark, Austria, Naples, and even Portugal. When Holland joined it England declared war on her. The purpose of the League,

86

presently joined by France and Spain, was to enunciate certain new principles in International Law in regard to blockade and the trade of neutrals during war-time. But England, though she was fighting the world, was not yet beaten. Gibraltar, invested from 1779 by the combined forces of France and Spain, was heroically defended by General Elliot, and on January 16th, 1780, Admiral Rodney won a great victory against the Spaniards off Cape St. Vincent. Having brought succour to hard-pressed Gibraltar, Rodney sailed for the West Indies. By the end of 1780 a series of victories won by Clinton, culminating in the capture of Charleston, had brought back great parts of the southern colonies to their allegiance. But the end of the fratricidal strife was by that time in sight. Lord Cornwallis, commanding in Virginia, was cooped up with a small force on the Peninsula of Yorktown, and by a combined movement between Washington and a French fleet under de Grasse was compelled to surrender. Yorktown was virtually the end of the war; but before peace was concluded Rodney struck a blow in the West Indies which in Froude's glowing words " sounded over the world and saved for Britain her ocean sceptre." On April 12th, 1782, off Martinique, Rodney engaged de Grasse and by brilliant seamanship annihilated the French fleet. " On that memorable day," adds Froude, " was the English Empire saved. Peace followed, but it was peace with honour." [1] Public opinion in England had, meanwhile, begun to weaken, despite the dying appeal of Lord Chatham against disruption. On March 20th, 1782, Lord North insisted on the acceptance of his resignation. Lord Rockingham, who succeeded him, died in July 1782; Lord Shelburne came in, and in the following year peace was concluded. Rodney's victories had saved the West Indies, but Spain obtained Florida as well as Minorca. France recovered Pondicherry and four other towns in India, Senegal, and in North America the islands of St. Pierre and Miquelon, with certain fishing rights on the western coast. She also acquired Tobago and

[1] *The English in the West Indies*, pp. 13, 31.

St. Lucia. The American colonies achieved independence; the First British Empire was shattered.

Yet even in disaster there were compensations. The greatest was a lesson which needed to be learnt before England could build up an overseas Empire that would endure. Under the old colonial system, colonies were regarded primarily as estates to be worked for the benefit of the Mother Country. That conception was common to all colonizing countries. Yet even Adam Smith, while denouncing the trade policy of that day as a " manifest violation of the most sacred rights of mankind," was fain to admit that though the colonial policy of Great Britain was " dictated by the same mercantile spirit as that of other nations, it has upon the whole been less illiberal and oppressive than that of any of them." After the loss of the American colonies there could be no question of ignoring or even subordinating the rights and interests of dependent communities. England was constrained to act not in the spirit of an absolute owner but in that of a trustee.

Chapter Eight

The Second British Empire

THE NAPOLEONIC WARS

THE year 1783 appeared to contemporaries to close *The Remnants* a volume: we can see that it only ended a chapter. *of the First* The First Empire had indeed been shattered into *Empire* fragments, but the fragments that remained were not inconsiderable. Our immediate duty is to pick them up.

The West Indies had been saved by Rodney. The only serious loss in that region was Tobago, and that loss was not permanent. Warren Hastings had saved the embryonic British Empire in India. In Europe, though Minorca was lost, Gibraltar, thanks to Elliot and Rodney, was saved. In North America there still remained to us Newfoundland, the Maritime Provinces, and Quebec—but Quebec, though ruled from England, was a French colony. Many oversea possessions, then, Great Britain retained, and most of these were commercially valuable; but of colonies proper, great fields for the expansion of the British race, we had, in 1783, practically none.

Two other results of the American Revolution, omitted of set purpose in the preceding chapters, must now be briefly noticed.

The first concerned Ireland. The successful revolt of the *Agitation in* American colonies gave a powerful impulse to the reform *Ireland* movement in Ireland. That movement hardly touched Celtic Ireland; it was confined almost entirely to the colonists of British descent, and they, with few exceptions, were Protestants. Between the position of the Anglo-Irish colonists in Ireland and the British colonists in America there was much in common. Both acknowledged the sovereignty of the British Crown; both repudiated the right of the British Parliament to interfere in their domestic

89

affairs; both were anxious to get rid of the commercial restrictions imposed upon them by England and maintained in the interests of the English manufacturers. The successful resistance of the American colonies naturally encouraged the hopes of the Anglo-Irish.

In another way the American war reacted upon Ireland. The war put a severe strain upon the military and naval resources of Great Britain. Ireland was denuded of British troops, and its coasts, owing to the preoccupation of the British navy, were left open to the attacks of American privateers. In particular, the exploits of Paul Jones created a panic in Ireland. With a small squadron he hovered round the coasts in 1778, and in 1789 actually captured a ship of war in Belfast Lough.

The Irish Volunteers

The Irish Protestants resolved to arm in their own defence, and nearly 100,000 volunteers were ultimately enrolled. Like Cromwell's Ironsides, the volunteers had their " adjutators," and from defence they went on to politics. Organized in a representative Convention, they demanded equality of trade with England and legislative independence for the Irish Parliament.

Legislative Independence

England was not in a position to resist their demands. Henry Grattan, their most eloquent champion in the Irish Parliament, moved the fateful resolution which asserted that while the Crown of Ireland was inseparably united with that of England, Ireland was by right a distinct Kingdom, and that her King, Lords, and Commons alone had the right to bind Ireland. To that resolution effect was given by legislation in the English and in the Irish Parliament: the " Grattan Constitution " came into operation, and until 1800 Ireland was united with England only through the Executive controlled by the Crown.

The Rebellion and the Union

Thus far the " Irish " movement had been mainly confined to Protestants, who desired " Home Rule " but not separation. But the outbreak of the Revolution in France reacted powerfully upon Catholic and Celtic, as well as upon Protestant, Ireland. In 1791 the Society of United Irishmen was formed. Their object was separation. In 1798 rebellion, fomented by the French republicans, broke out. The rebellion was crushed, but it had revealed the dangers inherent in the Grattan Constitution, and in 1800 that experiment was brought to an end by the Legislative Union. The Irish Parliament was abolished and Irish members were, for the first time since Cromwell's day, brought into the Imperial Parliament at Westminster.

So much for the effect of the American Revolution upon *Domestic* Ireland. Another effect of it was to stimulate the demand *Reform in England* for reform in England. The mitigation of the criminal code, the abolition of the slave trade, though not of negro slavery, economical reform (actually accomplished in 1782 by Burke), above all, Parliamentary reform—all these questions were arousing attention in England, and to movement of opinion in their favour the American Revolution gave a powerful impulse.

In 1780 the Duke of Richmond introduced a Bill which anticipated all the demands subsequently embodied in the People's Charter. The Bill was rejected, and the outbreak of the Revolution in France postponed for a quarter of a century all consideration of domestic reform.

Meanwhile, revolutions of another kind were transforming *The Industrial* the social and industrial aspect of Great Britain, and were *and Agrarian Revolutions* destined to exercise a decisive effect upon the character of the Second Colonial Empire.

Down to the middle of the eighteenth century and beyond it, England was a country of farms, of villages, and small market-towns. The population was scanty and scattered. Of the eight and a half million people in Great Britain only about twenty per cent lived in towns; the vast majority lived on the land, and by the land which was mostly cultivated on the " open field " system. Not, indeed, wholly by the land; for between industrial and agricultural society there was no sharp distinction. Every cottage had its spinning-wheel; most of the farms had a hand-loom as well.

This social system was shattered by the coincidence of the *A New* Industrial Revolution and the long French war. Machinery *England* supplanted hand labour; industry was dragged out of the cottages into factories; the factories were aggregated into towns; a rapidly increasing population had to be fed and clothed. The open fields could neither feed nor clothe them. The enclosure movement, already initiated, with many other reforms in agriculture, by reforming landlords and scientific farmers, proceeded at a greatly accelerated pace; rents rose rapidly, farmers made (during the war) large profits; but money, though forthcoming, could not compensate the peasantry for the loss of their rights of Common.

In fine, from the Napoleonic wars there emerged a new England: an England of industrial towns; of factories, forges, and mines; of rapidly expanding overseas trade; of banks and financial houses; of capitalist farmers and capitalist manufacturers; of landless labourers and an urban proletariat. Upon this new England a new British Empire was based.[1]

A New Empire

The new Empire developed upon several distinct lines. The most important line led to the peaceful settlement by British men and women of vast areas, unclaimed by any European Power, and inhabited, if at all, very sparsely by aborigines. Such areas were found in North America and Australia, and settlement in those regions has led to the trial of a great and unique political experiment. The great Dominions of Canada, Australia, and New Zealand have by successive stages been admitted to the privileges, and endowed with the responsibilities, of self-government, and are now partners with the Motherland in the British Commonwealth of Nations. So also is South Africa, though it reached the goal of self-government by a different route.

The Fruits of Conquest

A second category includes a large number of colonies which belong to the British Empire by right of conquest. Some of them, such as South Africa, Ceylon, and the Mauritius, were the prizes of the victory of Great Britain over European opponents; others, such as the Rhodesias,

[1] For the agrarian revolution cf. Marriott: *The English Land System* (Murray, 1914), and for the connection of Economics and Empire cf. Dr. Lilian Knowles: *Economic Development of the Overseas Empire*, 3 vols. (Routledge, 1924, 1930, 1936).

represent the spoils of " native " wars. The Constitutional classification will demand attention in a later chapter. For the present it is enough to say that most of the British possessions obtained by conquest, as well as some of those resulting from peaceful occupation, are broadly classed together as Crown colonies. Besides these Great Britain administers a number of Protectorates and Mandated Territories belonging to yet other categories, and there are not a few possessions which defy orderly classification.

Thus the Second Empire presents almost every variety of governmental form from military autocracy to unfettered democracy, with many examples of intermediate species. With all these the ensuing narrative must deal.

The First British Empire was broken up in 1783. Before Great Britain could devote herself to the development of the Second, she had to fight the final round in her duel with France. *The Napoleonic Wars*

The later stages of the American war gave France, as we have seen, an opportunity for revenge which she did not neglect. But for the luxury of revenge she paid dearly. The Revolution of 1789 was precipitated, if not partly caused, by the financial chaos in which France was involved by her intervention in the American war. On the Revolution there followed the Great European war. Into that war Great Britain was drawn most unwillingly, but, in the event, it developed into a duel between Napoleon, master of the Continent, and Great Britain, mistress of the seas. Into the details of that great conflict this narrative cannot enter, but one aspect of it, being of supreme importance in connection with the British Empire, cannot be ignored. *The French in India*

Though beaten by Clive and Coote in the Seven Years' war, France had never abandoned the hope of regaining her pre-eminence in India. She hoped to regain it by intrigues with the Native Powers. Of those Powers the most formidable were Hyder Ali, the brilliant military adventurer who had established his dominion in Mysore, the Nizam of Hyderabad, and the powerful Confederacy of the Marathas.

With them the English Company wrestled for supremacy in India for half a century—from the first war with Hyder Ali of Mysore in 1767 down to the final defeat of the Marathas in 1817.

Fortunately, during the most critical period of the contest the English Company in India was represented by Warren Hastings, Governor of Bengal from 1772 to 1774, and Governor-General from 1774 to 1785. While Great Britain was losing an Empire in the West, Warren Hastings, almost unaided, was winning for her an Empire in the East. As in the West, so in the East, the French did all in their power to assist those who fought against us. They had their agents still at the courts of Hyder Ali of Mysore and of the Nizam of Hyderabad. They encouraged those Princes to seize the opportunity, while England was girt with a ring of enemies in Europe and America, to drive her out of India. Thanks to Warren Hastings they failed. Two years after the acknowledgment of American Independence, Hastings left India. He left the Company indisputably first among the rival Powers in India, and on the high road to paramountcy over the whole subcontinent. Three years after his return he had to face the ordeal of an impeachment. The ordeal lasted seven years and forty-five days. Hastings, though honourably acquitted, emerged from it a broken and a ruined man. Such was his reward for pre-eminent service to the Empire, for the redemption of a continent. " The valour of others acquired, I gave shape and consistency to the dominion which you hold there. I preserved it . . . and you have rewarded me with confiscation, disgrace, and a life of impeachment." Bitter words, but true. Of course Hastings made mistakes, but every mistake was magnified into a crime by malignant enemies, and of the more serious allegations most have been disproved by the judicial examination of evidence by Sir John Strachey [1] and Sir James Fitzjames Stephen.[2]

On the foundations securely laid by Warren Hastings, Lord Cornwallis, Lord Wellesley, Lord Minto, and Lord

---

[1] *Hastings and the Rohilla War*, 1892.   [2] *Nuncomar and Impey*, 2 vols., 1885.

Moira (Hastings) built. When Lord Hastings left India in 1823 the East India Company was not only the first among rival Powers; it was the dominant Power in India and the Far East. The most critical years in that period were those of Lord Wellesley's rule (1798–1805). The struggle which by arms and diplomacy he waged in India formed an integral part of the world-war between England and Napoleon.

From the outset of his career Napoleon had fixed on England as the enemy. He had also made up his mind that Egypt was the nerve-centre of the British Empire; but India was ever " the proud goal of his ambition " (the phrase is Fournier's). As late as 1811 he was still confident of achieving it; but by 1813 his project of invading India by land had " receded into the distant and uncertain future "! " In order to ruin England utterly we must seize Egypt,— for through Egypt we come into touch with India; we shall reopen the old route through Suez and let the other—by the Cape of Good Hope—fall into disuse." So the young General Buonaparte had written to the Directory in August 1797. In concluding the Treaty of Campo Formio (October 1797) he took the first step towards his goal by annexing the Ionian Isles. " Corfu, Zante, and Cephalonia," he wrote, " are of greater interest to us than all Italy. . . . They make us masters both of the Adriatic and of the Levant." " Why should we not take Malta ? " The question was addressed to his friend Talleyrand, who cordially favoured the Egyptian project " as a possible chance of driving the English out of India."

Napoleon and the East

Lord Wellesley's forward policy in India, cordially supported by Lord Castlereagh when President of the Board of Control (1802–1806), must be judged in the light of Napoleon's designs.[1] The Nizam of Hyderabad had an army of fourteen thousand men, armed, trained, and disciplined on the French model and commanded by a Frenchman. Another Frenchman—de Boigne—had trained and organized the army of Sindhia, the most powerful Prince in the

Wellesley and Castlereagh

[1] For the relations of Wellesley and Castlereagh see Marriott: *Castlereagh* (Methuen, 1936), pp. 76–107.

Maratha Confederacy. But the most cordial friend of France and the most bitter and persistent enemy of England was Tipu, who in 1782 had succeeded his father Hyder Ali as Sultan of Mysore. Towards the end of 1797 Tipu, with statesmanlike grasp of the world situation, proposed to the French Republic an alliance with the object of expelling the English from India. Once that was accomplished the French were to have Bombay.

A small detachment of Frenchmen and half-castes was accordingly sent to India. They organized at Seringapatam a Jacobin Club under the presidency of "Citizen Tipu," planted a tree of liberty, and proclaimed the French Republic one and indivisible. These proceedings, farcical as in retrospect they appear, might have ended in tragedy for British India had Lord Wellesley neglected them. He dealt with the situation promptly.

The " Subsidiary System "

Having formed a league with the Nizam and the Marathas he isolated and crushed Tipu, who fell in the defence of Seringapatam (1799). The authority of the English Company was henceforward unquestioned in the Deccan. In addition to Mysore, Wellesley took over the administration of the Carnatic, Tanjore and the Nawabi of Surat, a great part of Oudh, and brought into the net of his " subsidiary " system the rest of Oudh, the territories of the Nizam, and much of the Maratha territory as well. The mission which he sent to Persia (1801) was the first step towards the establishment of British influence in that country and the control of the Persian Gulf. Had he not been overruled he would have added to the security of India by the conquest of the French islands of Bourbon and Mauritius. The acquisition of Ceylon in 1796 was due largely to the courageous if calculating enterprise of a Scottish Professor, Hugh Cleghorn.[1]

Wellesley was recalled in 1805. With the aid of his brothers, Arthur and Henry, he had not only made the British Company paramount in India, but had dispelled all real danger of an invasion by Napoleon.

[1] For this romantic story, cf. *The Cleghorn Papers*, Edinburgh, 1927 ; see *infra*, p. 346.

Meanwhile, Napoleon had been allowed to initiate his *French Expedition to Egypt, 1798–1799* favourite project. In April 1798 he was appointed to the command of the army of the East. When his troops embarked at Toulon he revealed to them his ultimate ambition. " You are," he said, " a wing of the Army of England." It was thus that he regarded the expedition.

He occupied Malta, without resistance from the Knights of St. John (June 10th, 1798), and on July 1st landed in Egypt. Within a month he was master of that country. But Nelson was on his track, and on August 1st annihilated the French fleet at the battle of the Nile. That great victory rendered Napoleon's position exceedingly precarious; and, though he made a brilliant expedition into Syria and inflicted a series of heavy defeats upon the Turks, he was quick to perceive that his victories were rendered barren by the British command of the sea. Moreover, the rapid development of events in France convinced him that the political pear was ripe. He must return to pick it. He left Egypt to Kleber, evaded the British fleet in the Mediterranean, and reached Paris on October 16th, 1799. The *coup d'état* of the Eighth Brumaire (November 9th) made him master of France.

England remained mistress of the seas. The field of her *British Capture of Colonies* operations was, moreover, extended by the declaration of war against Holland (after its occupation by France, 1795) and by Spain's declaration of war in the same year against England. The series of naval victories won by England was practically unbroken. Hood's victory over a French fleet off Toulon (1793) was less complete than it should have been, but it was followed by Howe's victory off Ushant (1794)—the famous " First of June." Mutinies at Spithead (April) and at the Nore (May) made 1797 an anxious year for the Admiralty, despite the victory of Nelson and Sir John Jarvis over the French and Spaniards off Cape St. Vincent (February 14th), and Admiral Duncan's over the Dutch off Camperdown in October. Meanwhile, French and Spanish islands in the West Indies were taken, and sometimes retaken, and in the East Indies we deprived the Dutch not

only of Ceylon, but of Malacca, Cochin, their new settlement on the Malabar coast, Banda, and Amboyna. At the instance of the Dutch Stadtholder, then a fugitive in England, we occupied Cape Colony (1795) lest it should fall into the hands of France. In 1797 we took Trinidad from Spain, and in 1800 the loss of Minorca was more than compensated by the capture of Malta.

In 1802, however, peace was temporarily restored by the Treaty of Amiens. To France, Spain, and Holland England restored all her conquests except Ceylon and Trinidad. Malta was to have been restored to the Knights of St. John, but in view of the threatening attitude of Napoleon the restoration was delayed. The delay was bitterly resented by Napoleon, and led to the renewal of the war in 1803.

British Naval Policy   Down to this point the administration of the Admiralty, despite brilliant victories won by the sailors, was open to serious criticism. The criticism applies, indeed, to Pitt's whole conduct of the war. " Like a bad chess player," says Mr. Goldwin Smith, " he ran over the board taking pawns, while the adversary was checking his King." But against such amateur criticism may be set the expert opinion of Captain Mahan, who completely vindicated both the statesmanship and the strategy of Pitt. Mahan admits, indeed, " serious mistakes of detail," but he insists that Pitt's general conception was sound, that security—his " great object "— was achieved with complete success.[1]

The war, after its renewal in 1803, became more and more a fight *à outrance* between England and Napoleon. Trafalgar decided it in our favour. Trafalgar forced Napoleon to play his last card—the Continental blockade. The blockade exasperated and estranged his allies and his dependent Kingdoms, involved Napoleon himself in the Peninsular war —the " Spanish ulcer " that gradually drained his strength, forced him to march to Moscow, and by inevitable stages led to his final overthrow at Waterloo.

[1] Mahan: *Influence of Sea Power upon the French Revolution and Empire, passim,* and especially chapter XIX.

The Treaties by which the war was ended were of momen- *The Peace* tous consequence to the Empire. Castlereagh, who *Settlement and the Empire* negotiated them on behalf of Great Britain, laid down explicitly the objects at which he aimed. A prolonged peace based upon general security and stability was the supreme object. France was not to be punished too severely for the sins of Napoleon, nor in such manner as to provoke her to a war of revenge. Holland and Belgium, united as the Kingdom of the Netherlands, were to interpose a strong barrier between France and Germany, and secure the safety of England. In the interests of humanity, and to placate the English abolitionists, the slave trade was to be suppressed as quickly as might be. Heligoland, Malta, and a Protectorate over the Ionian Isles were the only territorial acquisitions in Europe that England could show for her immense sacrifices in men and money; but not in Europe did she seek her compensations. Outside Europe she retained such colonial conquests as were vital to her naval strategy, and she insisted there must be no questioning of her maritime rights, particularly the right of search. In the East Indies the French were limited to a commercial occupation of their factories, and except for police purposes were not to maintain any military forces whatsoever. The question of European ascendancy in India was thus finally set at rest. Java was restored to the Dutch despite the strong protest of Sir Stamford Raffles, who had persuaded Lord Minto to undertake its conquest in 1810 and had since governed it with eminent success. So also were the Moluccas. But the Mauritius, taken from the French, was retained (together with the Seychelles), in order to safeguard Great Britain's route to the East. More important, in that regard, was Cape Colony, of which Holland was permanently deprived. She received, however, £6,000,000 in compensation for the loss.[1] Part of Dutch Guiana was also retained. In the West Indies, all conquests except St. Lucia and Tobago, together with Trinidad (captured by Great Britain from Spain in 1797), were

[1] See *infra*, p. 160.

restored to their previous owners. The two latter colonies were amalgamated in 1889.

The year 1814 had witnessed not only the conclusion of the First Treaty of Paris, but the signature of the Treaty of Ghent between Great Britain and the United States. Of the war which had broken out between them in 1812 the sole redeeming feature was the loyalty and gallantry displayed by the Canadians. To Canada, then, the story belongs.

Chapter Nine

The Canadas (1763–1847)

THE EMPIRE LOYALISTS. THE WAR OF 1812–1814. THE EVOLUTION OF COLONIAL SELF-GOVERNMENT

THE loss of the American colonies decided the fate of Canada. Canada, hitherto almost exclusively French, was henceforward to be predominantly British. *The United Empire Loyalists*

Great efforts had been made by Great Britain, during the negotiations for peace (1782–1783), to obtain tolerable conditions for those who, in the war, had espoused the British cause. Those efforts were warmly seconded by France. But all to no purpose: the Americans were obdurate, and persisted to the end in their spiteful treatment of those who until 1783 had been their compatriots. Some of these United Empire Loyalists were men of position and considerable substance. Their property was doubtless tempting to a bankrupt State, but none the less the conduct of the victors was as morally unworthy as it was politically unwise. The American war was, after all, a civil war. Moderation in victory, wise in all wars, is especially prudent in wars between brethren. How many good citizens the future United States lost by their intemperance cannot be precisely estimated. One estimate puts the number of Loyalists during the war at one-third of the whole population. Alexander Hamilton estimated that in 1775 only half the people were " Whigs," and that even in 1782 they did not number more than two-thirds. The Loyalists were strongest in New York colony, where they numbered 90,000 out of a total of 100,000, and of the migrants into Canada a third came from that colony. Many Loyalists had from 1775 onwards taken refuge in England.[1] For these refugees the British

---

[1] A. G. Bradley: *The United Empire Loyalists*, p. 117—an excellent book, to which these paragraphs owe much.

101

Government as well as private citizens did what they could, either in the form of temporary relief, or of pensions ranging from £50 to £200 a year. Even before the war ended some £40,000 a year was expended upon them. Nevertheless, the beneficiaries complained that their reception in England was chilly, and that the relief given to them was inadequate.

Migration to Nova Scotia

The refugees in England were only a trickle as compared with the flood that burst into Nova Scotia. Before 1783 over 3,000 Loyalists had drifted into that Province, most of them entirely destitute, and had been provided by the British Government with food, clothes, and shelter, as well as with loans and pensions on the same scale as those granted in England. The Loyalists found Nova Scotia inhabited by a mixed population, of whom perhaps half were Germans or Swiss while the rest were Puritans from New England— nearly 14,000 in all. After the Peace there was a sudden influx of some 30,000–35,000 people. Hasty preparations had been made for their arrival, but these preparations were inevitably inadequate, and great hardships were endured by the migrants. Anything, however, seemed to them preferable to transference to a foreign flag. Their one anxiety, as a contemporary correspondent wrote, was to "remove within the British territories in order to exculpate themselves from being accessory to the many Bloody and inhuman Cruelties perpetrated against the King's good subjects to the everlasting Infamy of the perpetrators of the Division of the British Empire." [1] "The people," wrote another contemporary, "are reduced, for the most part, to begging by the event of the War—and this uncultivated and rude country will require their utmost exertions for the bare subsistence of their Wives and children." Grants of land were made to them on a generous scale: to field officers 5,000 acres, to captains 3,000, to subalterns 2,000, and 200 to privates. But the land had to be cleared, and (in all but a few cases) shanties had to be built. The Government provided timber as well as stock, seed, and implements, together with rations

[1] Quoted in *The Times*.

102

for the first three years.   Yet all that was done amounted to no more than a mitigation of the sufferings the migrating Loyalists had to endure.

Between the new-comers and earlier settlers there arose, *New Bruns-* almost at once, a good deal of friction.   Consequently in *wick* 1784 the immigrants, who had mostly settled in the rich and beautiful valley of the St. John, established in that region a separate colony.   It received the name New Brunswick, and was placed under its own Governor, assisted by a nominated Council and an elected Assembly.   For its earliest officials the new colony could draw upon some of the ablest and most experienced of the Loyalists, and consequently it started its independent existence under auspices of exceptional promise.

Cape Breton Island, to which some 3,000 Loyalists found *Cape Breton* their way, also received a separate administration (1784) *and Prince* under a Lieutenant-Governor, but without a representative *Edward Islands* Assembly.[1]

Prince Edward Island had enjoyed a separate administration since 1768, but the whole island had been granted in considerable estates to about a dozen ex-officers of the British army.   After 1783 these proprietors, largely absentees, offered grants of land to the Loyalists on the same scale as the grants in Nova Scotia.   After they had worked them up into improved farms, questions were raised as to titles. Disputes ensued, and dragged on for many years.   Nevertheless, the Maritime Provinces as a whole prospered greatly during the half-century or more which followed on the Loyalist immigration.   In recent years, however, they have complained with some bitterness, and not groundlessly, that their economic interests have been subordinated to those of the larger units of the Canadian Federation.

Of those units the greatest is Ontario, then known as *Upper Canada* Upper Canada.   A large number of Loyalists settled from the first in that Province.   By 1795 they numbered 30,000, as compared with some 10,000 to 15,000 who had found a home in Lower Canada (Quebec).   In the latter Province,

---

[1] It was reannexed to Nova Scotia in 1820.

however, the immigrants formed only a small minority in a French population of about 150,000. In Upper Canada and in the Maritimes the American Loyalists were soon reinforced by emigrants from the Motherland, particularly from the Highlands of Scotland. Some years later (1804) the whole regiment of Glengarry Fencibles, led by their priest Father (Bishop) Macdonnall, with their families—one thousand souls in all—arrived in Canada and settled in the County of Glengarry, west of Montreal. They were welcomed by many compatriots already settled there. They have always retained their faith, and still form an important and easily recognizable section of the inhabitants of that district. After the Peace of 1815 there was a further and larger migration, including a large number of officers from Great Britain.

In all, the British Government spent £6,000,000 in assistance and compensation to the Empire Loyalists. One-third of it went to former inhabitants of New York. The amounts paid to individuals varied from £45,000 granted to Sir John Johnson down to £10 to £15 to humbler individuals. But the money was well spent. From 1783 down to the present day the Loyalist families have formed the most valuable element in the social, political, and economic life of all Canada east of the Rockies.

Constitutional Development, 1761–1791 The influx of the Loyalists and in particular the creation of Upper Canada necessitated a constitutional readjustment.

New France had been governed on the same lines as old France. Originally administered under charters granted to a succession of companies, Canada presently took the shape of a Royal Province with a Governor, Bishop, Intendent, and a Sovereign Council, which was the counterpart of a Provincial *Parlement* in the old country. Count Frontenac did summon a *States-General* in 1672, but was severely snubbed for his pains by Colbert. There was, in truth, neither need of nor desire for Representative Institutions of the English type. Economically and socially New France was organized on the seignorial system, which survived until 1854 and left a permanent impress upon the life of Lower Canada.

For several years after the British conquest Canada was governed under the *Régime Militaire*, and the English soldiers who ruled it won the hearts of the French Canadians by the paternal kindness of their administration. In 1764 the *Régime Militaire* was, however, superseded by the establishment of *Civil Government*. The Executive was vested in a Governor and Council, and it was proposed to call a Representative Assembly. The Roman Catholic Church and the French legal system were to be proscribed and the Anglican Church and English law were to take their place. In fine, the Home Government intended to transform Quebec into an English colony. General Murray (Governor 1764–1768) and the administrators on the spot, notably Sir Guy Carleton (Governor from 1768 to 1778 and again from 1786 to 1796), recognized that even if this were desirable it was impossible. The divergence of outlook between Westminster and Quebec resulted in great confusion in the administration of the colony. Only the common sense of the Governors and their determination not to allow the situation then developing in the English colonies to be reproduced in Quebec saved the latter from complete chaos, and perhaps deterred it from rebellion.

The position was clarified by the passing of the *Quebec Act*. The motives that inspired the Act have been variously construed. Were they beneficent or sinister? Was the Act passed to placate the French Canadians or to counteract the intrigues of the English colonies? Anyway, the Act reversed the policy of 1764. There was to be no Representative Assembly, but the Governor was to be assisted by an enlarged and nominated Council for which Roman Catholics were to be eligible. Taken as a whole, the Act undoubtedly went far to stabilize and perpetuate French influence in North America.[1] At the same time, it may well be argued that it saved Canada for the British Empire.

Régime Militaire

Quebec Act, 1774

[1] See *supra*, p. 84.

If, however, Carleton's cautious administration of the *Quebec Act* maintained the ascendancy of the French system, it also averted the absorption of Canada into the American Republic.

The influx of Loyalists created a new situation. The American Loyalists possessed, no less than the rebels, the instinct for " liberty " in the English sense, nor were they slow to demand in their new homes the political and legal systems to which they had been accustomed in the old. Nova Scotia had possessed a Representative Assembly since 1758, Prince Edward Island since 1773, and New Brunswick obtained it in 1784. In Canada the French had been well content without one; the British immigrants were not. Moreover, it soon became clear that the French and English were in many other respects ill-yoked partners. They were sharply divided in religion, in agricultural methods, and in regard to land-tenure. French land-tenure differed altogether from English, the two legal systems had nothing in common: in fine, the whole political and social outlook of the two peoples was fundamentally opposed. Pitt accordingly decided that it was necessary to separate Upper Canada from Quebec. There was indeed to be a Governor-in-Chief for the whole of Canada, but each Province was to have its own Lieutenant-Governor, assisted by an Executive Council nominated by and responsible to him. Each Province was also to have a Legislature of two Houses: a nominated Legislative Council and an elected Assembly. The Assembly was entrusted with powers of taxation but not with control over the Executive. In both Provinces the criminal code was to be that of England; English land-tenure was to be the rule in Upper Canada; in Lower Canada the French system was to continue unless English tenure was preferred by the grantee. In Upper Canada land was set aside for the " support and maintenance of a Protestant clergy," and parsonages were to be erected and maintained " according to the establishment of the Church of England." In Lower *The Constitu-* Canada the Catholic clergy were to have their tithes and *tional Act, 1791* dues as of old. The Act of 1791 also gave permission for the creation of a local hereditary nobility with the right to sit in the Legislative Councils. But Lord Dorchester (as Carleton had become) warned the Imperial Government that " the fluctuating state of prosperity (in Canada) would expose all hereditary honours to fall into disregard." He was right: the permission was never exercised, though in later years several Canadians, like Lord Strathcona, have been rewarded for eminent services to the Dominion and the Empire with peerages of the United Kingdom.

The *Constitutional Act* of 1791 was a statesman-like measure; it reflected great credit on Lord Dorchester, on Pitt, and on the Imperial Parliament, and it provided a model for the intermediate stage in the evolution of self-government throughout the Empire. In Canada, the Act gave, for some years, great satisfaction. Doctrinaires subsequently complained that a Responsible Executive was withheld; but for that experiment neither Province was ready—any more than the English Parliament had been ready in the fifteenth century. As time went on, however, various defects in the Act of 1791 were revealed, and contributed to the outbreak of the rebellion of 1837 in both provinces.

In the meantime the fortitude of both Canadas, no less than their loyalty to the British Crown, was subjected to a severe test.

On June 18th, 1812, the United States declared war upon Great Britain. The majority in favour of the declaration was small in both Houses of Congress. So strongly was it opposed by the Northern States that they threatened secession; but the " War-Hawks " of Kentucky were spoiling for a fight, and in other States there was a considerable party which welcomed an opportunity for manifesting gratitude towards France and for the complete and final extinction of British sovereignty on the American continent.

Lord Castlereagh, the Secretary of State for War and the Colonies, had as far back as 1807 foreseen the possibility of war, and had warned Lord Chatham (Master-General of

The War of 1812 1814

107

THE BRITISH EMPIRE

Ordnance) that though Canada would have to rely mainly
on its local militia for its own defence, it might be well to
send out 10,000 to 12,000 regular troops as a reinforcement.
Castlereagh thought it unlikely, however, that "if our navy
is alert and proper defensive exertions are made on our part
the Americans would attack in force, more especially in view
of the fact that the northern States of the Union . . . are
those which are least disposed to a contest with us." [1]
Castlereagh might have added a further reason for the attitude of the New England States. They were making great
profit out of the war by the supply of provisions, which being
exported via Halifax, (N.S.) or by the St. Lawrence, were
not only exempt from interference by British ships, but also
evaded the embargo imposed in 1807 by the American
Congress.

Napoleon's Continental System   Maritime rights, then, were the root of the trouble. After
Trafalgar the only weapon with which Napoleon could strike
at England was trade. Accordingly, in November 1806 he
issued from Berlin the first of a series of Decrees which built
up his *Continental System*. Those Decrees declared the
British Isles to be in a state of blockade; interdicted all trade
with England; ordered all British merchandise to be confiscated wherever found; and forbade the reception in France
or allied ports of any ship coming from Great Britain or her
colonies.

The Orders in Council   The British Government retorted by the *Orders in Council*
(January–November 1807), which declared a blockade of
all ports from which the British flag was excluded, insisted
upon the right of search, and forbade the sale of ships from
a belligerent to a neutral. Napoleon's *Decrees* and the *Orders
in Council* inflicted a terrible blow upon American trade.
Particularly did America resent and resist the right of
search, which was not always exercised with tenderness for
neutrals. In June 1807 the American frigate *Chesapeake*
refused to allow H.M.S. *Leopard* to search her. The
Leopard fired, killed three men, wounded others, and carried
off four seamen. One of them, an Englishman, was hanged

[1] *Castlereagh Correspondence*, VII, pp. 104–106.

108

as a deserter; the rest were Americans who having been impressed into the British service had escaped. Many British seamen had similarly escaped and taken service under the American flag. The British Government, therefore, while apologizing for the *Chesapeake* incident, refused to renounce the right of impressment. In 1809 the United States, by the *Non-Intercourse Act*, prohibited trade with England or France, but a year later the Act was withdrawn in favour of France, on Napoleon's announcement that he had rescinded the Decrees in favour of America. The announcement was a blind; and the Americans were deservedly punished by the seizure of all their ships and goods thus lured into French ports.

Relations between Great Britain and America became more and more strained, until on June 23rd, 1812, the British *Orders in Council* were unconditionally withdrawn. It was too late. On June 18th America had declared war.

At the outset the conditions looked greatly in favour of America. The population of the independent States— 3,000,000 at the time of the disruption—had by 1812 more than doubled. Canada had a population of only 600,000, and of these many were recent comers from America, and their attitude was doubtful. The hands of Great Britain were tied. Not until 1814, after the brilliant culmination of Wellington's campaigns in the Peninsula, could Great Britain reinforce the few regulars who in 1812 garrisoned Canada. In the summer of 1814 some 16,000 of Wellington's veterans reached Canada: but the war was then nearing its close.

Outbreak of War

The fighting had been almost entirely confined to the Niagara frontier and the district of the Great Lakes. The New England States had no stomach for the war, and the Maritimes were left unmolested. In the first year of the war the Canadians not only repelled the invaders but carried the war into America. These early successes were largely due to the promptitude and brilliant generalship of General Sir Isaac Brock, the administrator of Upper Canada. Unfortunately Brock was killed in a battle at Queenstown on October 13th, 1812, but his gallantry had already gone far to save Canada for the Empire.

The Naval War

On the whole, the American navy showed itself, especially on the Great Lakes, superior to the few frigates Great Britain could spare from Europe. The only naval engagement redounding to the credit of the British navy was the famous duel outside Boston harbour between the *Shannon*, a British frigate, and the *Chesapeake* (1813). A whole flotilla of boats, filled with the citizens of Boston, sailed out of the harbour to witness the expected triumph of the *Chesapeake*. But within fifteen minutes after the first shot was fired the British flag was hoisted in the *Chesapeake*: seventy of her seamen were killed, and her gallant captain lay dying. Captain Brooke, who commanded the *Shannon*, was disabled by wounds: so it fell to Lieutenant Wallis, a Nova Scotian by birth, to take the *Shannon* and her prize into Halifax, where an enthusiastic welcome greeted them (June 6th, 1813).

In order to divert American attention from Upper Canada, a joint naval and military expedition, under the command of Admiral Cochrane and General Ross, was sent in the summer of 1814 to harass the Southern States. Ross landed in Chesapeake Bay, defeated the American militia at Bladensburg Bay, occupied Washington, and, in reprisal for similar outrages at York (Toronto) and Newark, burnt the public buildings of the Federal capital. That act of vandalism left bitter memories and had no military significance. Ross, having re-embarked, made an unsuccessful assault upon Baltimore, where he lost 2,000 men and his own life. An attack on New Orleans (January 8th, 1815) was equally unsuccessful.

Treaty of Ghent

Before that attack was delivered Peace had, unknown to the combatants, been signed at Ghent (December 24th).

The war should never have been fought. The Peace settled nothing. The question of maritime rights was not mentioned in the Treaty. Nor, despite Mr. Wilson's emphasis on the freedom of the seas in the second of his " Fourteen Points," was it raised in 1919 at Paris. Great Britain insisted that the Indians who had been loyal to her in the war should be expressly included in the Peace, and agreed that the question of the boundary left unsettled in 1783 should be referred to two Commissioners, who, if they failed to agree, should nominate an umpire. They nominated the King of the Netherlands, but the Americans refused to accept his award, and the unsettled question brought the two countries to the brink of war in 1846.

If, however, the Peace settled nothing, the war had decided that, thanks to the gallantry of her own citizens, Canada should remain under the British flag. It did something more. It aroused the self-consciousness of a people destined to become a nation, predominantly British in blood and British in sympathies.

Yet within a generation both Canadas were in rebellion against the British Crown. *The Rebellions of 1837*

Of the causes operating to produce the rebellions of 1837 some were peculiar to one or other Province, some were common to both. In neither Province did the Act of 1791 provide a permanent solution of the constitutional problem. Not only did the Executive remain independent of the Legislature, but the Legislative Council or " Upper House," being nominated by the Governor, was more closely in touch with the Executive than with the elected Assembly, and was indeed to a large extent identical in personnel with the Executive Council. This led to conflict between the two branches of Legislature, particularly in the Lower Province, where the French Canadians complained that both the Executive and Legislative Councils were composed almost exclusively of English Protestants. In Upper Canada mistrust was engendered by the monopoly of office and influence enjoyed by an oligarchical clique popularly known as the " Family Compact." " The bench, the magistracy, the high offices of the Episcopal Church, and a great part of the legal profession," wrote Lord Durham, " are filled by adherents of this party . . . they have acquired nearly the whole of the waste lands of the Province,[1] and have monopolized most of the posts, great and small, in the

[1] *Report* (ed. Lucas), II, p. 148.

patronage of the Government." The monopoly enjoyed by the clique was in truth due to the high character and ability of their leaders. None the less, it was bound to excite envy, and was one of the exciting causes of discontent and ultimately of rebellion.

Still more bitter was the feeling against a similar monopoly in Lower Canada, intensified as it was in that Province by religious and racial jealousy. It was the racial antagonism that particularly surprised and most deeply impressed Lord Durham. " I expected to find a contest between a Government and a people. I found two nations warring in the bosom of a single State: I found a struggle not of principles but of races." [1] His analysis, though accurate as far as it went, was not exhaustive. In Lower Canada the contest was between a Government and a people. But the Government was English: the people were French.

Moreover, there was a constitutional principle at issue between the Legislative Assembly and the Executive. The conflict turned on the control of finance. The Home Government instructed the Provincial Executive to press the Assembly to make permanent provision for the expenses of the civil administration in the form of a Civil List. The Crown already obtained a revenue, independent of the Legislature, from rents and dues as well as from customs and licence duties. But these sources of revenue were insufficient. The Assembly not only refused to supplement them by a Civil List, but claimed also to control the Crown revenues, and to make all supplies dependent on annual votes.

There was friction also between the two Provinces on the question of finance. All customs duties were levied in Lower Canada; Upper Canada was at the mercy of its neighbour. To meet this difficulty the Imperial Parliament passed the *Canada Trade Act* (1822), which deprived the Quebec Legislature of the power to vary the customs duties to the detriment of Upper Canada. This Act was deeply resented by the Quebec Assembly, which resolved " That

[1] *Report* (ed. Lucas), II, p. 16.

to this Legislature alone appertains the right of distributing all monies levied in the Colonies." Still more strongly did Lower Canada resent the proposal to reunite the two Provinces. To represent their views the Assembly sent to London a deputation. It consisted of John Neilson, a journalist of Scottish birth, and Louis-Joseph Papineau, Speaker of the Assembly, a brilliant orator and an ardent champion of the French Canadians. The reunion proposal was, by their efforts, withdrawn: but on his return Papineau continued his violent attacks upon the Executive, and when in 1827 he was re-elected Speaker the Governor refused to confirm his election. The Assembly persisted, and a deadlock ensued. But when, in 1831, the Assembly refused to grant a Civil List, the Whig Ministry of 1830 made a complete surrender and placed all the revenues unconditionally at the disposal of the two local Legislatures. To this gesture Upper Canada responded by voting a Civil List. The Quebec Assembly, on the contrary, interpreted the concession as surrender, and put forward a demand (1835) for unconditional control of public revenue from all sources, and for an elected Legislative Council.

Upper Canada, no less than Lower, resented the dependence of the Legislative Council upon the Executive, but the special grievance of Upper Canada was the favour shown to the Episcopal Church in the apportionment of the " clergy reserves " and the endowment of forty-four rectories (1835). Of this favour great jealousy was manifested not only by the Scottish Presbyterians, who ultimately secured State recognition on the same footing as the Episcopalians, but also by the Methodists, who in numbers and influence far exceeded all the rest of the Protestants combined.

The leader of the malcontents in Upper Canada was William Lyon Mackenzie, an able but excitable Scottish journalist who in 1820 had emigrated to Canada and from 1824 to 1834 conducted the *Colonial Advocate*. In 1834 Mackenzie became the first Mayor of the city hitherto known as York but in that year rechristened Toronto.

Of the rebellion which broke out in October 1837

Mackenzie was the leader in the Upper Province, Papineau in the Lower. In Lower Canada the rebellion was almost entirely confined to the French inhabitants; it was discouraged by the Roman Catholic clergy, and opposed by the overwhelming majority of the British residents. In neither Province did the rebellion last three months, and before Christmas 1837 it had been without difficulty suppressed. Papineau was declared an " outlaw " and fled to the United States, but in 1847 returned under a general amnesty, and was elected to the United Legislature. In 1854, however, he retired into private life.

The rebellion in Upper Canada was crushed with even less difficulty. Mackenzie fled over the border, but returned in 1849, and from 1851 to 1859 he sat in Parliament. He died in 1861. His younger daughter married a Canadian lawyer and became the mother of William Lyon Mackenzie King, more than once Prime Minister of the Dominion.

The Durham Mission

Short-lived as the rebellions were, and easily as they were suppressed, the Imperial Government did not underrate their significance. In January 1838 it suspended the Constitution of 1791, and sent out as Governor-in-Chief and High Commissioner the Earl of Durham. Durham was a statesman of brilliant parts but quarrelsome temper, who as Lord Privy Seal in the Grey Ministry had been largely responsible for the Reform Bill of 1832. He arrived at Quebec on May 27th and left again for England on November 1st, and of his five months in Canada only eleven days were spent in the Upper Province. The Maritime Provinces and (for certain purposes) Newfoundland were included in Durham's Commission, but though he interviewed delegates from Nova Scotia, New Brunswick, and Prince Edward Island he did not visit those Provinces, and only three pages of the *Report* are devoted to them. Brief, however, as was Durham's stay in Canada, it sufficed to ruin his personal career. His arrogant temper and high-handed proceedings outraged local feeling and brought him into conflict with the Home Government. On June 25th he issued an Ordinance proclaiming an amnesty for all who had taken part in the late rebellion, with twenty-three exceptions. Eight persons who had pleaded guilty to high treason were deported to Bermuda, and fifteen others who had taken refuge in flight were forbidden to return to Canada on pain of death. Only two rebels were executed. The deportation to Bermuda was illegal; an outcry was raised against the Ordinance; the Home Government disallowed it, and Lord Durham, in deep dudgeon, resigned.

The famous *Report* which bears Lord Durham's name was *The Durham* dated January 31st, 1839; on July 28th, 1840, Lord Durham *Report* died. Of the *Report* a contemporary wit said: " Wakefield thought it; Buller wrote it; Durham signed it." Doubtless the two brilliant men who acted as Durham's secretaries had a share in its composition, perhaps a large share, but that it reflects the views of its reputed author there can be no question. In form and arrangement the *Report* is unsystematic; it gives evidence of the haste with which it was in fact composed. It plainly incorporates passages contributed by various hands. Nevertheless, every fresh perusal of the document must strengthen the conviction that here we have one of the most valuable State Papers ever penned on the government of Colonies and Dependencies. Its pages contain hardly a trace of the doctrinaire; they reflect the mind of a great statesman, determined to forgo theories, to face facts, and on the facts to base his recommendations for a prompt and practical solution of the problems presented to him.

At the base of the specific recommendations was the union *The Union* of the two Canadas. Lord Durham's first inclination was towards a federal system on the lines adopted in the United States, and this partly accounts for the emphasis he laid on the " establishment of a good system of municipal government," which he regarded as " a matter of vital importance." Federalism, however, he ultimately rejected in view of the necessity to " anglify " French Canada. " I entertain no doubt as to the national character which must be given to Lower Canada; it must be that of the British Empire; . . . that of the great race which must, in the lapse of no long period of time, be predominant over the whole North American continent." Lord Durham was naturally impressed by recent events, but he underrated the amazing fertility of the French stock and its political persistence. Still less could he foresee the unfortunate tendency to recruit the population of the Prairie Provinces from central and eastern Europe. His preference for a Legislative Union as opposed to a Federation was based upon considerations which in 1838 may well have seemed conclusive. But he did not omit to provide for the admission into the Union of " all or any of the other North American Colonies," if desired by their several Legislatures and approved by the United Legislature.

The Legislature

That Legislature was to be bicameral. The existing constitution of the Legislative Councils was eminently unsatisfactory, but Lord Durham admitted that the difficulty of creating an efficient Second Chamber in a colony was " very great." He rejected the idea of election for that Chamber, but suggested no alternative, contenting himself with the expression of a hope that Parliament would revise the existing Constitution of the Legislative Council and give it " such a character as would enable it by its tranquil and safe but effective working to act as a useful check on the popular branch of the Legislature." It were idle to pretend that his hope was fulfilled either under the Act of 1840 or under the Federal Constitution of 1867. The problem has in truth mocked the efforts of every would-be reformer.[1] As regards the Union in general, pessimists predicted it would endanger the connection of the Canadas with the Empire. Lord Durham refused to believe them. He was right. The Imperial connection he would have further strengthened by an Imperial subsidy to steamship communications between Great Britain and Halifax; he also advocated the construction (already mooted) of an intercolonial railway to connect the Maritime Provinces with Quebec, as well as the improvement of communications by rail, road,

[1] *Report*, p. 326, and cf. Marriott: *Second Chambers* (revised ed., Oxford, 1927), *passim*.

and water between the two Canadas.¹ Such developments were indeed essential to the promotion of emigration on any considerable scale from Great Britain to Canada. Durham insisted that the scale must be considerable but that the scheme must be most carefully devised; indiscriminate emigration would do nothing but harm.

Apart from these larger projects certain detailed recommendations were made. The independence of the Judicature was to be secured by the same means as in England; and the English practice was to be imitated in regard to money grants. Wakefield's influence on the *Report* may be discerned in the space devoted to the land question. The existing provisions in regard to clergy reserves and the application of the funds arising therefrom were to be repealed and the entire administration of the public lands was to be confided to an Imperial authority. This was a matter of vital interest alike to the Mother Country and the colonies. All the revenues of the Crown except those derived from public lands were to be at once surrendered to the United Legislature on the concession of an adequate Civil List. The refusal of a Civil List was, perhaps, justified in the absence of responsible government ; the concession of it was the natural condition and corollary of Responsibility.

The establishment of responsible government was, then, *A Responsible* the central and cardinal proposal of the *Durham Report*. *Executive* Nothing less could " ensure harmony, in place of collision, between the various powers of the State and bring the influence of public opinion to bear on every detail of public affairs." To establish it calls for " no change in the principles of government, no invention of a new constitutional theory." Quite otherwise. " It needs but to follow out consistently the principles of the British Constitution. . . . We are not now to consider the policy of establishing representative government in the North American Colonies. That had been irrevocably done. . . . I would not impair

¹ The first steam passage across the Atlantic was made by the *Royal William* in 1833. Regular sailings began in 1838; in 1840 the *Britannia*—the pioneer vessel of a famous line—sailed from Liverpool for Halifax. Its owner was a citizen of Halifax—one Mr. Cunard.

a single prerogative of the Crown. . . . But the Crown must
. . . submit to the necessary consequence of representative
institutions; and if it has to carry on the Government in
unison with a representative body, it must consent to carry
it on by means of those in whom that representative body
has confidence. . . . The Governor, as the representative
of the Crown, should be instructed that he must carry on
his Government by heads of departments in whom the
United Legislature shall have confidence; and that he must
look for no support from home in any contest with the
Legislature except on points involving strictly Imperial
interest."

A better description of the essentials of the Cabinet system
it would be difficult to find, but the Imperial interests were,
in Lord Durham's view, neither few nor unimportant. All
matters of purely internal government he proposed to place
in the hands of the colonists, but to reserve to the Imperial
Government the " constitution of the form of government—
the regulation of foreign relations, and of trade with the
Mother Country, the other British Colonies, and foreign
nations—the disposal of the public lands," and (inferen-
tially) defence.

Thirty years later Mr. Disraeli spoke regretfully of the
absence of these and similar reservations, and attributed the
neglect of Lord Durham's suggestions to the separatist im-
pulses of the Manchester School.[1] Yet, in a sense, the views
of the Whig Ministry in 1839 were less advanced than Lord
Durham's. To Poulett Thomson (Lord Sydenham), who
succeeded Lord Durham, Lord John Russell, as Colonial
Secretary, did indeed write (October 14th, 1839): " Your
Excellency . . . must be aware that there is no surer way of
earning the approbation of the Queen than by maintaining
the harmony of the Executive with the legislative authorities," but Russell either failed to appreciate the full import
of Durham's cardinal suggestion or deliberately refused to
sanction its application. On the contrary, he reiterated his
opinion, previously expressed, that the demand that colonial

---

[1] See *infra*, p. 209.

ministers of the Crown should be responsible to Parliament " is a condition which cannot be carried into effect in a colony—it is a condition which can only exist in one place, namely the seat of Empire." [1]

The *Union Act* of 1840 did not in fact contain any refer- *The Union Act, 1840* ence to a responsible Executive. Its primary object was the union of the Upper and Lower Provinces. The United Legislature was to consist of a Council, of not fewer than twenty persons nominated by the Crown for life and holding office on good behaviour, and an Assembly, the members of which were to possess property valued at not less than £500 and to be elected in equal numbers from the two old Provinces. The Speaker of the Council was to be nominated by the Governor, the Speaker of the Assembly to be elected by the assembly itself. There was to be a Civil List, upon which the expenses of Government, the salaries of judges, interest on the debt, and pensions were to be charged. All money bills were to originate with the Executive, but taxation (outside the Civil List) was to be controlled by the Legislature. English was to be the official language, but French translations were to be supplied at Government expense, and French was, in fact, freely used in debate. The status of the Churches was defined and the payment of their ministers provided for: but the first united Legislature passed an Act absolutely prohibiting free grants of land to any ecclesiastical body.

The absence of any provision for a Cabinet combined with *Lord Sydenham* the somewhat contradictory instructions of Lord John Russell rendered the position of Lord Sydenham [2] very difficult. But the first Governor-General of united Canada was a man of wide experience not only in commerce but in Cabinet administration. Better still, he was a man of the world, possessed of great social charm and infinite tact. All that a man could do to smooth the difficulties of a transitional period Lord Sydenham did. But it was not

[1] Cf. *Durham Report*, ed. Lucas, I, pp. 143 f., and III, pp. 332 f.; and Kennedy: *Constitution of Canada*, C. xiii.
[2] Poulett Thomson had been M.P. for Manchester and President of the Board of Trade in Lord Grey's Ministry. He was raised to the peerage in 1840.

Cabinet Government

until the governorship of Durham's son-in-law the Earl of Elgin (1847–1854) that the Cabinet system was definitely and finally accepted in principle and in practice adopted.[1] In 1847 formal instructions were sent to Lord Elgin " to act generally on the advice of the Executive Council and to receive as members of that body those who might be pointed out to him as entitled to be so by their possessing the confidence of the Assembly."

Upon Lord Elgin—his own son-in-law—Lord Durham's mantle had fortunately fallen. It was in the spirit of Lord Durham, if on the instructions of Earl Grey,[2] that the greatest of Canadian Governors acted. He was (in his own words) " possessed with the idea that it is possible to maintain on the soil of North America, and in the face of republican America, the British connection and British institutions, if you give the latter freely and trustingly." Freely and trustingly he gave them. The response was not withheld. Lord Elgin was justified. Responsible government not only saved Canada; it has preserved intact the Self-governing Empire.

[1] It was adopted in Nova Scotia and New Brunswick in 1848 and in Prince Edward Island in 1851.
[2] The third Earl Grey, Colonial Secretary 1846–1852.

Chapter Ten

Australia

FROM CONVICT SETTLEMENT TO SELF-GOVERNMENT (1788–1855)

C ANADA pointed the way. As regards consti- *Responsible* tutional development the rest of the British *Government* Dominions followed. By graduated steps all the more important colonies reached the goal of self-government, attained by Canada in 1840.

Throughout the first half of the Victorian era responsible government was almost universally regarded in England as the final stage of colonial development under the Crown. More than that; it was generally accepted as the indispensable prelude to independence. Neither in Canada nor in Australia was the former anticipation fulfilled; in none of the Dominions was the latter.

From Canada we turn to Australia. Nor is the transition from North America to the South Pacific so abrupt as might appear. British Canada and the Australian colonies owe their existence to a common cause—the secession of the United States. After the Declaration of Independence England could no longer transport her convicted criminals to the colonies. What was to be done with them ? The hulks moored in the Thames, as *Great Expectations* taught us, provided a temporary expedient. But owing to the operation of the abominable Penal Code the hulks were soon crowded *The Penal* to their utmost capacity, and beyond it. Some relief was *Code* afforded by the imposition of the death penalty. " The laws of our country," said Romilly in 1783, " may indeed be said to be written in blood." In 1785 no fewer than ninety-seven executions (twenty of them simultaneous) took place in London alone. For more than two hundred offences the death penalty could still be legally inflicted;

procedure was antiquated and ineffective; the innocent were sometimes convicted; the guilty frequently escaped. The severity of the law defeated its own object: it blunted the moral conscience of the nation; it obliterated the distinction between trivial and grave offences; it encouraged serious crime; it failed to deter the casual offender. Criminal procedure was reduced to a farce. Juries often refused to convict when conviction might cost the offender his life. Poachers, sheep-stealers, and shop-lifters were sentenced to death by the score, but rarely suffered the extreme penalty. Of 655 persons indicted for shop-lifting between 1805 and 1807, 113 were sentenced to death, but not in one case was the penalty enforced. On the other hand, over one hundred persons were, between 1811 and 1818, hanged for forgery. Not until Sir Robert Peel's tenure of the Home Office (1822–1827) was the system radically reformed and the Penal Code brought more closely into accord with modern ideas of crime and its punishment.

But in 1783 Peel's reforms were nearly half a century ahead. In the meantime some place had to be found for convicts. Some convicts were indeed desperate criminals, but many had, for quite trivial offences, been sentenced to transportation. This fact must be borne in mind in considering the " penal " origin of certain Australian colonies.

The Convict Problem A Committee of the House of Commons had been appointed in 1779 to consider the problem, and among the witnesses examined was a distinguished naturalist, Mr. (Sir) Joseph Banks, who for more than forty years (1778–1820) was President of the Royal Society. Banks suggested that Botany Bay on the coast of Australia would be a suitable site for the purpose the Committee had in view. That Banks was in a position to make the suggestion was due to one of the most intrepid of English discoverers.

Captain Cook James Cook (1728–1779) was the son of a Yorkshire farm hand. He ran away to sea, served in the merchant service, was transferred (1755) to the Royal Navy, and was present at the capture of Quebec. While stationed at Halifax he studied mathematics and soon manifested a remarkable talent for accurate observation. He was given the command of the schooner *Grenville*, and in 1763 surveyed the coast of Newfoundland and Labrador. In 1768 he received a commission as Lieutenant and was sent out by the Admiralty to the Pacific to observe the transit of Venus. The observation was successfully made from Tahiti (1769), and before returning home Cook sailed round New Zealand, surveyed the whole eastern coast of Australia, and took possession of it in the King's name. To the land hitherto known as New Holland he gave the name of New South Wales, from its fancied resemblance to the northern shore of the Bristol Channel. To whom the first discovery of Australia was due is uncertain, but it had been first disclosed to the world, early in the sixteenth century, by the Portuguese, who christened it Great Java, but failed to follow up the discovery. The Dutch explored the coasts in the seventeenth century, but like their predecessors they made no permanent settlements. William Dampier, famous as navigator and privateer, touched on the coast in 1689, but for all practical purposes Cook's survey was the beginning of the authentic history of Australia.

Having completed his survey Cook returned home in May 1771, only to be sent out again in 1772. In the course of the voyage, which lasted until July 1775, he settled for all time more than one question which had long puzzled geographers. A third voyage (1776–1779) was undertaken in order to attack the problem of the North West Passage from the Asiatic side. Cook discovered the Sandwich Islands, and thence reached the west coast of North America, touched at Nootka Sound, and entered the Behring Strait. His eastward progress being stopped by ice he returned to winter in the south, and at the Sandwich Islands met his death at the hands of the natives (February 14th, 1779).

Cook's death was a tragedy; but his fame is secure. If a man's life-work is to be measured by practical results, Cook's was not second to that of any English explorer.

The United Empire Loyalists

Without Joseph Banks those results might not, however, have matured. In 1783 the problem of the American Loyalists was at least as pressing as that of the English convicts, and in that year a plea for settling them in New South Wales was submitted to the Government. The author of the plea was the son of an American Loyalist, James Maria Matra. As a midshipman on the *Endeavour* Matra had come in contact with Banks, who concurred in his scheme. As regards the Loyalists the scheme came to nothing, but Pitt and Lord Sydney, then Secretary of State, seized on it as a solution of the convict problem.

Captain Arthur Phillip

Captain Arthur Phillip, R.N., who had seen service in the Seven Years' war, was selected to command the expedition and to act as Governor of the projected colony. The fleet, consisting of the frigate *Sirius*, an armed tender *Supply*, three store-ships carrying agricultural implements, clothing for the convicts and the troops, and provisions (supplemented at Capetown) for two years, left Spithead on May 13th, 1787, and reached Botany Bay on January 18th, 1788. A brief inspection satisfied Phillip that Botany Bay was an unsuitable site, and he decided, with a perspicuity abundantly justified, to make the settlement at Port Jackson, a few miles farther north. In that superb natural harbour, known to the world as Sydney, the fleet dropped anchor on January 26th, 1788.

New South Wales

The convicts landed at Port Jackson numbered 717, of whom 188 were women, and they were guarded by 191 marines under eighteen officers. Phillip was directed to occupy Norfolk Island, in order to prevent it from falling into the hands of any other European Power, and to that island some of the worst convicts were for many years deported. Nor were fears of competition groundless. Within a week of Phillip's arrival at Botany Bay two French ships appeared, though merely, it was explained, to get supplies of " wood and water." Their needs were courteously supplied, and they sailed away only to be wrecked off the New Hebrides. What would have happened had they arrived at Botany Bay a week sooner it is vain to conjecture.

Of Port Jackson Phillip reported enthusiastically. " This country," he declared, " will prove the most valuable acquisition Great Britain ever made," but in order to justify his prediction he besought the Government to recruit free settlers to whom convicts might be assigned as labourers. From 1793 onwards a few free settlers did periodically arrive, but for the first thirty years New South Wales was predominantly a convict settlement. Not until 1821 was it opened without restriction to free immigrants. In that year the total population of the colony was 23,939, of whom 9,451 were still serving as convicts, 1,307 had come as free settlers, 1,495 had been born in the colony, 3,255 were " emancipists," and some 2,500 were on ticket of leave and had received pardons, absolute or conditional. By 1841 the total population had risen to 130,856, of whom nearly 53,000 were free immigrants. The transportation of convicts to New South Wales was stopped by Order in Council in 1840, but for many years the merits and demerits of the system continued to be hotly debated both in England and in the colonies. The persistence of the controversy is demonstrated by the fact that in 1849 Western Australia had actually petitioned the Home Government that it might be made a regular penal settlement. During the next twenty years some 10,000 convicts were in fact sent out to Western Australia, and it is generally agreed that transportation rescued the colony from depression if not from collapse. By the middle 'sixties, however, the position had greatly improved, and in 1868 transportation was brought to an end. To an impudent demand for compensation for the loss of the convicts the Home Government very properly declined to accede.

To return to New South Wales. Captain Phillip, strong, just, and humane, performed his difficult task with conspicuous success, but in 1792 he was compelled by ill-health to retire. Between Phillip's departure and the appointment (1809) of Lachlan Macquarie as Governor, the colony was ruled by a succession of men who left little or no mark upon it. That is characteristic of Australia. It has owed less to rulers and politicians than to the pioneers in agriculture and industry. The primary interest, indeed, of Australian history lies not (until quite recently) in constitutional and political evolution, but in economic development and social experiment.

John Macarthur, 1767–1834

One of the most notable of Australia's benefactors was the man commonly acclaimed as " the father of New South Wales." John Macarthur was a hot-tempered Highland soldier who in 1790 went out to Sydney as Captain of the New South Wales Corps. Gifted with both shrewdness and vision, Macarthur quickly perceived the economic potentialities of the colony. By 1796 he had ten acres of land laid out in gardens and vineyards, a good deal of arable sown with wheat and maize, a fair stock of horses, cattle, goats, and swine, and, above all, 300 sheep. In 1797 he made a shrewd investment; he purchased some Spanish merino sheep bred in Cape Colony, and with them laid the foundations of Australia's most prosperous industry. The officers of the New South Wales Corps were a rough lot, who did not disdain to make money by a traffic in spirits, and in 1801 Macarthur quarrelled with his commanding officer, dangerously wounded him in a duel, and was sent under arrest to England to stand a court-martial. The court-martial was refused, but Macarthur having carried with him some specimens of his wool aroused the interest of English manufacturers as well as of the Colonial Office. He resigned his commission, and in 1805 returned to the colony, taking with him five merino rams and a ewe from the flock at Kew, and an order from Lord Camden, Secretary of State, authorizing him, on condition that he devoted himself to the production of fine wool, to select 5,000 acres of the most suitable land in the colony. " Keen as a razor and rapacious as a shark," Macarthur soon came into conflict with Governor Bligh, whose brief tenure of office (1806–1808) was brought to an end by a mutiny fomented by Macarthur, who became Secretary of the Provisional Government set up by the mutineers. From 1809–1817 Macarthur was exiled to England, but his farm was successfully carried on during his absence by his wife, and in 1817 he was permitted to return to New South Wales. In 1828 he was elected a member of the First Legislative Council of New South Wales; in 1834 his tempestuous career was ended by death.

With all his faults of temper Macarthur was a man of high *Wool* personal character, and the value of his services to his adopted country is literally immeasurable. Wool was the foundation on which its prosperity was built. Wool has brought Australia through more than one crisis, commercial and financial. About one-fourth (440,000 tons) of the world's total production of wool (1,700,000 tons) comes from Australia. Her wool exports in 1936–1937 were valued at £62,529,000, and of that total more than one-third (1,067,688 bales out of 2,794,137) was taken by the United Kingdom. The trade with England really began as far back as 1821, when twenty-seven bales of Australian wool were sold in Change Alley. The value of the wool produced since that date has been computed at no less than £1,700,000,000.

Well may Macarthur's name be honoured in Australia. *Governor* Hardly less honoured is that of Lachlan Macquarie, who *Macquarie* was Governor from 1809 to 1820. Before his arrival, Sydney, enclosed within a circlet of hills, had been regarded as a "natural gaol." In 1813, under the pressure of drought, however, the barrier formed by the Blue Mountains was surmounted, and beyond it were revealed almost boundless tracts of the finest sheep-grazing land in the world. Though the discovery was due to Gregory Blaxland, it was Macquarie who had the new country surveyed, constructed a road over the mountains, and so opened the way to a new era of prosperity for the colony.

Had Macquarie's views prevailed the wealth of the colony would have been mostly enjoyed by the "emancipists," whom he preferred as colonists to the free settlers, and still more to the mutinous and acquisitive officers of the New South Wales Corps, which soon after his arrival he disbanded. The penal settlement had, however, proved very expensive. During its first years it had cost the Government nearly £100,000 a year. Nevertheless, a Committee appointed by the House of Commons in 1812 reported that the system of transportation was " in a train entirely to answer the ends proposed by its establishment," and " cordially concurred " in Macquarie's policy of encouragement to the emancipists. Over eighty per cent of the convicts had been transported for quite trivial offences; the more dangerous men had from the first been sent to Norfolk Island. Originally occupied in 1788, Norfolk Island, though temporarily abandoned in 1814, was reoccupied as a penal settlement in 1824, and finally (1867) became the headquarters of the Melanesian Mission founded by George Augustus Selwyn, first Bishop of New Zealand, and one of the saintliest and wisest men ever sent into the mission-field by the Church of England.

Tasmania   Van Diemen's Land also relieved New South Wales of some of the worst of its criminals. Lying 120 miles south of Australia, Van Diemen's Land (rechristened Tasmania, after its Dutch discoverer, in 1855) was first revealed as an island by Surgeon Bass in 1795, and five years later was selected in preference to Port Phillip as a subsidiary penal settlement. In 1804 the worst element in its population was reinforced by the transference of the convicts from Norfolk Island, but not even they could permanently disfigure its native loveliness. Governor Macquarie twice visited the island and left his mark on it in the shape of good roads, impressive public buildings, and an improved social order.

Macquarie was convinced that the future of Tasmania, as of New South Wales, lay not with free settlers but with those, often more unfortunate than ineradicably wicked, who had come into conflict with the law at home. " There never," he wrote officially in 1818, " can be any . . . public advantage derived, from allowing any more settlers to come out at all." But economic forces were too strong for Macquarie. " The discovery," writes Professor Ernest Scott, " of the immense plains west of the (Blue) mountains made it impossible that New South Wales should continue to be nothing more than a convict settlement. Gregory Blaxland killed the convict system by breaking down the gaol walls. It was not merely a geographical discovery that he and his companions made; it was a profound social change." [1]

Governor Macquarie was relieved of office in 1821 and retired to England, where, three years later, he died. Macquarie's policy in regard to the exclusion of free immigrants, if generous in intention, was hopelessly shortsighted; nevertheless, the young colony owes him a considerable debt, and it needed not the ostentatious bestowal of his name to keep his memory alive.

Before Macquarie left Australia several difficult problems had begun to engage attention not only in the colony but at home. The most insistent were the interdependent problems of land settlement and labour supply. " The disposal of public lands in a new country has more influence on the prosperity of the people than any other branch of Government." The words are Lord Durham's, the sentiment is Wakefield's. *Land and Labour*

Edward Gibbon Wakefield was a man of limitless energy and enthusiasm. Born in 1796, he began life in the diplomatic service, eloped with a ward in Chancery at the age of twenty-two, and after her death abducted an heiress. For that crime he suffered three years' imprisonment, and might well have made his first acquaintance with Australia as a convict. Escaping that fate, Wakefield wrote, while in Newgate, *A Letter from Sydney . . . Together with the Outline of a System of Colonization* (London, 1829). Personal contact with returned convicts had given him a mass of intimate information which he utilized with such skill that his *Letter* was generally accepted as the first-hand narrative of an actual settler. The ideas adumbrated in the *Letter* were developed in his more famous work *The Art of Colonization* (1849). *Edward Gibbon Wakefield*

Wakefield's scheme was designed to solve simultaneously two problems : the lack of employment for agricultural

---

[1] Ap. C.H.B.E., vii, 3.

labourers in the old country, and the lack of labour in the colonies. Unemployment in England was, he believed, due to the unnatural stimulus given to industry and to population during the Napoleonic wars, and to the subsequent depression accentuated by the maladministration of the old Poor Law. Labour shortage in the colonies he attributed mainly to the ruinous policy adopted by them in regard to the allocation of waste lands. Settlers could still obtain for little or nothing an unlimited quantity of land without giving any guarantee that they could profitably utilize it. The result was that every labourer preferred, very naturally, to cultivate land not for a master but as a proprietor. That was not all. " Large tracts became the property of speculators who leave their lands unsettled and untouched. Deserts are thus interposed between settlements; the natural difficulties of communication are enhanced; the inhabitants are not merely scattered over a wide space of country, but are separated from each other by impassable wastes; the cultivator is cut off or far removed from a market in which to dispose of his surplus produce and to procure other commodities; and the greatest obstacles exist to co-operation in labour, to exchange, to the division of employment, to combination for Municipal or other public purposes. . . ." [1] This acute diagnosis, though embodied in Durham's *Report on Canada*, is undoubtedly from Wakefield's pen. On it he based his threefold prescription: Let all land in the colonies be sold at a " sufficient price," preferably by auction with a minimum limit fixed high enough to discourage its premature purchase by labourers who, for their first years in the colony, would be better employed at wages, or by speculators who have neither the means nor the wish to utilize it. The money thus obtained would provide a fund to assist the emigration of young paupers of both sexes in equal numbers. Any surplus might be devoted to the general expenses of administration in the colony concerned. By this ingenious device an exact proportion would, Wakefield claimed, be established and automatically main-

[1] *Durham Report*, II, p. 204.

tained between people and land. The larger the sum derived by the colonial Government from sales and rents, the more money available to assist emigration. "The Mother Country and the colony would become partners in a new trade—the creation of happy human beings; one country furnishing the raw material—that is the land, the dust of which man is made; the other furnishing the machinery—that is, men and women, to convert the un-peopled soil into living images of God." The results of Wakefield's ingenious theory will be presently disclosed.

Wakefield's *Letter from Sydney* was published in 1829. *Western* In the same year a British settlement was effected in Western *Australia* Australia. In 1827 Governor Darling, of New South Wales, suspicious of the presence of French vessels in Australian waters, despatched Captain (afterwards Admiral Sir James) Stirling to survey the country about the Swan River. His reports were so favourable that Darling recommended that a settlement should be founded. But the Home Government were reluctant to incur any expense, and only after striking a bargain with a group of private capitalists did they sanction the enterprise. Captain Fremantle was sent out to the Swan River and on May 2nd, 1829, took possession in the name of the Crown of "all that part of New Holland not included within the territory of New South Wales." In August 1829 Fremantle arrived with the first batch of settlers, and remained as Governor for ten years. The Colonial Office insisted that from the outset the enterprise must be self-supporting. Parties of emigrants containing a proportion of not less than five females to six males were to receive free grants of land at the rate of forty acres for every £3 of capital invested in public or private objects in the colony to the satisfaction of the Government. The offer was sufficiently attractive to bring 850 genuine settlers to the new colony within six months of its foundation. Many of the settlers were of good quality and fair substance; they brought in £45,000 of capital, and obtained £41,550 worth of land at 1s. 6d. an acre.

This promising start was followed, unfortunately, by a

hard struggle for survival. But in 1834 the Home Government came to the help of the colony by a grant-in-aid and a
supply of stores. Still, progress continued to be very slow.
By 1840 the population numbered only 2,300, and the land
sales were on an almost negligible scale. In desperation the
colony in 1849 petitioned the Home Government to convert
it into a regular penal settlement. The proposal was cordially welcomed in Whitehall. In 1850 the first batch of
convicts was sent out, accompanied by an equal number of
free settlers. From that moment the tide turned. The
colonists got the labour they so sorely needed, while Government establishments, with the expenditure rendered necessary thereby, diffused a sense of prosperity. The rigidity of
the land regulations was relaxed: sales rapidly increased,
and the leased area was immensely extended. In the decade
following 1850 the revenue of the colony rose from £11,792 to
£60,741, and other signs of prosperity proportionately multiplied. If the convicts had not literally saved the colony, their
advent had coincided with a welcome change in its fortunes.

South Australia   South Australia was specifically founded in order to test
by practical experiment the soundness of Wakefield's theory
of colonization. Though his name does not appear on the
prospectus of the South Australian Association (December
1833), its Committee was an exceptionally strong one, including as it did George Grote, Charles Buller, Nassau
Senior, Robert Torrens, and several influential Members of
Parliament. But if Wakefield's name was prudently withheld, the prospectus embodied his principles. It also conformed to the regulations laid down by Lord Goderich's
(Ripon's) Regulations of 1831. Those Regulations required
that henceforward all Crown lands in Australia must be sold
by public auction to the highest bidder, but with a minimum
price of 5s. per acre. In 1834 Parliament passed an Act to
establish the " British Province of South Australia," with the
proviso that £35,000 worth of land must be sold and a
guarantee fund of £20,000 raised before the Act came into
operation. Difficulties ensued, but in December 1836 a
start was made and South Australia, with its capital at

Adelaide, came into existence. The rebellion in the Canadas (1837) turned the tide of emigration towards Australia, and by 1841 15,000 people were already settled in South Australia, 250,000 acres had been sold and had realized nearly £230,000, 7,000 acres had been brought under cultivation, and the settlers possessed 200,000 sheep and 15,000 cattle. Great expense had, however, been incurred; and without the reluctant help of the Imperial Parliament the experiment, on the verge of success, might have collapsed. In 1841, however, the Colonial Office wisely sent out as Governor Captain George Grey, then a young man of less than thirty, who was destined to leave a name greatly honoured not only in Australia but in New Zealand and South Africa. By the enforcement of rigid economy, the reduction of the extravagant wages paid to Government employees, and in other ways, the young Governor, in the course of four years, placed the colony on a firm footing. To the rapid improvement two other things contributed: the discovery of vast copper deposits and of silver lead in the Murchison district, and the passing of the *Crown Lands Sales Act* (1842) by the Imperial Parliament. That Act, which applied to the whole of Australia, forbade the sale of Crown land (with a few exceptions) at less than £1 an acre, and allocated at least fifty per cent of the proceeds to the promotion of emigration. Wakefield was completely vindicated. In 1844 over 1,000 emigrants reached South Australia, and by 1850 the population exceeded 63,000. To the total export trade of £570,000, minerals contributed no less than £364,000. Since Grey's time more than £33,000,000 worth of copper has been produced in South Australia; but in the long run agriculture beat mining, the value of the agricultural products now (1937) amounting to £20,000,000 as against £2,700,000 obtained from minerals. To the remarkable prosperity of South Australia in early days a powerful impulse was given by the discovery of gold in Victoria (1851).

Only in that year did Victoria enter upon its independent *Victoria* existence. Originally part of New South Wales, Port

133

Phillip was first colonized by settlers from Tasmania. Their enterprise was not encouraged by the authorities at Sydney or in Whitehall, but in 1836 the Colonial Office, yielding to the logic of facts, threw the Port Phillip district open to settlement—a step which was soon followed by an agitation in favour of the separation of Victoria from New South Wales. Various industries were set up at Melbourne, rapidly developing into a populous and flourishing town, and both in arable farming and in sheep-breeding the Port Phillip district began to compete with the parent colony. An Act of 1850, while placing Victoria on the same constitutional footing as that enjoyed by New South Wales since 1842, evidently contemplated imminent separation.

Gold   In less than six weeks after the establishment of Victoria a rich find of gold was reported from Ballarat. A frenzied rush to the new gold-diggings ensued, and in half a decade the population of Victoria increased from some 70,000 to 330,000. For some years the gold-fields were the scene of wild confusion, and the local Executive was powerless to deal with the situation, though there was less disorder and less crime than might have been expected from a population so motley. By 1856 the Victorian gold-fields carried a population of 180,000, which produced gold to the value of £14,000,000 a year.[1] By 1861 both these figures were nearly halved. The first profusion of alluvial deposits had been quickly exhausted, and machine mining had replaced the pick and shovel of the individual digger. Meanwhile, the Government had been compelled (in 1855) to substitute an export duty of 2s. 6d. per ounce for the licence duty of 30s. a month, which had imposed such an unequal burden on the unlucky and the lucky. The wealth obtained by the lucky miners was not, however, monopolized by them. The gold discoveries gave an immense stimulus to all the main industries of Australia, notably to sheep-breeding, and in the decade 1851–1861 the total population increased from fewer than half a million to over 1,100,000. That of Victoria alone increased from 77,345 to 540,322.

[1] C.H.B.E., Vol. VII (1), chapter IX, p. 258.

Not less important was the impulse which gold gave to constitutional development.

During the first stage of its history New South Wales was a purely military government, under a Governor armed with dictatorial powers. The first Governors were sailors; a little later soldiers were frequently appointed; but before 1850 few civilians appear in the lists. Until 1814 the administration of justice, civil no less than criminal, was in the hands of the Governor, but in that year a step towards the separation of the Judicature and the Executive was taken by the creation of independent courts of civil jurisdiction. Under an Imperial Statute passed in 1823, two Supreme Courts, each with a Chief Justice and two other judges, were set up in New South Wales and Tasmania; in both colonies there were to be regular courts of Quarter Sessions, and the Governor was also empowered to set up, for the recovery of petty debts, local courts presided over by Commissioners, on the model of English County Courts. Criminal trials were to be conducted by a judge and seven military officers, but in civil suits the parties might agree to have a jury of twelve freeholders. In 1825 English law, statute, judge-made, and common law, became the law of the colony.

Constitutional Evolution in New South Wales

The changes effected by the Act of 1823 were not merely judicial. The Act also provided for the creation of a Legislative Council of five to seven members nominated by the Colonial Office. The Governor retained the sole right of initiating legislation, but all his proposals were to carry the certificate of the Chief Justice that the proposals were consistent with the laws of England " so far as the circumstances of the Colony will admit." The Governor also retained the right, in an emergency, to issue Ordinances, overriding the opposition, even if unanimous, of the Council. Nevertheless, restricted as were the powers of the Council, its mere existence was a step towards the limitation of autocracy, and it did gradually obtain a considerable measure of control over taxation. The Act of 1823 also provided for the setting up of similar institutions in Tasmania, the

Legislative Council

THE BRITISH EMPIRE

Government of which was in 1825 separated from that of New South Wales.

The process begun in 1823 was extended in 1828 by another Imperial Statute, which limited the powers of both the Chief Justice and the Governor, empowered the Crown to increase the members of the Legislative Council to fifteen, and hand over to it the raising and spending of the Customs revenue. Thenceforward, officials formed a minority of the Council. On the Judicial side the Act gave litigants the right of appeal in important cases to the Privy Council; it instituted circuit courts, and authorized the Crown to delegate to the Legislative Councils the power to extend trial by jury in both civil and criminal cases.

Executive Council   Meanwhile, the instructions issued to (Sir) Ralph Darling, on his appointment as Governor in 1825, provided for the creation of an Executive Council, on whose advice he was normally to act. The Council consisted entirely of officials, but its existence gave them a cohesion they had hitherto lacked, though the extent of their influence on the general administration of affairs depended largely on the will, and even the whim, of the Governor.

Representative Government   A further and important stage in the constitutional development was reached by the legislation of 1842. Of the two Acts passed in that year by the Imperial Parliament one dealt with land sales, and must be considered later; the other established representative institutions. The Legislative Council was to consist of twelve members nominated by the Crown and twenty-four elected by the inhabitants on a franchise based on a moderate property qualification. Emancipists were not excluded either from the electorate or the Legislature. Of the elected, six were allotted to the Port Phillip district. Of the nominated members, not more than half were to be officials (though officials might also stand for election), and they were to be appointed for the term of the Parliament, which, subject to dissolution, was to be five years. To the Governor (who was not to be a member of the Council) and the Council was given a general power of making laws " not repugnant to the law of England," but this power was not to extend to Bills affecting the salaries of officials, the constitution of the Council, the customs duties, or the sale or other appropriation of lands. A Civil List of £81,600 was set aside for salaries and administration expenses, of which £30,000 a year was to provide for public worship. There were also to be elective local Councils, with power to make by-laws, to manage roads and bridges and so forth; but this part of the Act was a failure.

New South Wales showed the way to the other Australian colonies. The Constitution of 1842 was devised for the parent colony, and was extended during the next ten years to other Australian colonies.

The Act of 1842 registered merely a stage in the constitu- *Responsible* tional evolution of Australia parallel with the *Canada Act* of *Government* 1791. The concession of responsible government to Canada naturally aroused similar aspirations in Australia. Consequently during the 'forties there was more or less persistent agitation. Of specific grievances the most prominent were the disposal of Crown lands and the withdrawal of the Civil List from the control of the local Legislature. But more fundamental, in Australia as in Canada, was the relation between the Legislature and the Executive. " There is but one way of preventing the collisions, which have thus unhappily commenced, from becoming permanent—to give the Legislative Council the necessary privileges of a representative body, which imply that control over the Ministers and Administration of the Colony which belongs to responsible government properly so called, and which can occasion the choice—as well as the removal—of the functionaries who are entrusted with the chief executive departments." So ran a Report of 1844. The language might have come from the pen of Lord Durham.

Lord Grey—grandson of the Prime Minister of 1830—was *Act of 1850* Colonial Secretary from 1846 to 1852, and devoted time and thought to the problems which arose in his Department.[1]

---

[1] Cf. his *The Colonial Policy of Lord John Russell's Administration*, 2 vols. (London, 1853).

His considered view was that the solution should, as far as possible, be left to the colonists themselves. He himself favoured the creation of a Federal Assembly, but the time for that solution had not come. Consequently the only remaining trace of Lord Grey's original proposal was the title of Governor-General, borne by the Governor of New South Wales until 1861, when it was quietly dropped. The *Australian Colonies Government Act* of 1850 was in the main an enabling Act. It established Victoria as a separate colony; it retained the Crown lands and the revenue derived therefrom under Imperial control; but it virtually remitted to the several Australian colonies the power of amending their constitutions. They acted promptly upon the powers thus granted. Before the end of 1854 New South Wales, Victoria, South Australia, and Tasmania had all submitted Constitutional Bills for the approval of the Crown. That approval was given in 1855. For their Legislatures all four colonies adopted the bicameral form; in all four the Executive ultimately became " responsible " in the English sense.

Western Australia was in a different position. Owing to its retention of a convict element in the population it was not until 1870 that a Legislative Council on the model of the New South Wales Council of 1823 could be established in Western Australia. But the intermediate stages leading up to complete self-government were abbreviated, and in 1890 the Government of Western Australia became " responsible."

Queensland   Queensland demands brief mention. Of that colony John Macarthur was the real if remote progenitor, for the Darling Downs provide one of the finest tracts of sheep-grazing land on the continent. Not, however, until 1859 was Queensland separated from New South Wales, and at the same time attained the dignity of responsible government.

Thus did all the six Australian colonies reach the goal of self-government. But Lord Grey's prescience was not at fault. No more for Australia than for Canada was responsible government the apex of constitutional development. For New Zealand, on the contrary, it was. But New Zealand demands a chapter to itself.

Chapter Eleven

New Zealand

"THE BRITAIN OF THE SOUTH"

"THE future home, as I believe it to be, of the greatest nation in the Pacific." So Froude wrote of New Zealand in 1885. In that prediction Australia is not likely to acquiesce; but few will question the accuracy of Lord Bryce's statement that "of all the British self-governing Dominions New Zealand is that best suited by climate to be a home for men of British stock." [1] Nevertheless, New Zealand may be treated, in relation to the main theme of the present work, with comparative brevity. "Happy the country," it has been said, "that has had no history." New Zealand has not lacked history, but, except for a series of Maori wars, its history has been relatively unperturbed if not uneventful. New Zealand has no near neighbours, friendly or the reverse; the nearest are one thousand two hundred miles away, and they are British. It is not, like Canada, divided by race, creed, and political tradition. It has no such obstinate native problem as that which still distracts South Africa. It still contains a large and increasing number of Maoris,[2] but of its European inhabitants all but a negligible fraction are of British stock, and mostly British stock of high quality. New Zealand has never had, like Australia, to consider the relations between free settlers and emancipists. Exquisite scenery, rich natural resources, a genial climate, and a fertile soil have continued to minister to its prosperity. Nothing that can make for human happiness has been denied to those fortunate islands. That they are remote from what has hitherto been the centre of world civilization is true; but

[1] *Modern Democracies*, II, p. 29 (1921).
[2] 84,474 in 1937 (against 52,751 in 1921) out of a total population of 1,587,211.

remoteness may not be to the ultimate disadvantage of New Zealand, and in any case it is a fact of rapidly diminishing significance.

The Missionaries

Captain Cook had rediscovered New Zealand in 1769 and had claimed it as a British possession, but his action was disallowed by the Imperial Government. After his day the islands were visited by navigators of various nationalities, by whalers and sealers, and traders came to it in quest of flax and timber. The Rev. Samuel Marsden, when chaplain to the convict settlement of New South Wales, was thus brought into contact with Maoris who manned many of the whaling and sealing vessels in those waters, and forming a high opinion of them resolved to convert them to Christianity. From 1814 onwards he frequently visited the islands and paved the way for George Augustus Selwyn, who became first Bishop of New Zealand in 1841, and for twenty-seven years devoted himself with apostolic zeal to the spread of Christianity among the islands of the Pacific.

Settlements

In the late 'thirties the " weary Titan " was exceptionally weary. Both Canadas were in rebellion in 1837, and to the settlements already effected in New South Wales and Van Diemen's Land the British Government had lately added two more in Western and South Australia. It had no wish for more colonies. But in New Zealand its hand was forced partly by the missionary enthusiasm of Marsden, partly by reports that two French companies were contemplating a settlement, and not least by the insistent pressure of Edward Gibbon Wakefield.

A trickle of British settlers, not of the best type, had already found their way to New Zealand; in 1839 the Commission of Governor Gipps was specifically amended to include the islands twelve hundred miles distant from his seat of Government at Sydney, and in 1840 Captain William Hobson was despatched as Lieutenant-Governor to New Zealand.

The Treaty of Waitangi

Hobson found himself at once confronted by the problem presented by a large native population. The Maoris were not only numerous but highly intelligent and, though war-

140

like, chivalrous and exceedingly tenacious of their rights, especially their rights in the soil. In February 1840 they concluded with the British representative the *Treaty of Waitangi*, by which they readily acknowledged the sovereignty of the Queen. In return Her Majesty extended to them her protection " and all the rights and privileges of British subjects." In particular she guaranteed to the chiefs and their peoples all their proprietary rights in their lands, forests, and fisheries, with the proviso that if they wished to alienate them Her Majesty should have the right of pre-emption at prices to be agreed upon. The document was signed by the Lieutenant-Governor on behalf of the Crown, and by forty-six of the principal chiefs in the presence of a large gathering of lesser chiefs. The terms of this Treaty formed, for a quarter of a century, the chief bone of contention between the settlers and the natives, and were the main contributory cause of a series of disastrous wars. But the Sovereignty of the Queen proclaimed over all the islands on May 21st, 1840, was never challenged. In August of the same year the Imperial Parliament passed a Statute to constitute New Zealand a separate colony. It was to have a Legislative Council consisting of the Governor and at least six other persons nominated by the Secretary of State, while the Governor and his three chief officials were to form an Executive Council.

The immediate problem was not, however, constitutional *The Maoris* but agrarian. For Councils and even Governors at Auckland the Maoris cared nothing: their chiefs were their rulers, the land was their land. Finding themselves circumscribed and regulated the Maoris naturally came into collision not only with " the Government " but still more with the agents of the New Zealand Company, which, despite much misgiving and hesitation, had in February 1841 received a charter from the Imperial Government. The Company was formed to carry into effect the principles of Edward Gibbon Wakefield, and the first batch of settlers was sent out under the command of his younger brother, Colonel William Wakefield. Land purchase and settlement inevitably brought the Company into conflict with natives, who believed the land to be their own and had no wish to alienate it. The rights of the Maoris were upheld by the missionaries; the English settlers advanced under the banner (sometimes besmirched) of " economic development and social progress "; the Government at Auckland honestly endeavoured, though with inadequate force, to give effect to its awards, and to hold the scales evenly between the disputants.

Sir George Grey

In 1845 the Government passed into the hands of that great administrator, Captain George Grey. He had saved South Australia; he came to perform an equal service to New Zealand.

His first duty was to crush the Maori insurrection; his second to make friends with them, flattering the chiefs and employing the tribesmen at tempting wages on public works. He insisted, indeed, that the Colonial Office should give him adequate military force, without which his conciliatory policy would only be interpreted as weakness; but he also enrolled a native constabulary force in order to familiarize the Maoris with English laws.

South Island

In regard to the land question, Grey was inflexible in maintaining the sanctity of rights conferred by Treaty, but he bought out the few Maoris in South Island, thus providing large tracts of land for settlers sent out by the New Zealand Company. Of their settlements the two most notable and successful were those in Otago, with its capital at Dunedin, and at Christchurch in Canterbury. Both were religious in origin. Dunedin was founded by a small group of Scottish Presbyterians in 1848, but until the discovery of gold in Otago in 1859 its progress was slow. By 1861 Otago had nearly 30,000 inhabitants. The Canterbury Association started under more influential auspices: the Archbishops of Canterbury (Sumner) and Dunedin (Whately), seven bishops, and Lord Shaftesbury being its patrons. Such patrons naturally attracted high-class emigrants: of the one thousand five hundred colonists who in 1850–1851 went out to establish Christchurch, no fewer than one-fourth were cabin passengers.

In South Island, then, all promised well, and the transference of the capital in 1865 from Auckland to Wellington was merely a recognition of political and economic facts.

In North Island, Grey's task was much more difficult. *North Island* His land policy unfortunately brought him into conflict with Wakefield, who in 1853 went out to New Zealand himself, and there made his permanent home until his death in 1862. The personal tension did not last long: at the end of the year 1853 Grey left New Zealand, to take up his appointment as Governor of Cape Colony.

Before leaving New Zealand Grey had drafted the new *Responsible* Constitution which with some amendments was enacted by *Government* the Imperial Parliament in 1852. The Constitution was almost federal in texture. The two Islands were divided into six Provinces, each of which was to have its own Superintendent and an elected Council with considerable though restricted powers of local legislation. The Central Government was to consist of a Governor, a Legislative Council, the members of which were to be nominated for life by the Governor, and a House of Representatives, elected on the same franchise as the Provincial Councils, and (subject to dissolution) for five years. Grey would have had the Legislative Council elected by the Provincial Councils, which would have given an even more strongly federal character to the Constitution, but he was overruled by Whitehall. As in the Canada Union Act, there was no mention of a responsible executive, but when the question was raised in the very first session (May 1854) of the new Parliament, Wakefield carried with only one dissentient a motion in favour of the immediate establishment of a responsible Ministry. The Home Government raised no objection in principle, and in 1856 the Executive was entrusted to a Cabinet on the English model.

Of constitutional changes since 1856 the most drastic *Provincial* was the abolition in 1875 of the Provincial Councils. Ever *Councils* since 1856 there had been incessant conflict between the "centralists" and the Provincial Councils (increased in

143

number to nine), and though an acute observer has remarked that " centralization will never give expression to the true nature of New Zealand " it may be that by 1875 the Provincial Councils had served their educative purpose, and that the cause of good administration was served by their abolition. A different aspect of the matter deserves a passing reference. If Grey's original suggestion had been adopted the Provincial Councils, entrenched in the Second Chamber, might well have survived, and have given to that nominated Chamber a strength and authority it has sadly lacked. Of all methods of constructing a Second Chamber nomination has proved the least satisfactory, especially where the nomination is for a limited period. Until 1891 the Legislative Council of New Zealand was nominated for life, but when the Liberal-Labour Government, coming into power in 1890, found its Bills rejected or emasculated by the Council it resolved to reduce the obstructive Chamber to impotence. The Council was " swamped," and now consists of thirty-eight members nominated only for seven years. Its Speaker receives only £720 a year, as against £900 paid to the same officer in the " Lower " House, and its members £315 a year as against £450. Grey's Federal " Senate " might also have imposed some check upon the socialistic legislation carried since 1935. The unitary Council has been powerless, even if so inclined, to do so. The House of Representatives has since 1867 included four Maori members, elected by four Maori constituencies, and it is customary to have one Maori in the Cabinet. The basis of election has since 1899 been adult suffrage, extended in 1893 to women, who since 1919 have also been eligible for election. Voting has long been by ballot, and the duration of Parliament has been shortened to four years. For a time the principle of second ballots was adopted.

The Second Chamber

Most of the changes effected since 1856 have, however (with the exceptions noted), been on matters of detail, and have harmonized with the movements common to most other democratic communities.

Meanwhile things had gone none too well since the setting

up of Responsible Government. Parliamentary Government is not in itself the high road to successful administration; it is not only most exacting in its demands upon the men called upon to work it, but is doomed to failure unless certain conditions are fulfilled. The most important conditions are a long apprenticeship in self-government, and a large measure of national unity and social solidarity. Until the British colonists had asserted their final and complete ascendancy over the Maoris—and that was not until the 'seventies—the latter condition was not fulfilled in New Zealand.

In 1861 Sir George Grey had been recalled to New Zealand as the one man capable of straightening out the tangle. His second term of government (1861–1867) proved that even he was unequal to the task. Though a Liberal to the core, deeply imbued with English traditions of self-government, Grey had in him too much of the autocrat to be a successful " constitutional " ruler. His relations with his Ministers were consequently none too easy. Yet it was at his suggestion that the Home Government handed over the control of Native Affairs to the Colonial Ministry. Responsibility for administration carried with it, however, responsibility for the military changes involved by the Maori wars. But the forces were largely Imperial forces and took their orders from the Horse Guards. That caused another embarrassment to Grey, whose relations with General Duncan Cameron, commanding the Imperial troops, were as uneasy as his relations with his Ministers. More uneasy than either were his relations with Downing Street, and in 1867 he was recalled somewhat abruptly by the Duke of Buckingham, Colonial Secretary in Lord Derby's Cabinet.

Sir George Grey's Second Term

New Zealand had not, however, seen the last of Sir George Grey. On his return to England he sought to enter the Imperial Parliament; but the Tories mistrusted him as a Radical, and he was too much of an Imperialist for the " Little Englanders," who still dominated the Liberal Party. So he abandoned the hope of a Parliamentary career at home and in 1871 returned to New Zealand as a private citizen.

In that situation he could not long remain. In 1874 he was returned to the House of Representatives, and as Member for Auckland strongly opposed the abolition of the Provincial Councils. The opposition, as we have seen, was in vain. In 1877, however, Grey became Prime Minister at the head of a Radical Cabinet. For a man who had been the Governor in an autocratic régime to become Prime Minister under Parliamentary government was a paradoxical situation. Nor was the experiment either successful or prolonged. Grey's Ministry was brought down by the commercial crisis of 1879, and, with some ingratitude, he was himself deposed from the leadership of the party. He remained in Parliament as a private Member for fourteen years, but he was never reconciled to his party, and in Parliament was rather a lonely and pathetic figure. One definite service, however, he performed: he founded a school of politicians and trained the scholars. His " Greyhounds " may be compared to Lord Milner's " Kindergarten." To inspire younger men is no small part of the proper task of statesmen of high character and conspicuous ability. Among such Sir George Grey was not the least. Another service deserves to be recorded. In 1891 Grey was sent to represent New Zealand at the Convention which met at Sydney to consider, not for the first time, the question of Australasian
Federation Federation. At an earlier Convention (1883) a Bill had been drafted to constitute a Federal Council of Australasia, and New Zealand then agreed to be represented on the Council. Opinion in New Zealand was, however, by no means unanimous, and in December 1884 the Governor, Sir W. Jervois, reported to the Colonial Office that the general feeling was opposed to " federation in the ordinary sense of the term, arising partly from the fact that the distance between New Zealand and Australia is too great and the climate too different to make any arrangement like that now existing in the Canadian Dominions desirable, and partly from the disagreement among the advocates of federation as to details, some desiring that the council should be a legislative, others a deliberative body."

At the Sydney Conference of 1891 Grey showed himself more interested in the question of colonial autonomy than of federation. Not that he was opposed to the federal principle. His record proved the contrary. While Governor of Cape Colony he had strongly advocated a federal union among the various territories subject to the British Crown in South Africa. His suggestion was rejected by the Colonial Office, but some of the wisest statesmen in South Africa subsequently acknowledged that Grey had been right, and that a policy of federation would have averted subsequent misfortunes in South Africa.[1]

Grey's attitude at Sydney in 1891 was due, then, not to the principle of federation but to the fears of New Zealand lest an Australasian Federation might ultimately lead to its separation from the British Empire. Had Imperial Federation, of which Sir George Grey was an enthusiastic advocate, materialized, his opposition to a Pacific Federation might have been overcome. At Sydney he actually proposed " that a system of Federation should be adopted to enable all parts of the British Empire to join in the common federation while each retained its own autonomy." But the prevailing opinion in New Zealand was undoubtedly expressed by John Ballance, Premier of the colony, who said: " The whole weight of the argument is against New Zealand entering into any federation except the federation with the Mother Country."

Three years after the Sydney Convention Grey left New Zealand for good. The remaining four years of his life were spent in England, where he was received with high honour, and sworn of the Privy Council. He died in 1898 and was very properly honoured with a public funeral and a burial in St. Paul's. Despite his wide vision and lofty ideals the record of Grey's long life is one of imperfect achievement. Yet in the three British colonies which he governed the memory of a great man will not soon be permitted to die.

Grey, like other Liberals of his day, was primarily concerned with the improvement of constitutional machinery,

[1] See *infra*, p. 169.

with questions of colonial autonomy, the relations of central and local government, federalism, and the like. It is not, however, for such things that the history of New Zealand has been notable; it is for the initiation of social and economic experiments.

Trade Cycles   In the course of a century, the colony has suffered the usual alternations of adversity and prosperity. For the first ten years of its existence New Zealand, particularly in North Island, had a severe struggle. But the discovery of gold in Victoria (1851) at once reacted favourably on New Zealand. There was a sudden demand for farm produce of every kind; prices rose rapidly, and prosperity was widely diffused. Even more marked was the effect when gold was discovered in Otago in 1861 and in Canterbury in 1865. Within twelve months the revenue of Otago advanced from £83,000 to £280,000, and public finance only reflected private prosperity.

Sir Julius Vogel   Before the 'seventies, however, the effects of the gold boom were exhausted, and when Julius Vogel became Colonial Treasurer the outlook was dark. Vogel had emigrated from England to Victoria during the first gold rush, but in 1861 deserted Ballarat for Otago; he was elected to the Provincial Council in 1862 and in the following year to the Legislative Council of the colony. From 1869 to 1876 he was almost continuously in office, and, though not always as Prime Minister, was the strongest force in the Government and inspired its policy. Gifted with courage and imagination, he rescued the colony from depression, and by methods which many condemned as unorthodox and even mischievous, he undoubtedly diffused throughout the community a sense of confidence and well-being. He raised large loans, and used the money to finance public works, to construct railways and roads, and to promote immigration. He set up the Public Trust Office, initiated a scheme for State life insurance, constructed the cable from New Zealand to Australia, improved shipping and mail facilities, and established a system of education, free, secular, and compulsory.

His policy certainly had the bad effect of encouraging wild speculation, especially in land, but his admirers claim that the money raised by loans was, for the most part, wisely spent. His critics gravely question the wisdom, pointing to the undeniable facts that he burdened a young and poor country with a heavy debt, and that a relatively brief period of prosperity was followed by fifteen years (1879–1894) of profound depression. Whether the depression can justly be attributed to Vogel's unorthodox methods, or to forces operating on a world-scale, is still a matter of controversy. In 1876 Vogel exchanged the Premiership of New Zealand for the office of Agent-General in London, but in 1884 he returned to New Zealand and took office as Colonial Treasurer under (Sir) Robert Stout. This time, however, he failed to lift the colony out of the depression into which it had again fallen. He ultimately retired to England, where, broken in health and reduced to poverty, he died in 1899.

A country endowed with splendid natural resources, with abundant land and a small population, might have been expected to keep on an even keel and avoid those vicissitudes of fortune incidental to old countries, with their delicately balanced industrial systems and their dense populations dependent upon overseas trade. The fact that New Zealand, in its brief history, had already suffered from them acutely, gave its politicians furiously to think—and (as some hold) to act rather recklessly.

New Zealand has been described as " the social laboratory *A Social* of the world." If that means that it was the first modern *Laboratory* community to make daring experiments in legislation designed to improve the condition of the poorer classes, the description is justified.

Attention was first directed to the land, which, despite *The State and* Wakefield's precautions, was largely monopolized by large *the Land* proprietors. Graduated taxation was imposed upon land and incomes in 1891; in 1892 a Department of Agriculture was set up to enable small farmers to benefit by the results of scientific research; and in 1894 the *Land for Settlements Act* gave the State powers to repurchase land at the Government valuation, and the *Advance to Settlers Act* enabled small farmers to borrow on easy terms from the State. The object of all this legislation was to substitute small farmers, holding 999-year leases from the Crown, for larger land-owners, on freehold tenure. The object was practically attained. In 1892 45,000 holders cultivated 10,000,000 acres. In 1903 the holders had been increased to 64,000 and the land cultivated by them to 13,000,000 acres. Between 1907 and 1927 the agrarian legislation of the 'nineties was almost completely reversed, and the reaction, supported by the clear preference of the small farmers for freehold tenure, continued until the economic blizzard swept through the world in 1930.

The Economic Blizzard and Labour Legislation The catastrophic fall in prices after 1930 caused widespread havoc in New Zealand, particularly among the primary producers. They hoped much from the World Economic Conference of 1933, and its complete failure reduced them almost to despair. The Ministry, headed by Mr. Forbes and Mr. Coates, fought the demon with great courage, and called, not in vain, for sacrifices from all classes. New Zealand struggled through; but it is not surprising that the glittering promises held out by the Labour Party at the election of 1935 should have given it a sweeping victory. Of the eighty seats in the House of Representatives they secured no fewer than fifty-three, and for the first time an avowedly Socialist Ministry came not only into office but into power under Mr. M. J. Savage.

Only with his agrarian policy are we for the moment concerned. In outline it is simple. The *Primary Products Marketing Act* (1936) set up a Marketing Department to handle the export and sale, primarily of dairy produce; it provided for the payment to the dairy farmer of a guaranteed price for his produce, while the consumer was to be protected by State control of retail prices. The entire produce of dairy farmers intended for export is purchased by the State at a uniform fixed price, and is sold by the State on the London market at the best price obtainable. The price is to be such as to " yield to the efficient producer sufficient return to maintain himself and his family in a reasonable standard of comfort." [1] Under the *United Wheat Growers Act* the State also fixes the price of wheat, flour, bread, and other products to the home consumer. The result of this bold experiment cannot yet (1938) be foreseen: it is watched with interest in England, and with mingled optimism and anxiety in New Zealand.

It was not agriculture only that demanded the attention of the Legislature in the last decades of the nineteenth century. Evidence abounds that labour employed in industry was, at that time, becoming class conscious. The legal recognition given to English trade unions in the 'seventies had its repercussion in New Zealand. An Act was passed in 1878 to provide for the registration of trade unions; the trade unionists held their first Congress in 1885, and a decision of the Arbitration Court set up under the Act of 1894 compelled employers to give " preference to unionists." An *Employer's Liability Act* had been passed in 1882; Truck Acts and other Acts of similar import were passed to protect workmen against fraud, and allegations in regard to sweating and the conditions of home work compelled the Government in 1889 to appoint a " Sweating Commission." Its report led to the legislation of 1891. A Factory Act had been passed as far back as 1873, and was greatly extended in scope by the Acts of 1891 and 1894.

The State and Industry

More important even than legislation was the creation in 1891 of a Labour Department under W. Pember Reeves as Minister. Born in New Zealand in 1857, Reeves entered the colonial Parliament in 1887, and more than any other man was responsible for the remarkable labour legislation of the 'nineties. He became Agent-General (later High Commissioner) for the colony in 1897, and resigned that position to become Director of the London School of Economics in 1908. His well-known book on *State Experiments in Australia and New Zealand* (1902) covers the greater part of the Premiership of Richard John Seddon. Seddon was described by Lord Bryce as " one of the most remarkable

W. Pember Reeves

---

[1] W. Nash: *Labour Rule in New Zealand*, p. 4.

leaders of the people modern democracy has produced," and in New Zealand was admiringly and affectionately known as " King Dick."

Born in Lancashire in 1845, Seddon emigrated to Australia in 1863 and made money as a storekeeper both at Ballarat and in Otago. Elected to the New Zealand Legislature in 1881, he became Premier in 1893 and held that office until his death in 1906. An ardent Imperialist, he was also responsible for that great mass of social legislation which owed much of its impulse to the women whom he enfranchised in 1893. A man of boundless energy, a superb party leader, and a most successful politician, Seddon was neither an acute thinker nor a creative legislator or administrator. His was the driving force; the brain was Reeves's.

The primary concern of both men was to maintain industrial peace. A great strike—the first in New Zealand—was begun in 1890 to prevent the use by the shipping companies of non-union labour. Stimulated by the success of the London dockers in the preceding year, it failed to achieve a like result. Nevertheless, despite immediate failure, it was largely responsible for the " *Workman's Charter* " of 1894.

The basis of that Act was the organization of employers as well as workmen. On the Conciliation Boards set up in each district, both parties were to be represented and to meet under an impartial chairman. After the reference of the dispute to a Board a strike or lock-out was illegal. Failing agreement the matter was referred to a Court of Arbitration, consisting of a Judge of the Supreme Court. The awards were enforceable by heavy financial penalties. Reeves anticipated that " ninety-nine cases out of a hundred " would be settled by the Conciliation Boards. He was mistaken. The disputes were almost invariably carried to the Court. The Boards were in fact abolished in 1901, only, however, to be restored seven years later. The latest enactment on this subject (1936) carried the principle still farther. The Arbitration Court is now required to fix

" basic rates of wages at a level sufficient to enable adult male workers to maintain a wife and three children, in a fair and reasonable standard of comfort." " All workers subject to an Arbitration Court Award or to an industrial agreement are, moreover, required to be members of a trade union." [1]

Opinions differ about the success of compulsory arbitration, but the principle, though variously applied, has long ago been accepted as an integral part of the industrial life of the Dominion. In the words of a careful commentator, it has " checked sweating, encouraged the numerical if not the fighting strength of the Unions, and consolidated the gains that were made possible to the workers by a period of recovery from prolonged depression," and the scope of its awards have been " extended to cover not only wages and hours, but working conditions . . . apprenticeships, holidays," and much else.[2]

Nevertheless, a question obtrudes itself: How far would such protection of labour have been possible without the protection of industry ? A young colony naturally relies largely upon a tariff for revenue, and a revenue tariff is easily extended to the protection of domestic industries. The Trade Union Congress at Dunedin demanded a Protective policy in 1885, and in 1888 the demand was, to a moderate extent, conceded. The principle was carried farther in the 'nineties, and still farther in 1907, 1921, and 1927. The Socialist Ministry now (1938) in power has made it clear that it will not hesitate to go much farther should the primary products of the Dominion not find extended markets abroad at remunerative prices. *Tariff Policy*

The present Ministry avowedly aims at establishing a complete and coherent system of State Socialism. Non-contributory Old Age Pensions had been introduced, in the face of violent opposition by Seddon, in 1898, and since then pensions have been increased in amount and extended to new categories of recipients. In 1936 the Savage Ministry raised the Old Age Pension to £1 a week, and *Old Age Pensions*

[1] Nash, *op. cit.*, p. 3. [2] J. B. Coudliffe, ap. C.H.B.E., p. 186.

153

established an invalid pension of a similar amount with an additional 10s. a week for the wives and for each dependent child. Deserted wives also receive pensions, and family allowances are made at the rate of 2s. a week for each dependent child in excess of two, in all cases where the income does not exceed £4 a week.

The State regulation of wages and hours of work was a logical corollary of the establishment of the Arbitration Court. The Savage Ministry has restored the principle of compulsion, abandoned during the Forbes-Coates régime. It has also conceded a forty-hour week without reduction of wages, and holidays with pay to all State employees, and it aims at extending the same principle to all workmen, for whom enrolment in trade unions will be compulsory.

The State has lately taken control of broadcasting, and to his other offices the Prime Minister has added that of Minister of Broadcasting. It has also taken steps to protect its railway monopoly against road competition. Besides the direct provision, on a modest scale, of working-class dwellings, the State also does the work done in England by voluntary Building and Benefit societies, as well as that of Insurance Companies.

Credit and Currency

The keystone of State Socialism is, however, the control of credit and currency. That has now been secured by the *Reserve Bank of New Zealand Amendment Act*. The Reserve Bank itself was set up in 1933 during the crisis that ensued on the economic blizzard, but until 1935 it enjoyed corporate independence and was not wholly under Government control. All restrictions upon Government action have now been removed, and the control of currency and credit is now wholly vested in the State.[1]

New Zealand and the Empire

The position of New Zealand in the Empire, its attitude towards federation, Australasian and Imperial, its external policy, above all, the superb service it rendered to the Empire in the Great War, are matters that will demand

[1] A detailed account of recent legislation will be found in the *New Zealand Official Year Book*, 1938, pp. 637–829.

attention later on. Meanwhile, two points need to be emphasized. On the one hand there is no reason to apprehend that the daring social experiment initiated in 1936 will in any degree impair the cordial attachment of New Zealand to the Commonwealth of which it forms so important a unit, or to the Crown which supplies the golden link of the Empire. That the experiment may accentuate the difficulty, already sufficiently formidable, of harmonizing the trade interest of the Dominion and the Motherland, is probable. But given genuine goodwill the difficulty will be surmounted. The other point is that to draw any conclusions as to the success or failure of the experiment now being made in New Zealand would be premature. Circumstances have, thus far, favoured it. While trade is good, revenue expanding, and prices high, no great harm may be done to the permanent interests of the community. What may happen when these conditions are reversed it were rash to prophesy.[1]

[1] Since this chapter was written (1938) a General Election has taken place in New Zealand. The Labour party gained some seats in the towns, but the general effect was to leave the political representation very much as it was before. The Labour party, under Mr. Savage, remains in power, and free to carry on the experiments initiated in 1936. By the *Social Security Act* (No. 7 of 1938) the rates of benefit quoted on pp. 153–4 *supra* have been in several cases increased. A substantial fall in the world price of some primary products, notably wool, has occurred. This threatens to justify the implicit warning in the last two sentences of the text.

Chapter Twelve

South Africa (1814–1884)

BRITONS AND BOERS

TO the British Empire the student of Politics owes a special debt of gratitude. Not since the days of ancient Greece has any political formation ever furnished the laboratory of Political Science with such profusion or such variety of material for analysis.

Alike to the scientific student and to the practical administrator South Africa presents problems peculiar to itself. Her problems differ widely from those of Australia and New Zealand. There is a much closer resemblance between those of South Africa and Canada. They would indeed be almost identical if the United States were inhabited by Indians, and if the Canadian Dominion were dominated by Quebec.

Governing Factors in South Africa Certain governing dominant factors in the problem must at the outset be emphasized. The first is the coexistence in South Africa of two European races, both of Low Dutch origin, but divided from each other by language, by economic interests, and most of all by a wide disparity in political and social development. The Boer of to-day has far more in common with the Englishman of the seventeenth century, a Puritan in creed, a countryman in outlook, than with the industrialized town-dwelling Briton of to-day.

Still more significant is the fact that the white people, Britons and Boers taken together, are a small minority in the Union of South Africa, numbering less than two millions in a population of over eight and a half millions, and that in British Africa as a whole the coloured people outnumber the white in vastly greater proportion. " The main drama of Africa," as Jan Hofmeyr has truly said, " is the struggle to avoid the occurrence of a tragic clash of colour."

There is a further complication in the problem. African natives are not the only non-Europeans: Asiatics have come to South Africa in large numbers. In Natal there are to-day almost as many Asiatics as Europeans; in the port of Durban they actually outnumber them.

Another fact, which has had an important influence upon South African history and politics, is that of the four Provinces in the Union two have been brought under British Sovereignty as a result of conquest after a long period of intermittent warfare.

A third Province, Cape Colony, first appears on the stage of history as an appendage of the East Indies, an incident of European enterprise in the Far East. The pioneers in that enterprise were, as we have seen, the Portuguese. It was they who discovered the Cape route to the East, and for a whole century they had a monopoly of opportunity in South Africa. They turned it to little account. Mozambique was seized by Vasco da Gama as he returned from his first voyage to India (1499): Portuguese mariners touched at Delagoa Bay (the name itself recalls the Portuguese capital in India) in 1502, and in 1505 they established a fort at Sofala just south of Beira. The murder of Almeida, one of the greatest of their Viceroys, by the Hottentots in Table Bay (1510) made them shy of South Africa, and although there was no European rival to dispute their ascendancy they were content to establish a few forts on the coast from the mouth of the Orange River on the west to that of the Limpopo on the east. Not until the latter years of the nineteenth century did Europe awake to the fact that the Portuguese held on the east coast a position of great strategic importance. Delagoa Bay, with the port of Lourenço Marques, was destined to prove a Naboth's vineyard to more than one European Power, but Portuguese East Africa still exists to obstruct the access of the Transvaal and of Rhodesia to the sea.

Portuguese Settlements

By the end of the sixteenth century the great days of Portugal were over. Portugal was absorbed into the Spanish monarchy in 1580, and the Portuguese possessions in the East consequently lay open to the attacks of Spain's enemies, the Dutch and the English. From that time onwards Dutch and English East Indiamen touched constantly at Table Bay. The first Englishmen to set foot on South African soil belonged to an expedition which left Plymouth on April 10th, 1591, under the command of Sir James Lancaster. " Going along the shore " (says a narrative of the voyage in Hakluyt) " we espied a goodly bay with an island lying to seawards of it, into which we did bear and found it very commodious for our ships to ride in." The bay was Table Bay. Nine years later the East India Company was formed, and thenceforward Table Bay became a regular place of call for English ships on the outward voyage. " In this place," writes an early voyager, " we had excellent good refreshing in so much that I think the like place is not to be found among savage people." It was " a goodly country inhabited by a most savage and beastly people as ever I think God created."

If it be asked why we never attempted permanent occupation of this important and salubrious spot, the answer is that we did. On June 24th, 1620, two English captains, Humphrey Fitzherbert and Andrew Shilling, in command of an expedition sent out by the East India Company, found themselves in Table Bay in the company of nine Dutch ships. Before leaving the Dutchmen hinted that the States-General of the Netherlands meant to take formal possession of this convenient port of call. Accordingly the Englishmen, fearing lest their countrymen in future " should be frustrated of watering but by license," determined to be beforehand with *English Occu-* the Dutch. On July 3rd, 1620, these two English captains *pation, 1620* by solemn proclamation " took quiet and peaceable possession of the bay of Saldania and of the whole continent adjoining so far as it was not occupied by any Christian Power in the name of their Sovereign, the high and mighty Prince James, by the grace of God King of Great Britain." But that timorous Prince declined to accept that fresh responsibility. Nor would the East India Company listen to the glowing reports brought home by their merchantmen.

Their resources as compared with those of the Dutch Company were very limited. They preferred to concentrate upon the East Indies, and consequently the Proclamation of July 3rd, 1620, was still-born: the title derived from prior occupation was surrendered.

It is interesting, though vain, to speculate how the whole history of European South Africa might have been altered had James I been less timorous and the English Company more enterprising. The Dutch, with their greater resources, showed less hesitation. In 1652 a Dutch expedition was sent out under the command of Jan van Riebeck, and the Cape of Good Hope was occupied and formally placed under the Governor-General and Council of India, with its seat of Government at Batavia.

For a century and a half Cape Castle was the " frontier- *Dutch* fortress " of the Dutch East Indies, but the Dutch made no *Possession* real effort to colonize in South Africa. Their little settlement provided fresh vegetables for ships trading to and from the East Indies, and thereby saved from the fatal scourge of scurvy many thousands of Dutch and English sailors. In this humane and not unprofitable work the Dutch settlers were much assisted by French Huguenots, some three hundred of whom took refuge in South Africa, to avoid persecution at the hands of Louis XIV (1686–1689). The Revocation of the Edict of Nantes proved an unalloyed blessing to the Protestant States of Europe—not least to England. Many of the Huguenots who found a home in South Africa came from some of the noblest houses in France, and from them not a few of the best families in South Africa are descended. They planted vines, grew corn, and taught the Dutch many useful arts. Their treatment, however, was exceedingly harsh, and they complained that " the great tyranny of the French monarchy from which they had fled had its counterpart in the policy of the petty despots who governed uncontrolled at the Cape of Good Hope."

It was not only the French Huguenots who suffered at the hands of the Dutch administration. The Dutch settlers were themselves the victims of the petty despotism exercised from Batavia. Before the end of the eighteenth century, however, the Dutch Company had become hopelessly corrupt and inefficient. Holland itself was conquered by the French Republic in 1795, and it was the Dutch Stadtholder, then a refugee in England, who advised the British Government to forestall a French conquest of Cape Colony. He sent orders to the Dutch Governor to welcome an English occupation as " an act of friendship and alliance " and as a protection against a French " invasion." Consequently, in September 1795 Capetown was occupied by a British force in the name of the Stadtholder, though not without some ineffectual resistance by the colonists.

The colony was restored to the " Batavian Republic " by the Treaty of Amiens (1802), but was reconquered in 1806 by Sir David Baird, and in 1814 was retained by Great Britain, who compensated the Dutch Government for its loss by a payment of £6,000,000 sterling. Thus did South Africa finally pass under British rule.

Not, however, until 1820 was any attempt made to transform it into a British colony. Lord Charles Somerset, who was Governor of Cape Colony for fifteen years (1814–1829), induced the Imperial Parliament to vote £50,000 towards the cost of establishing a British settlement. Of the 90,000 persons who offered themselves 5,000 were selected, and in 1820 they were planted round Algoa Bay, in the district west of the Fish River, which Somerset had recommended " as unrivalled in the world for beauty and fertility." These " Albany Settlers " provided the nucleus of British South Africa. From 1820 onwards there was a steady flow of migration from Great Britain, though it was at no time large until the discovery of gold and diamonds began to attract in large numbers a different type of settler. The eastern provinces of Cape Colony, centring on Port Elizabeth and Grahamstown, still remain more predominantly British and reproduce the characteristics of the homeland more faithfully than any other part of the colony.

Boers and Britons

Between the British settlers and the Boer farmers there was from the first little intercourse and virtually no fusion of blood. Nor are the reasons far to seek. The Boers were and are mostly farmers, living on large stock farms, and almost completely isolated not only from Britons but from each other. Deeply attached to their Calvinistic creed and immovable in adherence to their traditional manner of life and social customs, they were impatient of any kind of government control, and especially resentful of any interference between them and their Hottentot slaves.

The Albany Settlers had no slaves; the Boer farmers, who *Abolition of* relied mainly upon slaves for agricultural labour, possessed *Slavery* some 35,000 to 40,000, which were officially valued at £3,000,000. Slavery was abolished in 1833 by the Imperial Parliament. But of the £20,000,000 voted in compensation to slave-proprietors only £1,270,000 was allotted to the slave-owners in South Africa. Moreover, by an act of incredible folly and injustice, that sum, regarded by the Boers as wholly inadequate, was made payable only in London, where every claim had to be established by a procedure both expensive and to the Dutch farmers unintelligible. Agents had to be employed; speculators bought up the claims, and the money actually received in South Africa fell far short even of the allotted sum. So disgusted were the Boers that not a few refused to claim, and the unexpended balance was afterwards devoted to education in South Africa. Nor did the money loss represent the whole or main part of the hardship inflicted upon the Dutch farmer. Far more serious was the loss of essential labour. At one fell blow the farmers found themselves, in some districts at any rate, " totally deprived of every vestige of labour to improve or cultivate their farms or even to superintend or herd their flocks." [1]

Responsibility for the injury suffered by the Dutch slave- *Glenelg and* owners must rest ultimately upon Charles Grant (Lord *D'Urban* Glenelg), Colonial Secretary from 1835 to 1839. Glenelg was an ardent evangelical, a man of high principle, and a real philanthropist, but he was one of the most inefficient and weakly sentimental politicians who ever directed from Downing Street British Colonial policy. That he should

[1] Cloate: *Five Lectures on the Great Boer Trek* (1856).

have come into conflict with Sir Benjamin D'Urban, who was Governor at the Cape from 1834 to 1838, was less to D'Urban's discredit than to Glenelg's. D'Urban had been guilty of two crimes inexpiable in the eyes of a fervent disciple of the Manchester School and the Clapham Sect. He had extended the bounds of the British Empire and he had inflicted condign punishment on the " irreclaimable savages " and " merciless barbarians " who in overwhelming numbers had at Christmas 1834 poured over the eastern frontier of the colony and " in one week driven to utter destitution 7,000 of His Majesty's subjects," and laid waste one of the fairest and most fertile provinces of the Colony. (The descriptions are D'Urban's.)

The Kaffir War, 1834–1835   Sir Benjamin D'Urban, an old soldier of wide experience, himself directed an expedition against the Kaffirs in 1834–1835. The colony was cleared of invaders and a punitive expedition carried the war into Kaffirland. At the end of April, Hintsa, the paramount chief of the Kosas, surrendered to the British forces and peace was made. The eastern boundary of Cape Colony was extended to the Kei River, and the newly acquired territory was constituted as the province of Queen Adelaide.

But D'Urban had reckoned without Downing Street. From Downing Street Lord Glenelg indited the famous despatch which has caused his memory to be execrated alike by Britons and Boers in South Africa.[1] Glenelg, while admitting the " fatal imprudence " of the conduct of the Kaffirs, declared that they had " ample justification." He condemned and recalled a Governor who had the cordial support of both European races in the colony, and ordered the retrocession to the Kaffirs of the newly acquired province of Queen Adelaide. Sir Charles Lucas, commenting on the whole matter, while doing full justice to the exalted motives of Lord Glenelg, pertinently adds: " Few decisions have had more far-reaching results. . . . It was the beginning of

---

[1] Extracts from that historic despatch, described by the Editors as "academic nonsense," will be found in *Select Documents on British Colonial Policy* (ed. Bell and Morrell), where they occupy fourteen pages!

undoing in South Africa." [1] Unquestionably it was. Not only did it prolong the struggle between the Europeans and the Kaffirs for forty years, but it was a contributory cause of the Great Boer Trek and the establishment of the Transvaal Republic and the Orange Free State.

Relations between Britons and Boers, uneasy from the outset, had not been improved by the reforms, constitutional and judicial, carried through between 1825 and 1833. In particular, the Boers resented supersession of the familiar Landdrosts by Resident Magistrates, the abolition of the Burgher Senate in Capetown, and the local Boards of Heemraden, above all the substitution of English for Dutch as the official language of the Courts of Justice.

But these grievances, though irritating to the conservative *The Missionaries* farmers, were of small import compared with the perpetual interference of the missionaries between them and their slaves.

That the conduct of the missionaries, though inspired by compassion, should have been deeply resented was not unnatural. Nor were the missionaries themselves wholly blameless. Of the services rendered to Africa by such devoted men as Mackenzie and Maples, Robert Moffat and David Livingstone, it were impossible to speak too highly. It were vain to deny that there were too many instances of bitter prejudice, conspicuous tactlessness, and most reprehensible exaggeration. Moreover, the Boers, while loyal to their own Calvinistic creed, looked upon the British missionaries as part of a system which they regarded with growing aversion. All government they disliked; the British Government they came to detest. Accordingly they determined to go forth from the house of bondage and establish new homes in the country north of the Quathlamba Range. Two decades or more of inter-tribal wars among the Bantu tribes had made of that land a wilderness. Those were wars not of conquest but of mutual extermination. The country was cleared for the Boer migration.

To treks in search of new grazing-land the Boers had long *The Great Boer Trek* been accustomed[1]; but the Great Trek was much more

[1] *Historical Geography of the British Colonies*, IV (Part 1), p. 162.

than that. The story, full of romantic and pathetic incidents, must, however, be read elsewhere. Here it must suffice to say that between 1836 and 1838, groups of families, estimated in the aggregate at between five thousand and ten thousand, shook the dust of the Capetown Government off their feet and, with their wives and children, their household possessions and farming implements packed in ox-wagons, went forth to make for themselves new homes in the wilderness.

Natal Meanwhile, a large body of Boers under Piet Retief had made their way through the passes of the Drakensberg Mountains into Natal (1837–1838). More than ten years earlier a handful of English colonists had (1824) established themselves at Port Natal—so called because Vasco da Gama touched there on Christmas Day—*Dies Natalis*—in 1497. Twice had the English settlers been compelled to fly for their lives; twice they had returned, and in 1834 D'Urban forwarded to Whitehall a petition from British merchants at the Cape praying for " the formation of a Government establishment at Port Natal with an adequate military force for the protection of that place." The " weary Titan," faithful to the teaching of the Manchester School, refused to add to his burden. The petition was rejected. A similar refusal awaited a petition (1835) from " the householders of the town of D'Urban, Port Natal," for formal recognition as a regularly constituted colony.

Two years later Piet Retief and his companions arrived in Natal, and after a terrific struggle with the Zulus, under their crafty and bloodthirsty chief Dingaan, defeated them on the Tugela (December 16th, 1841, a day henceforward commemorated as " Dingaan's Day " [2]) and established themselves as the " Republic of Natal."

The Natal Boers applied (1841) for recognition from the

---

[1] *Boers* = the " frontier stockfarmers " who supplied the vast majority of the " trekkers." (Cf. E. A. Walker, ap. C.H.B.E. c. XIV, who combats the " traditional view " that the Trek was due to the abolition of slavery. The pastoralists, he says, " never had many slaves.")

[2] The centenary of the great Boer Trek was celebrated with picturesque elaboration in 1938. The celebration unfortunately recalled some bitter memories and also gave an impulse to Dutch nationalism in South Africa. Officially, however, due restraint was exercised, and British inhabitants wisely demonstrated their sympathy with the celebration.

British Government as an independent republic. The application excited alarm not only in Cape Colony, but also, though belatedly, in Downing Street. Independent Boer States west of the Drakensberg might be tolerated, but Natal touched the ocean; a Dutch republic established on the coast might establish embarrassing relations with European Powers unfriendly to England.

Moreover, ugly stories began to reach England of the treatment of the Zulus by the Boers. Exeter Hall raised its voice. Consequently, in 1842 Durban was reoccupied by British troops, and in the following year British Sovereignty was extended to Natal. The Boers protested and attacked Durban, but the British garrison repulsed the attack; Natal remained under the British flag. Of the Boers, some settled down under British rule, the irreconcilables sullenly recrossed the Drakensberg, where they established themselves in the country between the Orange and the Vaal. It was not long before their compatriots from Natal, led by Pretorius, followed their example. But they were not permitted to remain undisturbed. In 1848 Sir Harry Smith, who had lately returned to South Africa as Governor of Cape Colony, decided to annex the territory. The Boer settlers resisted the annexation, but were defeated at Boomplatz in August 1848, and a British Resident was placed in charge at Bloemfontein. Pretorius and his friends took refuge with their compatriots north of the Vaal.

The relations between the British Government at Capetown and the Boer emigrants to the Transvaal had never been defined. In the eyes of the Government the emigrants were British subjects who had simply removed from one part of British territory to another. In their own eyes they were free citizens of an independent Republic. The policy *British Policy* actively pursued during the next half-century by the British Government was as undignified as it was disastrous. After the Boer Trek two possible courses were open to it. On the one hand, the Government might have frankly recognized the secession of the emigrants and accepted, with such grace as was possible, the existence on South African soil of an independent Power of European descent. Or, alternatively, it might have made clear to the Boers from the outset that no other European Power would be permitted to establish itself in South Africa and that the Dutch farmers, wherever they might settle, must remain British subjects, though endowed with the largest measure of local self-government compatible with that condition.

Unfortunately neither policy was adopted; or rather each was adopted in turn. "Spasmodic violence alternating with impatient dropping of the reins; first severity and then indulgence, and then severity again, with no persisting with any one system—a process which drives nations mad as it drives children." Such was Froude's caustic summary of England's policy towards South Africa in the nineteenth century. Nor was it unfair.

The process started with concessions to the Boers. Seizing the opportunity of British preoccupation in a Kaffir war, Pretorius, then an outlaw beyond the Vaal, threatened in 1851 to raise an insurrection unless the independence of the Transvaal Boers were acknowledged. Not a man could be spared from the British forces to resist Pretorius's demand.

Sand River and Bloemfontein Conventions

Consequently, by the *Sand River Convention* (January 17th, 1852) Great Britain conceded to the "emigrant farmers beyond the Vaal the right . . . to Govern themselves without any interference on the part of Her Majesty the Queen's Government." On one condition did the British Government insist, that "no slavery is or shall be permitted or practised in the north of the Vaal River by the emigrant farmers." Difficulties soon arose on that point; but in the meantime Great Britain was involved in a war with the Basutos, whose territory bordered the eastern frontier of the Orange River Sovereignty. At the close of an arduous but indecisive campaign Colonel Sir Harry Cathcart, who in 1852 had succeeded Sir George Smith as Governor of Cape Colony, reported that unless 2,000 troops could be permanently stationed in the Orange River Sovereignty, that territory must be abandoned.

Abandonment appeared to Downing Street to be the preferable alternative. By a Convention concluded at Bloemfontein (February 23rd, 1854) the inhabitants of the territory between the Orange and Vaal Rivers were declared to be " finally freed from their allegiance to the British Crown," subject to the same proviso as to slavery as that imposed upon the Boers of the Transvaal. But the Bloemfontein Convention was, as a recent commentator has pointed out, a more " revolutionary " document than the Sand River Convention. The latter merely recognized facts; the Bloemfontein Convention meant " the withdrawal of an existing sovereignty against the wishes of many British subjects and in face of the apathy of many more." [1] For the next twenty years the British Government rigorously adhered to the principle of non-intervention in the affairs of the two Boer republics. Not until 1877 was the policy embodied in the Convention abruptly reversed.

In the meantime two important developments had taken place: Cape Colony had been endowed with responsible government and the period of " masterly inactivity " had been brought to an end by the extension of British Sovereignty to more than one native state in South Africa.

For twenty years after the conquest of South Africa the British administrators of the colony carried on the government by the machinery with which the Dutch inhabitants had long been familiar.[2] In 1811 a system of Itinerant Justices, strangely reminiscent of one of the great reforms of Henry II, was introduced. Like the Barons of Henry's Exchequer, the Justices acted both as Judges of Assize and as Commissioners, who supplied the central Government of Capetown with information about local affairs. The arrival of British colonists in 1820 necessitated a change. In 1825 an Advisory Council was appointed to assist the Governor, though under the autocratic rule of Lord Charles Somerset (1814–1829) the Council was of little effect. *Constitutional Development, 1833–1872*

The first important step towards self-government was taken in 1833, when an Executive Council, consisting of *Crown Colony Government*

[1] Walker, ap. C.H.B.E., p. 355.
[2] Cf. *Select Documents Illustrating South African History* (ed. G. W. Eybers, 1918).

officials, and a Legislative Council, in which the unofficial nominees might outnumber the officials by seven to four, were appointed. In view, however, of rapid constitutional developments in Canada, in Australia, and in New Zealand, the colonists in South Africa could not for long be content with so meagre a concession.[1] Accordingly a legislative body of two Chambers, both elected though for different terms and on a differentiating franchise, was, in 1853, set up. The control of the Civil List remained in the hands of the Governor, but the Legislature was invested with full discretion over the Customs, provided the discretion was not exercised for the purpose of imposing differentiating duties.

Responsible Government

The final stage was reached in 1872, when by a small majority, and not without misgivings, the traditional English system of an executive responsible to the local legislature was adopted in Cape Colony.[2] The circumstances of that colony differed greatly, as already explained, from those in Canada and Australasia. For reasons still to be examined, the experiment was, in South Africa, far more hazardous. Well had it been for the future of South Africa and of the Empire had more heed been paid to the alternative pressed upon the Imperial Government, many years earlier, by one of the greatest of colonial administrators.

Sir George Grey

Sir George Grey had been Governor and High Commissioner from 1854 to 1859, and though recalled in 1859 was reinstated in 1860, and retained office until his transference to New Zealand in 1861.

Sir George Grey found that the native problem was paramount in South Africa, though in his time it affected the Boer republics more acutely than the British colonies. Neither in the Transvaal nor in the Orange Free State were the Boers strong enough to deal with their native neighbours, and the Imperial Government, particularly when embarrassed by the Crimean war and the Indian Mutiny, did not deem it incumbent upon them to protect the independent republics.

[1] *Supra*, pp. 135 f.
[2] Natal reached the goal of responsibility, having passed through the same stages as the older colony, in 1893.

All their forces were wanted elsewhere, and in 1857 Grey did not hesitate to denude the Cape Colony of troops in order to save the situation in India. Those troops were the first Imperial reinforcements to reach the scene of the Mutiny, and enabled Colin Campbell to relieve Lucknow. That Grey could afford to take risks was due entirely to the wonderful influence he had obtained over the Kaffir chiefs. Before despatching the troops he summoned the chiefs to a conference and frankly told them that the Great Queen wanted her troops in India. He asked them to pledge their word not to give trouble in the absence of the troops. They gave the promise and kept it.

Meanwhile, there was developing in the Orange Free *Federation* State a movement in favour of federal union with the parent colony. It was cordially welcomed by Grey. He was convinced that the only path of safety for the whole of South Africa lay in some form of federation. In one of the ablest documents ever penned by a colonial Governor he laid his views before the Home Government. The latter had already commended to his consideration a scheme for the federation of the Cape, Natal, and Kaffaria. Grey had a wider vision: he wanted not only to federate the whole of South Africa but to associate with federation the immediate grant of self-government.[1] When, however, Grey brought the proposal of the Free State Boers before the Cape Parliament, contrary, be it admitted, to express instructions, he was summarily recalled.

Queen Victoria approved of Grey's objects—" the bringing the Kaffirs in British Kaffaria within the pale of the law so that they may know the blessings of it—and the reabsorption if possible of the Orange Free State "—and added: " to both these objects the efforts of the Government should be directed." [2]

Mr. Henry Labouchere (Colonial Secretary, 1855–1858) had other views. Like the rest of his School, he was an

[1] At a much later day the party known as the Federal Home Rulers advised the Asquith Government to " consult Sir George Grey "—of course, apocryphically. Cf. J. Milne in *Fortnightly Review* (June 1900).
[2] *Queen Victoria's Letters* (First series), III, p. 285.

obstinate separatist, and in July 1856 had the assurance to inform the Queen that "When Governor Sir George Grey went to the Cape all these questions had been finally disposed of." [1] Grey, then, was presumably the mischief-maker, but by the Queen's personal intervention he was restored [2] to his Governorship, though on condition that nothing more should be said about South African federation.

The condition was necessarily, though unfortunately, observed. The wisest of the Boers deplored the breakdown. "Had British Ministers in time past been wise enough to follow your advice, there would undoubtedly be to-day a British Dominion extending from Table Bay to the Zambesi." So Mr. F. W. Reitz, afterwards the Transvaal Secretary, wrote in 1893 to Sir George Grey.

The opportunity was missed. If neglected opportunity meant the loss of South Africa, what did it matter provided the Cape peninsula was retained for strategic purposes? The loss of the hinterland would but hasten the coming of the happy day when "those wretched Colonies" would no longer "hang like a millstone round our neck." Responsibilities once assumed are not, however, so lightly cast aside. The period of non-intervention was in fact drawing to a close, and forces too strong to be resisted were operating in the opposite direction.

Basutoland   In 1868 the Orange Free State, having with difficulty reduced the Basutos to submission, proposed to confiscate the most valuable portion of their territory. The British Government, in the general interest of South Africa, intervened. "Let me and my people rest and live under the large folds of the flag of England before I go hence." Such was the pathetic prayer of the famous Basuto chief Mosesh. The prayer was answered by the proclamation of British Sovereignty over Basutoland (1868). Three years later Basutoland was annexed to Cape Colony, but the colonial administration was not a success, and in 1884, in pursuance

[1] *Queen Victoria's Letters* (1st series), III, p. 256; and see Egerton: *Federations and Unions*, p. 71.
[2] By the Duke of Newcastle.

of the policy of direct Imperial control, Basutoland was transferred to the Imperial Government. Whether that Sovereignty shall now (1938) be virtually renounced in favour of the Union of South Africa is one of the most insistent questions to be faced in the self-governing Empire.

Hardly was the Basuto matter settled when a more com- *Diamonds* plicated question emerged on the western border of the Orange Free State. In 1870 diamonds were discovered in the country of which Kimberley is now the capital. The announcement of the discovery drew the usual crowd of adventurers to the district. The scenes of wild excitement and confusion already familiar to Australia and New Zealand were reproduced in South Africa. But with an added complication. To whom did the diamond fields belong? The Griqua chief Waterboer claimed them on behalf of his people; the Orange Free State coveted them, but offered to submit their claim to arbitration. Waterboer refused arbitration and preferred to place his territory under the British flag. British Sovereignty was accordingly proclaimed over Griqualand West. The Orange Free State protested, but eventually accepted £90,000 as compensation for the abandonment of their claim. Griqualand West was in 1880 annexed to Cape Colony, and its representatives took their place in the Cape Parliament (1880).

The acceptance of Griqualand West marked a turning- *Griqualand* point of immense significance in the history of British rule in *West* South Africa. New forces were operating not only in South Africa but in England, in other European countries, and, indeed, throughout the world. The era of *laissez-faire* was at an end. The era of *Weltpolitik* had arrived.

The northward movement initiated by the acquisition of Griqualand West carried British settlers to Bechuanaland and later on to Rhodesia, to the Zambesi, and the shores of Lake Tanganyika.

Nor were the social effects of the discovery of the diamond-fields less important than the political. " A new strain," as Sir Charles Lucas truly says, " entered into South African history when diamonds came to light at Kimberley. The digger, the capitalist, the company promoter, jostled the slow-moving Dutch farmer and quickened the pace of life. The dusty land where the stones were found was not a greater contrast to the glittering diamonds than were the conditions which mining brought to the stolid sobriety of a scattered pastoral people." [1] But this is looking ahead. These reactions were not fully revealed until the discovery of diamonds was followed by the discovery of gold in the Transvaal. That discovery was deferred for more than a decade; in the meantime many things of high significance had happened.

Lord Carnarvon

In 1874 the Conservative Party came into power in England. Their accession marked the close of the supremacy which for nearly half a century the Manchester School had exercised.

" In my opinion no Minister in the country will do his duty who neglects any opportunity of reconstructing as much as possible our Colonial Empire." So Disraeli had said two years before he came into power. The duty was not neglected. Disraeli appointed to the Colonial Office one of his ablest lieutenants. Lord Carnarvon was the man who had been officially responsible in 1867 for the enactment of a Federal Constitution for Canada. Though realizing how greatly the circumstances differed, he believed that " some form of federation " might solve many of the difficulties of South Africa.

The Native Question

Of these difficulties unquestionably the most obstinate and the most insistent arose from the relations between the independent Dutch republics and the native tribes by whom they were encircled. The natives were not without legitimate grievances. The explicit conditions on which the Transvaal and the Orange States had been handed over to the Boers, if observed doubtfully in the letter, were unquestionably violated in the spirit. In fact, if not in form, slavery survived. Moreover, the brutality with which natives were treated by the Boers, combined with the military weakness of the latter, provoked reprisals which in time constituted a

[1] *Op. cit.*, p. 246.

172

serious menace to the other European communities in South Africa. Particularly was this true of Natal, where " in one generation the natives had increased from less than 100,000 to more than 300,000, and at all times vastly outnumbered the Europeans." [1] " The key to South African politics is the question of the treatment of the Natives." So Sir Henry Barkly, Governor of Cape Colony (1870–1877), wrote to Lord Carnarvon in July 1874. Carnarvon agreed; but insisted that " half the cruelty and injustice to a native race arises from fear." The observation was just. But fear could be dissipated only if Natal and the Boer republics were strengthened by federation with the more powerful and more wealthy colony at the Cape.

Lord Carnarvon accordingly suggested that the several States of South Africa should be invited to a conference at Capetown to discuss these matters. Mr. Froude, the eminent historian, was sent out to represent the Colonial Office, but was received with extreme discourtesy by the Ministers at Capetown. Though the idea of federation found favour in many quarters, English and Dutch, throughout South Africa, the Cape Ministry, headed by (Sir) J. C. Molteno, puffed up by their recent accession to " Responsibility " and jealous of the " interference " of Downing Street, refused to meet Carnarvon's emissary at dinner, and cold-shouldered the whole project. The Conference never met. Froude returned to England empty-handed.

Despite his initial failure Carnarvon refused to acknowledge defeat. An informal conference at Downing Street (August 1876) did nothing to advance matters. Nevertheless, in 1877 the Imperial Parliament passed an Enabling Act which contained the outline of a complete Federal Constitution. Sir Bartle Frere, an administrator of great ability and ripe experience, was appointed in 1877 to succeed Sir Henry Barkly in South Africa and to carry the scheme into effect. Lord Carnarvon insisted, indeed, that " the action of all parties, whether in the British colonies or the Dutch States, must be spontaneous and uncontrolled," but

Sir Bartle Frere

[1] Hardinge: *Life of Lord Carnarvon*, II, p. 167.

he made no secret of his confident hope that Sir Bartle Frere would, within two years, be " the first Governor-General of (a federated) South Africa."

The hope was cruelly disappointed. Hardly had Frere reached Capetown (March 31st, 1877) when another trusted envoy of Lord Carnarvon's took a step which not only wrecked all hopes of federation but opened a new chapter of South African history. That chapter was not closed until the Treaty of Vereeniging was signed (1902).

Sir Theophilus Shepstone
No man had a longer or more intimate knowledge of native affairs in South Africa than Sir Theophilus Shepstone. In September 1876 Shepstone had been sent back to South Africa as Special Commissioner to the Transvaal, to enquire into the causes and circumstances of the wars between the Boers and their native neighbours. He was further authorized, should the circumstances demand it, and if it were desired by a substantial number of the inhabitants, to annex the whole or part of the Transvaal.

The Boers were at war with one chief, Sekukini, and had incurred the bitter enmity of two others, Cetewayo, King of the Zulus, and the Matabele chief, Lobengula. These warlike tribes were ready to annihilate the Boers. Shepstone decided that only annexation could save the Transvaal, and on April 12th, 1877, he took over its administration in the Queen's name, at the same time promising the Boers self-government under the Crown. The Boers protested against annexation and appealed to Lord Carnarvon to refuse his sanction. Lord Carnarvon upheld the decision of his agent.

Shepstone's prompt action undoubtedly saved the Boers, but it also brought the British Government face to face, in a more acute form than ever before, with the Native problem in South Africa. A series of disputes with the Zulus led in January 1879 to the outbreak of war with that powerful tribe. The war was brief but full of incident, tragic and heroic. A grievous disaster to a British force at Isandhlwana was redeemed by the heroic defence of Rorke's Drift. For nearly twelve hours two British subalterns, Bromhead and Chard, with 103 men of the South Wales

Borderers, held the Drift against 4,000 Zulus. They saved Natal. These incidents roused the British Cabinet to action. Sir Garnet Wolseley was sent out with large reinforcements. They arrived just as Lord Chelmsford, hitherto unsuccessful, was about to strike at Ulundi the blow that destroyed the Zulu army. Cetewayo, their chief, was captured, and the might of his people was overthrown. Before the year closed the power of Sekukini was also destroyed, and he himself joined Cetewayo in captivity.

The Boers could breathe freely. They had never ceased *Retrocession of* to protest against Shepstone's annexation, and now de- *the Transvaal* manded their country back. Despite persistent pressure from Sir Bartle Frere the Colonial Office had, with disastrous procrastination, failed to implement Shepstone's promise of self-government. The General Election of 1880 had brought Mr. Gladstone back to power, and consequently the Boers had good hopes that, armed with a legitimate grievance, their demand for retrocession would be conceded. It was; but not until the war of 1880–1881 had been fought and won by the Boers. A wholly inadequate British force, checked at Laing's Nek and at Ingogo, was disastrously defeated at Majuba Hill (February 26th, 1881). Sir Frederick Roberts was sent out with reinforcements, but arrived only in time to learn that a Convention had been concluded at Pretoria (March 23rd), recognizing, subject to the suzerainty of the Queen, the independence of the Transvaal. Three years later the Convention of London (1884) deleted all reference to suzerainty, and while reserving the control of external relations acknowledged the " South African Republic."

That was not the end of the matter.

Chapter Thirteen

The Watershed

THE MANCHESTER SCHOOL.
FREE TRADE IN THE WEST INDIES.
THE SHRINKAGE OF THE GLOBE.
THE ENGLISH IN EGYPT (1875–1904).

THE retrocession of the Transvaal was the expiring effort of the Manchester School. With the 'eighties there opened a new era in the history of England, of Europe, of the world.

Mutations of Colonial Policy

For precisely a century—from the surrender at Yorktown (1781) to the defeat at Majuba—the Imperial note had been as rarely heard in English politics as in English poetry. The impulse to colonization in its earliest stages had come, as we have seen, partly from economics and partly from religion. The lust for gold, a desire for high profits in trade, drove Englishmen to adventure life and fortune in the Far West and the Far East. Commercial companies established colonies in Virginia and factories in India. An irresistible desire to be allowed to worship God each after their own manner drove Puritans to New England and Catholics to Maryland.

Then, for a century, England and France fought 1or a great prize—world supremacy. Meanwhile, Economics began to dominate Politics. Of the new School Adam Smith was the prophet. His *Wealth of Nations* was published contemporaneously with the Declaration of American Independence (1776). Chatham rejoiced that the colonists had resisted the unjust impositions of the Motherland, but with his last breath protested against the concession of independence. Burke believed that the only ties between mother and daughter lands worth preserving were those provided " from common names, from kindred blood, from similar privileges and equal protection. These," he said in an

Adam Smith

176

immortal phrase, " are ties which though light as air are as strong as links of iron."

Those ties were snapped in 1783. Ten years later *Jeremy Bentham* Jeremy Bentham published his essay *Emancipate Your Colonies*. The adjuration was addressed primarily to Republican France, all of whose oversea possessions were before long " emancipated " by the British navy. But the advice, inspired by the conviction that " emancipation " would equally benefit a mother country and its colonies, was intended to apply to all colonial Powers.

For nearly a century Bentham exercised an immense influence over our colonial policy: his authority was hardly challenged. Sir George Cornewall Lewis's essay on *The Government of Dependencies* (1841) reflected more accurately than any other work the views of his generation. It echoed Bentham's voice. " If," wrote Lewis, " a dominant country understood the true nature of the advantages arising from the supremacy and dependence of the related communities, it would voluntarily recognize the legal independence of such of its own dependencies as were fit for independence; it would, by its political arrangements, study to prepare for independence those which were still unable to stand alone; and it would seek to promote colonization for the purpose of extending its trade rather than its empire, and without intending to maintain the dependence of its colonies beyond the time when they need its protection."

Cobden was the apostolic successor of Bentham. Free Trade was not only the most hopeful path to peace, it would help to rid us of the encumbrance of colonies. " The colonial system," he wrote, " with all its dazzling appeals to the passions of the people, can never be got rid of except by the indirect process of Free Trade, which will gradually and imperceptibly loose the bands which unite our colonies to us by a mistaken notion of self-interest."

Peel was destined to put into practice the principles of the *Free Trade* Manchester School; but the old mercantilist theory, and the policy based on it, died hard. The Navigation Laws and the policy of preferential rates had survived the Declaration of American Independence. The first inroad upon the traditional policy was made by an Act passed in 1822. The Act permitted the free exchange of food-stuffs and raw materials between any countries in America and the British colonies, and allowed the latter to export their produce direct to European ports—provided that the products were carried in British ships.

William Huskisson

William Huskisson, the disciple of Pitt and the colleague of Canning, carried the Free Trade policy much farther. The cosmopolitan and anti-Imperialist views of the Benthamite School were abhorrent to Huskisson. " England," he declared, " cannot afford to be little. She must be what she is or nothing." Economically, however, he was a convinced Free Trader, and, as President of the Board of Trade (1823–1827), gave effect to his convictions. Like his master Pitt, he negotiated reciprocity treaties, greatly reduced the customs duties on sugar, cotton and woollen goods, glass, paper, and other commodities, and removed vexatious restrictions on the home manufacture of linen and silk.[1] The principle of mutual Preference on Empire products, and protection for British shipping, was, however, maintained intact.

Sir Robert Peel

Peel carried Huskisson's policy to its logical conclusion by a series of fiscal reforms (1842–1846), culminating in the repeal of the Corn Laws. By the repeal of the Navigation Laws in 1849 Lord Grey [2] removed from the Statute-book the last trace of Mercantilism.

The Navigation Laws had been imposed in the interests of British shipping, naval and mercantile. They had effected their purpose. Throughout the nineteenth century the carrying trade of the world was largely in British hands; the supremacy of the British navy was unchallenged. The colonies had nothing to lose by the repeal of the Navigation Laws.

Slavery and Sugar

With the abolition of slavery and the removal of the pre-ferential duties on Empire produce it was otherwise.

---

[1] See for an admirable account of his work A. Brady: *William Huskisson and Liberal Reform*, Oxford, 1928.

[2] The third Earl Grey, Colonial Secretary in Lord John Russell's Ministry, 1846–1852.

Slavery and Preference were the dual foundations upon which the Second Colonial Empire had been built. Both were undermined in the first half of the nineteenth century. The Abolitionists won a notable victory in 1833; the tax-payers of Great Britain paid for that victory in cash. But, as in South Africa, so also in the West Indies, money could not compensate the slave-owners for the loss of slave labour. Between 1844 and 1860 all colonial preferences, the most important being that on sugar, were abolished.

The effect of the abolition of slavery and of Preference was *The West* especially disastrous to the West Indies. No part of the *Indies* Empire has suffered more frequent or more acute vicissitudes, political and economic, than those islands. For two centuries the European Powers played with them a game of battledore and shuttlecock. The prize for which the game was played was so highly accounted of in the eighteenth century that many people held, as we have seen, that French Canada was too dearly paid for in 1763 by the rendition of Guadeloupe. Pitt, when imposing an income-tax in 1798, calculated that of the incomes enjoyed in Great Britain those derived from the West Indies greatly surpassed those from all the other countries (including the thickly populated Ireland) outside Great Britain. Their prosperity depended, however, entirely upon cheap labour and dear sugar. The first was guaranteed by an ample supply of negro slaves; the second by the policy of mutual Preference.

To a large and growing body of opinion in England the *Abolition of* trade in African slaves had long been anathema. Castle- *Slavery* reagh by great efforts secured the adhesion of the Powers at the Congress of Vienna [1] (1814–1815) to the policy of abolishing the slave trade. But the cessation of the practice did not immediately follow upon acceptance of the principle. Great Britain had, indeed, abolished the slave trade in 1807, and the long and noble crusade of the Abolitionists was crowned, as already mentioned, with final victory in 1833. In point of compensation the West Indian planters came off

[1] Cf. Marriott: *Castlereagh*, chapter XV. England abolished the slave *trade* in 1806; *slavery* in 1833.

much better than the Dutch farmers in South Africa. The planters did receive the compensation voted by Parliament, and out of a total of £20,000,000 over £6,000,000 went to Jamaica, where there had been more than 300,000 slaves. The money represented about half the value of the emancipated negroes, but no money could compensate the owners for the loss of labour, though the blow was tempered for a while by a system of semi-servitude described as "apprenticeship" and more permanently by the importation, under indentures, of Asiatic labour, chiefly from India. Nevertheless, the emancipation of the slaves dealt the West Indies a blow from which, with the exception of Trinidad, they have never completely recovered.

Free Trade The Abolitionists had deprived the West Indies of cheap labour; the Free Traders cut their profits to the bone by the abolition of preferences. "England must be made a cheap place for the poor man." So Peel had insisted; but he did at least propose, in the interest of logic and of fair play for the planters, to retain the discrimination against slave-grown sugar. To the planters' natural indignation Lord John Russell discontinued discrimination. The West Indies, bereft of their slaves, had to face the competition of slave-grown sugar in the London market.

And not slave-grown sugar only. Napoleon had taught Europe that there was no need to depend on the tropics for sugar. Beetroot broke the monopoly of the cane. The development of economic nationalism in Europe (increasingly manifested since 1870) led not only to the protection of the home markets but to bounties on export which hit still harder the West Indian producer. For sugar dominated the market, and Jamaica and other West Indian islands sank deeper and deeper in the slough of depression.

Bananas They were eventually rescued from it by the development of a new culture, and by the advent to power in England of a great statesman with wide vision and clear aims. The sugar-cane gave place to the banana. Mr. Joseph Chamberlain declined the Chancellorship of the Exchequer in the Unionist Government of 1895 in order to devote himself to Imperial policy as Secretary of State for the Colonies.

His primary function he conceived to be the development of the neglected colonial estate. In one of the first speeches he addressed to the House of Commons as Secretary of State he said, " I regard many of our colonies as being in the condition of undeveloped estates which can never be developed without Imperial assistance." [1] His words applied primarily to Africa, yet in fact it was to the West Indies that Chamberlain gave first consideration.

In 1897 a Royal Commission was appointed to consider what could be done to save the islands from the bankruptcy which in many of them seemed imminent. As a result, an Imperial Department of Agriculture was set up and was followed later on by the establishment of a College in Trinidad to train men for tropical agriculture. A subsidy of £17,400 a year gave such stimulus to research and to commercial development that by 1911 it was withdrawn as superfluous. Loans were also granted at a low rate of interest for the improvement of transport facilities in the Crown colonies. Jamaica employed the £110,000 obtained therefrom to construct a railway from the coast to the highlands of the interior, and thus gave further encouragement to the production of the banana.

The island was no longer dependent exclusively on sugar. In 1895 sugar accounted for £3,200,000 out of a total export of £5,600,000. In 1911 total exports had risen to £7,100,000, to which sugar contributed less than half (£3,000,000). For this transformation bananas were mainly responsible. In 1885 no land was returned as being planted with bananas. In 1895 18,528 acres were so cultivated; and in 1915, 85,854. The area under coco-nuts more than doubled in the same period, from 4,628 acres (1895) to 11,058 (1915).[2] Meanwhile, sugar production had also been assisted by prohibiting the import (1903) of bounty-fed sugar. This killed the bounty system and increased the

---

[1] *Hansard*, August 22nd, 1895.
[2] Knowles: *Economic Development of the Overseas Empire*, pp. 128–130.

acreage under sugar in Jamaica from 28,871 in 1905 to 31,729 in 1915. To this improvement the reversal of fiscal policy in the Motherland further contributed. For that reversal the elder son of Joseph Chamberlain was responsible. Appropriately it fell to him in the Budget of 1919 to give Preference to colonial sugar and to other Empire commodities. Nevertheless, all is not well with the West Indies. In the present year (1938) there have been serious disturbances in Trinidad and in Jamaica, and yet another Royal Commission has been appointed to survey social and economic conditions in the West Indies.

Government   Nor can constitutional questions be excluded from the enquiry. In respect of government the Bahamas and the West Indies exhibit every possible variety. The Bahamas, Barbados, and Bermuda are highest in the scale, with wholly elected Legislative Assemblies and nominated Legislative Councils. Jamaica, Trinidad, Grenada, St. Lucia and St. Vincent, and the Leeward Islands, as well as the adjacent colonies of British Guiana and British Honduras, have partly elected Legislative Councils containing official majorities. Moreover, the Crown retains the power of legislating by Order in Council, and the Governors also possess virtually autocratic authority. But it is the fact that the West Indies afford the most striking illustration of the effect of Free Trade upon Imperial policy. That fact must be held responsible for this prolonged parenthesis.

Laissez-faire   To return. From the passing of the first Reform Bill (1832) to the enactment of the second (1867), the Manchester School was dominant in English politics. Their colonial policy may be reduced to a formula: self-government as a training for independence. Individuals like Sir William Molesworth, Lord Durham and his colleagues Gibbon Wakefield and Charles Buller, might dream of a different sequel to the policy they initiated, but they were in a negligible minority. " To ripen these (colonial) communities to the earliest possible maturity, social, political, commercial, to qualify them by all the appliances within the reach of the parent state for present self-government and eventual independence, is now the universally admitted aim of our Colonial policy." So Arthur Mills wrote in a widely influential book published in 1856. It was true. Statesmen like Lord Glenelg and Lord Granville shared that view with the permanent officials who advised them. Between 1837 and 1871 three men of exceptional ability, Sir James Stephen, Herman Merivale, and Sir Frederic Rogers (Lord Blachford) were successively responsible for the policy dictated from Downing Street. " I go very far with you in the desire to shake off all responsibly governed colonies." So Rogers wrote in 1865 to his colleague, Sir Henry Taylor. The Civil Servants and the politicians were backed by the philosophic historians. " What shall we give to England in place of her useless dependencies ? What shall we give to a man in place of his heavy burden or dangerous disease ? What but unencumbered strength and the vigour of returning health ? " [1]

Forces much stronger than the words of a doctrinaire were, however, already operating to disappoint their hopes. The globe was shrinking. " The cardinal fact of geography in the twentieth century is the shortening of distances and the shrinkage of the globe. . . . The result is that problems which a century ago or even fifty years ago were exclusively European now concern the whole world." General Smuts was right. The process had, however, already begun in the last decades of the nineteenth century. To that process several famous inventions powerfully contributed. The first was that of Sir Henry Bessemer, whose invention for the production of cheap steel substantially diminished the cost of ocean transport. From 1860 onwards the compound engine greatly economized the use of coal and enabled the steamship to displace the sailing ship even for ocean voyages. But the boilers were apt to be ruined by salt water; fresh water could not, owing to evaporation, be used more than once. Large storage-space for water was, therefore, essential, and left no room for bulky cargo. The perfecting of the surface condenser (1870) made it possible to pass the

Shrinkage of the Globe

[1] Goldwin Smith: *The Empire*, p. xix (Oxford, 1863).

same water through the boilers as often as need be. Space was thus made available for cargo and the working cost of steamers further reduced.[1] The opening of the Suez Canal (1869) shortened the voyage from London to Hong Kong by twenty-five per cent, and to Bombay by no less than forty.

" Man is of all kinds of luggage the most difficult to transport." So Adam Smith had written in 1776. If the impediments to the transport of both goods and men have been largely removed, still more impressive have been the improved facilities for communications. The first submarine cable connecting England and France was laid only in 1861, and that between England and America in 1865. To-day this method of communication has been supplemented by long-distance telephony and wireless telegraphy. But for inter-Imperial trade nothing has done so much as refrigeration and cold storage. The New Zealand Shipping Company adopted the use of refrigeration in 1882, and by that means mutton, lamb, and butter have been brought from the Australasian colonies to Great Britain in ever-increasing quantity and ever-improving quality. The British market is supplied, to the great advantage of our urban population, with fruit from all the Dominions and by dairy produce from most of them.

Thus distance has been almost eliminated by science.

Expansion of Europe

If the world has shrunk, Europe has expanded. The process was most obtrusive in Africa. The northern coast of that great continent has always belonged to the European system. In modern times France was the first to recognize this truth. Algeria has since 1830 passed gradually under the control of France, who in 1881 established, with Bismarck's encouragement, a Protectorate over Tunis. Nor did Bismarck miscalculate. Italy, deeply resentful of France's presence in Tunis, joined Germany and Austria-Hungary in the Triple Alliance. France and Italy have never, since then, been real friends. With a purpose equally

---

[1] *The Economic Development of the British Overseas Empire*: 3 vols., London, 1924, 1930. To that admirable work the wise reader will refer. The points here made are summarized from Marriott: *Modern England*, chapter I, and the whole subject is treated in much greater detail in Knowles : I. pp. 17–18.

184

amiable Bismarck encouraged England to remain in Egypt. For nearly twenty years France and England were bitterly estranged. So Bismarck divided his potential enemies. But in 1904 Great Britain recognized the predominant claims of France over Morocco: France recognized England's predominance in Egypt. In 1911 Italy conquered and annexed Tripoli. Thus the whole Mediterranean coast of Africa passed under European control.

In 1875 Great Britain, who had refused to participate in the construction of the canal through the isthmus of Suez, had suddenly awakened to the importance of the work accomplished by Lesseps. Thanks to the prompt action of Disraeli and the ready help of the Rothschilds, she then acquired the whole of the Khedive's interest (176,602 shares) in that undertaking. In 1876 the financial embarrassments of the Khedive Ismail compelled England and France to establish a Dual Control over Egypt. By 1879 Ismail's rule of tyranny and extravagance had become insupportable. In that year the Sultan of Turkey compelled him to abdicate, but his son Tewfik proved incapable of coping with the prevailing anarchy, and in 1882 Great Britain, deserted by France and the other Powers, was constrained to take action alone. Alexandria was bombarded by the British Fleet; Arabi, the leader of a nationalist movement, was defeated at Tel-el-Kebir, was captured, and deported to Ceylon.

England and Egypt

A British army was then stationed in Egypt to restore (in official phrase) the authority of the Khedive, and, though much has happened in the meantime, has not yet (1938) completely evacuated the country.

Although from the first it was never intended that the occupation should be other than temporary, circumstances inevitably prolonged it. Between 1883 and 1907 Lord Cromer, one of the greatest of British pro-consuls, effected a complete reorganization of the country. Not without interruptions. His own position was as anomalous as that of the country he represented. Technically only a British agent and Consul-General, he became virtually the ruler of the country. He was hampered by the jealousy of foreign colleagues in Cairo (particularly, until 1904, by those representing France) , and not less by complications connected with the Sudan.

The Sudan   For many years the Sudan had been, of all the provinces of Egypt, the most atrociously misgoverned. In 1883 the Sudanese, led by a fanatic who styled himself the Mahdi (the Messiah), revolted against their oppressors. The Egyptian Government despatched an English officer, General Hicks, to quell the insurrection, but Hicks was killed and the Egyptian force under his command was cut to pieces. The British Government declined the task of reconquering the Sudan, but scattered garrisons in the country could not be left to the tender mercies of the Mahdi. After much delay and with much hesitation General Charles Gordon was, on his own suggestion, despatched to rescue the garrison of Khartoum. He reached Khartoum, but found himself in turn besieged (February 1884). Not until August did the Gladstone Ministry decide to send out a relieving expedition. Sir Garnet Wolseley, who commanded it, made all possible haste, and on January 27th, 1885, came in sight of Khartoum. It was too late. Two days earlier the Mahdi had stormed the city and Gordon had been killed.

The British Government then decided, while retaining Suakin, the port of the Sudan on the Red Sea, to abandon to the Mahdi all the rest of the Nile valley south of Wadi Halfa.

For ten years the Sudan remained a prey to anarchy, and more than once threatened trouble to Egypt, but the threat was warded off by Egyptian forces under the command of General Grenfell and Colonel Kitchener. By the patient labours of those two officers the Egyptian army was completely reorganized, and by 1896 was judged to be ready for the accomplishment of a task—which, though deferred, was ultimately unavoidable—the reconquest of the Sudan.

Between 1896 and 1898 Kitchener carried out his plans with equal patience and skill, and on September 2nd, 1898,

Mahdism was finally annihilated by the great victory at Omdurman. Khartoum was immediately occupied, the British and Egyptian flags were hoisted side by side, and on the spot where Gordon had perished a solemn service was held in memory of a very perfect knight.

Hardly had General Kitchener occupied Khartoum when *Fashoda* the news reached him that a French expedition, commanded by Major Marchand, had arrived at Fashoda, and was prepared to dispute his further progress up the Nile.

As far back as March 1895 Sir Edward Grey, representing the Foreign Office in the House of Commons, had declared that the despatch of a French expedition to the Upper Nile would be regarded by Great Britain as an " unfriendly act." His warning was ignored. In 1896 Major Marchand was sent out to take command of an expeditionary force in the French Congo, and from there, in the face of almost insuperable difficulties, he pushed his way across central Africa and reached Fashoda just in time to forestall Kitchener's advance.

Courteously but firmly Kitchener denied Marchand's right to be at Fashoda. Marchand, however, stood his ground, and the dispute was referred to the home Governments. Lord Salisbury made it clear to the Quai d'Orsay that the Khedive's claim to all the lands ruled by the defeated Mahdi would be sustained by the whole force of Great Britain. So large a claim can be justified only if the fundamental issue is understood. To command the sources of the Nile was the supreme object of France and Germany no less than of Great Britain. The Nile meant not only the domination of Egypt but of the route to India and the Far East. Thus, in the autumn of 1898, England and France were on the brink of war; but war was happily averted by the firmness of Lord Salisbury and the good sense of the French, who recalled Marchand and concluded with Great Britain a comprehensive agreement. France was confirmed in possession of a great West African Empire, but acknowledged the rights of Great Britain over the whole Nile basin from the source of that river to its mouth. The road from Cairo to the Cape was still open. Incidentally, Fashoda, by one of the frequent parodoxes of politics, proved the prelude to the Anglo-French Entente of 1904.

To the successful negotiation of the Anglo-French Treaty many causes, with which this narrative is not concerned, contributed.[1] The basis of the agreement was an acknowledgment on the one side of England's paramount interest in Egypt and the Nile Valley, on the other of French interests in Morocco. But opportunity was also taken to clear up long-standing disputes between the two countries in all parts of the world: in Newfoundland; in the New Hebrides and Siam; in Madagascar and Zanzibar; and not least in West Africa, where Great Britain made important concessions to France on the Niger, on the Gambia, and in Guinea.

The French were not, however, our only neighbours in Africa.

[1] See Marriott: *History of Europe from 1815 to 1937* (3rd ed.), chapter XXI.

Chapter Fourteen

The Partition of Africa

BRITISH EXPANSION. THE BOER WAR. THE UNION OF SOUTH AFRICA

IN the last decades of the nineteenth century the attention of Europe was, in large measure, concentrated upon Africa. Much light had been thrown upon the dark recesses of that great continent by the ardour and persistent labours, the self-sacrifice and courage, of missionaries and explorers such as were Robert Moffat[1] and David Livingstone, Captain Speke and Colonel Grant, Sir Richard Burton, Sir Samuel Baker, and Sir H. M. Stanley.[2]

It was, however, the action of Belgium that precipitated *Partition of* the partition of the " Dark Continent." In 1879 Leopold II *Africa* persuaded Stanley to undertake a further exploration of the Congo basin, and the occupation of nearly 100,000 square miles of territory in that region eventually gave Belgium the third place among the European owners of Africa.

In the Congo region the Belgians had an active competitor in France, who emerged from the Partition of 1890 the largest of African Powers, with an area of nearly 400,000 square miles. But much of this was desert. Portugal, who prior to 1884 held the first place, now holds the fourth (with 788,000 square miles), but, thanks to the award of Marshal Macmahon in 1875, she still retains the valuable and much-coveted port of Lourenço Marques.

Much the most striking achievement, however, was that *The Germans* of Germany, who, though she had long taken her full share *in Africa* in the exploration of Africa, owned, prior to 1884, not one foot of territory on that continent. In the course of less

---

[1] 1795–1883.
[2] Livingstone's explorations were made between 1849 and 1873; Stanley's between 1871 and 1889.

than two years (1884–1885) Germany leapt into the third place with nearly 1,000,000 square miles of territory. She established a Protectorate over Damaraland and Namaqualand, a district afterwards known as South West Africa; she annexed, on the west coast, Togoland and the Cameroons, but the most important of her acquisitions was the great province which became known as German East Africa. With an area of 384,180 square miles, and a population believed to number nearly eight million persons, mostly belonging to strong fighting races, the province gave Germany a position of first-rate strategic importance.

British Advance in Africa

Yet, dramatic as was the entrance of Germany upon the colonial stage, her advance in Africa was less remarkable than the advance made by Great Britain after the rendition of the Transvaal (1884). Zululand, after an attempt to preserve peace between the chiefs by a British Resident, had been declared British territory in 1877, and with adjacent native territories was in 1897 annexed to Natal.

Bechuanaland Protectorate

Of still greater importance was the establishment (1885) of a British Protectorate over the huge central block of territory, Bechuanaland. Paul Kruger, who since 1883 had been President of the Transvaal Republic, had, from the first, cast longing eyes on a country in which a good many Transvaal Boers had settled. The Republic was, indeed, prohibited, by the Pretoria and London Conventions, from making any territorial encroachments upon its neighbours, but the advent of Germany excited Kruger's hope that in no long time he might be able to play off two great European Powers against each other and violate the Conventions with impunity.

Kruger was not alone in perceiving the importance of Bechuanaland. Cecil John Rhodes described it as the Suez Canal of South Africa, and his dream of an all-British route from the Cape to Cairo could never be realized if Bechuanaland were to pass under the control of any foreign Power. Moreover, the British Protectorate in Bechuanaland imposed an effective check upon the development of undue familiarity between Pretoria and the Germans in

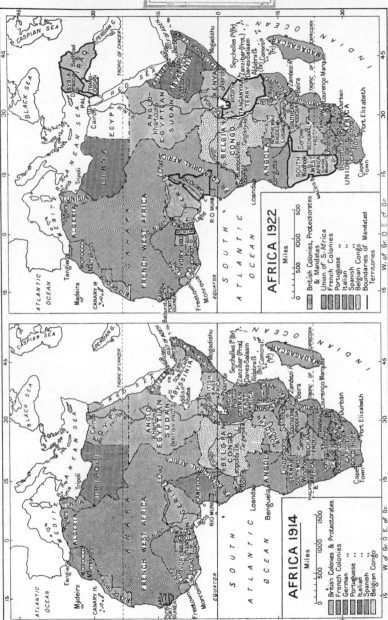

AFRICA IN 1914 AND 1922

the south-west. Cecil James Rhodes, the son of a Hert- *C. J. Rhodes*
fordshire parson, had gone out to South Africa in 1870, as
a lad of seventeen, and was one of the first to make a fortune
on the Kimberley diamond-field. He helped to establish
the great De Beers Company in 1880, and in the same year
entered the Cape Parliament. To his prescience the proclamation of the British Protectorate over Bechuanaland
was largely due.

In the expansion of the British Empire in Africa Chartered *Chartered*
Companies had begun in the 'eighties to play an important *Companies*
part. These companies had, in the seventeenth century,
been accepted as a valuable means of colonial and commercial development. But Adam Smith, sharing Burke's
abhorrence of the East India Company, denounced as wholly
inconsistent the functions of " trader and sovereign," and
his strictures went far to kill the system.

With great advantage, however, it was revived in the last
years of the nineteenth century. A chartered company was
admirably adapted to do pioneering work. It could take
risks and try experiments; the Crown, escaping initial
responsibility, could ultimately reap where the company had
sown. So it proved in Africa. The Royal Niger Company
was incorporated in 1886 and the Imperial British East
Africa Company in 1888.[1]

A century and a half before South Africa passed under the *West Africa*
Sovereignty of Great Britain, isolated points had been
occupied on the west coast. Down to the time when the
slave trade was abolished (1807), they were valued chiefly
as convenient centres for that nefarious traffic. Early in
the reign of Charles II (1662–64), forts and factories were
established on the Gold Coast and at the mouth of the
Gambia River and shiploads of slaves were sent from there *Gambia*
to the West Indies and the American colonies. After the
traffic in slaves was abolished, and before the new era of
European expansion had opened in the later years of the
nineteenth century, there were serious thoughts of abandon-
ing these pestilential possessions. Gambia was, however,

[1] See *infra*, p. 196.

placed under the administration of Sierra Leone in 1821, and was not separated from it until (1888) it became a Crown colony under an independent Government. It remains a mere islet in the vast ocean of French West Africa, but is a not-unimportant depot for the export of ground-nuts and palm-kernels. Much more important from an economic *Gold Coast* point of view is the Gold Coast Colony, which has an external trade of some £25,000,000 a year, including exports which represent more than half the world's supply of cocoa. Fifty-six per cent of the external trade is with the United Kingdom. The forts and factories on the Gold Coast passed backwards and forwards between various trading companies and the Crown, but were finally taken over by the Crown in 1843. Later on, the British Government bought out the contiguous Dutch and Danish forts, and, owing to attacks by the inland kingdom of Ashanti, were compelled to establish Protectorates over that country and the hinterland, now known as the Northern Territories. Like Gambia, the Gold Coast Colony is surrounded, save on its coast side, by French dominions.

Sierra Leone   In striking contrast to the history of Gambia and the Gold Coast is the history of Sierra Leone, which was bought by the British Government in 1787 from a native chief for the purpose of establishing a settlement for liberated negroes— primarily for those who had fought under the British flag in the American War of Secession. The strip of coast-land thus acquired not only gave us the finest harbour on the west coast of Africa, but provided a home for over one thousand negroes who had followed their masters to New Brunswick. Neither climatically, economically, socially, nor politically was New Brunswick suited to negroes, however touching their loyalty to the masters or to the Empire they had served. A body of philanthropists suggested to the Government their repatriation to Africa, and so Sierra Leone, with its capital of Freetown, came into being. The black Empire Loyalists were presently reinforced by slaves who were rescued at sea, or had escaped from the West Indies and the United States, and after 1807 the philan-

thropic company, to which in 1791 a charter of incorporation had been granted, transferred its rights to the Crown.
Sierra Leone is now a Crown colony with a partly elected
Legislature, and exercises a Protectorate over the adjoining
territory.

Of the British possession in West Africa, the Colony and *Nigeria*
Protectorate of Nigeria is much the largest and most important. Until the " scramble for Africa " began among
the European Powers the swamps on the delta of the Niger
offered no political temptations to any Government, but
the " Oil Rivers " area had for many years been exploited
by various traders, mainly for the sake of the palm-oil which
its forests yielded in profusion. When the scramble began,
Germany acquired Togoland and the Cameroons, but, a
British company, headed by Sir George Taubman Goldie,
was successful in establishing its title to Nigeria. A charter
was granted to the Royal Niger Company in 1888, but
fierce competition for possession of the hinterland continued between the English and the French until in 1898
their respective spheres were delimited. Two years later
the political jurisdiction of the Royal Niger Company was
transferred to the Crown, but the company continued its
activities as a commercial undertaking.

With the development of Nigeria, a territory about one-
third of the size of British India, two names will be im-
memorially associated. That of Sir Ronald Ross, who
effected the conquest of the mosquito, and that of Sir
Frederick (now Lord) Lugard, who has devoted some of
the best years of a long life to the extirpation of slavery in
tropical Africa. For some years he was engaged in that
humanitarian work in East Africa, but from 1894 until the
close of the World war he was (save for an interval of five
years spent as Governor of Hong Kong) employed in West
Africa. In 1897 he raised the West African Frontier Force
—a native army under British officers—and with their aid
he did much to secure the native chiefs of the interior against
the advances of France and Germany. By a series of Conventions between Great Britain and France (1890–1899) the

THE BRITISH EMPIRE

northern frontiers of Nigeria and the French sphere of influence were delimited, and Lugard and his West African Frontier Force were then compelled to undertake the effective occupation of the Moslem Emirates (1902–1903). The native chiefs were, as far as possible, confirmed in their authority over their tribesmen, but they had to accept British Residents, to put a stop to slave-raiding, to contribute to the expenses of administration, to maintain order, and to execute justice. When in 1907 Lugard left Africa to take up the Governorship of Hong Kong, he could already point to great improvements in the economic and social condition of the people. He returned in 1912 as Governor of North and South Nigeria, and when in 1914 the two Protectorates were amalgamated, Lugard became Governor-General of a united Nigeria, with its capital at Lagos, a former *entrepôt* of the slave trade, but acquired by the British Government in 1861 with a view of putting an end to that traffic.

East Africa

We pass from West to East Africa, which presents, in some respects, a marked contrast. East Africa has double the area of West Africa but less than half the population. Some small proportion of that population is in the highland areas British, and that proportion may increase. In West Africa there are no such areas suitable for the permanent settlement of the white man.

Aden, Perim, Socotra

Until the 'eighties, Eastern Equatorial Africa, though an object of ambition to the Khedive Ismail of Egypt, had come under the notice of Europe only through the devoted labours of explorers and missionaries. The Sultan of Zanzibar exercised jurisdiction over about a thousand miles of coast, nor were his claims over an ill-defined hinterland questioned by Europeans. In the early 'eighties, however, the Powers began to occupy strategic points on or off the coast of East Africa. Great Britain had long ago secured a station on the opposite shore at Aden (1837), and at Perim (1857). Socotra, occupied by the English East India Company in 1834, was declared a British Protectorate in 1886. Eritrea, with a coast-line of some seven hundred miles along the Red

194

Sea, passed into the keeping of Italy between 1882 and 1888, *Italians in East* as did Italian Somaliland. By a series of treaties with the *Africa* Somali Sultans, and Agreements with Great Britain and the rulers of Zanzibar and Abyssinia (1889–1905), Italy obtained Somaliland, and in 1925 Great Britain transferred to it a portion of Kenya Colony known as Jubaland, with the port of Kismayu. British Somaliland, opposite *British* Aden, was declared a British Protectorate in 1884, and its *Somaliland* limits were defined by treaties with France (1888), Italy (1894), and Abyssinia (1897). The town and territory of Obock, on the Red Sea, opposite Aden, were purchased by a Frenchman in 1857, but only in 1883 did France take formal possession of the patch of territory now known as French Somaliland, which included the important port of Jibuti. A French Protectorate over Madagascar was *French* recognized by the British Government in 1890, though *Somaliland and* not until 1896–1899 was that large island and its de- *Madagascar* pendencies brought into submission to the French Government.

Meanwhile, as we have already seen, the Germans had *Germans in* established themselves not only on the west coast (Togoland *Africa* and the Cameroons), but on Walfisch Bay (German South West Africa), and also in the territory now known as Tanganyika. So far as there was any "sovereignty" in the latter, it belonged to the Sultan of Zanzibar, whose independence was formally recognized by the British and French Governments in 1862. In 1878 the Sultan offered to lease all his territories on the mainland for seventy years to Sir William Mackinnon, Chairman of the British India Steam Navigation Company, well known not only as a keen and successful man of business but as a great philanthropist and Imperialist. The territory comprised over one million square miles, and included the Lakes Victoria Nyanza, Tanganyika, and Nyassa. The British Government refused to sanction this large addition to the Empire; but in 1885 the German Empire put in a claim to a considerable slice of this territory, and the claim was conceded by the Sultan of Zanzibar. The German and British spheres were delimited under a

series of agreements (1886–1890), and in 1887, within a few months of each other, the German Africa Company and the *British East Africa Company* British East Africa Association were formed. The latter, under the chairmanship of Mackinnon, was converted into a Chartered Company in 1888, and in 1890 Zanzibar was taken under British protection. In 1895 the Government bought out the territorial rights of the Company, and put the administration of the new East Africa Protectorate under the Foreign Office. Between 1896 and 1903 a railway was constructed between the important harbour of Mombasa and Lake Victoria Nyanza. White settlers followed in the track of the railway. In 1905 the control of the Protectorate was transferred to the Colonial Office, and in 1920 it became a Crown colony with the new title of Kenya. In addition to the Crown colony proper there is a strip of coast, which we expressly retained as a Protectorate. This strip included the harbour at Mombasa, and is known as the Kenya Protectorate.

Uganda Protectorate North of Tanganyika, bounded on the west by the Belgian Congo, and on the east by Kenya, lies the Protectorate of Uganda. This country was first revealed to Europeans by Burton and the missionaries in the 'sixties. After the acquisition of German East Africa, Germany threatened to absorb Uganda also and thus to obtain control of the Nile's sources, so vital to Egypt and the Sudan. The Anglo-German Treaty of 1890, however, assigned Uganda to Great Britain, and the Imperial British East Africa Company having secured the services of Captain (now Lord) Lugard, sent him to Uganda to administer the territory. With most inadequate resources Lugard asserted British claims, but the Home Government was impatient and, but for the urgent representations of Bishop Tucker and Lugard himself, would have abandoned the territory. In default the Government consented to send out Sir Gerald Portal to report on the situation. Portal reported strongly in favour of retention, and in 1894 Uganda was declared a British Protectorate.

Thus, as Lugard writes, " the continuous control of the

Nile from its sources in the Great Victoria and Albert Lakes was secured to the Empire." [1] In 1903 East Uganda was included in the East Africa Protectorate—now Kenya Colony—and three years later the control of the Uganda Protectorate was transferred from the Foreign Office to the Colonial Office. The completion of the Mombasa–Uganda Railway (1923) has opened up the territory, but the Uganda Protectorate will never be a white man's country, as part of Kenya Colony well may be.

Greatest of the African companies was that with which *British South Africa Company* the name of Rhodes will always be associated. Its sphere of operations was the vast Matabele-Mashonaland territory which was christened after him and is the standing memorial of his foresight and statesmanship.

Towards the end of the 'eighties Lobengula, the powerful ruler of the country, was the object of flattering attentions on the part of concession-hunters not English only but Germans, Portuguese, and Boers of the Transvaal. In 1888 the great chief, despite the ardent competition of other suitors, preferred to ally himself with the " Great White Queen." He engaged not to make any treaties or to cede any territory without the sanction of the Queen's representative, the High Commissioner of South Africa.

In 1889 the British South Africa Company received its charter from the Crown, and large powers were assigned to it over the territory extending from the Transvaal on the south to the Belgian Congo on the north, and bounded on the east and west by the Portuguese colonies.

Into this country Rhodes despatched an expedition, guided by the great traveller and hunter F. C. Selous, and commanded by Rhodes's physician and confidant Leander Starr Jameson. A friendly agreement was concluded with the Portuguese in 1891, but with the warlike Matabele there were serious collisions, and after several regrettable incidents Lobengula fled the country. The antagonism of his people was gradually overcome. With the Arab slave-traders in Northern Rhodesia the British also came into

[1] *Dual Mandate in Tropical Africa*, p. 21.

conflict, and only after a succession of hard blows struck at them was an end finally put to their nefarious activities. But we anticipate the sequence of events. To return.

Gold in the Transvaal

In the Transvaal things had been moving fast since 1884. Before that date there had been some gold discoveries in the Transvaal and in the borderlands it controlled, but it was only in that year that prospecting was rewarded on the Witwatersrand. What that discovery meant to a State which in 1877 had been bankrupt may be guessed from the fact that its revenue rose from less than £200,000 in 1885 to over £3,000,000 in 1898. But economic prosperity brought with it a crop of social and political complications. A crowd of adventurers, from many nations, was attracted to the Witwatersrand. Though ready to profit from the intrusion of financiers, engineers, and miners, the slow-moving, obstinate Dutch farmers, with Paul Kruger at their head, deeply resented their presence. By a series of enactments, the parliamentary franchise was denied to the men who provided nearly all the revenue of the republic. Thus the new city of Johannesburg developed as a community not merely of *Uitlanders*, but of political outlaws.

The Jameson Raid

To no counsels of prudence would President Kruger listen, and in 1895 the exasperated *Uitlanders* were foolish enough to attempt to take by force what was denied to reason. Rhodes, who in 1890 had become Premier of Cape Colony, was at the back of the revolutionary movement in the Transvaal. It was the capital blunder of his life. On December 29th, 1895, his friend Dr. Jameson, at the head of a force of 600 Chartered Company's police, with several Maxim guns, crossed the frontier between Bechuanaland and the Transvaal, but on January 2nd the whole force was surrounded by the Boers at Krugersdorp and forced to surrender. Sir Hercules Robinson, the High Commissioner at Capetown, had already ordered Jameson to withdraw, and, on hearing of the raid, himself hurried to the Transvaal and induced Jameson's confederates at Johannesburg to lay down their arms.

The whole scheme, foolishly conceived, had hopelessly

miscarried. Jameson and the leaders of the Raid were handed over for trial to the British Government, and on conviction were sentenced to short terms of imprisonment. The principal conspirators arrested in Johannesburg were tried in the Transvaal. Four of them (including Colonel Frank Rhodes, a brother of the Cape Premier) were sentenced to death, fifty-nine others were fined £2,000 apiece. The death-sentences were, on a vigorous protest from Mr. Chamberlain, commuted to fifteen years' imprisonment (afterwards reduced) and a fine in each case of £25,000.

The Jameson Raid, while replenishing the Transvaal Treasury, greatly embarrassed the British Government. Politically, the situation was redeemed by the foolish and flamboyant telegram despatched on January 3rd by the Kaiser William to President Kruger. Had the Portuguese Government not refused to permit the landing of German marines and guns at Lourenço Marques, Great Britain and Germany might have been at war in January 1896. Thanks to cool heads in England, and to the prompt despatch of naval and military reinforcements to the Cape, that danger was averted.

In the Transvaal, however, things went from bad to worse. In March 1899 a petition signed by 21,000 *Uitlanders*, recounting their grievances, was addressed to the Queen, and in May the British Government formally brought those grievances to the notice of Mr. Kruger and urged that they should be promptly redressed. Meanwhile in 1896 Rhodes had resigned the Premiership of the Cape, and in 1897 Mr. Chamberlain selected Mr. (afterwards Viscount) Milner to succeed Sir Hercules Robinson. On May 31st Milner met Kruger at Bloemfontein and endeavoured, though in vain, to persuade him to redress the grievances of which the *Uitlanders* justly complained. Kruger was adamant: he resented British intervention in the internal affairs of his independent Republic, and claimed that the last vestige of dependence should be obliterated by the specific renunciation of British suzerainty. In August Mr. Chamberlain warned the President that " the sands

Chamberlain and Milner

were running out." To that warning no heed was paid. On October 9th Mr. Kruger issued an ultimatum. The inevitable answer was war.

The South African War, 1899–1902

The war dragged on for nearly three years, but the military details are outside the scope of this narrative. The Boers, mobilizing a force of 40,000 to 50,000 men with extreme rapidity, invaded Natal, inflicted a terrible defeat on Sir Redvers Buller at Colenso (December 15th), and invested Ladysmith. Despite Buller's advice that that " untenable " position should be surrendered, Sir George White held on to it doggedly, and by his tenacity and gallantry redeemed the honour of British arms in Natal. On the western side General Gatacre was heavily repulsed in a night attack on Stormberg, on December 10th. On the 11th Lord Methuen, advancing by the railway to the relief of Kimberley, was, after several successful though costly engagements, defeated with heavy loss at Maggersfontein. That was one of the blackest weeks in British military history.

Roberts and Kitchener

Large reinforcements were, however, promptly sent out from England. Lord Roberts, with General Kitchener as Chief of his Staff, was put in command of them and landed at Capetown on January 10th, 1900. Lord Roberts was sixty-seven; he had lost his only son at Colenso, but with his arrival in South Africa the spirit of the scene changed instantaneously. The British forces were substantially reinforced by contingents from Australia, New Zealand, and Canada, as well as from several of the Crown colonies, the Federated Malay States, India, and Ceylon. The significance of the struggle was at least as keenly appreciated in the overseas Empire as in the homeland. Before it ended Australia had contributed more than 15,000 men, New Zealand more than 6,000, and Canada 5,762 to a victory which was largely theirs.

A succession of victories in the early months of 1900 caused great rejoicing throughout the Empire. General French in command of a large force of cavalry relieved Kimberley on February 16th; on the 27th (the anniversary of Majuba) he surrounded 4,000 Boers at Paardeberg and compelled them to surrender. Buller relieved Ladysmith on the 28th, and on March 13th Roberts himself entered Bloemfontein.

At Bloemfontein Lord Roberts halted for six weeks, in order to re-establish his transport after his rapid march, and to nurse his sick laid low with enteric. On May 1st he advanced from the Orange State into the Transvaal, entered Johannesburg on May 31st, and Pretoria on June 5th. Meanwhile, Mafeking, brilliantly defended since the first days of the war by Colonel (now Lord) Baden-Powell, was relieved by a mounted force under Colonel Mahon. The news of the relief of the little garrison was received in England with a wild enthusiasm, which has added a word to our vocabulary.

In his later years Lord Baden-Powell has done a service to the Empire greater even than his defence of Mafeking. Had the spirit of the Boy Scouts prevailed in 1900, the rejoicings over the relief of Mafeking, if not less whole-hearted, might have been more orderly.

With the defeat of the main Boer force at Diamond Hill on June 12th, the surrender of 4,000 Free State Boers on the Basutoland frontier, the occupation of every town of any importance in the Transvaal, and the flight of Paul Kruger to Europe via Lourenço Marques, Roberts seemed justified in declaring the war at an end. The Orange Free State had been formally annexed on May 28th, and the Transvaal on September 1st. On his departure from Pretoria (November 29th), Lord Roberts made over the command of the army to Lord Kitchener. Sir Alfred Milner became Governor of the Orange River Colony and of the Transvaal, in combination with the office of High Commissioner of South Africa. In December Lord Roberts left for home, arriving in England just in time (January 2nd) to bring the good news to his Sovereign. The old Queen rewarded her faithful servant with an earldom and the Garter, but on January 22nd, 1901, she herself passed away. The longest, perhaps the greatest, reign in all English history had ended.

In South Africa neither Milner nor Kitchener shared the

optimism of Lord Roberts. For nearly two more years
Louis Botha, De Wet, and Delarey continued to wage
guerrilla war with infinite resourcefulness and skill. But the
grim tenacity of Kitchener gradually bore down all resistance. Boer women and children were collected into con-
centration camps, and by a system of blockhouses the whole
country was slowly subdued. Kruger's personal appeal to
the European Powers for intervention entirely failed. Italy
and Portugal were, indeed, our only real friends, but warmly
as the other Powers sympathized with the Boers they were
not prepared to risk for their sake a war with the mistress
of the seas. The German Kaiser claimed from his grandmother credit for refusing to receive Mr. Kruger, and also
for refusing the latter's request for mediation. The Queen's
reply, described (not undeservedly) by a courtier as "worthy
of Queen Elizabeth," was a model of mingled courtesy,
sarcasm, and dignified self-reliance.[1]

The Treaty of Vereeniging King Edward VII was most anxious that formal
peace with the Boers should be concluded before his
coronation, and on May 31st, 1902, Articles of Peace were
signed.

By the Treaty of Vereeniging the burghers laid down their
arms and recognized Edward VII as their lawful Sovereign,
but both colonies were to have representative institutions,
leading up, as soon as might be, to complete self-government; no indemnity was imposed, and the British Government, with conspicuous generosity, promised £3,000,000 to
facilitate the resettlement of the burghers on their farms.
In the result, no less than £15,000,000 was expended in the
first two years on the work of reconstruction, and the British
Government also guaranteed a loan of £35,000,000.

The generosity was repaid. Thanks to Milner's genius
for administration, prisoners of war were quickly repatriated,
and a whole population was resettled on the soil. " I shall
live in the memories of men in this country, if I live at all,
in connexion with the great struggle to keep it within the
limits of the British Empire. . . . What I should prefer to

[1] See *Queen Victoria's Letters* (3rd series), Vol. III, pp. 507–509, 519–520.

be remembered by is the tremendous effort subsequent to the war not only to repair its ravages, but to restart those Colonies on a higher plane of civilization than they had ever previously attained." That history will ultimately respect Lord Milner's preference is certain, but on his retirement from South Africa (1905) he was violently attacked by a section of the Radical Party, and an address of appreciation from 370,000 of his English fellow-countrymen only partially atoned for that cruel wrong.

The attack was mainly due to Milner's assent to the demand of the mine-owners for the importation of Asiatic labour. *"Chinese Slavery"* The Transvaal possesses two great assets, wide pastures and rich gold deposits. Milner restored the pastoral industry, but he realized that the stability of the economic structure he sought to rear depended wholly upon the output of the mines. Unless they could be worked to full capacity the Transvaal would inevitably become a heavy charge upon the British taxpayer. But, of the 200,000 labourers required, the African natives would supply only 70,000. Mr. Chamberlain, on his memorable visit to South Africa in 1902–1903, had warned the Rand magnates that their demand for Asiatic labour would be hotly resisted both in the colony and at home, but Milner was convinced that recourse to that expedient, however distasteful, was unavoidable. An Ordinance to permit, under strict conditions, the importation of Asiatic labour was passed in 1904, but the Chinese coolies imported to the number of nearly 50,000 gave more trouble than they were worth. In the British General Election of 1906 the cry of " Chinese Slavery " was most disingenuously raised by Radical candidates and contributed greatly to the overwhelming victory of their party.[1]

Sir Henry Campbell-Bannerman, on coming into office as Prime Minister, found it impossible to abolish the employment of coolies at once, and could only prohibit further recruitment. By February 1910, however, the last batch of coolies had been repatriated.

[1] Mr. George Lansbury confessed his shame at having taken part in this "campaign of gross distortion and misrepresentation." *My Life* (1923), p. 202.

Self-govern-ment
Meanwhile, much had happened in South Africa. Crown colony government had been introduced into both the Boer colonies in 1902, and Mr. Alfred Lyttleton, who in 1903 succeeded Mr. Chamberlain as Colonial Secretary, drafted a new Constitution giving them a representative legislature but without a responsible executive. That Constitution never came into effect. In its stead, Campbell-Bannerman's Government embarked on what was acclaimed by its admirers as " a magnificent venture of faith." Responsible government of the accepted type was introduced into the Transvaal in 1906 and into the Orange River Colony in 1907, with the hope that that step would " in due time lead to the union of the interests of the whole of His Majesty's dominions in South Africa."

That hope was fulfilled more speedily than could have been anticipated. Lord Selborne, who in 1905 had succeeded Lord Milner as High Commissioner, reviewed the whole situation in a masterly State Paper comparable in significance with Lord Durham's historic *Report* on Canada.[1] The result was that in October 1908 delegates from each of the four Parliaments met in convention at Durban to frame a Constitution for South Africa.

Four problems confronted the Convention: the position of the native population; the need of labour for the mines, for industry, and for agriculture; the railway system and railway rates; and, closely connected with the last, the tariff question. The more closely these problems were studied the more clearly did the conclusion emerge that the solution of federation, adopted in Canada and Australia, was inapplicable to the peculiar conditions of South Africa. A scheme for Union was accordingly drafted, and by June 1909 had, after careful reconsideration, and with several amendments, been approved by the Legislatures of Cape Colony, the Transvaal, and the Orange River Colony, and by referendum in Natal.

The Union of South Africa
The Union of South Africa Act was passed, with the cordial goodwill of all parties, through the Imperial Parlia-

[1] Cmd. 3,564 (1907).

ment, and received the Royal Assent on September 20th, 1909. The Legislature of South Africa, consisting of the Crown and two Houses, is virtually Sovereign, being competent to amend even the Constitution itself. The Senate contains forty members, of whom thirty-two are elected (in equal numbers) by the four Provinces and eight by the Governor-General-in-Council—in other words, by the Ministry. Of the latter, four have to be selected " on the ground mainly of their thorough acquaintance . . . with the reasonable wants and wishes of the coloured races in South Africa." By the *Representation of the Natives Act* (1936) four additional Senators of European descent are elected by natives to represent them. The Senate possesses only a suspensive vote, which can be overridden by a majority obtained from a joint Session of the two Houses. The Assembly numbers 150 elected members, distributed among the four Provinces according to the number of their adult male Europeans. Natives are excluded from the franchise in all Provinces except in Cape Colony, where they return three European members.[1]

The Executive is, in the English sense, responsible and parliamentary. The Ministers forming the Executive Council must be members either of the Senate or the Assembly, and by custom are allowed to sit and speak, though not to vote, in both Houses. Their number must not exceed ten, exclusive (in practice) of one or two Ministers " without portfolio."

A Supreme Court was set up, but it is indicative of the

[1] The legislation of 1936, though very important, is rather complicated. Down to that year the natives, but in Cape Colony only, were included in the European voters' register. The Act of 1936 abrogated this privilege, but divided the Cape Provinces into three constituencies, in each of which the natives (separately enrolled) return one European member to the Assembly. Natives are also to be represented in the Senate by four additional (European) Senators, elected by electoral colleges, throughout the Union. A Native Representative Council was also established in 1936. This Council, numbering 22 in all, includes four natives nominated by the Governor-General and twelve elected members. Its functions are purely advisory.

By the *Native Trust and Land Act* (1936) an area equal in size to England and Wales is to be set aside for the exclusive settlement of natives.

The general principle of the above Acts may be described as " Economic segregation and more effective political representation."

unitary character of the South African Constitution that the function of the Court is merely, as in England, to interpret the law, not, as in America and Australia, to act as a guardian of the Constitution. From the Supreme Court an appeal lies to the Privy Council.

As befits the new Unitary State, the four original States have been reduced to the status of Provinces, with even less independence than the Provinces of the Federal Dominion of Canada, and still less than that enjoyed by the States of the Commonwealth of Australia.

No fewer than seventeen sections of the Union Act were devoted to the interdependent subjects of finance and railways.

Such in brief outline is the present Constitution of South Africa.[1] Of the questions that still await solution much the most difficult is the position of the natives both in the Union itself and in the Protectorates, for which the Imperial Crown still remains trustee. To that question, as well as to the question of the relations between the Union and the Imperial Government, further reference must presently be made. For the moment it must suffice to say that the experiment, initiated with conspicuous courage and unusual circumspection in 1909, has been attended with a remarkable, though not undeserved, measure of success.

[1] Further details will be found in Marriott: *The Mechanism of the Modern State* (Vol. I, chapter X), from which the above paragraphs are summarized. Reference may also be made to Marriott: *Modern England*, chapters VIII and XV.

Chapter Fifteen

Colonial Federalism.—I

THE DOMINION OF CANADA

N EITHER in Canada nor in the Australian Colonies did the attainment of responsible government mark the term of constitutional evolution. In Canada the Act of 1840 had united the Legislatures of Ontario and Quebec; in 1847 Lord Elgin initiated the experiment of responsible government.

An experiment it was. A responsible Executive is essential to the smooth working of Parliamentary Democracy. But there is no disguising the truth that the mechanism appropriate to that form of government is exceedingly delicate, and in unskilled or inexperienced hands is apt to get out of gear. Moreover, it can be worked successfully only if all the conditions are favourable. *Failure of the Union Act*

The first condition is an electorate reasonably homogeneous and agreed on fundamentals. Ontario and Quebec were in no sense homogeneous, and in several vital matters were violently opposed to each other. Quebec, almost solidly Catholic, was devotedly attached to the traditions inherited from pre-Revolution France. Ontario, with its large infusion of American loyalists, was Protestant in creed and progressive in temperament. Moreover, there was soon revealed a striking disparity in population. In 1841 Quebec outdistanced Ontario by 691,000 against 455,688. Twenty years later Ontario numbered 1,396,000 inhabitants while Quebec could count only 1,111,000. Consequently Ontario, which at the time of the *Union Act* had insisted on equal representation, began to agitate for readjustment in its favour. The French feared, and with good reason, that if representation were periodically readjusted to population, all that they valued—their *Upper and Lower Canada* educational system, their language, and their institutions—would be endangered.

The racial and religious antagonisms of the two peoples were reproduced in the United Legislature, and an absolute deadlock resulted. In ten years there were ten changes of Ministry. Cabinets, instead of conforming to the English principle of political homogeneity, had to recognize in their composition the prevailing dualism. Nor did repeated dissolutions produce the working majority essential to the success of parliamentary government.

It was typical of dualism that for some time the United Legislature had to sit alternately at Quebec and Toronto, to the great disadvantage of the business of the State. Ultimately the selection of a permanent capital was referred to Queen Victoria, who fixed on a lumber village superbly situated on the border of the two Provinces. On that site Ottawa, one of the most beautiful capitals in the world, has now been built.

Relations with the U.S.A. The adoption of Free Trade in England added to the difficulties of Canada. The Preference given to Canadian grain was withdrawn in 1849, and on lumber in 1860. Of what value was the connection with Great Britain? The separatist movement in Great Britain had its counterpart in Canada—but with a difference. Canada had a neighbour none too friendly towards a Canada under the British flag, but not averse from considering its inclusion in the Republic. In 1849 a society to promote annexation to the United States was formed in Upper Canada. Nearly 1,000 Montreal merchants issued a manifesto urging that " a peaceful and friendly separation from British connexion and a union upon equitable terms with the great North American Confederacy of Sovereign States " was the obvious solution for the troubles of Canada. The emphasis on " Sovereign States " indicates the direction in which the wind was blowing.

Boundary Questions After all, the boundary between the independent republics and the dependent colonies was invisible, and had lately been the subject of dispute between Great Britain and the

United States. The boundary between Maine and the adjacent British colonies had been settled by the Ashburton Treaty (1842) in a way that secured for Canada the communications between Quebec and the Maritime Provinces. More difficult was the definition of the frontier west of the Rockies. Vancouver Island, discovered by the famous English navigator of that name, in 1792, was granted to the Hudson's Bay Company in 1849. But in 1842 the U.S.A. laid claim to the whole of that portion of the Pacific Coast which lay between California (which then belonged to Mexico) and Alaska, then in the possession of Russia. Hence what was known as the Oregon Question. Had the American claim been conceded, Canada would have been cut off from the Pacific: British Columbia would never have come into existence. In 1844 the U.S.A. refused arbitration but on cooler reflection accepted it, and in 1846 the boundary was fixed at the 49th parallel, thus giving to Great Britain Vancouver Island and the whole of British Columbia, which (after the discovery of gold on the Fraser River) was constituted a Crown colony.

The trade question remained. In 1854 Canada con- *Tariffs* cluded a Reciprocity Treaty with the United States, and five years later established her right to commercial autonomy by increasing the custom duties on British goods. English manufacturers protested, but Alexander Galt, the finance Minister of Canada, unambiguously claimed that it was " the right of the people of Canada to decide for themselves both as to the mode and extent to which taxation shall be imposed." It was a perfectly fair retort to British Free *Fiscal* Traders, and the trade autonomy of the self-governing *Autonomy* colonies has never since been questioned. Disraeli, at a later date (1872), expressed his regret that self-government was not " conceded as part of a great policy of Imperial consolidation." " It ought," he added, " to have been accompanied with an Imperial tariff . . . and by a military Code which should have precisely defined the means and the responsibilities by which the Colonies should be

P 209

defended and by which, if necessary, this country should call for aid from the Colonies themselves."

Defence

Tariffs and defence were, indeed, closely associated. Three years after Canada's assertion of fiscal autonomy, the British House of Commons passed a resolution that the colonies must provide for their own internal security and should also be asked to share in their external defence. During the next few years relations between Great Britain and the U.S.A. were severely strained by incidents arising from the Civil War, and in 1866 a body of 800 Fenians

Fenian Raid

crossed the border into Canada in the mistaken belief (in the words of Joseph Howe) that they would find " in the Provinces the shortest way to Ireland." The raid was a complete fiasco, but it gave Mr. Seward, the American Secretary of State, an opportunity of intervening on behalf of the Fenian leaders taken prisoners on Canadian soil. This interference was regarded in England as the more offensive since Washington had been recently intriguing with Nova Scotia, with a view to discouraging their federal union with Canada.

The Fenian raid did nothing to postpone the withdrawal from Canada of Imperial troops. Except for the garrisons that were left in the important naval stations of Esquimalt and Halifax, Canada was by 1870 completely denuded of British forces.

On the other hand, the Fenian raid was a godsend to those Canadian statesmen—men like Sir John A. Macdonald, Sir A. T. Galt, George Brown, Sir Charles Tupper, Sir George Cartier, and others—who were becoming convinced that only confederation could cure the ills from which Canada was so manifestly suffering.

Towards Federation

The movement towards confederation was at once a centrifugal and a centripetal movement. As regards Upper and Lower Canada, federation would dissolve the ill-assorted union. On the other hand, as between both Canadas and the Maritime Provinces it would make for closer union. There was also the North West to be considered, and British Columbia far-distant and isolated, not to mention Newfoundland, which, asserting proudly its seniority, was condemned as an independent colony to poverty.

The subject of confederation was mooted to Bulwer Lytton, then Colonial Secretary, in 1858, but his attitude was discouraging. It was further considered in September 1862, at an inter-colonial conference at Quebec called primarily to discuss the question of an inter-colonial railway. The Duke of Newcastle, Bulwer Lytton's successor, accompanied the Prince of Wales on a memorable journey to Canada in 1860. That journey dispersed the doubts he had previously felt.

Meanwhile, a movement had developed towards union *The Maritimes* among the Maritimes, and in 1864 the Legislatures of Nova Scotia, New Brunswick, and Prince Edward Island sent delegates to discuss the project at a Convention at Charlottetown. Eight Canadian Ministers sought and obtained leave to attend the Charlottetown Convention, and urged the Maritimes to join Canada in promoting the larger scheme for the confederation of the whole of British North America.

From Charlottetown the conference adjourned to Quebec, where behind closed doors the delegates agreed upon seventy-two resolutions, which formed the basis of the scheme ultimately laid before the Imperial Parliament in 1865. The resolutions were passed by the Canadian Parliament by large majorities, and in 1866 delegates from both Canadas and Nova Scotia and New Brunswick met Lord Carnarvon, the new Colonial Secretary, in London, and, in conference with him, drafted the Bill. Lord Carnarvon was wholly sympathetic towards the scheme, being convinced that it was the only alternative to absorption by the United States, " and absorption in such a manner as to inflict on us war or great humiliation." [1]

Joseph Howe of Nova Scotia insisted, on the contrary, *Joseph Howe* that the confederation of Canada would be the prelude to absorption, and that absorption would mean the downfall of Great Britain. " How," he asked, " would it stand with these (British) islands ? When their only formidable

[1] Hardinge: *Life of the Fourth Earl of Carnarvon*, Vol. I, p. 294.

commercial rival ruled the whole continent of America from the Gulf of Mexico to Hudson Bay, when her mercantile marine was increased by a million tons of shipping, when England was left without a harbour of refuge, a spar or a ton of coal on the whole continent of America, when 4,000,000 British subjects had been drawn behind the Morrill Tariff, and every Loyal Irishman in British America had been converted into a Fenian, when the outposts of the enemy had been advanced 800 miles nearer to England by the possession of Nova Scotia and Newfoundland. . . ." [1]

A great orator and a brilliant controversialist, Howe was strongly in favour of Imperial Federation and also of the Federation of the Maritimes, but he was convinced that Canadian Confederation would mean the complete subordination of the Maritime Provinces to Ottawa, and would react disastrously on the British connection. Howe published a closely reasoned statement against confederation in September 1866. It is printed seemingly verbatim.[2]

Lord Carnarvon

As to the absorption of Canada by the U.S.A., Lord Carnarvon was nearer the truth than Joseph Howe; but about the Maritime Provinces Howe knew much more than Carnarvon, and his fears about their future have been largely justified by the event. Yet it is likely that they would have suffered much more under a separate confederation.

At the time, Howe's objections were overruled by Lord Carnarvon in the great speech in which he moved the second reading of the British North America Bill in the House of Lords on February 19th, 1867.[3] In neither House did the Bill encounter any serious opposition except from John Bright, who espoused the views of Joseph Howe. It received the Royal Assent on March 28th, and on July 1st of the same year the Dominion of Canada came legally into being.

British North America Act, 1867

The Executive remained vested in the Queen and her successors, who were to be represented in the Dominion by

---

[1] *The Speeches and Public Letters of Joseph Howe* (ed. Chisholm), Vol. II, p. 489 (Halifax, 1909).
[2] By Chisholm, Vol. II, pp. 468–1192. [3] *Speeches on Canada*, pp. 90–128.

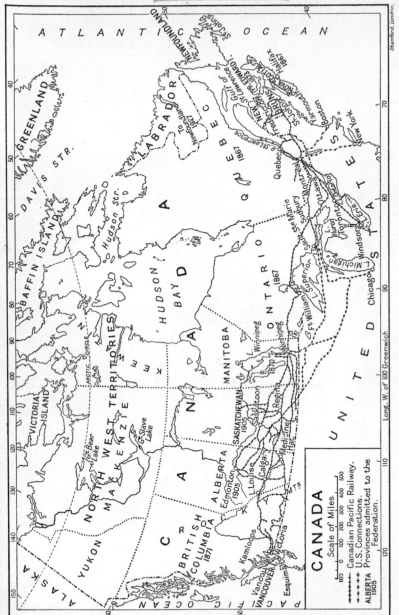

CANADA AND THE CANADIAN PACIFIC RAILWAY

Stanford, London.

CANADA

Scale of Miles

100   0   100 200 300 400 500

———— Canadian Pacific Railway.
++++++ U.S. Connections.
ALBERTA Provinces admitted to the
1905   Federation.

212]

a Governor-General with the customary powers of a " Constitutional " Sovereign, including the right to appoint and remove the Lieutenant-Governors of the constituent Provinces. There was to be a Privy Council of Canada, and it was assumed (though not expressed in the Act) that the Governor-General would act on the advice of a Parliamentary Cabinet. Legislative power was vested in the Queen, a *Executive and* Senate, and a House of Commons. The Canadian Senate *Legislature* was intended to embody, like that of the United States, the federal idea. Accordingly Quebec, Ontario, and the Maritime Provinces (Nova Scotia and New Brunswick) were each to be represented in it by twenty-four members, nominated for life by the Governor-General. After the accession of other Provinces the original scheme of distribution of Senatorial seats had to be modified. The Senate now consists of 96 members: Quebec and Ontario retain 24 apiece; Nova Scotia and New Brunswick 10 each; Prince Edward Island 4, British Columbia, Manitoba, Alberta, and Saskatchewan 6 apiece. The nomination system has not been a success. Devised originally with a view to an equal representation of Provincial groups, it has from the first been manipulated by party leaders to subserve party interests in the Federal Legislature.[1] The House of Commons has been similarly modified. Originally consisting of 181 members, it has now been enlarged to 245, of whom Ontario claim 82, Quebec 65, Saskatchewan 21, Manitoba and Alberta 17 apiece, British Columbia 16, Nova Scotia 12, New Brunswick 10, Prince Edward Island 4, and Yukon 1. Its duration is limited to five years. Money Bills can only be proposed by the Crown and must originate in the House of Commons. Otherwise the powers of the two Houses are nominally co-ordinate.

The judicial system in Canada follows the lines familiar *Judicature* in England. Judges of the Superior Courts are appointed by the Crown, their salaries are charged on the Civil List,

---

[1] For the position of the Canadian Senate, cf. Marriott: *Second Chambers* (ed. 1927); R. A. Mackay: *The Unreformed Senate of Canada* ; and Marriott: *Mechanism of the Modern State*, Vol. I, chapter IV, where the whole Constitution of 1867 is analysed in much greater detail.

and, as in England, they can be dismissed only on a joint address from both Houses of the Legislature. An appeal, criminal and civil, lies from any part of the Dominion to the Supreme Court of Canada, and from the latter, as well as from other courts, to the English Privy Council. The latter is still the ultimate Court of Appeal for 400,000,000 subjects of King George VI. Unlike the United States, Canada has no system of federal courts, and in particular it has no Supreme Court competent to interpret not merely the law, but the Constitution. The Canadian Constitution, like the English, is based on the theory of an omnipotent legislature.

Provincial Government

The relations between the Dominion and the Constituent Provinces are determined, however, by the Act of 1867.[1] Such relations form the crux of every federal Constitution. In Australia, as in the United States, the residue of power is vested in the States; in Canada the Provinces can exercise such powers only as are expressly delegated to them by the Constitution. That Constitution can be amended only by the Imperial Parliament, though by convention that Parliament acts only at the request of the Dominion. Between 1867 and 1930 seven such amendments were made.

In each of the Provinces there is a Lieutenant-Governor appointed by the Governor-General, a single-chamber Legislature, and an Executive responsible to the Legislature. Most of the Provincial Legislatures were originally bicameral, but in all the Legislative Council has been abolished. Four Provinces only, Ontario, Quebec, New Brunswick, and Nova Scotia, constituted in the first instance the Federal Dominion, but the Act of 1867 provided for the admission of other colonies or territories. Manitoba was the first Province to be carved out of the great North West Territory which with Rupert's Land was acquired by the Dominion in 1868. It was admitted to the Dominion in 1870, British Columbia and Vancouver having been united in 1866 were admitted to the Dominion in 1871, Prince Edward Island in 1873, and Alberta and Saskatchewan, also

[1] And subsequent amendments of that Act.

carved out of the territories of the old Hudson's Bay Company, in 1905. The remnant of the North West Territory was reconstituted in 1905, Yukon having been created a separate territory in 1898. These latter are administered by Commissioners.

The rights of the Provinces are guaranteed by the Acts of the Imperial Parliament. They are very jealously guarded, in some cases even aggressively asserted, as against the Federal Government, and are specifically recognized by seven of the Statutes of Westminster.

British Columbia made it a condition of its adhesion to the *The C.P.R.* Federal Dominion that a railway should be constructed to connect it with the Eastern Provinces. The Maritime Provinces had also stipulated that they should be linked up by rail with Ottawa. This line was opened in 1876, but the Maritimes are by no means satisfied with conditions of transport, which have not helped St. John and Halifax.

In regard to the transcontinental line, almost incredible difficulties, physical, financial, and political, were encountered, and were overcome only by the tenacity, skill, and courage of a small group of men, George Stephen (Lord Mountstephen), Sir William van Horne, and Donald Smith (Lord Strathcona). In 1881 the contract was concluded; on November 7th, 1885, in the Eagle Pass in the heart of the Rockies, the rail constructed from the east met the rail constructed from the west, and the last spike was driven by Donald Smith. The story of the Canadian Railway connecting Montreal with Vancouver, running for 2,500 miles through lands mainly uninhabited (in 1885) and crossing one of the great mountain ranges of the world, is nothing short of a romance. But it cannot be told here. Its significance is Imperial and strategic as well as commercial. Esquimalt, with a dry dock that will hold the biggest battleship afloat, looks forth over the Pacific, and its naval ratings can now, thanks to the superb railway system of Canada, be reinforced from Portsmouth within a fortnight. Canada now possesses nearly 60,000 miles of railways and 2,700 miles of internal navigable waterways. Thanks to those waterways ocean liners can now sail without breaking bulk from the Great Lakes, in the heart of Canada, to the Atlantic.

Newfoundland   The Act of 1867 contemplated the inclusion of Newfoundland in the federated Dominion of British North America. Newfoundland, however, preferred, in pride of birth, to remain in isolated independence. Even with the " Coast of Labrador," assigned to it by the decision of the Privy Council in 1927, Newfoundland contains less than 290,000 inhabitants, most of them very poor. In 1855 it was endowed with a responsible Government, but in 1934 a financial crisis compelled the colony to apply for help to the Imperial Government. This was granted, but on condition that self-government should be suspended and the administration be vested in Commissioners appointed in Whitehall.

Chapter Sixteen

Colonial Federalism.—II

THE COMMONWEALTH OF AUSTRALIA

FEDERATION was forced upon Canada by domestic *Australian* difficulties otherwise insuperable. A similar solution *Federation* was accepted by the Australian colonies owing to a growing recognition of external dangers accentuated by the unwelcome presence of European Powers in the Pacific.

Between 1854 and 1890 all the Australian colonies, as well as New Zealand, attained to the dignity of " responsible " government. But their material development, though substantial, was less rapid than their constitutional evolution. Of the three main prerequisites for development Australia possessed one—land—in superabundance, but lacked both capital and labour. Yet despite its abundance there has been no question which has demanded more attention from Australian Legislatures than the land. Again and again there has been a radical change of system in most of the colonies. As to capital Australia has frequently complained, and with some show of justice, that the City has been far more ready to develop industry by means of capital in foreign countries than in our own colonies. Without an adequate supply of British capital Australia refuses to admit, with our restrictions, British labour.

Labour has indeed been the crux of the economic pro- *Labour* blem. Australia, with a population largely concentrated in a few cities, has been particularly concerned to keep up the rate of wages. To this end immigration, not of foreigners only, has especially since the Act of 1901 been severely restricted. Even on the narrower economic ground the wisdom of this policy may be impugned. On a considera-tion of wider issues it would seem to be suicidal. *The Pacific*
Australia is no longer remote from Europe: to the coasts *Problem*

217

of Asia and the islands of the Indian Ocean it is very close. In those islands the Dutch have been dominant since the seventeenth century. But in 1814 they finally ceded Ceylon to Great Britain. In 1819 Singapore, then practically uninhabited but destined to become of great commercial and strategic importance, was acquired from the Sultan of Johore by Sir Stamford Raffles. In 1837 Singapore became the administrative centre for the Straits Settlements, which comprise, as well as Penang, ceded to the East India Company in 1786, Malacca (obtained from the Dutch in exchange for Sumatra in 1824), and Labuan (ceded to Great Britain in 1846). Later on, between 1874 and 1909, a group now known as the Federated Malay States became a British Protectorate and is governed by a High Commissioner. In 1909 Siam transferred to Great Britain all rights of suzerainty, protection, administration, and control over the four North Malay States: Kedah, Perlis, Trengganu, and Kelantan. The position, though somewhat anomalous, seems reasonably satisfactory, though it was the subject of enquiry by Lord Harlech (the Under-Secretary of State) in 1928, and in 1933 by Sir Samuel Wilson, Permanent Secretary. Lord Harlech summarized the position thus: " the Malays remain the subjects of the Mohammedan monarchies which they themselves established. Malay custom is not interfered with and the Malays play a large part in the government of their States; but . . . they have the assistance of a body of trained British Civil Servants."

Meanwhile, Hong Kong, an island at the mouth of the Canton River, had been acquired by Great Britain in 1841. The Fiji Islands were definitely annexed in 1874. In 1881 the Crown granted a charter to a British company which had already begun to exercise sovereign rights in North Borneo, and in 1888 the territory was formally recognized as a British Protectorate.

France in the Pacific   By that time the Australian colonies had other neighbours in the Pacific, and were increasingly apprehensive as to their activities. Both in Australia and in New Zealand we had,

THE PACIFIC OCEAN

as already indicated, anticipated a French occupation only by a hair's breadth. France was anxious to obtain a footing in the Pacific, and in 1843 the Society Islands, though discovered by a British navigator and Christianized by British missionaries, passed into the occupation of the French, who in 1880 annexed Tahiti also.

Of much greater concern to Australia were the activities of the French in the Western Pacific, particularly in New Caledonia and the New Hebrides. French missionaries had for some years been active in New Caledonia before the Government of Napoleon III annexed the island and its adjacent dependencies in 1853. Ten years later France established there a penal station, to which in the course of the next twenty years no fewer than 120,000 convicts were transported. New Caledonia is within 800 miles of Brisbane. Not a few convicts made their escape to the continent, and their presence greatly perturbed the Government and people. In 1888 the Australian Government made a strong protest to Whitehall against the carelessness which permitted many criminals of the worst type to escape from the penal settlement, but it was not until 1898 that France suspended transportation to New Caledonia.

The nuisance caused to the Australian Government by the convicts from New Caledonia quickened their apprehensions about the adjacent New Hebrides. In 1878 far-sighted Australian statesmen, pre-eminently (Sir) Julius Vogel, strongly urged that Great Britain should take possession both of the New Hebrides and of Samoa, but Lord Derby, then at the Foreign Office, was content with an assurance from France that she had no intention to annex. Australia had good reason to mistrust its sufficiency, and in 1883 Victoria urged the Imperial Government to annex all the Pacific islands between Fiji and New Guinea, including the New Hebrides. Lord Derby declined to act, though he did go so far as to promise that he would not consent to annexation by France without consulting the Australian colonies and securing conditions satisfactory to them.[1] In 1887

[1] A. and P., 1884–1885, LIV, 572, quoted ap. C.H.B.E., Vol. VII, 360.

Great Britain and France agreed to commit the policing of the islands to a joint commission of naval officers, without annexation by either Power. The matter was not, however, settled until the conclusion of the Anglo-French Agreement of 1904, in which the New Hebrides were included. As a result a *condominium* was established which, though cumbrous in operation, has kept convicts out, and has afforded protection to both Protestant and Roman Catholic missionaries.

Germany in the Pacific

In 1884 Germany also appeared in the Pacific. Rumours of her designs upon New Guinea had for some time past been current in Australia, but as lately as 1882 Lord Derby had declared that " he had no reason for supposing that Germany contemplated any scheme of colonization " in that direction. In 1883, however, Queensland, in order to force the hand of an apathetic and ill-informed Colonial Office, annexed New Guinea, but Lord Derby refused to countenance such unauthorized action. In 1884 Germany annexed the north-eastern coast of New Guinea, subsequently christened Kaiser Wilhelm's Land, and the group of islands collectively known as the Bismarck Archipelago. In 1886 she also established a virtual Protectorate over Samoa, where she came into conflict with the United States. Bismarck was, however, anxious to keep the peace in regions in which he took little interest; conferences were held between Great Britain, Germany, and the United States, with the result that the Samoan islands were placed under the joint control of the three Powers. This *condominium* worked badly, and in 1899 a troublesome situation was cleared up by the division of the Samoan group between Germany and the United States, Great Britain receiving her compensation elsewhere.

The U.S.A.

Though the United States had for many years past manifested an interest in the Sandwich Islands, it was not until 1898 that they were definitely annexed by that Power. In 1900 they were formally constituted the Territory of Hawaii. Part of the Samoan group had also, as we have seen, fallen into the keeping of the United States, and in 1898, as a result of the war against Spain, the

Philippine archipelago was transferred to her by the latter Power.

Thus before the close of the century the Pacific had become the scene of international rivalry, and the Australian colonies were in consequence increasingly uneasy. Very sparsely populated themselves, they looked across the Pacific at the shores of Asiatic countries teeming with population; they saw their own ramparts occupied by European Powers, who were possible competitors with the British Empire for world supremacy, while there was no obstacle to their ambitions except the British Navy.

This situation gave a powerful impulse to the movement *Federation* for a Federation between the several Australian colonies.

As long ago as 1847 Lord Grey, as Secretary of State, had drafted a scheme for a federal Constitution, and Bills to give effect to it were introduced into the Imperial Parliament in 1849 and again in 1850. But in view of strong opposition both at home and in the colonies they were withdrawn. The question was kept alive mainly through the persistence of Gavan Duffy, who, though deported from Ireland for his share in the rebellion of 1848, proved himself in Australia a prudent and far-sighted statesman. Not, however, until the events summarized in preceding paragraphs did the Australian colonies awake either to the need for more effective representation of the colonies in the Imperial economy, or for closer union among themselves.

In 1883 delegates from all the Australian colonies, as well as from New Zealand and Fiji, attended a conference at Sydney, and a scheme formulated by (Sir) Henry Parkes and (Sir) Samuel Griffith was enacted by the Imperial Parliament as the *Federal Council of Australasia Act* (1885). But the scheme was not a satisfactory one; New South Wales held aloof from it, and nothing was done. Nevertheless things were moving towards federation in Australia and were stimulated by the supine attitude of Whitehall. As Mr. Pember Reeves caustically but accurately says—" The air of icy superiority persistently worn by the Colonial Office, the Foreign Office, and the Admiralty when transacting

221

business with separate colonies did quite as much perhaps to irritate colonial leaders into speculating whether something big—say a federated continent—might not be required to impress the official mind at home."

The "something big" was ultimately achieved by the *Australian Commonwealth Act* passed by the Imperial Parliament in 1900. The Royal Assent to the last important Act of the reign was accompanied by the fervent prayer of the aged Queen that "the inauguration of the Commonwealth may ensure the increased prosperity of my loyal and beloved subjects in Australia."

Proof of their loyalty was at the moment being given by the presence of Australian and New Zealand contingents in South Africa. But, assuming fair consideration by the Imperial Government, it was never in doubt. The Act itself was the outcome of Conventions at Hobart (1895) and Adelaide (1897) and of a plebiscite taken in each colony. New Zealand refused to adhere to any federal scheme except a federation with the Mother Country.

The Commonwealth and the States

All the six Australian colonies approved and accepted it. Not, however, without safeguards for their independence. Large powers are indeed conceded to the Commonwealth exclusively, other enumerated powers are exercised concurrently, but all the residue of powers (a vital consideration in a federal Constitution) is vested in the States. The State Governors (unlike the Lieutenant-Governors of the Canadian Provinces) continue to be appointed directly by the Crown, and their Legislatures have the right, subject only to the veto of the Crown, to amend their several Constitutions. Relations between the Commonwealth and the States have not been free from friction, especially in relation to taxation, and one State—Western Australia—recently voted in favour of withdrawal. The legal aspect of the matter may be ambiguous, but in the present (1938) condition of world politics, the dissolution of the Commonwealth, or even the withdrawal of any constituent State, is obviously unthinkable.

The Legislature

Legislative power is vested in the Governor-General, a

Senate, and a House of Representatives. The Senate consists of thirty-six Members, six from each State. Equality of representation therein is regarded by the smaller States as the " sheet-anchor " of their rights and liberties, and no State can be deprived of its equal representation except by its own consent. Senators are directly elected by the people of the States voting under the method of the *scrutin de liste* as a single electorate. One result, perhaps unexpected, of this provision is that the Australian Senate has proved, unlike most Second Chambers, to be less conservative than the Lower House. Like most Second Chambers, the Senate has a " perpetual existence," as one-half of its Members, all of whom are elected for six years, retire every three years.

As regards finance, all Money Bills, carefully defined and limited, must originate in the Lower House. The Senate may reject but may not amend them, though the precautions against " tacking," or the introduction of any alien substance into a Money Bill, are unusually stringent and precise.

The federal Executive is based not upon the American *The Executive* but upon the English model, and consists of the Governor-General and a Cabinet responsible to the Legislature. Cabinet Ministers must be, or within three months of their appointment must become, Members of one or other House of the Legislature. This is a specific provision of the Constitution (64), and though based on the English convention it remained unique among the Constitutions of English-speaking peoples until it was copied in the *South Africa Union Act* of 1909.

The Judiciary is less unitary than in Canada, but less *The Judiciary* federal than that of the United States. An appeal lies from the State Courts to the federal Supreme Court ; appellate jurisdiction of the King-in-Council remains unimpaired. On this subject there was much discussion when the Draft Bill was before the Imperial Parliament. Joseph Chamberlain, who was in charge of the Bill, insisted that while the High Court of Australia was to be left " absolutely free to take its own course where Australian interests were solely and exclusively concerned," the right of appeal to the Privy Council was to be maintained in all cases where other than Australian interests were involved. Mr. Chamberlain had his way, and the principle for which, in the interests of the Empire as a whole, he fought is embodied in paragraph 74 of the Act. But difficulties soon revealed themselves in reference to the right, safeguarded in the Act, for an appeal from the *State* Courts direct to the Privy Council. The impasse was, however, ultimately resolved by an Act of the Federal Parliament (1907, No. 8). This Act abolished the concurrent jurisdiction of the State Courts in reference to questions affecting the constitutional rights and powers of the Commonwealth and the States *inter se*.[1]

Constitutional Revision

The jealous tenacity of the States was, however, most clearly manifested in the elaborate provision made in the *Commonwealth Act* for a revision of the Constitution. Proposed amendments may originate in either House, and having been passed through both Houses must be submitted to the electors in each State. They cannot become law until they have been approved by (i) a majority of States and (ii) a majority of the electors in the Commonwealth as a whole. Further, any amendment affecting the rights of any State in the Federal Legislature must obtain the approval of a majority of the electors in the State concerned. In the event of a disagreement between the two Houses of the federal Legislature in regard to revision the Governor-General may, after an interval, submit the matter to a referendum. Experience has shown, however, that projects so submitted are generally rejected.

On any question the Senate may force a dissolution. If, after a fresh election, the Lower House insists upon its original proposal the matter is determined by an absolute majority obtained from a joint sitting of the two Houses. Hence the great importance of the stipulation that the number of Members of the Lower House shall be " as nearly as

---

[1] On this complicated question see Egerton: *Federations*, p. 212 ; and, for much more detail on the Constitution as a whole, Marriott: *Mechanism of the Modern State*, Vol. I, chapter IX.

practicable twice the number of Senators." The Senators still number 36; the Lower House is constituted as follows: For New South Wales 28 members, Victoria 20, Queensland 10, South Australia 6, Western Australia and Tasmania 5 each, and from the Northern Territory 1, who may speak but not vote, except on a motion to disallow an ordinance emanating from the Territory. "The great lion in the path of the Constitution has been," wrote Sir G. A. Wade in 1919, "the problem of finance." The point did not escape the prescience of the framers of the Constitution, which contains no fewer than twenty-five clauses devoted to the subject of finance and trade. With this subject, especially in reference to the financial and fiscal relations between the Commonwealth and the component States, many if not most of the proposals submitted to a referendum have been concerned. The questions at issue are, however, too intricate for summary treatment, and the aspect of them is so constantly changing as to render quickly obsolete any observations upon them.

Behind all this formal machinery of the Constitution there is an institution of the greatest importance. With the local " caucus " British people are familiar; the parliamentary caucus is something different. It is a result of the ascendancy of the Labour Party in Australia, and it has its counterpart in the British Labour Party. Party discipline is exercised not only over candidates and constituencies but over elected Members. The latter must obey the resolutions of a parliamentary caucus which is itself the creature of the Trade Councils. Thus, whenever the Labour Party is in power the Trade Councils are in effect the real rulers of the country. So great was the importance which Lord Bryce, after close personal observation, attached to the parliamentary caucus that he said: " The dominance of the parliamentary caucus had been Australia's most distinctive contribution to the art of politics." *The Parliamentary Caucus*

Thus have the two great federal Dominions come into being under the Sovereignty of the Crown. Of the problems confronting them the most difficult perhaps is that which concerns the relations between the Federal Government and the component States or Provinces. To this problem further reference must be made. For the present it must suffice to say that great experiments in the science and art of Politics are being made both by Canada and Australia, and in both cases under conditions which should conduce ultimately to success.

Chapter Seventeen

Imperial Organization and Colonial Nationalism

CROSS-CURRENTS (1883–1911)

P RECEDING chapters have traced the progress of *Colonial* the four great Dominions to constitutional maturity: *Autonomy* to autonomy under a Constitution at once parliamentary and unitary in New Zealand; to a semi-federal Union in South Africa; to genuine federalism—though of different types—in Canada and Australia. Self-government was conceded to these distant dependencies under the impulse derived from the *laissez-faire* doctrines of the Manchester School, and the policy has undeniably justified itself, though not in the manner anticipated by its sponsors. The prophets of the Manchester School were confident that self-government would be the prelude to separation. That their hopes were falsified is due to the fact that, strong as have been the forces making for colonial nationalism, they have been counteracted by other forces operating in favour of Imperial integration.

To the scientific inventions which have gone far to *Nationalism,* annihilate distance and improve communications reference *Political and* has already been made. Political and economic develop- *Economic* ments have converged in a similar direction. Of the newly operating forces that of nationalism is the strongest. The formation of a federal Empire in Germany (1871) marked an important stage in the evolution of a German nation; in the same year Italy finally achieved national unity; the break-up of the Ottoman Empire permitted the submerged nationalities in the Balkans to acquire the status of virtually independent Nation-States. Thus, by the end of the 'seventies, the whole of Europe was almost exhaustively

227

parcelled out into Nation-States, self-governing and increasingly self-conscious.

The New Germany

Of the working of the new forces Germany afforded the most conspicuous illustration. Between 1871 and 1910 the population of Germany increased from 41,000,000 to nearly 65,000,000. Industrialization was making Germany, as it had long ago made England, a nation of town-dwellers. The urbanized population demanded food which a depleted countryside could inadequately supply; it demanded raw materials for its machines and markets for its surplus manufactured products, necessities which England largely obtained from her oversea possessions.

Hence, as already indicated, the scramble for Africa and the Pacific Islands. Plainly the globe was shrinking, and among the first to realize the shrinkage were, as we have seen, the British colonies in Australia. Deeply they resented the " intrusion " of France and Germany into the Pacific, and bitterly they reproached the apathy exhibited by Whitehall—notably by Lord Granville (Colonial Secretary, 1868–1870 and 1886) and Lord Derby (1882–1885) towards the " intruders."

History and Politics

Philosophical History rallied to the support of Politics. Until the 'seventies the " little Englanders " had dominated literature as they had dominated politics. Bentham and Cornewall Lewis, Grote, Goldwin Smith, and Freeman had had it almost all their own way, though Carlyle had in him elements of Imperialism. In 1883, however, J. R. Seeley published his lectures on *The Expansion of England*. Probably no book since Adam Smith's *Wealth of Nations* (1776) had exercised so immediate and profound an influence on British opinion. " The future," Seeley insisted, " is with the big States." An insular England stripped of her colonies would have no chance in the coming contest for *welt-macht* against the United States, Russia, or even Germany. But Great Britain still had it in her power to become a great World-State, if not the greatest among them. But she could hold that place among the Powers only if she followed the example of Germany, the United States, and her own

228

Dominion of Canada, and adopted the federal principle of government. Such was the pith of Seeley's argument, solidly reinforced by an appeal to history. J. A. Froude, who in 1892 succeeded his rival Freeman as Regius Professor of Modern History at Oxford, was also an ardent Imperialist, though less explicit than Seeley in exposition of a system. Froude's friend Lord Carnarvon had been at the Colonial Office from 1874 to 1878 and, as we have seen, had sent Froude to South Africa to convert the South African colonies to the principle of federation. His mission unfortunately failed, but his books *Oceana* (1886), *England in the West Indies* (1888), and *English Seamen in the Sixteenth Century* (1897), contributed powerfully to the rising tide of Imperialism. Besides the giants like Froude and Seeley there was a large group of publicists whose spade-work for the same cause deserves to be held in remembrance: men like F. P. de Labillière,[1] an indefatigable pioneer, Edward Jenkins,[2] Frederick Young,[3] J. Stanley Little,[4] and not least Sir George Parkin.[5] Parkin's lectures on Imperial Federation were credibly said to have " shifted the mind of England "; and as the first Secretary to the Rhodes Trustees he performed a service to the cause of Imperial unity the value of which cannot be over-estimated. Mention should, in this connection, be made also of the Poet-Laureate whose indignant outburst, suffixed (1872) to the dedication of his *Idylls of the King*, evoked the cordial gratitude of the Canadians conveyed to Tennyson in a characteristic letter from the Governor-General, Lord Dufferin. Thence onward Tennyson must be counted among the literary prophets of Imperialism.

Finally the politicians took action. In 1884 the Imperial Federation League came into being under very influential auspices. Promoted by such men as W. E. Forster, Lord Rosebery, Edward Stanhope, W. H. Smith, Sir Charles Tupper of Canada, and Sir Charles Gavan Duffy and Sir

Imperial Federation League

---

[1] *England and her Colonies* (1869), *Federal Britain* (1894).
[2] *Colonial and Imperial Unity* (1871). [3] *Imperial Federation* (1876).
[4] *A World Empire* (1879). [5] *Imperial Federation* (1892).

Henry Parkes of Australia, the League drew support from all parties. The League was content to obtain assent to principles without committing itself to any particular form of federation. " The Federation we aim at," said Lord Rosebery in 1888, " is the closest possible union of the various self-governing States ruled by the British Crown, consistently with that free national development which is the birthright of British subjects throughout the world—the closest union in sympathy, in external action and defence."

Words could not have been chosen to define more precisely the objects and the attitude of the League. That improved constitutional machinery would gradually be evolved was undoubtedly the hope of all Imperialists, but the League wisely refused to force the pace. Two matters were, however, pressing: some scheme of common defence and an " official acknowledgment of the right of the colonies to have a voice in the determination of foreign policy, especially when such policy directly affects their feelings or interests." These words are taken from a remarkable paper contributed by Mr. W. E. Forster, Chairman of the League, to the *Nineteenth Century* for February 1885. Australian statesmen were at that time, as we have seen, bitterly resentful (to quote the words used by Mr. Alfred Deakin [1] at the Imperial Conference of 1887) of " the disdain and indifference with which English enterprise (in the Pacific) was treated at the Colonial Office." Sir James Service, Premier of Victoria from 1883 to 1885, had recently complained that despite the concession of " responsible government " to the greater colonies they had " no representation whatever in the Imperial system," and that as regards foreign policy the Imperial Government remained " to all intents and purposes an unqualified autocracy."

That was true. The whole system was anachronistic and anomalous. The formation of the *Imperial Federation League* was, therefore, in the highest degree timely. For

[1] Australian statesman (1856–1919). Represented Victoria at the first Imperial Conference of 1887.

ten years it did educational and propagandist work of great value. Branches were formed not only in the United Kingdom but in Canada, Australia, and New Zealand; meetings were organized, literature distributed, and considerable enthusiasm aroused.[1] But the League ultimately foundered on the rock of Imperial Preference. Politically, Great Britain had effectually discarded the doctrines of the Manchester School; but, economically, their theories dominated commercial policy. It took a great war to shatter the citadel of Free Trade.

The League was dissolved in 1893, but not before it could *The* point to some positive achievements. Apart from the educa- *Imperial* tion of opinion it could claim a large share of responsibility *Institute* for the Exhibition (the " Colinderies " as it was nicknamed) held in 1886 to illustrate the products, manufactures, and art of the colonies and India. On May 4th, 1886, Queen Victoria opened it in state, and characteristically but not too felicitously referred to the Exhibition as "an impressive development of the idea which the Prince Consort had originated in 1851." It was not a development but an antithesis. The Exhibition of 1851 was the apotheosis of the Manchester School: it anticipated the triumph of internationalism. The "Colinderies" sprang from a different root; it reflected the sentiment of Imperial self-consciousness if not of Imperial self-sufficiency.

So satisfactory, however, were the financial results that a profit of over £30,000 was realized and formed the nucleus of a fund for the foundation of an Imperial Institute. On the suggestion of the Prince of Wales it was decided that this Institute, designed to illustrate in permanent form "the arts, manufactures, and commerce of the Queen's Colonial and Indian Empire," should form the chief national memorial of the Queen's Jubilee, which in 1887 was cele- *The Jubilee,* brated, with grateful hearts and deep-voiced rejoicing, by *1887*

[1] The present writer recalls with satisfaction the fact that he was responsible, with the help of Professors Bryce, Burrows, and Napier, the Hon. G. C. Brodrick, Warden of Merton, and others, for the founding of a branch in Oxford in 1886. *Imperial Federation*, July 1886, p. 187.

the many people of the far-flung Empire. The idea of the Institute was cordially acclaimed; generous contributions poured in, especially from the feudatory Princes of India; the Queen herself laid the foundation stone, with imposing ceremony, on July 4th, 1887; but the final result cruelly disappointed the hopes of the promoters. For some unexplained reason the Imperial Institute was from the outset a " frost."

Colonial
Conference

The Imperial Institute was not the only offspring of the League. Destined to more vigorous life was the Colonial Conference. In 1886 the Imperial Federation League sent a deputation to the Prime Minister to urge the Government to take advantage of the Jubilee celebrations to discuss personally with colonial statesmen the problems of imperial defence, inter-imperial communications, " and other means for securing the closer federation or union of all parts of the Empire." Lord Salisbury, though in guarded terms, assented to the suggestion, and on April 4th, 1887, the Conference met.

The subject of Federation was expressly excluded from the agenda; and though many of the colonial delegates, notably Sir Samuel Griffith of Queensland and J. H. Hofmeyr from South Africa, eagerly pressed for a resolution in favour of Imperial Preference, they were frustrated by the Colonial Secretary, Sir Henry Holland (afterwards Lord Knutsford), who, with an anxious eye upon the Liberal Unionists, kept the Conference off dangerous ground. As a result, the most fruitful discussions turned, as Lord Salisbury had hoped, upon the possibility of a *Kriegsverein*—a scheme of Imperial defence. Of these discussions the positive outcome was the agreement concluded with Australia. The Imperial Government undertook to maintain a strong squadron of cruisers and gunboats in the western Pacific, and the Australian colonies agreed to contribute £126,000 a year (increased in 1902 to £240,000) towards the expense of maintaining it; a general officer was to be sent to Australia to advise on military defence; Simon's Town was to be fortified by the Imperial Government; and the series of coaling stations was to be strengthened.[1] For the rest Alfred Deakin, the most interesting figure at the Conference, made, as already indicated, an outspoken and spirited attack upon the gross neglect by the Imperial Government of Australian interests in the Pacific, and insisted, like his colleague James Service, that the colonies were entitled to share in the shaping of a foreign policy so vitally important to them. " We hope," he said with emphasis, " that from this time forward colonial policy will be considered Imperial policy; that colonial interests will be considered and felt to be Imperial interests." [2]

The Conference of 1887, despite or perhaps by reason of some blunt speaking, was a notable success. For the first time the leading statesmen of the Empire were officially summoned to take counsel together on matters vital to the interests of the Empire as a whole; the colonial delegates saw England at its best, and witnessed a remarkable demonstration of loyalty towards the venerated occupant of the Imperial throne.

Nor was the Conference allowed to separate without a broad hint as to its possible evolution in the future. At the concluding session Sir Samuel Griffith, as " the oldest actual Minister present," gave expression to a thought which on this historic occasion was in many minds: " I consider that this Conference does comprise what may perhaps be called the rudimentary elements of a parliament; but it has been a peculiarity of our British institutions that those which have been found most durable are those which have grown up from institutions which were in the first instance of a rudimentary character. It is impossible to predicate now what form future conferences should take, or in what mode some day further effect would be given to their conclusions, but I think we may look forward to seeing this sort of informal Council of the Empire develop until it becomes a legislative body, at any rate a consultative body, and some day, perhaps, a legislative body under conditions that we

[1] For text of the agreement see *Proceedings of Conference*, cc. 5091, pp. 508–510.
[2] *Proceedings*, pp. 24–25.

cannot just now foresee." The Conference did, in fact, lay the foundation-stone of a political structure destined, we trust, to permanence. Yet ten years elapsed before the next Colonial Conference met in London.

Ottawa Conference, 1894

The gap was to some extent filled by a conference which, on the invitation of the Canadian Government, met at Ottawa in 1894. The Earl of Jersey, a former Governor of New South Wales (1891–1893), represented the Imperial Government, and representatives were also present from Canada, Cape Colony, New Zealand, and four of the Australian colonies. No political questions were discussed; the agenda was practically confined to the three subjects specified in the Canadian invitation: the construction of a submarine cable from Vancouver to Australia, the establishment of a quick mail service between Great Britain and Australasia via Canada, and the trade relations of the colonies with Great Britain and with one another. It was suggested that for the Pacific cable there should be a neutral landing-place in the Sandwich Islands (Hawaii), but those islands were formally annexed in 1898 by the United States. That scheme was therefore perforce abandoned. The cable was, however, ultimately laid (1902) from Vancouver to Auckland via Norfolk Island.

On the question of inter-Imperial trade the Conference resolved that any impediments imposed, by treaty or otherwise, on reciprocal trade arrangements between the different portions of the Empire should be removed, and recorded its belief in the advisability of such arrangements. The exceptional position of the Mother Country in respect of external trade was frankly recognized by colonial speakers, but the Conference resolved that " until the Mother Country can see her way to enter into Customs arrangements with her Colonies it is desirable that, when empowered to do so, the Colonies take steps to place each other's products on a more favourable Customs basis than is accorded to the products of foreign countries." It was not long before Canada herself made a beginning in this direction. But, before that, another Colonial Conference had met in London, and like

234

the first was coincident with a great event in the history of the Empire—the celebration of the completion of the sixtieth year of the Queen's reign.

The Conference of 1897 was memorable for many reasons, *Joseph* most of all for the fact that over its deliberations Mr. Joseph *Chamberlain* Chamberlain presided. Chamberlain, having made a great reputation as a local administrator in Birmingham, had entered Parliament in 1876, and had been admitted to the Cabinet in 1880. The succession to the Radical leadership seemed assured to him when, in 1886, he broke with Mr. Gladstone on the Irish question, acted as a Liberal Unionist in alliance with the Conservatives from 1886 onwards, and in 1895 became a member of Lord Salisbury's third Ministry. His choice of the Colonial Office, in preference even to the Treasury, was indicative of his rapidly growing interest in the Imperial problem, and he gave to the Office a place in the official hierarchy it had never hitherto occupied.

He had already discarded the rigid Free Trade views which at the time of the Free Trade agitation (*circ.* 1881) he had expounded with such vigour, and was moving towards the conclusion that a commercial union was the most promising method of approach to the political federation of the Empire. He was greatly impressed by the example of Germany. Speaking at the annual dinner of the Canada Club in 1896, he said, " We have a great example before us in the creation of the German Empire. How was that brought about ? You all recollect that, in the first instance, it commenced with the union of two States which now form that great Empire in a commercial *Zollverein*. They attracted the other States gradually—were joined by them for commercial purposes. A Council, or *Reichsrat*, was formed to deal with those commercial questions. Gradually in their discussions national objects and political interests were introduced, and so, from starting as it did on a purely commercial basis and for commercial interests, it developed until it became a bond of unity and the foundation of the German Empire."

On the same text Mr. Chamberlain preached to the Congress of Chambers of Commerce of the Empire which met in London in 1896. " If we had a commercial union throughout the Empire, of course there would have to be a Council of the Empire. . . . Gradually, therefore, by that prudent and experimental process by which all our greatest institutions have slowly been built up, we should, I believe, approach to a result which would be little, if at all, distinguished from a real federation of the Empire."

The Colonial Conference, 1897

Mr. Chamberlain's opening address at the Conference of 1897 marked an epoch in the history of Imperial copartnership. It was incomparably the boldest and frankest utterance to which colonial statesmen had ever listened from a responsible Minister of the Crown. " I feel," he said, " that there is a real necessity for some better machinery of consultation between the self-governing Colonies and the Mother Country, and it has sometimes struck me—I offer it now merely as a personal suggestion—that it might be feasible to create a great council of the Empire to which the Colonies would send representative plenipotentiaries—not mere delegates who were unable to speak in their name, without further reference to their respective Governments, but persons who by their position in the Colonies, by their representative character, and by their close touch with Colonial feeling, would be able upon all subjects submitted to them to give really effective and valuable advice. If such a council were created it would at once assume an immense importance, and it is perfectly evident that it might develop into something still greater. It might slowly grow to that Federal Council to which we must always look forward as our ultimate ideal."

Towards the attainment of that ideal no progress was in fact made at the Conference of 1897, though the *Report* made it clear that among some of the colonial Premiers there was a feeling that the present relations could not continue indefinitely. The general disposition of the delegates was, however, in favour of postponing the larger issue and concentrating upon issues which to the colonies appeared to be of more immediate importance. Accordingly, with the dissent only of Mr. Richard Seddon (New Zealand) and Sir E. Braddon (Tasmania), the following resolution was adopted : " The Prime Ministers here assembled are of opinion that the present political relations between the United Kingdom and the self-governing Colonies are generally satisfactory under the existing condition of things." [1] Rather more interest was evinced in the question of Imperial defence, but although the Imperial Government had repeatedly urged the colonies to make some contribution to the cost of the Imperial forces the response was tepid. The arrangement concluded in 1887 with Australia was confirmed, and the Cape Colony offered an " unconditional contribution of the cost of a first-class battleship "—a spontaneous offer which was gratefully accepted by the Home Government. A suggestion for the occasional interchange of military units was also approved.

The subject that was uppermost in the minds of the colonial delegates was, however, that of inter-Imperial trade. They wanted to persuade the Home Country to abandon Cobdenism and frankly adopt a policy of Imperial Preference. Many of the Conservative supporters of the Salisbury Government were as anxious as the colonies to go to all lengths in that direction. But Sir Michael Hicks Beach, a convinced Free Trader, was at the Treasury, and his views were shared by most of his Liberal Unionist colleagues. Mr. Chamberlain's ideal was an Imperial *Zollverein*, but the fiscal arrangements of the colonies rendered that solution impracticable. In the event, the Conference reaffirmed the request made at Ottawa for the " denunciation of any treaties that now hamper the commercial relations between Great Britain and her Colonies." Since 1894 the question had been brought to a practical issue by the offer of Canada to give a preference to the Mother Country. The Imperial Government accordingly decided to denounce

---

[1] *Proceedings*, p. 15. Only a brief report of the *Proceedings* was published (c. 8596, 1897). It contained a full report of the President's opening address and of an address by the First Lord of the Admiralty, Mr. Goschen, but for the rest, only a list of topics discussed and resolutions adopted.

the Treaties concluded with Belgium and the German *Zollverein* in 1862 and 1865 respectively. The Conference also pressed for the removal of all restrictions on the investment of trust funds in colonial stock, and recommended that the Conference should in future be periodically summoned. Personal consultation at regular intervals was, henceforward, to form a permanent part of the constitutional mechanism of the Empire.

On the whole, then, the tangible results of this Conference fell short of the hopes of its President. But the delegates were not ill-rewarded for their long journey. They had been privileged to play an honoured and conspicuous part in the pageantry which marked the culmination of the longest and greatest reign in English history. Before the next Conference met the Empire had become involved in an unfortunate and, in some senses, disastrous war. That the Imperial structure was unshaken by the South African war was due, as we have seen, to the splendid and spontaneous support given to the Motherland by the oversea branches of a united family.

Imperial Preference

Mr. Chamberlain was anxious to reward their loyalty by giving the colonies their heart's desire. His own conversion to the policy of Imperial Preference was now complete. He had been equally impressed by the hostility towards his country manifested during the South African war by foreign nations, and by the unshaken loyalty of the Empire. The recent crisis, as he truly said, had evoked " among the greater nations of the world . . . a passionate outburst which found expression in rejoicings at our reverses, in predictions about ultimate defeat, and in the grossest calumnies on the honour of our statesmen and the gallantry and humanity of our army." [1] How strongly contrasted with these sentiments were those manifested by the colonies! " During the whole of this time we have been supported and strengthened and encouraged and assisted by the men of our own blood and race. From the first day that struggle began, down to the other day when the terms of surrender

[1] At the Grocers' Hall, August 1st, 1901. (Boyd: *Speeches*, II, p. 71.)

238

were signed, we have had the affectionate regard and approval, we have had the active assistance, we have had the moral support of our fellow-subjects in all the possessions and dependencies of the British Crown." We had had more than their support. The death of the old Queen, the sudden illness which had struck down her son on the eve of his coronation, had evoked throughout the Empire a deep chord of sympathy. Manifestly there was among the British peoples, widely dispersed through the four quarters of the globe, a spiritual as well as a political unity: it even extended, in some degree, to the non-British members of the Empire. Small wonder that the eyes of the Colonial Secretary were opened to a wider vision of the Empire, and that he met his colleagues at the Conference of 1902 in a mood of exaltation and expectation.

The main subjects under discussion were, however, not sentimental but severely practical. Not the least practical was that of Imperial defence. With that question Sir Wilfrid Laurier, the Liberal Prime Minister of Canada, pointedly associated the question of admitting the colonies to political partnership in Imperial affairs. " If," he said, " you want our aid, call us to your Councils." " We do want your assistance," said Mr. Chamberlain, " in the administration of the vast Empire which is yours. The 'weary Titan' struggles under the too-vast orb of its fate. We have borne the burden for many years. We think it is time that our children should assist us to support it, and whenever you make the request to us, be very sure that we shall hasten gladly to call you to our Councils. If you are prepared at any time to take any share, any proportionate share, in the burdens of the Empire we are prepared to meet you with any proposal for giving to you a corresponding voice in the policy of the Empire." Dealing with specific schemes he ruled none out, but avowed his own preference—as a first step—for " the creation of a real Council of the Empire to which all questions of Imperial interest might be referred."

On the problem of Imperial defence he showed that naval and military expenditure worked out in the United Kingdom.

Conference of 1902

Imperial Defence

at £1 9s. 3d. per head per annum; in New South Wales at 3s. 5d.; in Victoria 3s. 3d.; in New Zealand 3s. 4d.; in the Cape and Natal between 2s. and 3s.; in Canada 2s. On this point the colonial response was prompt. The Australasian colonies agreed to raise their contribution for an improved Australasian squadron and the establishment of a branch of the Royal Naval Reserve from £126,000 to £200,000 a year; Cape Colony and Natal offered £50,000 and £35,000 a year respectively as an unconditional contribution towards the maintenance of the Navy; and Newfoundland undertook to provide £3,000 a year towards the branch of the Royal Naval Reserve hitherto maintained there by the Mother Country. Canada refused to participate, on the ground that it would be " an important departure from the principle of colonial self-government," but justly claimed that the value to the Empire of the Militia, entirely maintained at their own expense, had been demonstrated in South Africa, and promised to consider naval defence as well.

International Diplomacy An important point was raised by another resolution, which ran as follows: " That so far as may be consistent with the confidential negotiation of Treaties with Foreign Powers, the views of the Colonies affected should be obtained in order that they may be in a better position to give adhesion to such Treaties."

The principle was cautiously affirmed, but its significance was enhanced rather than diminished by the evident consideration for the susceptibilities of the Foreign Office, and the difficulties which surround the whole problem of Empire participation in foreign policy.

There remained, apart from such relatively minor matters as mail services and shipping subsidies, the all-important question of commercial relations within the Empire.

Empire Trade Mr. Chamberlain, emphasizing the unsatisfactory state of things then existing, expressed himself in favour of Free Trade within the Empire. But he was careful to add that he did not mean " the total abolition of custom duties within the Empire," which he recognized as impossible for countries which had to rely mainly on indirect taxation.

Canada had in 1900 increased the preference of twenty-five per cent granted to British goods in 1898 to thirty-three and one-third per cent. But the effect of it was disappointing. Despite the fact that the United Kingdom took eighty-five per cent of Canadian exports, the Canadian tariff still pressed with the greatest severity upon their best customer. Canada, on her part, demanded the exemption of their wheat and flour from the registration duty recently imposed by Parliament, but acute differences on the fiscal question in the Cabinet tied Chamberlain's hands. Thus Canada's ardent hopes were inevitably disappointed. Eventually, after long discussion, it was resolved that while Free Trade within the Empire was not at present practicable, it was desirable that the colonies should give a preference, " as far as their circumstances permit," to the products of the United Kingdom, and that the Imperial Government should be respectfully urged to grant " preferential treatment for the products and manufactures of the colonies either by exemption from, or reduction of, duties now or hereafter imposed."

The resolutions of the Conference constituted a definite challenge to the principle which for sixty years had inspired the fiscal policy of Great Britain. The issue thus raised was plainly of first-rate importance. Once raised it could not be indefinitely evaded, though for the moment it was evaded by Mr. Chamberlain's departure for South Africa.

For a Colonial Secretary to make an official visit to a British Dominion was without precedent. But it was Chamberlain's mission not to follow but to create precedents. The visit to South Africa, made with Lord Milner's " cordial approval," was a particularly happy one alike in its inception and its results.

Mr. Chamberlain's Mission to South Africa

Leaving England at the end of November in the cruiser *Good Hope*, Mr. and Mrs. Chamberlain visited Lord Cromer in Cairo, landed at Mombasa and made a trip on the Uganda Railway, attended a banquet given by the British residents at Zanzibar, and reached Durban on December 26th, 1902.

R 241

In the course of the next two months Chamberlain visited all the four colonies and made a series of speeches which were at once conciliatory and courageous. The supreme object of his mission was reconciliation; to persuade the Britons and Boers, capitalists and farmers, to live at peace with each other, and to labour for the well-being of the country they were henceforth to possess in common. But there was to be no misunderstanding. The war had decided the issue: " the British flag is and will be and must be paramount throughout South Africa." Yet " reconciliation should be easy. We hold out our hand and we ask the Dutch to take it frankly and in the spirit in which it is tendered." Politically, he looked forward to federation, but it must be reached by gradual stages. Economic reconstruction was the immediate task. Self-government would follow, but " not until their Boer friends had furnished them (the British Government) with some evidence of active loyalty." Self-government would prepare the way for federation. " Federation is a great aim, but it would be a great mistake to hasten it prematurely."

The visit was not devoid of jarring incidents—notably on questions of finance; but when on February 25th Mr. Chamberlain sailed from Capetown he could congratulate himself on a striking success achieved by a combination of cordiality and frankness.

A tumultuous welcome awaited him at home, but it could not atone for a bitter disappointment. During his absence in South Africa his colleagues had decided to repeal the registration duty of 1s. a quarter on imported wheat. The duty had produced a revenue of £2,000,000 without affecting the price of bread; but the strict Free Traders were alarmed lest even so minute a duty should open the door to a revival of Protection. Undoubtedly, the advocates of an inter-Imperial trade policy, both at home and in the Colonies, did regard the 1s. duty with the gratitude that hopes for more. *Obsta principiis* was the retort of the Free Traders.

Tariff Reform

In a speech at Birmingham (May 15th) Mr. Chamberlain

promptly took up the challenge; declared himself in favour of a complete and immediate reversal of the fiscal policy of this country. He urged that a preference should be given to colonial products, and that retaliatory duties should be imposed against those foreign countries which had erected tariff barriers against British goods.

Thus was the Tariff Reform campaign inaugurated. Its first effect was to split the Unionist party in twain and greatly to embarrass Mr. Balfour. Balfour was no dogmatic Free Trader, but neither was he a Protectionist; he leaned strongly towards the Imperialist views of Chamberlain and was ready to sacrifice " economic orthodoxy " (as then generally understood) in order to promote them. His paramount anxiety, however, was to avert the disruption of the party he led.

All his efforts to that end were unavailing. Mr. Chamberlain, as Colonial Secretary, and especially after his frank disclosure of his opinions to the colonial Premiers, could not, even temporarily, accept the exclusion of Tariff Reform from the party, and accordingly he resigned (September 9th, 1903). A few days later three Free Trade ministers, Lord Balfour of Burleigh, Mr. Ritchie, and Lord George Hamilton, in ignorance of Mr. Chamberlain's action, also resigned. On learning of it from the newspapers (Sept. 18th) they bitterly complained, with some justice, that they had been"jockeyed" into resignation, and got cold comfort from the fact that within a week or two the Duke of Devonshire joined them in exile.[1]

Mr. Balfour's agility availed him little: it still less availed his party. In December 1905 Mr. Balfour resigned; in January 1906 the Unionist Party was routed at the polls. *General Election of 1906*

Mr. Balfour was himself defeated (at Manchester), and his brother Gerald (now second Earl of Balfour), Mr. Alfred Lyttelton, who had succeeded Chamberlain at the Colonial Office, and most of the Tory leaders shared his fate. But both Chamberlains—father and son—were returned. Dur-

[1] The story of those days is told in detail in my *Modern England* (1934), pp. 191 f.

ing the two preceding years Chamberlain had carried on a vigorous campaign. He founded a Tariff Reform League on the lines of the Anti-Corn-Law League, and employed an army of statisticians to supply him with ammunition. He frankly confessed his abandonment of the Cobdenite doctrines of his political youth, but maintained that the economic conditions of the world had so entirely changed as to compel reconsideration of fiscal policy.

Mr. Chamberlain

But it was on the Imperial issue that Mr. Chamberlain concentrated his argument. "You cannot," he insisted, "weld the Empire together except by some form of commercial union." Political unity was his ultimate goal: an Imperial council to begin with, leading later, if it might be, to a complete and coherent federal Constitution. The experience of two Colonial Conferences and his recent tour in South Africa had, however, convinced him that commercial union was the necessary prelude to constitutional readjustment. Yet. England still needed many years of intensive education, not to add a period of commercial depression and a great war, before it was ready to abandon the doctrines of the Manchester School. Mr. Chamberlain never faltered, but the effort brought his active life to an abrupt and tragic termination.

On July 7th, 1906, Birmingham celebrated the seventieth birthday of its hero with great rejoicing. The celebrations closed with a great speech from the Senior Member for the city. The speech touched the highest note of Imperial patriotism: the set-back to the cause, though disheartening, was merely temporary: its ultimate triumph was certain:

"Others I doubt not, if not we,
The issue of our toil shall see."

Those were the last words ever uttered in public by Joseph Chamberlain. Two days later he had a paralytic stroke. He survived it for eight years, but though he retained control of his faculties and exercised them to further from his couch the cause he had so devotedly espoused, his active career was closed. The splendid vision vouchsafed to the great Imperial statesman has been at least partially realized. It is in the fitness of things that the two main instruments in its realization should have been the two stalwart sons sprung from his loins.

The Unionist débâcle of 1906 threw upon the Radical Government of Sir Henry Campbell-Bannerman the duty of organizing the Colonial Conference of 1907. Meeting under the auspices of a Government entirely out of sympathy with colonial ambitions, the atmosphere of that Conference was decidedly chilly. Mr. Lyttelton, who in 1905 had issued the invitations, had expressed the view that the time had come for transforming the " Colonial Conference " into an " Imperial Council " which should maintain continuity by the creation of a supplementary commission and a permanent secretariat. The colonial delegates made a determined effort to give effect to Mr. Lyttelton's suggestion, and to emancipate the " Conference " from the control of the Colonial Office. But the bureaucratic instincts of the Office prevailed against the wishes of the colonies, and the Conference had to be content with the following resolution:

Imperial Conference, 1907

" That it will be to the advantage of the Empire if a conference, to be called the *Imperial* Conference, is held every four years, at which questions of common interest may be discussed and considered as between *His Majesty's Government and his Governments of the self-governing Dominions beyond the Seas*. The Prime Minister of the United Kingdom will be *ex officio* President, and Prime Ministers of the self-governing Dominions *ex officio* members of the Conference. That it is desirable to establish a system by which the several Governments represented shall be kept informed during the periods between the Conferences in regard to matters which have been or may be subjects for discussion, by means of a permanent secretarial staff, charged, *under the direction of the Secretary of State for the Colonies*, with the duty of obtaining information for the use of the Conference, of attending to its resolutions, and of conducting correspondence on matters relating to its affairs."

Three points in the above text are worthy of note: (i) the term " Colonial " is definitely abandoned in favour of

" Imperial "; (ii) Dominion Ministers are for the first time referred to as " His Majesty's "; but (iii) the proposed permanent secretariat was still to be associated with the " Office." The first point explains itself. On the second there was an instructive and significant debate, indicative of the desire of the Dominion Ministers to be regarded as co-ordinate in status with " His Majesty's Government " at home, and as, equally with its members, " Servants of the King." The wording, as eventually adopted, was a rather clumsy but not insignificant compromise. Four years later Sir Wilfrid Laurier was able to claim that the discussions of 1907 " were productive of material and even important results," and it is interesting to note that in his opinion the most important of those results was " to substitute for the kind of ephemeral Colonial Conferences which had taken place before, a real Imperial system of periodical Conferences between the Government of His Majesty the King in the United Kingdom and (the precise phrase is noteworthy) the Governments of His Majesty the King in the Dominions beyond the Seas." [1] The third point represented, in one sense, a victory for the British bureaucracy, but at the same time it did not preclude an administrative advance. In 1908 the work of the Colonial Office was reorganized; Dominion affairs were separated from those of the Crown colonies and committed to a " Dominions Division." One other point in the proceedings of 1907 demands notice.

Australia and the Pacific Problem

The Australian delegates were again, as in 1887, gravely perturbed by the proceedings of the Foreign Office in regard to the problems of the Pacific. In 1906, after years of indecision, the British Government had suddenly, without consultation with the Australian Commonwealth or with New Zealand, concluded with France a Convention in regard to the New Hebrides. The whole transaction exhibited a flagrant disregard for the susceptibilities and interests of the people most closely concerned, and aroused bitter and just indignation amongst them. To this feeling Mr. Seddon, one of the most stout-hearted of Imperialists, gave vigorous

[1] *Minutes of Conference* of 1911, Cd. 5745, p. 24.

expression only a few hours before his lamented death (June 1906): " The Commonwealth and New Zealand Governments are incensed at the Imperial Government Conference fixing conditions of dual protectorate in the New Hebrides without first consulting the Colonies so deeply interested. The Imperial Government calls upon us now for advice upon what is already decided, making our difficulties very great. The entire subject is of vital importance to the Commonwealth and New Zealand. We ought to have been represented at the Conference. If anybody had been there for us who knew anything about the subject, the result would have been very different."

The outstanding figure at the Conference of 1907 was unquestionably that of Mr. Alfred Deakin, Premier of the Commonwealth. In a speech which re-echoed Seddon's last message to the Empire he referred to " the indifferent attitude of statesmen in this country to British interests in the Pacific "; to the time now past when " the anxiety of public men in this country was to avoid under any circumstances the assumption of more responsibilities and a great willingness to part with any they possessed "; to a feeling— " an exasperated feeling thus created in Australia—that British Imperial interests in that ocean have been mishandled from the first "; to the gross bungling of the Home Government in regard to New Guinea and the New Hebrides; to the misrepresentation of the Australians as a " grasping people," the truth being that " it is not a series of grasping annexations that we have been attempting, but a series of aggravated and exasperating losses which we have had to sustain "; and finally to the scandalous treatment of the Commonwealth in reference to the conclusion of the New Hebrides Convention. Mr. Deakin revived the memory of unfortunate incidents only, as he explained, " as warnings for the future and in order to explain the feeling that exists." To the indictment of the Home Government's procedure—their " take it or leave it " attitude—there was in reality no answer. Speeches such as Mr. Deakin's, so grave in substance, so admirable in restraint, at once

Alfred Deakin

reveal in lurid light the ineptitude of Whitehall, and compel admiration for the forbearance exhibited by the Dominions.

The blunder made by the Gladstone Government in 1884 had indeed, with singular fidelity to discredited precedent, been repeated by the Campbell-Bannerman Ministry in 1906, and the Home Government was within an ace of committing it again in 1915. Opportunity was also taken at the Conference of 1907 to discuss several detailed questions as to arms and ammunition (a point on which there was, nevertheless, considerable friction between the Canadian and Home Governments after the outbreak of war),[1] exchange of officers, cadets, military schools, and rifle clubs.

Subsidiary Conferences, 1907–1911

Before adjourning, the Conference resolved that " upon matters of importance requiring consultation between two or more Governments which cannot conveniently be postponed until the next Conference, or involving subjects of a minor character or such as call for detailed consideration, subsidiary conferences should be held between representatives of the Governments concerned specially chosen for the purpose." A Navigation Conference was accordingly held in 1907; Education Conferences in 1907 and 1911; a Copyright Conference in 1910, and a Surveyors' Conference in 1911. But of these subsidiary conferences the most important was one called to deal in 1909 with the question of naval and military defence. The Conference of 1907 had adopted the principle of the establishment of a general staff for the Empire, whose function was to study military science in all its branches; to collect and disseminate to the several Governments military information and intelligence ; to prepare schemes of defence on a common principle, and while not interfering with questions of command or administration to advise, at the request of any Government, as to the training, education, and war organization of the military forces of the Crown in every part of the Empire.

---

[1] Sir Sam Hughes, Minister of Militia in the Dominion, favoured the use of the Ross rifle, which had been rejected by the British War Office.

The Defence Conference which met in 1909 more than *Defence* justified its existence. It met in private, but Mr. Asquith *Conference, 1909* reported to the House that the Conference had agreed to recommend to their respective Governments a plan " for so organizing the forces of the Crown, wherever they are, that, while preserving the complete autonomy of each Dominion, should the Dominions desire to assist in the defence of the Empire in a real emergency, their forces could be rapidly combined into one homogeneous Imperial Army."

As regards naval defence, Canada decided to establish an auxiliary fleet, and undertook the maintenance of the dock-yards at Halifax and Esquimault. Australia also preferred to lay the foundations of her own fleet, purchasing for that purpose three cruisers and three destroyers from English firms. New Zealand, on the other hand, agreed to contribute a subsidy of £100,000 a year and a cruiser to a squadron of the new Pacific fleet. The latter was to consist of three units, one in the East Indies, one in the China Sea, one in Australian waters. It was further agreed that the personnel of the Australian and Canadian fleets should be trained and disciplined under regulations similar to those established in the Royal Navy, in order to allow of both interchange and union between the British and Dominion services; and, with the same object, that the standard of vessels and armaments should be uniform.

The Conference of 1909 was exceedingly timely, for since 1905 the international situation had gone from bad to worse. On March 31st, 1905, the German Emperor had visited Tangier, and had ostentatiously taken Morocco under his protection. Designed to demonstrate the hollowness of the *entente* recently (1904) concluded between England and France, it conspicuously failed in its amiable object. On the contrary, after the Conference that met at Algeciras (Jan. 1906), the *rapprochement* between Russia and England completed (1907), in German eyes, the " encirclement " of Germany. In 1908 Austria-Hungary brought Europe to the brink of war by annexing Bosnia and Herzegovina; in 1911 Germany brought it still nearer by the provocative despatch of the gunboat *Panther* to Agadir (July), and had not England ranged herself solidly behind France, war would almost certainly have broken out in August of that year.[1]

*Imperial
Conference
of 1911*
Such was the atmosphere in which the Conference of 1911 —for the first time officially " Imperial "—assembled. Nor were the cold blasts that blew from the Continent tempered by any increase of geniality on the part of the Home Government. To Sir Joseph Ward's resolution proposing the immediate formation of " an Imperial Council of State representative of all the self-governing parts of the Empire " and to be " in theory and in fact advisory to the Imperial Government on all questions affecting the interests of His Majesty's Dominions oversea," Mr. Asquith, as Prime Minister, opposed a frigid *non possumus*. The responsibility of the Imperial Government in foreign affairs, treaties, war and peace, must, he declared, remain exclusive and unimpaired. He categorically refused to " assent for a moment " to proposals which are so fatal to " the very fundamental conditions on which our Empire has been built up and carried on."

The edge of Asquith's blunt refusal was, however, turned by his announcement that he had just received a memorial from some three hundred Members of the House of Commons " belonging to various parties in the State " supporting the idea of a consultative Imperial Council.

Still more reassuring to the *amour propre* of the colonial delegates was the holding of a secret session of the Conference, at which Sir Edward Grey made a comprehensive and highly confidential disclosure respecting the diplomatic situation. Strictly confidential also was the discussion on Imperial defence, and the agreement resulting therefrom in regard to the co-operation of all the units of the Empire for military and naval purposes. Well might Mr. Andrew Fisher, Prime Minister of the Commonwealth, declare with fervour: " Hitherto, we have been negotiating with the Government of the United Kingdom at the portals

---

[1] These events are more fully treated in Marriott: *A History of Europe* (Methuen, Third ed., 1938), chapter XXI, to which the reader is respectfully referred.

of the household. You have thought it wise to take the representatives of the Dominions into the inner counsels of the nation, and frankly discuss with them the affairs of the Empire as they affect each and all of us. . . . I think no greater step has ever been taken or can be taken by any responsible advisers of the King."

Of the discussions subsequently made public the most important was that upon international agreements in general, and in particular upon the Declaration of London. That Declaration, embodying the new rules in regard to contraband decided upon at the Hague Conference of 1907, profoundly affected the position of the dominant sea-Power and its sea-Empire; but, apart from the merits, the Dominions held that, in a matter so closely affecting them, they ought to have been consulted. Consequently, on June 1st Mr. Fisher moved: " That it is regretted that the Dominions were not consulted prior to the acceptance by the British delegates of the terms of the Declaration of London. . . ." Upon that motion Sir Edward Grey spoke,[1] and on June 2nd the Conference resolved: " That this Conference, after hearing the Secretary of State for Foreign Affairs, cordially welcomes the proposals of the Imperial Government, viz.: (a) that the Dominions shall be afforded an opportunity of consultation when framing the instructions to be given to British delegates at future meetings of the Hague Conference, and that Conventions affecting the Dominions provisionally assented to at that Conference shall be circulated among the Dominion Governments for their consideration before any such Convention is signed; (b) that a similar procedure where time and opportunity and the subject-matter permit shall, as far as possible, be used when preparing instructions for the negotiations of other International Agreements affecting the Dominions."

The discussion was on a high plane, and in the course of it very serious objection was taken to the autocratic pro-

The Empire and International Agreements

---

[1] This speech, which will be found in *Minutes of Proceedings*, Cd. 5745, pp. 103–115, is quite distinct from the general survey of foreign affairs made *in camera* to the Committee of Defence.

cedure of the Home Government in reference to treaties which vitally concern the interests of the Dominions. Even General Botha, who throughout the Conference invariably spoke with characteristic modesty and marked consideration for the Home Government, was constrained, on this matter, to express his " profound conviction that it is in the highest interest of the Empire that the Imperial Government should not definitely bind itself by any promise or agreement with a foreign country which may affect a particular Dominion, without consulting the Dominion concerned." The sentiments of General Botha were the sentiments of all the self-governing Dominions. Nor did their misgivings lack justification. Nevertheless, there can be no question that the broad result of the Conference of 1911 conduced to a better understanding between Great Britain and the sister-nations. The discussions were frank almost to the verge of brutality; but confidence begot confidence. The comprehensive, precise, and accurate knowledge of the diplomatic situation which on dispersion the delegates carried back with them to their several Dominions necessarily involved a measure of responsibility. The status of dependency had been exchanged for that of partnership; the Dominions, when the crisis came, were not taken unawares. Their immediate and spontaneous participation in the war was the appropriate response to the confidence they had enjoyed.

Nevertheless, it could not be denied that the machinery of co-operation was still rudimentary, even though its haphazard development had been completely in harmony with British constitutional traditions, and with the instincts of a people as distrustful of theory as they are efficient in practice. A momentous question then remained: Would the machinery stand the strain, a severe and protracted strain? Would the " ties light as air " prove strong enough to hold the Commonwealth together through all the sufferings and sacrifices of a great war? The answer was not ambiguous.

Chapter Eighteen

The Empire at Bay

THE WORLD WAR

IN the evolution of the Empire the Great War marked a stage of supreme importance. The Dominions plunged into the war as Dependencies: they emerged from it as Nations.

The outbreak of the war threw into high relief the defects in the machinery of Imperial co-operation. But equally and simultaneously it revealed the fine spirit that could rise superior to all constitutional defects, the clearness of vision that instantly apprehended the great issues at stake, and the grim determination that once for all those issues should be decided in a sense consonant with the integrity of the Empire and the freedom for which it stands. *The Constitutional Position*

The constitutional position had been accurately stated by Sir Wilfrid Laurier in 1912:

" When England is at war, we are at war; but it does not follow that because we are at war we are actually in the conflict. . . . Why should we attempt to trifle with such questions as these ? Is it not a fact that our forces can go to war only by the action of this (Canadian) Parliament? " [1] Precisely. When the King of Great Britain and Ireland declares war he declares it as King of all the Britains and Emperor of India. The King's person is indivisible: the British Empire *vis-à-vis* the rest of the world is a unit. As a unit the Empire, on August 4th, 1914, went to war. Thus it came that, solely by the action of the Imperial Cabinet and the Imperial Parliament, all the units of the Empire were involved in war involuntarily; if not against their wills, at least without their wills. No British Dominion could have remained neutral in the war, except by renouncing its

[1] *Canadian House of Commons Debates*, December 12th, 1912.

allegiance to the King and formally severing its connection with the Empire. But although the sole responsibility for the declaration of war rested on the Imperial Government, and although that declaration created a state of war for the whole Empire, the active co-operation of the Dominions was entirely voluntary. No demand was made upon them for assistance, military, naval, or financial, and throughout the war their autonomy was scrupulously respected.[1]

Thus it was General Botha who decided the terms on which the German forces in South Africa laid down their arms, and it was Australian and New Zealand officers respectively who arranged the terms of the capitulation of German New Guinea and Samoa. The most sensitive of Dominion statesmen could hardly fail to be reassured by the policy pursued by the Imperial Government throughout the whole course of the war, as well as during the peace negotiations.

Colonial Co-operation

In no part of the Empire, except in South Africa, was there any hesitation to come forward with offers of assistance, still less to evade the legal responsibility of war. In South Africa General Botha's position was peculiar and difficult; he hesitated to commit his Government and for a time toyed with the idea of neutrality. Neutrality was legally and practically impossible. On August 5th Germany would have been as fully entitled to bombard Capetown or Durban as to bombard Portsmouth or Deal. Thus even in

South Africa

South Africa the Union Ministers accepted, as early as August 10th, 1914, the suggestion of the Imperial Government that they should promptly attack German South West Africa. Nor was the Legislature slow to support the action of the Executive. The House of Assembly, " fully recognizing the obligations of the Union as a portion of the British Empire," passed a humble address assuring His Majesty of " its loyal support in bringing to a successful issue the momentous conflict which had been forced upon him in defence of the principles of liberty and of international

[1] Keith: *Sovereignty of the British Dominions*, p. 314, and *War Government of the British Dominions*, p. 20.

honour, and of its whole-hearted determination to take all measures necessary for defending the interests of the Union and for co-operating with His Majesty's Imperial Government to maintain the security and integrity of the Empire." An amendment, proposed by General Hertzog, declaring that " an attack on German territory in South Africa would be in conflict with the interests of the Union and of the Empire," found only twelve supporters. But the Opposition were not content with verbal protest. Led by Christian De Wet and C. F. Beyers (who resigned his post as Commandant-General of the Union Defence Force), they raised a rebellion in October. With splendid moral courage General Botha himself took the field against " men who in the past have been our honoured leaders." The rebellion was sustained by some 10,000 men, but General Hertzog, though sympathizing with their attitude, was not among them. Before the end of December the rebellion was suppressed. Beyers had been drowned in the course of the campaign; De Wet was tried for treason and, though sentenced to six years' imprisonment, was after a few months released.

With his hands free from domestic disaffection, General *Conquest of* Botha in 1915 led an expedition into German South West *German South West* Africa. The campaign was arduous, but after some months' *Africa* fighting, marked by brilliant generalship, the Germans surrendered (July 9th) to General Botha, and the most important of their African colonies passed to the Union of South Africa. In addition to a large number of coloured and native troops, who were enlisted in labour brigades, South Africa contributed some 76,000 men to the armies of the Empire. Most of these fought under General Smuts in East Africa or in West Africa, but some 25,000 fought in Europe, and distinguished themselves on the Western Front.

Throughout the Empire the reaction to the European *The* situation was immediate. From all sides came offers of *Dominions and the* help. Canada promptly despatched 1,000,000 bags of flour *War* as a present to the Imperial Government, and by October 14th no fewer than 31,000 Canadian volunteers had reached England. They were followed by other large contingents, and before the end of the war Canada had raised no fewer than 628,462 men.

Australia was not a whit behind Canada. As early as August 3rd Mr. Hughes cabled to the Imperial Government that the Commonwealth was ready to despatch a force of 20,000 men. The first contingent actually left Australia on November 1st, 1914, and during the war no fewer than 329,883 splendid fighting men were sent overseas. New Zealand was equally prompt, and was at least as generous as Australia in its contribution to the common cause.

India played a part in the war not less important than that of the Dominions, though its constitutional and military position was entirely different.

India and the War

The army in India has always been maintained in a state of preparedness for war, but the military authorities, both in India and at home, had in view only frontier campaigns, or, at the worst, a possible attack by Russia or her allies on the North West Frontier. Consequently, the outbreak of the World war found India unprepared for military participation in distant theatres of war. In August 1914 there were, exclusive of the Indian Reserves, the Volunteers, and the Imperial Service Forces, about 235,000 men under arms in India: 75,000 were British and 160,000 formed the Indian army (with British officers and 341 British non-commissioned officers). When the call from Europe came, the response in India was immediate, spontaneous, and superb. On August 8th orders for mobilization were sent to Meerut and Lahore, and before the end of the month the Lahore Division had embarked. Owing to the lack of transports and escorts, the embarkation of the rest of the expeditionary force was delayed for some weeks. In a short time, however, all but eight of the regular British battalions and most of the batteries were withdrawn from India, and were replaced by twenty-nine Territorial field batteries and thirty-five Territorial battalions sent out from England.

On September 8th the Imperial Legislative Council met

at Simla, and the Viceroy conveyed to it a message from the King-Emperor. In reply, the Council passed, with enthusiasm and unanimity, a resolution affirming their "unswerving loyalty and enthusiastic devotion to their King-Emperor," and promising "unflinching support to the British Government." They expressed the opinion that "the people of India, in addition to the assistance now being afforded by India to the Empire, would wish to share in the heavy financial burden now imposed by the war on the United Kingdom." Such sentiments, while evidently sincere, were partly due to the anxiety of India not to be behind other "Dominions." "We aspire," said one Indian representative, "to colonial self-government, then we ought to emulate the example of the Colonials, and try to do what they are doing."

The ruling Princes were not behind the Government of British India in their professions of loyalty and promises of help. On September 8th the Viceroy telegraphed that "the Rulers of the Native States in India, who number several hundred in all, have with one accord rallied to the defence of the Empire and offered their personal services and the resources of their States for the War," and that from among the many Princes and nobles who had volunteered for active service he had selected some half-dozen Princes, including the Rulers of Patiala and Bikanir, Sir Partab Singh, and other cadets and nobles, and had accepted many offers of native contingents. He also reported that: *The Ruling Princes*

"The same spirit prevailed throughout British India. Hundreds of telegrams and letters had . . . come from communities and associations, religious, political, and social, of all classes and creeds, also from individuals offering their resources or asking for opportunity to prove their loyalty by personal service."

In the course of the war no fewer than 600,000 combatants (mostly Punjabis, Sikhs, Rajputs, and Gurkhas) and 474,000 non-combatants were sent overseas, and they distinguished themselves in nearly all the chief theatres of the war, notably in Mesopotamia, Palestine, Salonika, Gallipoli, and East Africa. The Bengali contribution to war service was negligible.

At this demonstration of Imperial unity the world stood amazed. Germany was not merely astonished but deeply chagrined. The German people had been beguiled into a confident anticipation that the first shot fired in a great European war would be the signal for the dissolution of England's " loosely compacted Empire." [1]

" We expected that British India would rise when the first shot was fired in Europe, but in fact thousands of Indians came to fight with the British against us. We anticipated that the whole British Empire would be torn in pieces, but the colonies appear to be united closer than ever with the Mother Country. We expected a triumphant rebellion in South Africa—it proved a fiasco."

Such was the lament of *Der Tag*. German philosophers could only attribute this to witchcraft; but, be that as it may, it proved to be in its consequences the most grave of all the miscalculations of German diplomacy.

The Empire's Contribution to Victory

The military history of the Great War lies outside the scope of this narrative. It must suffice to summarize the nature and extent of the contribution made by the overseas Empire. The extent of the sacrifice may be at least partially, if coldly, measured by statistics. Of the total of nearly 10,000,000 men who enlisted under the British flag, 3,284,743 came from the overseas Empire. Of the 947,023 who gave their lives for the common cause, 202,321 were from the colonies and India.

The first Canadian division landed in France in March, 1915, and by July 1st, 1916, there were nine colonial divisions on the Western Front alone. Conscription was adopted in Canada—not without resistance from the French Canadians, who might have been called to Europe by a double tie of patriotism—in 1917, and by the end of the war Canada had raised over half a million men, of whom 60,661 laid down their lives. Newfoundland also adopted compulsory service, but not until 1918, and by the time of the

---

[1] The phrase is Bernhardi's.

Armistice Newfoundland had recruited over 9,000 men, of whom 1,082 were killed or died of wounds. In addition over 3,000 Newfoundlanders joined the Canadian forces. The services rendered by the hardy fishermen from " Britain's oldest colony " as mine-sweepers was of inestimable value. Of the splendid courage shown by the Canadians in France, notably in the fierce battle for Vimy Ridge, it were almost impertinent to speak. It was only fitting, however, that the great soldier [1] who commanded them should have taken his title from that terrible engagement, and not less fitting that he should afterwards have been sent to Canada as Governor-General.

The courage displayed by the Canadians on the Western Front was at least equalled by the men from Australia and New Zealand forces, who earned undying fame on the Gallipoli peninsula, and not there only. Of the 329,862 Australians who came to Europe, 59,302 never returned. All the Australians were volunteers. Mr. Hughes attempted to impose conscription, but on a referendum his proposal was, by a very small majority, rejected, largely by the vote of the farmers and the influence of the Roman Catholic hierarchy. Nevertheless, the proportion of serving troops from Australia almost exactly equalled that of the Canadians, being 13·43 per cent of the male population, as against 13·48 in Canada.[2] The war cost the Commonwealth £600,000,000—a sum almost equal to the pre-war National Debt of the United Kingdom.

The contribution of New Zealand in man-power was proportionately even higher than that of Canada and Australia. It raised in all 112,223 men, or 19·35 per cent of its male population, and the New Zealanders suffered more than 50,000 casualties. Of all their men only 341 were taken prisoners. Such figures, apart from their splendid war record, would by themselves attest the superb courage they displayed. New Zealand, with a population

---

[1] Viscount Byng of Vimy.
[2] In the United Kingdom it was 25·36 per cent, or omitting the poor response from Ireland, 27·28 per cent.

of little over 1,000,000, incurred in the service of the Empire a debt of £81,500,000.

To the contribution made by India reference has already been made, but it may be added that included in the troops sent oversea were 26,000 officers and men of the Imperial Service Forces, and they lost in dead over 1,500 men. Of the Indian forces as a whole over 53,000 were killed or died of wounds. These losses were, as Lord Curzon truly said, " shattering." But he added:

" In the face of these trials and difficulties the cheerfulness, the loyalty, the good discipline, and intrepid courage of these denizens of another clime cannot be too highly praised."

The splendid contribution made by the overseas Empire to the common cause is the more remarkable in view of the fact that, excepting Africa, no part of that Empire was directly menaced by Germany. Protected by the British Navy, the Dominions, dependencies, and colonies might have pursued in security the even tenor of their way—doubtless with a profit to themselves relatively as large as that reaped by the United States.

Sea Power But the condition absolute of their security was British superiority at sea. That superiority was not immediately established. In home waters, indeed, the Admiralty was prepared for war. By 4 a.m. on August 4th the whole Fleet was mobilized and ready for action under Admiral Sir John Jellicoe; at 11 p.m. the historic order was issued: " Commence hostilities at once against Germany." In the outer seas, however, we were less prepared than Germany. The Germans had eight fast modern cruisers on foreign stations, and five gunboats. The *Scharnhorst*, the *Gneisenau*, the *Emden*, the *Nuremberg*, and the *Leipzig* were on the China station; the *Königsberg* was off East Africa; the *Dresden* and the *Karlsruhe* in the West Indies. These cruisers inflicted great damage upon us. Admiral von Tirpitz claimed, indeed, that " of enemy's goods and bottoms they destroyed more than double their own value " before they met their inevitable fate. His calculation was probably accurate.

Especially damaging to British merchant-shipping during *The Pacific* the first three months of the war was the activity of the *Emden* in the Pacific. Had it not been for our alliance with Japan, the situation in the Far East would have indeed been grave. Japan never hesitated as to the fulfilment of her obligations, though, even apart from the Treaty, the opportunity of revenge on Germany for the part she played in 1895 would probably have led to her intervention. On August 23rd, 1914, she declared war on Germany, and all the German possessions in the Pacific were swept up in the first months of the war. In that process the Australian colonies played an important part. On August 29th German Samoa was occupied by a force from New Zealand; in September the Bismarck Archipelago and German New Guinea fell to the Australians, and the Marshall and Caroline Islands to the Japanese. A force of 30,000 Japanese troops had, meantime, with some 2,000 British troops, attacked Kiaochow, which capitulated on November 7th. Three days later the *Emden* was at last hunted down and sunk off Cocos Island by the Australian cruiser *Sydney*. That was a brilliant achievement, but the naval resources of Australia and New Zealand were not equal to the task of transporting their troops to Europe. Nor could we spare ships for the purpose. Our Grand Fleet was fully occupied in home waters: we had to guard the Atlantic, and to a large extent the Mediterranean. It was the deliberate opinion of the statesmen both of Great Britain and of Australasia that the 1,600,000 troops from the Pacific Dominions and India could not have been safely transported across the oceans but for the assistance of our Japanese allies. " It was," said Lloyd George, " invaluable. It was one of the determining factors of the war." [1]

After the loss of her possessions in the Pacific, the German *Battle of* squadron made for home. Off the coast of Chile (whose *Coronel* neutrality was none too favourable to the Allies) Von Spee and his five cruisers fell in with a weak British squadron under Admiral Sir Charles Cradock. Cradock, though

[1] House of Commons *Official Debates*, August 18th, 1921, p. 1704.

without any hope of victory, determined to engage them (November 1st). *Good Hope* and *Monmouth* were sunk, the gallant Admiral going down with fourteen hundred officers and men. A fast but lightly armed cruiser, *Glasgow*, was sent off to warn the Falkland Islands, where *Canopus*, an old battleship, lay.[1]

The Sequel The disaster of Coronel was quickly retrieved. A squadron was promptly sent out from England under the command of Sir Doveton Sturdee, who, making all possible speed, arrived off the Falkland Isles on December 7th. On the very next day Sturdee fell in with Von Spee, and *Gneisenau, Scharnhorst, Leipzig,* and *Nuremberg* were sunk after a gallant fight; only *Dresden* escaped. The British loss was only seven men killed. *Dresden* was caught and sunk three months later.

Besides her cruisers Germany was expected to send out some forty armed merchantmen. Only five of them succeeded in leaving harbour. Of these the largest, *Kaiser Wilhelm der Grosse*, was sunk by *Highflyer* off the coast of Africa (August 26th); *Kap Trafalgar* was sunk by *Carmania* off the coast of Brazil after what has been described as "the finest single-ship action of the war" on September 14th; *Karlsruhe* was accidentally blown up; the other two were interned. Mr. Churchill, therefore, could boast that before the end of 1914 every one of the enemy ships on the high seas was "reduced to complete inactivity, sunk, or pinned in port."[2]

The German Colonies The German colonies lay at our mercy, though it was not until after a keen struggle that German East Africa was conquered.

West Africa gave comparatively little trouble. Togoland surrendered to a Franco-British force in the first month of the war, and at the peace was divided between the two Powers, about one-third of the colony (some 12,500 square miles) bordering on the Gold Coast territories being assigned to Great Britain and the remainder to France. The Cameroons were attacked, in August 1914, by French troops

[1] Built 1897: 13,500 tons. [2] *World Crisis*, p. 286.

from the French Congo and by a small British force from Nigeria in the same month. Not, however, until February 1916 was it finally conquered: an area of 33,000 square miles (out of 191,130), extending from the coast along the Nigerian frontier up to Lake Chad, was assigned to Great Britain, and the rest to France.

Of the African campaigns by far the most arduous and prolonged was that for the possession of German East Africa. Could Germany have held it with adequate naval as well as military forces, she would have threatened the British Empire's line of communications at a vital point. Our naval supremacy averted this danger; but Germany had made elaborate preparations to defend her own colony, and if occasion offered to attack British East Africa. General von Lettow-Vorbeck commanded a force of 3,000 Europeans and 12,000 well-equipped and well-disciplined Askaris. A British attack on Tanga was repulsed in November 1914, and not until General Smuts took over the command of the British forces at the beginning of 1916 was any effective progress made. Dar-es-Salaam was captured in September 1916, but another fourteen months of hard fighting was required before the Germans were cleared out of the colony. They took refuge in Portuguese East Africa, and thence, in the autumn of 1918, made their way into Northern Rhodesia; nor did they surrender until compelled to do so by the conclusion of the Armistice. *The Campaign in East Africa*

Rough and rapid as the foregoing summary has been, it will suffice to demonstrate the important part played by the British overseas Empire in the Great War. It also irresistibly suggests a further reflection. To the war record of the British Empire there is nothing comparable in the whole history of mankind. An Empire so " loosely compacted " that it was bound (according to the German analysis) to break into fragments at the first sound of the war-trumpet, had, in face of a grave menace, proved its solidarity. Burke was justified. The ties light as air had proved indestructible. They had held, in spite of the fact that the machinery of co-operation was lamentably old-fashioned and defective.

Nor were the Dominions, with all their loyalty to the Motherland, and despite their proud determination to play their full part in the defence of an Empire which was their heritage as much as that of insular Britons, blind to the deficiency in its mechanism.

Speaking at Winnipeg early in the war, Sir Robert Borden said: " It is impossible to believe that the existing status, so far as it concerns the control of foreign policy and extra-Imperial relations, can remain as it is to-day." " These pregnant events," he said in December 1915, " have already given birth to a new order. It is realized that great policies and questions which concern and govern the issues of peace and war cannot in future be assumed by the people of the British Islands alone." In language not less emphatic and more picturesque, Mr. Doherty, the Minister of Justice, spoke to similar purpose at Toronto: " Our recognition of this war as ours, our participation in it, spontaneous and voluntary as it is, determines absolutely once for all that we have passed from the status of the protected colony to that of the participating nation. The protected colony was rightly voiceless; the participating nation cannot continue so."

Australia and New Zealand re-echoed the voice of Canada. " There must be a change and it must be radical in its nature," declared Mr. Hughes. Mr. Fisher and Sir Joseph Ward spoke with similar emphasis, and the same point was driven home in England by Mr. Bonar Law: " It is not a possible arrangement that one set of men should contribute the lives and treasure of their people and should have no voice in the way in which those lives and that treasure are expended. That cannot continue. There must be a change."

The plea was irresistible and was not unheeded.

The change was not long delayed. The way was in fact prepared for it by another innovation. On taking office as Prime Minister in December 1916, Mr. Lloyd George set up a " War Cabinet " or " Directory." He had come to the conclusion that the war could not be carried to a successful issue by a "Sanhedrim"—a Cabinet of the time-honoured type. "The kind of craft," he said, "you have for river or canal traffic is not exactly the kind of vessel to construct for the high seas. I have no doubt that the old Cabinets were better adapted to navigate the Parliamentary river with its shoals and shifting sands and perhaps for a cruise in home waters—but a Cabinet of twenty-three was top-heavy for a gale. . . . It is true that in a multitude of counsellors there is wisdom. That was written for Oriental countries in peace times. You cannot run a war with a Sanhedrim."

Apart from the war the old Cabinet system was by many thoughtful politicians regarded as obsolescent. Unknown to the law, if not to the Constitution, the Cabinet had developed in characteristic English fashion. Its very existence depended on the will of an individual, himself without Constitutional status or salary, and by his personality efficiency was measured. Its procedure was hopelessly unbusinesslike, not to say haphazard. There was no order of business, no agenda, no minutes; and the only record of business done or decisions made was contained in the Prime Minister's letter, at the close of each meeting, to the Sovereign. "The Cabinet," said Lord Curzon, "often had the very haziest notion as to what its decisions were . . . cases frequently arose when the matter was left so much in doubt that a Minister went away and acted upon what he thought was a decision which subsequently turned out to be no decision at all, or was repudiated by his colleagues." [1] The system was evidently obsolescent even in a peace-time machine, much more under the stress of war.

Accordingly, Mr. Lloyd George superseded the Cabinet *The War Cabinet* by a "War Cabinet" or "Directory." For his Departmental Ministers (e.g. for Education and Trade) the Prime Minister went in some cases outside Parliament, though seats were presently found for the "experts" thus appointed.

The "Directory" itself was to consist of five members,

[1] House of Lords, *Official Report*, June 19th, 1919.

of whom only one was to be the head of an administrative department—Mr. Bonar Law, who was to be Chancellor of the Exchequer and lead the House of Commons. The other members were Lord Curzon, Mr. Lloyd George himself, Lord Milner, and Mr. Henderson; General Smuts was added to the Directory in June 1917. G. N. Barnes succeeded Henderson as representative of the Labour Party in the "Directory" in August 1917. The idea of this novel experiment was that half a dozen of the leading statesmen, relieved of all departmental responsibilities, should be free to give their whole time to the prosecution of the war. In practice this idea was imperfectly realized: much of the time of the "Directors" was given to the settlement of inter-departmental disputes.

Nevertheless, the new system was a great improvement on the old; and new methods of conducting business were introduced, all of which happily survived the restoration of the old Cabinet system in 1919.[1] Of these the most important were the preparation of an agenda and the circulation of papers in connection therewith, the keeping of minutes (under the strictest control and limitations), and above all the appointment of a secretary. The minutes were regularly sent to the King, a practice which (generally) relieved the Prime Minister of the duty of writing regular reports. The first Secretary was Colonel Sir Maurice Hankey, who had already proved his exceptional competence as Secretary to the Committee of Imperial Defence, and continued to act as Secretary to the restored Cabinet until 1938. No words can exaggerate the value of the services which he rendered to the State both during and after the war. Those services have secured for him an honoured place among the "makers" of a Constitution which in fact has never been "made."

The Committee of Imperial Defence

The appointment of Sir Maurice Hankey also maintained the continuity between the old Committee of Imperial

---

[1] For details of the work of the War Cabinet see *Reports* of the War Cabinet for 1917 and 1918 (Cd. 9005 and Cmd. 325); Marriott: *Mechanism of the Modern State*, Vol. II, pp. 80–84; and Jennings: *Cabinet Government*, pp. 232 f.

Defence and the new War Cabinet, much of whose procedure was adapted from the older institution.

The Committee of Imperial Defence, after existing as a somewhat nebulous body for ten years, had been reorganized with a small but permanent secretariat and staff in 1904. Its inception was largely due to the recommendations of Lord Esher, Sir John Fisher, and Sir George Clarke (afterwards Lord Sydenham of Combe). Clarke did considerable service as its first Secretary. Lord Esher became a " permanent member " of it in 1905. Minutes are taken and preserved and are available for reference by successive Committees. The Prime Minister became *ex-officio* chairman, and the other ordinary members are the Secretaries of State for Foreign Affairs, for the Dominions, for the Colonies, for India, for War, and for the Air, the First Lord of the Admiralty, the First Sea Lord, the Chief of the Imperial General Staff, the Chief of the Air Staff, the Directors of the Intelligence Departments of the War Office and the Admiralty, and the Chancellor of the Exchequer. The functions of the Committee are purely advisory, and their exercise depends wholly on the Prime Minister, who can summon to its meetings anyone he pleases. He was, however, expressly empowered to call for the attendance of any military or naval officers, or of other persons with administrative experience, whether they hold official positions or not. In particular the advice is sought of representatives of the Dominions. Lord Esher would have liked to see the Dominions regularly and permanently represented on the Committee, preferably by their Prime Ministers. They might, he suggested, visit London for that purpose, annually or at longest biannually in July.[1]

The Committee itself resolved in 1911 that Dominion Ministers appointed by their respective Governments should in future be invited to attend its meetings " when positions of naval and military defence affecting the oversea Dominions are under consideration." Canadian Ministers

[1] Esher: *The Committee of Imperial Defence*, p. vii, and *Journal and Letters*, Vol. II, *passim*.

did in fact attend some of the meetings in 1912, 1913, and 1914, and in 1913 Ministers from New Zealand and South Africa also attended. The organization of the Committee, in the conduct of which he took great personal interest, was the most important piece of constructive work (always excepting his Education Act of 1902) achieved during his Premiership by Mr. Balfour.[1]

In one sense, then, the Committee of Imperial Defence may be regarded as the progenitor of the Imperial War Cabinet, though the functions of the Committee were purely advisory. It had no executive powers: all decisions on matters of policy—indeed on every matter—were expressly reserved for the Cabinet. Nevertheless, its development was regarded with some jealousy on the part of those Cabinet Ministers who were not summoned to attend it.[2]

Soon after the outbreak of war the Committee of Imperial Defence was converted into a War Council. This Council was endowed with extended executive authority, and consisted, in addition to the Prime Minister, of five Cabinet Ministers and of the Service experts. Mr. Balfour, who at Mr. Asquith's request had served on one Sub-Committee of the C.I.D. from March 1913 till February 1914, became a member of the War Council on its formation,[3] and in January 1915 Lord Haldane and Sir Arthur Wilson were added to it.

All this was in the natural order of developments. Much more significant was the decision to create an Imperial Cabinet.

Imperial War Cabinet

The Prime Ministers of the Dominions and representatives of India were, in December 1916, invited by the Home Government to visit England " to attend a series of special and continuous meetings of the War Cabinet, in order to consider urgent questions affecting the prosecution of the war, the possible conditions on which, in agreement with our allies, we could assent to its termination, and the

---

[1] For convenience this paragraph describes the later, not the original, composition of the Committee, on which see also Esher: *Journal*, Vol. III, pp. 14 f.
[2] Fitzroy: *Memoirs*, Vol. II, p. 539 *ap.* (Jennings, p. 231).
[3] Dugdale: *Life of Balfour*, Vol. I, pp. 104, 125.

problems which will then immediately arise." The invitation was accepted; and the Imperial War Cabinet, consisting of the five members of the British War Directory; the Secretaries of State for Foreign Affairs, India, and the Colonies; three representatives of Canada, two of New Zealand, one of South Africa, and one of Newfoundland, met for the first time in March 1917. Three representatives of India were also present to advise the Secretary of State.

The Constitutional status of the Imperial War Cabinet was unequivocal. Speaking as leader of the House of Lords (February 7th, 1917) Lord Curzon said:

" The representatives are not coming here to endeavour to construct a brand-new Constitution for the British Empire. The capacity in which they come, however, does constitute a remarkable forward step in the constitutional evolution of the Empire. They are not coming as members of an Imperial Conference of the old style. They are coming as members for the time being of the Sovereign body of the British Empire. This seems to me the greatest step ever taken in recognizing the relations of the Dominions and ourselves on a basis of equality. . . . The War Cabinet is for a purpose being expanded into an Imperial Council."

Sir Robert Borden, Prime Minister of Canada, was equally explicit, and equally emphatic in his appreciation of the significance of the new departure. Speaking in the Dominion House of Commons after his return from the first meeting of the new Cabinet he said:

" Everyone has realized the somewhat anomalous position of the Empire in respect of questions which concern foreign policy and foreign relations. It is abundantly clear that it is those questions in which are involved the issues of peace and war, and it is equally clear that in the event of a great war threatening in any way the existence of our Empire or its interests, the self-governing Dominions are at war when the Mother Country is at war, and must inevitably take their part, and therefore they are concerned with the causes out of which war may arise. . . .

" The very nature of events arising out of the war make

it absolutely necessary that the Overseas Dominions should have a voice, and having that voice it was natural, and more than that, necessary, that they should be assembled in an Imperial War Cabinet.

" For the first time in the Empire's history (April 1917) there have been sitting in London two Cabinets, both properly constituted and both exercising well-defined powers. Over each of them the Prime Minister of the United Kingdom presides. One of them is designated as the ' War Cabinet,' which chiefly devotes itself to such questions touching the prosecution of the war as primarily concern the United Kingdom. The other is designated as the ' Imperial War Cabinet,' which has a wider purpose, jurisdiction, and personnel. To its deliberations have been summoned representatives of all the Empire's self-governing Dominions. We meet there on terms of equality under the Presidency of the First Minister of the United Kingdom; we meet there as equals, although Great Britain presides, *primus inter pares*. Ministers from six nations sit around the council board, all of them responsible to their respective Parliaments and to the people of the countries which they represent. Each nation has its voice upon questions of common concern and highest importance as the deliberations proceed; each preserves unimpaired its perfect autonomy, its self-government, and the responsibility of its Ministers to their own electorate. For many years the thought of statesmen and students in every part of the Empire has centred around the question of future constitutional relations; it may be that now, as in the past, the necessity imposed by great events has given the answer. . . .

" . . . With the constitution of that Cabinet a new era has dawned and a new page of history has been written. . . ."[1]

Thus for two months in the spring of 1917 the Empire did actually possess a real Imperial Executive if only in embryo. " The British Cabinet," said Mr. Lloyd George, " became for the time being an Imperial War Cabinet. While it was

[1] Borden in Dominion House of Commons, May 18th, 1917. *The War and the Future*, pp. 141–145.

in session its overseas members had access to all the information which was at the disposal of His Majesty's Government, and occupied a status of absolute equality with that of the members of the British War Cabinet." So completely successful, indeed, had the experiment proved, so serviceable to all its members and to the Empire, that on May 17th, 1917, the Prime Minister informed the House of Commons that the Imperial War Cabinet had unanimously resolved that " the procedure ought not to be allowed to fall into desuetude. Consequently it had been decided to hold an annual Imperial Cabinet," and the hope was expressed that it would become " an accepted convention of the British Constitution." [1]

A second session of the Imperial War Cabinet was held from June 11th to July 30th, 1918. The Prime Ministers of Canada, New Zealand, and Newfoundland again attended ; General Smuts represented South Africa, and Australia, unrepresented in 1917 owing to a General Election, was represented by the Prime Minister of the Commonwealth and by Sir Joseph Cooke, the Minister of the Navy. India, too, was represented by the Secretary of State, by the Maharajah of Patiala as " the spokesman of the Princes of India," and by Sir S. P. (afterwards Lord) Sinha, who was " deputed to this country as the representative of the people of India."

Nor did the Empire Cabinet of 1918 differ from its predecessor only in composition. Its scope and competence were extended to cover the whole field of Imperial policy, and its machinery was elaborated.

It was formally resolved that henceforward the Premiers *Machinery* of the Dominions should have the right (on questions only of Cabinet importance) to communicate directly with the Prime Minister of the United Kingdom and he with them.

Another point of great importance was also dealt with by formal resolution. The experience of the period between the adjournment of the first session (May 1917) and the

[1] House of Commons *Official Report*, May 17th, 1917.

271

meeting of the second (June 1918) sufficed to demonstrate the practical inconvenience resulting from the fact that while the Prime Ministers of the Dominions could only attend the Imperial War Cabinet for a few weeks in the year, matters of the greatest importance from the point of view of the common interest inevitably arose, and had to be decided in the interval between the sessions. The natural remedy for this defect lay in giving the Imperial War Cabinet continuity by the presence in London of oversea Ministers definitely nominated to represent the Prime Ministers in their absence. Consequently, the following resolution was adopted: " In order to secure continuity in the work of the Imperial War Cabinet and a permanent means of consultation during the war on the more important questions of common interest, the Prime Minister of each Dominion has the right to nominate a Cabinet Minister either as a resident or visitor in London to represent him at meetings of the Imperial War Cabinet to be held regularly between the Plenary sessions." It was also decided that arrangements should be made for the representation of India at these meetings.

Before that resolution could take effect the military collapse of the Central Powers—unexpectedly rapid and complete—brought the war to an end, and precipitated the summoning of a Peace Conference at Paris. At that Conference the Imperial War Cabinet virtually reappeared as the " British Empire Delegation."

Imperial War Conferences

In the meantime, however, discussions of great significance had taken place at the Imperial War Conference, which in the spring of 1917 sat side by side with the Imperial War Cabinet.

As regards the representatives of the Dominions and India, the personnel of the two bodies was identical. The members of the British War Cabinet did not, however, attend the Conference which met at the Colonial Office under the presidency of the Secretary of State, Mr. Walter Long. As a rule the Imperial Cabinet and the Imperial Conference met on alternate days, the latter being concerned with non-war problems, or questions connected with the war but of lesser importance. A great part of the proceedings was of a highly confidential character, and entirely unsuitable for publication, at any rate during the war, but extracts from the Minutes of Proceedings and some of the resolutions adopted were promptly published. Of those resolutions by far the most significant was the famous Resolution (IX) on the Constitution of the Empire. Adopted, apparently with unanimity, on April 16th, it finally ran as follows: " The Imperial War Conference are of opinion that the readjustment of the constitutional relations of the component parts of the Empire is too important and intricate a subject to be dealt with during the War and that it should form the subject of a special Imperial Conference to be summoned as soon as possible after the cessation of hostilities. They deem it their duty, however, to place on record their view that any such readjustment, while thoroughly preserving all existing powers of self-government and complete control of domestic affairs, should be based upon a full recognition of the Dominions as autonomous nations of an Imperial Commonwealth, and of India as an important portion of the same, should recognize the right of the Dominions and India to an adequate voice in foreign policy and in foreign relations, and should provide effective arrangements for continuous consultation in all important matters of common Imperial concern, and for such necessary concerted action, founded on consultation, as the several Governments may determine."

General Smuts bluntly said that the adoption of this resolution, which he nevertheless cordially supported, " negatived by implication the idea of a future Imperial Parliament and a future Imperial Executive."[1] The Conference of 1926 proved his prescience.

A second Imperial War Conference met in the summer of 1918, and, as in 1917, its meetings alternated with meetings of the Imperial War Cabinet. So far as appears from the published *Minutes* the constitutional problem was not even

---

[1] *Report*, Cd. 8566, p. 47.

approached. Questions of naturalization, of demobilization, of inter-Imperial communications, of emigration, of the treatment of British Indians in the Dominions, of the supply of raw materials, and similar topics, were dealt with in detail, but as hostilities had not yet ceased the problem of constitutional relations was deferred. The Conference broke up on July 26th; the Imperial War Cabinet held its last meeting on July 30th; its members dispersed.

During the next three months events developed rapidly. By the end of October the great military machine of Germany was broken into fragments; her allies fell away from her; her fleet mutinied; revolution broke out; on November 9th her Emperor fled for safety to Holland; on November 11th " cease fire " was sounded, and an Armistice was signed. The summoning of the Peace Conference recalled most of the Dominion Ministers to London, and by November 20th the Imperial Cabinet, though not complete in personnel until the close of the year, was again in formal session. At least twelve meetings were held before the migration to Paris, and at one very important meeting (December 3rd) M. Clemenceau and General Foch, representatives of France, and Signor Orlando and Baron Sonnino, representing Italy, were present. But the imminence of the Peace Conference overshadowed all other matters. From the supreme crisis of the war the Empire had safely emerged: problems, hardly less critical, confronted the peace-makers in Paris.

Chapter Nineteen

The Post-War Empire (1919–1926)

THE PEACE CONFERENCE AND AFTER

I MPORTANT as was the war in its effect upon *The Peace* Imperial relations, the significance of the Peace *Conference* Conference was even greater.

The status of the Dominions was the subject of earnest discussion at the Imperial War Cabinet in London before the Conference met. It was ultimately agreed that each Dominion should have separate representation equal to that of the smaller Allied Powers, and that, in addition, the British Empire should be represented by five delegates selected from day to day from a panel made up of representatives of the United Kingdom and the Dominions.

The Conference assembled in Paris on January 12th, *Representa-* 1919, and when the question of procedure was discussed, *tion of the* strong objection was taken by other Allied representatives *Dominions* to the exceptionally strong representation of the British Empire. Had the Dominions been represented at Paris only in and by the British Empire Delegation it might have made for simplicity of procedure, for the avoidance of friction at the moment, and of complications both internal and external in the future. Had that course been adopted the Peace Conference would still have formed, as General Smuts claims that it did form, " one of the most important landmarks in the history of the Empire." But with such a position the Dominions were not content. " It was abundantly clear to my colleague and myself that Australia must have separate representation at the Peace Conference. Consider the vastness of the Empire and the diversity of interests represented. Look at it geographically, industrially, or how you will, and it will be seen that no one can speak for Australia but those who speak as representatives of Australia herself." [1] So spake Mr. Hughes in the Commonwealth House of Representatives. Other Dominion Premiers have spoken—since they were free to speak—to the same effect; but the specific claim of the Dominions, and the ground on which it was based, was most clearly expressed in a telegram from the Canadian Cabinet to Sir Robert Borden, who was at the time sitting in the Imperial War Cabinet: " In view of war efforts of Dominions other nations entitled to representation at Conference should recognize unique character of British Commonwealth composed of group of free nations under one sovereign, and that provision should be made for special representation of those nations at Conference, even though it may be necessary that in any final decision reached they should speak with one voice " (December 4th, 1918). The other members of the Conference could not, as General Smuts subsequently pointed out, " realize the new situation arising, and that the British Empire, instead of being one central Government, consisted of a league of free States, free, equal, and working together for the great ideals of human government." [2]

Stated thus bluntly the situation might perhaps have created surprise if not alarm in the minds of other people besides the Allied representatives. But the Dominions had their way. In the Plenary Conference, Australia, Canada, and South Africa were each represented by two delegates, being treated as small nations on the same level as Greece, Portugal, Poland, or Roumania; New Zealand was represented by one. The Dominions in the aggregate were also entitled to be included in the British Empire Delegation of five members. Nor was the part which they played on this Delegation insignificant or subordinate. On the contrary, the leader of the British House of Commons emphatically insisted that just as in the Imperial War Cabinet the Dominion representatives " took in every respect an equal part in all that concerned the conduct of the war; so in

[1] Commonwealth of Australia, *Parliamentary Debates*, No. 87, p. 12168. The whole of Mr. Hughes's speech on the Peace Treaty will repay the most careful perusal.
[2] Quoted by Duncan Hall: *The British Commonwealth of Nations*, pp. 183–184.

Paris, in the last few months, they have, as members of the British Empire Delegation, taken a part as great as that of any member, except perhaps the Prime Minister, in moulding the Treaty of Peace." [1]

Well might General Smuts acclaim the Paris Conference as one of the most important landmarks in the history of the Empire. It is indeed impossible to read the debates on the Peace Treaty in the Legislatures of Canada and Australia [2] respectively without becoming acutely conscious of the fact that, profoundly as the Dominions were interested in the actual terms of the Treaty of Versailles, they were even more interested in the new status accorded to their representatives alike in the negotiations precedent to the signature of the Treaty, and in the League of Nations. That status—cordially conceded by the Imperial Government but somewhat reluctantly recognized by the Allied and Associated Powers —was succinctly and accurately defined by a speaker in the Commonwealth Parliament: "The Empire," said Mr. Burchell, "to-day stands in the position of a league of nations within the League of Nations." [3]

With the European settlement effected or attempted in 1919, this narrative is not concerned. With the colonial settlement it is otherwise; and it would be unfair to the Dominions were the impression to be conveyed that their insistence upon their new status was due either to constitutional pedantry or to political contumacy. Vital issues were at stake, and the Dominions were not prepared to entrust them to any delegates except such as were directly responsible to the Dominion Parliaments.

Among those issues not the least vital was raised by the disposition of the colonies which had formerly belonged to Germany in Africa and in the Pacific.

By Articles 118 and 119 of the Treaty of Versailles, *Mandates* Germany renounced in favour of the principal Allied and

---

[1] Speech by Mr. Bonar Law to the Empire Parliamentary Association, May 16th, 1919; quoted Duncan Hall: *op. cit.*, p. 189.
[2] The Debates in the Parliament of the Union of South Africa are not officially reported.
[3] Commonwealth of Australia, *Parliamentary Debates*, No. 90, p. 12586.

Associated Powers all her rights over her overseas possessions. There was, however, a strong feeling among the
Allies that whatever Power should be entrusted with the
government of territories inhabited by backward peoples,
the task should be undertaken, not for purposes of political
aggrandizement or commercial exploitation, but in the
spirit of trusteeship. An Englishman may be forgiven for
saying that the spirit which has in the main, despite occasional backsliding, inspired the colonial administration of
Great Britain was henceforward to govern the relations
between European rulers and their non-European subjects.
This intention was embodied in Article XXII of the Covenant of the League of Nations, which laid down that " to
those colonies and territories which as a consequence of the
late war have ceased to be under the Sovereignty of the
States which formerly governed them, and which are
inhabited by peoples not yet able to stand by themselves
under the strenuous conditions of the modern world, there
should be applied the principle that the well-being and
development of such peoples form a sacred trust of civilization." It further suggested that the best way of giving
effect to this principle is that " the tutelage of such peoples
should be entrusted to advanced nations who by reason of
their resources, their experience, or their geographical
position can best undertake this responsibility, and who are
willing to accept it, and that this tutelage should be exercised
by them as Mandatories of the League." The character
of the Mandate must, however, differ "according to the
stage of the development of the people, the geographical
situation of the territory, its economic conditions and
other similar circumstances." So the Powers in Conference decreed. Would the "Mandate" principle work
in the Pacific? The Australasian representatives were
doubtful.

*The Pacific
Islands*

" One of the most striking features of the Conference,"
said Mr. Hughes, the Premier of the Australian Commonwealth, " was the appalling ignorance of every nation as to
the affairs of every other nation—its geographical, racial,

historical conditions, or traditions."[1] The safety of Australia, so her sons consistently maintained, demanded that the great rampart of islands stretching around the north-east of Australia should be held by the Australian Dominion or by some Power (if there be one ?) in whom they have absolute confidence. At Paris Mr. Hughes made a great fight to obtain the direct control of them; worsted in that fight by Mr. Wilson's formulas, Australia was forced to accept the principle of the Mandate, but her representatives were careful to insist that the Mandate should be in a form consistent not only with their national safety but with their " economic, industrial, and general welfare."

In plain English that meant the maintenance of a " White Australia " and a preferential tariff. On both points Australia found herself in direct conflict with Japan, but, despite the formal protest and reservation of the latter, the Mandates for the ex-German possessions in the Pacific were issued in the form desired by the British Dominions, i.e. in the same form (" C ") as that accepted for South West Africa.

The islands north of the Equator, namely the Marshall, Caroline, Pelew, and Ladrone Islands, went to Japan, as did Kiaochow; those south of the Equator to the British Empire or its Dominions: the Bismarck Archipelago, German New Guinea, and those of the Solomon Islands formerly belonging to Germany, to Australia,[2] German Samoa to New Zealand,[3] and Nauru to the British Empire [4] —in all cases under Mandate.

The position in Africa differed widely from that in the Pacific.

In the ultimate settlement South West Africa was assigned *South West Africa* by the Principal Allied and Associated Powers to His Britannic Majesty, to be administered on his behalf by the Government of the Union of South Africa under a Mandate approved by the Council of the League of Nations.

South West Africa was indicated, like the South Pacific

[1] Commonwealth of Australia, *Parliamentary Debates*, No. 87, pp. 12, 173.
[2] Cmd. 1201 (1921).　　　[3] *Ibid.*, 1203.　　　[4] *Ibid.*, Zo4.

islands, in Article XXII of the Covenant as one of the territories which " owing to the sparseness of their popula-tion, or their small size, or their remoteness from the centres of civilization, or their geographical contiguity to the territory of the Mandatory and other circumstances, can be best administered under the laws of the Mandatory as integral portions of its territory, subject to the safeguards above mentioned in the interests of the indigenous popula-tion." The Mandate was accordingly issued in the form prescribed for Class C territories. It enjoins upon the Mandatory the duty of promoting to the utmost " the material and moral well-being and the social progress of the inhabitants "; it prohibits slavery, the sale of intoxicants to natives, the establishment of military or naval bases; and provides for complete freedom of conscience, and facilities for missionaries and ministers of all creeds. The Mandatory is further required to make an annual report to the Council of the League, containing full information with regard to the territory, and indicating the measures taken to fulfil the obligations the Mandatory has assumed.[1]

East Africa Of the African campaigns none, as we have seen, had been so arduous or prolonged as that for the possession of German East Africa. At the Peace Settlement it would naturally have become the prize of the conquerors, but in consequence of strong protests from Belgium was ultimately divided between the two Powers. The British portion, now known as Tanganyika Territory, lying immediately to the south of the Kenya colony (formerly the British East Africa Protectorate), has a coast-line of 620 miles, extending from the mouth of the Umba to Cape Delgado, an area of some 384,180 square miles, and an estimated pre-war native population of about 6,500,000. The rest of German East Africa—the provinces of Ruanda and Urundi, together with the country round Lake Kivu—was conferred upon Belgium. A strip on the east of the Belgian portion has, however, been reserved to Great Britain to facilitate the construction of the Cape to Cairo Railway.

[1] For the terms of the Mandate see Cmd. 1209 (1921).

Tanganyika, Togoland, and the Cameroons are all held by their respective assignees under Mandate from the League of Nations. These Mandates, however, unlike that for the South West Protectorate, belong not to Class C, but to Class B, which differs in two important respects from the former. On the one hand, the " mandated colony " does not become an integral portion of the territory of the Mandatory; on the other, the Mandates secure "equal opportunities for the trade and commerce of other members of the League." No such provision is contained either in the Mandate for South West Africa or in those for the Pacific Islands. The insertion of such a provision would plainly have proved too embarrassing to the Union of South Africa in the one case; to Australia and New Zealand in the other. The Mandates in Class B also provide more specifically and elaborately for the protection of the natives "from abuse and measures of fraud and force by the careful supervision of labour contracts and the recruiting of labour." [1]

Portugal put in a claim to a share in the repartition of Africa, but except for a slight readjustment of frontiers on the East Coast it was disallowed.

The general result of the partition may be summarized *Partition of* as follows: out of the 12,500,000 persons who were in 1914 *Africa* living under the German flag in Africa, forty-two per cent have been transferred to the guardianship of the British Empire, thirty-three per cent to that of France, and twenty-five per cent to Belgium. The settlement would seem in the main to accord with the principle laid down by Mr. Wilson, who insisted that there should be " a free, open-minded, and absolutely impartial adjustment of all Colonial claims, based upon a strict observance of the principle that in determining all such questions of sovereignty the interests of the populations concerned must have equal weight with the equitable claims of the Government whose title is to be determined." For the protection of those interests in the future, every possible security was taken in the Mandates as approved by the Council of the League of Nations.

[1] East Africa Cmd. 1284; West Africa Cmd. 1350 (1921).

The Turkish Vilayets

The Turkish vilayets of Palestine, Mesopotamia, and Syria were, evidently, in a very different position from the colonies taken from Germany in Africa. They were communities which (in the words of the Covenant) had " reached a stage of development where their existence as independent nations can be provisionally recognized, subject to the rendering of administrative advice and assistance by a Mandatory until such time as they are able to stand alone." Moreover, a few days after the conclusion of the armistice with Turkey, the British and French Governments had issued a joint declaration, stating their aim to be " the complete and final enfranchisement of the peoples so long oppressed by the Turks, and the establishment of national governments and administrations drawing their authority from the initiative and free choice of native populations." The Mandates were accordingly issued in a form (" A ") in accordance with these principles.

Palestine

Conquered by British forces during the war, Palestine remained in their occupation until July 1st, 1920; as from that date the country passed under the rule of a British High Commissioner, Sir Herbert Samuel. Under the Treaty of Sèvres, Turkey renounced all rights and title over the country in favour of the Principal Allied Powers, who conferred the Mandate upon Great Britain. In accordance with Mr. Balfour's declaration of November 2nd, 1917, Great Britain undertook to place the country under such conditions, political, administrative, and economic, as would secure the establishment of " a national home for the Jewish people," develop self-governing institutions, and safeguard the civil and religious rights of all the inhabitants of Palestine, irrespective of race and religion. English, Arabic, and Hebrew were to be the official languages of Palestine, and the most stringent precautions were taken for securing freedom of conscience and equality of commercial privileges.[1] How little those precautions have availed, recent and painful history has proved.

Mesopotamia

In Mesopotamia or Iraq the situation was complicated by

[1] Cmd. 1509 (1921).

282

the delays interposed by the events in the Near East already related. In May 1920 the British Government announced their acceptance of a Mandate from the League of Nations over Iraq. In October Sir Percy Cox reached Basra as High Commissioner, and a Provisional Council of State was appointed. In 1921 the Emir Feisal, son of Hussein, the ex-King of the Hedjaz, was elected King of Iraq, and an Arab Administration was set up. In 1924 a Constituent Assembly drafted a Constitution. This provided for a Limited Monarchy, a Legislature of two Houses—a Senate of twenty nominated members and a Lower House of eighty-eight deputies, with an Executive responsible to the Legislature. With the State thus newly constituted the British Government concluded a Treaty, which was to remain in force only until Iraq was admitted as an independent Sovereign State to membership of the League of Nations. To secure that admission the British Government undertook to use its good offices. Meanwhile, the path of the Mandatory Power was not a smooth one. The Turks made trouble on the north-eastern frontier, and it was not until 1926 that by a Treaty concluded at Angora the Turks agreed to the inclusion of the vilayet of Mosul in Iraq, subject to a share in the royalties on Mosul oil. There were troubles also on the Arabian frontier, and difficulties not a few to be encountered in Iraq itself. Gradually, however, under the strong and patient administration of Sir Percy Cox (High Commissioner, 1920–1923) and Sir Henry Dobbs (High Commissioner and Consul-General, 1923–1929), order was evolved out of chaos. An Iraqui Civil Service was organized; an efficient police-force set up; communications by rail, road, and air rapidly improved; the natural resources of the country developed, and schools and hospitals provided. The work done by British officials in Iraq is not indeed unworthy of comparison with that accomplished, under Lord Cromer, in Egypt. That work was consummated when in 1932 the Mandate was determined, and Iraq admitted as an independent State to membership in the League of Nations. The new State was, however, required as a condition of the withdrawal of the Mandate to enter into certain guarantees for the protection of foreigners and minorities.[1]

The Mandates Commission

The Mandatory is required, whatever the form of the Mandate, to make an annual report to the Council of the League of Nations, which exercises supervision over all the Mandatories by means of a Permanent Mandates Commission. This Commission consists of ten members, representing the three Mandatory and seven non-Mandatory States. Besides the annual reports it also receives memorials and petitions from the indigenous inhabitants of Mandated territories, or others interested in them. The functions of the Commission are, therefore, of a peculiarly delicate character, though they are purely advisory, and the Commission can rely on no sanction save the force of international public opinion.[2]

Egypt

It remains to add a few words on the settlement in Egypt. Except during the period from 1914 to 1922 Egypt proper has never formed part of the British Empire, though Great Britain had been in occupation since 1882. England's " special position " in Egypt, due not only to the military occupation, but still more to the regeneration work of Lord Cromer, was recognized in the Anglo-French Agreement of 1904. From the day when war broke out it was realized that of all the vital points in our " far-flung battle-line " perhaps the most vital was the Suez Canal. Consequently, as soon as the Ottoman Empire had definitely aligned itself on the side of the Central Empires it was deemed wise to depose the reigning Khedive of Egypt, Abbas II, and to replace him by his uncle Hussein Kamel. Turkish sovereignty was denounced; Egypt was declared a British Protectorate, and Cyprus was definitely annexed to the Empire (1914).

During the war discontent became acute among all classes in Egypt. The fellaheen were conscripted for labour

---

[1] Cmd. 2672 (1926).
[2] For the Mandate system generally cf. Lord Lugard: *Edinburgh Review*, Vol. 238, pp. 398–408, and the same writer in *Ency. Brit.*, New Volumes, Vol. II.

battalions, and their oppressors the middlemen, though growing fat on war profits, were not less discontented than the fellaheen. After the conclusion of the war, discontent was intensified. The revival of Turkey under Mustapha Kemal Pasha, and the prevalent insistence on "self-determination," aroused among the Egyptian intelligentsia nationalist aspirations. Especially did they resent the fact that, while the principle of "self-determination" was applied to Mesopotamia and Arabia, it was not extended to more advanced people like themselves. Of this feeling the insurrection of 1919 was the result. The insurrection was easily suppressed, but it was followed by the despatch to Egypt of a Mission of Enquiry, headed by Lord Milner. The Mission was boycotted. Lord Milner, however, subsequently reached an agreement with Zaghlul Pasha, the leader of the Egyptian nationalists, and in February 1922 the British Government declared the Protectorate to be at an end and Egypt to be " an independent sovereign State." On March 15th, 1922, the Sultan assumed the title of His Majesty King Fuad, and proclaimed Egypt a Monarchy.

Independence was, however, qualified by certain important reservations, which the nationalists have from the first, and not illogically, declared to be incompatible with " sovereignty." The Declaration reserved four matters absolutely to the discretion of the British Government: (i) The security of the communications of the British Empire in Egypt; (ii) The defence of Egypt against all foreign aggression or interference, direct or indirect ; (iii) The protection of foreign interests in Egypt and the protection of minorities ; (iv) The status of the Sudan. Pending the conclusion of Agreements on these points the *status quo* was to remain intact.

Years of negotiation, more than once interrupted by tragic events in Egypt, ensued. But at last in 1936 the " military occupation " was superseded by a " permanent military defensive alliance." The complete sovereignty of Egypt is acknowledged, but the Treaty also recognizes the paramount interest of the British Empire in the Suez Canal, entrusts its defence to British troops, and maintains the Anglo-Egyptian *condominium* over the Sudan which had been, as already indicated, conquered and regenerated by Great Britain. By a civil service mainly British the Sudan is still administered; and though the British Protectorate over Egypt has been denounced, British civil servants (though in greatly diminished numbers) and British troops are still in that country.

To return to the Dominions.

Post-war Reaction

Ardent Imperialists had, as we have seen, prepared in 1917 to sing their *Nunc Dimittis*. The first step towards the fulfilment of their ambitions had been taken; the final goal seemed well within sight. On the executive side of government the structure was complete; an Imperial Cabinet had come into being, and, though initiated as a war-time experiment, was to form, henceforward, a permanent part of the machinery of Empire.

The rejoicings of the Hamiltonian School were premature. Things did not work out as they were justified in anticipating. They ought, perhaps, to have paid less attention to the resolution of the Imperial Cabinet and more to that of the Imperial Conference.[1] The terms of Resolution IX were perhaps designedly balanced, not to say ambiguous. But there was no ambiguity, as we have seen, in the position taken up by the Dominion delegates at the Paris Conference. Centrifugal forces were plainly dominant, and were encouraged by the " national " status accorded, however unwillingly, to the Dominions by the League of Nations.

Imperial Conference, 1921

The constitutional question receded into the background during the next two years (1919–1921). Statesmen in the Dominions, as at home, were tired, and preoccupied with domestic questions. The question of Imperial defence seemed to lose its urgency when the German navy was sunk at Scapa Flow, and Lord Jellicoe's mission to the Dominions (1919) met with a chilly response. Japan was still the ally of Great Britain; Germany was disarmed.

The Conference of 1917, while definitely rejecting the

---

[1] *Supra*, p. 273.

federal solution, had, in set terms, postponed a decision on the constitutional problem. Consequently, a certain ambiguity intruded itself in the invitation sent to the Dominions to attend " the Imperial Conference in June (1921) on the lines of the Imperial War Cabinet meetings which had taken place in 1917 and 1918. . . ." The intention unquestionably was that the Dominion delegates should come and sit side by side with statesmen of the homeland in the *Cabinet* promised by the resolution of the Imperial War Cabinet of 1917. Thus, in April 1921, Winston Churchill, then Secretary of State for the Colonies, definitely said: " This was a very important year in the life of the British Empire, for it would see the first peace meeting of the Imperial Cabinet. It would not be like the old Imperial Conferences, but a meeting of the regular Imperial Cabinet." [1]

Was Mr. Churchill mistaken ? Was the meeting of 1921 to be a " Cabinet " or a " Conference," or something distinct from either ? Before the meeting took place all the Dominions had made it clear that it was not to be a Cabinet endowed with executive authority. Constitutionally, their position was unassailable. An executive Cabinet involves and implies, according to English tradition and practice, responsibility to a representative legislature. Was a Centralized Executive in London to be responsible to the Legislatures in Ottawa, Canberra, Capetown, Wellington, and St. John's, as well as to the Parliament at Westminster ? [2] Such a distributed responsibility would be evidently impossible. But if so, what became of a " Cabinet " ?

Clearly, then, the Dominions questioned the wisdom, and in some quarters even doubted the good faith, of the authorities in Downing Street. " At the moment there is a clamorous nationalism which through its organs seeks to create the impression that Downing Street is plotting to destroy the

---

[1] Quoted by Dawson: *Dominion Status*, p. 213. Mr. Dawson also quotes other contemporary statements to a similar effect, including one from an article in the *Edinburgh Review* for April 1921 by J. A. R. Marriott, M.P.

[2] I had urged this point very strongly both in the article " The Organization of the Empire " (*Edinburgh Review*, April 1921), and previously with more detail in *The Nineteenth Century and After* (September 1917): " Federalism, a Vanished Dream ? "

autonomy of Canada." So the Canadian correspondent of *The Times* reported on January 3rd, 1921. The impression was, of course, grotesquely untrue, but the mere mention of it indicates the atmosphere in which the meeting of 1921 took place.

Cabinet or Conference ? If that meeting was not a " Cabinet " on the new model, neither was it a " Conference " of the ordinary type. The difficulty of terminology was timorously and clumsily shelved, if not solved, by the official report, which was given out as *A Summary of the Proceedings at a Conference of Prime Ministers and Representatives of the United Kingdom, the Dominions, and India.* The larger constitutional question was not, however, evaded, and eventually the following resolution was adopted: " The Prime Ministers of the United Kingdom and the Dominions, having carefully considered the recommendations of the Imperial War Conference of 1917, that a special Imperial Conference should be summoned as soon as possible after the War to consider the constitutional relations of the component parts of the Empire, have reached the following conclusions: (*a*) Continuous consultation, to which the Prime Ministers attach no less importance than the Imperial War Conference of 1917, can only be secured by a substantial improvement in the communications between the component parts of the Empire. Having regard to the constitutional developments since 1917, no advantage is to be gained by holding a constitutional Conference. (*b*) The Prime Ministers of the United Kingdom and the Dominions and the Representatives of India should aim at meeting annually, or at such longer intervals as may prove feasible. (*c*) The existing practice of direct communication between the Prime Ministers of the United Kingdom and the Dominions, as well as the right of the latter to nominate Cabinet Ministers to represent them in consultation with the Prime Minister of the United Kingdom, are maintained."

These conclusions were regarded by Federalists as lamentably reactionary, but in reporting to the House of Commons on August 18th, Mr. Lloyd George characteristically put a good face upon them. " The general feeling was," he said, " that it would be a mistake to lay down any rules or to embark upon definitions as to what the British Empire meant. . . . You are defining life itself when you are defining the British Empire. You cannot do it, and therefore . . . we came to the conclusion that we would have no constitutional conference." [1] Mr. Hughes was even more explicit: " It is now admitted that a Constitutional Conference is not necessary, and that any attempt to set out in writing what are or should be the constitutional relations between the Dominions and the Mother Country would be fraught with very great danger to the Empire. The question of a Constitutional Conference, or any attempt at reduction of the Constitution to writing, may be therefore regarded as having been finally disposed of."

The meeting was not, then, to be regarded as a " Constitutional Conference," nor was any such Conference to be held in future. But, whatever its technical designation, it is clear from the *Official Report* that the meeting of 1921 was both a Conference and a Cabinet. Between June 20th and August 5th, " thirty-four plenary meetings took place," and " apart from the plenary meetings, the Prime Ministers of the United Kingdom and the Dominions met on eleven occasions." Plainly the latter meetings were " Cabinets " in all but name; Mr. Lloyd George referred to them in the House of Commons as " meetings of the Imperial Cabinet ": they were held in secret; no reports, except in the most general terms, were issued, but the decisions taken were regularly reported, as in the case of domestic Cabinets, to the King. Under whatever designation it sat, the meeting of 1921 decided questions of supreme moment to the Empire, and Mr. Lloyd George did not exaggerate when he said: " The whole course of human affairs has been altered because the British Empire has been proved to be a fact, and not, what a good many people who knew nothing about it imagined, a fiction." [2]

Apart from constitutional issues the outstanding signi- *Empire Foreign Policy*

[1] *Official Report*, Vol. 146, pp. 1701–1702. [2] *Hansard*, Vol. 146, pp. 1698–1702.

ficance of the meeting of 1921 was the series of discussions on the external affairs of the Empire. " Since the war," as Mr. Lloyd George said on a later occasion, " the Dominions have been given equal rights with Great Britain in the control of the foreign policy of the Empire. . . . The machinery must remain here. . . . The instrument of that foreign policy of the Empire is the British Foreign Office. That has been accepted by all the Dominions as inevitable. But they claim a voice in determining the lines of our future policy. . . . The sole control of Britain over foreign policy is now vested in the Empire as a whole. That is a new fact. . . . Joint control means joint responsibility." [1]

The Foreign Secretary, Lord Curzon, was equally explicit: " In former days the policy of Great Britain was the foreign policy of Great Britain alone. Now it is the foreign policy of the whole Empire. . . . In the various Imperial Conferences . . . a foreign policy for the whole Empire was framed."

The Anglo-Japanese Alliance

Of the questions connected with foreign affairs, the most important discussed in 1921 was that of the Anglo-Japanese Alliance. With that question, then, a conference, which met on the invitation of the United States at Washington

The Washington Conference

in November 1921, was largely concerned. The avowed and primary purpose of this Conference was to devise some means of arresting the ruinous competition in naval armaments. Great Britain accepted an invitation to attend on behalf of the British Empire, but requested Canada, Australia, New Zealand, and India to nominate delegates to attend along with the British representatives. That was not enough for the Dominions. They must receive separate invitations and attend the Conference on the same status as that accorded to them at Paris. That status they ultimately obtained: South Africa was, at its own request, represented by the chief British delegate, Mr. Balfour, but he signed the Treaties twice, once as representing the Empire and a second time as representing South Africa. The Dominions, accordingly, had their way; their

[1] *Hansard*, Vol. 149, pp. 28–30.

international position was recognized and safeguarded. The outcome of the Conference was twofold: a Four Power Treaty between Great Britain, France, Japan, and the United States to guarantee peace in the Pacific, and a Five Power Treaty, to which Italy also adhered, for the limitation of naval armaments. The Four Power Treaty superseded the Anglo-Japanese Alliance, to the great satisfaction of the United States, to which it had of late become an object of grave, though groundless, suspicion. Canada had also desired the termination of the Anglo-Japanese Alliance; Australia, to her subsequent regret, acquiesced in it; in Great Britain opinion was sharply divided. All parties desired to gratify the United States, but Japan had admittedly rendered conspicuous service to the British Empire in the war; to denounce the Alliance as soon as the war was won was, to say the least, an ungraceful act, and the conduct of Great Britain was deeply and not unreasonably resented in Japan. The consequences of that resentment are not exhausted yet. At the lowest, the Washington Conference had demonstrated the unity of the Empire and had respected the *amour-propre* of the Dominions.

Much more difficult and disquieting was the situation *Chanak* created by Mr. Lloyd George's mishandling of Near Eastern *Crisis* affairs. The cession of Smyrna to the Greeks, by the Treaty of Sèvres (1920), had aroused bitter resentment among the Turkish "nationalists," and, led by Mustapha Kemal Pasha, they turned upon the Greeks in Asia Minor, swept them into the sea, and delivered Smyrna over to fire and sword. Then, flushed with their bloody and unexpected victory over their hereditary foes, they advanced on the Dardanelles, entered the zone neutralized under the Peace Treaties, and actually came within fighting distance of the British garrison which from Chanak held the southern shore of the Straits. France withdrew her troops; Italy, who hated the Greeks, intimated that, in the event of war, no help was to be expected from her; Great Britain faced the Kemalists alone.

To that pass had the pro-Greek policy of Mr. Lloyd George, combined with the faithlessness of the French, brought Europe. In panic he appealed to the Dominions (September 15th), inviting them to send contingents for " the defence of interests for which they have already made enormous sacrifices, and of soil which is hallowed by immortal memories of the Anzacs." The characteristically clever appeal to the Anzacs evoked an immediate promise of help from New Zealand; Australia also promised " if circumstances required it to send a contingent of Australian troops." Mr. Hughes took the line which he defended in a subsequent debate: " When Britain is at war we are at war," but added, " this view is not entertained by all the Dominions." South Africa was relieved of embarrassment by the opportune absence of General Smuts in the wilds of Zululand; by the time he had returned the crisis was over and there was no longer any call for the intervention of the Union. Canada's answer was highly significant. Mr. Mackenzie King, the Premier, justly complained that there had been no warning of an impending crisis, no previous consultation with the Dominions in accordance with the resolutions of the 1921 Conference. " Public opinion in Canada," he added, " would demand the authorization of Parliament as a necessary preliminary to the despatch of a contingent to participate in the conflict in the Near East." He also requested that he might receive " the fullest information to be communicated to Parliament." [1] In brief: if Great Britain were at war, Canada would technically be at war, but *participation* was another matter, which could only be authorized by the Dominion Parliament. That was and that remains the constitutional position. In the event, war in the Near East was averted, though narrowly, by the combined firmness and tact of Sir Charles Harington, the Allied Commander-in-Chief at Constantinople.

Treaty of Lausanne

Mr. Lloyd George's handling of the Near Eastern crisis

---

[1] *Australian House of Representatives Debates*, July 30th, 1923; and *Canadian House of Commons Debates*, February 1st, 1923, both quoted by Dawson: *op. cit.*, pp. 236–245.

left Canada in an ugly temper, which was not improved by the circumstances attending the conclusion of the Treaty of Lausanne. After prolonged negotiations, carried through with patience and skill by Lord Curzon, that Treaty was eventually signed on July 24th, 1923. The terms were the best that could, under embarrassing circumstances, be extorted from a Turkey which had suddenly and unexpectedly converted defeat into victory. The Dominions were kept regularly informed as to the progress of the negotiations, but they were not invited to take part in them. Their exclusion was understood to have been due to the pressure of France, but it had, nevertheless, a lamentable effect upon the feelings, if not the action, of Canada.

Before the Conference met at Lausanne, Mr. Lloyd George's Ministry had resigned, though Lord Curzon remained at the Foreign Office, under Mr. Bonar Law and also under his successor, Mr. Baldwin. When the Treaty of Lausanne was submitted to Parliament for approval (April 1924), Mr. Ramsay MacDonald was both Prime Minister and Foreign Secretary. It was not, however, these rapid Ministerial changes that affected the attitude of Canada towards the international relations of the Empire. That attitude was briefly and bluntly set forth in the telegram with which the correspondence on the subject concluded (March 25th, 1924). " Canadian Government not having been invited to send representatives to the Lausanne Conference, and not having participation in the proceedings of the Conference either directly or indirectly, and not being for this reason a signatory to the Treaty on behalf of Canada . . . my Ministers do not feel that they are in a position to recommend to Parliament approval of the Peace Treaty with Turkey and the Convention thereto.[1] Without the approval of Parliament they feel that they are not warranted in signifying concurrence in the ratification of the Treaty and Convention. With respect to ratification, however, they will not take exception to such course as His

---

[1] I.e. the " Straits Convention," for which see debates thereon, *Hansard*, April 1st and 9th, 1924.

Majesty's Government may deem it advisable to recommend." [1]

That telegram, blunt as it sounds, was completely consonant with the position which Mr. Mackenzie King had from the first taken up, and it was wholly logical. Speaking for Canada he had made it clear that, though Canada did not resent exclusion from the Conference of Lausanne, the extent to which the Dominion might be bound by the " proceedings of the Conference or by the provisions of any Treaty arising therefrom, must be a question for the decision of the Canadian Parliament."

The Halibut Fisheries

Canada had, in the meantime, taken a significant step. On March 2nd, 1923, she had concluded with the United States a Treaty designed to protect the halibut fisheries in the Northern Pacific. The Treaty admittedly concerned only the two signatories: but treaties are a ticklish matter, and it is not unfair to suggest that, in concluding it, Mr. Mackenzie King was still feeling the smart of Lausanne. The Halibut Treaty was negotiated between Mr. Hughes, the American Secretary of State, and Mr. Lapointe, the Canadian Minister of Fisheries, who had been sent from Ottawa to conclude it. The British Ambassador at Washington claimed to act as a co-signatory with the Canadian envoy, and his claim was upheld by the Colonial Office. But Canada definitely repudiated it. The Treaty should be signed only by the two Powers immediately concerned. It was. The King issued full powers to Mr. Lapointe; the British Ambassador was excluded, though the Senate of the United States assented to the Treaty subject to its ratification " as between the United States and Great Britain." [2]

Imperial Conference, 1923

Thus an awkward corner was turned. But that it had called for adroit driving was plain, and it was under the

[1] Governor-General (Viscount Byng) to Dominions Secretary (J. H. Thomas), ap. Cmd. 2146 (1924), which contains the correspondence with the Canadian Government, October 27th, 1922, to March 25th, 1924.
[2] See Cmd. 2377, and on the whole question cf. Marriott: " Empire Foreign Policy " in the *Fortnightly Review* for May 1923, and Keith's *Responsible Government*, pp. 897 f.

shadow of the Halibut Treaty and the Chanak Crisis that the Imperial Conference of 1923 met. To that Conference Lord Curzon made an elaborate apology for the Treaty of Lausanne, but did not touch (so far as appears from the Official Report) on the point of most interest to the Conference—Imperial co-operation. Nor did the Conference suggest any improvement in the machinery of consultation in reference to the foreign policy of the Empire.[1]

The Conference did, however, consider the problem of *Treaty-making* treaties, and recommended " for the acceptance of the Governments of the Empire represented that a regular procedure should be observed in the negotiation, signature, and ratification of international agreements." The procedure was textually set forth [2]: the general effect was to regularize and confirm the procedure adopted by Canada in the conclusion of the Halibut Fisheries Treaty. The Conference specifically recognized the right of any Dominion to negotiate a treaty, but it affirmed the principle that no treaty should be negotiated by any one Government of the Empire without regard to its possible effect on other parts of the Empire, or the Empire as a whole, and that there should be a full interchange of views, before and during negotiations, between all the Dominions. Bilateral treaties imposing obligations on one part of the Empire only were to be signed by its representative; in other cases by the representatives of all the Dominions concerned. This decision was undoubtedly a concession to Dominion Nationalism; it emphasized " in the highest degree the separate character of the Dominions." One link with the Imperial Executive only remained. The full powers and the instruments of ratification were still issued with the King's signature affixed on the strength of a warrant countersigned by the British Secretary of State. In March 1931 the Irish Free State (which had

---

[1] That question was, however, raised by Mr. Ramsay MacDonald in a despatch of June 23rd, 1924, but the Baldwin Ministry which came into office in November 1924 declined to summon a special Constitutional Conference to discuss the matter; see Cmd. 2301 (1925).

[2] At Imperial Conference, 1923, Cmd. 1987 and 1988 (1923).

been for the first time admitted to an Imperial Conference in 1923) snapped even that slender link by securing the King's assent to a new procedure whereby the necessary documents were to be issued by him solely on the advice of Ireland. But the Irish Free State is, happily, *sui generis.*

Dominion Diplomacy

Closely connected with the question of treaty-making was that of separate diplomatic representation at foreign courts. In this matter also the Irish Free State created a precedent by securing in 1924 separate diplomatic representation at Washington. In notifying the new departure to the U.S. Government, the British Government emphasized the point that it did " not denote any departure from the principle of the diplomatic unity of the Empire." That is as it may be. Canada followed suit by appointing ministers to Washington in 1926, to Paris in 1928, and to Tokyo in 1929. In the latter year the Union of South Africa appointed Ministers to Washington, The Hague, and Rome. Australia and New Zealand have frowned upon the new departure, rightly regarding it as a menace, though not as yet a serious one, to Imperial unity.

Imperial Economic Conference, 1923

The proceedings of the Imperial Conference of 1923 were entirely overshadowed by those of the Imperial Economic Conference, which also met in October and November 1923 and was attended not only by the Prime Ministers of the Dominions (in some but not in all cases as official delegates), but by representatives of all the important public departments, notably the Colonial Office, the Board of Trade (whose President was Chairman), the Treasury, and the Board of Agriculture. A series of very important resolutions was adopted dealing with such matters as oversea settlement within the Empire,[1] Imperial co-operation in respect of commercial intelligence, the provision and dissemination of up-to-date statistics, Empire Imperial communications by sea and air, cables and wireless, Empire currency and exchange, economic defence, forestry, the import and export of livestock (especially Canadian cattle),

[1] Cf. *Record of Proceedings*, Cmd. 2009 (1924), pp. 136–150.

and other matters. But the question which excited most interest was the development of Imperial resources by conceding a preference to Empire goods. To the great satisfaction of the Dominions, the Imperial Government enumerated a detailed list of preferential rates which they proposed to submit to Parliament, and the Conference reaffirmed with emphasis the resolution on Imperial Preference passed by the Imperial War Conference of 1917.[1]

The defeat of the Conservative Government in January 1924 delayed action on many of the resolutions adopted at the Economic Conference of 1923, and led to the repeal by the MacDonald Government of all Imperial preferences and even of the McKenna duties.[2] Mr. Baldwin, however, returned to office in November, and almost his first act was to set up an Imperial Economic Committee, consisting of *Imperial Economic Committee* members with practical experience, nominated not only by the Home Government but all the Dominions, the India Office, the Colonial Office, and Southern Rhodesia. The Committee was charged to consider the methods of preparing for market and marketing within the United Kingdom the food products of the overseas parts of the Empire, with a view to increasing the consumption of such products in the United Kingdom in preference to imports from foreign countries, and to promote the interests of both producers and consumers. A million pounds a year was allocated for the purposes of the Committee, which produced a number of exceedingly valuable Reports. Further emphasis was given to this policy by the appointment in May 1926 of the Empire Marketing Board. The purpose of the Board was to im- *Empire Marketing Board* prove the marketing, and stimulate the consumption in this country, firstly of home produce, and secondly of the produce of the Empire overseas. This was done by an elaborate publicity and educational campaign, by making grants to appropriate bodies for scientific research into problems of production and marketing, and by other methods of a similar kind. The Board did a considerable amount of

[1] On the Economic Conference see Cmd. 2009 (1924).
[2] Imposed in 1915. See Mallet: *British Budgets*, Vol. I, 73.

good, but, as some thought, at disproportionate expense, and under the economic stress of 1932 it was dissolved.

Preference   The Baldwin Government, which remained in office from 1924 to 1929, restored the McKenna duties, with the accompanying preferences, and considerably extended both the amount and the range of the preference given to Empire products. It also passed (1925) a new *Safeguarding of Industries Act*, under which duties of a definitely protective character were imposed on a considerable range of articles. In every case preference was given to Empire products as against those of foreign origin. These duties, it was claimed, besides producing a substantial revenue, greatly assisted home manufacturers, without raising prices to the consumer. Best of all, so far from retarding they actually stimulated the export of the " safeguarded " commodities.

The next Imperial Conference met in 1926, but in the meantime the League of Nations had attempted by the *Draft Treaty of National Assistance* (1923) and by the *General Protocol* (1924) to involve Great Britain and the Empire in further responsibilities. From the assumption of those dangerous responsibilities we were saved largely by the vehement opposition of the Dominions. In 1925, however, the Imperial Government concluded with France and Germany and other Powers an agreement which was acclaimed at the time as a triumph for friendly diplomacy, but which imposed a serious obligation on the British Government.

The Locarno Pact   From sharing in that obligation the Dominions were specifically exempted. They had not been invited to the Conference at Locarno, and in the resulting Treaty the United Kingdom deliberately acted in isolation. Article IX expressly provided that the Treaty should impose " no obligation upon any of the British Dominions or upon India, unless the Government of such Dominion, or of India, signifies its acceptance thereof." No Government was in a hurry to do so, and General Smuts was not alone in expressing a fear that Locarno had given a further impetus to " centrifugal forces at work in the Empire." [1]

[1] Speech at Pretoria, *The Times*, November 12th, 1925.

Germany has presumably tossed the Locarno Treaty, to which she was a party, on to the dust-heap. But at the time it was regarded by most Imperialists as having dealt a grievous blow at the principle of the diplomatic solidarity of the Empire. It was not the last blow of its kind.

Chapter Twenty

Dominion Status

INTER-IMPERIAL RELATIONS (1926–1936).
THE STATUTE OF WESTMINSTER

Imperial Conference, 1926

THE centrifugal forces analysed in the preceding chapter received a further impetus from the Imperial Conference of 1926. In the whole series of Conferences that was, in a constitutional sense, the most important. The tide, as we have seen, had recently been running strongly towards disintegration. The Peace Conference at Paris; the new national status of the Dominions recognized in the final Covenant of the League of Nations, and emphasized at the meetings at Geneva; the Imperial Conferences of 1917 and 1921; the Washington Conference of 1922; the Chanak Crisis; the Treaty of Lausanne; the cold douche administered to the policy of Imperial Preference in 1924; the Locarno Treaty of 1925—blow after blow had fallen upon the ardent Federationists. There were some doughty

Personnel champions at the Conference of 1926. Mr. Bruce represented Australia; Mr. Coates, New Zealand; Lord Birkenhead, as Secretary of State, and the Maharajah of Burdwan represented India; Sir Austen Chamberlain and Mr. Amery were among the representatives of Great Britain. But too much attention was perhaps paid in the Conference to the susceptibilities of South Africa, represented by General Hertzog and Mr. Havenger, and to those of the Irish Free State. Canada's demand for separate diplomatic representation in foreign capitals, and the circumstances attendant upon the conclusion of the Halibut Treaty, to say nothing of her attitude towards the Chanak imbroglio, had, moreover, revealed a new and disturbing temper in Canadian politics.

Constitutional Relations

Almost the first business of the Conference was to appoint

a Committee " to investigate all the questions on the agenda affecting inter-Imperial Relations." The Report of that Committee is already historic; it opens with this significant statement: " The Committee are of opinion that nothing would be gained by attempting to lay down a Constitution for the British Empire. . . . There is, however," it proceeds, " one most important element in it which, from a strictly constitutional point of view, has now, as regards all vital matters, reached its full development—we refer to the group of self-governing communities composed of Great Britain and the Dominions. Their position and mutual relation may be readily defined. *They are autonomous Communities* *within the British Empire, equal in status, in no way subordinate* *one to another in any aspect of their domestic or external affairs,* *though united by a common allegiance to the Crown and freely* *associated as members of the British Commonwealth of Nations.* The Decisive Formula

Every self-governing member of the Empire is now the master of its destiny. In fact, if not always in form, it is subject to no compulsion whatever. But no account, however accurate, of the negative relation in which Great Britain and the Dominions stand to each other can do more than express a portion of the truth. The British Empire is not founded upon negatives. It depends essentially, if not formally, on positive ideals. . . . And though every Dominion is now and must always remain the sole judge of the nature and extent of its co-operation, no common cause will, in our opinion, be thereby imperilled. Equality of status, so far as Britain and the Dominions are concerned, is thus the root principle governing our inter-Imperial relations." There follows a sentence which seems to demand an Athanasius for its interpretation. " But the principles of equality and similarity, appropriate to *status*, do not universally extend to function. Here we require something more than immutable dogmas."

Of the specific recommendations of the Report the first concerns the Royal title, which, by an Act passed in 1927, was amended to run as follows: " George V, by the Grace of God, of Great Britain, Ireland and the British Dominions The Royal Title beyond the Seas King, Defender of the Faith, Emperor of India."

Passing from the Crown to its local representatives, the Report dealt with the position of the Governors-General, as follows:

Appointment of Governors-General   " In our opinion it is an essential consequence of the equality of status existing among the members of the British Commonwealth of Nations that the Governor-General of a Dominion is the representative of the Crown, holding in all essential respects the same position in relation to the administration of public affairs in the Dominion as is held by His Majesty the King in Great Britain, and that he is not the representative or agent of His Majesty's Government in Great Britain or of any department of that Government. It seemed to us to follow that the practice, whereby the Governor-General is the formal official channel of communication between His Majesty's Government in Great Britain and his Governments in the Dominions, might be regarded as no longer wholly in accordance with the constitutional position of the Governor-General. It was thought that the recognized official channel of communication should be, in future, between Government and Government direct."

This paragraph raised several important questions. Interrogated in the House of Commons as to whether in fact there had been, since the Conference, any change in the status of the Governors-General, or in their relation either to the Dominion Ministers or to the Imperial Ministers; Mr. Amery, the Secretary of State, replied:

" No, the change in the status of the Governor-General from an agent and instrument of the British Government to the representative of the Crown in a Dominion, and nothing else, was a change which, like the whole of the changes in our constitutional evolution, has taken place gradually over a long period of years, and was in substance the consummation of many years before the present Conference took place. All that the late Conference did was to suggest that the purely historic survival by which communication from the British Government to its partner Governments went via the

Governor-General's office—as it had done in the old days when the Governor-General still was, as the Governor of a Crown Colony is, the agent and instrument of the British Government—should be eliminated and the position brought up to date with present-day facts." [1]

If, however, the Governor-General of a self-governing Dominion was no longer to be the representative or agent of His Majesty's Government in Great Britain, or " of any department of that Government," the question naturally arose: On whose advice was the King to act in appointing him ? That question was answered as regards Australia by the following announcement issued, on December 2nd, 1930, not from Downing Street but from Australia House: " His Majesty the King on the recommendation of the Right Hon. J. H. Scullin, Prime Minister of Australia, has appointed the Right Hon. Sir Isaac Alfred Isaacs to the office of Governor-General for the Commonwealth of Australia." This announcement strikingly illustrated the constitutional change effected by a mere resolution of the Imperial Conference—a body devoid of legislative competence. An Australian paper described the incident as an " opportunity to sever the nexus with the British Government." Happily, the opportunity was not taken, but the precedent set by Mr. Scullin—a precedent not likely to be followed in Australia—was followed by General Hertzog in South Africa. In 1931 General Hertzog recommended the appointment of Sir Patrick Duncan as Governor-General. That the appointment was not unsuitable and was widely approved does not, however, furnish any argument in favour of a change which may have mischievous consequences in the future. As things were before the superfluous definition of 1926, no appointment to the office of the King's Representative in a Dominion was ever likely to be made without previous consultation with the Dominion concerned. That procedure, parallel with that followed in the case of Ambassadors, would have given ample security against the appointment of misfits.

[1] *Hansard*, June 29th, col. 540.

Legislative Relations

The next matters with which the Report dealt were connected with the operation of Dominion legislation, in particular His Majesty's " powers of disallowance " of the enactments of Dominion Legislatures; the reservation of Dominion legislation for the signification of His Majesty's pleasure; and the legislative competence of the Imperial Parliament (" the Parliament at Westminster," as the Report significantly termed it), and the Dominion Parliaments respectively. The Conference wisely concluded in reference to these matters that " the issues involved were so complex that . . . it would be necessary to obtain expert guidance as a preliminary to further consideration by His Majesty's Governments in Great Britain and the Dominions."

Committee of Experts, 1927

That expert guidance was obtained from a conference specially convened in 1929, and consisting mainly of lawyers and permanent officials from the United Kingdom and the Dominions.

The Committee of experts made certain recommendations which formed the basis of the *Statute of Westminster* (1931). As they were practically incorporated in that Statute, reference to its provisions may be conveniently anticipated.

In regard to " disallowance," or the right of the Crown, on the advice of Ministers of the United Kingdom, to annul an Act passed by a Dominion Legislature, the Conference agreed that it could no longer be exercised. The right had, in fact, not been exercised in relation to Canada since 1873, to New Zealand since 1867, and never to the Commonwealth of Australia or the Union of South Africa. Nevertheless, for certain technical reasons, the Conference did not recommend the specific abolition of the right. The Imperial Parliament concurred in the agreement of the Conference, and the *Statute of Westminster* consequently contains no direct reference to this right, nor to the power hitherto exercised by colonial Governors of " reserving " assent to Bills passed by their several legislatures, until they had consulted and received instructions from Whitehall.

Much more difficult and obscure, and at the same time

more practically important, was the problem of extra- *The Statute of Westminster, 1931*
territorial legislation. In this matter the *Statute of West-*
minster, following the cautious and non-committal recommendation of the Report, simply " declared and enacted
that the Parliament of a Dominion has full power to make
laws having extra-territorial operation " (section 3).

The Statute (by sections 5 and 6) removed all doubts as
to the unfettered power of a Dominion Legislature to make
laws in relation to merchant shipping, and also repealed,
though only as regards future enactments, the *Colonial Laws
Validity Act* of 1865. That Act affirmed the principle that
an Act of a colonial Legislature was not void, although repugnant to the law of England, *unless it contravened an Act of
the Imperial Parliament made directly* applicable to the colony
in question. The italicized words were held to impair
equality of status affirmed by the *Statute of Westminster.* The
Act of 1865 was, therefore, repealed.

Equality was even more specifically affirmed by the re-
pudiation of the right of the Imperial Parliament to legislate
for a Dominion " otherwise than at the request and with
the consent of that Dominion " (Preamble and section 4).
But the Expert Conference of 1929 was not allowed to forget,
and the Imperial Conference of 1930 reminded Whitehall,
that there are self-governing States in the Commonwealth
of Australia; and that even the Canadian Provinces have
rights which cannot be ignored. The rights of these units,
as well as those of New Zealand, were accordingly safeguarded by sections 7, 8, and 9 of the *Statute of Westminster.*

Reference has been repeatedly made in preceding para- *Dominion Status*
graphs to " Dominions " and " Dominion status." But
what is a " Dominion " ? To that important question the
only answer vouchsafed by the *Statute of Westminster* is that
in future Acts of Parliament the term " Colony " " shall not
include a Dominion or any Province or State forming part
of a Dominion " (11) and that a Dominion is one of the
existing six Dominions (1). This is in truth definition *per
enumerationem,* and it may well cause embarrassment to a legal

tribunal, such as the Permanent Court of International Justice, which now has jurisdiction in the case of a dispute between a "Dominion" and a "Dominion," or between a "Dominion" and the United Kingdom.

In view of these provisions the question obtrudes itself whether any remnant of Imperial unity survives the enactment of the *Statute of Westminster*. That question may most conveniently be answered in connection with the crisis which suddenly developed in December 1936.[1]

To return to the Conference of 1926. The definition of the constitutional status of Great Britain and the Dominions was of such transcendent importance as to overshadow all other matters under discussion. Attention was, however, also given to the conduct of foreign affairs, to defence, to treaty-making powers, to the vexed question of the representation of the different parts of the Empire at International Conferences, and to the conditions governing appeals from judgments in the Dominions to the Judicial Committee of the Privy Council. As to the last, no decisive action was taken, but it was made clear that the Imperial Government desired only that the question should in each case be decided " in accordance with the wishes of the part of the Empire primarily affected." In the sphere of foreign affairs, and of defence, it was frankly recognized that " the major share of responsibility rests now and must for some time continue to rest with His Majesty's Government in Great Britain." In the matter of inter-Imperial trade, a tribute was paid to the value of and work done by the Imperial Economic Committee established as a result of the Conference of 1923, and to that of the Empire Marketing Board. For the rest there was evidence of " a strong desire on the part of all the Governments represented to concert methods for encouraging the further development of Empire trade." On this high note the Conference of 1926 ended.

Imperial Conference, 1930

The discussion at the next conference was set in a different key. Mr. Snowden, an uncompromising Free Trader, was by then installed, though not too securely, at the Treasury,

[1] *Infra*, p. 310, and see Marriott: *This Realm of England*, pp. 386–387.

and made no secret of his hope " that he might remain there long enough to sweep away all the existing preferences."

Yet it was with the purpose of promoting the economic unity of the Empire that the delegates from the Dominions came together in 1930. The Dominions, like the United Kingdom, were in the throes of an economic and financial crisis, and saw no hope of emerging therefrom except by closer co-operation within the Empire. Of that co-operation Mr. R. B. Bennett, Prime Minister of Canada, was an ardent advocate. His personality entirely dominated the Conference of 1930, and gave it whatever importance it possessed. Certain " agreed conclusions of a general nature " (the phrase is significant) were reached on arbitration, disarmament, and other matters connected with the problem of international peace. It was also agreed to maintain the policy of establishing a permanent naval base at Singapore, but to suspend further expenditure on the work for five years. Only Mr. Bennett, however, saved the Conference of 1930 from being a fiasco, if not a disaster. In a series of impassioned speeches he insisted on the urgent necessity of putting into effective and immediate operation a large scheme of Empire Preference. " The day," he said, " is now at hand when the peoples of the Empire must decide, once for all, whether our welfare lies in closer economic union or whether it does not. . . . Delay is hazardous. . . . The time for action has come."

Other representatives of the Dominions expressed similar views in language hardly less vigorous. But their views made no impression on the Socialist Government, which had come into office in 1929. The preferential tariff solution was definitely turned down, and the Conference was saved from a disastrous breakdown only by adopting the suggestion of Mr. Bennett that " the Economic Section of the Conference be adjourned to meet at Ottawa . . . within the next twelve months." [1]

For that Conference the way was cleared by the advent

Mr. R. B. Bennett

[1] Cmd. 3717 (1930), p. 44.

to power (August 1931) of a National Government. From 1931 to 1937 Mr. Neville Chamberlain was Chancellor of the Exchequer, and with general approval carried through a fiscal revolution which completely reversed the Free Trade policy to which since 1842 Great Britain had steadfastly adhered.

A Bill to deal with the abnormal importation of "dumped" articles was introduced on November 17th, and three days later had received the Royal Assent. On the same day the Board of Trade exercised the powers conferred upon it by the Act and issued a list of twenty-three classes of commodities to be subject from November 25th to a duty of fifty per cent. That was an emergency measure.

On February 4th, 1931, Mr. Neville Chamberlain, as Chancellor of the Exchequer, proposed to the House of Commons a measure comparable in importance with those carried by Sir Robert Peel between 1842 and 1846. The Import Duties Bill was deliberately intended to effect a fiscal revolution, and its second reading was passed (February 16th) by 451 votes to 73. The objects of the Bill were to correct the adverse balance of trade, no longer corrected by shipping profits and the interest on foreign investments; to maintain the value of the pound sterling, and to ensure consumers against a rise in the cost of living; to provide further revenue; to stimulate home industry and reduce unemployment; to provide a basis for negotiation with foreign countries; and, above all, to facilitate the granting of preferences to the other units of the Empire. These objects it was hoped to attain by imposing a basic duty of ten per cent upon all imported goods not specifically exempted, and, if so advised by an Import Duties Advisory Committee to be set up under the Bill, an additional duty upon other commodities. The Bill received the Royal Assent on February 29th, and on the following day the general tariff came into force. No duties were to be levied on Empire goods until after the Ottawa Conference at earliest.

The Economic section of the Imperial Conference of *Ottawa* 1930, adjourned on Mr. Bennett's motion, met under his *Conference, 1932* chairmanship at Ottawa in 1932. The high hopes with which the delegates reassembled were, however, imperfectly realized. Even in an Empire, which though united in sentiment was physically dispersed, economic interests are apt to be divergent. Nevertheless, after a good deal of hard bargaining, a number of bilateral agreements were reached between Great Britain, India, Southern Rhodesia, and all the Dominions,[1] as well as between the Dominions and Colonies. Great Britain agreed to continue the policy adopted by the Act of 1932, to impose duties on imported wheat and other food-stuffs, with a preference to the Empire, and to institute a quota for bacon and later for mutton and beef. The Dominions undertook to grant increased preference to Empire products, and, in the case of manufactured goods, to accept the principle that (subject to special consideration in the case of " infant " industries) protective duties " should not exceed such a level as would give British producers full opportunity of reasonable competition on the basis of economical and efficient production." [2] Between 1932 and 1937 a number of subsidiary committees and conferences were held, among them a Wheat Conference in 1933, a Conference of Empire Statisticians (at Ottawa) in 1935, and a Conference to promote co-operation and collaboration in Industrial and Agricultural Research in 1936.

The Coronation ceremonies in 1937 afforded an oppor- *Imperial* tunity for another full conference. This conference was *Conference, 1937* mainly concerned with measures of Imperial strategy and defence. The occasion was taken for a detailed review of the state of defence in each of the Dominions, and close consideration was given to the ways in which the several Governments could co-operate each with the other in measures for the security of each member of the Commonwealth and Empire.

---

[1] Except, of course, the Irish Free State—if that is to be reckoned a " Dominion."
[2] For details cf. Cmd. 4175, p. 62.

To the confidential deliberations of the Conference of 1937, as to the Coronation ceremony, additional solemnity was given by thankful recognition of the fact that the Empire had recently emerged unshaken in structure and united in sentiment from what might have been a great catastrophe.

Abdication of King Edward VIII

Within five years after the enactment of the *Statute of Westminster* the strength of the base on which, in fact if not in law, the whole structure rested was subjected to a crucial test. In 1935 the whole Empire had joined in the manifestations of loyalty to the Imperial Throne and affection for its occupants evoked by the Silver Jubilee. Equally sincere and not less universal was the Empire's mourning when in 1936 King George V passed away. Preparations for the Coronation of his successor were already well advanced when the thunderbolt fell. King Edward VIII would never be crowned. On December 3rd, 1936, the whole Empire was astounded by the news that the King proposed to contract a marriage which seemed to his people incongruous and which his Ministers could not approve. The Prime Minister announced to Parliament that the Imperial Government was not prepared to introduce legislation to enable the King to marry the lady of his choice without giving her the position of Queen. At the King's wish Mr. Baldwin communicated immediately with the Dominion Premiers and consulted the Opposition leaders at home. It soon became manifest that the whole Empire preferred to accept the painful alternative offered by the King. Events moved with such rapidity that on December 10th the King announced to Parliament his " final and irrevocable decision to abdicate." On the same day Mr. Baldwin introduced a Bill " to give effect to his Majesty's declaration of abdication and for purposes connected therewith." On the 11th the Bill passed through all its stages, and received the Royal Assent. Thereupon King Edward VIII ceased to reign; the Duke of York, his next brother, became King, and on December 12th was proclaimed King as George VI.

Only with the Imperial significance of these painful events is this narrative concerned.

The Preamble to the *Statute of Westminster* contained these words: " Inasmuch as the Crown is the symbol of the free association of the members of the British Commonwealth of Nations, and as they are united by a common allegiance to the Crown, it would be in accord with the established constitutional position of all the members of the Commonwealth in relation to one another that any alteration in the law touching the Succession to the Throne or the Royal Style and Titles shall hereafter require the assent as well of the Parliaments of all the Dominions as of the Parliament of the United Kingdom."

Consequently, the Preamble to the *Act of Abdication* recited: " Whereas His Majesty . . . has been pleased to declare that He is irrevocably determined to renounce the Throne for Himself and His Descendants . . . and has signified His desire that effect thereto should be given immediately ; And whereas, following upon the communication to His Dominions of His Majesty's said declaration and desire, the Dominion of Canada pursuant to the provisions of section 4 of the *Statute of Westminster*, 1931, has requested and consented to the enactment of this Act, and the Commonwealth of Australia, the Dominion of New Zealand and the Union of South Africa have assented thereto: Be it therefore enacted, etc. . . ."

Section 4 of the *Statute of Westminster* provides that " no Act of the Parliament of the United Kingdom passed after the commencement of this Act shall extend or be deemed to extend to a Dominion as part of the law of that Dominion unless it is expressly declared in that Act that that Dominion has requested and consented to the enactment thereof." Canada had adopted the *Statute of Westminster*; hence her " *request*." For Australia and New Zealand, which had not adopted the Act, " assent " sufficed. The assent of South Africa was assured, but in view of a certain ambiguity introduced by the *Status of the Union Act*, 1934, its assent was based not on section 4, which required " request," but simply on the Preamble.

These, however, are matters for lawyers to argue and

explain.[1] For the historian it must suffice to record the fact
that to the crucial test imposed by the abdication crisis the
new Imperial Constitution reacted triumphantly. More
than that. The crisis and its outcome emphasized the truth
that the Crown is not merely the symbol of a free association
of British nations, but the sole legal link which binds them
together. If the British Commonwealth of Nations remains
in law a unity, it is the Crown that unites. Thus there has
opened a new era in the long history of the English Monarchy, and to the King is offered a further opportunity of
service to the Commonwealth. As a Canadian statesman
eloquently said: " We have demonstrated not only to everyone in our own Dominions but to all the world the granite
strength of the British Constitution enshrined as it is in
the British Throne." [2]

[1] The legal question involved is ably argued by W. Ivor Jennings, ap. the
Political Quarterly (Vol. VIII, No. 2), and by John Foster in *The Nineteenth
Century and After* for February 1937.
[2] Mr. Lapointe.

Chapter Twenty-one

The Government of India

FOR British India, as for the rest of the Empire, the *British* Great War was a critical period. Among the political *India* formations of the world India occupies a unique place. Neither in the ancient nor the modern era has there ever been any country in a position exactly parallel. India, with an area of 1,805,000 square miles, is twenty times as big as Great Britain; it has over 350 millions of inhabitants speaking no fewer than 222 recognized vernaculars ; it is divided by diversities of race, and comprises no fewer than 2,300 castes. Thus India presents to its rulers a problem of exceptional complexity. Of the total area of India, more than a third (700,000 square miles) lies within the boundaries not of British India but of the Native States, which, *The* 562 in number, vary in size from States like Kashmir and *Feudatory* Hyderabad (each of which is bigger than England) down *States* to properties of a few acres. One hundred and eight of these States are sufficiently important to entitle their rulers to sit by individual right in the Chamber of Princes. Some of them enjoy " constitutional government," others are autocracies; few of them are superior in antiquity to the British Raj: most of them, like the British Raj, arose, in the eighteenth century, on the ruins of the Mogul Empire. All now acknowledge the suzerainty of the King-Emperor. It is, however, with the evolution of the British Empire in India that this chapter is primarily concerned.

Englishmen originally settled in India merely as mer- *The East* chants. Their position there was defined, and their conduct *India* was regulated, by a charter granted to a commercial com- *Company* pany by Queen Elizabeth (1600).

That Company became in the course of a century (1757–1857) the paramount power in India. But the entrance of

313

a Chartered Company upon the field of Indian politics compelled the interference of the Crown. The resources of the
Company were quite inadequate to sustain the expenses of
government. Consequently, in return for a loan, Parliament claimed a measure of political responsibility. Lord
North's *Regulating Act* (1773) was the first of a series of
Statutes by which the government of India, at first shared
between the Company and the Crown, was ultimately
transferred to the Crown. Dual control was carried a stage
farther by Pitt's *India Act* of 1784, which, while leaving
patronage and commercial direction in the hands of the
Company, with its headquarters in Leadenhall Street,
vested the government of British India in a Ministerial
Department, known as the Board of Control. The President of the Board was a Cabinet Minister, and in fact, if not
in name, a Secretary of State for India.

*India under
the Crown*

The Dual system was brought to an end by the Mutiny.
By the *Government of India Act* (1858) the Queen of England assumed the direct Sovereignty over two-thirds of the
subcontinent of India; over the native Princes, who still
ruled the remaining third, she became Suzerain. To her
immediate subjects, and to the Feudatory Princes, the
Queen addressed a Proclamation which not only enunciated
admirable sentiments but contained passages which have
been construed—and rightly—as solemn pledges. Two
possess special significance. After disclaiming any intention
to interfere with the religious faith or observances of the
Indian peoples, and promising " to all alike the equal and
impartial protection of the law," the Queen's Proclamation
proceeded: " It is our further will that, so far as may be, our
subjects of whatever class or creed be fully and freely admitted
to any offices the duties of which they may be qualified by
their education, abilities, and integrity duly to discharge."
Those words made an impression upon the minds of educated natives which nothing will efface.

*The Crown
and the
Princes*

Even more specific was the pledge to the Princes:
" We desire no extension of our present territorial possessions; and while we will permit no aggression upon our

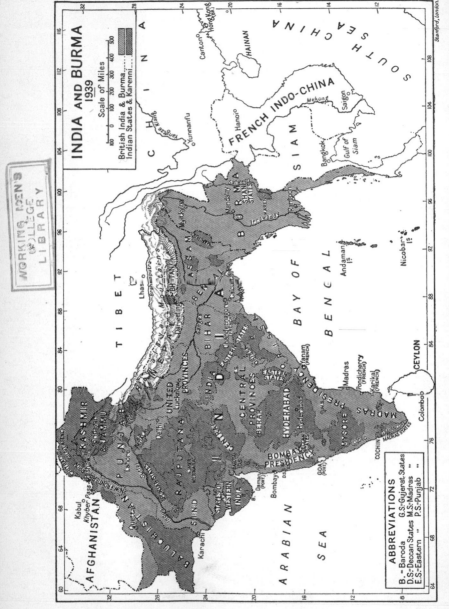

INDIA AND BURMA
1939

Scale of Miles

British India & Burma.
Indian States & Karenni.

ABBREVIATIONS

B. = Baroda   G.S=Gujerat States
D.S.=Deccan States   M.S.=Madras   "
E.S.=Eastern   "   P.S.=Punjab   "

Stanford, London.

INDIA AND BURMA, 1939

dominions or our rights to be attempted with impunity, we shall sanction no encroachment on those of others. We shall respect the rights, dignity, and honour of native princes as our own; and we desire that they, as well as our own subjects, should enjoy that prosperity and that social advancement which can only be secured by internal peace and good government."

Both in the letter and in the spirit that promise was scrupulously fulfilled. The Princes quickly came to understand that the Queen meant what she said; that the period of conquest and expansion was at an end; that the Chiefs might look forward to a period of stabilization and tranquillity; that, if they were no longer permitted to engage in their wonted occupation and attack their neighbours, their neighbours would no longer be allowed to attack them. The Sovereign Power, while prohibiting attack, was bound to accept the responsibility for defence. In fine, it imposed on all alike the *Pax Britannica*. But if the Suzerain guaranteed the thrones of the Princes, she was bound also to secure the well-being of their subjects. Rights involve duties; privileges must not be enjoyed at the expense of subjects deprived of the only effective check upon despotism. This was the " fundamental postulate " of the new order, and its implications were gradually realized by the Feudatories, though not until they had been brought home by one or two cases in which persistent misgovernment was punished by deprivation. Deprivation was not, however, followed (as in the days of John Company) by annexation. The sceptre was invariably restored to a native successor.

The promises to the natives of British India were implemented not less scrupulously than those made to the Princes. The fulfilment of promises assumed many forms, but three stand out conspicuously: increased facilities for education, the admission of natives to the Civil Service, and a series of steps in the direction of self-government.

It is now generally admitted that the educational system *Education* initiated by Macaulay in his famous Minute of 1835 was mistaken in its conception and disastrous in its results. Sir

315

Charles Wood, as President of the Board, drafted in 1854 a scheme designed to correct the worst of Macaulay's blunders; Lord Mayo (Viceroy 1869–1872) entirely reversed the policy of infiltration from above, but it was reserved for Lord Curzon (1895–1905) to devise a comprehensive scheme which should finally eradicate the effects of the initial mistake, and devise a scheme of education really suited to the needs of a people the vast majority of whom remained entirely illiterate. Yet the results were disappointingly meagre, alike in the fields of elementary, secondary, and, most of all, university education. The Sadler Commission (1919) made some important recommendations for the improvement of university education, particularly in Bengal; but the Simon Commission (1930) was constrained to emphasize its inherent weaknesses. The universities are now overcrowded with men who " are not profiting either intellectually or materially by their university training; many, too easily admitted, fall by the way, having wasted precious years of youth; many succeed in obtaining the coveted B.A. degree, only to find that the careers for which alone it fits them are hopelessly congested. Many of these half-educated and wholly disillusioned youths consequently remain unemployed, with results upon the political and social life of the country too obvious to call for emphasis." Clearly, then, the failure of English administrators in the field of education has been due to excess rather than to lack of zeal, or of benevolence.

The Civil Service

The English rulers of India have been genuinely anxious to open to Indians every avenue for advancement. Of those avenues the Civil Service was the most obvious. The Charter Act of 1833 had opened the Service to Indians, but little came of the opening until in 1853 the system of open competition was adopted. The conditions of service were revised in favour of Indians by the *Civil Service Act* of 1861. But little came of this Act, or of subsequent attempts made in 1870 and 1880 to give reality to these concessions, and only about sixty Indians had been appointed when in 1891 the system was again changed. Still Indians complained that the progress of Indianization was lamentably slow.

During the war recruiting in England was suspended, and the *Indian Government Act* of 1919 revolutionized the whole position. But that Act, so far from satisfying Indian aspirations, served rather to stimulate anti-British agitation in India. The impression was given that the English were " packing up," and that within a measurable distance of time there would not be an English soldier or an English civilian left in India. The impression was strengthened by the permission given to All-India Service officers to retire, prematurely, on a proportionate pension. Of that permission the result was that the Government of India was suddenly deprived of the services of a large proportion of its most valuable and most experienced officers. This was a serious matter. Moreover, recruiting, suspended during the war, was not resumed after its close. Oxford had been for sixty years one of the principal recruiting centres for the " Indian Civil." During the five years before the war it contributed nearly a hundred and twenty recruits to that Service. During the years 1921–1923 the aggregate was only ten. So it was at Cambridge, and elsewhere.

A Commission appointed (1923), under the chairmanship of Lord Lee of Fareham, attempted to restore the balance. Their recommendations meant, in effect, that in the " transferred " sphere of the Provincial Governments, the whole administration would be staffed by Indians, and that in the superior posts of the Civil Service and in the Police, the proportion of Englishmen and Indians would, by a gradual process, attain approximate equality by the year 1939.

Nor has constitutional evolution lagged behind reforms in education and in the Civil Service. On the contrary, the transference of British India to the Crown has been followed by a series of measures which, by their progressive and cumulative effect, have gone far to transfer political responsibility from the Imperial Crown and Parliament to the Indian peoples. *Constitutional Evolution*

Indian Councils Act, 1861

Of these measures the first was the *Indian Councils Act* of 1861, which modified the composition of the Governor-General's Council, or Executive, and remodelled the legislative system of British India.

The Act also restored the right of legislation to the Presidency Councils of Madras and Bombay, and led to the establishment of a Council in Bengal (1862), in the North West Provinces and Oudh (1886), in the Punjab (1897), and in due course in Burma and various other provinces.

The Judiciary

The year 1861 was further memorable for the passing of the Indian High Courts Act, which abolished the old Sadr Adalat (courts generally inherited by the Company from their native predecessors), and set up new High Courts of Judicature in Calcutta, Madras, and Bombay.

Local Government

In the sphere of Central government there is no important development to record between the measure of 1861 and the legislation devised by Lord Dufferin and carried into effect by Lord Lansdowne as Viceroy in 1892. The viceroyalty of Lord Ripon (1880–1884) was, however, distinguished by an important reform in local government. A full generation of Indians had by this time enjoyed the advantages of a " Western " education; not a few Indians had studied the working of English political institutions at first hand; many of them had imbibed the political philosophy of Mill, and had come to share the Englishman's conviction that " liberty " was inseparable from parliamentary government. Indians were seeking and finding employment in the public services and at the Bar, and some had been promoted to the Bench. But this did not satisfy their ambitions: they desired for the people of their own races a larger measure of self-government. With this aspiration Lord Ripon was in sympathy. But he wisely began with local government. Between 1883 and 1885 a series of Acts was passed to establish District Boards and subordinate bodies, and to extend the powers of municipal corporations. So far as possible an elective and non-official element was to be introduced, but wide discretionary powers were conferred upon the local authorities in order that they might apply the general principle with some regard to local conditions and necessities. Lord Ripon was under no illusions as to the probable effect of his reforms. " It is not," he confessed, " primarily with a view to improvements in administration that this measure is brought forward. It is chiefly desirable as a measure of political and popular education."

Both in India and at home these measures were regarded with not a little apprehension; but the opposition to them was negligible compared with that aroused by a Bill, generally known as the Ilbert Bill,[1] which proposed to remove from the Code of Criminal Procedure " at once and completely every judicial disqualification based merely on race distinctions." Racial feelings were bitterly aroused, especially among the non-official classes, by the suggestion that Europeans should be put at the mercy of native judges, and in face of the agitation which sprang up, the Government withdrew the Bill. A compromise was, however, reached in 1884, by which Europeans charged before a District Magistrate or Sessions Judge might claim a mixed jury, not less than half the members of which were to be Europeans or Americans.

Amid the angry tumult aroused by the Ilbert Bill, an event of much greater importance was almost ignored. In 1885, during the brilliant viceroyalty of Lord Dufferin, there met for the first time a National Congress representing the most advanced section of educated Indian opinion. *Lord Dufferin, Viceroy 1884–1888* How far the Congress was, or is, representative of any class, except that to which we had ourselves given a quasi-national character by the common use of the English tongue, it is difficult to say. Certain it is, however, that from its first meeting in 1885 down to the present day, the Congress has gathered a large number of adherents, who with ever-increasing vehemence have demanded the concession of a Constitution framed on the model of Western democracy, with a representative and elected Legislature and an Executive responsible thereto.

Lord Dufferin, while determined to suppress incendiary *The Indian Congress*

[1] Sir C. Ilbert was legal member of Council under Lord Ripon.

agitation, declared himself in favour of giving " a wider share in the administration of public affairs to such Indian gentlemen as by their influence, their acquirements, and the confidence they inspire in their fellow-countrymen are marked out as fitted to assist with their counsels the responsible rulers of the country." He expressly disclaimed any idea of establishing a parliamentary system for British India, but devised a scheme for the "liberalization of the provincial councils as political institutions." Elected members were to be introduced into them but to remain in a minority; the paramount control of policy was to be left in the hands of the provincial Governments.

Indian Councils Act, 1892

These principles were frankly though cautiously applied in the Act of 1892, passed by Lord Cross, and carried into effect by Lord Lansdowne (1888–1894). The Legislative Councils, both central and provincial, were considerably enlarged, and the official element was reduced. An official majority was, indeed, retained, but, as regards the unofficial minority, the principle of election was virtually admitted, though the term itself was studiously avoided. To these reconstituted Councils additional functions were entrusted. An annual budget was to be laid before them, and they were to have the right of discussing, though not of voting upon, it. The right of interpolating the Executive members, denied to the Councils in 1861, was now conferred upon them.

The advance thus registered was substantial; though it failed, of course, to satisfy the more ardent spirits in the Congress Party, who maintained a more or less continuous agitation. " A wave of political unrest," to use Mr. John (Lord) Morley's words, " was indeed slowly sweeping over India. Revolutionary voices, some moderate, others extreme, grew articulate and shrill, and claims or aspirations for extending the share of the people in their own government took more organized shape."

Unrest in India

" Political unrest " is one of those political euphemisms under which is concealed a multitude of ambiguities. For

nearly half a century the British Raj has been confronted
with an agitation whose precise character is not easily determined. Were India a " nation," it would be accurate to
describe it as a " national " movement, but any element of
" nationalism " which it possesses must be ascribed solely
to the policy consistently pursued by Great Britain. Hand
in hand with the process of unification has gone a policy of
political evolution—the introduction into India of the
political institutions familiar to Englishmen in their European
home.

Wholly benevolent as were the motives that inspired this
policy, it undoubtedly diffused a sense of instability in India.
That feeling was stimulated by external events. The reverses suffered by the Italians in Abyssinia in 1887 and 1893
caused some excitement in the Indian bazaars. The
defeats inflicted upon British forces in the earlier stages of
the South African War caused much more. But more
important than either was the defeat of Russia at the hands
of Japan (1904-1905). The repercussion of that momentous war was felt throughout the whole continent of Asia,
and, indeed, in all parts of the world where coloured races
were in contact with whites. Most of all was it felt in India,
where the Japanese victory was craftily represented as a
blow to the prestige not of Russia only, but of all the
Western peoples, not excepting, of course, the English.

The Russo-Japanese war coincided with the closing year *Lord*
of Lord Curzon's viceroyalty. That statesman's career in *Curzon,*
India had in it an element of tragedy. No Viceroy ever *1899-1905*
entered upon his high office with more complete equipment
or more generous hopes. No man ever devoted himself to
a task, great or humble, with more tireless industry. There
was indeed hardly any sphere of administration into which
he did not penetrate; hardly any feature of Indian life on
which he did not leave the impress of his own individuality:
defence and frontier policy, education, agriculture, irrigation, finance, and industry; art, archæology, and architec-
ture; game preservation and the preservation of historical
monuments; sanitation, precautions against famine and

plague, and what not. But the detailed story of these activities must be read elsewhere.[1] Ambitious Lord Curzon unquestionably was, and autocratic; but the main-spring of his multifarious activities was zeal for the public service, and genuine love for the people he ruled. Deep, especially, was his solicitude for the well-being of those patient, kindly, inarticulate millions who drew their scanty subsistence from the cultivation of the soil. Towards the " national " aspirations of the " politicians " he was less sympathetic; though he welcomed and encouraged their co-operation. " We are ordained to walk here in the same track together for many a long day to come. You cannot do without us. We should be impotent without you. Let the Englishman and the Indian accept the consecration of a union that is so mysterious as to have in it something of the divine, and let our common ideal be a united country and a happier people." These words, spoken at Calcutta in 1902, expressed Curzon's innermost conviction. Yet he left India a deeply dis-illusioned man. His educational policy and his scheme for the partition of Bengal were alike regarded as reflections upon Bengali character, and the latter policy was reversed in 1911. But even more damaging to the prestige, both of Curzon and of British power in India, were the circum-stances which led to his resignation (November 1905). That Curzon was right in thinking that to combine in one person the offices of Commander-in-Chief and Military Member of Council involved an undue subordination of the civil to the military power, and that the India Office was unwise in supporting the soldier against the Viceroy, is now generally admitted. Nor can it be doubted that the super-session of Lord Curzon, the strongest and proudest of recent Viceroys, dealt a serious blow at the prestige of his office and sensibly diminished the respect due to the King-Emperor whom he represented.

The Morley-Minto Régime

Hardly had Lord Curzon been succeeded as Viceroy by Lord Minto, when the advent of a Radical Ministry, with

[1] E.g. in *The India We Served*, by Sir W. R. Laurence, who was Private Secretary to Lord Curzon (1928), or Lord Ronaldshay's *Life of Curzon*.

Lord Morley at the India Office, gave fresh hope to the
" nationalists " in India. A religious revival among the
Hindus stimulated and sanctified preparation for armed insurrection. A campaign of violence and assassination was
launched, and many innocent victims paid with their lives
for the weak benevolence of the new régime. Neither the
visit in the winter of 1905–1906 of the then Prince and
Princess of Wales, who were received with immense enthusiasm, nor the fact that the new Viceroy and the new
Secretary of State were known to be contemplating a further
instalment of constitutional reform, seriously interrupted
the campaign of violence. To get rid of the foreign government by any means effectual for the purpose was incul-
cated as a religious duty.

The Imperial Government was seriously alarmed. In
1907 and 1908 legislation was passed on the lines familiar
in Irish " Coercion " Acts, and in the latter year Bal
Gangadhar Tilak, a Poona Brahman, who stood forth as
the leader of the extremists, was tried and sentenced to six
years' imprisonment.

Such was the atmosphere in which the constitutional
reforms known as the Morley-Minto reforms were launched.

They were prepared by a Royal Proclamation. On *Proclamation*
November 2nd, 1908, being the fiftieth anniversary of the *of King*
assumption of the government of India by the Crown, *Edward VII*
King Edward VII addressed to the Princes and Peoples of *(1908)*
India a Proclamation. Looking back on the " labours of the
past half-century with clear gaze and good conscience,"
the King-Emperor noted the splendid fight against the
" calamities of Nature," drought and plague; the wonderful
material advance that India had made; the impartial administration of law; and the unswerving loyalty of the
Feudatory Princes and Ruling Chiefs whose " rights and
privileges have been respected, preserved, and guarded."
He referred to the paramount duty of repressing " with a
stern arm guilty conspiracies that have no just cause and no
serious aim " and are abhorrent to the great mass of the
Indian peoples, and declared that such conspiracies would

323

not be suffered to interrupt the task of " building up the fabric of security and order." " From the first," he added, " the principle of representative institutions began to be gradually introduced, and the time has come when . . . that principle may be prudently extended. Important classes among you, representing ideas that have been fostered and encouraged by British rule, claim equality of citizenship, and a greater share in legislation and government. The politic satisfaction of such a claim will strengthen, not impair, existing authority and power. Administration will be all the more efficient, if the officers who conduct it have greater opportunities of contact with those whom it affects and with those who influence and reflect common opinion about it."

In accord with these principles the *Indian Councils Act* (1909) was passed. Lord Morley expressly disclaimed the intention of setting up parliamentary government in India, yet his Act has generally and rightly been regarded as a step in that direction.

Indian Councils Act, 1909

All the Legislative Councils, central and provincial, were henceforth to be composed of three classes of members: (*a*) nominated official members; (*b*) nominated non-official members; (*c*) elected members. Separate representation was also guaranteed to Mohammedans. Not only the size but the functions of the Councils were enlarged. They were invested with power to move, and to vote on, resolutions, not only on the budget, but on any matter of general public interest; though the Executive Government was not bound to act on such resolutions. As regards the Executive Councils, the maximum number of ordinary members in Madras and Bombay was raised from two to four. In 1910 the Secretary of State appointed a Hindu barrister, Mr. (afterwards Lord) Sinha, as legal member of the Viceroy's Council, and, on his resignation, a Mohammedan gentleman, Mr. Syed Ali Imam. Two Indian gentlemen had in 1907 been appointed members of the Council of India.

Lord Morley claimed for his measures that they marked the " opening of a very important chapter in the history of

Great Britain and India "; but whither, if not towards the parliamentary government he deprecated, did that chapter tend ?

That was a question for the future to answer. For the moment, the operation of the Morley-Minto reforms was overshadowed by the visit to India of the King-Emperor, George V, and the Queen. On December 7th, 1911, Their Majesties made their State entry into the capital of the Mogul Emperors, and on the 12th, with stately and superb ceremonial, the great Coronation Durbar was held. The King-Emperor announced a series of administrative changes consequential upon the " modification " of Lord Curzon's partition of Bengal; the creation of a Governor-in-Council for the freshly delimited Province of Bengal; a Lieutenant-Governorship for the new Province of Bihar, Orissa, and Chota Nagpur, with a capital at Patna; and a Chief Com-missionership for Assam. But these were matters of relatively small importance. Great was the sensation when the King-Emperor announced that the capital of the Indian Empire was presently to be transferred from Calcutta to Delhi, and that the supreme Government was to be established in a new city planned (and now built) on a scale of dazzling magnificence. As to the wisdom and the motives of the transference of the seat of government, opinion was and is sharply divided.

Three years after the King-Emperor's announcements the whole Imperial fabric of which he is the corner-stone was shaken to its foundations by the shock of world war.

Of the contribution made by India to the war effort of the Empire mention has already been made. The contribution was the more significant in view of the fact that the military organization of India had been planned only to maintain internal peace, to meet tribal outbreaks on the frontier, and to repel a continental invasion. For participation in a European war India was not prepared, and she deserves the more credit for the ready response made to the demands of the Imperial Government.

Unfortunately, the splendid spirit manifested in India in

The Coronation Durbar, 1911

India and the War

the early days of the war was not maintained until its close. " The War," as Sir Valentine Chirol said, " lasted too long and was too remote (from the Indian people). . . . The sick and wounded from Mesopotamia brought home too often tales of mismanagement and defeat, startlingly corroborated by the thunderbolt of the Kut surrender. . . . If England had been reluctant at first to credit Kitchener's prophecy that the war would last three years, Indians were still more at a loss to understand why victory should be so slow to come to Great Britain and her powerful allies, and they began to doubt whether it would come at all."

Revolutionary Agitation

During the first two years of war there had been an almost complete cessation of outrages or even disorder in India. The exception, curiously enough, was provided by the Punjab, whose peasants supplied half the combatants in the expeditionary forces. The immediate cause of the outbreak was the return to India of some Sikhs and Punjabi Moslems who had been refused permission by the Canadian authorities to land at Vancouver. Inflamed by propaganda literature circulated by Indian revolutionary societies in the United States, they returned to India, bent upon making trouble for the British Government. For some ten months (October 1914 to August 1915) the Punjab was the scene of a serious revolutionary outbreak, eventually quelled by the courage and resource of the Lieutenant-Governor, Sir Michael O'Dwyer, loyally supported by the great majority of the inhabitants, as well as by the Rulers of the Native States in the Punjab. The lull that ensued was temporary and delusive. In 1914 B. G. Tilak had been released on the expiration of his sentence. In the following year the Congress meeting at Cawnpore endorsed the demand formulated by Tilak and Mrs. Annie Besant for " Home Rule within the Empire," and in 1917 elected Mrs. Besant to the presidential chair.

Declaration of August 20th, 1917

This was the moment chosen by the British Government for the historic announcement made to Parliament on August 20th.

" The policy of His Majesty's Government," so the

Declaration ran, " with which the Government of India are in complete accord, is that of the increasing association of Indians in every branch of the administration, and the gradual development of self-governing institutions with a view to the progressive realization of responsible government in India as an integral part of the British Empire. They have decided that substantial steps in this direction should be taken as soon as possible. . . . I would add that progress in this policy can only be achieved by successive stages. The British Government and the Government of India, on whom the responsibility lies for the welfare and advancement of the Indian peoples, must be judges of the time and measure of such advance, and they must be guided by the co-operation received from those upon whom new opportunities of service will thus be conferred, and by the extent to which it is found that confidence can be reposed in their sense of responsibility."

As was only to be expected, public attention fastened upon the crucial words " responsible government," while the second and conditioning paragraph was at the time and subsequently ignored.

The Declaration was made to the House of Commons by Mr. E. S. Montagu, who had only just succeeded Sir Austen Chamberlain as Secretary of State for India; but, since he was not a member of the War Cabinet, his responsibility for the Declaration was less than that of Lord Curzon, who was a member and whose pen had drafted the critical words. Yet except for the words " responsible government," now used officially for the first time in relation to India, the resolution differed little in wording from that of successive Statutes and Proclamations from 1833 onwards. The resolution came, however, at a moment when the whole British Empire was fain to acknowledge a deep debt of gratitude to the fighting peoples of India. Unfortunately, it was interpreted in India not as a graceful acknowledgment of their loyal co-operation, but as a concession to the Congress politicians, to whom the Empire owed nothing and meant nothing.

The impression made by the Declaration was accentuated by the Report (April 1918) made to Parliament by the Viceroy and the Secretary of State, who had visited India in the preceding winter.

The Report contained a number of detailed recommendations for the future government of India, subsequently embodied in the Act of 1919. One sentence, almost parenthetical, revealed the spirit in which the Report was drafted: " We believe profoundly that . . . nationhood within the Empire represents something better than anything India has hitherto attained: that the placid pathetic contentment of the masses is not the soil on which Indian nationhood will grow, and that in deliberately disturbing it we are working for her highest good."

It might have been anticipated that a Report designed to disturb contentment would at least placate the extremists. It did nothing of the kind. On the contrary, the Congress Party declared that the Montagu-Chelmsford scheme meant for India " perpetual slavery which can only be broken by a revolution." They proceeded to break it. Meanwhile, they embarked upon an agitation which gave to an attractive but inscrutable personality a welcome opportunity.

Mr. Gandhi Mr. Gandhi seized it with consummate ability. In February 1919 he launched his Civil Disobedience Campaign—an advance upon passive resistance—and this was followed, almost immediately, by renewed outbreaks at Delhi, Ahmedabad, Amritsar, and other places. At Amritsar, near Lahore, a formidable rising was quelled by the drastic action taken by General Dyer. The Amritsar incident was (in Carlyle's phrase) no " rose-water surgery," but it may be that, though it cost hundreds of lives, it saved thousands; that, even if General Dyer temporarily lost his head and finally his job, he saved a Province. Anyway, the scale of the disturbances may be judged by the fact that in connection with the outrages in Lahore and Amritsar no fewer than 2,500 persons were brought to trial, and 1,800 were convicted. With the help of martial law order was gradually restored.

Meanwhile, the Imperial Parliament proceeded to embody in the *Government of India Act* (1919) the recommendations of the Montagu-Chelmsford Report. The changes introduced by that Act into the Supreme Government of India, though considerable, were relatively unimportant. The Government remained in fact an autocracy tempered by a bicameral legislature. *Government of India Act, 1919*

The changes effected in the provincial Governments were based upon the principle of diarchy, or a division of the functions of government into two sections, one dealing with subjects—such as local self-government, education, public health, excise, agriculture, fisheries, weights and measures, public works, and like matters—the administration of which was " transferred " to Ministers chosen from and responsible to the elected local legislature or Legislative Councils: the other with subjects—such as justice and police—reserved for the exclusive jurisdiction of the Governor and his Executive Council.

The new constitution was formally inaugurated on February 21st, 1921, at Delhi by H.R.H. the Duke of Connaught, on behalf of the King-Emperor.

The persistent agitation in British India naturally caused some disquietude among the rulers of the Indian States. In the whole Empire there is no more loyal element than these rulers, but the efforts of the Montagu-Chelmsford régime to disturb the contentment of the Indian peasantry, even if only partially successful, inevitably reacted upon the subjects of the native Princes. Accordingly, at their request, a small Committee was, in 1927, appointed (i) to report upon the relationship between the Paramount Power and the Indian States, and (ii) to enquire into the financial and economic relations between British India and the States and to . . . make " recommendations . . . for their adjustment." The Report, published in 1929, did not give complete satisfaction to the Princes; but it was made clear that the Princes would continue to enjoy complete autonomy " so long as they governed their people well," and that they would not be handed over to a new Indian *The Indian States Committee*

329

"Dominion" without their own consent. This was the vital point.

Almost simultaneously with the appointment of the Indian States Committee, the Royal Commission, provided for in the Act of 1919, was appointed, under the chairmanship of Sir John Simon—a distinguished lawyer and former Home Secretary—to enquire into "the working of the system of government, the growth of education, and the development of representative institutions in British India," and to report "as to whether and to what extent it is desirable to establish the principle of responsible government, or to extend, modify, or restrict the degree of responsible government then existing therein."

The Simon Commission, after two prolonged visits to India, laid before Parliament (June 1930) an invaluable and exhaustive Report, containing, on the one hand, a comprehensive survey, historical and analytical, of conditions in British India, and on the other, a series of carefully devised and detailed proposals. Those proposals were, however, superseded by the scheme of 1935. Consequently they ceased to possess anything more than an academic interest.[1]

In the course of their investigations the Commissioners had become more and more "impressed by the impossibility of considering the constitutional problems of British India without taking into account the relations between British India and the Indian States." They accordingly suggested "the setting up of some sort of conference, after the Reports of the Statutory Commission and the Indian Central Committee have been made, considered, and published . . . and that in this conference His Majesty's Government should meet both representatives of British India and representatives of the States." Mr. Ramsay MacDonald, having consulted the leaders of the other parties, concurred.[2] Accordingly, before the scheme was submitted to Parliament the whole subject was meticulously

---

[1] The curious will find them, together with further details on the whole subject, in Marriott: *The English in India*, pp. 280 f.
[2] MacDonald had, for the second time, become Prime Minister in 1929.

discussed in a series of Round Table Conferences (September *Round* 1930 to March 1933), which were attended by Indian representatives, as well as by English statesmen of all parties. Three small Committees had also been sent to India to investigate and report upon the three subjects of the franchise, finance, and the Indian States.[1]   After the third session of the Round Table Conference, the reconsidered and revised proposals of the Government were embodied in a second White Paper.[2]   A Joint Select Committee of Lords and Commons was then appointed, "with power to call into consultation representatives of the Indian States and British India," to consider the proposals   It sat under the chairmanship of the Marquis of Linlithgow, now (1938) Viceroy of India, and after holding159 meetings reported its approval of the proposals.

Round Table Conferences

Never, it can be confidently said, has any great constitutional measure been submitted to Parliament after more prolonged, careful, and detailed consideration and reconsideration.   The resulting Bill was piloted through the House of Commons with great patience and skill by Sir Samuel Hoare, and in 1935 received the Royal Assent.

The Act of 1935, which reconstructs both the Central and the provincial Governments, rests on three main foundations: (i) All-India Federation; (ii) Provincial autonomy; and (iii) "Responsibility with safeguards."   The whole of India—the Feudatory States as well as British India—is to be united into a Federal Empire.   The units are to be formed of (i) the Governor's Provinces of British India and (ii) such Feudatory States as shall accede to the scheme.   But the All-India Federation cannot come into existence until the rulers of States representing at least one-half of the aggregate population of the States, and entitled to at least half the seats in the Upper Federal Chamber, have presented an Address to the Crown praying for the establishment of the

India Act, 1935

---

[1] Reports Cmd. 4068, 4069, and 4103 of 1932.   A small Committee headed by Sir Harcourt Butler had previously (1929) reported on the relations between the Crown and the Indian Princes.

[2] Cmd. 4268 ; the first White Paper (Cmd. 3972) was issued in 1931.

Federation. Thus the key of the situation is held by the more important ruling Princes.

Assuming their accession, the Federal Legislature will consist of two Chambers: the Upper (Council of State) containing 260 members, 104 representing the States and 156 elected on a high franchise to represent British India; the Lower Chamber (Federal Assembly) containing 250 members elected by the Provincial Legislatures of British India, and 125 States representatives. The Executive will be vested in the Governor-General, as representing the King-Emperor, and he will act generally on the advice of a Council of Ministers responsible to the Legislature. Certain departments, however—foreign affairs and defence—the Viceroy will administer through Ministers personally and exclusively responsible to himself, and in certain other matters he may act otherwise than on the advice of his " responsible " Ministers.

The machinery of the Central Government is (save for the federal element) reproduced in the autonomous Provinces: the Governor will, in certain spheres, act (like the Governor-General) on his own responsibility, but, in most, on that of Ministers responsible to the Legislature, which in six of the most important Provinces will be bicameral, and in the rest unicameral.

The Act also provides for the creation of a Federal Court, whose chief function is to adjudicate in disputes between the autonomous Provinces, and also (when the Federal Constitution comes into existence) between the Indian States with one another or with the Federation. An appeal will, however, lie as of right in all cases to the Privy Council. The Federal Court inaugurated in December 1937 has begun to function under its first Chief Justice, Sir Maurice Gwyer, an English lawyer of varied experience and great distinction.

For the rest, the Act is not yet (1938) in full operation. The new provincial Government and Legislatures came into being in 1937. But not without a serious hitch. In seven out of the eleven Provinces, the Congress Party, having obtained majorities, refused to form Ministries unless the Governors pledged themselves not to use the special powers conferred upon them by the Constitution. A deadlock ensued; and, though it has been temporarily resolved, the fear persists that it may recur with Ministries belonging to a Party pledged to work for the complete severance of the British connection.

The more important part of the Act of 1935 has not yet (1938) come into being. It depends, as already indicated, on the willingness of the Princes to come into the Federation.

Very great pressure has been put upon them to induce *The Act* them to do so at the earliest possible moment. But in each *and the* case the Instrument of Accession is to be a matter of indi- *Princes* vidual negotiation between the Indian Ruler and the Crown. That is not the only obstacle. If many of the rulers are mistrustful of federation, so also is the Indian Congress, which dreads the prospect of being faced in the Federal Legislation by powerful blocks of what it derisively describes as " Palace Nominees." Accordingly it insists, as a condition precedent alike to its own consent to federation and to the admission of the States, that the latter should democratize their own Constitutions. The States are at present for the most part autocracies, some of them benevolent, some of them the reverse. If the wishes of the Congress Party prevail they must all consent to " approximate to the Provinces in the establishment of responsible government, civil liberties, and method of election to the Federal House."

It is safe to assume that the Government of India will offer every encouragement to the recalcitrant States to fulfil the conditions imposed by the Congress. For the moment, however, the Constitution of 1935 remains a torso.

Forty years ago Sir William Hunter, distinguished both as an Indian administrator and as an historian, used words which are as true to-day as they were when first uttered. " In thinking of her work in India Great Britain may look back proudly, but she must also anxiously look forward." In the interval many experiments, always generous in intention, if not invariably successful, have been tried. British brains, British enterprise, and British capital have transformed the face of the country. Means of communication have been improved out of recognition. Irrigation works on a stupendous scale have brought over 30,000,000 acres under cultivation, and have thus greatly added to the agricultural wealth of a people who still live mainly by agriculture. The standard of living, though still low, has steadily risen, and subsistence has more than kept pace with a rapid increase in population. Above all, famines, which by their regular recurrence had formerly presented a perennial problem to successive administrators, have been virtually eliminated. This great task has been achieved by improved sanitation (much resented by the beneficiaries), by canalization, by irrigation, by the development of means of transport, and particularly by carefully devised schemes for relief work. Despite all this, there is still much discontent, especially among politically minded Indians. As a rebuke to such ingratitude the words of a broad-minded Moslem, Sir Syed Ahmed, deserve to be recalled : " Be not unjust to that nation which is ruling over you, and think on this—how upright is her rule. Of such benevolence as the English Government shows to the foreign nations under her rule, there is no example in the history of the world."

Great Britain may indeed " look back proudly "; can she look forward confidently ?

Chapter Twenty-two

The Colonial Empire

SURVEY AND SUMMARY

P RECEDING chapters have concentrated attention mainly upon the Dominions and India. But the British Empire, oceanic in origin and dispersed throughout the world, is not more remarkable for its geographical distribution than for the extraordinary variety of its constitutional forms. Of that Empire it remains to take a brief survey.

The Empire falls geographically into six great groups: *Geographical* (1) the European, with the United Kingdom itself, the Isle *Groups* of Man, the Channel Islands, and the strategical points in the Mediterranean—Gibraltar, Malta, and Cyprus (Asia); (2) the American, including, besides the great Dominion of Canada, Newfoundland and Labrador, British Guiana, Honduras, the Falkland Islands, and the Bermudas; (3) the Australasian, including the Commonwealth of Australia, New Zealand, Fiji, New Guinea, and other islands in the South Pacific held under Mandates; (4) the African, including, in addition to the four united colonies and the Rhodesias, Nigeria, Gambia, Sierra Leone, and the Gold Coast, and (on the east coast), Kenya, as well as various Protectorates and Mandated Territories; and Mauritius and the Seychelles in the Indian Ocean; (5) the Asiatic, including, besides India itself and Burma, Ceylon, Hong Kong, the Straits Settlements, the Malay States, Labuan, North Borneo, and Sarawak; and finally (6) the West Indian Islands, of which the most important are Jamaica, the Bahamas, Barbados, Trinidad and Tobago, the Windward and Leeward Islands.

Constitutionally, the categories are less clear-cut, but the *Constitutional* overseas possessions of the Crown fall broadly into two main *Categories* divisions: the Dominions and the Colonies.

335

According to legal definition the term *colony* includes " any part of His Majesty's dominions exclusive of the British Islands (i.e. the United Kingdom, the Channel Islands, and the Isle of Man), and of British India." [1] The term is thus equally applicable, in a legal sense, on the one hand to Hong Kong, a trading station, Gibraltar, a fortress, and Ascension, which is administered not by the Colonial Office but by the Board of Admiralty, in whose books it was until 1922 " rated " as a man-of-war; and, on the other, to Canada, South Africa, Australia, and New Zealand. These latter have, however, repudiated the term " colony," with its supposed implication of inferiority and subordination; they are designated as Dominions, and since 1925 have been administered by the Dominions Office. In view of the mixed company to which they were consigned by the Interpretation Act of 1889, their susceptibility was not wonderful, and in any case has been respected. Otherwise, there would be much to be said for confining the term " colony " to those lands which, alike by their expanse, their emptiness, and their climate, offer almost illimitable fields for the expansion of the British race, and consigning all other units of the Empire to the category of dependencies.

The constitutional status of the colonies is infinitely various. Some colonies are virtually self-governing, and only just fall short of complete " Dominion status "; others shade off gradually, down to the lowest constitutional grade of pure autocracies. A brief enumeration must accordingly suffice.

Northern Ireland

Northern Ireland is in a class apart, and its internal administration with a Governor, bicameral Legislature, and an Executive responsible thereto is indistinguishable from that of a Dominion; but it still forms part of the United Kingdom; it is still represented in the Imperial Parliament, and admits the jurisdiction of the Home Office. Certain subjects, such as defence, external trade, and coinage, are still reserved to the Imperial Government. Ulster owes this unique position to its acceptance of the legislation of 1920,

[1] Interpretation Act, 1889 (52 & 53 Vic., c. 63, § 18 (1, 3)).

which dissolved the Union consummated in 1800. By the Act of Union Ireland had been admitted to full partnership, political and commercial, with Great Britain; the Protestant minority received a guarantee for the maintenance of the Established Church, and to the Roman Catholics hopes of complete religious and civil equality were held out. Not until 1829, however, were those hopes realized, and then only as the result of renewed agitation. The Protestant Church itself was disestablished and disendowed in 1869, and between 1870 and 1905 a series of agrarian measures was passed, the ultimate effect of which was to transfer the ownership of the land in Ireland from the landlords to the tenants. Still agitation persisted. Mr. Gladstone had attempted in 1886, and again in 1893, to pass a Home Rule Bill for Ireland, but unsuccessfully; and not until 1914 was a Home Rule Act, passed under the new procedure of the Parliament Act, put upon the Statute-book. By that time the Great War had broken out, and when in September 1914 the Royal Assent was given to the Bill, an agreed measure was simultaneously passed suspending the operation of the Act during the continuance of the war. Before the (legal) termination of the war was reached the Act of 1914 was repealed and superseded by the *Act for the Better Government of Ireland* (1920).

This latter Act, a product of coalition government, was, *Government* as regards Southern Ireland, still-born. Ever since the *of Ireland Act, 1920* rebellion which broke out at Easter 1916 Southern Ireland had been in the grip of the Sinn Fein Party. Nor were they induced to relax it by the passing of the Act of 1920. That Act provided for the establishment, at Belfast and Dublin respectively, of two Parliaments, with Executives responsible thereto, and each Parliament was to contribute twenty members to an all-Ireland Council, which was intended to form the nucleus for an all-Ireland Parliament. The Act never operated in Southern Ireland; the Irish Nationalists resented from the first the idea of partition; a still more extreme party would accept nothing short of an Irish republic.

z   337

Ulster

Northern Ireland—the six Ulster counties of Antrim, Armagh, Down, Fermanagh, Londonderry, and Tyrone, with the Boroughs of Belfast and Londonderry—accepted and have loyally and successfully worked the semi-federal scheme already described. To Ulster it seemed at least preferable to subordination to a Dublin Parliament. Southern Ireland adopted the principle of non-co-operation, refused to work the Act, and carried on a guerrilla war against the forces of the Crown. In July 1921, however, a truce was proclaimed, and the Sinn Fein leaders accepted an invitation to negotiate with the Government in London. After much haggling the offer of " Dominion status," with certain con-

Southern Ireland

ditions, was accepted. In December 1921 a treaty was signed, and on March 31st, 1922, a Bill embodying its terms received the Royal Assent. Ireland was to enjoy full Dominion status, under the style of the Irish Free State, and to form, under the British Crown, a member of the British Commonwealth of nations; the six counties of Ulster retaining the right, immediately exercised, to contract out of it. Southern Ireland did not, in terms, repudiate the " Treaty," but the development of events in that portion of the island has left the constitutional position so ambiguous that it would serve no good purpose at present (1938) to attempt to define it.

The Home Islands

Conquered by the Norsemen in the ninth century, the Isle of Man was ruled by them until its conquest by the Scots in the thirteenth. From the fifteenth onwards it formed part of the English realm, but was held of the Crown by the House of Stanley and the Duke of Atholl successively, until, in 1765, the Crown assumed direct control.

Like Northern Ireland, the Isle of Man is under the jurisdiction of the Home Office. The Island retains indeed its own historic Legislature, but control over both the Legislature and the Executive is exercised by the Home Secretary, acting, for the most part, through the Lieutenant-Governor. The Legislature of the Court of Tynwald consists of two branches: a small Legislative Council and the

House of Keys. The Council consists of eleven members, including the Lieutenant-Governor, the Bishop, the Attorney-General, and the two Deemsters.

The Channel Islands are still ruled by the Crown as Duke of Normandy, and upon the customs of that Duchy the law of the Island is based. Both Jersey and Guernsey have their own Constitutions, but both resemble that of Mediaeval France more closely than that of Modern England. The " States " of Guernsey legislate for the adjacent islands, including Sark and Alderney, but all are subject to the legislative supremacy of the Imperial Parliament. The Crown also claims the right to legislate by Order in Council, but such Orders are registered in the local Courts of Justice, thus recalling the *Lits de justice* of the Parlement of Paris.

From the United Kingdom and its adjoining islands we *The* pass to the Mediterranean. The western approach to that *Mediterranean* still vital sea-route is guarded by Gibraltar. Conquered by Sir George Rooke in 1704, it was besieged for three years and seven months by a combined force of French and Spaniards (1779–1783) but was heroically defended by General Eliot, and has ever since remained in British hands.

Gibraltar is a purely military outpost, and constitution- *Gibraltar* ally is included in the lowest category. It has no Legislative Council, and is administered by a Governor, who is invariably a distinguished soldier and commands the garrison. That the Mediterranean is one of the vital arteries of the Empire is not open to doubt, but the place of " the Rock " in the general schemes of Imperial defence is a matter of debate among experts. Among them are some who would gladly see Gibraltar exchanged for Ceuta, but that and similar questions must be left to expert strategists; the historian must be content to record the historical facts.

Malta, the half-way house on the Mediterranean route, *Malta* is in every sense in a very different position from Gibraltar. Surrendered to the British navy in 1800, it was retained at the Peace of 1814, and the superb harbour of Valetta has made it an ideal base for the Mediterranean fleet. Constitutionally it has had a chequered history, and the variations reflect not only the restlessness of an alien population under British rule but the dual position of the island in the Empire. Under the Constitution granted in 1921 the Governor became the constitutional head of an administration with a bicameral Legislature and an Executive which, as regards internal affairs, was almost " responsible." The control of external trade, of the naval, military, and air forces, and of all matters such as postal and telegraphic communications, which concern defence as much as civil convenience, were reserved to the representative of the Imperial Government. The position was admittedly anomalous, and to ambitious Nationalists was doubtless irritating. With its arsenal and dockyard Malta occupies too important a place in the scheme of Imperial defence for any risks to be taken. Consequently, the Constitution was in 1933 suspended, and Malta again became a Crown colony. On July 29th, 1938, however, it was officially announced in the Imperial Parliament that a limited measure of self-government is to be restored, and the hope is that a new Legislative Council will enable the people to be associated through elected representatives with the government of the colony. It is not, however, considered likely that " within any period which can at present be foreseen " responsible government will be restored. It is indeed imperative that the Governor of a great fortress should be clothed with the powers essential for its defence.

Newfound-land
Parenthetically we may observe that Newfoundland, our " oldest colony," has, like Malta, also fallen, temporarily, from its high estate.

Troubles, political and financial, overtook that Dominion in 1932, and in 1933 it requested the Imperial Government to send out a Royal Commission to investigate the position. As a result, Newfoundland was in 1934 temporarily reduced to the status of a Crown colony; the Government was vested in a Governor, assisted by six Commissioners (three of whom were specially sent out from England); and the colony was saved from imminent bankruptcy by a three per cent loan guaranteed by the Imperial Government. Since then, recovery, though not rapid, has been steady, and is likely to be assisted by the development, with the aid of British capital, of the paper-making industry.

Cyprus, also, has been in trouble of late. Handed over *Cyprus* to the " occupation " of Great Britain in 1878, that island was not formally dissevered from the Ottoman Empire and annexed to the British Empire until 1914. Had Great Britain given to Cyprus a tithe of the intelligent attention given, since 1911, by Italy to Rhodes, the condition of affairs would now be very different. Cyprus has, in fact, been rather discreditably neglected. The Italians in Rhodes, while careful to preserve all that makes the island historically interesting and to exploit its archaeological treasures, have also made it a tourist resort and have attracted many holiday-makers both from Egypt and from Europe. There is no reason why Cyprus should not be made equally attractive, both to invalids and to pleasure-seekers, nor is it inferior to Rhodes in archaeological interest. But in Cyprus, as in Rhodes, these matters are plainly subsidiary to strategical considerations. From 1925 to 1931 Cyprus possessed an Executive Council and a Legislative Council, containing an electoral majority. Serious rioting occurred, however, in 1931, and since that time all powers, legislative as well as executive, have been vested in the Governor.

The Cypriot Nationalists are now demanding a Constitution on the lines of that enjoyed by Malta before 1933.

Passing from Europe into Asiatic waters we must notice *The Sudan* in passing the curious constitutional status of the Sudan, the conquest of which has already been described. Though Egypt has become an independent State, the Anglo-Egyptian Sudan is still legally under a *condominium* of Great Britain and Egypt. Practically, the administration is British, though efforts are being made, and with increasing success, to associate the Sudanese with the work of the British officials. For this task the Sudanese have been equipped mainly by the admirable education provided for them at the Gordon Memorial College at Khartoum. Supreme civil and military authority is vested in the

Governor-General, who is technically appointed by Egyptian decree, though practically on the nomination of the English Foreign Office.

Of the islands guarding the ocean route to India and the Far East mention has been already made, though it should be added that with the coming into force (April 1st, 1937) of the *India Act* of 1935, Aden ceased to be a part of British India and became a Crown colony under a Governor assisted by an Executive Council. It is strongly fortified and garrisoned, and is increasingly important as an air base.

Malaya
Infinitely more important is Singapore, the possession of which the Empire owes to one of those intrepid adventurers who, despite official discouragement, have built up, stone by stone, the structure as it confronts the world to-day.

But for Sir Stamford Raffles, Singapore would to-day undoubtedly belong to the Dutch East Indies. In 1819, however, Raffles obtained permission from the English East India Company, whose servant he was, to establish, by agreement with the Malay Chief of Johore, a trading post on Singapore island, at that time a swampy and almost uninhabited island. Raffles had also been mainly responsible for the acquisition of Java, had temporarily administered it, and had given it up at the Peace of 1814 with great reluctance. In Singapore he sought compensation for the abandonment of Java, and fully was his foresight justified. Malacca was obtained from the Dutch in 1824 in exchange for Sumatra, and the whole peninsula thus passed under British control. In 1837 Singapore became the administrative centre for the " Straits Settlements," as they were officially named—Singapore, Malacca, and Penang. By subsequent treaties the native rulers accepted British Residents as " advisers," and by a treaty concluded in 1909 Siam transferred to Great Britain all rights of suzerainty, protection, administration, and control of the four North Malay States: Kedah, Perlis, Trengganu, and Kelantan. Thus, as the late Parliamentary Under-Secretary of State for the Colonies wrote: " The Malays remain the subjects of the Mohammedan monarchies which they themselves estab-

342

lished. Malay custom is not interfered with and the Malays play a large part in the government of their States; but . . . they have the assistance of a body of trained British Civil Servants to guide and assist the development and administration of their countries." [1]

Meanwhile, between 1874 and 1909, Perak, Selangor, *F.M.S.* Pahang, and a group of small States known as the Negri Sembilan (Nine States) were federated, and became a British Protectorate with the title of the Federated Malay States under a British High Commissioner, who is also Governor of the Straits Settlements. Johore, like the four non-federated northern States mentioned above, remains outside the Federation; but in 1885 the Sultan placed the foreign relations of his State under British control; a British adviser, to assist the Sultan in his internal administration, was appointed in 1910, and additional British officials in 1914. Johore is not technically a part of the British Empire.

Important as these possessions are from an economic point of view, their place in the Imperial system is primarily due to the construction of a great dockyard and the establishment of a naval and air base on the island of Singapore.

The island is only twenty-six miles by fourteen miles in *Singapore* size, but situated at south of the Malay Peninsula and on the Johore straits it occupies, as Sir Robert (Viscount) Horne told the House of Commons, " one of the most important places on the earth's surface, so far as we are concerned, and so far as our interests go. It dominates seas on the perimeter of which you have Australia and New Zealand and India, territories which represent three-fourths of all the British territories in the world, and which carry three-fourths of all the populations over which the King reigns. These seas in which Singapore is carrying every year £1,000,000,000 worth of cargo to Great Britain . . . They carry practically all the rubber that comes to us, practically all the jute, all the hemp, all the wool, all the zinc ore, and many other commodities which are of the first essential

---

[1] Report on Malaya by the Right Hon. W. Ormsby-Gore, M.P. (Cmd. 3235, p. 9.)

to our ordinary manufacturing industries. At any day of the year there would be afloat upon that sea something over £150,000,000 worth of ships and cargo belonging to Great Britain." [1]

At this vital point it was in 1921 decided, to the great satisfaction of the Dominions, especially Australia and New Zealand, to establish a first-rate naval base. Work was started in 1922; the Socialist Party suspended it in 1924, but it was happily resumed with some help from New Zealand and Hong Kong and Malaya, in 1925 ; and though temporarily checked by a second Socialist Government in 1929, it has, by British brains and British capital, been carried to a successful issue. When the dockyard is completed it will have cost £11,000,000, almost the whole of which has been provided by the British taxpayer. In addition, the fortifications have been modernized and greatly strengthened, barracks for an increased garrison have been built, and a great military aerodrome has been constructed on a site adjacent to the base. The new graving dock was formally opened with impressive ceremony on February 14th, 1938.

It is the hope of all men of goodwill that these elaborate precautions will deter any potential enemy from disturbing the peace of the Pacific.

Another important outpost of the Empire, Hong Kong, was acquired as the result of the Chinese war of 1841–1842; Wei-Hai-Wei [2] in 1898; the island of Labuan, near Borneo, *Borneo* became a Crown colony in 1847; but in Borneo itself the position was and remains almost Gilbertian. Sir James Brooke, an ex-officer of the Indian army, visited Sarawak in 1840, helped to suppress a rebellion then in progress, and was appointed Governor of the country by the Sultan. He rooted out piracy along the coasts, and eventually became Sovereign of Sarawak, a position which became hereditary in his family. [3] The British Government appointed him

---

[1] *Hansard*, March 25th, 1924 (Vol. 171, p. 1186).
[2] Retroceded 1930.
[3] The present Rajah, third in descent from Rajah Brooke, is H.H. Sir Charles Vyner Brooke, G.C.M.G. He succeeded in 1917.

Governor of Labuan and Consul-General of Borneo, but his own principality of Sarawak he retained as an independent sovereignty. In 1888, however, the external relations of the country were placed under the control of the Foreign Office.

In 1881 the Crown granted a charter to a British company which had already begun to exercise sovereign rights in North Borneo, and in 1888 the territory was formally recognized as a British Protectorate. In North Borneo the measure of control exercised by the Colonial Office stops short of that exercised over Protectorates in the full sense of the term. It remains as a unique survival of Chartered Company administration, though, like Sarawak, Malaya, the Friendly (or Tonga) Islands, and Zanzibar, it is technically described as a " Protected State." [1] *North Borneo Company*

Before leaving the Far East it remains to add something about the position in the Imperial system of Burma and Ceylon. *Burma*

When in 1823 Lord Amherst became Governor-General of India, the eastern frontiers of Bengal were threatened by the advance of the Kingdom of Burma. Though the intermediate tribes had indeed been taken under British protection, the precaution proved inadequate to defend them against the encroachments of their neighbours. Consequently, in 1824, the Governor-General was compelled to declare war. The expedition was delayed because the Bengal Sepoys refused to forfeit their caste by crossing the " black water." The ensuing mutiny—a premonition of the events of 1857—was easily suppressed, and the expedition eventually penetrated to Ava, where Lord Amherst dictated terms of peace. The King of Burma agreed to recognize an English Protectorate over Upper Assam, Cachar, and Manipur, and to cede the Maritime Provinces of Arakan and Tenasserim. Thus a " non-Indian people was for the first time brought within the jurisdiction of the Indian Empire." [2]

[1] The distinction between a " Protectorate " and a " Protected State " is clearly explained by Professor Berriedale Keith : *The Governments of the British Empire*, p. 35 (Macmillan, 1935).
[2] Lyall : *British Dominion in India*.

That did not end the trouble. Pegu was annexed by Lord Dalhousie after a second Burma war in 1852, and in 1886 Lord Dufferin completed Lord Dalhousie's work. King Thibaw, an oriental despot of the worst type, was deposed, and his kingdom was annexed to British India. The country, with an area larger than that of France, was, however, reduced to obedience only after two years of harassing guerrilla warfare. Once conquered, it was rapidly brought into a state of high administrative efficiency by a band of skilled civilians. Burma was raised to the status of a Lieutenant-Governorship in 1897, and in 1923 was, under the Act of 1919, constituted a Governor's Province.

The Simon Commission recognized that Burma and India are " different countries," that Burma's " political union with India is based neither upon geographical connection nor racial affinity," least of all upon community of economic interest. Accordingly they recommended that Burma should be immediately separated from British India. To that recommendation the Act of 1935 gave effect : on April 1st, 1937, Burma was formally separated from India and now enjoys " responsible government " of the usual type, with a bicameral Legislature and an Executive responsible thereto, though powers parallel with those exercised by the Governor-General of India are vested in the Governor.[1] Experience has already proved (1938) that this precaution was not superfluous.

Ceylon   Ceylon, unlike Burma, has never been part of British India. Occupied by the Portuguese in 1505, Ceylon remained in their hands until it was captured by the Dutch in 1656, and by the Dutch East India Company the island was administered until 1796.

The capture of Ceylon in 1796, largely by the ingenuity of Dr. Hugh Cleghorn, an enterprising professor from St. Andrews, is one of the most romantic incidents in the long struggle between Great Britain and Revolutionary France. Colombo was at that time defended mainly by a mercenary

[1] For details of the Constitution see Keith: *The Governments of the British Empire*, pp. 601 f.

Swiss regiment in the pay of the Dutch Company. Cleghorn, who as a good linguist was then engaged in secret
service work on the continent, conceived the ingenious idea
of purchasing the regiment from the Comte de Meulon, its
proprietor, and carried de Meulon himself off to Ceylon to
superintend the completion of the bargain.[1] The Swiss
regiment was transferred to the British service, and in
February 1796 Colombo and all the other Dutch Indepen-
dencies in Ceylon surrendered to the force despatched from
Madras under Colonel Stuart. Ceylon was temporarily
administered by the East India Company, but in 1802 it
became a Crown colony under the direct government of the
Colonial Office, and so continued after the final annexation
of the island to Great Britain by the Peace of 1814. Modi-
fications in the Crown Colony Constitution were effected in
a popular direction in 1910, 1920, and 1923. The progress
of the nationalist agitation in India gave an impulse to a
similar agitation among the Low Country Sinhalese and
Tamil societies, who formed, on the Indian model, a
National Congress, and demanded that at least half the
Executive Council and a majority of the Legislative Council
should be Ceylonese. These demands were mostly conceded
in 1923, but the concessions gave no satisfaction. The
machinery of government was creaking ominously, when in
1927 a Special Commission was sent out to Ceylon, under
the chairmanship of the Earl of Donoughmore, to report
on the working of the Constitution and make suggestions
for its amendment.

Their Report was most discouraging. "The existing Constitution is," they reported, "reducing the Government to
impotence, without providing any means of training the
unofficial members in the assumption of executive responsibility," and has on the whole proved "detrimental to the
best interests of the country." [2]

Accordingly they recommended a frank acceptance of

The Donoughmore Constitution, 1931

---

[1] The thrilling story may be read in *The Cleghorn Papers* (ed. Neil) (A. & C. Black, 1927).
[2] Cmd. 3131 (1928), p. 28.

347

the principle of " responsible " Government, but proposed
to apply the principle in an unusual form. The parliamentary
franchise was to be extended to all males over twenty-one
years of age and to all females over thirty, thus increasing
the electorate from 204,997 to 2,175,000, of whom one-
third would be women. Communal representation was to
be abolished, and the qualification for membership of the
Legislature was to be the same as that for the electorate,
except that members were to be literate in English and not
to hold any public office under the Crown in the island.
Then came the bold and even startling innovation. The
Executive and the Legislative Councils were to be abolished
and replaced by a State Council of sixty-one members,
which " would deal with administrative as well as legislative
matters and would sit therefore in executive as well as
legislative session." The Party system seemed to the
Commissioners to be wholly inapplicable to Ceylon, and a
parliamentary Executive of the English type was consequently ruled out. Each of the fifty elected members of the
State Council was to become a member also of one of
the Executive Committees charged with the supervision of
the Departments of Government. The seven Chairmen of
Committees were, together with the three Officers of State,
to form a Board of Ministers under the chairmanship of the
Chief Secretary. The Chief Secretary was to be in charge
of external affairs, defence, and the public services, the
Treasurer (Financial Secretary) in charge of finance, and
the Attorney-General (or Legal Secretary) in charge of the
Legal Department. These three Officers of State were to
be appointed by the Governor and to have no vote,
either at the Board of Ministers or in the Council, though
sitting and speaking in both bodies.

The Commissioners, in fine, based their scheme on the
model of the London County Council rather than on that
of a parliamentary Democracy, though the Board of
Ministers was remotely to resemble a Cabinet, if without
collective responsibility or a common allegiance to a Party.
" Ministers " were to be responsible individually and solely

to the State Council. The Governor's function was to be " supervising rather than executive," though he was to have " the unqualified right to refuse or reserve his assent both in executive and legislative matters," or himself to carry out such measures on certifying that his action was " of paramount importance to the public interest." [1]

The recommendations of the Commission were immediately accepted by the Imperial Government, and came into being in 1931.[2]

The Constitution drafted by the Donoughmore Commission was admittedly experimental, and there is an acute difference of opinion as to the measure of success it has attained. If the safeguards have not proved entirely illusory, their application by the Governor has evoked profound dissatisfaction among the Sinhalese who control the machine. The Committee system, adopted in order to give security and a share in administration to the minority communities, has failed to effect that purpose, and has otherwise worked disastrously. The minorities look to the Governor for protection, and desire only that the safeguards should be made more effective. The majority resent the safeguards and demand such revision of the Constitution as shall curtail the power of the Governor and the Officers of State, and shall give them " responsible government " in the Dominion sense.

The issue is at present (1938) uncertain and the future exceedingly obscure.

Neither Ceylon nor Burma, though self-governing colonies, is technically a Dominion. Nor is Southern Rhodesia. Originally administered by the British South Africa Company, it soon outgrew its swaddling clothes, but the transition from the rule of the Chartered Company to that of the Crown was neither rapid nor easy. *Southern Rhodesia*

During the South African war Rhodesia was temporarily cut off from all communications with Britons in the south,

---

[1] Cmd. 3131 (1928) and Cmd. 3419 (1929).
[2] Cmd. 3862 (1931), and generally see L. A. Mills: *Ceylon under British Rule* (Oxford, 1933).

349

but volunteers from Rhodesia gave a good account of themselves, as they did later in the Great War. Cecil Rhodes, on whom the whole burden of administration had really rested, died in 1902, and after his death the Company proved unequal to its task. The administration of a rapidly developing colony was necessarily expensive: the Company was plunging deeper and deeper into debt; the shareholders were disappointed at the lack of dividends; the settlers felt increasingly aggrieved by their exclusion from a share in the government of the colony. A Legislative Council containing a minority of (four) elected members had been set up by Order in Council in 1898, and after further agitation the elected members obtained a majority (1909). That did not deter them from making a notable contribution to the campaign in East Africa in 1914–1918. Nearly five thousand men out of the scanty white population volunteered for service, and many thousands of natives showed their appreciation of British rule both as combatants and as auxiliaries.

After the war there was a strong movement in Southern Rhodesia in favour of Responsible Government. The Government of South Africa was, on the contrary, anxious to incorporate it in the Union. General Smuts offered generous terms both to the Company and to the settlers to induce them to come in. A plebiscite was, however, taken in October 1922 and showed majorities of 8,774 votes against incorporation and 5,989 in favour of Responsible Government. Accordingly Southern Rhodesia was in 1923 formally annexed to the British Crown, with a constitution of the usual type—a bicameral Legislature and an Executive responsible thereto. The Company retained its mineral rights and other commercial assets, and received a cash payment of £3,750,000 in respect of unalienated lands.

Though endowed with Responsible Government, Southern Rhodesia has not yet been promoted to " Dominion status " (whatever that undefined description implies). It possesses, however, all the attributes of a Dominion, and is, in fact, administered not by the Colonial Office but by the Office set up in 1925 to deal with Dominion affairs. Accordingly, Southern Rhodesia finds itself, in this respect, in the august company of the Dominion of Canada, the Commonwealth of Australia, the Union of South Africa, and New Zealand. It was not, however, included in the enumeration set forth in the *Statute of Westminster*, which contains the nearest approach to a definition (if only *per enumerationem*) of " Dominion status " to be found in British constitutional law.

Northern Rhodesia, with a population of 10,000 Euro- *Northern* peans and nearly 1,400,000 natives, is in a totally different *Rhodesia* position from Southern Rhodesia. In 1924 it was transferred to the Crown and was endowed with a Constitution, but of the Crown colony type—a Governor and Legislative Council with an official majority.

Of the acquisition of South West Africa and of East Africa, mention has already been made. The final result is that from Capetown to the Upper Nile there is now a solid block of British territory, with a continuous coast-line from Walfisch Bay to Mombasa, broken only by Portuguese territory in Mozambique. This block affords a microcosm, in a constitutional sense, of the overseas Empire, with its self-governing Dominions (the Union of South Africa and Southern Rhodesia), the Crown colonies of Northern Rhodesia and Kenya, the Uganda and Basutoland Protectorates, not to mention two different types of " Mandated " Territories in South West Africa and Tanganyika.

There is, however, one factor common to the Union *The Dual* of South Africa, to the Mandated Territories, and to all *in Africa* the colonies and Protectorates intermediate between these extremes. The enormous preponderance of natives over Europeans dominates the whole position in Africa. Even in the Union, Europeans number only two millions out of a total population of nine and a half millions; in Basutoland less than 1,500 out of some 575,000; in Bechuanaland, 1,900 out of 265,000; in Swaziland 2,700 out of 155,000; in

351

South West Africa 31,000 out of 360,000; in Southern Rhodesia 57,000 out of 1,310,000; in Northern Rhodesia only 10,000 out of 1,367,000; in Kenya 18,000 out of three and a quarter millions; while in the other British possessions in Africa the white inhabitants are a mere fragment of the whole. This dominating fact has suggested to thoughtful observers and experienced officials the principle of the " Dual Mandate."

That phrase (which we owe to Lord Lugard) and the principle it enshrines represent, on the one hand, a reaction against the policy of the indiscriminate " Europeanization " of conquered peoples, and on the other, the fulfilment of the obligations of Trusteeship. Those obligations are twofold. Our primary duty in Africa, as elsewhere, is admittedly towards the native inhabitants of the territories acquired. But there is another. The British Empire holds its vast possessions in trust on behalf of civilization, and in particular on behalf of the industrialized countries which are increasingly dependent upon tropical lands and peoples for the supply of essential raw material, as well as for markets in which to sell their own manufactured goods.

This principle of trusteeship applies, of course, to British administration in all parts of the world, but its obligations are specially obtrusive in Africa, where there is a teeming population which can under no circumstances be Europeanized to their own benefit, but are entitled to receive every consideration from their European rulers for their well-being, moral and intellectual, physical and economic.

In different parts of Africa the problem, though essentially integral, presents itself in varying aspects, and with less or greater degree of intensity.

The Native Problem In South Africa it not only lies at the root of the Native problem in the Union itself but also dominates the problem of the Protectorates. As to the first, Sir Patrick Duncan and General Hertzog, like everyone else entitled to speak for the Dominions, have made it unmistakably clear that the European minority are determined not to be governed

by the native majority, being convinced that " the supremacy of the white man's rule in South Africa is essential if he
is to retain either his birthright or his civilization." On
this point the skilled European workman is wholly in agreement with his employer, and he refuses to work alongside
the native as an equal, still less under his supervision.
Only in the Cape Colony are natives admitted to the
parliamentary franchise, and not even there are they
admitted to Parliament. There is in truth an unshakable
determination that throughout the Union the white man
shall remain dominant.

This attitude materially affects the question as to the *The South African Protectorates*
incorporation of the three Protectorates, Swaziland, Basuto-
land, and Bechuanaland. Their incorporation in the
Union was undoubtedly contemplated by the Act of 1909.
A specific scheme was actually embodied in a schedule to
the Act. That incorporation is ardently desired by the
Europeans in the Union and in the Protectorates is undeniable. But the assent of the Imperial Government is
required, and they are solemnly pledged not to give that
assent against the wishes of the Protectorates. That the
natives in the Protectorates view the idea of incorporation
with apprehension can hardly be doubted. The deadlock,
then, would appear to be complete.

There is a further point. The South African Government
holds that the Union is deeply concerned in the policy pursued by the Imperial Government in regard to the natives in
other parts of Africa. They contend that whatever the policy
may be, it is bound to have repercussions in the Union.
That being so, the Union Government claims that it ought
in courtesy, if not by right, to be consulted in the matter.
The claim is not unreasonable; but though the problem is
in one sense integral, the solutions attempted must, under
the varying conditions in different parts of Africa, be
equally various. The general principle has never been
better stated than by Lord Lugard: " Here then is the true
conception of the inter-relation of colour: Complete uniformity in ideals, absolute equality in the paths of knowledge

and culture, equal opportunity for those who strive, equal administration for those who achieve; in matters social and racial a separate path, each pursuing his own inherited traditions, preserving his own race purity and race pride; equality in things spiritual, agreed difference in the physical and material." [1]

Those are wise words. Frequent and distressing lapses from the ideals they indicate have, of course, occurred in British administration; yet it may fairly be claimed that towards those ideals British policy has invariably striven. The constitutional destiny of the several parts of this vast continent may be uncertain; but meanwhile, the claims put forward on humanitarian grounds by Lord Lugard are, in respect of tropical Africa, unquestionably justified. " We have," he writes, " added to the prosperity and wealth of these lands and checked famine and disease. We have put an end to the awful misery of the slave trade and inter-tribal war, to human sacrifice and the ordeals of the witch doctor." [2]

That proud claim cannot be denied. But an implicit question remains unanswered: How can the civilization of tropical Africa be most effectively promoted in the future? One solution of the problem may be ruled out at once. " The idea that the African if left to himself—a thing impossible in modern international conditions—will by himself evolve into the ' gentle savage ' of Rousseau's imagination is an assumption untenable in the light of history "—and, be it added, of experience. So Lord Harlech wrote in his Report on West Africa in 1926. [3]

There remain then the two alternatives: to attempt to Europeanize the African, or by preserving all that is good in native law, customs, and perhaps even religion, make him a good African citizen. All the most thoughtful and experienced administrators are agreed that the latter is, and for many years to come must be, the preferable alternative. Individual Africans may, with advantage to themselves and

[1] Lugard : *Dual Mandate*, p. 21.   [2] *Op. cit.*, p. 610.
[3] Cmd. 2744 (1926), p. 13.

354

their fellows, be endowed with a European civilization, but for the mass of the people,

> " The fluttered folk and wild,
> Half-devil and half-child,"

the best that can be done is to give them strong and just government, and as far as possible without a sudden breach between the past and the present, without violence to their habits and traditions—in fine, to make them good Africans instead of spurious Europeans.

Chapter Twenty-three

Epilogue

RETROSPECT AND PROSPECT

CONCLUSIONS, in both senses of the word, are manifestly inappropriate to this work. Expository not argumentative, it has attempted merely to tell a story which is still evidently unfinished and always to be " continued in our next." For the British Empire is an edifice upon which it is hoped the coping-stone may never be placed. Nevertheless, a final glance at the structure as it exists to-day may suggest certain problems that will have to be faced as the building proceeds.

Of those problems some are special to particular Dominions and colonies, others are common to the Empire as a whole.

Canada

For nearly a decade Canada, owing chiefly to the low price obtainable for her wheat, has suffered from economic depression, and that depression has accentuated a constitutional problem which has never been completely solved.

The Federal Government and the Provinces

In all federal States the most obstinate problem is the relation between the Federal or Central Government and the component States or Provinces. The problem is apt to become acute, as recent history has shown, whether the residual powers are vested, as in the U.S.A., in the States, or, as in Canada, in the Dominion. The question has lately been raised in Canada from two opposite sides. On the one hand, certain Provincial Governments, including those of Ontario, New Brunswick, and British Columbia, denied the validity of various Statutes dealing with industrial and social matters (" the New Deal ") enacted by the Federal Legislature on the initiative of Mr. R. B. Bennett's Government in 1934 and 1935. The constitutional issue was further complicated by the fact that the Statutes were passed in

356

accordance with conventions adopted at Geneva under the terms of the Treaty of Versailles, but that complication (though learnedly argued before the Judicial Committee of the Privy Council) must not divert attention from the broader issue. That issue lay between the Dominion and the Provincial Parliaments in Canada. On appeal to the Judicial Committee of the Privy Council the issue was decided in favour of the Provinces, and thus Mr. Bennett's "New Deal" was invalidated. Lord Atkin, in giving judgment (January 28th, 1937), said that "the legislative powers (in Canada) remained distributed. . . . While the ship of State now sailed on larger ventures and into foreign waters she still retained the watertight compartments which were an essential part of her original structure." (The Act of 1867.)

The same truth was enforced from the opposite quarter when the Ottawa Government put the brake upon Mr. Aberhart's "Social Credit" policy adopted in Alberta. Three Acts passed in 1937 by the Alberta Legislature have been declared by the Supreme Court of Canada to be *ultra vires*. Mr. Aberhart has appealed to the Privy Council, which will presently decide between Ottawa and Alberta.

Meanwhile a Royal Commission has been appointed in Canada to report upon the whole question at issue between the Federal Government and the Provinces. The Commission has not yet (September 1938) reported. Should Canada ultimately decide upon a revision of her Constitution the Imperial Parliament will, as a matter of course, give effect to her wishes. That the matter is grave may be judged from the warning words of Mr. Meighen, who, speaking in the Senate at Ottawa, said (May 18th, 1938) that Canada was "on the edge of a crisis which portended disintegration."

Another constitutional issue has been accentuated by these domestic differences in Canada. In February 1938 a Bill was introduced in the Dominion Parliament for the abolition of appeals to the Privy Council. It was con- *Canada and the Privy Council* tended that the judgments of the Privy Council had gone far to undermine the basic character of Canadian Federalism, with the result that " they now had a decentralized federalism with the residue of legislative power in the Provinces." Into the merits of the dispute we cannot enter, but that there is considerable dissatisfaction in Canada in regard to the appellate jurisdiction of the Privy Council is not disputable.

Australia

Nor is that dissatisfaction confined to Canada. The Australian Constitution, as we have seen, differs in important respects from that of Canada. Australia can, for example, amend its own Constitution without even a nominal reference to the Imperial Parliament, though elaborate precautions are provided against its doing so without the assent both of the component States and of the people of the Commonwealth as a whole.[1] Moreover, the residue of powers is vested not in the Commonwealth but in the States, whose constitutional position was further safeguarded by section IX of the *Statute of Westminster*. Neither the provisions of the *Commonwealth Act* nor those of the *Statute of Westminster* have availed to avert disputes between the Commonwealth and the States. Financial and commercial relations have been the most fertile source of disputes, and

Western Australia : Proposed Secession

in June 1934 the Parliament of Western Australia went so far as to pass an Act in favour of secession from the Commonwealth.[2] Fortified by a State Referendum, Western Australia then petitioned the Imperial Parliament praying it to pass legislation or otherwise " to effectuate the withdrawal of the people of Western Australia from the Federal Commonwealth," and to restore Western Australia to " its former status as a separate and distinct self-governing colony in the British Empire." The Imperial Parliament, while affirming its legal competence to amend the *Commonwealth Act*, decided that " it would not be constitutionally proper for it to legislate for the internal affairs of any Dominion or

---

[1] See *supra*, pp. 225 f.
[2] See on the whole question Carraway: *The Failure of Federalism in Australia* (Oxford, 1930).

self-governing State or Colony." Accordingly it declined to receive the petition.[1]

Western Australia remains, therefore, a component State of the Commonwealth, which has done its best to meet the grievances of which that State originally, and not unreasonably, complained. But so jealous are the States of the Central Authority that the Commonwealth has on several recent occasions been defeated on Referendum in attempting to obtain powers which to many impartial observers seem essential to the well-being, if not to the security, of Australia as a whole.[2]

Both the Commonwealth and States have frequently had recourse to the Privy Council, though such appeals are not regarded with universal favour. One or two examples must suffice. In 1932 the Privy Council decided a particularly interesting constitutional point, raised by the action of the State Legislature of New South Wales in abolishing its Second Chamber. The High Court of Australia had confirmed the finding of the Supreme Court of New South Wales that the Bill introduced by the Lang (Labour) Government, and passed by both Houses of the State Parliament, could not legally be presented for the Royal Assent until it had been submitted to the people of the State by Referendum. Thereupon the Lang Government appealed to the Privy Council, which in June 1932 confirmed the judgments of the two Australian Courts. The New South Wales Legislative Council was originally a nominated body, and as such was a particularly weak Second Chamber, being liable to be swamped by successive Governments in their respective interests. Consequently, in 1933, after the defeat of the Lang Government at the polls, the Legislative Council was, as a result of a Referendum, reconstituted. It now consists of sixty members elected jointly by both Houses of the State Parliament. Members are elected for twelve years, but one-fourth of them retire triennially. The history of this incident, in each of its successive phases, has

Australia and the Privy Council

---

[1] Report of Joint Select Committee (May 1935).
[2] E.g. the Aviation Case (1936).

a constitutional significance extending far beyond the limits of New South Wales or even of Australia.[1] Another case referred to the decision of the Judicial Committee (the " Dried Fruit Case," *James* v. *The Commonwealth*), had a twofold significance, economic and constitutional. Section 92 of the *Commonwealth Act* declared " trade, commerce, and intercourse among the States, whether by means of internal carriage or ocean navigation, shall be absolutely free." The Privy Council held in 1936 that the Commonwealth Acts restricting inter-State trade in dried fruit were invalid, as contravening that section. That judgment not only struck at the root of the marketing policy of the Commonwealth Government, but maintained constitutional limitations upon federal powers in economic matters. It affords, moreover, one more illustration of the strong feeling of the States, especially the smaller and less industrialized States, against any extension of federal powers.

Yet with all this it is clear that the forces which at the close of the nineteenth century induced the separate colonies to accept federation are to-day operating with ever-increasing strength.

Defence   Of those forces the strongest was and is the relative defencelessness even of a federated Australia in view of changing conditions in the Pacific. The Pacific is no longer outside the orbit of *Weltpolitik*. It might easily become the scene of a world-conflict. It is not, then, remarkable that both Australia and New Zealand should recently have given increased attention to problems of national defence. The Australian navy includes four, and the New Zealand navy two cruisers, besides smaller craft; both Dominions have small air forces, and both provide military training, on a voluntary basis, for their manhood. The defence expenditure of Australia, though less than a third of that of Great Britain, is nearly four times per head greater than that of Canada. In no Dominion, however, is the expenditure on

[1] On the problem generally see Marriott: *Second Chambers* (2nd ed., Oxford, 1927) ; and see especially p. 107, where correction as above is needed.

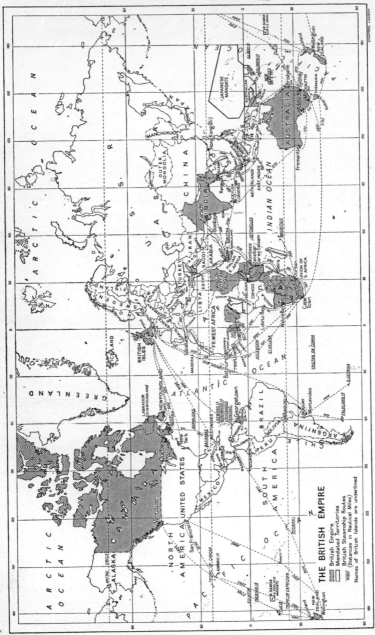

THE BRITISH EMPIRE AND MANDATED TERRITORIES, 1938

THE BRITISH EMPIRE

British Empire
Mandated Territories
British Steamship Routes
(Distances in Nautical Miles)
Names of British Islands are underlined

defence adequate: they all rely for security upon the Royal Navy. Technically, indeed, each Dominion is responsible for its own defence, and any contribution it may choose to make towards the maintenance of what may be strictly termed an " Imperial " navy is entirely at its own discretion. Nevertheless, the last Imperial Conference (1937) showed a deepened sense of the responsibility of each member of the Commonwealth for the safety of the whole.

Closely, indeed inextricably, connected with the problem *Foreign* of Empire defence is that of foreign policy. No Dominion *Policy* can be expected to share with the Motherland the responsibility for defence, unless it has a share in shaping the policy which may necessitate active participation in war. Loud was the insistence on this elementary truth during the Great War of 1914-1918. The Dominions, as we have seen, demanded, quite justly, admission to the inner councils of the Empire. They obtained admission, and on a basis of complete equality. But no sooner was the war ended than they shrank from the responsibility entailed by membership of an Imperial Cabinet. The difficulties which beset the creation of an Imperial Executive are admittedly formidable, perhaps insuperable; but the defects of the existing machinery are lamentably conspicuous. Enlightened statesmen in the Dominions are at least as conscious of the existing deficiency and the potential danger as statesmen of the homeland. Among the former, Mr. Menzies, at present (1938) Attorney-General of Australia, has been particularly outspoken and helpful on this matter. That Dominion Governments should be kept regularly informed by the Imperial Government is not, he insists, enough: they must also be systematically consulted—not after but before important decisions on policy are taken. " If," he said (June 21st, 1938), " we are to have one voice of the British people—and I am a believer in one voice, not six voices, of the British people—and if that one voice is to speak with clarity and with a proper authority in the world, we must devote ourselves increasingly to the problem of finding out how we can accelerate and complete the process of consulta-

361

tion between the British Government here and those other British Governments which are to be found in the self-governing communities of the Commonwealth. . . . We should be directing our minds to see how far it can be made possible to consult every Dominion at the right moment and with a mind which is open until that Dominion has spoken."

That is only sober sense: but it is not always easy to give effect to its promptings. Science has already done much to solve the problem of Empire consultation, as the experience of December 1936 conclusively proved. But the problem (to adapt Lord Melbourne's famous warning) is that " if the units of the Empire do not hang together they will beyond doubt hang separately."

Migration   Not unconnected with the problem of Imperial defence, but raising even wider issues, is that of the redistribution of the white population of the Empire.

The late Lord Northcliffe, on visiting Australia in 1922, was invited to give his views frankly about the country. He did. He declared himself to be " profoundly impressed by its magnitude, its profuse wealth . . . its emptiness and its defencelessness." He was " staggered," he said, " by the indifference of the Australian people to the vital question of population. . . . The key to your white Australian ideal is population. You must increase your slender garrison by the multiplication of your people. The world will not tolerate an empty Australia. This continent must carry its full quota of people . . . you have no option. Tens of millions of people will come to you whether you like it or not. You cannot hold up the human flood by a restriction clause in an Act of Parliament."

Lord Northcliffe's blunt words were much resented at the time, but in 1931 his warning was in substance repeated by Sir Raphael Cilento, the Director-General of Health and Medical Services in Australia. He reminded his fellow-countrymen that the birth-rate of Australia is one of the lowest in the world, the natural increase for 1931 being half that of 1891. He regarded a period of increased pressure in the Pacific as imminent and inevitable. The population of Japan proper would, he reckoned, increase from its present figure (92,000,000) to 113,000,000 by the time England and the United States would reach the period of stalemate. For Australia, with two persons to the square mile against 352 in Japan, the alternative, he concluded, was " immigration or ultimate invasion."

The external menace to Canada is more remote than to Australia, but in respect of density of population her position is not much better. With three persons to the square mile she compares with thirteen in New Zealand, with 483 in the United Kingdom, with 701 in England proper, and with 366 in Germany.

The figures for both Dominions need, however, to be corrected. The Astor Committee on Empire migration, reporting in 1933 (Cmd. 4075), pertinently pointed out that physiographical considerations render considerable areas of Canada and Australia unsuitable for permanent white settlement. Deducting these areas the average density of Canada would be not 3 but 7·25, and of Australia not 2 but 3·75. Even so, the figures are sufficiently ominous. They are rendered the more ominous by the practical cessation of migration. During the years 1900–1914 emigration from the United Kingdom was on a very large scale, the peak being reached in the years 1910–1913, when the Old Country was reinforcing the overseas Empire at the rate of 304,000 [1] per annum, or an aggregate of 1,217,710. All this migration took place with a minimum of assistance from the State.[2]

During the Great War migration naturally ceased. When it was resumed in 1919 it was with State assistance, generous but not too carefully discriminating, given primarily to enable ex-Service men to settle in the Dominions. Lack of discrimination and selection involved suffering to individuals

---

[1] These figures are *gross*. The *net* emigration to the Empire was about 200,000 per annum.
[2] A small amount of assistance was given to the " 1820 " settlers in South Africa, to the New Zealand Colonization Company, and to the Selkirk Scheme in Canada (Cmd. 4689).

and great embarrassment to the Dominions. As a result the stream, though maintained (1919–1922) at an average of 180,000, tended to become sluggish.

Empire Settlement Act, 1922

Consequently, in 1922, the *Empire Settlement Act* was passed, after conferences between the Governments of the United Kingdom, Canada, Australia, and New Zealand. The Act empowered the British Government to co-operate with the Dominion Governments, or with public or private organizations, such as the Church Army, the Salvation Army, Dr. Barnardo's Homes, etc., in carrying out agreed schemes for the assistance of suitable persons who wished to settle overseas. The Imperial Government undertook to subsidize schemes up to a maximum of £3,000,000 a year, and the Dominions agreed to contribute £1 for £1 of the sum spent on assisted migration.

For the first seven years things went fairly well. Nearly 300,000 persons were in that period assisted to migrate, mostly to Australia, but a large number also went to Canada, about 40,000 to New Zealand, and a few to South Africa. But with the onset of the " economic blizzard " (1929) there was a set-back; the total sum authorized under the Act was £43,500,000; the actual expenditure down to the end of 1936 was only £6,105,417. Economic depression, which paradoxically operates not as a stimulus but as a deterrent to emigration, was primarily responsible for this pitiable result. Primarily, but not solely. Careless selection of migrants had done great harm both in the Dominions and at home, where every case of a misfit is industriously advertised. The Dominions became suspicious that the United Kingdom wished to solve her most obdurate social problem by shipping unemployables off to the Dominions. This suspicion, though groundless, was particularly operative in Australia, where, though the need for population was greatest, the trade unions were very powerful, and held tenaciously to the " lump of labour " fallacy.

Voluntary Agencies

The voluntary societies—the Salvation Army, the Church Army, Dr. Barnardo's Homes, and others—continued, even during the days of depression, to do magnificent work for

364

children. And for children and young unmarried women the demand of the Dominions has never ceased. Among voluntary agencies special mention should be made of the scheme initiated by Kingsley Fairbridge, an Oxford Rhodes Scholar. In 1913 Fairbridge and his wife started a farm school at Pinjarra in Western Australia,[1] and so successful did the scheme prove that other Fairbridge schools have already been established on Vancouver Island (B.C.), in New South Wales, and in Victoria, and other schools on the same principle are contemplated elsewhere. *Fairbridge Farm Schools*

There are other encouraging features in the present situation. In 1937 the Imperial Parliament extended the *Empire Settlement Act* for a further period of fifteen years. The maximum expenditure in any one year is, indeed, cut down from £3,000,000 to £1,500,000 (a sum which experience has unhappily proved to be more than sufficient), but the State aid to voluntary societies is increased from fifty to seventy-five per cent. Still more encouraging are the unmistakable manifestations of renewed interest in Empire settlement on the side of the Dominions. Of this a specially welcome indication is the passing of a State Insurance Act by the Commonwealth of Australia (July 1938). The Act will for the first time make possible a mutual arrangement entitling emigrants from Great Britain to retain their health insurance and pension rights. This is a concession of the first importance, and should the example of Australia be followed by other Dominions, one of the most formidable deterrents to emigration from this country will be removed. As long ago as 1926 an Inter-Departmental Committee [2] recognized that the cumulative effect of the social services was " to counteract to an appreciable extent the attractions of the life of independence offered in the Dominions." Since 1926 this deterrent influence has operated with steadily intensifying force. Prospective beneficiaries are naturally reluctant to sacrifice their investments in health insurance, *National Insurance and Migration*

---

[1] For particulars see Ruby Fairbridge: *Pinjarra* (Oxford, 1937), and Annual Reports of the Fairbridge Farm Schools.
[2] Cmd. 2608 (1926).

unemployment, and pensions schemes. The aggregate of those investments is very large. If, by mutual arrangements, the prospective participants in the accumulated funds are enabled to retain their rights, one of the greatest obstacles to emigration will be removed, a powerful stimulus will be given to the economic activities of the Dominions, and an important contribution will be made towards solving the problem of Imperial defence.

Unsolved Problems

Many other problems await solution alike in the Dominions, in India, and in the colonial Empire. Will it be possible to satisfy the demands of coloured labour in the West Indies without destroying the industries on which their subsistence depends ? Is a West Indian federation feasible or desirable ? Is closer union possible or desirable between the British possessions in East Africa, or between Northern and Southern Rhodesia ? Can the extreme nationalists in South Africa be persuaded to abstain from pin-pricks (such as the Flag question) which irritate loyalists without advancing their own ambitions ? Can we devise more effective machinery for continuous consultations between the partners in the Commonwealth ?

Not that the existing machinery has hitherto failed in a real emergency. Despite vain talk about the " right of secession," the forces which, on balance, tend to integration are, if less obtrusive, immensely strong.

Bonds of Empire

Among the ties " light as air " passing reference should be made to the development of personal relations by the visits of politicians belonging to various Inter-Parliamentary Associations; to the tours arranged for schoolboys and schoolgirls; and most important of all perhaps to the scholarships provided for colonial students at Oxford by the munificence of Cecil Rhodes. But why does not some benefactor, with purse as deep and vision as broad as Cecil Rhodes', found scholarships at colonial universities and schools for English lads and lasses ? There is already on a small scale an interchange of teachers; an interchange of students would be at least as valuable.

More substantial bonds are in process of being forged.

THE PRIVY COUNCIL

Science has removed almost every impediment to continuous consultation between the several Governments of the Empire; the Imperial Conference gains in utility at each successive meeting; the value of the Judicial Committee of the Privy Council, though not uncriticized and admittedly *The Privy Council* not an ideal Court of Appeal for the Empire, is widely appreciated. It is, as Lord Hewart lately said, " a significant and conspicuous symbol of the unity of the British Dominions involving not the faintest hint or suggestion of subordination." " No fallacy," he added, " could be more complete or more gratuitous than that which assumes or implies that appeal to the Privy Council is an appeal to England from some other part of the British Commonwealth of Nations. The existence of the Judicial Committee as the final Imperial Court of Appeal in high questions of legal principle means, and ought to mean, that some of the best and most experienced legal minds in the British Empire, no matter from what quarter they may severally come, are ready and willing to be applied to the most important topics of legal principle which may have given rise to serious controversy in one of the Dominions. The learning, experience, and wisdom of the whole are brought to bear in the interests of any particular part. On a recent occasion no fewer than five distinguished judges from different parts of the British Dominions, contributing their learning to the common stock, were actually sitting in court in Downing Street as members of the Judicial Committee of the Privy Council." [1]

" No other Court in the world's history," wrote another high authority, " has possessed so wide a sphere or so august a position. No other Court can compare with it in the variety of laws it has to administer." " Apart," said Lord Macmillan, " from the numerous cases arising on the terms of Dominion and Indian Statutes and Colonial Ordinances, many of the Indian appeals raise intricate questions of Hindu or of Moslem law, cases from Quebec must be decided according to the Civil Code founded on French law, and cases from Mauritius also involve French law. Roman-

[1] Speaking at Johannesburg on August 26th, 1936 (*The Times*, August 27th).

367

Dutch law is applied in appeals from South Africa, Ceylon, and British Guiana; the ancient customs of Normandy are invoked in appeals from the Channel Islands, and there are still, it is said, some vestiges of old Spanish law in Trinidad, while primitive native customs have to be considered in cases from some of the Colonies and Protectorates." [1] All these appeals are still addressed to " The King's Most Excellent Majesty in Council."

The Crown   Yet important as the Judicial Committee is as a " symbol of unity under the Throne," and impressive as is the position of the Crown as the arbiter of Justice throughout a quarter of the world, the political function, legally and constitutionally assigned to the King-Emperor, is even more significant. " The Crown is the symbol of the free association of the members of the British Commonwealth of Nations. They are united by a common allegiance to the Crown." So runs the Preamble to the *Statute of Westminster*. But the function of the Crown in the Empire is not confined to the Dominions, it extends to India, to the colonies, and all other " possessions." And in all these spheres of authority the significance of the Crown has, in these latter days, admittedly increased. " The importance of the Crown in our Constitution is not a diminishing but an increasing factor." So spake Mr. Balfour in paying tribute to the late Queen Victoria in 1901. His words crystallized into a sentence the sober judgment of one of the most thoughtful critics in contemporary politics. The development observable under Queen Victoria has proceeded rapidly under her successors. Nor has the recognition of that truth been confined to the King's subjects at the heart of the Empire. General Smuts spoke for the whole British Commonwealth when he propounded his famous dilemma: " How are you going to keep this Commonwealth of Nations together ? . . . There are two potent factors that you must rely upon for the future. The first is your hereditary Kingship, the other is our Conference system. . . . You cannot make a republic of the British Commonwealth of Nations. . . . The theory of the

[1] Lord Macmillan, in *The Times*, August 14th, 1933.

Constitution is that the King is not your King but the King of all of us, ruling over every part of the whole Commonwealth . . . and if his place should be taken by anybody else, that somebody would have to be elected under a process which it will pass the wit of man to devise." [1]

Yet the British Monarchy, nay, the Empire itself, are but means to an end, instruments fashioned for some high purpose. Mr. Baldwin gave exalted expression to this thought when, at the opening of the Imperial Conference of 1923, he said:

" The British Empire has often been described as the product of accidents. It is, in fact, the natural and spontaneous product not of its own necessities only, but of those of mankind. . . . Our ever-increasing control of natural forces has so knit the nations together that whatever affects one for good or ill affects them all. They are as organs of one body. . . . Like a network of steel embedded in concrete this Commonwealth holds more than itself together . . . but steel of the wrong temper may be as brittle as glass. The only element which can give a tensile quality to human ties is a sense of duty in men to each other. . . . The British Empire cannot live for itself alone. Its strength as a Commonwealth of Nations will grow so far as its members unite to bear on their shoulders the burdens of those weaker and less fortunate than themselves." [2]

Most thoughtful Englishmen share Mr. Baldwin's conviction. More impressive because more impartial are the opinions of foreign critics. Great Frenchmen have always been particularly generous in their appreciation of the Imperial achievements of Great Britain—particularly of her work in India. Some ninety years ago Alexis de Tocqueville wrote: " There never has been anything so extraordinary under the sun as the conquest and still more the government of India by the English; nothing which from all points of the globe so much attracts the eyes of mankind to that little island whose very name was to the Greeks unknown." " For every man who believes in the legitimate progress of

Some Foreign Tributes

---

[1] *War-Time Speeches*, p. 34.   [2] Cmd. 1988 (1923), pp. 10–11.

the human race what a consoling and marvellous spectacle is that of the English dominion in India!" So wrote the Comte de Montalembert in 1855. Much more recently (June 1938) yet another Frenchman, M. André Thérive, wrote: " England proves by her example what civilization is. Instead of ceaselessly seeking a theory of it, she is content to practise it." Yet even more remarkable, as coming from a highly critical German professor, is this tribute from the pen of Dr. Wilhelm Dibelius: " England," he wrote, " is the single country in the world that, looking after its own interest with meticulous care, has at the same time something to give to others; the single country where patriotism does not represent a threat or challenge to the rest of the world; the single country that invariably summons the most progressive, idealistic, and efficient forces in other nations to co-operate with it. . . . Britain is the solitary great Power with a national programme which, while egotistic through and through, at the same time promises to the world as a whole something which the world passionately desires—order, progress, and eternal peace." [1]

Whether this remarkable tribute to his country is deserved, it is hardly for an Englishman to say. Nor is it for him to decide whether England's achievement is due to the accidents of fortune or to an altruistic policy deliberately adopted, and, on the whole, steadily pursued. That in the Imperial sphere England has obtained a unique position is, plainly, indisputable. To that success many things have contributed: the geographical position of the island home of the race; a population with a genius for seamanship and a love of adventure; the early realization of national unity in England; the gradual evolution of a Constitution, designed to reconcile order and liberty, at once strong and flexible, and adaptable to the needs of Englishmen in their scattered homes throughout the world; an early start in the race for industrial and commercial supremacy and the urge derived therefrom towards the acquisition of tropical possessions, yielding raw materials and offering markets; and, not least,

[1] *England* (E.T.), pp. 103–109.

a sensitive conscience and a genuine desire, if imperfectly attained, to administer impartial justice and to promote the peace of the world. Some great words written at the crisis of the Great War (1917) may at another solemn moment [1] be recalled: " The root of their success has not been their material or military but their moral strength; and it is the moral quality in the British Empire which has confounded its domestic critics and its foreign foes. Unity is a form of selfishness unless it is spontaneous, and British Empire means a sacrifice of self. It is a communion of service which makes the British Empire one, and will make a Commonwealth of nations; and we achieve atonement by bearing one another's burdens and understanding one another's minds."[2]

An Englishman would fain believe that these words are true.

[1] Written on Michaelmas Day (September 29th, 1938).
[2] *Times Literary Supplement*, June 7th, 1917.

APPENDIX A

LIST OF BOOKS

A FULL and carefully articulated bibliography will be found in the several volumes of the *Cambridge History of the British Empire*, 8 vols. (Cambridge, 1929). The following is only a small selection from a large number of modern works, and a still smaller selection from a vast collection of official publications.

(i) Official :
Some important Parliamentary Papers.
Correspondence re Colonial Representatives in London (Cc. 24, 51) (1870).
Proceedings of Colonial (and Imperial) Conferences, Conf. of 1887 (Cc. 5091) (1887); *Ottawa, 1894* (C. 7553) (1894); *Conf. of 1897* (C. 8596) (1897); *Conf. of 1902* (Cmd. 1597, 1723) (1903); *Empire Trade* (C. 8449) (1897); *Future Organization* (Cd. 2785) (1906); *Conf. of 1907* (Cdd. 3337, 3340); *Conf. of 1911* (Cd. 5273 (1910), 5513 (1910), Cdd. 5741, 5745, 5746); *Conf. of 1917* (Cd. 8566); *Conf. of 1918* (Cd. 9177); *Conf. of 1921* (Cmd. 1474); *Conf. of 1923* (Cmd. 1987, 1988); *Imp. Econ. Conf., 1923* (Cmd. 1990); *Imp. Econ. Conf., 1924* (Cmd. 2009, 2084, 2115) ; *Conf. of 1926* (Cmd. 2768, 2759) ; *Conf. of 1930* (Cmd. 3716, 3717, 3718). *Imp. Econ. Conf. Ottawa, 1932* (Cmd. 4174, 4175, 4178 (1932)). *Conf. of 1937* (Cmd. 5482).
Second Chambers in the Dominions (lxvi, 81 of 1910).
Treaty Making Powers of Dominions (lxvi, 129 of 1910).
Committee of Imperial Defence (Cd. 6560 of 1912 and Cd. 7347 of 1914).
Dominions Royal Commission, 1914–17 (Cd. 8462 of 1917).
Imperial Preference (Cd. 8482 of 1917–18).
Imperial Customs Conference, 1921 (Cmd. 1231 of 1921).
Imperial Shipping Committee, Reports (1920–2) (1932).
Imperial Economic Committee, Reports (Cmd. 2493, 4499 of 1925 and 24 more down to 1932).
Report of Conference on Dominion Legislation (1930) (Cmd. 3479 of 1930).
Statute of Westminster (22 & 23 George V, c. 4).
The Colonial Empire in 1937–38 (Cmd. 5760 of 1938).
Reports on *Nigeria* (468 of 1920): *West Indies* (Cmd. 1679 of 1922); *West Africa* (Cmd. 2744 of 1926); *East Africa* (Cmd. 2387 of 1925); *Closer Union of Eastern and Central African Dependencies* (Cmd. 3234 of 1929); *Malaya, Ceylon, and Java* (Cmd. 3235 of 1928); *Ceylon Constitution* (Cmd. 3131 of 1928); *Kenya Land Commission* (Précis of) (Cmd. 4580 of 1934).
See also *Statistical Abstract of British Oversea Dominions, etc.* (H.M.S.O., Annual).

(ii) Some General Works:
L. S. Amery: *The Empire in the New Era* (1928).
—— *A Plan of Action* (1932).
(ed. K. N. Bell and W. P. Morrell): Documents on *British Colonial Policy, 1830–60*, 1928.

Lord Bryce: *Modern Democracies* (1921).
W. A. Carruthers: *Emigration from the British Isles* (1929).
(ed. E. T. Cook): *The Empire and the World* (1937).
—— *The King and the Imperial Crown* (1936).
V. Cornish: *Geography of Imperial Defence* (1922).
L. Curtis: *Problem of the Commonwealth* (1916).
R. M. Dawson: *The Development of Dominion Status, 1900–36* (1937).
A. G. Dewey: *The Dominions and Diplomacy*, 2 vols. (1929).
H. E. Egerton: *British Colonial Policy* (1920).
—— *In the Nineteenth Century* (1923).
—— *Federations and Unions in the British Empire*, Texts, etc. (1911).
H. V. Evatt: *The King and His Dominion Governors* (1936).
J. A. Froude: *Oceania* (1886).
H. D. Hall. *The British Commonwealth of Nations* (1920).
W. P. Hall: *Empire to Commonwealth* (1929).
F. J. C. Hearnshaw: *Democracy in the British Empire* (1920).
B. Holland: *Imperium et Libertas* (1901).
R. Jebb : *Studies in Colonial Nationalism* (1905).
—— *The Britannic Question* (1913).
A. B. Keith: *Responsible Government in the Dominions* (1912).
—— *Imperial Unity and the Dominions* (1916).
—— *Dominion Home Rule, 1921.*
—— *The Constitution, etc., of the Empire* (1925).
—— *The Sovereignty of the British Dominions* (1929).
—— *The Constitutional Law of the British Dominions* (1933); and other works.
—— (ed.) *Selected Speeches and Documents on British Colonial Policy, 1763–1917*, 2 vols. (1918).
L. C. A. Knowles : *The Economic Development of the British Overseas Empire*, 3 vols. (1924–36).
F. P. de Labillière: *Federal Britain* (1894).
S. Leacock: *Economic Prosperity in the British Empire* (1930).
Sir C. P. Lucas: *Greater Rome and Greater Britain* (1912).
Sir H. Luke: *Cyprus Under the Turks* (Oxford, 1929).
J. A. R. Marriott: *Mechanism of the Modern State*, Vol. I (1927).
—— *Empire Settlement* (1927).
Lord Milner: *Constructive Imperialism* (1908).
C. W. J. Orr: *Cyprus Under British Rule* (1918).
(ed. Palmer): *Consultation and Co-operation in the British Commonwealth* (1934).
A. G. Scholes: *Education for Empire Settlement* (1932).
R. L. Schuyler: *Parliament and the British Empire* (N.Y., 1929).
Sir J. R. Seeley: *The Expansion of England* (1884).
R. Stokes: *New Imperial Ideas* (1930).
(ed. Toynbee): *British Commonwealth Relations* (1934).
J. E. Tyler: *The Struggle for Imperial Unity, 1868–95* (1938).
J. A. Williamson: *A History of British Expansion*, 2 vols. (1930).
B. Worsfold: *The Empire on the Anvil* (1916).

(iii) The First Colonial Empire:
Sir W. W. Hunter: *History of British India*, 2 vols. (1900).
J. A. Froude: *English Seamen in the Sixteenth Century.*

373

R. Hakluyt: *Voyages*, 8 vols. (1926–8).

S. Purchas: *Pilgrims*, 20 vols. (ed. Raleigh, 1907).

C. R. Beazley: *John and Sebastian Cabot* (1898).

—— *The Dawn of Modern Geography*, 3 vols. (1897).

Sir J. Corbett: *Drake and the Tudor Navy*, 2 vols. (1898).

J. A. Williamson, *Maritime Enterprise, 1485–1558* (1913).

—— *Age of Drake* (1937).

C. M. Andrews: *The Colonial Period* (1912).

—— *Colonial Self-Government, 1652–89* (1904).

J. A. Doyle: *The English in America*, 5 vols. (1882, etc.).

H. C. Lodge: *Short History of the English Colonies in America* (N.Y., 1881).

R. J. Thwaites: *The Colonies, 1492–1750* (1891).

A. A. Ettinger: *J. E. Oglethorpe* (1936).

G. L. Beer: *The Commercial Policy of England towards the American Colonies* (N.Y., 1893).

—— *British Colonial Policy, 1754–65* (N.Y. 1907).

G. B. Hertz: *The Old Colonial System* (1905).

Sir J. S. Corbett : *England in the Seven Years War*, 2 Vols. (1908).

A. T. Mahan: *Influence of Sea Power upon History.*

A. G. Bradley: *Fight with France for North America* (1900).

F. Parkman: *Montcalm and Wolfe* (1884).

S. G. Fisher: *The Struggle for American Independence*, 2 vols. (1908).

Sir G. O. Trevelyan: *The American Revolution*, 4 vols. (1899).

W. E. H. Lecky: *History of England*, Vol. III, chapter XII (1882).

A. Smith : *Wealth of Nations, 1776* (1882).

Lord Bryce : *The American Commonwealth*, 2 vols. (1889).

E. Burke : *Speeches on American Taxation.*

S. Johnson : *Taxation No Tyranny.*

Sparks : *Life of Washington.*

(iv) Canada :

The Canada Year Book (Annual) (Official).

W. P. M. Kennedy: *Documents of the Canadian Constitution* (1918).

—— *The Nature of Canadian Federalism*, 1921.

—— *The Constitution of Canada* (1923).

G. M. Wrong and others: *The Federation of Canada 1867–1917* (1917).

A. Short and A. G. Doughty: *Documents of the Constitutional History of Canada, 1759–91* (Ottawa, 1918).

(ed. J. H. Rose and others) : *Cambridge History of the British Empire* (1930), Vol. VI.

R. Coupland: *The Quebec Act* (1925).

A. G. Bradley: *The United Empire Loyalists* (1932).

W. S. Wallace: *The United Empire Loyalists* (1914).

Sir R. Borden: *Canadian Constitutional Studies* (1922); *The War and the Future* (1917).

Sir J. G. Bourinot : *Federal Government* (1889).

—— *Canada* (1922).

Earl of Carnarvon: *Speeches on Canadian Affairs* (1902).

(ed. J. A. Chisholm): *The Speeches and Public Letters of Joseph Howe*, 2 vols. (Halifax, Canada, 1909).

APPENDIX A

G. R. Parkin: *The Great Dominion* (1895).
H. B. Willson: *Life of Lord Strathcona* (1915).
Sir C. Tupper: *Recollections of Sixty Years* (1914).
E. M. Saunders: *Life of Sir C. Tupper*, 2 vols. (1916).
J. S. Ewart: *The Kingdom Papers* (1912).
Canada in the Great World War (various writers), 6 vols. (Toronto, 1917–21).
R. A. Mackay: *The Unreformed Senate of Canada* (1926).
(ed. Sir C. P. Lucas): *The Empire at War*, Vol. II (1921–6).
Lord Beaverbrook: *Canada in Flanders*, 3 vols. (1916–18).
J. Pope: *Memorials of Sir John Macdonald, 1894, Correspondence of* (n.d.).
P. E. Corbett and H. A. Smith: *Canada and World Politics* (1928).
O. D. Skelton: *Life and Letters of Sir W. Laurier*, 2 vols. (1921).
—— *Life and Times of Sir A. Galt* (1920).
Lord Bryce: *Modern Democracies*, chapter xxiii (1921).

(v) Australasia :
Australian Commonwealth Year Book (Annual) (Official).
(ed. F. Watson): *Historical Records of Australia* (1914–24).
(ed. J. H. Rose and others): *Cambridge History of the British Empire*, Vol. VII, Parts I and II (1933).
H. R. Evatt: *Federalism in Australia* (1918).
B. R. Wise: *The Making of the Australian Commonwealth* (1913).
R. Kerr: *The Law of the Australian Constitution* (1925).
—— *The Case of the People of Western Australia for Secession* (Perth, W.A., 1934).
A. W. Jose: *History of Australasia* (1921).
Sir T. A. Coghlan: *Progress of Australasia in the XIXth Century* (1903).
—— *Labour and Industry in Australia, 1788–1901*, 4 vols. (1918).
E. Jenks: *A History of the Australasian Colonies* (1912).
C. E. Lyne: *Life of Sir H. Parkes* (1897).
W. P. Reeves: *State Experiments in Australia and New Zealand* (1902).
E. Lewin: *The Commonwealth of Australia* (1917).
Sir C. G. Wade: *Australia* (1918).
W. H. Moore: *The Constitution of the Commonwealth* (1910).
Sir J. Quick: *Legislative Powers of Commonwealth and States* (1919).
—— and R. R. Garran: *Annotated Constitution of the Commonwealth* (1901).
A. P. Canaway: *The Failure of Federalism in Australia* (1930).
Sir J. Kirwan: *An Empty Land* (1934).
Sir Ian Hamilton: *Gallipoli Diary*, 2 vols. (1920).
(ed. C. P. Lucas): *The Empire of War*, Vol. III (1921–6).
Sir J. Monash: *The Australians in France* (1923).
A. P. Wavell: *The Palestine Campaign* (1928).
(ed. Bean) : *Official History of Australia in the War of 1914–18* (Sydney, 1921–   ).

New Zealand :
New Zealand Official Year Book (Annual) (Official).
Sir R. Stout: *New Zealand* (1911).
J. Hight and J. D. Bamford: *The Constitutional Law and History of New Zealand* (1914).
(ed. Rose and others): The Cambridge *History of the British Empire*, Vol. VII, Pt. II (1933).

(ed. Bean) : *Official History of New Zealand's Effort in the Great War,* 4 vols. (Wellington, 1919–   ).
E. Best: *The Maori,* 2 vols. (Wellington, 1925).
A. J. Harrop: *E. J. Wakefield* (1928).
E. J. Wakefield: *Adventures in New Zealand, 1839–44* (1845).
G. C. Henderson: *Grey* (1907).
R. C. Mills: *Wakefield Experiment in Empire Building* (1915).
Lord Bryce: *Modern Democracies,* Vol. II, chapter liii (1921).
R. Taylor: *The Past and Present of New Zealand* (1868).
Hon. W. P. Reeves: *The Fortunate Isles* (Wellington, 1897).

(vi) Africa :
South Africa:
Year Book of the Union of South Africa (Annual) (Official).
J. H. Hofmeyr: *South Africa* (1931).
J. C. Smuts: *Africa and Some World Problems* (1930).
V. R. Markham: *South Africa Past and Present* (1900).
—— *The New Era in South Africa* (1904).
Lord Carnarvon: *Speeches on the Affairs of West and South Africa* (1903).
Lord Buxton: *General Botha* (1924).
B. Williams: *Cecil Rhodes* (1921).
Sir L. Michel: *Life of Rhodes,* 2 vols. (1910).
W. B. Worsfold: *The Union of South Africa* (1912).
—— *Lord Methuen's Work in South Africa* (1917).
The Government of South Africa (Central News Agency, South Africa), 2 vols. (1908).
L. Curtis: *The Framework of Union* (1908).
Earl of Selborne: *Memorandum on Federation* (a State Paper of the first importance) (Cmd. 3564, 1907).
R. H. Brand: *The Union of South Africa* (1909).
M. Nathan: *The South African Commonwealth* (1919).

East and West Africa:
Marjory R. Dilley: *British Policy in Kenya Colony* (1938).
C. W. Hobley: *Kenya, from Chartered Company to Crown Colony* (1929).
E. Huxley: *White Man's Country. Lord Delamere and the Making of Kenya,* 2 vols. (1935).
W. H. Ingrams: *Zanzibar, Its History and its People.*
Sir H. Johnston: *The Uganda Protectorate,* 2 vols. (1902).
Report of the East Africa Commission, (1925) (Cmd. 2387).
Report of W. Ormsby-Gore on West Africa (1926) (Cmd. 2744).
Reports on British Sphere of the Cameroons (1922) (Cmd. 1647).

Partition of Africa :
Sir C. Lucas: *The Partition and Colonization of Africa* (1922).
E. Banning: *Le partage politique de l'Afrique* (1885–8).
J. S. Keltie: *The Partition of Africa* (1895).
V. Deville: *Partage de l'Afrique* (1898).
G. Hanotaux: *Le Partage de l'Afrique* (1890–8).
H. A. Gibbons: *The New Map of Africa* (1890–8).
Lord Lugard: *The Dual Mandate in Africa.*

APPENDIX A

F. M. Anderson and A. S. Hershey: *Handbook for the Diplomatic History of Africa 1870–1914.*
E. Lewin: *The Germans and Africa* (1938).
Mauritius:
W. H. Ingrams: *Short History of Mauritius* (1931).

(vii) Egypt :
Egypt No. 1 (1921) Milner Mission Report (Cmd. 1131) ; No. 4 (1921) (Cmd. 1555) ; No. 1 (1922) (Cmd. 1592); (1924) (Cmd. 2269); No. 1 (1928) (Cmd. 3050).
Reports by H.M. High Commissioner.
Papers (1882), (1884–5), (1897) *on Egypt and the Soudan* (Annual, H.M.S.O.).
Lord Cromer : *Annual Reports in Blue Books.*
—— *Modern Egypt* (1908).
—— *Abbas II* (1915).
Lord Milner: *England in Egypt* (1892).
D. A. Cameron: *Egypt in the Nineteenth Century* (1898).
Sir A. Colvin: *The Making of Modern Egypt* (1906).
Sir R. Wingate: *Mahdism and the Egyptian Soudan* (1891).
A. E. Hake: *Gordon's Journals at Khartoum* (1885).
G. W. Steevens: *With Kitchener to Khartoum* (1898).
Sir D. M. Wallace: *Egypt and the Egyptian Question* (1883).
J. A. R. Marriott: *England since Waterloo* (1913).
—— *A History of Europe, 1815–1923* (1931).
—— *Modern England* (1934)
Lord Morley: *Gladstone*, Vol. III (1903).
G. Buckle: *Disraeli*, Vols. V and VI (1920).
Lord Zetland: *Lord Cromer* (1932).
Lord Lloyd: *Egypt since Cromer*, 2 vols. (1933–4).
Sir I. Malcolm: *The Suez Canal* (1921).
Sir A. Wilson: *The Suez Canal* (1931).
Sir W. Hayter: *Recent Constitutional Developments in Egypt* (1924).
Lord Fitzmaurice: *Life of Lord Granville* (1905).

(viii) The East Indies.
The Moral and Material Progress of India (Annual).
India Office List (Annual).
Montagu-Chelmsford Report, Cd. 9109 (1918).
Civil Services in India, Cmd. 2128 (1924).
Indian States Committees (H. Butler), Cmd. 3302 (1929).
Statutory Commission (Simon), Cmd. 3568, 3569 (1929).
Round Table Conference, Cmd. 3772 (1931).
Round Table Conference, Cmd. 3972 (1931).
Proposals for Indian Constitutional Reform, Cmd. 4268 (1933).
Government of India Act (1935).
(ed. A. B. Keith): *Speeches and Documents on Indian Policy,* 2 vols. (1922).
Viscount Morley: *Indian Speeches* (1909).
—— *Recollections,* 2 vols. (1917).
(ed. Sir T. Raleigh): *Lord Curzon in India* (Speeches) (1906).
J. A. R. Marriott: *The English in India* (1932).
The British Crown and the Indian States (P. S. King, 1829).

Sir C. Ilbert: *The Government of India* (1915).
Sir W. W. Hunter: *The India of the Queen* (1903).
Sir A. Lyall: *Life of the Marquess of Dufferin*, 2 vols. (1905).
Lord Zetland: *Life of Lord Curzon*, 3 vols. (1928).
Lord Newton : *Lord Lansdowne* (1929).
Sir R. Craddock: *The Dilemma in India* (1929).
Sir T. B. Sapru: *The Indian Constitution* (1926).
M. E. Darling: *Rusticus Loquitur* (1930).
Sir H. Butler: *India Insistent* (1931).
Sir V. Lovett: *History of the Indian National Movement* (1920).
—— *India* (1923).
Sir V. Chivol: *Indian Unrest* (1910).
—— *India Old and New* (1926).
Sir W. Lawrence: *The India We Served* (1929).

Burma and Ceylon:
Sir G. Scott: *Burma from the Earliest Times to the Present Day* (1924).
Sir H. T. White: *Burma* (Cambridge, 1923).
A. Gibson: *Ceylon* (1929).
Ceylon Report of the Special Commission on the Constitution (1928, Cmd. 3131).
(ed. W. Neil) : *The Colonial Office List* (Annual).
Ceylon: *Correspondence Regarding the Constitution* (1929) (Cmd. 3419).
L. A. Mills: *Ceylon under British Rule 1795–1932* (1933).
The Cleghorn Papers (1927).
Sir George Barrow: *Ceylon Past and Present* (1857).
H. W. Codrington: *A Short History of Ceylon* (1926).
Sir West Ridgeway: *Administration of the Affairs of Ceylon, 1896–1903* (Colombo, 1903).
(ix) British Malaya, etc.
Colonial Secretary's Annual Report.
Straits Settlements Blue Book (Annual).
R. L. German: *Handbook to British Malaya* (1935).
Ashley Gibson: *The Malay Peninsula* (1928).
Hartland: *Economic Conditions in Malaya* (1935).
C. P. Lucas: *Historical Geography of the British Colonies*, Vol. I (Oxford, 1906).
Sir F. Swettenham: *British Malaya* (1929).
A. K. Terrell: *Malayan Legislation and Its Future* (1932).
S. Baring Gould: *History of Sarawak 1839–1908* (1909).
Sir S. St. John: *Life of Sir Charles Brooke, Raja of Sarawak* (1879).
L. A. Mills: *British Malaya, 1824–67* (1925).
Report of the Hon. W. Ormsby-Gore on Malaya, Ceylon, and Java (1928 Cmd. 3235).
(x) The West Indies :
Report of Visit of the Hon. E. F. L. Wood, M.P., to the West Indies and British Guiana, 1921–2 (Cmd. 1679), (1922).
Sir C. Lucas: *Historical Geography of the British Colonies*, Vol. II, (1905).
W. L. Mathieson: *British Slavery and its Abolition* (1926).
F. W. Pitman: *Development of the British West Indies, 1700–63* (Yale, 1917).
J. A. Froude: *The English in the West Indies* (1888).
H. Wrong: *The Government of the West Indies* (1923).

APPENDIX B

LIST OF REVIEW ARTICLES ON IMPERIAL TOPICS

BY J. A. R. MARRIOTT

A Great Anglo-Indian: Sir William Hunter and His Work. Fortnightly Review, June 1900.
The Imperial Note in Victorian Poetry. Nineteenth Century, August 1900.
Ireland Under Queen Victoria. Fortnightly Review, March 1901.
The House of Lords as an Imperial Senate. Fortnightly Review, June 1907.
Why Halt Ye? Nineteenth Century, May 1911.
The Key of the Empire. Nineteenth Century, November 1911.
The Third Edition of Home Rule. Nineteenth Century, May 1912.
The Evolution of Colonial Self-Government. Fortnightly Review, September 1912.
A Family Council. Nineteenth Century, May 1915.
The Problem of the Commonwealth. Nineteenth Century, January 1917.
British Federalism : A Vanished Dream? Nineteenth Century, September 1917.
The New Orientation of History. Nineteenth Century, April 1918.
The Problem of Federalism. Nineteenth Century, June 1919.
The Fourth Home Rule Bill. Fortnightly Review, April 1920.
The Heel of Achilles. Nineteenth Century, June 1920.
Empire Partnership. Fortnightly Review, December 1921.
England, Ireland and Ulster. Fortnightly Review, July 1922.
Empire Foreign Policy. Fortnightly Review, May 1923.
The Organization of the Empire. Edinburgh Review, April 1921.
The Egyptian Factor in European Diplomacy. Edinburgh Review, July 1924.
The Imperial Parliament in the Empire. Nineteenth Century, September 1927.
A Glimpse of Canada. Fortnightly Review, February 1929.
The British Empire and Foreign Relations. Edinburgh Review, April 1929.
Making a Constitution for India. Fortnightly Review, May 1931.
A Constitution for a Continent. Fortnightly Review, May 1931.
India : The Task Ahead. Fortnightly Review, October 1931.
The Crown Imperial. Quarterly Review, April 1937.
Population and Prosperity (Empire Migration). Nineteenth Century, May 1937.
British Foreign Policy. Quarterly Review, October 1937.

INDEX

INDEX

383

LIST OF BOOKS BY THE SAME AUTHOR

The Makers of Modern Italy. Macmillan, 1889. (New and Enlarged Edition (Clarendon Press), 1931. 2nd Edition, 1937.)

The Life and Times of Lucius Cary, Viscount Falkland. Methuen, 1907. (Out of print.)

The Remaking of Modern Europe. Methuen, 1909. (21st Edition revised 1933.)

Second Chambers. Clarendon Press, 1910. (New Edition revised 1927.)

English Political Institutions. Clarendon Press, 1910. (4th Edition, with additional chapters, 1938.)

England Since Waterloo. Methuen, 1913. (10th Edition, 1935.)

The French Revolution of 1848 in Its Economic Aspects. Clarendon Press, 1913.

The English Land System. Murray, 1914.

The Evolution of Prussia (with Sir C. G. Robertson). Clarendon Press, 1915. (5th and Revised Edition, 1937.)

The Eastern Question. Clarendon Press, 1917. (3rd Edition revised 1924.)

English History in Shakespeare. Chapman & Hall, 1918. (2nd Edition, 1919.) (Out of print.)

The European Commonwealth. Clarendon Press, 1918.

Europe and Beyond. Methuen, 1921. (4th Edition revised 1933.)

Economics and Ethics. Methuen, 1923. (Cheap Edition, 1937.)

The Mechanism of the Modern State. 2 vols. Clarendon Press, 1927.

Empire Settlement. Clarendon Press, 1927.

How We Are Governed. Clarendon Press, 1928. (4th Edition revised 1936.)

The Crisis of English Liberty. Clarendon Press, 1930.

The History of Modern Europe 1815–1920. Methuen, 1930. (3rd Edition revised to 1937, 1938.)

How We Live. Clarendon Press, 1930. (New and Revised Edition, 1938.)

The English in India. Clarendon Press, 1932.

Life of John Colet. Methuen, 1933.

Oxford: Its Place in National History. Clarendon Press, 1933.

Queen Victoria and Her Ministers. Murray, 1933.

Modern England, 1885–1932. Methuen, 1934. (2nd Edition.)

Dictatorship and Democracy. Clarendon Press, 1935. (2nd Edition, 1937.)

Twenty-Five Years of the Reign of King George V. Methuen, 1935.

Castlereagh. Methuen, 1936.

Life of R. F. Horton (with A. Peel). Allen & Unwin, 1937.

Commonwealth or Anarchy. P. Allan, 1937.

This Realm of England. Blackie, 1938.